50 HUMOROUS STORIES

JEROME K. JEROME

EONN PUBLISHING

CONTENTS

TOLD AFTER SUPPER

Introductory	3
Now The Stories Came To Be Told	9
Teddy Biffles' Story	15
Interlude--The Doctor's Story	19
The Haunted Mill Or The Ruined Home	21
Interlude	25
The Ghost Of The Blue Chamber	27
A Personal Explanation	31
My Own Story	33

TOMMY AND CO.

Story The First	43
Story The Second	69
Story The Third	87
Story The Fourth	109
Story The Fifth	131
Story The Sixth	153
Story The Seventh	183

THE OBSERVATIONS OF HENRY

The Ghost of the Marchioness of Appleford	213
The Uses And Abuses Of Joseph	227
The Surprise Of Mr. Milberry	239
The Probation Of James Wrench	251
The Wooing of Tom Sleight's Wife	265

JOHN INGERFIELD AND OTHER STORIES

To The Gentle Reader	279
In Remembrance of John Ingerfield, and of Anne, His Wife	281
The Woman Of The Saeter	307
Variety Patter	321
Silhouettes	331
The Lease of the «Cross Keys»	341

MALVINA OF BRITTANY AND OTHER STORIES

Malvina of Brittany	349
The Street Of The Blank Wall	403
His Evening Out	427
The Lesson	451
Sylvia Of The Letters	465
The Fawn Gloves	493

SKETCHES IN LAVENDER, BLUE AND GREEN

Sketches In Lavender, Blue And Green	505
Reginald Blake, Financier and Cad	507
An Item of Fashionable Intelligence	517
Blase Billy	535
The Choice Of Cyril Harjohn	547
The Materialisation Of Charles And Mivanway	559
Portrait Of A Lady	571
The Man Who Would Manage	583
The Man Who Lived For Others	591
A Man Of Habit	599
The Absent-Minded Man	607
A Charming Woman	615
Whibley's Spirit	621
The Man Who Went Wrong	629

The Hobby Rider	639
Dick Dunkerman's Cat	655
The Minor Poet's Story	663
The Degeneration Of Thomas Henry	673
The City Of The Sea	679
Driftwood	685

TOLD AFTER SUPPER

INTRODUCTORY

It was Christmas Eve.

I begin this way because it is the proper, orthodox, respectable way to begin, and I have been brought up in a proper, orthodox, respectable way, and taught to always do the proper, orthodox, respectable thing; and the habit clings to me.

Of course, as a mere matter of information it is quite unnecessary to mention the date at all. The experienced reader knows it was Christmas Eve, without my telling him. It always is Christmas Eve, in a ghost story,

Christmas Eve is the ghosts' great gala night. On Christmas Eve they hold their annual fete. On Christmas Eve everybody in Ghostland who IS anybody--or rather, speaking of ghosts, one should say, I suppose, every nobody who IS any nobody--comes out to show himself or herself, to see and to be seen, to promenade about and display their winding-sheets and grave-clothes to each other, to criticise one another's style, and sneer at one another's complexion.

"Christmas Eve parade," as I expect they themselves term it, is a function, doubtless, eagerly prepared for and looked forward to throughout Ghostland, especially the swagger set, such as the murdered Barons, the crime-stained Countesses, and the Earls who came over with the Conqueror, and assassinated their relatives, and died raving mad.

Hollow moans and fiendish grins are, one may be sure, energetically practised up. Blood-curdling shrieks and marrow-freezing gestures are probably rehearsed for weeks beforehand. Rusty chains and gory daggers are over-hauled, and put into good working order; and sheets and shrouds, laid carefully by from the previous year's show, are taken down and shaken out, and mended, and aired.

Oh, it is a stirring night in Ghostland, the night of December the twenty-fourth!

Ghosts never come out on Christmas night itself, you may have noticed. Christmas Eve, we suspect, has been too much for them; they are not used to excitement. For about a week after Christmas Eve, the gentlemen ghosts, no doubt, feel as if they were all head, and go about making solemn resolutions to themselves that they will stop in next Christmas Eve; while lady spectres are contradictory and snappish, and liable to burst into tears and leave the room hurriedly on being spoken to, for no perceptible cause whatever.

Ghosts with no position to maintain--mere middle-class ghosts--occasionally, I believe, do a little haunting on off-nights: on Allhallows Eve, and at Midsummer; and some will even run up for a mere local event--to celebrate, for instance, the anniversary of the hanging of somebody's grandfather, or to prophesy a misfortune.

He does love prophesying a misfortune, does the average British ghost. Send him out to prognosticate trouble to somebody, and he is happy. Let him force his way into a peaceful home, and turn the whole house upside down by foretelling a funeral, or predicting a bankruptcy, or hinting at a coming disgrace, or some other terrible disaster, about which nobody in their senses want to know sooner they could possibly help, and the prior knowledge of which can serve no useful purpose whatsoever, and he feels that he is combining duty with pleasure. He would never forgive himself if anybody in his family had a trouble and he had not been there for a couple of months beforehand, doing silly tricks on the lawn, or balancing himself on somebody's bed-rail.

Then there are, besides, the very young, or very conscientious ghosts with a lost will or an undiscovered number weighing heavy on their minds, who will haunt steadily all the year round; and also the fussy ghost, who is indignant at having been buried in the dust-bin or in the village pond, and who never gives the parish a single night's quiet until somebody has paid for a first-class funeral for him.

But these are the exceptions. As I have said, the average orthodox ghost does his one turn a year, on Christmas Eve, and is satisfied.

Why on Christmas Eve, of all nights in the year, I never could myself understand. It is invariably one of the most dismal of nights to be out in--cold, muddy, and wet. And besides, at Christmas time, everybody has quite enough to put up with in the way of a houseful of living relations, without wanting the ghosts of any dead ones mooning about the place, I am sure.

There must be something ghostly in the air of Christmas--something about the close, muggy atmosphere that draws up the ghosts, like the dampness of the summer rains brings out the frogs and snails.

And not only do the ghosts themselves always walk on Christmas Eve, but live people always sit and talk about them on Christmas Eve. Whenever five or six English-speaking people meet round a fire on Christmas Eve, they start telling each other ghost stories. Nothing satisfies us on Christmas Eve but to hear each other tell authentic anecdotes about spectres. It is a genial, festive season, and we love to muse upon graves, and dead bodies, and murders, and blood.

There is a good deal of similarity about our ghostly experiences; but this of course is not our fault but the fault ghosts, who never will try any new performances, but always will keep steadily to old, safe business. The consequence is that, when you have been at one Christmas Eve party, and heard six people relate their adventures with spirits, you do not require to hear any more ghost stories. To listen to any further ghost stories after that would be like sitting out two farcical comedies, or taking in two comic journals; the repetition would become wearisome.

There is always the young man who was, one year, spending the

Christmas at a country house, and, on Christmas Eve, they put him to sleep in the west wing. Then in the middle of the night, the room door quietly opens and somebody--generally a lady in her nightdress--walks slowly in, and comes and sits on the bed. The young man thinks it must be one of the visitors, or some relative of the family, though he does not remember having previously seen her, who, unable to go to sleep, and feeling lonesome, all by herself, has come into his room for a chat. He has no idea it is a ghost: he is so unsuspicious. She does not speak, however; and, when he looks again, she is gone!

The young man relates the circumstance at the breakfast-table next morning, and asks each of the ladies present if it were she who was his visitor. But they all assure him that it was not, and the host, who has grown deadly pale, begs him to say no more about the matter, which strikes the young man as a singularly strange request.

After breakfast the host takes the young man into a corner, and explains to him that what he saw was the ghost of a lady who had been murdered in that very bed, or who had murdered somebody else there--it does not really matter which: you can be a ghost by murdering somebody else or by being murdered yourself, whichever you prefer. The murdered ghost is, perhaps, the more popular; but, on the other hand, you can frighten people better if you are the murdered one, because then you can show your wounds and do groans.

Then there is the sceptical guest--it is always 'the guest' who gets let in for this sort of thing, by-the-bye. A ghost never thinks much of his own family: it is 'the guest' he likes to haunt who after listening to the host's ghost story, on Christmas Eve, laughs at it, and says that he does not believe there are such things as ghosts at all; and that he will sleep in the haunted chamber that very night, if they will let him.

Everybody urges him not to be reckless, but he persists in his foolhardiness, and goes up to the Yellow Chamber (or whatever colour the haunted room may be) with a light heart and a candle, and wishes them all good-night, and shuts the door.

Next morning he has got snow-white hair.

He does not tell anybody what he has seen: it is too awful.

There is also the plucky guest, who sees a ghost, and knows it is a ghost, and watches it, as it comes into the room and disappears through the wainscot, after which, as the ghost does not seem to be coming back, and there is nothing, consequently, to be gained by stopping awake, he goes to sleep.

He does not mention having seen the ghost to anybody, for fear of frightening them--some people are so nervous about ghosts,--but determines to wait for the next night, and see if the apparition appears again.

It does appear again, and, this time, he gets out of bed, dresses himself and does his hair, and follows it; and then discovers a secret passage leading from the bedroom down into the beer-cellar,- -a passage which, no doubt, was not unfrequently made use of in the bad old days of yore.

After him comes the young man who woke up with a strange sensation in the middle of the night, and found his rich bachelor uncle standing by his bedside. The rich uncle smiled a weird sort of smile and vanished. The young man immediately got up and looked at his watch. It had stopped at half-past four, he having forgotten to wind it.

He made inquiries the next day, and found that, strangely enough, his rich uncle, whose only nephew he was, had married a widow with eleven children at exactly a quarter to twelve, only two days ago,

The young man does not attempt to explain the circumstance. All he does is to vouch for the truth of his narrative.

And, to mention another case, there is the gentleman who is returning home late at night, from a Freemasons' dinner, and who, noticing a light issuing from a ruined abbey, creeps up, and looks through the keyhole. He sees the ghost of a 'grey sister' kissing the ghost of a brown monk, and is so inexpressibly shocked and frightened that he faints on the spot, and is discovered there the next morning, lying in a heap against the door, still speechless, and with his faithful latch-key clasped tightly in his hand.

All these things happen on Christmas Eve, they are all told of on Christmas Eve. For ghost stories to be told on any other evening than the evening of the twenty-fourth of December would be impossible in English society as at present regulated. Therefore, in introducing the sad but authentic ghost stories that follow hereafter, I feel that it is unnecessary to inform the student of Anglo-Saxon literature that the date on which they were told and on which the incidents took place was--Christmas Eve.

Nevertheless, I do so.

NOW THE STORIES CAME TO BE TOLD

It was Christmas Eve! Christmas Eve at my Uncle John's; Christmas Eve (There is too much 'Christmas Eve' about this book. I can see that myself. It is beginning to get monotonous even to me. But I don't see how to avoid it now.) at No. 47 Laburnham Grove, Tooting! Christmas Eve in the dimly-lighted (there was a gas-strike on) front parlour, where the flickering fire-light threw strange shadows on the highly coloured wall-paper, while without, in the wild street, the storm raged pitilessly, and the wind, like some unquiet spirit, flew, moaning, across the square, and passed, wailing with a troubled cry, round by the milk-shop.

We had had supper, and were sitting round, talking and smoking.

We had had a very good supper--a very good supper, indeed. Unpleasantness has occurred since, in our family, in connection with this party. Rumours have been put about in our family, concerning the matter generally, but more particularly concerning my own share in it, and remarks have been passed which have not so much surprised me, because I know what our family are, but which have pained me very much. As for my Aunt Maria, I do not know when I shall care to see her again. I should have thought Aunt Maria might have known me better.

But although injustice--gross injustice, as I shall explain later on--has been done to myself, that shall not deter me from doing justice to others; even to those who have made unfeeling insinuations. I will do justice to Aunt Maria's hot veal pasties, and toasted lobsters, followed by her own special make of cheesecakes, warm (there is no sense, to my thinking, in cold cheesecakes; you lose half the flavour), and washed down by Uncle John's own particular old ale, and acknowledge that they were most tasty. I did justice to them then; Aunt Maria herself could not but admit that.

After supper, Uncle brewed some whisky-punch. I did justice to that also; Uncle John himself said so. He said he was glad to notice that I liked it.

Aunt went to bed soon after supper, leaving the local curate, old Dr. Scrubbles, Mr. Samuel Coombes, our member of the County Council, Teddy Biffles, and myself to keep Uncle company. We agreed that it was too early to give in for some time yet, so Uncle brewed another bowl of punch; and I think we all did justice to that--at least I know I did. It is a passion with me, is the desire to do justice.

We sat up for a long while, and the Doctor brewed some gin-punch later on, for a change, though I could not taste much difference myself. But it was all good, and we were very happy--everybody was so kind.

Uncle John told us a very funny story in the course of the evening. Oh, it WAS a funny story! I forget what it was about now, but I know it amused me very much at the time; I do not think I ever laughed so much in all my life. It is strange that I cannot recollect that story too, because he told it us four times. And it was entirely our own fault that he did not tell it us a fifth. After that, the Doctor sang a very clever song, in the course of which he imitated all the different animals in a farmyard. He did mix them a bit. He brayed for the bantam cock, and crowed for the pig; but we knew what he meant all right.

I started relating a most interesting anecdote, but was somewhat surprised to observe, as I went on, that nobody was paying the slightest attention to me whatever. I thought this rather rude of them at first, until it dawned upon me that I was talking to myself all the time, instead of out aloud, so that, of course, they did not know that I was telling them a tale at all, and were probably puzzled to understand the meaning of my animated expression and eloquent gestures. It was a most curious mistake for any one to make. I never knew such a thing happen to me before.

Later on, our curate did tricks with cards. He asked us if we had ever seen a game called the "Three Card Trick." He said it was an artifice by means of which low, unscrupulous men, frequenters of race-meetings and such like haunts, swindled foolish young fellows out of their money. He said it was a very simple trick to do: it all depended on the quickness of the hand. It was the quickness of the hand deceived the eye.

He said he would show us the imposture so that we might be warned against it, and not be taken in by it; and he fetched Uncle's pack of cards from the tea-caddy, and, selecting three cards from the pack, two plain cards and one picture card, sat down on the hearthrug, and explained to us what he was going to do.

He said: "Now I shall take these three cards in my hand--so--and let you all see them. And then I shall quietly lay them down on the rug, with the backs uppermost, and ask you to pick out the picture card. And you'll think you know which one it is." And he did it.

Old Mr. Coombes, who is also one of our churchwardens, said it was the middle card.

"You fancy you saw it," said our curate, smiling.

"I don't 'fancy' anything at all about it," replied Mr. Coombes, "I tell you it's the middle card. I'll bet you half a dollar it's the middle card."

"There you are, that's just what I was explaining to you," said our curate, turning to the rest of us; "that's the way these foolish young fellows that I was speaking of are lured on to lose their money. They make sure they know the card, they fancy they saw it. They don't grasp the idea that it is the quickness of the hand that has deceived their eye."

He said he had known young men go off to a boat race, or a cricket match, with pounds in their pocket, and come home, early in the afternoon, stone broke; having lost all their money at this demoralising game.

He said he should take Mr. Coombes's half-crown, because it would teach Mr. Coombes a very useful lesson, and probably be the means of saving Mr. Coombes's money in the future; and he should give the two-and-sixpence to the blanket fund.

"Don't you worry about that," retorted old Mr. Coombes. "Don't you take the half-crown OUT of the blanket fund: that's all."

And he put his money on the middle card, and turned it up.

Sure enough, it really was the queen!

We were all very much surprised, especially the curate.

He said that it did sometimes happen that way, though--that a man did sometimes lay on the right card, by accident.

Our curate said it was, however, the most unfortunate thing a man could do for himself, if he only knew it, because, when a man tried and won, it gave him a taste for the so-called sport, and it lured him on into risking again and again; until he had to retire from the contest, a broken and ruined man.

Then he did the trick again. Mr. Coombes said it was the card next the coal-scuttle this time, and wanted to put five shillings on it.

We laughed at him, and tried to persuade him against it. He would listen to no advice, however, but insisted on plunging.

Our curate said very well then: he had warned him, and that was all that he could do. If he (Mr. Coombes) was determined to make a fool of himself, he (Mr. Coombes) must do so.

Our curate said he should take the five shillings and that would put things right again with the blanket fund.

So Mr. Coombes put two half-crowns on the card next the coal-scuttle and turned it up.

Sure enough, it was the queen again!

After that, Uncle John had a florin on, and HE won.

And then we all played at it; and we all won. All except the curate, that is. He had a very bad quarter of an hour. I never knew a man have such hard luck at cards. He lost every time.

We had some more punch after that; and Uncle made such a

funny mistake in brewing it: he left out the whisky. Oh, we did laugh at him, and we made him put in double quantity afterwards, as a forfeit.

Oh, we did have such fun that evening!

And then, somehow or other, we must have got on to ghosts; because the next recollection I have is that we were telling ghost stories to each other.

TEDDY BIFFLES' STORY

Teddy Biffles told the first story, I will let him repeat it here in his own words.

(Do not ask me how it is that I recollect his own exact words--whether I took them down in shorthand at the time, or whether he had the story written out, and handed me the MS. afterwards for publication in this book, because I should not tell you if you did. It is a trade secret.)

Biffles called his story -

JOHNSON AND EMILY OR THE FAITHFUL GHOST (Teddy Biffles' Story)

I was little more than a lad when I first met with Johnson. I was home for the Christmas holidays, and, it being Christmas Eve, I had been allowed to sit up very late. On opening the door of my little bedroom, to go in, I found myself face to face with Johnson, who was coming out. It passed through me, and uttering a long low wail of misery, disappeared out of the staircase window.

I was startled for the moment--I was only a schoolboy at the time, and had never seen a ghost before,--and felt a little nervous about going to bed. But, on reflection, I remembered that it was only sinful people that spirits could do any harm to, and so tucked myself up, and went to sleep.

In the morning I told the Pater what I had seen.

"Oh yes, that was old Johnson," he answered. "Don't you be frightened of that; he lives here." And then he told me the poor thing's history.

It seemed that Johnson, when it was alive, had loved, in early life, the daughter of a former lessee of our house, a very beautiful girl, whose Christian name had been Emily. Father did not know her other name.

Johnson was too poor to marry the girl, so he kissed her good-bye, told her he would soon be back, and went off to Australia to make his fortune.

But Australia was not then what it became later on. Travellers through the bush were few and far between in those early days; and, even when one was caught, the portable property found upon the body was often of hardly sufficiently negotiable value to pay the simple funeral expenses rendered necessary. So that it took Johnson nearly twenty years to make his fortune.

The self-imposed task was accomplished at last, however, and then, having successfully eluded the police, and got clear out of the Colony, he returned to England, full of hope and joy, to claim his bride.

He reached the house to find it silent and deserted. All that the neighbours could tell him was that, soon after his own departure, the family had, on one foggy night, unostentatiously disappeared, and that nobody had ever seen or heard anything of them since, although the landlord and most of the local tradesmen had made searching inquiries.

Poor Johnson, frenzied with grief, sought his lost love all over the world. But he never found her, and, after years of fruitless effort, he returned to end his lonely life in the very house where, in the happy bygone days, he and his beloved Emily had passed so many blissful hours.

He had lived there quite alone, wandering about the empty

rooms, weeping and calling to his Emily to come back to him; and when the poor old fellow died, his ghost still kept the business on.

It was there, the Pater said, when he took the house, and the agent had knocked ten pounds a year off the rent in consequence.

After that, I was continually meeting Johnson about the place at all times of the night, and so, indeed, were we all. We used to walk round it and stand aside to let it pass, at first; but, when we grew at home with it, and there seemed no necessity for so much ceremony, we used to walk straight through it. You could not say it was ever much in the way.

It was a gentle, harmless, old ghost, too, and we all felt very sorry for it, and pitied it. The women folk, indeed, made quite a pet of it, for a while. Its faithfulness touched them so.

But as time went on, it grew to be a bit a bore. You see it was full of sadness. There was nothing cheerful or genial about it. You felt sorry for it, but it irritated you. It would sit on the stairs and cry for hours at a stretch; and, whenever we woke up in the night, one was sure to hear it pottering about the passages and in and out of the different rooms, moaning and sighing, so that we could not get to sleep again very easily. And when we had a party on, it would come and sit outside the drawing-room door, and sob all the time. It did not do anybody any harm exactly, but it cast a gloom over the whole affair.

"Oh, I'm getting sick of this old fool," said the Pater, one evening (the Dad can be very blunt, when he is put out, as you know), after Johnson had been more of a nuisance than usual, and had spoiled a good game of whist, by sitting up the chimney and groaning, till nobody knew what were trumps or what suit had been led, even. "We shall have to get rid of him, somehow or other. I wish I knew how to do it."

"Well," said the Mater, "depend upon it, you'll never see the last of him until he's found Emily's grave. That's what he is after. You find Emily's grave, and put him on to that, and he'll stop there. That's the only thing to do. You mark my words."

The idea seemed reasonable, but the difficulty in the way was that we none of us knew where Emily's grave was any more than the ghost of Johnson himself did. The Governor suggested palming off some other Emily's grave upon the poor thing, but, as luck would have it, there did not seem to have been an Emily of any sort buried anywhere for miles round. I never came across a neighbourhood so utterly destitute of dead Emilies.

I thought for a bit, and then I hazarded a suggestion myself.

"Couldn't we fake up something for the old chap?" I queried. "He seems a simple-minded old sort. He might take it in. Anyhow, we could but try."

"By Jove, so we will," exclaimed my father; and the very next morning we had the workmen in, and fixed up a little mound at the bottom of the orchard with a tombstone over it, bearing the following inscription:-

SACRED TO THE MEMORY OF EMILY HER LAST WORDS WERE - "TELL JOHNSON I LOVE HIM"

"That ought to fetch him," mused the Dad as he surveyed the work when finished. "I am sure I hope it does."

It did!

We lured him down there that very night; and--well, there, it was one of the most pathetic things I have ever seen, the way Johnson sprang upon that tombstone and wept. Dad and old Squibbins, the gardener, cried like children when they saw it.

Johnson has never troubled us any more in the house since then. It spends every night now, sobbing on the grave, and seems quite happy.

"There still?" Oh yes. I'll take you fellows down and show you it, next time you come to our place: 10 p.m. to 4 a.m. are its general hours, 10 to 2 on Saturdays.

INTERLUDE--THE DOCTOR'S STORY

It made me cry very much, that story, young Biffles told it with so much feeling. We were all a little thoughtful after it, and I noticed even the old Doctor covertly wipe away a tear. Uncle John brewed another bowl of punch, however, and we gradually grew more resigned.

The Doctor, indeed, after a while became almost cheerful, and told us about the ghost of one of his patients.

I cannot give you his story. I wish I could. They all said afterwards that it was the best of the lot--the most ghastly and terrible--but I could not make any sense of it myself. It seemed so incomplete.

He began all right and then something seemed to happen, and then he was finishing it. I cannot make out what he did with the middle of the story.

It ended up, I know, however, with somebody finding something; and that put Mr. Coombes in mind of a very curious affair that took place at an old Mill, once kept by his brother-in-law.

Mr. Coombes said he would tell us his story, and before anybody could stop him, he had begun.

Mr Coombes said the story was called -

THE HAUNTED MILL OR THE RUINED HOME

(MR. COOMBES'S STORY)

Well, you all know my brother-in-law, Mr. Parkins (began Mr. Coombes, taking the long clay pipe from his mouth, and putting it behind his ear: we did not know his brother-in-law, but we said we did, so as to save time), and you know of course that he once took a lease of an old Mill in Surrey, and went to live there.

Now you must know that, years ago, this very mill had been occupied by a wicked old miser, who died there, leaving--so it was rumoured- -all his money hidden somewhere about the place. Naturally enough, every one who had since come to live at the mill had tried to find the treasure; but none had ever succeeded, and the local wiseacres said that nobody ever would, unless the ghost of the miserly miller should, one day, take a fancy to one of the tenants, and disclose to him the secret of the hiding-place.

My brother-in-law did not attach much importance to the story, regarding it as an old woman's tale, and, unlike his predecessors, made no attempt whatever to discover the hidden gold.

"Unless business was very different then from what it is now," said my brother-in-law, "I don't see how a miller could very well have saved anything, however much of a miser he might have been: at all events, not enough to make it worth the trouble of looking for it."

Still, he could not altogether get rid of the idea of that treasure.

One night he went to bed. There was nothing very extraordinary about that, I admit. He often did go to bed of a night. What WAS remarkable, however, was that exactly as the clock of the village church chimed the last stroke of twelve, my brother-in-law woke up with a start, and felt himself quite unable to go to sleep again.

Joe (his Christian name was Joe) sat up in bed, and looked around.

At the foot of the bed something stood very still, wrapped in shadow.

It moved into the moonlight, and then my brother-in-law saw that it was the figure of a wizened little old man, in knee-breeches and a pig-tail.

In an instant the story of the hidden treasure and the old miser flashed across his mind.

"He's come to show me where it's hid," thought my brother-in-law; and he resolved that he would not spend all this money on himself, but would devote a small percentage of it towards doing good to others.

The apparition moved towards the door: my brother-in-law put on his trousers and followed it. The ghost went downstairs into the kitchen, glided over and stood in front of the hearth, sighed and disappeared.

Next morning, Joe had a couple of bricklayers in, and made them haul out the stove and pull down the chimney, while he stood behind with a potato-sack in which to put the gold.

They knocked down half the wall, and never found so much as a four- penny bit. My brother-in-law did not know what to think.

The next night the old man appeared again, and again led the way into the kitchen. This time, however, instead of going to the fire-place, it stood more in the middle of the room, and sighed there.

"Oh, I see what he means now," said my brother-in-law to himself; "it's under the floor. Why did the old idiot go and stand up against the stove, so as to make me think it was up the chimney?"

They spent the next day in taking up the kitchen floor; but the only thing they found was a three-pronged fork, and the handle of that was broken.

On the third night, the ghost reappeared, quite unabashed, and for a third time made for the kitchen. Arrived there, it looked up at the ceiling and vanished.

"Umph! he don't seem to have learned much sense where he's been to," muttered Joe, as he trotted back to bed; "I should have thought he might have done that at first."

Still, there seemed no doubt now where the treasure lay, and the first thing after breakfast they started pulling down the ceiling. They got every inch of the ceiling down, and they took up the boards of the room above.

They discovered about as much treasure as you would expect to find in an empty quart-pot.

On the fourth night, when the ghost appeared, as usual, my brother-in-law was so wild that he threw his boots at it; and the boots passed through the body, and broke a looking-glass.

On the fifth night, when Joe awoke, as he always did now at twelve, the ghost was standing in a dejected attitude, looking very miserable. There was an appealing look in its large sad eyes that quite touched my brother-in-law.

"After all," he thought, "perhaps the silly chap's doing his best. Maybe he has forgotten where he really did put it, and is trying to remember. I'll give him another chance."

The ghost appeared grateful and delighted at seeing Joe prepare to follow him, and led the way into the attic, pointed to the ceiling, and vanished.

"Well, he's hit it this time, I do hope," said my brother-in-law; and next day they set to work to take the roof off the place.

It took them three days to get the roof thoroughly off, and all they found was a bird's nest; after securing which they covered up the house with tarpaulins, to keep it dry.

You might have thought that would have cured the poor fellow of looking for treasure. But it didn't.

He said there must be something in it all, or the ghost would never keep on coming as it did; and that, having gone so far, he would go on to the end, and solve the mystery, cost what it might.

Night after night, he would get out of his bed and follow that spectral old fraud about the house. Each night, the old man would indicate a different place; and, on each following day, my brother-in-law would proceed to break up the mill at the point indicated, and look for the treasure. At the end of three weeks, there was not a room in the mill fit to live in. Every wall had been pulled down, every floor had been taken up, every ceiling had had a hole knocked in it. And then, as suddenly as they had begun, the ghost's visits ceased; and my brother-in-law was left in peace, to rebuild the place at his leisure.

"What induced the old image to play such a silly trick upon a family man and a ratepayer?" Ah! that's just what I cannot tell you.

Some said that the ghost of the wicked old man had done it to punish my brother-in-law for not believing in him at first; while others held that the apparition was probably that of some deceased local plumber and glazier, who would naturally take an interest in seeing a house knocked about and spoilt. But nobody knew anything for certain.

INTERLUDE

We had some more punch, and then the curate told us a story.

I could not make head or tail of the curate's story, so I cannot retail it to you. We none of us could make head or tail of that story. It was a good story enough, so far as material went. There seemed to be an enormous amount of plot, and enough incident to have made a dozen novels. I never before heard a story containing so much incident, nor one dealing with so many varied characters.

I should say that every human being our curate had ever known or met, or heard of, was brought into that story. There were simply hundreds of them. Every five seconds he would introduce into the tale a completely fresh collection of characters accompanied by a brand new set of incidents.

This was the sort of story it was:-

"Well, then, my uncle went into the garden, and got his gun, but, of course, it wasn't there, and Scroggins said he didn't believe it."

"Didn't believe what? Who's Scroggins?"

"Scroggins! Oh, why he was the other man, you know--it was wife."

"WHAT was his wife--what's SHE got to do with it?"

"Why, that's what I'm telling you. It was she that found the hat.

She'd come up with her cousin to London--her cousin was my sister-in-law, and the other niece had married a man named Evans, and Evans, after it was all over, had taken the box round to Mr. Jacobs', because Jacobs' father had seen the man, when he was alive, and when he was dead, Joseph--"

"Now look here, never you mind Evans and the box; what's become of your uncle and the gun?"

"The gun! What gun?"

"Why, the gun that your uncle used to keep in the garden, and that wasn't there. What did he do with it? Did he kill any of these people with it--these Jacobses and Evanses and Scrogginses and Josephses? Because, if so, it was a good and useful work, and we should enjoy hearing about it."

"No--oh no--how could he?--he had been built up alive in the wall, you know, and when Edward IV spoke to the abbot about it, my sister said that in her then state of health she could not and would not, as it was endangering the child's life. So they christened it Horatio, after her own son, who had been killed at Waterloo before he was born, and Lord Napier himself said--"

"Look here, do you know what you are talking about?" we asked him at this point.

He said "No," but he knew it was every word of it true, because his aunt had seen it herself. Whereupon we covered him over with the tablecloth, and he went to sleep.

And then Uncle told us a story.

Uncle said his was a real story.

THE GHOST OF THE BLUE CHAMBER

(MY UNCLE'S STORY)

"I don't want to make you fellows nervous," began my uncle in a peculiarly impressive, not to say blood-curdling, tone of voice, "and if you would rather that I did not mention it, I won't; but, as a matter of fact, this very house, in which we are now sitting, is haunted."

"You don't say that!" exclaimed Mr. Coombes.

"What's the use of your saying I don't say it when I have just said it?" retorted my uncle somewhat pettishly. "You do talk so foolishly. I tell you the house is haunted. Regularly on Christmas Eve the Blue Chamber [they called the room next to the nursery the 'blue chamber,' at my uncle's, most of the toilet service being of that shade] is haunted by the ghost of a sinful man--a man who once killed a Christmas wait with a lump of coal."

"How did he do it?" asked Mr. Coombes, with eager anxiousness. "Was it difficult?"

"I do not know how he did it," replied my uncle; "he did not explain the process. The wait had taken up a position just inside the front gate, and was singing a ballad. It is presumed that, when he opened his mouth for B flat, the lump of coal was thrown by the sinful man from one of the windows, and that it went down the wait's throat and choked him."

"You want to be a good shot, but it is certainly worth trying," murmured Mr. Coombes thoughtfully.

"But that was not his only crime, alas!" added my uncle. "Prior to that he had killed a solo cornet-player."

"No! Is that really a fact?" exclaimed Mr. Coombes.

"Of course it's a fact," answered my uncle testily; "at all events, as much a fact as you can expect to get in a case of this sort.

"How very captious you are this evening. The circumstantial evidence was overwhelming. The poor fellow, the cornet-player, had been in the neighbourhood barely a month. Old Mr. Bishop, who kept the 'Jolly Sand Boys' at the time, and from whom I had the story, said he had never known a more hard-working and energetic solo cornet-player. He, the cornet-player, only knew two tunes, but Mr. Bishop said that the man could not have played with more vigour, or for more hours in a day, if he had known forty. The two tunes he did play were "Annie Laurie" and "Home, Sweet Home"; and as regarded his performance of the former melody, Mr. Bishop said that a mere child could have told what it was meant for.

"This musician--this poor, friendless artist used to come regularly and play in this street just opposite for two hours every evening. One evening he was seen, evidently in response to an invitation, going into this very house, BUT WAS NEVER SEEN COMING OUT OF IT!"

"Did the townsfolk try offering any reward for his recovery?" asked Mr. Coombes.

"Not a ha'penny," replied my uncle.

"Another summer," continued my uncle, "a German band visited here, intending--so they announced on their arrival--to stay till the autumn.

"On the second day from their arrival, the whole company, as fine and healthy a body of men as one could wish to see, were invited to dinner by this sinful man, and, after spending the whole of the next twenty-four hours in bed, left the town a broken and dyspeptic crew; the parish doctor, who had attended them, giving it as his opinion that it was doubtful if they would, any of them, be fit to play an air again."

"You--you don't know the recipe, do you?" asked Mr. Coombes.

"Unfortunately I do not," replied my uncle; "but the chief ingredient was said to have been railway refreshment-room pork-pie.

"I forget the man's other crimes," my uncle went on; "I used to know them all at one time, but my memory is not what it was. I do not, however, believe I am doing his memory an injustice in believing that he was not entirely unconnected with the death, and subsequent burial, of a gentleman who used to play the harp with his toes; and that neither was he altogether unresponsible for the lonely grave of an unknown stranger who had once visited the neighbourhood, an Italian peasant lad, a performer upon the barrel- organ.

"Every Christmas Eve," said my uncle, cleaving with low impressive tones the strange awed silence that, like a shadow, seemed to have slowly stolen into and settled down upon the room, "the ghost of this sinful man haunts the Blue Chamber, in this very house. There, from midnight until cock-crow, amid wild muffled shrieks and groans and mocking laughter and the ghostly sound of horrid blows, it does fierce phantom fight with the spirits of the solo cornet- player and the murdered wait, assisted at intervals, by the shades of the German band; while the ghost of the strangled harpist plays mad ghostly melodies with ghostly toes on the ghost of a broken harp.

Uncle said the Blue Chamber was comparatively useless as a sleeping-apartment on Christmas Eve.

"Hark!" said uncle, raising a warning hand towards the ceiling, while we held our breath, and listened; "Hark! I believe they are at it now--in the BLUE CHAMBER!"

THE BLUE CHAMBER

I rose up, and said that I would sleep in the Blue Chamber.

Before I tell you my own story, however--the story of what happened in the Blue Chamber--I would wish to preface it with -

A PERSONAL EXPLANATION

I feel a good deal of hesitation about telling you this story of my own. You see it is not a story like the other stories that I have been telling you, or rather that Teddy Biffles, Mr. Coombes, and my uncle have been telling you: it is a true story. It is not a story told by a person sitting round a fire on Christmas Eve, drinking whisky punch: it is a record of events that actually happened.

Indeed, it is not a 'story' at all, in the commonly accepted meaning of the word: it is a report. It is, I feel, almost out of place in a book of this kind. It is more suitable to a biography, or an English history.

There is another thing that makes it difficult for me to tell you this story, and that is, that it is all about myself. In telling you this story, I shall have to keep on talking about myself; and talking about ourselves is what we modern-day authors have a strong objection to doing. If we literary men of the new school have one praiseworthy yearning more ever present to our minds than another it is the yearning never to appear in the slightest degree egotistical.

I myself, so I am told, carry this coyness--this shrinking reticence concerning anything connected with my own personality, almost too far; and people grumble at me because of it. People come to me and say -

"Well, now, why don't you talk about yourself a bit? That's what we want to read about. Tell us something about yourself."

But I have always replied, "No." It is not that I do not think the subject an interesting one. I cannot myself conceive of any topic more likely to prove fascinating to the world as a whole, or at all events to the cultured portion of it. But I will not do it, on principle. It is inartistic, and it sets a bad example to the younger men. Other writers (a few of them) do it, I know; but I will not--not as a rule.

Under ordinary circumstances, therefore, I should not tell you this story at all. I should say to myself, "No! It is a good story, it is a moral story, it is a strange, weird, enthralling sort of a story; and the public, I know, would like to hear it; and I should like to tell it to them; but it is all about myself--about what I said, and what I saw, and what I did, and I cannot do it. My retiring, anti-egotistical nature will not permit me to talk in this way about myself."

But the circumstances surrounding this story are not ordinary, and there are reasons prompting me, in spite of my modesty, to rather welcome the opportunity of relating it.

As I stated at the beginning, there has been unpleasantness in our family over this party of ours, and, as regards myself in particular, and my share in the events I am now about to set forth, gross injustice has been done me.

As a means of replacing my character in its proper light--of dispelling the clouds of calumny and misconception with which it has been darkened, I feel that my best course is to give a simple, dignified narration of the plain facts, and allow the unprejudiced to judge for themselves. My chief object, I candidly confess, is to clear myself from unjust aspersion. Spurred by this motive--and I think it is an honourable and a right motive--I find I am enabled to overcome my usual repugnance to talking about myself, and can thus tell -

MY OWN STORY

As soon as my uncle had finished his story, I, as I have already told you, rose up and said that *I* would sleep in the Blue Chamber that very night.

"Never!" cried my uncle, springing up. "You shall not put yourself in this deadly peril. Besides, the bed is not made."

"Never mind the bed," I replied. "I have lived in furnished apartments for gentlemen, and have been accustomed to sleep on beds that have never been made from one year's end to the other. Do not thwart me in my resolve. I am young, and have had a clear conscience now for over a month. The spirits will not harm me. I may even do them some little good, and induce them to be quiet and go away. Besides, I should like to see the show."

Saying which, I sat down again. (How Mr. Coombes came to be in my chair, instead of at the other side of the room, where he had been all the evening; and why he never offered to apologise when I sat right down on top of him; and why young Biffles should have tried to palm himself off upon me as my Uncle John, and induced me, under that erroneous impression, to shake him by the hand for nearly three minutes, and tell him that I had always regarded him as father,--are matters that, to this day, I have never been able to fully understand.)

They tried to dissuade me from what they termed my foolhardy enterprise, but I remained firm, and claimed my privilege. I was 'the guest.' 'The guest' always sleeps in the haunted chamber on Christmas Eve; it is his perquisite.

They said that if I put it on that footing, they had, of course, no answer; and they lighted a candle for me, and accompanied me upstairs in a body.

Whether elevated by the feeling that I was doing a noble action, or animated by a mere general consciousness of rectitude, is not for me to say, but I went upstairs that night with remarkable buoyancy. It was as much as I could do to stop at the landing when I came to it; I felt I wanted to go on up to the roof. But, with the help of the banisters, I restrained my ambition, wished them all good- night, and went in and shut the door.

Things began to go wrong with me from the very first. The candle tumbled out of the candlestick before my hand was off the lock. It kept on tumbling out of the candlestick, and every time I picked put it up and put it in, it tumbled out again: I never saw such a slippery candle. I gave up attempting to use the candlestick at last, and carried the candle about in my hand; and, even then, it would not keep upright. So I got wild and threw it out of window, and undressed and went to bed in the dark.

I did not go to sleep,--I did not feel sleepy at all,--I lay on my back, looking up at the ceiling, and thinking of things. I wish I could remember some of the ideas that came to me as I lay there, because they were so amusing. I laughed at them myself till the bed shook.

I had been lying like this for half an hour or so, and had forgotten all about the ghost, when, on casually casting my eyes round the room, I noticed for the first time a singularly contented-looking phantom, sitting in the easy-chair by the fire, smoking the ghost of a long clay pipe.

I fancied for the moment, as most people would under similar circumstances, that I must be dreaming. I sat up, and rubbed my eyes.

No! It was a ghost, clear enough. I could see the back of the chair through his body. He looked over towards me, took the shadowy pipe from his lips, and nodded.

The most surprising part of the whole thing to me was that I did not feel in the least alarmed. If anything, I was rather pleased to see him. It was company.

I said, "Good evening. It's been a cold day!"

He said he had not noticed it himself, but dared say I was right.

We remained silent for a few seconds, and then, wishing to put it pleasantly, I said, "I believe I have the honour of addressing the ghost of the gentleman who had the accident with the wait?"

He smiled, and said it was very good of me to remember it. One wait was not much to boast of, but still, every little helped.

I was somewhat staggered at his answer. I had expected a groan of remorse. The ghost appeared, on the contrary, to be rather conceited over the business. I thought that, as he had taken my reference to the wait so quietly, perhaps he would not be offended if I questioned him about the organ-grinder. I felt curious about that poor boy.

"Is it true," I asked, "that you had a hand in the death of that Italian peasant lad who came to the town once with a barrel-organ that played nothing but Scotch airs?"

He quite fired up. "Had a hand in it!" he exclaimed indignantly. "Who has dared to pretend that he assisted me? I murdered the youth myself. Nobody helped me. Alone I did it. Show me the man who says I didn't."

I calmed him. I assured him that I had never, in my own mind, doubted that he was the real and only assassin, and I went on and asked him what he had done with the body of the cornet-player he had killed.

He said, "To which one may you be alluding?"

"Oh, were there any more then?" I inquired.

He smiled, and gave a little cough. He said he did not like to appear to be boasting, but that, counting trombones, there were seven.

"Dear me!" I replied, "you must have had quite a busy time of it, one way and another."

He said that perhaps he ought not to be the one to say so, but that really, speaking of ordinary middle-society, he thought there were few ghosts who could look back upon a life of more sustained usefulness.

He puffed away in silence for a few seconds, while I sat watching him. I had never seen a ghost smoking a pipe before, that I could remember, and it interested me.

I asked him what tobacco he used, and he replied, "The ghost of cut cavendish, as a rule."

He explained that the ghost of all the tobacco that a man smoked in life belonged to him when he became dead. He said he himself had smoked a good deal of cut cavendish when he was alive, so that he was well supplied with the ghost of it now.

I observed that it was a useful thing to know that, and I made up my mind to smoke as much tobacco as ever I could before I died.

I thought I might as well start at once, so I said I would join him in a pipe, and he said, "Do, old man"; and I reached over and got out the necessary paraphernalia from my coat pocket and lit up.

We grew quite chummy after that, and he told me all his crimes. He said he had lived next door once to a young lady who was learning to play the guitar, while a gentleman who practised on the bass-viol lived opposite. And he, with fiendish cunning, had introduced these two unsuspecting young people to one another, and had persuaded them to elope with each other against their parents' wishes, and take their musical instruments with them; and they had done so, and, before the honeymoon was over, SHE had broken his head with the bass-viol, and HE had tried to cram the guitar down her throat, and had injured her for life.

My friend said he used to lure muffin-men into the passage and then stuff them with their own wares till they burst and died. He said he had quieted eighteen that way.

Young men and women who recited long and dreary poems at evening parties, and callow youths who walked about the streets late at night, playing concertinas, he used to get together and poison in batches of ten, so as to save expense; and park orators and temperance lecturers he used to shut up six in a small room with a glass of water and a collection-box apiece, and let them talk each other to death.

It did one good to listen to him.

I asked him when he expected the other ghosts--the ghosts of the wait and the cornet-player, and the German band that Uncle John had mentioned. He smiled, and said they would never come again, any of them.

I said, "Why; isn't it true, then, that they meet you here every Christmas Eve for a row?"

He replied that it WAS true. Every Christmas Eve, for twenty-five years, had he and they fought in that room; but they would never trouble him nor anybody else again. One by one, had he laid them out, spoilt, and utterly useless for all haunting purposes. He had finished off the last German-band ghost that very evening, just before I came upstairs, and had thrown what was left of it out through the slit between the window-sashes. He said it would never be worth calling a ghost again.

"I suppose you will still come yourself, as usual?" I said. "They would be sorry to miss you, I know."

"Oh, I don't know," he replied; "there's nothing much to come for now. Unless," he added kindly, "YOU are going to be here. I'll come if you will sleep here next Christmas Eve."

"I have taken a liking to you," he continued; "you don't fly off, screeching, when you see a party, and your hair doesn't stand on end. You've no idea," he said, "how sick I am of seeing people's hair standing on end."

He said it irritated him.

Just then a slight noise reached us from the yard below, and he started and turned deathly black.

"You are ill," I cried, springing towards him; "tell me the best thing to do for you. Shall I drink some brandy, and give you the ghost of it?"

He remained silent, listening intently for a moment, and then he gave a sigh of relief, and the shade came back to his cheek.

"It's all right," he murmured; "I was afraid it was the cock."

"Oh, it's too early for that," I said. "Why, it's only the middle of the night."

"Oh, that doesn't make any difference to those cursed chickens," he replied bitterly. "They would just as soon crow in the middle of the night as at any other time--sooner, if they thought it would spoil a chap's evening out. I believe they do it on purpose."

He said a friend of his, the ghost of a man who had killed a water-rate collector, used to haunt a house in Long Acre, where they kept fowls in the cellar, and every time a policeman went by and flashed his bull's-eye down the grating, the old cock there would fancy it was the sun, and start crowing like mad; when, of course, the poor ghost had to dissolve, and it would, in consequence, get back home sometimes as early as one o'clock in the morning, swearing fearfully because it had only been out for an hour.

I agreed that it seemed very unfair.

"Oh, it's an absurd arrangement altogether," he continued, quite angrily. "I can't imagine what our old man could have been thinking of when he made it. As I have said to him, over and over again, 'Have a fixed time, and let everybody stick to it--say four o'clock in summer, and six in winter. Then one would know what one was about.'"

"How do you manage when there isn't any cock handy?" I inquired.

He was on the point of replying, when again he started and listened. This time I distinctly heard Mr. Bowles's cock, next door, crow twice.

"There you are," he said, rising and reaching for his hat; "that's the sort of thing we have to put up with. What IS the time?"

I looked at my watch, and found it was half-past three.

"I thought as much," he muttered. "I'll wring that blessed bird's neck if I get hold of it." And he prepared to go.

"If you can wait half a minute," I said, getting out of bed, "I'll go a bit of the way with you."

"It's very good of you," he rejoined, pausing, "but it seems unkind to drag you out."

"Not at all," I replied; "I shall like a walk." And I partially dressed myself, and took my umbrella; and he put his arm through mine, and we went out together.

Just by the gate we met Jones, one of the local constables.

"Good-night, Jones," I said (I always feel affable at Christmas-time).

"Good-night, sir," answered the man a little gruffly, I thought. "May I ask what you're a-doing of?"

"Oh, it's all right," I responded, with a wave of my umbrella; "I'm just seeing my friend part of the way home."

He said, "What friend?"

"Oh, ah, of course," I laughed; "I forgot. He's invisible to you. He is the ghost of the gentleman that killed the wait. I'm just going to the corner with him."

"Ah, I don't think I would, if I was you, sir," said Jones severely. "If you take my advice, you'll say good-bye to your friend here, and go back indoors. Perhaps you are not aware that you are walking about with nothing on but a night-shirt and a pair of boots and an opera-hat. Where's your trousers?"

I did not like the man's manner at all. I said, "Jones! I don't wish to have to report you, but it seems to me you've been drinking. My trousers are where a man's trousers ought to be--on his legs. I distinctly remember putting them on."

"Well, you haven't got them on now," he retorted.

"I beg your pardon," I replied. "I tell you I have; I think I ought to know."

"I think so, too," he answered, "but you evidently don't. Now you come along indoors with me, and don't let's have any more of it."

Uncle John came to the door at this point, having been awaked, I suppose, by the altercation; and, at the same moment, Aunt Maria appeared at the window in her nightcap.

I explained the constable's mistake to them, treating the matter as lightly as I could, so as not to get the man into trouble, and I turned for confirmation to the ghost.

He was gone! He had left me without a word--without even saying good-bye!

It struck me as so unkind, his having gone off in that way, that I burst into tears; and Uncle John came out, and led me back into the house.

On reaching my room, I discovered that Jones was right. I had not put on my trousers, after all. They were still hanging over the bed-rail. I suppose, in my anxiety not to keep the ghost waiting, I must have forgotten them.

Such are the plain facts of the case, out of which it must, doubtless, to the healthy, charitable mind appear impossible that calumny could spring.

But it has.

Persons--I say 'persons'--have professed themselves unable to understand the simple circumstances herein narrated, except in the light of explanations at once misleading and insulting. Slurs have been cast and aspersions made on me by those of my own flesh and blood.

But I bear no ill-feeling. I merely, as I have said, set forth this statement for the purpose of clearing my character from injurious suspicion.

THE END

TOMMY AND CO.

STORY THE FIRST

PETER HOPE PLANS HIS PROSPECTUS

"Come in!" said Peter Hope.

Peter Hope was tall and thin, clean-shaven but for a pair of side whiskers close-cropped and terminating just below the ear, with hair of the kind referred to by sympathetic barbers as "getting a little thin on the top, sir," but arranged with economy, that everywhere is poverty's true helpmate. About Mr. Peter Hope's linen, which was white though somewhat frayed, there was a self- assertiveness that invariably arrested the attention of even the most casual observer. Decidedly there was too much of it--its ostentation aided and abetted by the retiring nature of the cut- away coat, whose chief aim clearly was to slip off and disappear behind its owner's back. "I'm a poor old thing," it seemed to say. "I don't shine--or, rather, I shine too much among these up-to-date young modes. I only hamper you. You would be much more comfortable without me." To persuade it to accompany him, its proprietor had to employ force, keeping fastened the lowest of its three buttons. At every step, it struggled for its liberty. Another characteristic of Peter's, linking him to the past, was his black silk cravat, secured by a couple of gold pins chained together. Watching him as he now sat writing, his long legs encased in tightly strapped grey trousering, crossed beneath the table, the lamplight falling on his fresh-complexioned face, upon the shapely hand that steadied the half-written sheet, a stranger might have rubbed his eyes, wondering by what hallucination he thus found himself in presence seemingly of some young beau belonging to the early 'forties; but looking closer, would have seen the many wrinkles.

"Come in!" repeated Mr. Peter Hope, raising his voice, but not his eyes.

The door opened, and a small, white face, out of which gleamed a pair of bright, black eyes, was thrust sideways into the room.

"Come in!" repeated Mr. Peter Hope for the third time. "Who is it?"

A hand not over clean, grasping a greasy cloth cap, appeared below the face.

"Not ready yet," said Mr. Hope. "Sit down and wait."

The door opened wider, and the whole of the figure slid in and, closing the door behind it, sat itself down upon the extreme edge of the chair nearest.

"Which are you--Central News or Courier?" demanded Mr. Peter Hope, but without looking up from his work.

The bright, black eyes, which had just commenced an examination of the room by a careful scrutiny of the smoke-grimed ceiling, descended and fixed themselves upon the one clearly defined bald patch upon his head that, had he been aware of it, would have troubled Mr. Peter Hope. But the full, red lips beneath the turned-up nose remained motionless.

That he had received no answer to his question appeared to have escaped the attention of Mr. Peter Hope. The thin, white hand moved steadily to and fro across the paper. Three more sheets were added to those upon the floor. Then Mr. Peter Hope pushed back his chair and turned his gaze for the first time upon his visitor.

To Peter Hope, hack journalist, long familiar with the genus Printer's Devil, small white faces, tangled hair, dirty hands, and greasy caps were common objects in the neighbourhood of that buried rivulet, the Fleet. But this was a new species. Peter Hope sought his spectacles, found them after some trouble under a heap of newspapers, adjusted them upon his high, arched nose, leant forward, and looked long and up and down.

"God bless my soul!" said Mr. Peter Hope. "What is it?"

The figure rose to its full height of five foot one and came forward slowly.

Over a tight-fitting garibaldi of blue silk, excessively decollete, it wore what once had been a boy's pepper-and-salt jacket. A worsted comforter wound round the neck still left a wide expanse of throat showing above the garibaldi. Below the jacket fell a long, black skirt, the train of which had been looped up about the waist and fastened with a cricket-belt.

"Who are you? What do you want?" asked Mr. Peter Hope.

For answer, the figure, passing the greasy cap into its other hand, stooped down and, seizing the front of the long skirt, began to haul it up.

"Don't do that!" said Mr. Peter Hope. "I say, you know, you--"

But by this time the skirt had practically disappeared, leaving to view a pair of much-patched trousers, diving into the right-hand pocket of which the dirty hand drew forth a folded paper, which, having opened and smoothed out, it laid upon the desk.

Mr. Peter Hope pushed up his spectacles till they rested on his eyebrows, and read aloud--"'Steak and Kidney Pie, 4d.; Do. (large size), 6d.; Boiled Mutton--'"

"That's where I've been for the last two weeks," said the figure,--"Hammond's Eating House!"

The listener noted with surprise that the voice--though it told him as plainly as if he had risen and drawn aside the red rep curtains, that outside in Gough Square the yellow fog lay like the ghost of a dead sea--betrayed no Cockney accent, found no difficulty with its aitches.

"You ask for Emma. She'll say a good word for me. She told me so."

"But, my good--" Mr. Peter Hope, checking himself, sought again the assistance of his glasses. The glasses being unable to decide the point, their owner had to put the question bluntly:

"Are you a boy or a girl?"

"I dunno."

"You don't know!"

"What's the difference?"

Mr. Peter Hope stood up, and taking the strange figure by the shoulders, turned it round slowly twice, apparently under the impression that the process might afford to him some clue. But it did not.

"What is your name?"

"Tommy."

"Tommy what?"

"Anything you like. I dunno. I've had so many of 'em."

"What do you want? What have you come for?"

"You're Mr. Hope, ain't you, second floor, 16, Gough Square?"

"That is my name."

"You want somebody to do for you?"

"You mean a housekeeper!"

"Didn't say anything about housekeeper. Said you wanted somebody to do for you--cook and clean the place up. Heard 'em talking about it in the shop this afternoon. Old lady in green bonnet was asking Mother Hammond if she knew of anyone."

"Mrs. Postwhistle--yes, I did ask her to look out for someone for me. Why, do you know of anyone? Have you been sent by anybody?"

"You don't want anything too 'laborate in the way o' cooking? You was a simple old chap, so they said; not much trouble."

"No--no. I don't want much--someone clean and respectable. But why couldn't she come herself? Who is it?"

"Well, what's wrong about me?"

"I beg your pardon," said Mr. Peter Hope.

"Why won't I do? I can make beds and clean rooms--all that sort o' thing. As for cooking, I've got a natural aptitude for it. You ask Emma; she'll tell you. You don't want nothing 'laborate?"

"Elizabeth," said Mr. Peter Hope, as he crossed and, taking up the poker, proceeded to stir the fire, "are we awake or asleep?"

Elizabeth thus appealed to, raised herself on her hind legs and dug her claws into her master's thigh. Mr. Hope's trousers being thin, it was the most practical answer she could have given him.

"Done a lot of looking after other people for their benefit," continued Tommy. "Don't see why I shouldn't do it for my own."

"My dear--I do wish I knew whether you were a boy or a girl. Do you seriously suggest that I should engage you as my housekeeper?" asked Mr. Peter Hope, now upright with his back to the fire.

"I'd do for you all right," persisted Tommy. "You give me my grub and a shake-down and, say, sixpence a week, and I'll grumble less than most of 'em."

"Don't be ridiculous," said Mr. Peter Hope.

"You won't try me?"

"Of course not; you must be mad."

"All right. No harm done." The dirty hand reached out towards the desk, and possessing itself again of Hammond's Bill of Fare, commenced the operations necessary for bearing it away in safety.

"Here's a shilling for you," said Mr. Peter Hope.

"Rather not," said Tommy. "Thanks all the same."

"Nonsense!" said Mr. Peter Hope.

"Rather not," repeated Tommy. "Never know where that sort of thing may lead you to."

"All right," said Mr. Peter Hope, replacing the coin in his pocket. "Don't!"

The figure moved towards the door.

"Wait a minute. Wait a minute," said Mr. Peter Hope irritably.

The figure, with its hand upon the door, stood still.

"Are you going back to Hammond's?"

"No. I've finished there. Only took me on for a couple o' weeks, while one of the gals was ill. She came back this morning."

"Who are your people?"

Tommy seemed puzzled. "What d'ye mean?"

"Well, whom do you live with?"

"Nobody."

"You've got nobody to look after you--to take care of you?"

"Take care of me! D'ye think I'm a bloomin' kid?"

"Then where are you going to now?"

"Going? Out."

Peter Hope's irritation was growing.

"I mean, where are you going to sleep? Got any money for a lodging?"

"Yes, I've got some money," answered Tommy. "But I don't think much o' lodgings. Not a particular nice class as you meet there. I shall sleep out to-night. 'Tain't raining."

Elizabeth uttered a piercing cry.

"Serves you right!" growled Peter savagely. "How can anyone help treading on you when you will get just between one's legs. Told you of it a hundred times."

The truth of the matter was that Peter was becoming very angry with himself. For no reason whatever, as he told himself, his memory would persist in wandering to Ilford Cemetery, in a certain desolate corner of which lay a fragile little woman whose lungs had been but ill adapted to breathing London fogs; with, on the top of her, a still smaller and still more fragile mite of humanity that, in compliment to its only relative worth a penny-piece, had been christened Thomas--a name common enough in all conscience, as Peter had reminded himself more than once. In the name of common sense, what had dead and buried Tommy Hope to do with this affair? The whole thing was the veriest sentiment, and sentiment was Mr. Peter Hope's abomination. Had he not penned articles innumerable pointing out its baneful influence upon the age? Had he not always condemned it, wherever he had come across it in play or book? Now and then the suspicion had crossed Peter's mind that, in spite of all this, he was somewhat of a sentimentalist himself--things had suggested this to him. The fear had always made him savage.

"You wait here till I come back," he growled, seizing the astonished Tommy by the worsted comforter and spinning it into the centre of the room. "Sit down, and don't you dare to move." And Peter went out and slammed the door behind him.

"Bit off his chump, ain't he?" remarked Tommy to Elizabeth, as the sound of Peter's descending footsteps died away. People had a way of addressing remarks to Elizabeth. Something in her manner invited this.

"Oh, well, it's all in the day's work," commented Tommy cheerfully, and sat down as bid.

Five minutes passed, maybe ten. Then Peter returned, accompanied by a large, restful lady, to whom surprise--one felt it instinctively--had always been, and always would remain, an unknown quantity.

Tommy rose.

"That's the--the article," explained Peter.

Mrs. Postwhistle compressed her lips and slightly tossed her head. It was the attitude of not ill-natured contempt from which she regarded most human affairs.

"That's right," said Mrs. Postwhistle; "I remember seeing 'er there--leastways, it was an 'er right enough then. What 'ave you done with your clothes?"

"They weren't mine," explained Tommy. "They were things what Mrs. Hammond had lent me."

"Is that your own?" asked Mrs. Postwhistle, indicating the blue silk garibaldi.

"Yes."

"What went with it?"

"Tights. They were too far gone."

"What made you give up the tumbling business and go to Mrs. 'Ammond's?"

"It gave me up. Hurt myself."

"Who were you with last?"

"Martini troupe."

"And before that?"

"Oh! heaps of 'em."

"Nobody ever told you whether you was a boy or a girl?"

"Nobody as I'd care to believe. Some of them called me the one, some of them the other. It depended upon what was wanted."

"How old are you?"

"I dunno."

Mrs. Postwhistle turned to Peter, who was jingling keys.

"Well, there's the bed upstairs. It's for you to decide."

"What I don't want to do," explained Peter, sinking his voice to a confidential whisper, "is to make a fool of myself."

"That's always a good rule," agreed Mrs. Postwhistle, "for those to whom it's possible."

"Anyhow," said Peter, "one night can't do any harm. To-morrow we can think what's to be done."

"To-morrow" had always been Peter's lucky day. At the mere mention of the magic date his spirits invariably rose. He now turned upon Tommy a countenance from which all hesitation was banished.

"Very well, Tommy," said Mr. Peter Hope, "you can sleep here to-night. Go with Mrs. Postwhistle, and she'll show you your room."

The black eyes shone.

"You're going to give me a trial?"

"We'll talk about all that to-morrow." The black eyes clouded.

"Look here. I tell you straight, it ain't no good."

"What do you mean? What isn't any good?" demanded Peter.

"You'll want to send me to prison."

"To prison!"

"Oh, yes. You'll call it a school, I know. You ain't the first that's tried that on. It won't work." The bright, black eyes were flashing passionately. "I ain't done any harm. I'm willing to work. I can keep myself. I always have. What's it got to do with anybody else?"

Had the bright, black eyes retained their expression of passionate defiance, Peter Hope might have retained his common sense. Only Fate arranged that instead they should suddenly fill with wild tears. And at sight of them Peter's common sense went out of the room disgusted, and there was born the history of many things.

"Don't be silly," said Peter. "You didn't understand. Of course I'm going to give you a trial. You're going to 'do' for me. I merely meant that we'd leave the details till to-morrow. Come, housekeepers don't cry."

The little wet face looked up.

"You mean it? Honour bright?"

"Honour bright. Now go and wash yourself. Then you shall get me my supper."

The odd figure, still heaving from its paroxysm of sobs, stood up.

"And I have my grub, my lodging, and sixpence a week?"

"Yes, yes; I think that's a fair arrangement," agreed Mr. Peter Hope, considering. "Don't you, Mrs. Postwhistle?"

"With a frock--or a suit of trousers--thrown in," suggested Mrs. Postwhistle. "It's generally done."

"If it's the custom, certainly," agreed Mr. Peter Hope. "Sixpence a week and clothes."

And this time it was Peter that, in company with Elizabeth, sat waiting the return of Tommy.

"I rather hope," said Peter, "it's a boy. It was the fogs, you know. If only I could have afforded to send him away!"

Elizabeth looked thoughtful. The door opened.

"Ah! that's better, much better," said Mr. Peter Hope. "'Pon my word, you look quite respectable."

By the practical Mrs. Postwhistle a working agreement, benefiting both parties, had been arrived at with the long-trained skirt; while an ample shawl arranged with judgment disguised the nakedness that lay below. Peter, a fastidious gentleman, observed with satisfaction that the hands, now clean, had been well cared for.

"Give me that cap," said Peter. He threw it in the glowing fire. It burned brightly, diffusing strange odours.

"There's a travelling cap of mine hanging up in the passage. You can wear that for the present. Take this half-sovereign and get me some cold meat and beer for supper. You'll find everything else you want in that sideboard or else in the kitchen. Don't ask me a hundred questions, and don't make a noise," and Peter went back to his work.

"Good idea, that half-sovereign," said Peter. "Shan't be bothered with 'Master Tommy' any more, don't expect. Starting a nursery at our time of life. Madness." Peter's pen scratched and spluttered. Elizabeth kept an eye upon the door.

"Quarter of an hour," said Peter, looking at his watch. "Told you so." The article on which Peter was now engaged appeared to be of a worrying nature.

"Then why," said Peter, "why did he refuse that shilling? Artfulness," concluded Peter, "pure artfulness. Elizabeth, old girl, we've got out of this business cheaply. Good idea, that half-sovereign." Peter gave vent to a chuckle that had the effect of alarming Elizabeth.

But luck evidently was not with Peter that night.

"Pingle's was sold out," explained Tommy, entering with parcels; "had to go to Bow's in Farringdon Street."

"Oh!" said Peter, without looking up.

Tommy passed through into the little kitchen behind. Peter wrote on rapidly, making up for lost time.

"Good!" murmured Peter, smiling to himself, "that's a neat phrase. That ought to irritate them."

Now, as he wrote, while with noiseless footsteps Tommy, unseen behind him, moved to and fro and in and out the little kitchen, there came to Peter Hope this very curious experience: it felt to him as if for a long time he had been ill--so ill as not even to have been aware of it--and that now he was beginning to be himself again; consciousness of things returning to him. This solidly furnished, long, oak-panelled room with its air of old-world dignity and repose--this sober, kindly room in which for more than half his life he had lived and worked--why had he forgotten it? It came forward greeting him with an amused smile, as of some old friend long parted from. The faded photos, in stiff, wooden frames upon the chimney-piece, among them that of the fragile little woman with the unadaptable lungs.

"God bless my soul!" said Mr. Peter Hope, pushing back his chair. "It's thirty years ago. How time does fly! Why, let me see, I must be--"

"D'you like it with a head on it?" demanded Tommy, who had been waiting patiently for signs.

Peter shook himself awake and went to his supper.

A bright idea occurred to Peter in the night. "Of course; why didn't I think of it before? Settle the question at once." Peter fell into an easy sleep.

"Tommy," said Peter, as he sat himself down to breakfast the next morning. "By-the-by," asked Peter with a puzzled expression, putting down his cup, "what is this?"

"Cauffee," informed him Tommy. "You said cauffee."

"Oh!" replied Peter. "For the future, Tommy, if you don't mind, I will take tea of a morning."

"All the same to me," explained the agreeable Tommy, "it's your breakfast."

"What I was about to say," continued Peter, "was that you're not looking very well, Tommy."

"I'm all right," asserted Tommy; "never nothing the matter with me."

"Not that you know of, perhaps; but one can be in a very bad way, Tommy, without being aware of it. I cannot have anyone about me that I am not sure is in thoroughly sound health."

"If you mean you've changed your mind and want to get rid of me--" began Tommy, with its chin in the air.

"I don't want any of your uppishness," snapped Peter, who had wound himself up for the occasion to a degree of assertiveness that surprised even himself. "If you are a thoroughly strong and healthy person, as I think you are, I shall be very glad to retain your services. But upon that point I must be satisfied. It is the custom," explained Peter. "It is always done in good families. Run round to this address"-- Peter wrote it upon a leaf of his notebook--"and ask Dr. Smith to come and see me before he begins his round. You go at once, and don't let us have any argument."

"That is the way to talk to that young person--clearly," said Peter to himself, listening to Tommy's footsteps dying down the stairs.

Hearing the street-door slam, Peter stole into the kitchen and brewed himself a cup of coffee.

Dr. Smith, who had commenced life as Herr Schmidt, but who in consequence of difference of opinion with his Government was now an Englishman with strong Tory prejudices, had but one sorrow: it was that strangers would mistake him for a foreigner. He was short and stout, with bushy eyebrows and a grey moustache, and looked so fierce that children cried when they saw him, until he patted them on the head and addressed them as "mein leedle frent" in a voice so soft and tender that they had to leave off howling just to wonder where it came from. He and Peter, who was a vehement Radical, had been cronies for many years, and had each an indulgent contempt for the other's understanding, tempered by a sincere affection for one another they would have found it difficult to account for.

"What tink you is de matter wid de leedle wench?" demanded Dr. Smith, Peter having opened the case. Peter glanced round the room. The kitchen door was closed.

"How do you know it's a wench?"

The eyes beneath the bushy brows grew rounder. "If id is not a wench, why dress it--"

"Haven't dressed it," interrupted Peter. "Just what I'm waiting to do--so soon as I know."

And Peter recounted the events of the preceding evening.

Tears gathered in the doctor's small, round eyes. His absurd sentimentalism was the quality in his friend that most irritated Peter.

"Poor leedle waif!" murmured the soft-hearted old gentleman. "Id was de good Providence dat guided her--or him, whichever id be."

"Providence be hanged!" snarled Peter. "What was my Providence doing--landing me with a gutter-brat to look after?"

"So like you Radicals," sneered the doctor, "to despise a fellow human creature just because id may not have been born in burble and fine linen."

"I didn't send for you to argue politics," retorted Peter, controlling his indignation by an effort. "I want you to tell me whether it's a boy or a girl, so that I may know what to do with it."

"What mean you to do wid id?" inquired the doctor.

"I don't know," confessed Peter. "If it's a boy, as I rather think it is, maybe I'll be able to find it a place in one of the offices- -after I've taught it a little civilisation."

"And if id be a girl?"

"How can it be a girl when it wears trousers?" demanded Peter. "Why anticipate difficulties?"

Peter, alone, paced to and fro the room, his hands behind his back, his ear on the alert to catch the slightest sound from above.

"I do hope it is a boy," said Peter, glancing up.

Peter's eyes rested on the photo of the fragile little woman gazing down at him from its stiff frame upon the chimney-piece. Thirty years ago, in this same room, Peter had paced to and fro, his hands behind his back, his ear alert to catch the slightest sound from above, had said to himself the same words.

"It's odd," mused Peter--"very odd indeed."

The door opened. The stout doctor, preceded at a little distance by his watch-chain, entered and closed the door behind him.

"A very healthy child," said the doctor, "as fine a child as any one could wish to see. A girl."

The two old gentlemen looked at one another. Elizabeth, possibly relieved in her mind, began to purr.

"What am I to do with it?" demanded Peter.

"A very awkward bosition for you," agreed the sympathetic doctor.

"I was a fool!" declared Peter.

"You haf no one here to look after de leedle wench when you are away," pointed out the thoughtful doctor.

"And from what I've seen of the imp," added Peter, "it will want some looking after."

"I tink--I tink," said the helpful doctor, "I see a way out!"

"What?"

The doctor thrust his fierce face forward and tapped knowingly with his right forefinger the right side of his round nose. "I will take charge of de leedle wench."

"You?"

"To me de case will not present de same difficulties. I haf a housekeeper."

"Oh, yes, Mrs. Whateley."

"She is a goot woman when you know her," explained the doctor. "She only wants managing."

"Pooh!" ejaculated Peter.

"Why do you say dat?" inquired the doctor.

"You! bringing up a headstrong girl. The idea!"

"I should be kind, but firm."

"You don't know her."

"How long haf you known her?"

"Anyhow, I'm not a soft-hearted sentimentalist that would just ruin the child."

"Girls are not boys," persisted the doctor; "dey want different treatment."

"Well, I'm not a brute!" snarled Peter. "Besides, suppose she turns out rubbish! What do you know about her?"

"I take my chance," agreed the generous doctor.

"It wouldn't be fair," retorted honest Peter.

"Tink it over," said the doctor. "A place is never home widout de leedle feet. We Englishmen love de home. You are different. You haf no sentiment."

"I cannot help feeling," explained Peter, "a sense of duty in this matter. The child came to me. It is as if this thing had been laid upon me."

"If you look upon id dat way, Peter," sighed the doctor.

"With sentiment," went on Peter, "I have nothing to do; but duty-- duty is quite another thing." Peter, feeling himself an ancient Roman, thanked the doctor and shook hands with him.

Tommy, summoned, appeared.

"The doctor, Tommy," said Peter, without looking up from his writing, "gives a very satisfactory account of you. So you can stop."

"Told you so," returned Tommy. "Might have saved your money."

"But we shall have to find you another name."

"What for?"

"If you are to be a housekeeper, you must be a girl."

"Don't like girls."

"Can't say I think much of them myself, Tommy. We must make the best of it. To begin with, we must get you proper clothes."

"Hate skirts. They hamper you."

"Tommy," said Peter severely, "don't argue."

"Pointing out facts ain't arguing," argued Tommy. "They do hamper you. You try 'em."

The clothes were quickly made, and after a while they came to fit; but the name proved more difficult of adjustment. A sweet-faced, laughing lady, known to fame by a title respectable and orthodox, appears an honoured guest to-day at many a literary gathering. But the old fellows, pressing round, still call her "Tommy."

The week's trial came to an end. Peter, whose digestion was delicate, had had a happy thought.

"What I propose, Tommy--I mean Jane," said Peter, "is that we should get in a woman to do just the mere cooking. That will give you more time to--to attend to other things, Tommy--Jane, I mean."

"What other things?" chin in the air.

"The--the keeping of the rooms in order, Tommy. The--the dusting."

"Don't want twenty-four hours a day to dust four rooms."

"Then there are messages, Tommy. It would be a great advantage to me to have someone I could send on a message without feeling I was interfering with the housework."

"What are you driving at?" demanded Tommy. "Why, I don't have half enough to do as it is. I can do all--"

Peter put his foot down. "When I say a thing, I mean a thing. The sooner you understand that, the better. How dare you argue with me! Fiddle-de-dee!" For two pins Peter would have employed an expletive even stronger, so determined was he feeling.

Tommy without another word left the room. Peter looked at Elizabeth and winked.

Poor Peter! His triumph was short-lived. Five minutes later, Tommy returned, clad in the long, black skirt, supported by the cricket belt, the blue garibaldi cut decollete, the pepper-and-salt jacket, the worsted comforter, the red lips very tightly pressed, the long lashes over the black eyes moving very rapidly.

"Tommy" (severely), "what is this tomfoolery?"

"I understand. I ain't no good to you. Thanks for giving me a trial. My fault."

"Tommy" (less severely), "don't be an idiot."

"Ain't an idiot. 'Twas Emma. Told me I was good at cooking. Said I'd got an aptitude for it. She meant well."

"Tommy" (no trace of severity), "sit down. Emma was quite right. Your cooking is--is promising. As Emma puts it, you have aptitude. Your--perseverance, your hopefulness proves it."

"Then why d'ye want to get someone else in to do it?"

If Peter could have answered truthfully! If Peter could have replied:

"My dear, I am a lonely old gentleman. I did not know it until--until the other day. Now I cannot forget it again. Wife and child died many years ago. I was poor, or I might have saved them. That made me hard. The clock of my life stood still. I hid away the key. I did not want to think. You crept to me out of the cruel fog, awakened old dreams. Do not go away any more"--perhaps Tommy, in spite of her fierce independence, would have consented to be useful; and thus Peter might have gained his end at less cost of indigestion. But the penalty for being an anti-sentimentalist is that you must not talk like this even to yourself. So Peter had to cast about for other methods.

"Why shouldn't I keep two servants if I like?" It did seem hard on the old gentleman.

"What's the sense of paying two to do the work of one? You would only be keeping me on out of charity." The black eyes flashed. "I ain't a beggar."

"And you really think, Tommy--I should say Jane, you can manage the--the whole of it? You won't mind being sent on a message, perhaps in the very middle of your cooking. It was that I was thinking of, Tommy--some cooks would."

"You go easy," advised him Tommy, "till I complain of having too much to do."

Peter returned to his desk. Elizabeth looked up. It seemed to Peter that Elizabeth winked.

The fortnight that followed was a period of trouble to Peter, for Tommy, her suspicions having been aroused, was sceptical of "business" demanding that Peter should dine with this man at the club, lunch with this editor at the Cheshire Cheese. At once the chin would go up into the air, the black eyes cloud threateningly. Peter, an unmarried man for thirty years, lacking experience, would under cross-examination contradict himself, become confused, break down over essential points.

"Really," grumbled Peter to himself one evening, sawing at a mutton chop, "really there's no other word for it--I'm henpecked."

Peter that day had looked forward to a little dinner at a favourite restaurant, with his "dear old friend Blenkinsopp, a bit of a gourmet, Tommy--that means a man who likes what you would call elaborate cooking!"--forgetful at the moment that he had used up "Blenkinsopp" three days before for a farewell supper, "Blenkinsopp" having to set out the next morning for Egypt. Peter was not facile at invention. Names in particular had always been a difficulty to him.

"I like a spirit of independence," continued Peter to himself. "Wish she hadn't quite so much of it. Wonder where she got it from."

The situation was becoming more serious to Peter than he cared to admit. For day by day, in spite of her tyrannies, Tommy was growing more and more indispensable to Peter. Tommy was the first audience that for thirty years had laughed at Peter's jokes; Tommy was the first public that for thirty years had been convinced that Peter was the most brilliant journalist in Fleet Street; Tommy was the first anxiety that for thirty years had rendered it needful that Peter each night should mount stealthily the creaking stairs, steal with shaded candle to a bedside. If only Tommy wouldn't "do" for him! If only she could be persuaded to "do" something else.

Another happy thought occurred to Peter.

"Tommy--I mean Jane," said Peter, "I know what I'll do with you."

"What's the game now?"

"I'll make a journalist of you."

"Don't talk rot."

"It isn't rot. Besides, I won't have you answer me like that. As a Devil--that means, Tommy, the unseen person in the background that helps a journalist to do his work--you would be invaluable to me.

It would pay me, Tommy--pay me very handsomely. I should make money out of you."

This appeared to be an argument that Tommy understood. Peter, with secret delight, noticed that the chin retained its normal level.

"I did help a chap to sell papers, once," remembered Tommy; "he said I was fly at it."

"I told you so," exclaimed Peter triumphantly. "The methods are different, but the instinct required is the same. We will get a woman in to relieve you of the housework."

The chin shot up into the air.

"I could do it in my spare time."

"You see, Tommy, I should want you to go about with me--to be always with me."

"Better try me first. Maybe you're making an error."

Peter was learning the wisdom of the serpent.

"Quite right, Tommy. We will first see what you can do. Perhaps, after all, it may turn out that you are better as a cook." In his heart Peter doubted this.

But the seed had fallen upon good ground. It was Tommy herself that manoeuvred her first essay in journalism. A great man had come to London--was staying in apartments especially prepared for him in St. James's Palace. Said every journalist in London to himself: "If I could obtain an interview with this Big Man, what a big thing it would be for me!" For a week past, Peter had carried everywhere about with him a paper headed: "Interview of Our Special Correspondent with Prince Blank," questions down left-hand column, very narrow; space for answers right-hand side, very wide. But the Big Man was experienced.

"I wonder," said Peter, spreading the neatly folded paper on the desk before him, "I wonder if there can be any way of getting at him--any dodge or trick, any piece of low cunning, any plausible lie that I haven't thought of."

"Old Man Martin--called himself Martini--was just such another," commented Tommy. "Come pay time, Saturday afternoon, you just couldn't get at him--simply wasn't any way. I was a bit too good for him once, though," remembered Tommy, with a touch of pride in her voice; "got half a quid out of him that time. It did surprise him."

"No," communed Peter to himself aloud, "I don't honestly think there can be any method, creditable or discreditable, that I haven't tried." Peter flung the one-sided interview into the wastepaper-basket, and slipping his notebook into his pocket, departed to drink tea with a lady novelist, whose great desire, as stated in a postscript to her invitation, was to avoid publicity, if possible.

Tommy, as soon as Peter's back was turned, fished it out again.

An hour later in the fog around St. James's Palace stood an Imp, clad in patched trousers and a pepper-and-salt jacket turned up about the neck, gazing with admiring eyes upon the sentry.

"Now, then, young seventeen-and-sixpence the soot," said the sentry, "what do you want?"

"Makes you a bit anxious, don't it," suggested the Imp, "having a big pot like him to look after?"

"Does get a bit on yer mind, if yer thinks about it," agreed the sentry.

"How do you find him to talk to, like?"

"Well," said the sentry, bringing his right leg into action for the purpose of relieving his left, "ain't 'ad much to do with 'im myself, not person'ly, as yet. Oh, 'e ain't a bad sort when yer know 'im."

"That's his shake-down, ain't it?" asked the Imp, "where the lights are."

"That's it," admitted sentry. "You ain't an Anarchist? Tell me if you are."

"I'll let you know if I feel it coming on," the Imp assured him.

Had the sentry been a man of swift and penetrating observation--which he wasn't--he might have asked the question in more serious a tone. For he would have remarked that the Imp's black eyes were resting lovingly upon a rain-water-pipe, giving to a skilful climber easy access to the terrace underneath the Prince's windows.

"I would like to see him," said the Imp.

"Friend o' yours?" asked the sentry.

"Well, not exactly," admitted the Imp. "But there, you know, everybody's talking about him down our street."

"Well, yer'll 'ave to be quick about it," said the sentry. 'E's off tonight."

Tommy's face fell. "I thought it wasn't till Friday morning."

"Ah!" said the sentry, "that's what the papers say, is it?" The sentry's voice took unconsciously the accent of those from whom no secret is hid. "I'll tell yer what yer can do," continued the sentry, enjoying an unaccustomed sense of importance. The sentry glanced left, then right. "'E's a slipping off all by 'imself down to Osborne by the 6.40 from Waterloo. Nobody knows it--'cept, o' course, just a few of us. That's 'is way all over. 'E just 'ates- -"

A footstep sounded down the corridor. The sentry became statuesque.

At Waterloo, Tommy inspected the 6.40 train. Only one compartment indicated possibilities, an extra large one at the end of the coach next the guard's van. It was labelled "Reserved," and in the place of the usual fittings was furnished with a table and four easy-chairs. Having noticed its position, Tommy took a walk up the platform and disappeared into the fog.

Twenty minutes later, Prince Blank stepped hurriedly across the platform, unnoticed save by half a dozen obsequious officials, and entered the compartment reserved for him. The obsequious officials bowed. Prince Blank, in military fashion, raised his hand. The 6.40 steamed out slowly.

Prince Blank, who was a stout gentleman, though he tried to disguise the fact, seldom found himself alone. When he did, he generally indulged himself in a little healthy relaxation. With two hours' run to Southampton before him, free from all possibility of intrusion, Prince Blank let loose the buttons of his powerfully built waistcoat, rested his bald head on the top of his chair, stretched his great legs across another, and closed his terrible, small eyes.

For an instant it seemed to Prince Blank that a draught had entered into the carriage. As, however, the sensation immediately passed away, he did not trouble to wake up. Then the Prince dreamed that somebody was in the carriage with him--was sitting opposite to him. This being an annoying sort of dream, the Prince opened his eyes for the purpose of dispelling it. There was somebody sitting opposite to him--a very grimy little person, wiping blood off its face and hands with a dingy handkerchief. Had the Prince been a man capable of surprise, he would have been surprised.

"It's all right," assured him Tommy. "I ain't here to do any harm. I ain't an Anarchist."

The Prince, by a muscular effort, retired some four or five inches and commenced to rebutton his waistcoat.

"How did you get here?" asked the Prince.

"'Twas a bigger job than I'd reckoned on," admitted Tommy, seeking a dry inch in the smeared handkerchief, and finding none. "But that don't matter," added Tommy cheerfully, "now I'm here."

"If you do not wish me to hand you over to the police at Southampton, you had better answer my questions," remarked the Prince drily.

Tommy was not afraid of princes, but in the lexicon of her harassed youth "Police" had always been a word of dread.

"I wanted to get at you."

"I gather that."

"There didn't seem any other way. It's jolly difficult to get at you. You're so jolly artful."

"Tell me how you managed it."

"There's a little bridge for signals just outside Waterloo. I could see that the train would have to pass under it. So I climbed up and waited. It being a foggy night, you see, nobody twigged me. I say, you are Prince Blank, ain't you?"

"I am Prince Blank."

"Should have been mad if I'd landed the wrong man."

"Go on."

"I knew which was your carriage--leastways, I guessed it; and as it came along, I did a drop." Tommy spread out her arms and legs to illustrate the action. "The lamps, you know," explained Tommy, still dabbing at her face--"one of them caught me."

"And from the roof?"

"Oh, well, it was easy after that. There's an iron thing at the back, and steps. You've only got to walk downstairs and round the corner, and there you are. Bit of luck your other door not being locked. I hadn't thought of that. Haven't got such a thing as a handkerchief about you, have you?"

The Prince drew one from his sleeve and passed it to her. "You mean to tell me, boy--"

"Ain't a boy," explained Tommy. "I'm a girl!"

She said it sadly. Deeming her new friends such as could be trusted, Tommy had accepted their statement that she really was a girl. But for many a long year to come the thought of her lost manhood tinged her voice with bitterness.

"A girl!"

Tommy nodded her head.

"Umph!" said the Prince; "I have heard a good deal about the English girl. I was beginning to think it exaggerated. Stand up."

Tommy obeyed. It was not altogether her way; but with those eyes beneath their shaggy brows bent upon her, it seemed the simplest thing to do.

"So. And now that you are here, what do you want?"

"To interview you."

Tommy drew forth her list of questions.

The shaggy brows contracted.

"Who put you up to this absurdity? Who was it? Tell me at once."

"Nobody."

"Don't lie to me. His name?"

The terrible, small eyes flashed fire. But Tommy also had a pair of eyes. Before their blaze of indignation the great man positively quailed. This type of opponent was new to him.

"I'm not lying."

"I beg your pardon," said the Prince.

And at this point it occurred to the Prince, who being really a great man, had naturally a sense of humour, that a conference conducted on these lines between the leading statesman of an

Empire and an impertinent hussy of, say, twelve years old at the outside, might end by becoming ridiculous. So the Prince took up his chair and put it down again beside Tommy's, and employing skilfully his undoubted diplomatic gifts, drew from her bit by bit the whole story.

"I'm inclined, Miss Jane," said the Great Man, the story ended, "to agree with our friend Mr. Hope. I should say your metier was journalism."

"And you'll let me interview you?" asked Tommy, showing her white teeth.

The Great Man, laying a hand heavier than he guessed on Tommy's shoulder, rose. "I think you are entitled to it."

"What's your views?" demanded Tommy, reading, "of the future political and social relationships--"

"Perhaps," suggested the Great Man, "it will be simpler if I write it myself."

"Well," concurred Tommy; "my spelling is a bit rocky."

The Great Man drew a chair to the table.

"You won't miss out anything--will you?" insisted Tommy.

"I shall endeavour, Miss Jane, to give you no cause for complaint," gravely he assured her, and sat down to write.

Not till the train began to slacken speed had the Prince finished. Then, blotting and refolding the paper, he stood up.

"I have added some instructions on the back of the last page," explained the Prince, "to which you will draw Mr. Hope's particular attention. I would wish you to promise me, Miss Jane, never again to have recourse to dangerous acrobatic tricks, not even in the sacred cause of journalism."

"Of course, if you hadn't been so jolly difficult to get at--"

"My fault, I know," agreed the Prince. "There is not the least doubt as to which sex you belong to. Nevertheless, I want you to promise me. Come," urged the Prince, "I have done a good deal for you--more than you know."

"All right," consented Tommy a little sulkily. Tommy hated making promises, because she always kept them. "I promise."

"There is your Interview." The first Southampton platform lamp shone in upon the Prince and Tommy as they stood facing one another. The Prince, who had acquired the reputation, not altogether unjustly, of an ill-tempered and savage old gentleman, did a strange thing: taking the little, blood-smeared face between his paws, he kissed it. Tommy always remembered the smoky flavour of the bristly grey moustache.

"One thing more," said the Prince sternly--"not a word of all this. Don't open your mouth to speak of it till you are back in Gough Square."

"Do you take me for a mug?" answered Tommy.

They behaved very oddly to Tommy after the Prince had disappeared. Everybody took a deal of trouble for her, but none of them seemed to know why they were doing it. They looked at her and went away, and came again and looked at her. And the more they thought about it, the more puzzled they became. Some of them asked her questions, but what Tommy really didn't know, added to what she didn't mean to tell, was so prodigious that Curiosity itself paled at contemplation of it.

They washed and brushed her up and gave her an excellent supper; and putting her into a first-class compartment labelled "Reserved," sent her back to Waterloo, and thence in a cab to Gough Square, where she arrived about midnight, suffering from a sense of self- importance, traces of which to this day are still discernible.

Such and thus was the beginning of all things. Tommy, having talked for half an hour at the rate of two hundred words a minute, had suddenly dropped her head upon the table, had been aroused with difficulty and persuaded to go to bed. Peter, in the deep easy-chair before the fire, sat long into the night. Elizabeth, liking quiet company, purred softly. Out of the shadows crept to Peter Hope an old forgotten dream--the dream of a wonderful new Journal, price one penny weekly, of which the Editor should come to be one Thomas Hope, son of Peter Hope, its honoured Founder and Originator: a powerful Journal that should supply a long-felt want, popular, but at the same time elevating--a pleasure to the public, a profit to its owners. "Do you not remember me?" whispered the Dream. "We had long talks together. The morning and the noonday pass. The evening still is ours. The twilight also brings its promise."

Elizabeth stopped purring and looked up surprised. Peter was laughing to himself.

STORY THE SECOND

WILLIAM CLODD APPOINTS HIMSELF MANAGING DIRECTOR

Mrs. Postwhistle sat on a Windsor-chair in the centre of Rolls Court. Mrs. Postwhistle, who, in the days of her Hebehood, had been likened by admiring frequenters of the old Mitre in Chancery Lane to the ladies, somewhat emaciated, that an English artist, since become famous, was then commencing to popularise, had developed with the passing years, yet still retained a face of placid youthfulness. The two facts, taken in conjunction, had resulted in an asset to her income not to be despised. The wanderer through Rolls Court this summer's afternoon, presuming him to be familiar with current journalism, would have retired haunted by the sense that the restful-looking lady on the Windsor-chair was someone that he ought to know. Glancing through almost any illustrated paper of the period, the problem would have been solved for him. A photograph of Mrs. Postwhistle, taken quite recently, he would have encountered with this legend: "BEFORE use of Professor Hardtop's certain cure for corpulency." Beside it a photograph of Mrs. Postwhistle, then Arabella Higgins, taken twenty years ago, the legend slightly varied: "AFTER use," etc. The face was the same, the figure--there was no denying it--had undergone decided alteration.

Mrs. Postwhistle had reached with her chair the centre of Rolls

Court in course of following the sun. The little shop, over the lintel of which ran: "Timothy Postwhistle, Grocer and Provision Merchant," she had left behind her in the shadow. Old inhabitants of St. Dunstan-in-the-West retained recollection of a gentlemanly figure, always in a very gorgeous waistcoat, with Dundreary whiskers, to be seen occasionally there behind the counter. All customers it would refer, with the air of a Lord High Chamberlain introducing debutantes, to Mrs. Postwhistle, evidently regarding itself purely as ornamental. For the last ten years, however, no one had noticed it there, and Mrs. Postwhistle had a facility amounting almost to genius for ignoring or misunderstanding questions it was not to her taste to answer. Most things were suspected, nothing known. St. Dunstan-in-the-West had turned to other problems.

"If I wasn't wanting to see 'im," remarked to herself Mrs. Postwhistle, who was knitting with one eye upon the shop, "'e'd a been 'ere 'fore I'd 'ad time to clear the dinner things away; certain to 'ave been. It's a strange world."

Mrs. Postwhistle was desirous for the arrival of a gentleman not usually awaited with impatience by the ladies of Rolls Court--to wit, one William Clodd, rent-collector, whose day for St. Dunstan- in-the-West was Tuesday.

"At last," said Mrs. Postwhistle, though without hope that Mr. Clodd, who had just appeared at the other end of the court, could possibly hear her. "Was beginning to be afraid as you'd tumbled over yerself in your 'urry and 'urt yerself."

Mr. Clodd, perceiving Mrs. Postwhistle, decided to abandon method and take No. 7 first.

Mr. Clodd was a short, thick-set, bullet-headed young man, with ways that were bustling, and eyes that, though kind, suggested trickiness.

"Ah!" said Mr. Clodd admiringly, as he pocketed the six half-crowns that the lady handed up to him. "If only they were all like you, Mrs. Postwhistle!"

"Wouldn't be no need of chaps like you to worry 'em," pointed out Mrs. Postwhistle.

"It's an irony of fate, my being a rent-collector, when you come to think of it," remarked Mr. Clodd, writing out the receipt. "If I had my way, I'd put an end to landlordism, root and branch. Curse of the country."

"Just the very thing I wanted to talk to you about," returned the lady--"that lodger o' mine."

"Ah! don't pay, don't he? You just hand him over to me. I'll soon have it out of him."

"It's not that," explained Mrs. Postwhistle. "If a Saturday morning 'appened to come round as 'e didn't pay up without me asking, I should know I'd made a mistake--that it must be Friday. If I don't 'appen to be in at 'alf-past ten, 'e puts it in an envelope and leaves it on the table."

"Wonder if his mother has got any more like him?" mused Mr. Clodd. "Could do with a few about this neighbourhood. What is it you want to say about him, then? Merely to brag about him?"

"I wanted to ask you," continued Mrs. Postwhistle, "'ow I could get rid of 'im. It was rather a curious agreement."

"Why do you want to get rid of him? Too noisy?"

"Noisy! Why, the cat makes more noise about the 'ouse than 'e does. 'E'd make 'is fortune as a burglar."

"Come home late?"

"Never known 'im out after the shutters are up."

"Gives you too much trouble then?"

"I can't say that of 'im. Never know whether 'e's in the 'ouse or isn't, without going upstairs and knocking at the door."

"Here, you tell it your own way," suggested the bewildered Clodd. "If it was anyone else but you, I should say you didn't know your own business."

"'E gets on my nerves," said Mrs. Postwhistle. "You ain't in a 'urry for five minutes?"

Mr. Clodd was always in a hurry. "But I can forget it talking to you," added the gallant Mr. Clodd.

Mrs. Postwhistle led the way into the little parlour.

"Just the name of it," consented Mr. Clodd. "Cheerfulness combined with temperance; that's the ideal."

"I'll tell you what 'appened only last night," commenced Mrs. Postwhistle, seating herself the opposite side of the loo-table. "A letter came for 'im by the seven o'clock post. I'd seen 'im go out two hours before, and though I'd been sitting in the shop the whole blessed time, I never saw or 'eard 'im pass through. E's like that. It's like 'aving a ghost for a lodger. I opened 'is door without knocking and went in. If you'll believe me, 'e was clinging with 'is arms and legs to the top of the bedstead--it's one of those old-fashioned, four-post things--'is 'ead touching the ceiling. 'E 'adn't got too much clothes on, and was cracking nuts with 'is teeth and eating 'em. 'E threw a 'andful of shells at me, and making the most awful faces at me, started off gibbering softly to himself."

"All play, I suppose? No real vice?" commented the interested Mr. Clodd.

"It will go on for a week, that will," continued Mrs. Postwhistle-- "'e fancying 'imself a monkey. Last week he was a tortoise, and was crawling about on his stomach with a tea-tray tied on to 'is back. 'E's as sensible as most men, if that's saying much, the moment 'e's outside the front door; but in the 'ouse--well, I suppose the fact is that 'e's a lunatic."

"Don't seem no hiding anything from you," Mrs. Postwhistle remarked Mr. Clodd in tones of admiration. "Does he ever get violent?"

"Don't know what 'e would be like if 'e 'appened to fancy 'imself something really dangerous," answered Mrs. Postwhistle. "I am a bit nervous of this new monkey game, I don't mind confessing to you-- the things that they do according to the picture-books. Up to now, except for imagining 'imself a mole, and taking all his meals underneath the carpet, it's been mostly birds and cats and 'armless sort o' things I 'aven't seemed to mind so much."

"How did you get hold of him?" demanded Mr. Clodd. "Have much trouble in finding him, or did somebody come and tell you about him?"

"Old Gladman, of Chancery Lane, the law stationer, brought 'im 'ere one evening about two months ago--said 'e was a sort of distant relative of 'is, a bit soft in the 'ead, but perfectly 'armless-- wanted to put 'im with someone who wouldn't impose on 'im. Well, what between 'aving been empty for over five weeks, the poor old gaby 'imself looking as gentle as a lamb, and the figure being reasonable, I rather jumped at the idea; and old Gladman, explaining as 'ow 'e wanted the thing settled and done with, got me to sign a letter."

"Kept a copy of it?" asked the business-like Clodd.

"No. But I can remember what it was. Gladman 'ad it all ready. So long as the money was paid punctual and 'e didn't make no disturbance and didn't fall sick, I was to go on boarding and lodging 'im for seventeen-and-sixpence a week. It didn't strike me as anything to be objected to at the time; but 'e payin' regular, as I've explained to you, and be'aving, so far as disturbance is concerned, more like a Christian martyr than a man, well, it looks to me as if I'd got to live and die with 'im."

"Give him rope, and possibly he'll have a week at being a howling hyaena, or a laughing jackass, or something of that sort that will lead to a disturbance," thought Mr. Clodd, "in which case, of course, you would have your remedy."

"Yes," thought Mrs. Postwhistle, "and possibly also 'e may take it into what 'e calls is 'ead to be a tiger or a bull, and then perhaps before 'e's through with it I'll be beyond the reach of remedies."

"Leave it to me," said Mr. Clodd, rising and searching for his hat. "I know old Gladman; I'll have a talk with him."

"You might get a look at that letter if you can," suggested Mrs. Postwhistle, "and tell me what you think about it. I don't want to spend the rest of my days in a lunatic asylum of my own if I can 'elp it."

"You leave it to me," was Mr. Clodd's parting assurance.

The July moon had thrown a silver veil over the grimness of Rolls Court when, five hours later, Mr. Clodd's nailed boots echoed again upon its uneven pavement; but Mr. Clodd had no eye for moon or stars or such-like; always he had things more important to think of.

"Seen the old 'umbug?" asked Mrs. Postwhistle, who was partial to the air, leading the way into the parlour.

"First and foremost commenced," Mr. Clodd, as he laid aside his hat, "it is quite understood that you really do want to get rid of him? What's that?" demanded Mr. Clodd, a heavy thud upon the floor above having caused him to start out of his chair.

"'E came in an hour after you'd gone," explained Mrs. Postwhistle, "bringing with him a curtain pole as 'e'd picked up for a shilling in Clare Market. 'E's rested one end upon the mantelpiece and tied the other to the back of the easy-chair--'is idea is to twine 'imself round it and go to sleep upon it. Yes, you've got it quite right without a single blunder. I do want to get rid of 'im"

"Then," said Mr. Clodd, reseating himself, "it can be done."

"Thank God for that!" was Mrs. Postwhistle's pious ejaculation.

"It is just as I thought," continued Mr. Clodd. "The old innocent-- he's Gladman's brother-in-law, by the way--has got a small annuity. I couldn't get the actual figure, but I guess it's about sufficient to pay for his keep and leave old Gladman, who is running him, a very decent profit. They don't want to send him to an asylum. They can't say he's a pauper, and to put him into a private establishment would swallow up, most likely, the whole of his income. On the other hand, they don't want the bother of looking after him themselves. I talked pretty straight to the old man--let him see I understood the business; and--well, to cut a long story short, I'm willing to take on the job, provided you really want to have done with it, and Gladman is willing in that case to let you off your contract."

Mrs. Postwhistle went to the cupboard to get Mr. Clodd a drink. Another thud upon the floor above--one suggestive of exceptional velocity--arrived at the precise moment when Mrs. Postwhistle, the tumbler level with her eye, was in the act of measuring.

"I call this making a disturbance," said Mrs. Postwhistle, regarding the broken fragments.

"It's only for another night," comforted her Mr. Clodd. "I'll take him away some time to-morrow. Meanwhile, if I were you, I should spread a mattress underneath that perch of his before I went to bed. I should like him handed over to me in reasonable repair."

"It will deaden the sound a bit, any'ow," agreed Mrs. Postwhistle.

"Success to temperance," drank Mr. Clodd, and rose to go.

"I take it you've fixed things up all right for yourself," said Mrs. Postwhistle; "and nobody can blame you if you 'ave. 'Eaven bless you, is what I say."

"We shall get on together," prophesied Mr. Clodd. "I'm fond of animals."

Early the next morning a four-wheeled cab drew up at the entrance to Rolls Court, and in it and upon it went away Clodd and Clodd's Lunatic (as afterwards he came to be known), together with all the belongings of Clodd's Lunatic, the curtain-pole included; and there appeared again behind the fanlight of the little grocer's shop the intimation: "Lodgings for a Single Man," which caught the eye a few days later of a weird-looking, lanky, rawboned laddie, whose language Mrs. Postwhistle found difficulty for a time in comprehending; and that is why one sometimes meets to-day worshippers of Kail Yard literature wandering disconsolately about St. Dunstan-in-the-West, seeking Rolls Court, discomforted because it is no more. But that is the history of the "Wee Laddie," and this of the beginnings of William Clodd, now Sir William Clodd, Bart., M.P., proprietor of a quarter of a hundred newspapers, magazines, and journals: "Truthful Billy" we called him then.

No one can say of Clodd that he did not deserve whatever profit his unlicensed lunatic asylum may have brought him. A kindly man was William Clodd when indulgence in sentiment did not interfere with business.

"There's no harm in him," asserted Mr. Clodd, talking the matter over with one Mr. Peter Hope, journalist, of Gough Square. "He's just a bit dotty, same as you or I might get with nothing to do and all day long to do it in. Kid's play, that's all it is. The best plan, I find, is to treat it as a game and take a hand in it. Last week he wanted to be a lion. I could see that was going to be awkward, he roaring for raw meat and thinking to prowl about the house at night. Well, I didn't nag him--that's no good. I just got a gun and shot him. He's a duck now, and I'm trying to keep him one: sits for an hour beside his bath on three china eggs I've bought him. Wish some of the sane ones were as little trouble."

The summer came again. Clodd and his Lunatic, a mild-looking little old gentleman of somewhat clerical cut, one often met with arm-in-arm, bustling about the streets and courts that were the scene of Clodd's rent-collecting labours. Their evident attachment to one another was curiously displayed; Clodd, the young and red-haired, treating his white-haired, withered companion with fatherly indulgence; the other glancing up from time to time into Clodd's face with a winning expression of infantile affection.

"We are getting much better," explained Clodd, the pair meeting Peter Hope one day at the corner of Newcastle Street. "The more we are out in the open air, and the more we have to do and think about, the better for us--eh?"

The mild-looking little old gentleman hanging on Clodd's arm smiled and nodded.

"Between ourselves," added Mr. Clodd, sinking his voice, "we are not half as foolish as folks think we are."

Peter Hope went his way down the Strand.

"Clodd's a good sort--a good sort," said Peter Hope, who, having in his time lived much alone, had fallen into the habit of speaking his thoughts aloud; "but he's not the man to waste his time. I wonder."

With the winter Clodd's Lunatic fell ill.

Clodd bustled round to Chancery Lane.

"To tell you the truth," confessed Mr. Gladman, "we never thought he would live so long as he has."

"There's the annuity you've got to think of," said Clodd, whom his admirers of to-day (and they are many, for he must be a millionaire by this time) are fond of alluding to as "that frank, outspoken Englishman." "Wouldn't it be worth your while to try what taking him away from the fogs might do for him?"

Old Gladman seemed inclined to consider the question, but Mrs. Gladman, a brisk, cheerful little woman, had made up her mind.

"We've had what there is to have," said Mrs. Gladman. "He's seventy-three. What's the sense of risking good money? Be content."

No one could say--no one ever did say--that Clodd, under the circumstances, did not do his best. Perhaps, after all, nothing could have helped. The little old gentleman, at Clodd's suggestion, played at being a dormouse and lay very still. If he grew restless, thereby bringing on his cough, Clodd, as a terrible black cat, was watching to pounce upon him. Only by keeping very quiet and artfully pretending to be asleep could he hope to escape the ruthless Clodd.

Doctor William Smith (ne Wilhelm Schmidt) shrugged his fat shoulders. "We can do noding. Dese fogs of ours: id is de one ting dat enables the foreigner to crow over us. Keep him quiet. De dormouse--id is a goot idea."

That evening William Clodd mounted to the second floor of 16, Gough Square, where dwelt his friend, Peter Hope, and knocked briskly at the door.

"Come in," said a decided voice, which was not Peter Hope's.

Mr. William Clodd's ambition was, and always had been, to be the owner or part-owner of a paper. To-day, as I have said, he owns a quarter of a hundred, and is in negotiation, so rumour goes, for seven more. But twenty years ago "Clodd and Co., Limited," was but in embryo. And Peter Hope, journalist, had likewise and for many a long year cherished the ambition to be, before he died, the owner or part-owner of a paper. Peter Hope to-day owns nothing, except perhaps the knowledge, if such things be permitted, that whenever and wherever his name is mentioned, kind thoughts arise unbidden--that someone of the party will surely say: "Dear old Peter! What a good fellow he was!" Which also may be in its way a valuable possession: who knows? But twenty years ago Peter's horizon was limited by Fleet Street.

Peter Hope was forty-seven, so he said, a dreamer and a scholar. William Clodd was three-and-twenty, a born hustler, very wide awake. Meeting one day by accident upon an omnibus, when Clodd lent Peter, who had come out without his purse, threepence to pay his fare with; drifting into acquaintanceship, each had come to acquire a liking and respect for the other. The dreamer thought with wonder of Clodd's shrewd practicability; the cute young man of business was lost in admiration of what seemed to him his old friend's marvellous learning. Both had arrived at the conclusion that a weekly journal with Peter Hope as editor, and William Clodd as manager, would be bound to be successful.

"If only we could scrape together a thousand pounds!" had sighed Peter.

"The moment we lay our hands upon the coin, we'll start that paper. Remember, it's a bargain," had answered William Clodd.

Mr. William Clodd turned the handle and walked in. With the door still in his hand he paused to look round the room. It was the first time he had seen it. His meetings hitherto with Peter Hope had been chance rencontres in street or restaurant. Always had he been curious to view the sanctuary of so much erudition.

A large, oak-panelled room, its three high windows, each with a low, cushioned seat beneath it, giving on to Gough Square. Thirty-five years before, Peter Hope, then a young dandy with side whiskers close-cropped and terminating just below the ear; with wavy, brown hair, giving to his fresh-complexioned face an appearance almost girl-ish; in cut-away blue coat, flowered waistcoat, black silk cravat secured by two gold pins chained together, and tightly strapped grey trouserings, had, aided and abetted by a fragile little lady in crinoline and much-flounced skirt, and bodice somewhat low, with corkscrew curls each movement of her head set ringing, planned and furnished it in accordance with the sober canons then in vogue, spending there-upon more than they should, as is to be expected from the young to whom the future promises all things. The fine Brussels carpet! A little too bright, had thought the shaking curls. "The colours will tone down, miss--ma'am." The shopman knew. Only by the help of the round island underneath the massive Empire table, by excursions into untrodden corners, could Peter recollect the rainbow floor his feet had pressed when he was twenty-one. The noble bookcase, surmounted by Minerva's bust. Really it was too expensive. But the nodding curls had been so obstinate. Peter's silly books and papers must be put away in order; the curls did not intend to permit any excuse for untidiness. So, too, the handsome, brass-bound desk; it must be worthy of the beautiful thoughts Peter would pen upon it. The great sideboard, supported by two such angry-looking mahogany lions; it must be strong to support the weight of silver clever Peter would one day purchase to place upon it. The few oil paintings in their heavy frames. A solidly furnished, sober apartment; about it that subtle atmosphere of dignity one finds but in old rooms long undisturbed, where one seems to read upon the walls: "I, Joy and Sorrow, twain in one, have dwelt here." One item only there was that seemed out of place among its grave surroundings--a guitar, hanging from the wall, ornamented with a ridiculous blue bow, somewhat faded.

"Mr. William Clodd?" demanded the decided voice.

Clodd started and closed the door.

"Guessed it in once," admitted Mr. Clodd.

"I thought so," said the decided voice. "We got your note this afternoon. Mr. Hope will be back at eight. Will you kindly hang up your hat and coat in the hall? You will find a box of cigars on the mantelpiece. Excuse my being busy. I must finish this, then I'll talk to you."

The owner of the decided voice went on writing. Clodd, having done as he was bid, sat himself in the easy-chair before the fire and smoked. Of the person behind the desk Mr. Clodd could see but the head and shoulders. It had black, curly hair, cut short. It's only garment visible below the white collar and red tie might have been a boy's jacket designed more like a girl's, or a girl's designed more like a boy's; partaking of the genius of English statesmanship, it appeared to be a compromise. Mr. Clodd remarked the long, drooping lashes over the bright, black eyes.

"It's a girl," said Mr. Clodd to himself; "rather a pretty girl."

Mr. Clodd, continuing downward, arrived at the nose.

"No," said Mr. Clodd to himself, "it's a boy--a cheeky young beggar, I should say."

The person at the desk, giving a grunt of satisfaction, gathered together sheets of manuscript and arranged them; then, resting its elbows on the desk and taking its head between its hands, regarded Mr. Clodd.

"Don't you hurry yourself," said Mr. Clodd; "but when you really have finished, tell me what you think of me."

"I beg your pardon," apologised the person at the desk. "I have got into a habit of staring at people. I know it's rude. I'm trying to break myself of it."

"Tell me your name," suggested Mr. Clodd, "and I'll forgive you."

"Tommy," was the answer--"I mean Jane."

"Make up your mind," advised Mr. Clodd; "don't let me influence you. I only want the truth."

"You see," explained the person at the desk, "everybody calls me Tommy, because that used to be my name. But now it's Jane."

"I see," said Mr. Clodd. "And which am I to call you?"

The person at the desk pondered. "Well, if this scheme you and Mr. Hope have been talking about really comes to anything, we shall be a good deal thrown together, you see, and then I expect you'll call me Tommy--most people do."

"You've heard about the scheme? Mr. Hope has told you?"

"Why, of course," replied Tommy. "I'm Mr. Hope's devil."

For the moment Clodd doubted whether his old friend had not started a rival establishment to his own.

"I help him in his work," Tommy relieved his mind by explaining. "In journalistic circles we call it devilling."

"I understand," said Mr. Clodd. "And what do you think, Tommy, of the scheme? I may as well start calling you Tommy, because, between you and me, I think the idea will come to something."

Tommy fixed her black eyes upon him. She seemed to be looking him right through.

"You are staring again, Tommy," Clodd reminded her. "You'll have trouble breaking yourself of that habit, I can see."

"I was trying to make up my mind about you. Everything depends upon the business man."

"Glad to hear you say so," replied the self-satisfied Clodd.

"If you are very clever-- Do you mind coming nearer to the lamp? I can't quite see you over there."

Clodd never could understand why he did it--never could understand why, from first to last, he always did what Tommy wished him to do; his only consolation being that other folks seemed just as helpless. He rose and, crossing the long room, stood at attention before the large desk, nervousness, to which he was somewhat of a stranger, taking possession of him.

"You don't LOOK very clever."

Clodd experienced another new sensation--that of falling in his own estimation.

"And yet one can see that you ARE clever."

The mercury of Clodd's conceit shot upward to a point that in the case of anyone less physically robust might have been dangerous to health.

Clodd held out his hand. "We'll pull it through, Tommy. The Guv'nor shall find the literature; you and I will make it go. I like you."

And Peter Hope, entering at the moment, caught a spark from the light that shone in the eyes of William Clodd and Tommy, whose other name was Jane, as, gripping hands, they stood with the desk between them, laughing they knew not why. And the years fell from old Peter, and, again a boy, he also laughed he knew not why. He had sipped from the wine-cup of youth.

"It's all settled, Guv'nor!" cried Clodd. "Tommy and I have fixed things up. We'll start with the New Year."

"You've got the money?"

"I'm reckoning on it. I don't see very well how I can miss it."

"Sufficient?"

"Just about. You get to work."

"I've saved a little," began Peter. "It ought to have been more, but somehow it isn't."

"Perhaps we shall want it," Clodd replied; "perhaps we shan't. You are supplying the brains."

The three for a few moments remained silent.

"I think, Tommy," said Peter, "I think a bottle of the old Madeira- -"

"Not to-night," said Clodd; "next time."

"To drink success," urged Peter.

"One man's success generally means some other poor devil's misfortune," answered Clodd.

"Can't be helped, of course, but don't want to think about it to-night. Must be getting back to my dormouse. Good night."

Clodd shook hands and bustled out.

"I thought as much," mused Peter aloud.

"What an odd mixture the man is! Kind--no one could have been kinder to the poor old fellow. Yet all the while-- We are an odd mixture, Tommy," said Peter Hope, "an odd mixture, we men and women." Peter was a philosopher.

The white-whiskered old dormouse soon coughed himself to sleep for ever.

"I shall want you and the missis to come to the funeral, Gladman," said Mr. Clodd, as he swung into the stationer's shop; "and bring Pincer with you. I'm writing to him."

"Don't see what good we can do," demurred Gladman.

"Well, you three are his only relatives; it's only decent you should be present," urged Clodd. "Besides, there's the will to be read. You may care to hear it."

The dry old law stationer opened wide his watery eyes.

"His will! Why, what had he got to leave? There was nothing but the annuity."

"You turn up at the funeral," Clodd told him, "and you'll learn all about it. Bonner's clerk will be there and will bring it with him. Everything is going to be done comme il faut, as the French say."

"I ought to have known of this," began Mr. Gladman.

"Glad to find you taking so much interest in the old chap," said Clodd. "Pity he's dead and can't thank you."

"I warn you," shouted old Gladman, whose voice was rising to a scream, "he was a helpless imbecile, incapable of acting for himself! If any undue influence--"

"See you on Friday," broke in Clodd, who was busy.

Friday's ceremony was not a sociable affair. Mrs. Gladman spoke occasionally in a shrill whisper to Mr. Gladman, who replied with grunts. Both employed the remainder of their time in scowling at Clodd. Mr. Pincer, a stout, heavy gentleman connected with the House of Commons, maintained a ministerial reserve. The undertaker's foreman expressed himself as thankful when it was over. He criticised it as the humpiest funeral he had ever known; for a time he had serious thoughts of changing his profession.

The solicitor's clerk was waiting for the party on its return from Kensal Green. Clodd again offered hospitality. Mr. Pincer this time allowed himself a glass of weak whisky-and-water, and sipped it with an air of doing so without prejudice. The clerk had one a little stronger, Mrs. Gladman, dispensing with consultation, declined shrilly for self and partner. Clodd, explaining that he always followed legal precedent, mixed himself one also and drank "To our next happy meeting." Then the clerk read.

It was a short and simple will, dated the previous August. It appeared that the old gentleman, unknown to his relatives, had died possessed of shares in a silver mine, once despaired of, now prospering. Taking them at present value, they would produce a sum well over two thousand pounds. The old gentleman had bequeathed five hundred pounds to his brother-in-law, Mr. Gladman; five hundred pounds to his only other living relative, his first cousin, Mr. Pincer; the residue to his friend, William Clodd, as a return for the many kindnesses that gentleman had shown him.

Mr. Gladman rose, more amused than angry.

"And you think you are going to pocket that one thousand to twelve hundred pounds. You really do?" he asked Mr. Clodd, who, with legs stretched out before him, sat with his hands deep in his trousers pockets.

"That's the idea," admitted Mr. Clodd.

Mr. Gladman laughed, but without much lightening the atmosphere. "Upon my word, Clodd, you amuse me--you quite amuse me," repeated Mr. Gladman.

"You always had a sense of humour," commented Mr. Clodd.

"You villain! You double-dyed villain!" screamed Mr. Gladman, suddenly changing his tone. "You think the law is going to allow you to swindle honest men! You think we are going to sit still for you to rob us! That will--" Mr. Gladman pointed a lank forefinger dramatically towards the table.

"You mean to dispute it?" inquired Mr. Clodd.

For a moment Mr. Gladman stood aghast at the other's coolness, but soon found his voice again.

"Dispute it!" he shrieked. "Do you dispute that you influenced him?--dictated it to him word for word, made the poor old helpless idiot sign it, he utterly incapable of even understanding--"

"Don't chatter so much," interrupted Mr. Clodd. "It's not a pretty voice, yours. What I asked you was, do you intend to dispute it?"

"If you will kindly excuse us," struck in Mrs. Gladman, addressing Mr. Clodd with an air of much politeness, "we shall just have time, if we go now, to catch our solicitor before he leaves his office."

Mr. Gladman took up his hat from underneath his chair.

"One moment," suggested Mr. Clodd. "I did influence him to make that will. If you don't like it, there's an end of it."

"Of course," commenced Mr. Gladman in a mollified tone.

"Sit down," suggested Mr. Clodd. "Let's try another one." Mr. Clodd turned to the clerk. "The previous one, Mr. Wright, if you please; the one dated June the 10th."

An equally short and simple document, it bequeathed three hundred pounds to Mr. William Clodd in acknowledgment of kindnesses received, the residue to the Royal Zoological Society of London, the deceased having been always interested in and fond of animals. The relatives, "Who have never shown me the slightest affection or given themselves the slightest trouble concerning me, and who have already received considerable sums out of my income," being by name excluded.

"I may mention," observed Mr. Clodd, no one else appearing inclined to break the silence, "that in suggesting the Royal Zoological Society to my poor old friend as a fitting object for his benevolence, I had in mind a very similar case that occurred five years ago. A bequest to them was disputed on the grounds that the testator was of unsound mind. They had to take their case to the House of Lords before they finally won it."

"Anyhow," remarked Mr. Gladman, licking his lips, which were dry, "you won't get anything, Mr. Clodd--no, not even your three-hundred pounds, clever as you think yourself. My brother-in-law's money will go to the lawyers."

Then Mr. Pincer rose and spoke slowly and clearly. "If there must be a lunatic connected with our family, which I don't see why there should be, it seems to me to be you, Nathaniel Gladman."

Mr. Gladman stared back with open mouth. Mr. Pincer went on impressively.

"As for my poor old cousin Joe, he had his eccentricities, but that was all. I for one am prepared to swear that he was of sound mind in August last and quite capable of making his own will. It seems to me that the other thing, dated in June, is just waste paper."

Mr. Pincer having delivered himself, sat down again. Mr. Gladman showed signs of returning language.

"Oh! what's the use of quarrelling?" chirped in cheery Mrs. Gladman. "It's five hundred pounds we never expected. Live and let live is what I always say."

"It's the damned artfulness of the thing," said Mr. Gladman, still very white about the gills.

"Oh, you have a little something to thaw your face," suggested his wife.

Mr. and Mrs. Gladman, on the strength of the five hundred pounds, went home in a cab. Mr. Pincer stayed behind and made a night of it with Mr. Clodd and Bonner's clerk, at Clodd's expense.

The residue worked out at eleven hundred and sixty-nine pounds and a few shillings. The capital of the new company, "established for the purpose of carrying on the business of newspaper publishers and distributors, printers, advertising agents, and any other trade and enterprise affiliated to the same," was one thousand pounds in one pound shares, fully paid up; of which William Clodd, Esquire, was registered proprietor of four hundred and sixty-three; Peter Hope, M.A., of 16, Gough Square, of also four hundred and sixty-three; Miss

Jane Hope, adopted daughter of said Peter Hope (her real name nobody, herself included, ever having known), and generally called Tommy, of three, paid for by herself after a battle royal with William Clodd; Mrs. Postwhistle, of Rolls Court, of ten, presented by the promoter; Mr. Pincer, of the House of Commons, also of ten (still owing for); Dr. Smith (ne Schmidt) of fifty; James Douglas Alexander Calder McTear (otherwise the "Wee Laddie"), residing then in Mrs. Postwhistle's first floor front, of one, paid for by poem published in the first number: "The Song of the Pen."

Choosing a title for the paper cost much thought. Driven to despair, they called it Good Humour.

STORY THE THIRD

GRINDLEY JUNIOR DROPS INTO THE POSITION OF PUBLISHER

Few are the ways of the West Central district that have changed less within the last half-century than Nevill's Court, leading from Great New Street into Fetter Lane. Its north side still consists of the same quaint row of small low shops that stood there--doing perhaps a little brisker business--when George the Fourth was King; its southern side of the same three substantial houses each behind a strip of garden, pleasant by contrast with surrounding grimness, built long ago--some say before Queen Anne was dead.

Out of the largest of these, passing through the garden, then well cared for, came one sunny Sunday morning, some fifteen years before the commencement proper of this story, one Solomon Appleyard, pushing in front of him a perambulator. At the brick wall surmounted by wooden railings that divides the garden from the court, Solomon paused, hearing behind him the voice of Mrs. Appleyard speaking from the doorstep.

"If I don't see you again until dinner-time, I'll try and get on without you, understand. Don't think of nothing but your pipe and forget the child. And be careful of the crossings."

Mrs. Appleyard retired into the darkness. Solomon, steering the perambulator carefully, emerged from Nevill's Court without accident. The quiet streets drew Solomon westward. A vacant seat beneath the shade overlooking the Long Water in Kensington Gardens invited to rest.

"Piper?" suggested a small boy to Solomon. "Sunday Times, 'Server?"

"My boy," said Mr. Appleyard, speaking slowly, "when you've been mewed up with newspapers eighteen hours a day for six days a week, you can do without 'em for a morning. Take 'em away. I want to forget the smell of 'em."

Solomon, having assured himself that the party in the perambulator was still breathing, crossed his legs and lit his pipe.

"Hezekiah!"

The exclamation had been wrung from Solomon Appleyard by the approach of a stout, short man clad in a remarkably ill-fitting broad-cloth suit.

"What, Sol, my boy?"

"It looked like you," said Solomon. "And then I said to myself: 'No; surely it can't be Hezekiah; he'll be at chapel.'"

"You run about," said Hezekiah, addressing a youth of some four summers he had been leading by the hand. "Don't you go out of my sight; and whatever you do, don't you do injury to those new clothes of yours, or you'll wish you'd never been put into them. The truth is," continued Hezekiah to his friend, his sole surviving son and heir being out of earshot, "the morning tempted me. 'Tain't often I get a bit of fresh air."

"Doing well?"

"The business," replied Hezekiah, "is going up by leaps and bounds- -leaps and bounds. But, of course, all that means harder work for me. It's from six in the morning till twelve o'clock at night."

"There's nothing I know of," returned Solomon, who was something of a pessimist, "that's given away free gratis for nothing except misfortune."

"Keeping yourself up to the mark ain't too easy," continued Hezekiah; "and when it comes to other folks! play's all they think of.

Talk religion to them--why, they laugh at you! What the world's coming to, I don't know. How's the printing business doing?"

"The printing business," responded the other, removing his pipe and speaking somewhat sadly, "the printing business looks like being a big thing. Capital, of course, is what hampers me--or, rather, the want of it. But Janet, she's careful; she don't waste much, Janet don't."

"Now, with Anne," replied Hezekiah, "it's all the other way-- pleasure, gaiety, a day at Rosherville or the Crystal Palace-- anything to waste money."

"Ah! she was always fond of her bit of fun," remembered Solomon.

"Fun!" retorted Hezekiah. "I like a bit of fun myself. But not if you've got to pay for it. Where's the fun in that?"

"What I ask myself sometimes," said Solomon, looking straight in front of him, "is what do we do it for?"

"What do we do what for?"

"Work like blessed slaves, depriving ourselves of all enjoyments. What's the sense of it? What--"

A voice from the perambulator beside him broke the thread of Solomon Appleyard's discourse. The sole surviving son of Hezekiah Grindley, seeking distraction and finding none, had crept back unperceived. A perambulator! A thing his experience told him out of which excitement in some form or another could generally be obtained. You worried it and took your chance. Either it howled, in which case you had to run for your life, followed--and, unfortunately, overtaken nine times out of ten--by a whirlwind of vengeance; or it gurgled: in which case the heavens smiled and halos descended on your head. In either event you escaped the deadly ennui that is the result of continuous virtue. Master Grindley, his star having pointed out to him a peacock's feather lying on the ground, had, with one eye upon his unobservant parent, removed the complicated coverings sheltering Miss Helvetia Appleyard from the world, and anticipating by a quarter of a century the prime enjoyment of British youth, had set to work to tickle that lady on the nose. Miss Helvetia Appleyard awakened, did precisely what the tickled British maiden of to-day may be relied upon to do under corresponding circumstances: she first of all took swift and comprehensive survey of the male thing behind the feather. Had he been displeasing in her eyes, she would, one may rely upon it, have anteceded the behaviour in similar case of her descendant of to-day--that is to say, have expressed resentment in no uncertain terms. Master Nathaniel Grindley proving, however, to her taste, that which might have been considered impertinence became accepted as a fit and proper form of introduction. Miss Appleyard smiled graciously--nay, further, intimated desire for more.

"That your only one?" asked the paternal Grindley.

"She's the only one," replied Solomon, speaking in tones less pessimistic.

Miss Appleyard had with the help of Grindley junior wriggled herself into a sitting posture. Grindley junior continued his attentions, the lady indicating by signs the various points at which she was most susceptible.

"Pretty picture they make together, eh?" suggested Hezekiah in a whisper to his friend.

"Never saw her take to anyone like that before," returned Solomon, likewise in a whisper.

A neighbouring church clock chimed twelve. Solomon Appleyard, knocking the ashes from his pipe, arose.

"Don't know any reason myself why we shouldn't see a little more of one another than we do," suggested Grindley senior, shaking hands.

"Give us a look-up one Sunday afternoon," suggested Solomon. "Bring the youngster with you."

Solomon Appleyard and Hezekiah Grindley had started life within a few months of one another some five-and-thirty years before. Likewise within a few hundred yards of one another, Solomon at his father's bookselling and printing establishment on the east side of the High Street of a small Yorkshire town; Hezekiah at his father's grocery shop upon the west side, opposite. Both had married farmers' daughters. Solomon's natural bent towards gaiety Fate had corrected by directing his affections to a partner instinct with Yorkshire shrewdness; and with shrewdness go other qualities that make for success rather than for happiness. Hezekiah, had circumstances been equal, might have been his friend's rival for Janet's capable and saving hand, had not sweet-tempered, laughing Annie Glossop--directed by Providence to her moral welfare, one must presume--fallen in love with him. Between Jane's virtues and Annie's three hundred golden sovereigns Hezekiah had not hesitated a moment. Golden sovereigns were solid facts; wifely virtues, by a serious-minded and strong-willed husband, could be instilled--at all events, light-heartedness suppressed. The two men, Hezekiah urged by his own ambition, Solomon by his wife's, had arrived in London within a year of one another: Hezekiah to open a grocer's shop in Kensington, which those who should have known assured him was a hopeless neighbourhood. But Hezekiah had the instinct of the money-maker. Solomon, after looking about him, had fixed upon the roomy, substantial house in Nevill's Court as a promising foundation for a printer's business.

That was ten years ago. The two friends, scorning delights, living laborious days, had seen but little of one another. Light-hearted Annie had borne to her dour partner two children who had died. Nathaniel George, with the luck supposed to wait on number three, had lived on, and, inheriting fortunately the temperament of his mother, had brought sunshine into the gloomy rooms above the shop in High Street, Kensington. Mrs. Grindley, grown weak and fretful, had rested from her labours.

Mrs. Appleyard's guardian angel, prudent like his protege, had waited till Solomon's business was well established before despatching the stork to Nevill's Court, with a little girl. Later had sent a boy, who, not finding the close air of St. Dunstan to his liking, had found his way back again; thus passing out of this story and all others. And there remained to carry on the legend of the Grindleys and the Appleyards only Nathaniel George, now aged five, and Janet Helvetia, quite a beginner, who took lift seriously.

There are no such things as facts. Narrow-minded folk--surveyors, auctioneers, and such like--would have insisted that the garden between the old Georgian house and Nevill's Court was a strip of land one hundred and eighteen feet by ninety-two, containing a laburnum tree, six laurel bushes, and a dwarf deodora. To Nathaniel George and Janet Helvetia it was the land of Thule, "the furthest boundaries of which no man has reached." On rainy Sunday afternoons they played in the great, gloomy pressroom, where silent ogres, standing motionless, stretched out iron arms to seize them as they ran. Then just when Nathaniel George was eight, and Janet Helvetia four and a half, Hezekiah launched the celebrated "Grindley's Sauce." It added a relish to chops and steaks, transformed cold mutton into a luxury, and swelled the head of Hezekiah Grindley--which was big enough in all conscience as it was--and shrivelled up his little hard heart. The Grindleys and the Appleyards visited no more. As a sensible fellow ought to have seen for himself, so thought Hezekiah, the Sauce had altered all things. The possibility of a marriage between their children, things having remained equal, might have been a pretty fancy; but the son of the great Grindley, whose name in three-foot letters faced the world from every hoarding, would have to look higher than a printer's daughter. Solomon, a sudden and vehement convert to the principles of mediaeval feudalism, would rather see his only child, granddaughter of the author of The History of Kettlewell and other works, dead and buried than married to a grocer's son, even though he might inherit a fortune made out of poisoning the public with a mixture of mustard and sour beer. It was many years before Nathaniel George and Janet Helvetia met one another again, and when they did they had forgotten one another,

Hezekiah S. Grindley, a short, stout, and pompous gentleman, sat under a palm in the gorgeously furnished drawing-room of his big house at Notting Hill. Mrs. Grindley, a thin, faded woman, the despair of her dressmaker, sat as near to the fire as its massive and imposing copper outworks would permit, and shivered. Grindley junior, a fair-haired, well-shaped youth, with eyes that the other sex found attractive, leant with his hands in his pockets against a scrupulously robed statue of Diana, and appeared uncomfortable.

"I'm making the money--making it hand over fist. All you'll have to do will be to spend it," Grindley senior was explaining to his son and heir.

"I'll do that all right, dad."

"I'm not so sure of it," was his father's opinion. "You've got to prove yourself worthy to spend it. Don't you think I shall be content to have slaved all these years merely to provide a brainless young idiot with the means of self-indulgence. I leave my money to somebody worthy of me. Understand, sir?--somebody worthy of me."

Mrs. Grindley commenced a sentence; Mr. Grindley turned his small eyes upon her. The sentence remained unfinished.

"You were about to say something," her husband reminded her.

Mrs. Grindley said it was nothing.

"If it is anything worth hearing--if it is anything that will assist the discussion, let's have it." Mr. Grindley waited. "If not, if you yourself do not consider it worth finishing, why have begun it?"

Mr. Grindley returned to his son and heir. "You haven't done too well at school--in fact, your school career has disappointed me."

"I know I'm not clever," Grindley junior offered as an excuse.

"Why not? Why aren't you clever?"

His son and heir was unable to explain.

"You are my son--why aren't you clever? It's laziness, sir; sheer laziness!"

"I'll try and do better at Oxford, sir--honour bright I will!"

"You had better," advised him his father; "because I warn you, your whole future depends upon it. You know me. You've got to be a credit to me, to be worthy of the name of Grindley--or the name, my boy, is all you'll have."

Old Grindley meant it, and his son knew that he meant it. The old Puritan principles and instincts were strong in the old gentleman--formed, perhaps, the better part of him. Idleness was an abomination to him; devotion to pleasure, other than the pleasure of money-making, a grievous sin in his eyes. Grindley junior fully intended to do well at Oxford, and might have succeeded. In accusing himself of lack of cleverness, he did himself an injustice. He had brains, he had energy, he had character. Our virtues can be our stumbling-blocks as well as our vices. Young Grindley had one admirable virtue that needs, above all others, careful controlling: he was amiability itself. Before the charm and sweetness of it, Oxford snobbishness went down. The Sauce, against the earnest counsel of its own advertisement, was forgotten; the pickles passed by. To escape the natural result of his popularity would have needed a stronger will than young Grindley possessed. For a time the true state of affairs was hidden from the eye of Grindley senior. To "slack" it this term, with the full determination of "swotting" it the next, is always easy; the difficulty beginning only with the new term. Possibly with luck young Grindley might have retrieved his position and covered up the traces of his folly, but for an unfortunate accident. Returning to college with some other choice spirits at two o'clock in the morning, it occurred to young Grindley that trouble might be saved all round by cutting out a pane of glass with a diamond ring and entering his rooms, which were on the ground-floor, by the window. That, in mistake for his own, he should have selected the bedroom of the College Rector was a misfortune that might have occurred to anyone who had commenced the evening on champagne and finished it on whisky. Young Grindley, having been warned already twice before, was "sent down." And then, of course, the whole history of the three wasted years came out. Old Grindley in his study chair having talked for half an hour at the top of his voice, chose, partly by reason of physical necessity, partly by reason of dormant dramatic instinct, to speak quietly and slowly.

"I'll give you one chance more, my boy, and one only. I've tried you as a gentleman--perhaps that was my mistake. Now I'll try you as a grocer."

"As a what?"

"As a grocer, sh-g-r-o-c-e-r--grocer, a man who stands behind a counter in a white apron and his shirt-sleeves; who sells tea and sugar and candied peel and such-like things to customers--old ladies, little girls; who rises at six in the morning, takes down the shutters, sweeps out the shop, cleans the windows; who has half an hour for his dinner of corned beef and bread; who puts up the shutters at ten o'clock at night, tidies up the shop, has his supper, and goes to bed, feeling his day has not been wasted. I meant to spare you. I was wrong. You shall go through the mill as I went through it. If at the end of two years you've done well with your time, learned something--learned to be a man, at all events--you can come to me and thank me."

"I'm afraid, sir," suggested Grindley junior, whose handsome face during the last few minutes had grown very white, "I might not make a very satisfactory grocer. You see, sir, I've had no experience."

"I am glad you have some sense," returned his father drily. "You are quite right. Even a grocer's business requires learning. It will cost me a little money; but it will be the last I shall ever spend upon you. For the first year you will have to be apprenticed, and I shall allow you something to live on. It shall be more than I had at your age--we'll say a pound a week. After that I shall expect you to keep yourself."

Grindley senior rose. "You need not give me your answer till the evening. You are of age. I have no control over you unless you are willing to agree. You can go my way, or you can go your own."

Young Grindley, who had inherited a good deal of his father's grit, felt very much inclined to go his own; but, hampered on the other hand by the sweetness of disposition he had inherited from his mother, was unable to withstand the argument of that lady's tears, so that evening accepted old Grindley's terms, asking only as a favour that the scene of his probation might be in some out-of-the- way neighbourhood where there would be little chance of his being met by old friends.

"I have thought of all that," answered his father. "My object isn't to humiliate you more than is necessary for your good. The shop I have already selected, on the assumption that you would submit, is as quiet and out-of-the-way as you could wish. It is in a turning off Fetter Lane, where you'll see few other people than printers and caretakers. You'll lodge with a woman, a Mrs. Postwhistle, who seems a very sensible person. She'll board you and lodge you, and every Saturday you'll receive a post-office order for six shillings, out of which you'll find yourself in clothes. You can take with you sufficient to last you for the first six months, but no more. At the end of the year you can change if you like and go to another shop, or make your own arrangements with Mrs. Postwhistle. If all is settled, you go there to-morrow. You go out of this house to-morrow in any event."

Mrs. Postwhistle was a large, placid lady of philosophic temperament. Hitherto the little grocer's shop in Rolls Court, Fetter Lane, had been easy of management by her own unaided efforts; but the neighbourhood was rapidly changing. Other grocers' shops were disappearing one by one, making way for huge blocks of buildings, where hundreds of iron presses, singing day and night, spread to the earth the song of the Mighty Pen. There were hours when the little shop could hardly accommodate its crowd of customers. Mrs. Postwhistle, of a bulk not to be moved quickly, had, after mature consideration, conquering a natural disinclination to change, decided to seek assistance.

Young Grindley, alighting from a four-wheeled cab in Fetter Lane, marched up the court, followed by a weak-kneed wastrel staggering under the weight of a small box. In the doorway of the little shop, young Grindley paused and raised his hat.

"Mrs. Postwhistle?"

The lady, from her chair behind the counter, rose slowly.

"I am Mr. Nathaniel Grindley, the new assistant."

The weak-kneed wastrel let fall the box with a thud upon the floor. Mrs. Postwhistle looked her new assistant up and down.

"Oh!" said Mrs. Postwhistle. "Well, I shouldn't 'ave felt instinctively it must be you, not if I'd 'ad to pick you out of a crowd. But if you tell me so, why, I suppose you are. Come in."

The weak-kneed wastrel, receiving to his astonishment a shilling, departed.

Grindley senior had selected wisely. Mrs. Postwhistle's theory was that although very few people in this world understood their own business, they understood it better than anyone else could understand it for them. If handsome, well-educated young gentlemen, who gave shillings to wastrels, felt they wanted to become smart and capable grocers' assistants, that was their affair. Her business was to teach them their work, and, for her own sake, to see that they did it. A month went by. Mrs. Postwhistle found her new assistant hard-working, willing, somewhat clumsy, but with a smile and a laugh that transformed mistakes, for which another would have been soundly rated, into welcome variations of the day's monotony.

"If you were the sort of woman that cared to make your fortune," said one William Clodd, an old friend of Mrs. Postwhistle's, young Grindley having descended into the cellar to grind coffee, "I'd tell you what to do. Take a bun-shop somewhere in the neighbourhood of a girls' school, and put that assistant of yours in the window. You'd do a roaring business."

"There's a mystery about 'im," said Mrs. Postwhistle.

"Know what it is?"

"If I knew what it was, I shouldn't be calling it a mystery," replied Mrs. Postwhistle, who was a stylist in her way.

"How did you get him? Win him in a raffle?"

"Jones, the agent, sent 'im to me all in a 'urry. An assistant is what I really wanted, not an apprentice; but the premium was good, and the references everything one could desire."

"Grindley, Grindley," murmured Clodd. "Any relation to the Sauce, I wonder?"

"A bit more wholesome, I should say, from the look of him," thought Mrs. Postwhistle.

The question of a post office to meet its growing need had long been under discussion by the neighbourhood. Mrs. Postwhistle was approached upon the subject. Grindley junior, eager for anything that might bring variety into his new, cramped existence, undertook to qualify himself.

Within two months the arrangements were complete. Grindley junior divided his time between dispensing groceries and despatching telegrams and letters, and was grateful for the change.

Grindley junior's mind was fixed upon the fashioning of a cornucopia to receive a quarter of a pound of moist. The customer, an extremely young lady, was seeking to hasten his operations by tapping incessantly with a penny on the counter. It did not hurry him; it only worried him. Grindley junior had not acquired facility in the fashioning of cornucopias--the vertex would invariably become unrolled at the last moment, allowing the contents to dribble out on to the floor or counter. Grindley junior was sweet-tempered as a rule, but when engaged upon the fashioning of a cornucopia, was irritable.

"Hurry up, old man!" urged the extremely young lady. "I've got another appointment in less than half an hour."

"Oh, damn the thing!" said Grindley junior, as the paper for the fourth time reverted to its original shape.

An older lady, standing behind the extremely young lady and holding a telegram-form in her hand, looked indignant.

"Temper, temper," remarked the extremely young lady in reproving tone.

The fifth time was more successful. The extremely young lady went out, commenting upon the waste of time always resulting when boys were employed to do the work of men. The older lady, a haughty person, handed across her telegram with the request that it should be sent off at once.

Grindley junior took his pencil from his pocket and commenced to count.

"Digniori, not digniorus," commented Grindley junior, correcting the word, "datur digniori, dative singular." Grindley junior, still irritable from the struggle with the cornucopia, spoke sharply.

The haughty lady withdrew her eyes from a spot some ten miles beyond the back of the shop, where hitherto they had been resting, and fixed them for the first time upon Grindley junior.

"Thank you," said the haughty lady.

Grindley junior looked up and immediately, to his annoyance, felt that he was blushing. Grindley junior blushed easily--it annoyed him very much.

The haughty young lady also blushed. She did not often blush; when she did, she felt angry with herself.

"A shilling and a penny," demanded Grindley junior.

The haughty young lady counted out the money and departed.

Grindley junior, peeping from behind a tin of Abernethy biscuits, noticed that as she passed the window she turned and looked back. She was a very pretty, haughty lady. Grindley junior rather admired dark, level brows and finely cut, tremulous lips, especially when combined with a mass of soft, brown hair, and a rich olive complexion that flushed and paled as one looked at it.

"Might send that telegram off if you've nothing else to do, and there's no particular reason for keeping it back," suggested Mrs. Postwhistle.

"It's only just been handed in," explained Grindley junior, somewhat hurt.

"You've been looking at it for the last five minutes by the clock," said Mrs. Postwhistle.

Grindley junior sat down to the machine. The name and address of the sender was Helvetia Appleyard, Nevill's Court.

Three days passed--singularly empty days they appeared to Grindley junior. On the fourth, Helvetia Appleyard had occasion to despatch another telegram--this time entirely in English.

"One-and-fourpence," sighed Grindley junior.

Miss Appleyard drew forth her purse. The shop was empty.

"How did you come to know Latin?" inquired Miss Appleyard in quite a casual tone.

"I picked up a little at school. It was a phrase I happened to remember," confessed Grindley junior, wondering why he should be feeling ashamed of himself.

"I am always sorry," said Miss Appleyard, "when I see anyone content with the lower life whose talents might, perhaps, fit him for the higher." Something about the tone and manner of Miss Appleyard reminded Grindley junior of his former Rector. Each seemed to have arrived by different roads at the same philosophical aloofness from the world, tempered by chastened interest in human phenomena. "Would you like to try to raise yourself--to improve yourself--to educate yourself?"

An unseen little rogue, who was enjoying himself immensely, whispered to Grindley junior to say nothing but "Yes," he should.

"Will you let me help you?" asked Miss Appleyard. And the simple and heartfelt gratitude with which Grindley junior closed upon the offer proved to Miss Appleyard how true it is that to do good to others is the highest joy.

Miss Appleyard had come prepared for possible acceptance. "You had better begin with this," thought Miss Appleyard. "I have marked the passages that you should learn by heart. Make a note of anything you do not understand, and I will explain it to you when-- when next I happen to be passing."

Grindley junior took the book--Bell's Introduction to the Study of the Classics, for Use of Beginners--and held it between both hands. Its price was ninepence, but Grindley junior appeared to regard it as a volume of great value.

"It will be hard work at first," Miss Appleyard warned him; "but you must persevere. I have taken an interest in you; you must try not to disappoint me."

And Miss Appleyard, feeling all the sensations of a Hypatia, departed, taking light with her and forgetting to pay for the telegram. Miss Appleyard belonged to the class that young ladies who pride themselves on being tiresomely ignorant and foolish sneer at as "blue-stockings"; that is to say, possessing brains, she had felt the necessity of using them. Solomon Appleyard, widower, a sensible old gentleman, prospering in the printing business, and seeing no necessity for a woman regarding herself as nothing but a doll, a somewhat uninteresting plaything the newness once worn off, thankfully encouraged her. Miss Appleyard had returned from Girton wise in many things, but not in knowledge of the world, which knowledge, too early acquired, does not always make for good in young man or woman. A serious little virgin, Miss Appleyard's ambition was to help the human race. What more useful work could have come to her hand than the raising of this poor but intelligent young grocer's assistant unto the knowledge and the love of higher things. That Grindley junior happened to be an exceedingly good-looking and charming young grocer's assistant had nothing to do with the matter, so Miss Appleyard would have informed you. In her own reasoning she was convinced that her interest in him would have been the same had he been the least attractive of his sex. That there could be danger in such relationship never occurred to her.

Miss Appleyard, a convinced Radical, could not conceive the possibility of a grocer's assistant regarding the daughter of a well-to-do printer in any other light than that of a graciously condescending patron. That there could be danger to herself! you would have been sorry you had suggested the idea. The expression of lofty scorn would have made you feel yourself contemptible.

Miss Appleyard's judgment of mankind was justified; no more promising pupil could have been selected. It was really marvellous the progress made by Grindley junior, under the tutelage of Helvetia Appleyard. His earnestness, his enthusiasm, it quite touched the heart of Helvetia Appleyard. There were many points, it is true, that puzzled Grindley junior. Each time the list of them grew longer. But when Helvetia Appleyard explained them, all became clear. She marvelled herself at her own wisdom, that in a moment made darkness luminous to this young man; his rapt attention while she talked, it was most encouraging. The boy must surely be a genius. To think that but for her intuition he might have remained wasted in a grocer's shop! To rescue such a gem from oblivion, to polish it, was surely the duty of a conscientious Hypatia. Two visits--three visits a week to the little shop in Rolls Court were quite inadequate, so many passages there were requiring elucidation. London in early morning became their classroom: the great, wide, empty, silent streets; the mist-curtained parks, the silence broken only by the blackbirds' amorous whistle, the thrushes' invitation to delight; the old gardens, hidden behind narrow ways. Nathaniel George and Janet Helvetia would rest upon a seat, no living creature within sight, save perhaps a passing policeman or some dissipated cat. Janet Helvetia would expound. Nathaniel George, his fine eyes fixed on hers, seemed never to tire of drinking in her wisdom.

There were times when Janet Helvetia, to reassure herself as to the maidenly correctness of her behaviour, had to recall quite forcibly the fact that she was the daughter of Solomon Appleyard, owner of the big printing establishment; and he a simple grocer. One day, raised a little in the social scale, thanks to her, Nathaniel George would marry someone in his own rank of life. Reflecting upon the future of Nathaniel George, Janet Helvetia could not escape a shade of sadness. It was difficult to imagine precisely the wife she would have chosen for Nathaniel George. She hoped he would do nothing foolish. Rising young men so often marry wives that hamper rather than help them.

One Sunday morning in late autumn, they walked and talked in the shady garden of Lincoln's Inn. Greek they thought it was they had been talking; as a matter of fact, a much older language. A young gardener was watering flowers, and as they passed him he grinned. It was not an offensive grin, rather a sympathetic grin; but Miss Appleyard didn't like being grinned at. What was there to grin at? Her personal appearance? some gaucherie in her dress? Impossible. No lady in all St. Dunstan was ever more precise. She glanced at her companion: a clean-looking, well-groomed, well-dressed youth. Suddenly it occurred to Miss Appleyard that she and Grindley junior were holding each other's hand. Miss Appleyard was justly indignant.

"How dare you!" said Miss Appleyard. "I am exceedingly angry with you. How dare you!"

The olive skin was scarlet. There were tears in the hazel eyes.

"Leave me this minute!" commanded Miss Appleyard.

Instead of which, Grindley junior seized both her hands.

"I love you! I adore you! I worship you!" poured forth young Grindley, forgetful of all Miss Appleyard had ever told him concerning the folly of tautology.

"You had no right," said Miss Appleyard.

"I couldn't help it," pleaded young Grindley. "And that isn't the worst."

Miss Appleyard paled visibly. For a grocer's assistant to dare to fall in love with her, especially after all the trouble she had taken with him! What could be worse?

"I'm not a grocer," continued young Grindley, deeply conscious of crime. "I mean, not a real grocer."

And Grindley junior then and there made a clean breast of the whole sad, terrible tale of shameless deceit, practised by the greatest villain the world had ever produced, upon the noblest and most beautiful maiden that ever turned grim London town into a fairy city of enchanted ways.

Not at first could Miss Appleyard entirely grasp it; not till hours later, when she sat alone in her own room, where, fortunately for himself, Grindley junior was not, did the whole force and meaning of the thing come home to her. It was a large room, taking up half of the top story of the big Georgian house in Nevill's Court; but even as it was, Miss Appleyard felt cramped.

"For a year--for nearly a whole year," said Miss Appleyard, addressing the bust of William Shakespeare, "have I been slaving my life out, teaching him elementary Latin and the first five books of Euclid!"

As it has been remarked, it was fortunate for Grindley junior he was out of reach. The bust of William Shakespeare maintained its irritating aspect of benign philosophy.

"I suppose I should," mused Miss Appleyard, "if he had told me at first--as he ought to have told me--of course I should naturally have had nothing more to do with him. I suppose," mused Miss Appleyard, "a man in love, if he is really in love, doesn't quite know what he's doing. I suppose one ought to make allowances. But, oh! when I think of it--"

And then Grindley junior's guardian angel must surely have slipped into the room, for Miss Appleyard, irritated beyond endurance at the philosophical indifference of the bust of William Shakespeare, turned away from it, and as she did so, caught sight of herself in the looking-glass. Miss Appleyard approached the glass a little nearer. A woman's hair is never quite as it should be. Miss Appleyard, standing before the glass, began, she knew not why, to find reasons excusing Grindley junior. After all, was not forgiveness an excellent thing in woman? None of us are quite perfect. The guardian angel of Grindley junior seized the opportunity.

That evening Solomon Appleyard sat upright in his chair, feeling confused. So far as he could understand it, a certain young man, a grocer's assistant, but not a grocer's assistant--but that, of course, was not his fault, his father being an old brute--had behaved most abominably; but not, on reflection, as badly as he might have done, and had acted on the whole very honourably, taking into consideration the fact that one supposed he could hardly help it. Helvetia was, of course, very indignant with him, but on the other hand, did not quite see what else she could have done, she being not at all sure whether she really cared for him or whether she didn't; that everything had been quite proper and would not have happened if she had known it; that everything was her fault, except most things, which weren't; but that of the two she blamed herself entirely, seeing that she could not have guessed anything of the kind. And did he, Solomon Appleyard, think that she ought to be very angry and never marry anybody else, or was she justified in overlooking it and engaging herself to the only man she felt she could ever love?

"You mustn't think, Dad, that I meant to deceive you. I should have told you at the beginning--you know I would--if it hadn't all happened so suddenly."

"Let me see," said Solomon Appleyard, "did you tell me his name, or didn't you?"

"Nathaniel," said Miss Appleyard. "Didn't I mention it?"

"Don't happen to know his surname, do you," inquired her father.

"Grindley," explained Miss Appleyard--"the son of Grindley, the Sauce man."

Miss Appleyard experienced one of the surprises of her life. Never before to her recollection had her father thwarted a single wish of her life. A widower for the last twelve years, his chief delight had been to humour her. His voice, as he passionately swore that never with his consent should his daughter marry the son of Hezekiah Grindley, sounded strange to her. Pleadings, even tears, for the first time in her life proved fruitless.

Here was a pretty kettle of fish! That Grindley junior should defy his own parent, risk possibly the loss of his inheritance, had seemed to both a not improper proceeding. When Nathaniel George had said with fine enthusiasm: "Let him keep his money if he will; I'll make my own way; there isn't enough money in the world to pay for losing you!" Janet Helvetia, though she had expressed disapproval of such unfilial attitude, had in secret sympathised. But for her to disregard the wishes of her own doting father was not to be thought of. What was to be done?

Perhaps one Peter Hope, residing in Gough Square hard by, might help young folks in sore dilemma with wise counsel. Peter Hope, editor and part proprietor of Good Humour, one penny weekly, was much esteemed by Solomon Appleyard, printer and publisher of aforesaid paper.

"A good fellow, old Hope," Solomon would often impress upon his managing clerk. "Don't worry him more than you can help; things will improve. We can trust him."

Peter Hope sat at his desk, facing Miss Appleyard. Grindley junior sat on the cushioned seat beneath the middle window. Good Humour's sub-editor stood before the fire, her hands behind her back.

The case appeared to Peter Hope to be one of exceeding difficulty.

"Of course," explained Miss Appleyard, "I shall never marry without my father's consent."

Peter Hope thought the resolution most proper.

"On the other hand," continued Miss Appleyard, "nothing shall induce me to marry a man I do not love." Miss Appleyard thought the probabilities were that she would end by becoming a female missionary.

Peter Hope's experience had led him to the conclusion that young people sometimes changed their mind.

The opinion of the House, clearly though silently expressed, was that Peter Hope's experience, as regarded this particular case, counted for nothing.

"I shall go straight to the Governor," explained Grindley junior, "and tell him that I consider myself engaged for life to Miss Appleyard. I know what will happen--I know the sort of idea he has got into his head. He will disown me, and I shall go off to Africa."

Peter Hope was unable to see how Grindley junior's disappearance into the wilds of Africa was going to assist the matter under discussion.

Grindley junior's view was that the wilds of Africa would afford a fitting background to the passing away of a blighted existence.

Peter Hope had a suspicion that Grindley junior had for the moment parted company with that sweet reasonableness that otherwise, so Peter Hope felt sure, was Grindley junior's guiding star.

"I mean it, sir," reasserted Grindley junior. "I am--" Grindley junior was about to add "well educated"; but divining that education was a topic not pleasing at the moment to the ears of Helvetia Appleyard, had tact enough to substitute "not a fool. I can earn my own living; and I should like to get away."

"It seems to me--" said the sub-editor.

"Now, Tommy--I mean Jane," warned her Peter Hope. He always called her Jane in company, unless he was excited. "I know what you are going to say. I won't have it."

"I was only going to say--" urged the sub-editor in tone of one suffering injustice.

"I quite know what you were going to say," retorted Peter hotly. "I can see it by your chin. You are going to take their part--and suggest their acting undutifully towards their parents."

"I wasn't," returned the sub-editor. "I was only--"

"You were," persisted Peter. "I ought not to have allowed you to be present. I might have known you would interfere."

"--going to say we are in want of some help in the office. You know we are. And that if Mr. Grindley would be content with a small salary--"

"Small salary be hanged!" snarled Peter.

"--there would be no need for his going to Africa."

"And how would that help us?" demanded Peter. "Even if the boy were so--so headstrong, so unfilial as to defy his father, who has worked for him all these years, how would that remove the obstacle of Mr. Appleyard's refusal?"

"Why, don't you see--" explained the sub-editor.

"No, I don't," snapped Peter.

"If, on his declaring to his father that nothing will ever induce him to marry any other woman but Miss Appleyard, his father disowns him, as he thinks it likely--"

"A dead cert!" was Grindley junior's conviction.

"Very well; he is no longer old Grindley's son, and what possible objection can Mr. Appleyard have to him then?"

Peter Hope arose and expounded at length and in suitable language the folly and uselessness of the scheme.

But what chance had ever the wisdom of Age against the enthusiasm of Youth, reaching for its object. Poor Peter, expostulating, was swept into the conspiracy. Grindley junior the next morning stood before his father in the private office in High Holborn.

"I am sorry, sir," said Grindley junior, "if I have proved a disappointment to you."

"Damn your sympathy!" said Grindley senior. "Keep it till you are asked for it."

"I hope we part friends, sir," said Grindley junior, holding out his hand.

"Why do you irate me?" asked Grindley senior. "I have thought of nothing but you these five-and-twenty years."

"I don't, sir," answered Grindley junior. "I can't say I love you. It did not seem to me you--you wanted it. But I like you, sir, and I respect you. And--and I'm sorry to have to hurt you, sir."

"And you are determined to give up all your prospects, all the money, for the sake of this--this girl?"

"It doesn't seem like giving up anything, sir," replied Grindley junior, simply.

"It isn't so much as I thought it was going to be," said the old man, after a pause. "Perhaps it is for the best. I might have been more obstinate if things had been going all right. The Lord has chastened me."

"Isn't the business doing well, Dad?" asked the young man, with sorrow in his voice.

"What's it got to do with you?" snapped his father. "You've cut yourself adrift from it. You leave me now I am going down."

Grindley junior, not knowing what to say, put his arms round the little old man.

And in this way Tommy's brilliant scheme fell through and came to naught. Instead, old Grindley visited once again the big house in Nevill's Court, and remained long closeted with old Solomon in the office on the second floor. It was late in the evening when Solomon opened the door and called upstairs to Janet Helvetia to come down.

"I used to know you long ago," said Hezekiah Grindley, rising. "You were quite a little girl then."

Later, the troublesome Sauce disappeared entirely, cut out by newer flavours. Grindley junior studied the printing business. It almost seemed as if old Appleyard had been waiting but for this. Some six months later they found him dead in his counting-house. Grindley junior became the printer and publisher of Good Humour.

STORY THE FOURTH

MISS RAMSBOTHAM GIVES HER SERVICES

To regard Miss Ramsbotham as a marriageable quantity would have occurred to few men. Endowed by Nature with every feminine quality calculated to inspire liking, she had, on the other hand, been disinherited of every attribute calculated to excite passion. An ugly woman has for some men an attraction; the proof is ever present to our eyes. Miss Ramsbotham was plain but pleasant looking. Large, healthy in mind and body, capable, self-reliant, and cheerful, blessed with a happy disposition together with a keen sense of humour, there was about her absolutely nothing for tenderness to lay hold of. An ideal wife, she was an impossible sweetheart. Every man was her friend. The suggestion that any man could be her lover she herself would have greeted with a clear, ringing laugh.

Not that she held love in despite; for such folly she was possessed of far too much sound sense. "To have somebody in love with you--somebody strong and good," so she would confess to her few close intimates, a dreamy expression clouding for an instant her broad, sunny face, "why, it must be just lovely!" For Miss Ramsbotham was prone to American phraseology, and had even been at some pains, during a six months' journey through the States (whither she had been commissioned by a conscientious trade journal seeking reliable information concerning the condition of female textile workers) to acquire a slight but decided American accent. It was her one affectation, but assumed, as one might feel certain, for a practical and legitimate object.

"You can have no conception," she would explain, laughing, "what a help I find it. 'I'm 'Muriken' is the 'Civis Romanus sum' of the modern woman's world. It opens every door to us. If I ring the bell and say, 'Oh, if you please, I have come to interview Mr. So- and-So for such-and-such a paper,' the footman looks through me at the opposite side of the street, and tells me to wait in the hall while he inquires if Mr. So-and-So will see me or not. But if I say, 'That's my keerd, young man. You tell your master Miss Ramsbotham is waiting for him in the showroom, and will take it real kind if he'll just bustle himself,' the poor fellow walks backwards till he stumbles against the bottom stair, and my gentleman comes down with profuse apologies for having kept me waiting three minutes and a half.

"'And to be in love with someone," she would continue, "someone great that one could look up to and honour and worship--someone that would fill one's whole life, make it beautiful, make every day worth living, I think that would be better still. To work merely for one's self, to think merely for one's self, it is so much less interesting."

Then, at some such point of the argument, Miss Ramsbotham would jump up from her chair and shake herself indignantly.

"Why, what nonsense I'm talking," she would tell herself, and her listeners. "I make a very fair income, have a host of friends, and enjoy every hour of my life. I should like to have been pretty or handsome, of course; but no one can have all the good things of this world, and I have my brains. At one time, perhaps, yes; but now--no, honestly I would not change myself."

Miss Ramsbotham was sorry that no man had ever fallen in love with her, but that she could understand.

"It is quite clear to me." So she had once unburdened herself to her bosom friend. "Man for the purposes of the race has been given two kinds of love, between which, according to his opportunities and temperament, he is free to choose: he can fall down upon his knees and adore physical beauty (for Nature ignores entirely our mental side), or he can take delight in circling with his protecting arm the weak and helpless. Now, I make no appeal to either instinct. I possess neither the charm nor beauty to attract--"

"Beauty," reminded her the bosom friend, consolingly, "dwells in the beholder's eye."

"My dear," cheerfully replied Miss Ramsbotham, "it would have to be an eye of the range and capacity Sam Weller frankly owned up to not possessing--a patent double-million magnifying, capable of seeing through a deal board and round the corner sort of eye--to detect any beauty in me. And I am much too big and sensible for any man not a fool ever to think of wanting to take care of me.

"I believe," remembered Miss Ramsbotham, "if it does not sound like idle boasting, I might have had a husband, of a kind, if Fate had not compelled me to save his life. I met him one year at Huyst, a small, quiet watering-place on the Dutch coast. He would walk always half a step behind me, regarding me out of the corner of his eye quite approvingly at times. He was a widower--a good little man, devoted to his three charming children. They took an immense fancy to me, and I really think I could have got on with him. I am very adaptable, as you know. But it was not to be. He got out of his depth one morning, and unfortunately there was no one within distance but myself who could swim. I knew what the result would be. You remember Labiche's comedy, Les Voyage de Monsieur Perrichon? Of course, every man hates having had his life saved, after it is over; and you can imagine how he must hate having it saved by a woman. But what was I to do? In either case he would be lost to me, whether I let him drown or whether I rescued him. So, as it really made no difference, I rescued him. He was very grateful, and left the next morning.

"It is my destiny. No man has ever fallen in love with me, and no man ever will. I used to worry myself about it when I was younger. As a child I hugged to my bosom for years an observation I had overheard an aunt of mine whisper to my mother one afternoon as they sat knitting and talking, not thinking I was listening. 'You never can tell,' murmured my aunt, keeping her eyes carefully fixed upon her needles; 'children change so. I have known the plainest girls grow up into quite beautiful women. I should not worry about it if I were you--not yet awhile.' My mother was not at all a bad-looking woman, and my father was decidedly handsome; so there seemed no reason why I should not hope. I pictured myself the ugly duckling of Andersen's fairy-tale, and every morning on waking I would run straight to my glass and try to persuade myself that the feathers of the swan were beginning at last to show themselves." Miss Ramsbotham laughed, a genuine laugh of amusement, for of self-pity not a trace was now remaining to her.

"Later I plucked hope again," continued Miss Ramsbotham her confession, "from the reading of a certain school of fiction more popular twenty years ago than now. In these romances the heroine was never what you would call beautiful, unless in common with the hero you happened to possess exceptional powers of observation. But she was better than that, she was good. I do not regard as time wasted the hours I spent studying this quaint literature. It helped me, I am sure, to form habits that have since been of service to me. I made a point, when any young man visitor happened to be staying with us, of rising exceptionally early in the morning, so that I always appeared at the breakfast-table fresh, cheerful, and carefully dressed, with, when possible, a dew-besprinkled flower in my hair to prove that I had already been out in the garden. The effort, as far as the young man visitor was concerned, was always thrown away; as a general rule, he came down late himself, and generally too drowsy to notice anything much. But it was excellent practice for me. I wake now at seven o'clock as a matter of course, whatever time I go to bed. I made my own dresses and most of our cakes, and took care to let everybody know it. Though I say it who should not, I play and sing rather well. I certainly was never a fool. I had no little brothers and sisters to whom to be exceptionally devoted, but I had my cousins about the house as much as possible, and damaged their characters, if anything, by over-indulgence. My dear, it never caught even a curate! I am not one of those women to run down men; I think them delightful creatures, and in a general way I find them very intelligent. But where their hearts are concerned it is the girl with the frizzy hair, who wants two people to help her over the stile, that is their idea of an angel. No man could fall in love with me; he couldn't if he tried. That I can understand; but"-- Miss Ramsbotham sunk her voice to a more confidential tone--"what I cannot understand is that I have never fallen in love with any man, because I like them all."

"You have given the explanation yourself," suggested the bosom friend--one Susan Fossett, the "Aunt Emma" of The Ladies' Journal, a nice woman, but talkative. "You are too sensible."

Miss Ramsbotham shook her head, "I should just love to fall in love. When I think about it, I feel quite ashamed of myself for not having done so."

Whether it was this idea, namely, that it was her duty, or whether it was that passion came to her, unsought, somewhat late in life, and therefore all the stronger, she herself would perhaps have been unable to declare. Certain only it is that at over thirty years of age this clever, sensible, clear-seeing woman fell to sighing and blushing, starting and stammering at the sounding of a name, as though for all the world she had been a love-sick girl in her teens.

Susan Fossett, her bosom friend, brought the strange tidings to Bohemia one foggy November afternoon, her opportunity being a tea- party given by Peter Hope to commemorate the birthday of his adopted daughter and sub-editor, Jane Helen, commonly called Tommy. The actual date of Tommy's birthday was known only to the gods; but out of the London mist to wifeless, childless Peter she had come the evening of a certain November the eighteenth, and therefore by Peter and his friends November the eighteenth had been marked upon the calendar as a day on which they should rejoice together.

"It is bound to leak out sooner or later," Susan Fossett was convinced, "so I may as well tell you: that gaby Mary Ramsbotham has got herself engaged."

"Nonsense!" was Peter Hope's involuntary ejaculation.

"Precisely what I mean to tell her the very next time I see her," added Susan.

"Who to?" demanded Tommy.

"You mean 'to whom.' The preeposition governs the objective case," corrected her James Douglas McTear, commonly called "The Wee Laddie," who himself wrote English better than he spoke it.

"I meant 'to whom,'" explained Tommy.

"Ye didna say it," persisted the Wee Laddie.

"I don't know to whom," replied Miss Ramsbotham's bosom friend, sipping tea and breathing indignation. "To something idiotic and incongruous that will make her life a misery to her."

Somerville, the briefless, held that in the absence of all data such conclusion was unjustifiable.

"If it had been to anything sensible," was Miss Fossett's opinion, "she would not have kept me in the dark about it, to spring it upon me like a bombshell. I've never had so much as a hint from her until I received this absurd scrawl an hour ago."

Miss Fossett produced from her bag a letter written in pencil.

"There can be no harm in your hearing it," was Miss Fossett's excuse; "it will give you an idea of the state of the poor thing's mind."

The tea-drinkers left their cups and gathered round her. "Dear Susan," read Miss Fossett, "I shall not be able to be with you to-morrow. Please get me out of it nicely. I can't remember at the moment what it is. You'll be surprised to hear that I'm ENGAGED-- to be married, I mean, I can hardly REALISE it. I hardly seem to know where I am. Have just made up my mind to run down to Yorkshire and see grandmamma. I must do SOMETHING. I must TALK to SOMEBODY and--forgive me, dear--but you ARE so sensible, and just now--well I don't FEEL sensible. Will tell you all about it when I see you--next week, perhaps. You must TRY to like him. He is SO handsome and REALLY clever--in his own way. Don't scold me. I never thought it possible that ANYONE could be so happy. It's quite a different sort of happiness to ANY other sort of happiness. I don't know how to describe it. Please ask Burcot to let me off the ante-quarian congress. I feel I should do it badly. I am so thankful he has NO relatives--in England. I should have been so TERRIBLY nervous. Twelve hours ago I could not have DREAMT of it, and now I walk on tiptoe for fear of waking up. Did I leave my chinchilla at your rooms? Don't be angry with me. I should have told you if I had known. In haste. Yours, Mary."

"It's dated from Marylebone Road, and yesterday afternoon she did leave her chinchilla in my rooms, which makes me think it really must be from Mary Ramsbotham. Otherwise I should have my doubts," added Miss Fossett, as she folded up the letter and replaced it in her bag.

"Id is love!" was the explanation of Dr. William Smith, his round, red face illuminated with poetic ecstasy. "Love has gone to her-- has dransformed her once again into the leedle maid."

"Love," retorted Susan Fossett, "doesn't transform an intelligent, educated woman into a person who writes a letter all in jerks, underlines every other word, spells antiquarian with an 'e,' and Burcott's name, whom she has known for the last eight years, with only one 't.' The woman has gone stark, staring mad!"

"We must wait until we have seen him," was Peter's judicious view. "I should be so glad to think that the dear lady was happy."

"So should I," added Miss Fossett drily.

"One of the most sensible women I have ever met," commented William Clodd. "Lucky man, whoever he is. Half wish I'd thought of it myself."

"I am not saying that he isn't," retorted Miss Fossett. "It isn't him I'm worrying about."

"I preesume you mean 'he,'" suggested the Wee Laddie. "The verb 'to be'--"

"For goodness' sake," suggested Miss Fossett to Tommy, "give that man something to eat or drink. That's the worst of people who take up grammar late in life. Like all converts, they become fanatical."

"She's a ripping good sort, is Mary Ramsbotham," exclaimed Grindley junior, printer and publisher of Good Humour. "The marvel to me is that no man hitherto has ever had the sense to want her."

"Oh, you men!" cried Miss Fossett. "A pretty face and an empty head is all you want."

"Must they always go together?" laughed Mrs. Grindley junior, nee Helvetia Appleyard.

"Exceptions prove the rule," grunted Miss Fossett.

"What a happy saying that is," smiled Mrs. Grindley junior. "I wonder sometimes how conversation was ever carried on before it was invented."

"De man who would fall in love wid our dear frent Mary," thought Dr. Smith, "he must be quite egsceptional."

"You needn't talk about her as if she was a monster--I mean were," corrected herself Miss Fossett, with a hasty glance towards the Wee Laddie. "There isn't a man I know that's worthy of her."

"I mean," explained the doctor, "dat he must be a man of character- -of brain. Id is de noble man dat is attracted by de noble woman."

"By the chorus-girl more often," suggested Miss Fossett.

"We must hope for the best," counselled Peter. "I cannot believe that a clever, capable woman like Mary Ramsbotham would make a fool of herself."

"From what I have seen," replied Miss Fossett, "it's just the clever people--as regards this particular matter--who do make fools of themselves."

Unfortunately Miss Fossett's judgment proved to be correct. On being introduced a fortnight later to Miss Ramsbotham's fiance, the impulse of Bohemia was to exclaim, "Great Scott! Whatever in the name of--" Then on catching sight of Miss Ramsbotham's transfigured face and trembling hands Bohemia recollected itself in time to murmur instead: "Delighted, I'm sure!" and to offer mechanical congratulations. Reginald Peters was a pretty but remarkably foolish-looking lad of about two-and-twenty, with curly hair and receding chin; but to Miss Ramsbotham evidently a promising Apollo. Her first meeting with him had taken place at one of the many political debating societies then in fashion, attendance at which Miss Ramsbotham found useful for purposes of journalistic "copy." Miss Ramsbotham, hitherto a Radical of pronounced views, he had succeeded under three months in converting into a strong supporter of the Gentlemanly Party. His feeble political platitudes, which a little while before she would have seized upon merrily to ridicule, she now sat drinking in, her plain face suffused with admiration. Away from him and in connection with those subjects--somewhat numerous--about which he knew little and cared less, she retained her sense and humour; but in his presence she remained comparatively speechless, gazing up into his somewhat watery eyes with the grateful expression of one learning wisdom from a master.

Her absurd adoration--irritating beyond measure to her friends, and which even to her lover, had he possessed a grain of sense, would have appeared ridiculous--to Master Peters was evidently a gratification. Of selfish, exacting nature, he must have found the services of this brilliant woman of the world of much practical advantage. Knowing all the most interesting people in London, it was her pride and pleasure to introduce him everywhere. Her friends put up with him for her sake; to please her made him welcome, did their best to like him, and disguised their failure. The free entry to a places of amusement saved his limited purse. Her influence, he had instinct enough to perceive, could not fail to be of use to him in his profession: that of a barrister. She praised him to prominent solicitors, took him to tea with judges' wives, interested examiners on his behalf. In return he overlooked her many disadvantages, and did not fail to let her know it. Miss Ramsbotham's gratitude was boundless.

"I do so wish I were younger and better looking," she sighed to the bosom friend. "For myself, I don't mind; I have got used to it. But it is so hard on Reggie. He feels it, I know he does, though he never openly complains."

"He would be a cad if he did," answered Susan Fossett, who having tried conscientiously for a month to tolerate the fellow, had in the end declared her inability even to do more than avoid open expression of cordial dislike. "Added to which I don't quite see of what use it would be. You never told him you were young and pretty, did you?"

"I told him, my dear," replied Miss Ramsbotham, "the actual truth. I don't want to take any credit for doing so; it seemed the best course. You see, unfortunately, I look my age. With most men it would have made a difference. You have no idea how good he is. He assured me he had engaged himself to me with his eyes open, and that there was no need to dwell upon unpleasant topics. It is so wonderful to me that he should care for me--he who could have half the women in London at his feet."

"Yes, he's the type that would attract them, I daresay," agreed Susan Fossett. "But are you quite sure that he does?--care for you, I mean."

"My dear," returned Miss Ramsbotham, "you remember Rochefoucauld's definition. 'One loves, the other consents to be loved.' If he will only let me do that I shall be content. It is more than I had any right to expect."

"Oh, you are a fool," told her bluntly her bosom friend.

"I know I am," admitted Miss Ramsbotham; "but I had no idea that being a fool was so delightful."

Bohemia grew day by day more indignant and amazed. Young Peters was not even a gentleman. All the little offices of courtship he left to her. It was she who helped him on with his coat, and afterwards adjusted her own cloak; she who carried the parcel, she who followed into and out of the restaurant. Only when he thought anyone was watching would he make any attempt to behave to her with even ordinary courtesy. He bullied her, contradicted her in public, ignored her openly. Bohemia fumed with impotent rage, yet was bound to confess that so far as Miss Ramsbotham herself was concerned he had done more to make her happy than had ever all Bohemia put together. A tender light took up its dwelling in her eyes, which for the first time it was noticed were singularly deep and expressive. The blood, of which she possessed if anything too much, now came and went, so that her cheeks, in place of their insistent red, took on a varied pink and white. Life had entered her thick dark hair, giving to it shade and shadow.

The woman began to grow younger. She put on flesh. Sex, hitherto dormant, began to show itself; femininities peeped out. New tones, suggesting possibilities, crept into her voice. Bohemia congratulated itself that the affair, after all, might turn out well.

Then Master Peters spoiled everything by showing a better side to his nature, and, careless of all worldly considerations, falling in love himself, honestly, with a girl at the bun shop. He did the best thing under the circumstances that he could have done: told Miss Ramsbotham the plain truth, and left the decision in her hands.

Miss Ramsbotham acted as anyone who knew her would have foretold. Possibly, in the silence of her delightful little four-roomed flat over the tailor's shop in Marylebone Road, her sober, worthy maid dismissed for a holiday, she may have shed some tears; but, if so, no trace of them was allowed to mar the peace of mind of Mr. Peters. She merely thanked him for being frank with her, and by a little present pain saving them both a future of disaster. It was quite understandable; she knew he had never really been in love with her. She had thought him the type of man that never does fall in love, as the word is generally understood--Miss Ramsbotham did not add, with anyone except himself--and had that been the case, and he content merely to be loved, they might have been happy together. As it was--well, it was fortunate he had found out the truth before it was too late. Now, would he take her advice?

Mr. Peters was genuinely grateful, as well he might be, and would consent to any suggestion that Miss Ramsbotham might make; felt he had behaved shabbily, was very much ashamed of himself, would be guided in all things by Miss Ramsbotham, whom he should always regard as the truest of friends, and so on.

Miss Ramsbotham's suggestion was this: Mr. Peters, no more robust of body than of mind, had been speaking for some time past of travel. Having nothing to do now but to wait for briefs, why not take this opportunity of visiting his only well-to-do relative, a Canadian farmer. Meanwhile, let Miss Peggy leave the bun shop and take up her residence in Miss Ramsbotham's flat. Let there be no engagement--merely an understanding. The girl was pretty, charming, good, Miss Ramsbotham felt sure; but--well, a little education, a little training in manners and behaviour would not be amiss, would it? If, on returning at the end of six months or a year, Mr. Peters was still of the same mind, and Peggy also wishful, the affair would be easier, would it not?

There followed further expressions of eternal gratitude. Miss Ramsbotham swept all such aside. It would be pleasant to have a bright young girl to live with her; teaching, moulding such an one would be a pleasant occupation.

And thus it came to pass that Mr. Reginald Peters disappeared for a while from Bohemia, to the regret of but few, and there entered into it one Peggy Nutcombe, as pretty a child as ever gladdened the eye of man. She had wavy, flaxen hair, a complexion that might have been manufactured from the essence of wild roses, the nose that Tennyson bestows upon his miller's daughter, and a mouth worthy of the Lowther Arcade in its days of glory. Add to this the quick grace of a kitten, with the appealing helplessness of a baby in its first short frock, and you will be able to forgive Mr. Reginald Peters his faithlessness. Bohemia looked from one to the other--from the fairy to the woman--and ceased to blame. That the fairy was as stupid as a camel, as selfish as a pig, and as lazy as a nigger Bohemia did not know; nor--so long as her figure and complexion remained what it was--would its judgment have been influenced, even if it had. I speak of the Bohemian male.

But that is just what her figure and complexion did not do. Mr. Reginald Peters, finding his uncle old, feeble, and inclined to be fond, deemed it to his advantage to stay longer than he had intended. Twelve months went by. Miss Peggy was losing her kittenish grace, was becoming lumpy. A couple of pimples--one near the right-hand corner of her rosebud mouth, and another on the left-hand side of her tip-tilted nose--marred her baby face. At the end of another six months the men called her plump, and the women fat. Her walk was degenerating into a waddle; stairs caused her to grunt. She took to breathing with her mouth, and Bohemia noticed that her teeth were small, badly coloured, and uneven. The pimples grew in size and number. The cream and white of her complexion was merging into a general yellow. A certain greasiness of skin was manifesting itself. Babyish ways in connection with a woman who must have weighed about eleven stone struck Bohemia as incongruous. Her manners, judged alone, had improved. But they had not improved her. They did not belong to her; they did not fit her. They sat on her as Sunday broadcloth on a yokel. She had learned to employ her "h's" correctly, and to speak good grammar. This gave to her conversation a painfully artificial air. The little learning she had absorbed was sufficient to bestow upon her an angry consciousness of her own invincible ignorance.

Meanwhile, Miss Ramsbotham had continued upon her course of rejuvenation. At twenty-nine she had looked thirty-five; at thirty-two she looked not a day older than five-and-twenty. Bohemia felt that should she retrograde further at the same rate she would soon have to shorten her frocks and let down her hair. A nervous excitability had taken possession of her that was playing strange freaks not only with her body, but with her mind. What it gave to the one it seemed to take from the other. Old friends, accustomed to enjoy with her the luxury of plain speech, wondered in vain what they had done to offend her. Her desire was now towards new friends, new faces. Her sense of humour appeared to be departing from her; it became unsafe to jest with her. On the other hand, she showed herself greedy for admiration and flattery. Her former chums stepped back astonished to watch brainless young fops making their way with her by complimenting her upon her blouse, or whispering to her some trite nonsense about her eyelashes. From her work she took a good percentage of her brain power to bestow it on her clothes. Of course, she was successful. Her dresses suited her, showed her to the best advantage. Beautiful she could never be, and had sense enough to know it; but a charming, distinguished-looking woman she had already become. Also, she was on the high road to becoming a vain, egotistical, commonplace woman.

It was during the process of this, her metamorphosis, that Peter Hope one evening received a note from her announcing her intention of visiting him the next morning at the editorial office of Good Humour. She added in a postscript that she would prefer the interview to be private.

Punctually to the time appointed Miss Ramsbotham arrived. Miss Ramsbotham, contrary to her custom, opened conversation with the weather. Miss Ramsbotham was of opinion that there was every possibility of rain. Peter Hope's experience was that there was always possibility of rain.

"How is the Paper doing?" demanded Miss Ramsbotham.

The Paper--for a paper not yet two years old--was doing well. "We expect very shortly--very shortly indeed," explained Peter Hope, "to turn the corner."

"Ah! that 'corner,'" sympathised Miss Ramsbotham.

"I confess," smiled Peter Hope, "it doesn't seem to be exactly a right-angled corner. One reaches it as one thinks. But it takes some getting round--what I should describe as a cornery corner."

"What you want," thought Miss Ramsbotham, "are one or two popular features."

"Popular features," agreed Peter guardedly, scenting temptation, "are not to be despised, provided one steers clear of the vulgar and the commonplace."

"A Ladies' Page!" suggested Miss Ramsbotham--"a page that should make the woman buy it. The women, believe me, are going to be of more and more importance to the weekly press."

"But why should she want a special page to herself?" demanded Peter Hope. "Why should not the paper as a whole appeal to her?"

"It doesn't," was all Miss Ramsbotham could offer in explanation.

"We give her literature and the drama, poetry, fiction, the higher politics, the--"

"I know, I know," interrupted Miss Ramsbotham, who of late, among other failings new to her, had developed a tendency towards impatience; "but she gets all that in half a dozen other papers. I have thought it out." Miss Ramsbotham leaned further across the editorial desk and sunk her voice unconsciously to a confidential whisper. "Tell her the coming fashions. Discuss the question whether hat or bonnet makes you look the younger. Tell her whether red hair or black is to be the new colour, what size waist is being worn by the best people. Oh, come!" laughed Miss Ramsbotham in answer to

Peter's shocked expression; "one cannot reform the world and human nature all at once. You must appeal to people's folly in order to get them to listen to your wisdom. Make your paper a success first. You can make it a power afterwards."

"But," argued Peter, "there are already such papers--papers devoted to--to that sort of thing, and to nothing else."

"At sixpence!" replied the practical Miss Ramsbotham. "I am thinking of the lower middle-class woman who has twenty pounds a year to spend on dress, and who takes twelve hours a day to think about it, poor creature. My dear friend, there is a fortune in it. Think of the advertisements."

Poor Peter groaned--old Peter, the dreamer of dreams. But for thought of Tommy! one day to be left alone to battle with a stony-eyed, deaf world, Peter most assuredly would have risen in his wrath, would have said to his distinguished-looking temptress, "Get thee behind me, Miss Ramsbotham. My journalistic instinct whispers to me that your scheme, judged by the mammon of unrighteousness, is good. It is a new departure. Ten years hence half the London journals will have adopted it. There is money in it. But what of that? Shall I for mere dross sell my editorial soul, turn the temple of the Mighty Pen into a den of--of milliners! Good morning, Miss Ramsbotham. I grieve for you. I grieve for you as for a fellow-worker once inspired by devotion to a noble calling, who has fallen from her high estate. Good morning, madam."

So Peter thought as he sat tattooing with his finger-tips upon the desk; but only said -

"It would have to be well done."

"Everything would depend upon how it was done," agreed Miss Ramsbotham. "Badly done, the idea would be wasted. You would be merely giving it away to some other paper."

"Do you know of anyone?" queried Peter.

"I was thinking of myself," answered Miss Ramsbotham.

"I am sorry," said Peter Hope.

"Why?" demanded Miss Ramsbotham. "Don't you think I could do it?"

"I think," said Peter, "no one could do it better. I am sorry you should wish to do it--that is all."

"I want to do it," replied Miss Ramsbotham, a note of doggedness in her voice.

"How much do you propose to charge me?" Peter smiled.

"Nothing."

"My dear lady--"

"I could not in conscience," explained Miss Ramsbotham, "take payment from both sides. I am going to make a good deal out of it. I am going to make out of it at least three hundred a year, and they will be glad to pay it."

"Who will?"

"The dressmakers. I shall be one of the most stylish women in London," laughed Miss Ramsbotham.

"You used to be a sensible woman," Peter reminded her.

"I want to live."

"Can't you manage to do it without--without being a fool, my dear."

"No," answered Miss Ramsbotham, "a woman can't. I've tried it."

"Very well," agreed Peter, "be it so."

Peter had risen. He laid his shapely, white old hand upon the woman's shoulder. "Tell me when you want to give it up. I shall be glad."

Thus it was arranged. Good Humour gained circulation and--of more importance yet--advertisements; and Miss Ramsbotham, as she had predicted, the reputation of being one of the best-dressed women in London. Her reason for desiring such reputation Peter Hope had shrewdly guessed. Two months later his suspicions were confirmed. Mr. Reginald Peters, his uncle being dead, was on his way back to England.

His return was awaited with impatience only by the occupants of the little flat in the Marylebone Road; and between these two the difference of symptom was marked. Mistress Peggy, too stupid to comprehend the change that had been taking place in her, looked forward to her lover's arrival with delight. Mr. Reginald Peters, independently of his profession, was in consequence of his uncle's death a man of means. Miss Ramsbotham's tutelage, which had always been distasteful to her, would now be at an end. She would be a "lady" in the true sense of the word--according to Miss Peggy's definition, a woman with nothing to do but eat and drink, and nothing to think of but dress. Miss Ramsbotham, on the other hand, who might have anticipated the home-coming of her quondam admirer with hope, exhibited a strange condition of alarmed misery, which increased from day to day as the date drew nearer.

The meeting--whether by design or accident was never known--took place at an evening party given by the proprietors of a new journal. The circumstance was certainly unfortunate for poor Peggy, whom Bohemia began to pity. Mr. Peters, knowing both women would be there and so on the look-out, saw in the distance among the crowd of notabilities a superbly millinered, tall, graceful woman, whose face recalled sensations he could not for the moment place. Chiefly noticeable about her were her exquisite neck and arms, and the air of perfect breeding with which she moved, talking and laughing, through the distinguished, fashionable throng. Beside her strutted, nervously aggressive, a vulgar, fat, pimply, shapeless young woman, attracting universal attention by the incongruity of her presence in the room. On being greeted by the graceful lady of the neck and arms, the conviction forced itself upon him that this could be no other than the once Miss Ramsbotham, plain of face and indifferent of dress, whose very appearance he had almost forgotten. On being greeted gushingly as "Reggie" by the sallow-complexioned, over-dressed young woman he bowed with evident astonishment, and apologised for a memory that, so he assured the lady, had always been to him a source of despair.

Of course, he thanked his stars--and Miss Ramsbotham--that the engagement had never been formal. So far as Mr. Peters was concerned, there was an end to Mistress Peggy's dream of an existence of everlasting breakfasts in bed. Leaving the Ramsbotham flat, she returned to the maternal roof, and there a course of hard work and plain living tended greatly to improve her figure and complexion;

so that in course of time, the gods smiling again upon her, she married a foreman printer, and passes out of this story.

Meanwhile, Mr. Reginald Peters--older, and the possessor, perhaps, of more sense--looked at Miss Ramsbotham with new eyes, and now not tolerated but desired her. Bohemia waited to assist at the happy termination of a pretty and somewhat novel romance. Miss Ramsbotham had shown no sign of being attracted elsewhere. Flattery, compliment, she continued to welcome; but merely, so it seemed, as favourable criticism. Suitors more fit and proper were now not lacking, for Miss Ramsbotham, though a woman less desirable when won, came readily to the thought of wooing. But to all such she turned a laughing face.

"I like her for it," declared Susan Fossett; "and he has improved--there was room for it--though I wish it could have been some other. There was Jack Herring--it would have been so much more suitable. Or even Joe, in spite of his size. But it's her wedding, not ours; and she will never care for anyone else."

And Bohemia bought its presents, and had them ready, but never gave them. A few months later Mr. Reginald Peters returned to Canada, a bachelor. Miss Ramsbotham expressed her desire for another private interview with Peter Hope.

"I may as well keep on the Letter to Clorinda," thought Miss Ramsbotham. "I have got into the knack of it. But I will get you to pay me for it in the ordinary way."

"I would rather have done so from the beginning," explained Peter.

"I know. I could not in conscience, as I told you, take from both sides. For the future--well, they have said nothing; but I expect they are beginning to get tired of it."

"And you!" questioned Peter.

"Yes. I am tired of it myself," laughed Miss Ramsbotham. "Life isn't long enough to be a well-dressed woman."

"You have done with all that?"

"I hope so," answered Miss Ramsbotham.

"And don't want to talk any more about it?" suggested Peter.

"Not just at present. I should find it so difficult to explain."

By others, less sympathetic than old Peter, vigorous attempts were made to solve the mystery. Miss Ramsbotham took enjoyment in cleverly evading these tormentors. Thwarted at every point, the gossips turned to other themes. Miss Ramsbotham found interest once again in the higher branches of her calling; became again, by slow degrees, the sensible, frank, 'good sort' that Bohemia had known, liked, respected--everything but loved.

Years later, to Susan Fossett, the case was made clear; and through Susan Fossett, a nice enough woman but talkative, those few still interested learned the explanation.

"Love," said Miss Ramsbotham to the bosom friend, "is not regulated by reason. As you say, there were many men I might have married with much more hope of happiness. But I never cared for any other man. He was not intellectual, was egotistical, possibly enough selfish. The man should always be older than the woman; he was younger, and he was a weak character. Yet I loved him."

"I am glad you didn't marry him," said the bosom friend.

"So am I," agreed Miss Ramsbotham.

"If you can't trust me," had said the bosom friend at this point, "don't."

"I meant to do right," said Miss Ramsbotham, "upon my word of honour I did, in the beginning."

"I don't understand," said the bosom friend.

"If she had been my own child," continued Miss Ramsbotham, "I could not have done more--in the beginning. I tried to teach her, to put some sense into her. Lord! the hours I wasted on that little idiot! I marvel at my own patience. She was nothing but an animal. An animal! she had only an animal's vices. To eat and drink and sleep was her idea of happiness; her one ambition male admiration, and she hadn't character enough to put sufficient curb upon her stomach to retain it. I reasoned with her, I pleaded with her, I bullied her. Had I persisted I might have succeeded by sheer physical and mental strength in restraining her from ruining herself. I was winning. I had made her frightened of me. Had I gone on, I might have won. By dragging her out of bed in the morning, by insisting upon her taking exercise, by regulating every particle of food and drink she put into her mouth, I kept the little beast in good condition for nearly three months. Then, I had to go away into the country for a few days; she swore she would obey my instructions. When I came back I found she had been in bed most of the time, and had been living chiefly on chocolate and cakes. She was curled up asleep in an easy-chair, snoring with her mouth wide open, when I opened the door. And at sight of that picture the devil came to me and tempted me. Why should I waste my time, wear myself out in mind and body, that the man I loved should marry a pig because it looked like an angel? 'Six months' wallowing according to its own desires would reveal it in its true shape. So from that day I left it to itself. No, worse than that- -I don't want to spare myself--I encouraged her. I let her have a fire in her bedroom, and half her meals in bed. I let her have chocolate with tablespoonfuls of cream floating on the top: she loved it. She was never really happy except when eating. I let her order her own meals. I took a fiendish delight watching the dainty limbs turning to shapeless fat, the pink-and-white complexion growing blotchy. It is flesh that man loves; brain and mind and heart and soul! he never thinks of them. This little pink-and-white sow could have cut me out with Solomon himself. Why should such creatures have the world arranged for them, and we not be allowed to use our brains in our own defence? But for my looking-glass I might have resisted the temptation, but I always had something of the man in me: the sport of the thing appealed to me. I suppose it was the nervous excitement under which I was living that was changing me. All my sap was going into my body. Given sufficient time, I might meet her with her own weapons, animal against animal. Well, you know the result: I won. There was no doubt about his being in love with me. His eyes would follow me round the room, feasting on me. I had become a fine animal. Men desired me, Do you know why I refused him? He was in every way a better man than the silly boy I had fallen in love with; but he came back with a couple of false teeth: I saw the gold setting one day when he opened his mouth to laugh. I don't say for a moment, my dear, there is no such thing as love--love pure, ennobling, worthy of men and women, its roots in the heart and nowhere else. But that love I had missed; and the other! I saw it in its true light. I had fallen in love with him because he was a pretty, curly-headed boy. He had fallen in love with Peggy when she was pink-and-white and slim. I shall always see the look that came into his eyes when she spoke to him at the hotel, the look of disgust and loathing. The girl was the same; it was only her body that had grown older. I could see his eyes fixed upon my arms and neck. I had got to grow old in time, brown skinned, and wrinkled. I thought of him, growing bald, fat--"

"If you had fallen in love with the right man," had said Susan Fossett, "those ideas would not have come to you."

"I know," said Miss Ramsbotham. "He will have to like me thin and in these clothes, just because I am nice, and good company, and helpful. That is the man I am waiting for."

He never came along. A charming, bright-eyed, white-haired lady occupies alone a little flat in the Marylebone Road, looks in occasionally at the Writers' Club. She is still Miss Ramsbotham.

Bald-headed gentlemen feel young again talking to her: she is so sympathetic, so big-minded, so understanding. Then, hearing the clock strike, tear themselves from her with a sigh, and return home--some of them--to stupid shrewish wives.

STORY THE FIFTH

JOEY LOVEREDGE AGREES--ON CERTAIN TERMS--TO JOIN THE COMPANY

The most popular member of the Autolycus Club was undoubtedly Joseph Loveredge. Small, chubby, clean-shaven, his somewhat longish, soft, brown hair parted in the middle, strangers fell into the error of assuming him to be younger than he really was. It is on record that a leading lady novelist--accepting her at her own estimate--irritated by his polite but firm refusal to allow her entrance into his own editorial office without appointment, had once boxed his ears, under the impression that he was his own office-boy. Guests to the Autolycus Club, on being introduced to him, would give to him kind messages to take home to his father, with whom they remembered having been at school together. This sort of thing might have annoyed anyone with less sense of humour. Joseph Loveredge would tell such stories himself, keenly enjoying the jest--was even suspected of inventing some of the more improbable. Another fact tending to the popularity of Joseph Loveredge among all classes, over and above his amiability, his wit, his genuine kindliness, and his never-failing fund of good stories, was that by care and inclination he had succeeded in remaining a bachelor. Many had been the attempts to capture him; nor with the passing of the years had interest in the sport shown any sign of diminution. Well over the frailties and distempers so dangerous to youth, of staid and sober habits, with an ever- increasing capital invested in sound securities, together with an ever-increasing income from his pen, with a tastefully furnished house overlooking Regent's Park, an excellent and devoted cook and house-keeper, and relatives mostly settled in the Colonies, Joseph Loveredge, though inexperienced girls might pass him by with a contemptuous sniff, was recognised by ladies of maturer judgment as a prize not too often dangled before the eyes of spinsterhood. Old foxes--so we are assured by kind-hearted country gentlemen-- rather enjoy than otherwise a day with the hounds. However that may be, certain it is that Joseph Loveredge, confident of himself, one presumes, showed no particular disinclination to the chase. Perhaps on the whole he preferred the society of his own sex, with whom he could laugh and jest with more freedom, to whom he could tell his stories as they came to him without the trouble of having to turn them over first in his own mind; but, on the other hand, Joey made no attempt to avoid female company whenever it came his way; and then no cavalier could render himself more agreeable, more unobtrusively attentive. Younger men stood by, in envious admiration of the ease with which in five minutes he would establish himself on terms of cosy friendship with the brilliant beauty before whose gracious coldness they had stood shivering for months; the daring with which he would tuck under his arm, so to speak, the prettiest girl in the room, smooth down as if by magic her hundred prickles, and tease her out of her overwhelming sense of her own self-importance. The secret of his success was, probably, that he was not afraid of them. Desiring nothing from them beyond companionableness, a reasonable amount of appreciation for his jokes--which without being exceptionally stupid they would have found it difficult to withhold--with just sufficient information and intelligence to make conversation interesting, there was nothing about him by which they could lay hold of him. Of course, that rendered them particularly anxious to lay hold of him. Joseph's lady friends might, roughly speaking, be divided into two groups: the unmarried, who wanted to marry him to themselves; and the married, who wanted to marry him to somebody else. It would be a social disaster, the latter had agreed among themselves, if Joseph Loveredge should never wed.

"He would make such an excellent husband for poor Bridget."

"Or Gladys. I wonder how old Gladys really is?"

"Such a nice, kind little man."

"And when one thinks of the sort of men that ARE married, it does seem such a pity!"

"I wonder why he never has married, because he's just the sort of man you'd think WOULD have married."

"I wonder if he ever was in love."

"Oh, my dear, you don't mean to tell me that a man has reached the age of forty without ever being in love!"

The ladies would sigh.

"I do hope if ever he does marry, it will be somebody nice. Men are so easily deceived."

"I shouldn't be surprised myself a bit if something came of it with Bridget. She's a dear girl, Bridget--so genuine."

"Well, I think myself, dear, if it's anyone, it's Gladys. I should be so glad to see poor dear Gladys settled."

The unmarried kept their thoughts more to themselves. Each one, upon reflection, saw ground for thinking that Joseph Loveredge had given proof of feeling preference for herself. The irritating thing was that, on further reflection, it was equally clear that Joseph Loveredge had shown signs of preferring most of the others.

Meanwhile Joseph Loveredge went undisturbed upon his way. At eight o'clock in the morning Joseph's housekeeper entered the room with a cup of tea and a dry biscuit. At eight-fifteen Joseph Loveredge arose and performed complicated exercises on an indiarubber pulley, warranted, if persevered in, to bestow grace upon the figure and elasticity upon the limbs. Joseph Loveredge persevered steadily, and had done so for years, and was himself contented with the result, which, seeing it concerned nobody else, was all that could be desired. At half-past eight on Mondays, Wednesdays, and Fridays, Joseph Loveredge breakfasted on one cup of tea, brewed by himself; one egg, boiled by himself; and two pieces of toast, the first one spread with marmalade, the second with butter. On Tuesdays, Thursdays, and Saturdays Joseph Loveredge discarded eggs and ate a rasher of bacon. On Sundays Joseph Loveredge had both eggs and bacon, but then allowed himself half an hour longer for reading the paper. At nine-thirty Joseph Loveredge left the house for the office of the old-established journal of which he was the incorruptible and honoured City editor. At one-forty-five, having left his office at one-thirty, Joseph Loveredge entered the Autolycus Club and sat down to lunch. Everything else in Joseph's life was arranged with similar preciseness, so far as was possible with the duties of a City editor. Monday evening Joseph spent with musical friends at Brixton. Friday was Joseph's theatre night. On Tuesdays and Thursdays he was open to receive invitations out to dinner; on Wednesdays and Saturdays he invited four friends to dine with him at Regent's Park. On Sundays, whatever the season, Joseph Loveredge took an excursion into the country. He had his regular hours for reading, his regular hours for thinking. Whether in Fleet Street, or the Tyrol, on the Thames, or in the Vatican, you might recognise him from afar by his grey frock-coat, his patent- leather boots, his brown felt hat, his lavender tie. The man was a born bachelor. When the news of his engagement crept through the smoky portals of the Autolycus Club nobody believed it.

"Impossible!" asserted Jack Herring. "I've known Joey's life for fifteen years. Every five minutes is arranged for. He could never have found the time to do it."

"He doesn't like women, not in that way; I've heard him say so," explained Alexander the Poet. "His opinion is that women are the artists of Society--delightful as entertainers, but troublesome to live with."

"I call to mind," said the Wee Laddie, "a story he told me in this verra room, barely three months agone: Some half a dozen of them were gong home together from the Devonshire. They had had a joyous evening, and one of them--Joey did not notice which--suggested their dropping in at his place just for a final whisky. They were laughing and talking in the dining-room, when their hostess suddenly appeared upon the scene in a costume--so Joey described it--the charm of which was its variety. She was a nice-looking woman, Joey said, but talked too much; and when the first lull occurred, Joey turned to the man sitting nighest to him, and who looked bored, and suggested in a whisper that it was about time they went.

"'Perhaps you had better go,' assented the bored-looking man. 'Wish I could come with you; but, you see, I live here.'"

"I don't believe it," said Somerville the Briefless. "He's been cracking his jokes, and some silly woman has taken him seriously."

But the rumour grew into report, developed detail, lost all charm, expanded into plain recital of fact. Joey had not been seen within the Club for more than a week--in itself a deadly confirmation. The question became: Who was she--what was she like?

"It's none of our set, or we should have heard something from her side before now," argued acutely Somerville the Briefless.

"Some beastly kid who will invite us to dances and forget the supper," feared Johnny Bulstrode, commonly called the Babe. "Old men always fall in love with young girls."

"Forty," explained severely Peter Hope, editor and part proprietor of Good Humour, "is not old."

"Well, it isn't young," persisted Johnny.

"Good thing for you, Johnny, if it is a girl," thought Jack Herring. "Somebody for you to play with. I often feel sorry for you, having nobody but grown-up people to talk to."

"They do get a bit stodgy after a certain age," agreed the Babe.

"I am hoping," said Peter, "it will be some sensible, pleasant woman, a little over thirty. He is a dear fellow, Loveredge; and forty is a very good age for a man to marry."

"Well, if I'm not married before I'm forty--" said the Babe.

"Oh, don't you fret," Jack Herring interrupted him--"a pretty boy like you! We will give a ball next season, and bring you out, if you're good--get you off our hands in no time."

It was August. Joey went away for his holiday without again entering the Club. The lady's name was Henrietta Elizabeth Doone. It was said by the Morning Post that she was connected with the Doones of Gloucestershire.

Doones of Gloucestershire--Doones of Gloucestershire mused Miss Ramsbotham, Society journalist, who wrote the weekly Letter to Clorinda, discussing the matter with Peter Hope in the editorial office of Good Humour. "Knew a Doon who kept a big second-hand store in Euston Road and called himself an auctioneer. He bought a small place in Gloucestershire and added an 'e' to his name. Wonder if it's the same?"

"I had a cat called Elizabeth once," said Peter Hope.

"I don't see what that's got to do with it."

"No, of course not," agreed Peter. "But I was rather fond of it. It was a quaint sort of animal, considered as a cat--would never speak to another cat, and hated being out after ten o'clock at night."

"What happened to it?" demanded Miss Ramsbotham.

"Fell off a roof," sighed Peter Hope. "Wasn't used to them."

The marriage took place abroad, at the English Church at Montreux. Mr. and Mrs. Loveredge returned at the end of September. The Autolycus Club subscribed to send a present of a punch-bowl, left cards, and waited with curiosity to see the bride. But no invitation arrived. Nor for a month was Joey himself seen within the Club. Then, one foggy afternoon, waking after a doze, with a cold cigar in his mouth, Jack Herring noticed he was not the only occupant of the smoking-room. In a far corner, near a window, sat Joseph Loveredge reading a magazine. Jack Herring rubbed his eyes, then rose and crossed the room.

"I thought at first," explained Jack Herring, recounting the incident later in the evening, "that I must be dreaming. There he sat, drinking his five o'clock whisky-and-soda, the same Joey Loveredge I had known for fifteen years; yet not the same. Not a feature altered, not a hair on his head changed, yet the whole face was different; the same body, the same clothes, but another man. We talked for half an hour; he remembered everything that Joey Loveredge had known. I couldn't understand it. Then, as the clock struck, and he rose, saying he must be home at half-past five, the explanation suddenly occurred to me: JOEY LOVEREDGE WAS DEAD; THIS WAS A MARRIED MAN."

"We don't want your feeble efforts at psychological romance," told him Somerville the Briefless. "We want to know what you talked about. Dead or married, the man who can drink whisky-and-soda must be held responsible for his actions. What's the little beggar mean by cutting us all in this way? Did he ask after any of us? Did he leave any message for any of us? Did he invite any of us to come an see him?"

"Yes, he did ask after nearly everybody; I was coming to that. But he didn't leave any message. I didn't gather that he was pining for old relationships with any of us."

"Well, I shall go round to the office to-morrow morning," said Somerville the Briefless, "and force my way in if necessary. This is getting mysterious."

But Somerville returned only to puzzle the Autolycus Club still further. Joey had talked about the weather, the state of political parties, had received with unfeigned interest all gossip concerning his old friends; but about himself, his wife, nothing had been gleaned. Mrs. Loveredge was well; Mrs. Loveredge's relations were also well. But at present Mrs. Loveredge was not receiving.

Members of the Autolycus Club with time upon their hands took up the business of private detectives. Mrs. Loveredge turned out to be a handsome, well-dressed lady of about thirty, as Peter Hope had desired. At eleven in the morning, Mrs. Loveredge shopped in the neighbourhood of the Hampstead Road. In the afternoon, Mrs. Loveredge, in a hired carriage, would slowly promenade the Park, looking, it was noticed, with intense interest at the occupants of other carriages as they passed, but evidently having no acquaintances among them. The carriage, as a general rule, would call at Joey's office at five, and Mr. and Mrs. Loveredge would drive home. Jack Herring, as the oldest friend, urged by the other members, took the bull by the horns and called boldly. On neither occasion was Mrs. Loveredge at home.

"I'm damned if I go again!" said Jack. "She was in the second time, I know. I watched her into the house. Confound the stuck-up pair of them!"

Bewilderment gave place to indignation. Now and again Joey would creep, a mental shadow of his former self, into the Club where once every member would have risen with a smile to greet him. They gave him curt answers and turned away from him. Peter Hope one afternoon found him there alone, standing with his hands in his pockets looking out of window. Peter was fifty, so he said, maybe a little older; men of forty were to him mere boys. So Peter, who hated mysteries, stepped forward with a determined air and clapped Joey on the shoulder.

"I want to know, Joey," said Peter, "I want to know whether I am to go on liking you, or whether I've got to think poorly of you. Out with it."

Joey turned to him a face so full of misery that Peter's heart was touched. "You can't tell how wretched it makes me," said Joey. "I didn't know it was possible to feel so uncomfortable as I have felt during these last three months."

"It's the wife, I suppose?" suggested Peter.

"She's a dear girl. She only has one fault."

"It's a pretty big one," returned Peter. "I should try and break her of it if I were you."

"Break her of it!" cried the little man. "You might as well advise me to break a brick wall with my head. I had no idea what they were like. I never dreamt it."

"But what is her objection to us? We are clean, we are fairly intelligent--"

"My dear Peter, do you think I haven't said all that, and a hundred things more? A woman! she gets an idea into her head, and every argument against it hammers it in further. She has gained her notion of what she calls Bohemia from the comic journals. It's our own fault, we have done it ourselves. There's no persuading her that it's a libel."

"Won't she see a few of us--judge for herself? There's Porson--why Porson might have been a bishop. Or Somerville--Somerville's Oxford accent is wasted here. It has no chance."

"It isn't only that," explained Joey; "she has ambitions, social ambitions. She thinks that if we begin with the wrong set, we'll never get into the right. We have three friends at present, and, so far as I can see, are never likely to have any more. My dear boy, you'd never believe there could exist such bores. There's a man and his wife named Holyoake. They dine with us on Thursdays, and we dine with them on Tuesdays. Their only title to existence consists in their having a cousin in the House of Lords; they claim no other right themselves. He is a widower, getting on for eighty. Apparently he's the only relative they have, and when he dies, they talk of retiring into the country. There's a fellow named Cutler, who visited once at Marlborough House in connection with a charity. You'd think to listen to him that he had designs upon the throne. The most tiresome of them all is a noisy woman who, as far as I can make out, hasn't any name at all. 'Miss Montgomery' is on her cards, but that is only what she calls herself. Who she really is! It would shake the foundations of European society if known. We sit and talk about the aristocracy; we don't seem to know anybody else. I tried on one occasion a little sarcasm as a corrective-- recounted conversations between myself and the Prince of Wales, in which I invariably addressed him as 'Teddy.' It sounds tall, I know, but those people took it in. I was too astonished to undeceive them at the time, the consequence is I am a sort of little god to them. They come round me and ask for more. What am I to do? I am helpless among them. I've never had anything to do before with the really first-prize idiot; the usual type, of course, one knows, but these, if you haven't met them, are inconceivable. I try insulting them; they don't even know I am insulting them. Short of dragging them out of their chairs and kicking them round the room, I don't see how to make them understand it."

"And Mrs. Loveredge?" asked the sympathetic Peter, "is she--"

"Between ourselves," said Joey, sinking his voice to a needless whisper, seeing he and Peter were the sole occupants of the smoking-room--"I couldn't, of course, say it to a younger man--but between ourselves, my wife is a charming woman. You don't know her."

"Doesn't seem much chance of my ever doing so," laughed Peter.

"So graceful, so dignified, so--so queenly," continued the little man, with rising enthusiasm. "She has only one fault--she has no sense of humour."

To Peter, as it has been said, men of forty were mere boys.

"My dear fellow, whatever could have induced you--"

"I know--I know all that," interrupted the mere boy. "Nature arranges it on purpose. Tall and solemn prigs marry little women with turned-up noses. Cheerful little fellows like myself--we marry serious, stately women. If it were otherwise, the human race would be split up into species."

"Of course, if you were actuated by a sense of public duty--"

"Don't be a fool, Peter Hope," returned the little man. "I'm in love with my wife just as she is, and always shall be. I know the woman with a sense of humour, and of the two I prefer the one without. The Juno type is my ideal. I must take the rough with the smooth. One can't have a jolly, chirpy Juno, and wouldn't care for her if one could."

"Then are you going to give up all your old friends?"

"Don't suggest it," pleaded the little man. "You don't know how miserable it makes me--the mere idea. Tell them to be patient. The secret of dealing with women, I have found, is to do nothing rashly." The clock struck five. "I must go now," said Joey. "Don't misjudge her, Peter, and don't let the others. She's a dear girl. You'll like her, all of you, when you know her. A dear girl! She only has that one fault."

Joey went out.

Peter did his best that evening to explain the true position of affairs without imputing snobbery to Mrs. Loveredge. It was a difficult task, and Peter cannot be said to have accomplished it successfully. Anger and indignation against Joey gave place to pity. The members of the Autolycus Club also experienced a little irritation on their own account.

"What does the woman take us for?" demanded Somerville the Briefless. "Doesn't she know that we lunch with real actors and actresses, that once a year we are invited to dine at the Mansion House?"

"Has she never heard of the aristocracy of genius?" demanded Alexander the Poet.

"The explanation may be that possibly she has seen it," feared the Wee Laddie.

"One of us ought to waylay the woman," argued the Babe--"insist upon her talking to him for ten minutes. I've half a mind to do it myself."

Jack Herring said nothing--seemed thoughtful.

The next morning Jack Herring, still thoughtful, called at the editorial offices of Good Humour, in Crane Court, and borrowed Miss Ramsbotham's Debrett. Three days later Jack Herring informed the Club casually that he had dined the night before with Mr. and Mrs. Loveredge. The Club gave Jack Herring politely to understand that they regarded him as a liar, and proceeded to demand particulars.

"If I wasn't there," explained Jack Herring, with unanswerable logic, "how can I tell you anything about it?"

This annoyed the Club, whose curiosity had been whetted. Three members, acting in the interests of the whole, solemnly undertook to believe whatever he might tell them. But Jack Herring's feelings had been wounded.

"When gentlemen cast a doubt upon another gentleman's veracity--"

"We didn't cast a doubt," explained Somerville the Briefless. "We merely said that we personally did not believe you. We didn't say we couldn't believe you; it is a case for individual effort. If you give us particulars bearing the impress of reality, supported by details that do not unduly contradict each other, we are prepared to put aside our natural suspicions and face the possibility of your statement being correct."

"It was foolish of me," said Jack Herring. "I thought perhaps it would amuse you to hear what sort of a woman Mrs. Loveredge was like--some description of Mrs. Loveredge's uncle. Miss Montgomery, friend of Mrs. Loveredge, is certainly one of the most remarkable women I have ever met. Of course, that isn't her real name. But, as I have said, it was foolish of me. These people--you will never meet them, you will never see them; of what interest can they be to you?"

"They had forgotten to draw down the blinds, and he climbed up a lamp-post and looked through the window," was the solution of the problem put forward by the Wee Laddie.

"I'm dining there again on Saturday," volunteered Jack Herring. "If any of you will promise not to make a disturbance, you can hang about on the Park side, underneath the shadow of the fence, and watch me go in. My hansom will draw up at the door within a few minutes of eight."

The Babe and the Poet agreed to undertake the test.

"You won't mind our hanging round a little while, in case you're thrown out again?" asked the Babe.

"Not in the least, so far as I am concerned," replied Jack Herring. "Don't leave it too late and make your mother anxious."

"It's true enough," the Babe recounted afterwards. "The door was opened by a manservant and he went straight in. We walked up and down for half an hour, and unless they put him out the back way, he's telling the truth."

"Did you hear him give his name?" asked Somerville, who was stroking his moustache.

"No, we were too far off," explained the Babe. "But--I'll swear it was Jack--there couldn't be any mistake about that."

"Perhaps not," agreed Somerville the Briefless.

Somerville the Briefless called at the offices of Good Humour, in Crane Court, the following morning, and he also borrowed Miss Ramsbotham's Debrett.

"What's the meaning of it?" demanded the sub-editor.

"Meaning of what?"

"This sudden interest of all you fellows in the British Peerage."

"All of us?"

"Well, Herring was here last week, poring over that book for half an hour, with the Morning Post spread out before him. Now you're doing the same thing."

"Ah! Jack Herring, was he? I thought as much. Don't talk about it, Tommy. I'll tell you later on."

On the following Monday, the Briefless one announced to the Club that he had received an invitation to dine at the Loveredges' on the following Wednesday. On Tuesday, the Briefless one entered the Club with a slow and stately step. Halting opposite old Goslin the porter, who had emerged from his box with the idea of discussing the Oxford and Cambridge boat race, Somerville, removing his hat with a sweep of the arm, held it out in silence. Old Goslin, much astonished, took it mechanically, whereupon the Briefless one, shaking himself free from his Inverness cape, flung it lightly after the hat, and strolled on, not noticing that old Goslin, unaccustomed to coats lightly and elegantly thrown at him, dropping the hat, had caught it on his head, and had been, in the language of the prompt-book, "left struggling." The Briefless one, entering the smoking-room, lifted a chair and let it fall again with a crash, and sitting down upon it, crossed his legs and rang the bell.

"Ye're doing it verra weel," remarked approvingly the Wee Laddie. "Ye're just fitted for it by nature."

"Fitted for what?" demanded the Briefless one, waking up apparently from a dream.

"For an Adelphi guest at eighteenpence the night," assured him the Wee Laddie. "Ye're just splendid at it."

The Briefless one, muttering that the worst of mixing with journalists was that if you did not watch yourself, you fell into their ways, drank his whisky in silence. Later, the Babe swore on a copy of Sell's Advertising Guide that, crossing the Park, he had seen the Briefless one leaning over the railings of Rotten Row, clad in a pair of new kid gloves, swinging a silver-headed cane.

One morning towards the end of the week, Joseph Loveredge, looking twenty years younger than when Peter had last seen him, dropped in at the editorial office of Good Humour and demanded of Peter Hope how he felt and what he thought of the present price of Emma Mines.

Peter Hope's fear was that the gambling fever was spreading to all classes of society.

"I want you to dine with us on Sunday," said Joseph Loveredge. "Jack Herring will be there. You might bring Tommy with you."

Peter Hope gulped down his astonishment and said he should be delighted; he thought that Tommy also was disengaged. "Mrs. Loveredge out of town, I presume?" questioned Peter Hope.

"On the contrary," replied Joseph Loveredge, "I want you to meet her."

Joseph Loveredge removed a pile of books from one chair and placed them carefully upon another, after which he went and stood before the fire.

"Don't if you don't like," said Joseph Loveredge; "but if you don't mind, you might call yourself, just for the evening--say, the Duke of Warrington."

"Say the what?" demanded Peter Hope.

"The Duke of Warrington," repeated Joey. "We are rather short of dukes. Tommy can be the Lady Adelaide, your daughter."

"Don't be an ass!" said Peter Hope.

"I'm not an ass," assured him Joseph Loveredge. "He is wintering in Egypt. You have run back for a week to attend to business. There is no Lady Adelaide, so that's quite simple."

"But what in the name of--" began Peter Hope.

"Don't you see what I'm driving at?" persisted Joey. "It was Jack's idea at the beginning. I was frightened myself at first, but it is working to perfection. She sees you, and sees that you are a gentleman. When the truth comes out--as, of course, it must later on--the laugh will be against her."

"You think--you think that'll comfort her?" suggested Peter Hope.

"It's the only way, and it is really wonderfully simple. We never mention the aristocracy now--it would be like talking shop. We just enjoy ourselves. You, by the way, I met in connection with the movement for rational dress. You are a bit of a crank, fond of frequenting Bohemian circles."

"I am risking something, I know," continued Joey; "but it's worth it. I couldn't have existed much longer. We go slowly, and are very careful. Jack is Lord Mount-Primrose, who has taken up with anti-vaccination and who never goes out into Society. Somerville is Sir Francis Baldwin, the great authority on centipedes. The Wee Laddie is coming next week as Lord Garrick, who married that dancing-girl, Prissy Something, and started a furniture shop in Bond Street. I had some difficulty at first. She wanted to send out paragraphs, but I explained that was only done by vulgar persons-- that when the nobility came to you as friends, it was considered bad taste. She is a dear girl, as I have always told you, with only one fault. A woman easier to deceive one could not wish for. I don't myself see why the truth ever need come out-- provided we keep our heads."

"Seems to me you've lost them already," commented Peter; "you're overdoing it."

"The more of us the better," explained Joey; "we help each other. Besides, I particularly want you in it. There's a sort of superior Pickwickian atmosphere surrounding you that disarms suspicion."

"You leave me out of it," growled Peter.

"See here," laughed Joey; "you come as the Duke of Warrington, and bring Tommy with you, and I'll write your City article."

"For how long?" snapped Peter. Incorruptible City editors are not easily picked up.

"Oh, well, for as long as you like."

"On that understanding," agreed Peter, "I'm willing to make a fool of myself in your company."

"You'll soon get used to it," Joey told him; "eight o'clock, then, on Sunday; plain evening dress. If you like to wear a bit of red ribbon in your buttonhole, why, do so. You can get it at Evans', in Covent Garden."

"And Tommy is the Lady--"

"Adelaide. Let her have a taste for literature, then she needn't wear gloves. I know she hates them." Joey turned to go.

"Am I married?" asked Peter.

Joey paused. "I should avoid all reference to your matrimonial affairs if I were you," was Joey's advice. "You didn't come out of that business too well."

"Oh! as bad as that, was I? You don't think Mrs. Loveredge will object to me?"

"I have asked her that. She's a dear, broad-minded girl. I've promised not to leave you alone with Miss Montgomery, and Willis has had instructions not to let you mix your drinks."

"I'd have liked to have been someone a trifle more respectable," grumbled Peter.

"We rather wanted a duke," explained Joey, "and he was the only one that fitted in all round."

The dinner a was a complete success. Tommy, entering into the spirit of the thing, bought a new pair of open-work stockings and assumed a languid drawl. Peter, who was growing forgetful, introduced her as the Lady Alexandra; it did not seem to matter, both beginning with an A. She greeted Lord Mount-Primrose as "Billy," and asked affectionately after his mother. Joey told his raciest stories. The Duke of Warrington called everybody by their Christian names, and seemed well acquainted with Bohemian society-- a more amiable nobleman it would have been impossible to discover. The lady whose real name was not Miss Montgomery sat in speechless admiration. The hostess was the personification of gracious devotion.

Other little dinners, equally successful, followed. Joey's acquaintanceship appeared to be confined exclusively to the higher circles of the British aristocracy--with one exception: that of a German baron, a short, stout gentleman, who talked English well, but with an accent, and who, when he desired to be impressive, laid his right forefinger on the right side of his nose and thrust his whole face forward. Mrs. Loveredge wondered why her husband had not introduced them sooner, but was too blissful to be suspicious. The Autolycus Club was gradually changing its tone. Friends could no longer recognise one another by the voice. Every corner had its solitary student practising high-class intonation. Members dropped into the habit of addressing one another as "dear chappie," and, discarding pipes, took to cheap cigars. Many of the older habitues resigned.

All might have gone well to the end of time if only Mrs. Loveredge had left all social arrangements in the hands of her husband--had not sought to aid his efforts. To a certain political garden- party, one day in the height of the season, were invited Joseph Loveredge and Mrs. Joseph Loveredge, his wife. Mr. Joseph Loveredge at the last moment found himself unable to attend. Mrs. Joseph Loveredge went alone, met there various members of the British aristocracy. Mrs. Joseph Loveredge, accustomed to friendship with the aristocracy, felt at her ease and was natural and agreeable. The wife of an eminent peer talked to her and liked her. It occurred to Mrs. Joseph Loveredge that this lady might be induced to visit her house in Regent's Park, there to mingle with those of her own class.

"Lord Mount-Primrose, the Duke of Warrington, and a few others will be dining with us on Sunday next," suggested Mrs. Loveredge. "Will not you do us the honour of coming? We are, of course, only simple folk ourselves, but somehow people seem to like us."

The wife of the eminent peer looked at Mrs. Loveredge, looked round the grounds, looked at Mrs. Loveredge again, and said she would like to come. Mrs. Joseph Loveredge intended at first to tell her husband of her success, but a little devil entering into her head and whispering to her that it would be amusing, she resolved to keep it as a surprise, to be sprung upon him at eight o'clock on Sunday. The surprise proved all she could have hoped for.

The Duke of Warrington, having journalistic matters to discuss with Joseph Loveredge, arrived at half-past seven, wearing on his shirt-front a silver star, purchased in Eagle Street the day before for eight-and-six. There accompanied him the Lady Alexandra, wearing the identical ruby necklace that every night for the past six months, and twice on Saturdays, "John Strongheart" had been falsely accused of stealing. Lord Garrick, having picked up his wife (Miss Ramsbotham) outside the Mother Redcap, arrived with her on foot at a quarter to eight. Lord Mount-Primrose, together with Sir Francis Baldwin, dashed up in a hansom at seven-fifty. His Lordship, having lost the toss, paid the fare. The Hon. Harry Sykes (commonly called "the Babe") was ushered in five minutes later. The noble company assembled in the drawing-room chatted blithely while waiting for dinner to be announced. The Duke of Warrington was telling an anecdote about a cat, which nobody appeared to believe. Lord Mount-Primrose desired to know whether by any chance it might be the same animal that every night at half-past nine had been in the habit of climbing up his Grace's railings and knocking at his Grace's door. The Honourable Harry was saying that, speaking of cats, he once had a sort of terrier--when the door was thrown open and Willis announced the Lady Mary Sutton.

Mr. Joseph Loveredge, who was sitting near the fire, rose up. Lord Mount-Primrose, who was standing near the piano, sat down. The Lady Mary Sutton paused in the doorway. Mrs. Loveredge crossed the room to greet her.

"Let me introduce you to my husband," said Mrs. Loveredge. "Joey, my dear, the Lady Mary Sutton. I met the Lady Mary at the O'Meyers' the other day, and she was good enough to accept my invitation. I forgot to tell you."

Mr. Loveredge said he was delighted; after which, although as a rule a chatty man, he seemed to have nothing else to say. And a silence fell.

Somerville the Briefless--till then. That evening has always been reckoned the starting-point of his career. Up till then nobody thought he had much in him--walked up and held out his hand.

"You don't remember me, Lady Mary," said the Briefless one. "I met you some years ago; we had a most interesting conversation--Sir Francis Baldwin."

The Lady Mary stood for a moment trying apparently to recollect. She was a handsome, fresh-complexioned woman of about forty, with frank, agreeable eyes. The Lady Mary glanced at Lord Garrick, who was talking rapidly to Lord Mount-Primrose, who was not listening, and who could not have understood even if he had been, Lord Garrick, without being aware of it, having dropped into broad Scotch. From him the Lady Mary glanced at her hostess, and from her hostess to her host.

The Lady Mary took the hand held out to her. "Of course," said the Lady Mary; "how stupid of me! It was the day of my own wedding, too. You really must forgive me. We talked of quite a lot of things. I remember now."

Mrs. Loveredge, who prided herself upon maintaining old-fashioned courtesies, proceeded to introduce the Lady Mary to her fellow-guests, a little surprised that her ladyship appeared to know so few of them. Her ladyship's greeting of the Duke of Warrington was accompanied, it was remarked, by a somewhat curious smile. To the Duke of Warrington's daughter alone did the Lady Mary address remark.

"My dear," said the Lady Mary, "how you have grown since last we met!"

The announcement of dinner, as everybody felt, came none too soon.

It was not a merry feast. Joey told but one story; he told it three times, and twice left out the point. Lord Mount-Primrose took sifted sugar with pate de foie gras and ate it with a spoon. Lord Garrick, talking a mixture of Scotch and English, urged his wife to give up housekeeping and take a flat in Gower Street, which, as he pointed out, was central. She could have her meals sent in to her and so avoid all trouble. The Lady Alexandra's behaviour appeared to Mrs. Loveredge not altogether well-bred. An eccentric young noblewoman Mrs. Loveredge had always found her, but wished on this occasion that she had been a little less eccentric. Every few minutes the Lady Alexandra buried her face in her serviette, and shook and rocked, emitting stifled sounds, apparently those of acute physical pain. Mrs. Loveredge hoped she was not feeling ill, but the Lady Alexandra appeared incapable of coherent reply. Twice during the meal the Duke of Warrington rose from the table and began wandering round the room; on each occasion, asked what he wanted, had replied meekly that he was merely looking for his snuff-box, and had sat down again. The only person who seemed to enjoy the dinner was the Lady Mary Sutton.

The ladies retired upstairs into the drawing-room. Mrs. Loveredge, breaking a long silence, remarked it as unusual that no sound of merriment reached them from the dining-room. The explanation was that the entire male portion of the party, on being left to themselves, had immediately and in a body crept on tiptoe into Joey's study, which, fortunately, happened to be on the ground floor. Joey, unlocking the bookcase, had taken out his Debrett, but appeared incapable of understanding it. Sir Francis Baldwin had taken it from his unresisting hands; the remaining aristocracy huddled themselves into a corner and waited in silence.

"I think I've got it all clearly," announced Sir Francis Baldwin, after five minutes, which to the others had been an hour. "Yes, I don't think I'm making any mistake. She's the daughter of the Duke of Truro, married in '53 the Duke of Warrington, at St. Peter's, Eaton Square; gave birth in '55 to a daughter, the Lady Grace Alexandra Warberton Sutton, which makes the child just thirteen. In '63 divorced the Duke of Warrington. Lord Mount-Primrose, so far as I can make out, must be her second cousin. I appear to have married her in '66 at Hastings. It doesn't seem to me that we could have got together a homelier little party to meet her even if we had wanted to."

Nobody spoke; nobody had anything particularly worth saying. The door opened, and the Lady Alexandra (otherwise Tommy) entered the room.

"Isn't it time," suggested the Lady Alexandra, "that some of you came upstairs?"

"I was thinking myself," explained Joey, the host, with a grim smile, "it was about time that I went out and drowned myself. The canal is handy."

"Put it off till to-morrow," Tommy advised him. "I have asked her ladyship to give me a lift home, and she has promised to do so. She is evidently a woman with a sense of humour. Wait till after I have had a talk with her."

Six men, whispering at the same time, were prepared with advice; but Tommy was not taking advice.

"Come upstairs, all of you," insisted Tommy, "and make yourselves agreeable. She's going in a quarter of an hour."

Six silent men, the host leading, the two husbands bringing up the rear, ascended the stairs, each with the sensation of being twice his usual weight. Six silent men entered the drawing-room and sat down on chairs. Six silent men tried to think of something interesting to say.

Miss Ramsbotham--it was that or hysterics, as she afterwards explained--stifling a sob, opened the piano. But the only thing she could remember was "Champagne Charlie is my Name," a song then popular in the halls. Five men, when she had finished, begged her to go on. Miss Ramsbotham, speaking in a shrill falsetto, explained it was the only tune she knew. Four of them begged her to play it again. Miss Ramsbotham played it a second time with involuntary variations.

The Lady Mary's carriage was announced by the imperturbable Willis. The party, with the exception of the Lady Mary and the hostess, suppressed with difficulty an inclination to burst into a cheer. The Lady Mary thanked Mrs. Loveredge for a most interesting evening, and beckoned Tommy to accompany her. With her disappearance, a wild hilarity, uncanny in its suddenness, took possession of the remaining guests.

A few days later, the Lady Mary's carriage again drew up before the little house in Regent's Park. Mrs. Loveredge, fortunately, was at home. The carriage remained waiting for quite a long time. Mrs. Loveredge, after it was gone, locked herself in her own room. The under-housemaid reported to the kitchen that, passing the door, she had detected sounds indicative of strong emotion.

Through what ordeal Joseph Loveredge passed was never known. For a few weeks the Autolycus Club missed him. Then gradually, as aided by Time they have a habit of doing, things righted themselves. Joseph Loveredge received his old friends; his friends received Joseph Loveredge. Mrs. Loveredge, as a hostess, came to have only one failing--a marked coldness of demeanour towards all people with titles, whenever introduced to her.

STORY THE SIXTH

"THE BABE" APPLIES FOR SHARES

People said of the new journal, Good Humour--people of taste and judgment, that it was the brightest, the cleverest, the most literary penny weekly that ever had been offered to the public. This made Peter Hope, editor and part-proprietor, very happy. William Clodd, business manager, and also part-proprietor, it left less elated.

"Must be careful," said William Clodd, "that we don't make it too clever. Happy medium, that's the ideal."

People said--people of taste and judgment, that Good Humour was more worthy of support than all the other penny weeklies put together. People of taste and judgment even went so far, some of them, as to buy it. Peter Hope, looking forward, saw fame and fortune coming to him.

William Clodd, looking round about him, said -

"Doesn't it occur to you, Guv'nor, that we're getting this thing just a trifle too high class?"

"What makes you think that?" demanded Peter Hope.

"Our circulation, for one thing," explained Clodd. "The returns for last month--"

"I'd rather you didn't mention them, if you don't mind," interrupted Peter Hope; "somehow, hearing the actual figures always depresses me."

"Can't say I feel inspired by them myself," admitted Clodd.

"It will come," said Peter Hope, "it will come in time. We must educate the public up to our level."

"If there is one thing, so far as I have noticed," said William Clodd, "that the public are inclined to pay less for than another, it is for being educated."

"What are we to do?" asked Peter Hope.

"What you want," answered William Clodd, "is an office-boy."

"How will our having an office-boy increase our circulation?" demanded Peter Hope. "Besides, it was agreed that we could do without one for the first year. Why suggest more expense?"

"I don't mean an ordinary office-boy," explained Clodd. "I mean the sort of boy that I rode with in the train going down to Stratford yesterday."

"What was there remarkable about him?"

"Nothing. He was reading the current number of the Penny Novelist. Over two hundred thousand people buy it. He is one of them. He told me so. When he had done with it, he drew from his pocket a copy of the Halfpenny Joker--they guarantee a circulation of seventy thousand. He sat and chuckled over it until we got to Bow."

"But--"

"You wait a minute. I'm coming to the explanation. That boy represents the reading public. I talked to him. The papers he likes best are the papers that have the largest sales. He never made a single mistake. The others--those of them he had seen--he dismissed as 'rot.' What he likes is what the great mass of the journal-buying public likes. Please him--I took his name and address, and he is willing to come to us for eight shillings a week--and you please the people that buy. Not the people that glance through a paper when it is lying on the smoking-room table, and tell you it is damned good, but the people that plank down their penny. That's the sort we want."

Peter Hope, able editor, with ideals, was shocked--indignant. William Clodd, business man, without ideals, talked figures.

"There's the advertiser to be thought of," persisted Clodd. "I don't pretend to be a George Washington, but what's the use of telling lies that sound like lies, even to one's self while one's telling them? Give me a genuine sale of twenty thousand, and I'll undertake, without committing myself, to convey an impression of forty. But when the actual figures are under eight thousand--well, it hampers you, if you happen to have a conscience.

"Give them every week a dozen columns of good, sound literature," continued Clodd insinuatingly, "but wrap it up in twenty-four columns of jam. It's the only way they'll take it, and you will be doing them good--educating them without their knowing it. All powder and no jam! Well, they don't open their mouths, that's all."

Clodd was a man who knew how to get his way. Flipp--spelled Philip--Tweetel arrived in due course of time at 23, Crane Court, ostensibly to take up the position of Good Humour's office-boy; in reality, and without his being aware of it, to act as its literary taster. Stories in which Flipp became absorbed were accepted. Peter groaned, but contented himself with correcting only their grosser grammatical blunders; the experiment should be tried in all good faith. Humour at which Flipp laughed was printed. Peter tried to ease his conscience by increasing his subscription to the fund for destitute compositors, but only partially succeeded. Poetry that brought a tear to the eye of Flipp was given leaded type. People of taste and judgment said Good Humour had disappointed them. Its circulation, slowly but steadily, increased.

"See!" cried the delighted Clodd; "told you so!"

"It's sad to think--" began Peter.

"Always is," interrupted Clodd cheerfully. "Moral--don't think too much."

"Tell you what we'll do," added Clodd. "We'll make a fortune out of this paper. Then when we can afford to lose a little money, we'll launch a paper that shall appeal only to the intellectual portion of the public. Meanwhile--"

A squat black bottle with a label attached, standing on the desk, arrested Clodd's attention.

"When did this come?" asked Clodd.

"About an hour ago," Peter told him.

"Any order with it?"

"I think so." Peter searched for and found a letter addressed to "William Clodd, Esq., Advertising Manager, Good Humour." Clodd tore it open, hastily devoured it.

"Not closed up yet, are you?"

"No, not till eight o'clock."

"Good! I want you to write me a par. Do it now, then you won't forget it. For the 'Walnuts and Wine' column."

Peter sat down, headed a sheet of paper: 'For W. and W. Col.'

"What is it?" questioned Peter--"something to drink?"

"It's a sort of port," explained Clodd, "that doesn't get into your head."

"You consider that an advantage?" queried Peter.

"Of course. You can drink more of it."

Peter continued to write: 'Possesses all the qualities of an old vintage port, without those deleterious properties--' "I haven't tasted it, Clodd," hinted Peter.

"That's all right--I have."

"And was it good?"

"Splendid stuff. Say it's 'delicious and invigorating.' They'll be sure to quote that."

Peter wrote on: 'Personally I have found it delicious and--' Peter left off writing. "I really think, Clodd, I ought to taste it. You see, I am personally recommending it."

"Finish that par. Let me have it to take round to the printers. Then put the bottle in your pocket. Take it home and make a night of it."

Clodd appeared to be in a mighty hurry. Now, this made Peter only the more suspicious. The bottle was close to his hand. Clodd tried to intercept him, but was not quick enough.

"You're not used to temperance drinks," urged Clodd. "Your palate is not accustomed to them."

"I can tell whether it's 'delicious' or not, surely?" pleaded Peter, who had pulled out the cork.

"It's a quarter-page advertisement for thirteen weeks. Put it down and don't be a fool!" urged Clodd.

"I'm going to put it down," laughed Peter, who was fond of his joke. Peter poured out half a tumblerful, and drank--some of it.

"Like it?" demanded Clodd, with a savage grin.

"You are sure--you are sure it was the right bottle?" gasped Peter.

"Bottle's all right," Clodd assured him. "Try some more. Judge it fairly."

Peter ventured on another sip. "You don't think they would be satisfied if I recommended it as a medicine?" insinuated Peter--"something to have about the house in case of accidental poisoning?"

"Better go round and suggest the idea to them yourself. I've done with it." Clodd took up his hat.

"I'm sorry--I'm very sorry," sighed Peter. "But I couldn't conscientiously--"

Clodd put down his hat again with a bang. "Oh! confound that conscience of yours! Don't it ever think of your creditors? What's the use of my working out my lungs for you, when all you do is to hamper me at every step?"

"Wouldn't it be better policy," urged Peter, "to go for the better class of advertiser, who doesn't ask you for this sort of thing?"

"Go for him!" snorted Clodd. "Do you think I don't go for him? They are just sheep. Get one, you get the lot. Until you've got the one, the others won't listen to you."

"That's true," mused Peter. "I spoke to Wilkinson, of Kingsley's, myself. He advised me to try and get Landor's. He thought that if I could get an advertisement out of Landor, he might persuade his people to give us theirs."

"And if you had gone to Landor, he would have promised you theirs provided you got Kingsley's."

"They will come," thought hopeful Peter. "We are going up steadily. They will come with a rush."

"They had better come soon," thought Clodd. "The only things coming with a rush just now are bills."

"Those articles of young McTear's attracted a good deal of attention," expounded Peter. "He has promised to write me another series."

"Jowett is the one to get hold of," mused Clodd. "Jowett, all the others follow like a flock of geese waddling after the old gander. If only we could get hold of Jowett, the rest would be easy."

Jowett was the proprietor of the famous Marble Soap. Jowett spent on advertising every year a quarter of a million, it was said. Jowett was the stay and prop of periodical literature. New papers that secured the Marble Soap advertisement lived and prospered; the new paper to which it was denied languished and died. Jowett, and how to get hold of him; Jowett, and how to get round him, formed the chief topic of discussion at the council-board of most new papers, Good Humour amongst the number.

"I have heard," said Miss Ramsbotham, who wrote the Letter to Clorinda that filled each week the last two pages of Good Humour, and that told Clorinda, who lived secluded in the country, the daily history of the highest class society, among whom Miss Ramsbotham appeared to live and have her being; who they were, and what they wore, the wise and otherwise things they did--"I have heard," said Miss Ramsbotham one morning, Jowett being as usual the subject under debate, "that the old man is susceptible to female influence."

"What I have always thought," said Clodd. "A lady advertising-agent might do well. At all events, they couldn't kick her out."

"They might in the end," thought Peter. "Female door-porters would become a profession for muscular ladies if ever the idea took root."

"The first one would get a good start, anyhow," thought Clodd.

The sub-editor had pricked up her ears. Once upon a time, long ago, the sub-editor had succeeded, when all other London journalists had failed, in securing an interview with a certain great statesman. The sub-editor had never forgotten this--nor allowed anyone else to forget it,

"I believe I could get it for you," said the sub-editor.

The editor and the business-manager both spoke together. They spoke with decision and with emphasis.

"Why not?" said the sub-editor. "When nobody else could get at him, it was I who interviewed Prince--"

"We've heard all about that," interrupted the business-manager. "If I had been your father at the time, you would never have done it."

"How could I have stopped her?" retorted Peter Hope. "She never said a word to me."

"You could have kept an eye on her."

"Kept an eye on her! When you've got a girl of your own, you'll know more about them."

"When I have," asserted Clodd, "I'll manage her."

"We know all about bachelor's children," sneered Peter Hope, the editor.

"You leave it to me. I'll have it for you before the end of the week," crowed the sub-editor.

"If you do get it," returned Clodd, "I shall throw it out, that's all."

"You said yourself a lady advertising-agent would be a good idea," the sub-editor reminded him.

"So she might be," returned Clodd; "but she isn't going to be you."

"Why not?"

"Because she isn't, that's why."

"But if--"

"See you at the printer's at twelve," said Clodd to Peter, and went out suddenly.

"Well, I think he's an idiot," said the sub-editor.

"I do not often," said the editor, "but on this point I agree with him. Cadging for advertisements isn't a woman's work."

"But what is the difference between--"

"All the difference in the world," thought the editor.

"You don't know what I was going to say," returned his sub.

"I know the drift of it," asserted the editor.

"But you let me--"

"I know I do--a good deal too much. I'm going to turn over a new leaf."

"All I propose to do --"

"Whatever it is, you're not going to do it," declared the chief. "Shall be back at half-past twelve, if anybody comes."

"It seems to me--" But Peter was gone.

"Just like them all," wailed the sub-editor. "They can't argue; when you explain things to them, they go out. It does make me so mad!"

Miss Ramsbotham laughed. "You are a downtrodden little girl, Tommy."

"As if I couldn't take care of myself!" Tommy's chin was high up in the air.

"Cheer up," suggested Miss Ramsbotham. "Nobody ever tells me not to do anything. I would change with you if I could."

"I'd have walked into that office and have had that advertisement out of old Jowett in five minutes, I know I would," bragged Tommy. "I can always get on with old men."

"Only with the old ones?" queried Miss Ramsbotham.

The door opened. "Anybody in?" asked the face of Johnny Bulstrode, appearing in the jar.

"Can't you see they are?" snapped Tommy.

"Figure of speech," explained Johnny Bulstrode, commonly called "the Babe," entering and closing the door behind him.

"What do you want?" demanded the sub-editor.

"Nothing in particular," replied the Babe.

"Wrong time of the day to come for it, half-past eleven in the morning," explained the sub-editor.

"What's the matter with you?" asked the Babe.

"Feeling very cross," confessed the sub-editor.

The childlike face of the Babe expressed sympathetic inquiry.

"We are very indignant," explained Miss Ramsbotham, "because we are not allowed to rush off to Cannon Street and coax an advertisement out of old Jowett, the soap man. We feel sure that if we only put on our best hat, he couldn't possibly refuse us."

"No coaxing required," thought the sub-editor. "Once get in to see the old fellow and put the actual figures before him, he would clamour to come in."

"Won't he see Clodd?" asked the Babe.

"Won't see anybody on behalf of anything new just at present, apparently," answered Miss Ramsbotham. "It was my fault. I was foolish enough to repeat that I had heard he was susceptible to female charm. They say it was Mrs. Sarkitt that got the advertisement for The Lamp out of him. But, of course, it may not be true."

"Wish I was a soap man and had got advertisements to give away," sighed the Babe.

"Wish you were," agreed the sub-editor.

"You should have them all, Tommy."

"My name," corrected him the sub-editor, "is Miss Hope."

"I beg your pardon," said the Babe. "I don't know how it is, but one gets into the way of calling you Tommy."

"I will thank you," said the sub-editor, "to get out of it."

"I am sorry," said the Babe.

"Don't let it occur again," said the sub-editor.

The Babe stood first on one leg and then on the other, but nothing seemed to come of it. "Well," said the Babe, "I just looked in, that's all. Nothing I can do for you?"

"Nothing," thanked him the sub-editor.

"Good morning," said the Babe.

"Good morning," said the sub-editor.

The childlike face of the Babe wore a chastened expression as it slowly descended the stairs. Most of the members of the Autolycus Club looked in about once a day to see if they could do anything for Tommy. Some of them had luck. Only the day before, Porson--a heavy, most uninteresting man--had been sent down all the way to Plaistow to inquire after the wounded hand of a machine-boy. Young Alexander, whose poetry some people could not even understand, had been commissioned to search London for a second-hand edition of Maitland's Architecture. Since a fortnight nearly now, when he had been sent out to drive away an organ that would not go, Johnny had been given nothing.

Johnny turned the corner into Fleet Street feeling bitter with his lot. A boy carrying a parcel stumbled against him.

"Beg yer pardon--" the small boy looked up into Johnny's face, "miss," added the small boy, dodging the blow and disappearing into the crowd.

The Babe, by reason of his childlike face, was accustomed to insults of this character, but to-day it especially irritated him. Why at twenty-two could he not grow even a moustache? Why was he only five feet five and a half? Why had Fate cursed him with a pink-and-white complexion, so that the members of his own club had nicknamed him "the Babe," while street-boys as they passed pleaded with him for a kiss? Why was his very voice, a flute-like alto, more suitable-- Suddenly an idea sprang to life within his brain. The idea grew. Passing a barber's shop, Johnny went in.

"'Air cut, sir?" remarked the barber, fitting a sheet round Johnny's neck.

"No, shave," corrected Johnny.

"Beg pardon," said the barber, substituting a towel for the sheet. "Do you shave up, sir?" later demanded the barber.

"Yes," answered Johnny.

"Pleasant weather we are having," said the barber.

"Very," assented Johnny.

From the barber's, Johnny went to Stinchcombe's, the costumier's, in Drury Lane.

"I am playing in a burlesque," explained the Babe. "I want you to rig me out completely as a modern girl."

"Peeth o' luck!" said the shopman. "Goth the very bundle for you. Juth come in."

"I shall want everything," explained the Babe, "from the boots to the hat; stays, petticoats--the whole bag of tricks."

"Regular troutheau there," said the shopman, emptying out the canvas bag upon the counter. "Thry 'em on."

The Babe contented himself with trying on the costume and the boots.

"Juth made for you!" said the shopman.

A little loose about the chest, suggested the Babe.

"Thath's all right," said the shopman. "Couple o' thmall towelths, all thath's wanted."

"You don't think it too showy?" queried the Babe.

"Thowy? Sthylish, thath's all."

"You are sure everything's here?"

"Everythinkth there. 'Thept the bit o' meat inthide," assured him the shopman.

The Babe left a deposit, and gave his name and address. The shopman promised the things should be sent round within an hour. The Babe, who had entered into the spirit of the thing, bought a pair of gloves and a small reticule, and made his way to Bow Street.

"I want a woman's light brown wig," said the Babe to Mr. Cox, the perruquier.

Mr. Cox tried on two. The deceptive appearance of the second Mr. Cox pronounced as perfect.

"Looks more natural on you than your own hair, blessed if it doesn't!" said Mr. Cox.

The wig also was promised within the hour. The spirit of completeness descended upon the Babe. On his way back to his lodgings in Great Queen Street, he purchased a ladylike umbrella and a veil.

Now, a quarter of an hour after Johnny Bulstrode had made his exit by the door of Mr. Stinchcombe's shop, one, Harry Bennett, actor and member of the Autolycus Club, pushed it open and entered. The shop was empty. Harry Bennett hammered with his stick and waited. A piled-up bundle of clothes lay upon the counter; a sheet of paper, with a name and address scrawled across it, rested on the bundle. Harry Bennett, given to idle curiosity, approached and read the same. Harry Bennett, with his stick, poked the bundle, scattering its items over the counter.

"Donth do thath!" said the shopman, coming up. "Juth been putting 'em together."

"What the devil," said Harry Bennett, "is Johnny Bulstrode going to do with that rig-out?"

"How thoud I know?" answered the shopman. "Private theathricals, I suppoth. Friend o' yourth?"

"Yes," replied Harry Bennett. "By Jove! he ought to make a good girl. Should like to see it!"

"Well arthk him for a ticket. Donth make 'em dirty," suggested the shopman.

"I must," said Harry Bennett, and talked about his own affairs.

The rig-out and the wig did not arrive at Johnny's lodgings within the hour as promised, but arrived there within three hours, which was as much as Johnny had expected. It took Johnny nearly an hour to dress, but at last he stood before the plate-glass panel of the wardrobe transformed. Johnny had reason to be pleased with the result. A tall, handsome girl looked back at him out of the glass- -a little showily dressed, perhaps, but decidedly chic.

"Wonder if I ought to have a cloak," mused Johnny, as a ray of sunshine, streaming through the window, fell upon the image in the glass. "Well, anyhow, I haven't," thought Johnny, as the sunlight died away again, "so it's no good thinking about it."

Johnny seized his reticule and his umbrella and opened cautiously the door. Outside all was silent. Johnny stealthily descended; in the passage paused again. Voices sounded from the basement. Feeling like an escaped burglar, Johnny slipped the latch of the big door and peeped out. A policeman, pasting, turned and looked at him. Johnny hastily drew back and closed the door again. Somebody was ascending from the kitchen. Johnny, caught between two terrors, nearer to the front door than to the stairs, having no time, chose the street. It seemed to Johnny that the street was making for him. A woman came hurriedly towards him. What was she going to say to him? What should he answer her? To his surprise she passed him, hardly noticing him. Wondering what miracle had saved him, he took a few steps forward. A couple of young clerks coming up from behind turned to look at him, but on encountering his answering stare of angry alarm, appeared confused and went their way. It began to dawn upon him that mankind was less discerning than he had feared. Gaining courage as he proceeded, he reached Holborn. Here the larger crowd swept around him indifferent.

"I beg your pardon," said Johnny, coming into collision with a stout gentleman.

"My fault," replied the stout gentleman, as, smiling, he picked up his damaged hat.

"I beg your pardon," repeated Johnny again two minutes later, colliding with a tall young lady.

"Should advise you to take something for that squint of yours," remarked the tall young lady with severity.

"What's the matter with me?" thought Johnny. "Seems to be a sort of mist--" The explanation flashed across him. "Of course," said Johnny to himself, "it's this confounded veil!"

Johnny decided to walk to the Marble Soap offices. "I'll be more used to the hang of things by the time I get there if I walk," thought Johnny. "Hope the old beggar's in."

In Newgate Street, Johnny paused and pressed his hands against his chest. "Funny sort of pain I've got," thought Johnny. "Wonder if I should shock them if I went in somewhere for a drop of brandy?"

"It don't get any better," reflected Johnny, with some alarm, on reaching the corner of Cheapside. "Hope I'm not going to be ill. Whatever--" The explanation came to him. "Of course, it's these damned stays! No wonder girls are short-tempered, at times."

At the offices of the Marble Soap, Johnny was treated with marked courtesy. Mr. Jowett was out, was not expected back till five o'clock. Would the lady wait, or would she call again? The lady decided, now she was there, to wait. Would the lady take the easy-chair? Would the lady have the window open or would she have it shut? Had the lady seen The Times?

"Or the Ha'penny Joker?" suggested a junior clerk, who thereupon was promptly sent back to his work.

Many of the senior clerks had occasion to pass through the wait-ing- room. Two of the senior clerks held views about the weather which they appeared wishful to express at length. Johnny began to enjoy himself. This thing was going to be good fun. By the time the slamming of doors and the hurrying of feet announced the advent of the chief, Johnny was looking forward to his interview.

It was briefer and less satisfactory than he had anticipated. Mr. Jowett was very busy--did not as a rule see anybody in the afternoon; but of course, a lady-- Would Miss--"

"Montgomery."

"Would Miss Montgomery inform Mr. Jowett what it was he might have the pleasure of doing for her?"

Miss Montgomery explained.

Mr. Jowett seemed half angry, half amused.

"Really," said Mr. Jowett, "this is hardly playing the game. Against our fellow-men we can protect ourselves, but if the ladies are going to attack us--really it isn't fair."

Miss Montgomery pleaded.

"I'll think it over," was all that Mr. Jowett could be made to promise. "Look me up again."

"When?" asked Miss Montgomery.

"What's to-day?--Thursday. Say Monday." Mr. Jowett rang the bell. "Take my advice," said the old gentleman, laying a fatherly hand on Johnny's shoulder, "leave business to us men. You are a handsome girl. You can do better for yourself than this."

A clerk entered, Johnny rose.

"On Monday next, then," Johnny reminded him.

"At four o'clock," agreed Mr. Jowett. "Good afternoon."

Johnny went out feeling disappointed, and yet, as he told himself, he hadn't done so badly. Anyhow, there was nothing for it but to wait till Monday. Now he would go home, change his clothes, and get some dinner. He hailed a hansom.

"Number twenty-eight--no. Stop at the Queen's Street corner of Lincoln's Inn Fields," Johnny directed the man.

"Quite right, miss," commented the cabman pleasantly. "Corner's best--saves all talk."

"What do you mean?" demanded Johnny.

"No offence, miss," answered the man. "We was all young once."

Johnny climbed in. At the corner of Queen Street and Lincoln's Inn Fields, Johnny got out. Johnny, who had been pondering other matters, put his hand instinctively to where, speaking generally, his pocket should have been; then recollected himself.

"Let me see, did I think to bring any money out with me, or did I not?" mused Johnny, as he stood upon the kerb.

"Look in the ridicule, miss," suggested the cabman.

Johnny looked. It was empty.

"Perhaps I put it in my pocket," thought Johnny.

The cabman hitched his reins to the whip-socket and leant back.

"It's somewhere about here, I know, I saw it," Johnny told himself. "Sorry to keep you waiting," Johnny added aloud to the cabman.

"Don't you worry about that, miss," replied the cabman civilly; "we are used to it. A shilling a quarter of an hour is what we charge."

"Of all the damned silly tricks!" muttered Johnny to himself.

Two small boys and a girl carrying a baby paused, interested.

"Go away," told them the cabman. "You'll have troubles of your own one day."

The urchins moved a few steps further, then halted again and were joined by a slatternly woman and another boy.

"Got it!" cried Johnny, unable to suppress his delight as his hand slipped through a fold. The lady with the baby, without precisely knowing why, set up a shrill cheer. Johnny's delight died away; it wasn't the pocket-hole. Short of taking the skirt off and turning it inside out, it didn't seem to Johnny that he ever would find that pocket.

Then in that moment of despair he came across it accidentally. It was as empty as the reticule!

"I am sorry," said Johnny to the cabman, "but I appear to have come out without my purse."

The cabman said he had heard that tale before, and was making preparations to descend. The crowd, now numbering eleven, looked hopeful. It occurred to Johnny later that he might have offered his umbrella to the cabman; at least it would have fetched the eighteen-pence. One thinks of these things afterwards. The only idea that occurred to him at the moment was that of getting home.

"'Ere, 'old my 'orse a minute, one of yer," shouted the cabman.

Half a dozen willing hands seized the dozing steed and roused it into madness.

"Hi! stop 'er!" roared the cabman.

"She's down!" shouted the excited crowd.

"Tripped over 'er skirt," explained the slatternly woman. "They do 'amper you."

" No, she's not. She's up again!" vociferated a delighted plumber, with a sounding slap on his own leg. "Gor blimy, if she ain't a good 'un!"

Fortunately the Square was tolerably clear and Johnny a good runner. Holding now his skirt and petticoat high in his left hand, Johnny moved across the Square at the rate of fifteen miles an hour. A butcher's boy sprang in front of him with arms held out to stop him. The thing that for the next three months annoyed that butcher boy most was hearing shouted out after him "Yah! who was knocked down and run over by a lidy?" By the time Johnny reached the Strand, via Clement's Inn, the hue and cry was far behind. Johnny dropped his skirts and assumed a more girlish pace. Through Bow Street and Long Acre he reached Great Queen Street in safety. Upon his own doorstep he began to laugh. His afternoon's experience had been amusing; still, on the whole, he wasn't sorry it was over. One can have too much even of the best of jokes. Johnny rang the bell.

The door opened. Johnny would have walked in had not a big, raw- boned woman barred his progress.

"What do you want?" demanded the raw-boned woman.

"Want to come in," explained Johnny.

"What do you want to come in for?"

This appeared to Johnny a foolish question. On reflection he saw the sense of it. This raw-boned woman was not Mrs. Pegg, his landlady. Some friend of hers, he supposed.

"It's all right," said Johnny, "I live here. Left my latchkey at home, that's all."

"There's no females lodging here," declared the raw-boned lady. "And what's more, there's going to be none."

All this was very vexing. Johnny, in his joy at reaching his own doorstep, had not foreseen these complications. Now it would be necessary to explain things. He only hoped the story would not get round to the fellows at the club.

"Ask Mrs. Pegg to step up for a minute," requested Johnny.

"Not at 'ome," explained the raw-boned lady.

"Not--not at home?"

"Gone to Romford, if you wish to know, to see her mother."

"Gone to Romford?"

"I said Romford, didn't I?" retorted the raw-boned lady, tartly.

"What--what time do you expect her in?"

"Sunday evening, six o'clock," replied the raw-boned lady.

Johnny looked at the raw-boned lady, imagined himself telling the raw-boned lady the simple, unvarnished truth, and the raw-boned lady's utter disbelief of every word of it. An inspiration came to his aid.

"I am Mr. Bulstrode's sister," said Johnny meekly; "he's expecting me."

"Thought you said you lived here?" reminded him the raw-boned lady.

"I meant that he lived here," replied poor Johnny still more meekly. "He has the second floor, you know."

"I know," replied the raw-boned lady. "Not in just at present."

"Not in?"

"Went out at three o'clock."

"I'll go up to his room and wait for him," said Johnny.

"No, you won't," said the raw-boned lady.

For an instant it occurred to Johnny to make a dash for it, but the raw-boned lady looked both formidable and determined. There would be a big disturbance--perhaps the police called in. Johnny had often wanted to see his name in print: in connection with this affair he somehow felt he didn't.

"Do let me in," Johnny pleaded; "I have nowhere else to go."

"You have a walk and cool yourself," suggested the raw-boned lady. "Don't expect he will be long."

"But, you see--"

The raw-boned lady slammed the door.

Outside a restaurant in Wellington Street, from which proceeded savoury odours, Johnny paused and tried to think.

"What the devil did I do with that umbrella? I had it--no, I didn't. Must have dropped it, I suppose, when that silly ass tried to stop me. By Jove! I am having luck!"

Outside another restaurant in the Strand Johnny paused again. "How am I to live till Sunday night? Where am I to sleep? If I telegraph home--damn it! how can I telegraph? I haven't got a penny. This is funny," said Johnny, unconsciously speaking aloud; "upon my word, this is funny! Oh! you go to--."

Johnny hurled this last at the head of an overgrown errand-boy whose intention had been to offer sympathy.

"Well, I never!" commented a passing flower-girl. "Calls 'erself a lidy, I suppose."

"Nowadays," observed the stud and button merchant at the corner of Exeter Street, "they make 'em out of anything."

Drawn by a notion that was forming in his mind, Johnny turned his steps up Bedford Street. "Why not?" mused Johnny. "Nobody else seems to have a suspicion. Why should they? I'll never hear the last of it if they find me out. But why should they find me out? Well, something's got to be done."

Johnny walked on quickly. At the door of the Autolycus Club he was undecided for a moment, then took his courage in both hands and plunged through the swing doors.

"Is Mr. Herring--Mr. Jack Herring--here?"

"Find him in the smoking-room, Mr. Bulstrode," answered old Goslin, who was reading the evening paper.

"Oh, would you mind asking him to step out a moment?"

Old Goslin looked up, took off his spectacles, rubbed them, put them on again.

"Please say Miss Bulstrode--Mr. Bulstrode's sister."

Old Goslin found Jack Herring the centre of an earnest argument on Hamlet--was he really mad?

"A lady to see you, Mr. Herring," announced old Goslin.

"A what?"

"Miss Bulstrode--Mr. Bulstrode's sister. She's waiting in the hall."

"Never knew he had a sister," said Jack Herring, rising.

"Wait a minute," said Harry Bennett. "Shut that door. Don't go." This to old Goslin, who closed the door and returned. "Lady in a heliotrope dress with a lace collar, three flounces on the skirt?"

"That's right, Mr. Bennett," agreed old Goslin.

"It's the Babe himself!" asserted Harry Bennett.

The question of Hamlet's madness was forgotten.

"Was in at Stinchcombe's this morning," explained Harry Bennett; "saw the clothes on the counter addressed to him. That's the identical frock. This is just a 'try on'--thinks he's going to have a lark with us."

The Autolycus Club looked round at itself.

"I can see verra promising possibilities in this, provided the thing is properly managed," said the Wee Laddie, after a pause.

"So can I," agreed Jack Herring. "Keep where you are, all of you. 'Twould be a pity to fool it,"

The Autolycus Club waited. Jack Herring re-entered the room.

"One of the saddest stories I have ever heard in all my life," explained Jack Herring in a whisper. "Poor girl left Derbyshire this morning to come and see her brother; found him out--hasn't been seen at his lodgings since three o'clock; fears something may have happened to him. Landlady gone to Romford to see her mother; strange woman in charge, won't let her in to wait for him."

"How sad it is when trouble overtakes the innocent and helpless!" murmured Somerville the Briefless.

"That's not the worst of it," continued Jack. "The dear girl has been robbed of everything she possesses, even of her umbrella, and hasn't got a sou; hasn't had any dinner, and doesn't know where to sleep."

"Sounds a bit elaborate," thought Porson.

"I think I can understand it," said the Briefless one. "What has happened is this. He's dressed up thinking to have a bit of fun with us, and has come out, forgetting to put any money or his latchkey in his pocket. His landlady may have gone to Romford or may not. In any case, he would have to knock at the door and enter into explanations. What does he suggest--the loan of a sovereign?"

"The loan of two," replied Jack Herring.

"To buy himself a suit of clothes. Don't you do it, Jack. Providence has imposed this upon us. Our duty is to show him the folly of indulging in senseless escapades."

"I think we might give him a dinner," thought the stout and sympathetic Porson.

"What I propose to do," grinned Jack, "is to take him round to Mrs. Postwhistle's. She's under a sort of obligation to me. It was I who got her the post office. We'll leave him there for a night, with instructions to Mrs. P. to keep a motherly eye on him. To-morrow he shall have his 'bit of fun,' and I guess he'll be the first to get tired of the joke."

It looked a promising plot. Seven members of the Autolycus Club gallantly undertook to accompany "Miss Bulstrode" to her lodgings. Jack Herring excited jealousy by securing the privilege of carrying her reticule. "Miss Bulstrode" was given to understand that anything any of the seven could do for her, each and every would be delighted to do, if only for the sake of her brother, one of the dearest boys that ever breathed--a bit of an ass, though that, of course, he could not help. "Miss Bulstrode" was not as grateful as perhaps she should have been. Her idea still was that if one of them would lend her a couple of sovereigns, the rest need not worry themselves further. This, purely in her own interests, they declined to do. She had suffered one extensive robbery that day already, as Jack reminded her. London was a city of danger to the young and inexperienced. Far better that they should watch over her and provide for her simple wants. Painful as it was to refuse a lady, a beloved companion's sister's welfare was yet dearer to them. "Miss Bulstrode's" only desire was not to waste their time. Jack Herring's opinion was that there existed no true Englishman who would grudge time spent upon succouring a beautiful maiden in distress.

Arrived at the little grocer's shop in Rolls Court, Jack Herring drew Mrs. Postwhistle aside.

"She's the sister of a very dear friend of ours," explained Jack Herring.

"A fine-looking girl," commented Mrs. Postwhistle.

"I shall be round again in the morning. Don't let her out of your sight, and, above all, don't lend her any money," directed Jack Herring.

"I understand," replied Mrs. Postwhistle.

"Miss Bulstrode" having despatched an excellent supper of cold mutton and bottled beer, leant back in her chair and crossed her legs.

"I have often wondered," remarked Miss Bulstrode, her eyes fixed upon the ceiling, "what a cigarette would taste like."

"Taste nasty, I should say, the first time," thought Mrs. Postwhistle, who was knitting.

"Some girls, so I have heard," remarked Miss Bulstrode, "smoke cigarettes."

"Not nice girls," thought Mrs. Postwhistle.

"One of the nicest girls I ever knew," remarked Miss Bulstrode, "always smoked a cigarette after supper. Said it soothed her nerves."

"Wouldn't 'ave thought so if I'd 'ad charge of 'er," said Mrs. Postwhistle.

"I think," said Miss Bulstrode, who seemed restless, "I think I shall go for a little walk before turning in."

"Perhaps it would do us good," agreed Mrs. Postwhistle, laying down her knitting.

"Don't you trouble to come," urged the thoughtful Miss Bulstrode. "You look tired."

"Not at all," replied Mrs. Postwhistle. "Feel I should like it."

In some respects Mrs. Postwhistle proved an admirable companion. She asked no questions, and only spoke when spoken to, which, during that walk, was not often. At the end of half an hour, Miss Bulstrode pleaded a headache and thought she would return home and go to bed. Mrs. Postwhistle thought it a reasonable idea.

"Well, it's better than tramping the streets," muttered Johnny, as the bedroom door was closed behind him, "and that's all one can say for it. Must get hold of a smoke to-morrow, if I have to rob the till.

What's that?" Johnny stole across on, tiptoe. "Confound it!" said Johnny, "if she hasn't locked the door!"

Johnny sat down upon the bed and took stock of his position. "It doesn't seem to me," thought Johnny, "that I'm ever going to get out of this mess." Johnny, still muttering, unfastened his stays. "Thank God, that's off!" ejaculated Johnny piously, as he watched his form slowly expanding. "Suppose I'll be used to them before I've finished with them."

Johnny had a night of dreams.

For the whole of next day, which was Friday, Johnny remained "Miss Bulstrode," hoping against hope to find an opportunity to escape from his predicament without confession. The entire Autolycus Club appeared to have fallen in love with him.

"Thought I was a bit of a fool myself," mused Johnny, "where a petticoat was concerned. Don't believe these blithering idiots have ever seen a girl before."

They came in ones, they came in little parties, and tendered him devotion. Even Mrs. Postwhistle, accustomed to regard human phenomena without comment, remarked upon it.

"When you are all tired of it," said Mrs. Postwhistle to Jack Herring, "let me know."

"The moment we find her brother," explained Jack Herring, "of course we shall take her to him."

"Nothing like looking in the right place for a thing when you've finished looking in the others," observed Mrs. Postwhistle.

"What do you mean?" demanded Jack.

"Just what I say," answered Mrs. Postwhistle.

Jack Herring looked at Mrs. Postwhistle. But Mrs. Postwhistle's face was not of the expressive order.

"Post office still going strong?" asked Jack Herring.

"The post office 'as been a great 'elp to me," admitted Mrs. Postwhistle; "and I'm not forgetting that I owe it to you."

"Don't mention it," murmured Jack Herring.

They brought her presents--nothing very expensive, more as tokens of regard: dainty packets of sweets, nosegays of simple flowers, bottles of scent. To Somerville "Miss Bulstrode" hinted that if he really did desire to please her, and wasn't merely talking through his hat--Miss Bulstrode apologised for the slang, which, she feared, she must have picked up from her brother--he might give her a box of Messani's cigarettes, size No. 2. The suggestion pained him. Somerville the Briefless was perhaps old-fashioned. Miss Bulstrode cut him short by agreeing that he was, and seemed disinclined for further conversation.

They took her to Madame Tussaud's. They took her up the Monument. They took her to the Tower of London. In the evening they took her to the Polytechnic to see Pepper's Ghost. They made a merry party wherever they went.

"Seem to be enjoying themselves!" remarked other sightseers, surprised and envious.

"Girl seems to be a bit out of it," remarked others, more observant.

"Sulky-looking bit o' goods, I call her," remarked some of the ladies.

The fortitude with which Miss Bulstrode bore the mysterious disappearance of her brother excited admiration.

"Hadn't we better telegraph to your people in Derbyshire?" suggested Jack Herring.

"Don't do it," vehemently protested the thoughtful Miss Bulstrode; "it might alarm them. The best plan is for you to lend me a couple of sovereigns and let me return home quietly."

"You might be robbed again," feared Jack Herring. "I'll go down with you."

"Perhaps he'll turn up to-morrow," thought Miss Bulstrode. "Expect he's gone on a visit."

"He ought not to have done it," thought Jack Herring, "knowing you were coming."

"Oh! he's like that," explained Miss Bulstrode.

"If I had a young and beautiful sister--" said Jack Herring.

"Oh! let's talk of something else," suggested Miss Bulstrode. "You make me tired."

With Jack Herring, in particular, Johnny was beginning to lose patience. That "Miss Bulstrode's" charms had evidently struck Jack Herring all of a heap, as the saying is, had in the beginning amused Master Johnny. Indeed--as in the seclusion of his bedchamber over the little grocer's shop he told himself with bitter self-reproach--he had undoubtedly encouraged the man. From admiration Jack had rapidly passed to infatuation, from infatuation to apparent imbecility. Had Johnny's mind been less intent upon his own troubles, he might have been suspicious. As it was, and after all that had happened, nothing now could astonish Johnny. "Thank Heaven," murmured Johnny, as he blew out the light, "this Mrs. Postwhistle appears to be a reliable woman."

Now, about the same time that Johnny's head was falling thus upon his pillow, the Autolycus Club sat discussing plans for their next day's entertainment.

"I think," said Jack Herring, "the Crystal Palace in the morning when it's nice and quiet."

"To be followed by Greenwich Hospital in the afternoon," suggested Somerville.

"Winding up with the Moore and Burgess Minstrels in the evening," thought Porson.

"Hardly the place for the young person," feared Jack Herring. "Some of the jokes--"

"Mr. Brandram gives a reading of Julius Caesar at St. George's Hall," the Wee Laddie informed them for their guidance.

"Hallo!" said Alexander the Poet, entering at the moment. "What are you all talking about?"

"We were discussing where to take Miss Bulstrode to-morrow evening," informed him Jack Herring.

"Miss Bulstrode," repeated the Poet in a tone of some surprise. "Do you mean Johnny Bulstrode's sister?"

"That's the lady," answered Jack. "But how do you come to know about her? Thought you were in Yorkshire."

"Came up yesterday," explained the Poet. "Travelled up with her."

"Travelled up with her?"

"From Matlock Bath. What's the matter with you all?" demanded the Poet. "You all of you look--"

"Sit down," said the Briefless one to the Poet. "Let's talk this matter over quietly."

Alexander the Poet, mystified, sat down.

"You say you travelled up to London yesterday with Miss Bulstrode. You are sure it was Miss Bulstrode?"

"Sure!" retorted the Poet. "Why, I've known her ever since she was a baby."

"About what time did you reach London?"

"Three-thirty."

"And what became of her? Where did she say she was going?"

"I never asked her. The last I saw of her she was getting into a cab. I had an appointment myself, and was--I say, what's the matter with Herring?"

Herring had risen and was walking about with his head between his hands.

"Never mind him. Miss Bulstrode is a lady of about--how old?"

"Eighteen--no, nineteen last birthday."

"A tall, handsome sort of girl?"

"Yes. I say, has anything happened to her?"

"Nothing has happened to her," assured him Somerville. "SHE'S all right. Been having rather a good time, on the whole."

The Poet was relieved to hear it.

"I asked her an hour ago," said Jack Herring, who was still holding his head between his hands as if to make sure it was there, "if she thought she could ever learn to love me. Would you say that could be construed into an offer of marriage?"

The remainder of the Club was unanimously of opinion that, practically speaking, it was a proposal.

"I don't see it," argued Jack Herring. "It was merely in the nature of a remark."

The Club was of opinion that such quibbling was unworthy of a gentleman.

It appeared to be a case for prompt action. Jack Herring sat down and then and there began a letter to Miss Bulstrode, care of Mrs. Postwhistle.

"But what I don't understand--" said Alexander the Poet.

"Oh! take him away somewhere and tell him, someone," moaned Jack Herring. "How can I think with all this chatter going on?"

"But why did Bennett--" whispered Porson.

"Where is Bennett?" demanded half a dozen fierce voices.

Harry Bennett had not been seen all day.

Jack's letter was delivered to "Miss Bulstrode" the next morning at breakfast-time. Having perused it, Miss Bulstrode rose and requested of Mrs. Postwhistle the loan of half a crown.

"Mr. Herring's particular instructions were," explained Mrs. Postwhistle, "that, above all things, I was not to lend you any money."

"When you have read that," replied Miss Bulstrode, handing her the letter, "perhaps you will agree with me that Herring is--an ass."

Mrs. Postwhistle read the letter and produced the half-crown.

"Better get a shave with part of it," suggested Mrs. Postwhistle. "That is, if you are going to play the fool much longer."

"Miss Bulstrode" opened his eyes. Mrs. Postwhistle went on with her breakfast.

"Don't tell them," said Johnny; "not just for a little while, at all events."

"Nothing to do with me," replied Mrs. Postwhistle.

Twenty minutes later, the real Miss Bulstrode, on a visit to her aunt in Kensington, was surprised at receiving, enclosed in an envelope, the following hastily scrawled note:-

"Want to speak to you at once--ALONE. Don't yell when you see me. It's all right. Can explain in two ticks.--Your loving brother, JOHNNY."

It took longer than two ticks; but at last the Babe came to an end of it.

"When you have done laughing," said the Babe.

"But you look so ridiculous," said his sister.

"THEY didn't think so," retorted the Babe. "I took them in all right. Guess you've never had as much attention, all in one day."

"Are you sure you took them in?" queried his sister.

"If you will come to the Club at eight o'clock this evening," said the Babe, "I'll prove it to you. Perhaps I'll take you on to a theatre afterwards--if you're good."

The Babe himself walked into the Autolycus Club a few minutes before eight and encountered an atmosphere of restraint.

"Thought you were lost," remarked Somerville coldly.

"Called away suddenly--very important business," explained the Babe. "Awfully much obliged to all you fellows for all you have been doing for my sister. She's just been telling me."

"Don't mention it," said two or three.

"Awfully good of you, I'm sure," persisted the Babe. "Don't know what she would have done without you."

A mere nothing, the Club assured him. The blushing modesty of the Autolycus Club at hearing of their own good deeds was touching. Left to themselves, they would have talked of quite other things. As a matter of fact, they tried to.

"Never heard her speak so enthusiastically of anyone as she does of you, Jack," said the Babe, turning to Jack Herring.

"Of course, you know, dear boy," explained Jack Herring, "anything I could do for a sister of yours--"

"I know, dear boy," replied the Babe; "I always felt it."

"Say no more about it," urged Jack Herring.

"She couldn't quite make out that letter of yours this morning," continued the Babe, ignoring Jack's request. "She's afraid you think her ungrateful."

"It seemed to me, on reflection," explained Jack Herring, "that on one or two little matters she may have misunderstood me. As I wrote her, there are days when I don't seem altogether to quite know what I'm doing."

"Rather awkward," thought the Babe.

"It is," agreed Jack Herring. "Yesterday was one of them."

"She tells me you were most kind to her," the Babe reassured him.

"She thought at first it was a little uncivil, your refusing to lend her any money. But as I put it to her --"

"It was silly of me," interrupted Jack. "I see that now. I went round this morning meaning to make it all right. But she was gone, and Mrs. Postwhistle seemed to think I had better leave things as they were. I blame myself exceedingly."

"My dear boy, don't blame yourself for anything. You acted nobly," the Babe told him. "She's coming here to call for me this evening on purpose to thank you."

"I'd rather not," said Jack Herring.

"Nonsense," said the Babe.

"You must excuse me," insisted Jack Herring. "I don't mean it rudely, but really I'd rather not see her."

"But here she is," said the Babe, taking at that moment the card from old Goslin's hand. "She will think it so strange."

"I'd really rather not," repeated poor Jack.

"It seems discourteous," suggested Somerville.

"You go," suggested Jack.

"She doesn't want to see me," explained Somerville.

"Yes she does," corrected him the Babe.

"I'd forgotten, she wants to see you both."

"If I go," said Jack, "I shall tell her the plain truth."

"Do you know," said Somerville, "I'm thinking that will be the shortest way."

Miss Bulstrode was seated in the hall. Jack Herring and Somerville both thought her present quieter style of dress suited her much better.

"Here he is," announced the Babe, in triumph. "Here's Jack Herring and here's Somerville. Do you know, I could hardly persuade them to come out and see you. Dear old Jack, he always was so shy."

Miss Bulstrode rose. She said she could never thank them sufficiently for all their goodness to her. Miss Bulstrode seemed quite overcome. Her voice trembled with emotion.

"Before we go further, Miss Bulstrode," said Jack Herring, "it will be best to tell you that all along we thought you were your brother, dressed up as a girl."

"Oh!" said the Babe, "so that's the explanation, is it? If I had only known--" Then the Babe stopped, and wished he hadn't spoken.

Somerville seized him by the shoulders and, with a sudden jerk, stood him beside his sister under the gas-jet.

"You little brute!" said Somerville. "It was you all along." And the Babe, seeing the game was up, and glad that the joke had not been entirely on one side, confessed.

Jack Herring and Somerville the Briefless went that night with Johnny and his sister to the theatre--and on other nights. Miss Bulstrode thought Jack Herring very nice, and told her brother so. But she thought Somerville the Briefless even nicer, and later, under cross-examination, when Somerville was no longer briefless, told Somerville so himself.

But that has nothing to do with this particular story, the end of which is that Miss Bulstrode kept the appointment made for Monday afternoon between "Miss Montgomery" and Mr. Jowett, and secured thereby the Marble Soap advertisement for the back page of Good Humour for six months, at twenty-five pounds a week.

STORY THE SEVENTH

DICK DANVERS PRESENTS HIS PETITION

William Clodd, mopping his brow, laid down the screwdriver, and stepping back, regarded the result of his labours with evident satisfaction.

"It looks like a bookcase," said William Clodd. "You might sit in the room for half an hour and never know it wasn't a bookcase."

What William Clodd had accomplished was this: he had had prepared, after his own design, what appeared to be four shelves laden with works suggestive of thought and erudition. As a matter of fact, it was not a bookcase, but merely a flat board, the books merely the backs of volumes that had long since found their way into the paper-mill. This artful deception William Clodd had screwed upon a cottage piano standing in the corner of the editorial office of Good Humour. Half a dozen real volumes piled upon the top of the piano completed the illusion. As William Clodd had proudly remarked, a casual visitor might easily have been deceived.

"If you had to sit in the room while she was practising mixed scales, you'd be quickly undeceived," said the editor of Good Humour, one Peter Hope. He spoke bitterly.

"You are not always in," explained Clodd. "There must be hours when she is here alone, with nothing else to do. Besides, you will get used to it after a while."

"You, I notice, don't try to get used to it," snarled Peter Hope. "You always go out the moment she commences."

"A friend of mine," continued William Clodd, "worked in an office over a piano-shop for seven years, and when the shop closed, it nearly ruined his business; couldn't settle down to work for want of it."

"Why doesn't he come here?" asked Peter Hope. "The floor above is vacant."

"Can't," explained William Clodd. "He's dead."

"I can quite believe it," commented Peter Hope.

"It was a shop where people came and practised, paying sixpence an hour, and he had got to like it--said it made a cheerful background to his thoughts. Wonderful what you can get accustomed to."

"What's the good of it?" demanded Peter Hope.

"What's the good of it!" retorted William Clodd indignantly. "Every girl ought to know how to play the piano. A nice thing if when her lover asks her to play something to him--"

"I wonder you don't start a matrimonial agency," sneered Peter Hope. "Love and marriage--you think of nothing else."

"When you are bringing up a young girl--" argued Clodd.

"But you're not," interrupted Peter; "that's just what I'm trying to get out of your head. It is I who am bringing her up. And between ourselves, I wish you wouldn't interfere so much."

"You are not fit to bring up a girl."

"I've brought her up for seven years without your help. She's my adopted daughter, not yours. I do wish people would learn to mind their own business."

"You've done very well --"

"Thank you," said Peter Hope sarcastically. "It's very kind of you. Perhaps when you've time, you'll write me out a testimonial."

"--up till now," concluded the imperturbable Clodd. "A girl of eighteen wants to know something else besides mathematics and the classics. You don't understand them."

"I do understand them," asserted Peter Hope. "What do you know about them? You're not a father."

"You've done your best," admitted William Clodd in a tone of patronage that irritated Peter greatly; "but you're a dreamer; you don't know the world. The time is coming when the girl will have to think of a husband."

"There's no need for her to think of a husband, not for years," retorted Peter Hope. "And even when she does, is strumming on the piano going to help her?"

"I tink--I tink," said Dr. Smith, who had hitherto remained a silent listener, "our young frent Clodd is right. You haf never quite got over your idea dat she was going to be a boy. You haf taught her de tings a boy should know."

"You cut her hair," added Clodd.

"I don't," snapped Peter.

"You let her have it cut--it's the same thing. At eighteen she knows more about the ancient Greeks and Romans than she does about her own frocks."

"De young girl," argued the doctor, "what is she? De flower dat makes bright for us de garden of life, de gurgling brook dat murmurs by de dusty highway, de cheerful fire--"

"She can't be all of them," snapped Peter, who was a stickler for style. "Do keep to one simile at a time."

"Now you listen to plain sense," said William Clodd. "You want--we all want--the girl to be a success all round."

"I want her--" Peter Hope was rummaging among the litter on the desk. It certainly was not there. Peter pulled out a drawer-two drawers. "I wish," said Peter Hope, "I wish sometimes she wasn't quite so clever."

The old doctor rummaged among dusty files of papers in a corner. Clodd found it on the mantelpiece concealed beneath the hollow foot of a big brass candlestick, and handed it to Peter.

Peter had one vice--the taking in increasing quantities of snuff, which was harmful for him, as he himself admitted. Tommy, sympathetic to most masculine frailties, was severe, however, upon this one.

"You spill it upon your shirt and on your coat," had argued Tommy. "I like to see you always neat. Besides, it isn't a nice habit. I do wish, dad, you'd give it up."

"I must," Peter had agreed. "I'll break myself of it. But not all at once--it would be a wrench; by degrees, Tommy, by degrees."

So a compromise had been compounded. Tommy was to hide the snuff- box. It was to be somewhere in the room and to be accessible, but that was all. Peter, when self-control had reached the breaking-point, might try and find it. Occasionally, luck helping Peter, he would find it early in the day, when he would earn his own bitter self-reproaches by indulging in quite an orgie. But more often Tommy's artfulness was such that he would be compelled, by want of time, to abandon the search. Tommy always knew when he had failed by the air of indignant resignation with which he would greet her on her return. Then perhaps towards evening, Peter, looking up, would see the box open before his nose, above it, a pair of reproving black eyes, their severity counterbalanced by a pair of full red lips trying not to smile. And Peter, knowing that only one pinch would be permitted, would dip deeply.

"I want her," said Peter Hope, feeling with his snuff-box in his hand more confidence in his own judgment, "to be a sensible, clever woman, capable of earning her own living and of being independent; not a mere helpless doll, crying for some man to come and take care of her."

"A woman's business," asserted Clodd, "is to be taken care of."

"Some women, perhaps," admitted Peter; "but Tommy, you know very well, is not going to be the ordinary type of woman. She has brains; she will make her way in the world."

"It doesn't depend upon brains," said Clodd. "She hasn't got the elbows."

"The elbows?"

"They are not sharp enough. The last 'bus home on a wet night tells you whether a woman is capable of pushing her own way in the world. Tommy's the sort to get left on the kerb."

"She's the sort," retorted Peter, "to make a name for herself and to be able to afford a cab. Don't you bully me!" Peter sniffed self-assertiveness from between his thumb and finger.

"Yes, I shall," Clodd told him, "on this particular point. The poor girl's got no mother."

Fortunately for the general harmony the door opened at the moment to admit the subject of discussion.

"Got that Daisy Blossom advertisement out of old Blatchley," announced Tommy, waving triumphantly a piece of paper over her head.

"No!" exclaimed Peter. "How did you manage it?"

"Asked him for it," was Tommy's explanation.

"Very odd," mused Peter; "asked the old idiot for it myself only last week. He refused it point-blank."

Clodd snorted reproof. "You know I don't like your doing that sort of thing. It isn't proper for a young girl--"

"It's all right," assured him Tommy; "he's bald!"

"That makes no difference," was Clodd's opinion.

"Yes it does," was Tommy's. "I like them bald."

Tommy took Peter's head between her hands and kissed it, and in doing so noticed the tell-tale specks of snuff.

"Just a pinch, my dear," explained Peter, "the merest pinch."

Tommy took up the snuff-box from the desk. "I'll show you where I'm going to put it this time." She put it in her pocket. Peter's face fell.

"What do you think of it?" said Clodd. He led her to the corner. "Good idea, ain't it?"

"Why, where's the piano?" demanded Tommy.

Clodd turned in delighted triumph to the others.

"Humbug!" growled Peter.

"It isn't humbug," cried Clodd indignantly. "She thought it was a bookcase--anybody would. You'll be able to sit there and practise by the hour," explained Clodd to Tommy. "When you hear anybody coming up the stairs, you can leave off."

"How can she hear anything when she--" A bright idea occurred to Peter. "Don't you think, Clodd, as a practical man," suggested Peter insinuatingly, adopting the Socratic method, "that if we got her one of those dummy pianos--you know what I mean; it's just like an ordinary piano, only you don't hear it?"

Clodd shook his head. "No good at all. Can't tell the effect she is producing."

"Quite so. Then, on the other hand, Clodd, don't you think that hearing the effect they are producing may sometimes discourage the beginner?"

Clodd's opinion was that such discouragement was a thing to be battled with.

Tommy, who had seated herself, commenced a scale in contrary motion.

"Well, I'm going across to the printer's now," explained Clodd, taking up his hat. "Got an appointment with young Grindley at three. You stick to it. A spare half-hour now and then that you never miss does wonders. You've got it in you." With these encouraging remarks to Tommy, Clodd disappeared.

"Easy for him," muttered Peter bitterly. "Always does have an appointment outside the moment she begins."

Tommy appeared to be throwing her very soul into the performance. Passers-by in Crane Court paused, regarded the first-floor windows of the publishing and editorial offices of Good Humour with troubled looks, then hurried on.

"She has--remarkably firm douch!" shouted the doctor into Peter's ear. "Will see you--evening. Someting--say to you."

The fat little doctor took his hat and departed. Tommy, ceasing suddenly, came over and seated herself on the arm of Peter's chair.

"Feeling grumpy?" asked Tommy.

"It isn't," explained Peter, "that I mind the noise. I'd put up with that if I could see the good of it."

"It's going to help me to get a husband, dad. Seems to me an odd way of doing it; but Billy says so, and Billy knows all about everything."

"I can't understand you, a sensible girl, listening to such nonsense," said Peter. "It's that that troubles me."

"Dad, where are your wits?" demanded Tommy. "Isn't Billy acting like a brick? Why, he could go into Fleet Street to half a dozen other papers and make five hundred a year as advertising-agent--you know he could. But he doesn't. He sticks to us. If my making myself ridiculous with that tin pot they persuaded him was a piano is going to please him, isn't it common sense and sound business, to say nothing of good nature and gratitude, for me to do it? Dad, I've got a surprise for him. Listen." And Tommy, springing from the arm of Peter's chair, returned to the piano.

"What was it?" questioned Tommy, having finished. "Could you recognise it?"

"I think," said Peter, "it sounded like-- It wasn't 'Home, Sweet Home,' was it?"

Tommy clapped her hands. "Yes, it was. You'll end by liking it yourself, dad. We'll have musical 'At Homes.'"

"Tommy, have I brought you up properly, do you think?"

"No dad, you haven't. You have let me have my own way too much. You know the proverb: 'Good mothers make bad daughters.' Clodd's right; you've spoilt me, dad. Do you remember, dad, when I first came to you, seven years ago, a ragged little brat out of the streets, that didn't know itself whether 'twas a boy or a girl? Do you know what I thought to myself the moment I set eyes on you? 'Here's a soft old juggins; I'll be all right if I can get in here!' It makes you smart, knocking about in the gutters and being knocked about; you read faces quickly."

"Do you remember your cooking, Tommy? You 'had an aptitude for it,' according to your own idea."

Tommy laughed. "I wonder how you stood it."

"You were so obstinate. You came to me as 'cook and housekeeper,' and as cook and housekeeper, and as nothing else, would you remain. If I suggested any change, up would go your chin into the air. I dared not even dine out too often, you were such a little tyrant. The only thing you were always ready to do, if I wasn't satisfied, was to march out of the house and leave me. Wherever did you get that savage independence of yours?"

"I don't know. I think it must have been from a woman--perhaps she was my mother; I don't know--who used to sit up in the bed and cough, all night it seemed to me. People would come to see us-- ladies in fine clothes, and gentlemen with oily hair. I think they wanted to help us. Many of them had kind voices. But always a hard look would come into her face, and she would tell them what even then I knew to be untrue--it was one of the first things I can recollect--that we had everything we wanted, that we needed no help from anyone. They would go away, shrugging their shoulders. I grew up with the feeling that seemed to have been burnt into my brain, that to take from anybody anything you had not earned was shameful. I don't think I could do it even now, not even from you. I am useful to you, dad--I do help you?"

There had crept a terror into Tommy's voice. Peter felt the little hands upon his arm trembling.

"Help me? Why, you work like a nigger--like a nigger is supposed to work, but doesn't. No one--whatever we paid him--would do half as much. I don't want to make your head more swollen than it is, young woman, but you have talent; I am not sure it is not genius." Peter felt the little hands tighten upon his arm.

"I do want this paper to be a success; that is why I strum upon the piano to please Clodd. Is it humbug?"

"I am afraid it is; but humbug is the sweet oil that helps this whirling world of ours to spin round smoothly. Too much of it cloys: we drop it very gently."

"But you are sure it is only humbug, Tommy?" It was Peter's voice into which fear had entered now. "It is not that you think he understands you better than I do--would do more for you?"

"You want me to tell you all I think of you, and that isn't good for you, dad--not too often. It would be you who would have swelled head then."

"I am jealous, Tommy, jealous of everyone that comes near you. Life is a tragedy for us old folks. We know there must come a day when you will leave the nest, leave us voiceless, ridiculous, flitting among bare branches. You will understand later, when you have children of your own. This foolish talk about a husband! It is worse for a man than it is for the woman. The mother lives again in her child: the man is robbed of all."

"Dad, do you know how old I am?--that you are talking terrible nonsense?"

"He will come, little girl."

"Yes," answered Tommy, "I suppose he will; but not for a long while--oh, not for a very long while. Don't. It frightens me."

"You? Why should it frighten you?"

"The pain. It makes me feel a coward. I want it to come; I want to taste life, to drain the whole cup, to understand, to feel. But that is the boy in me. I am more than half a boy, I always have been. But the woman in me: it shrinks from the ordeal."

"You talk, Tommy, as if love were something terrible."

"There are all things in it; I feel it, dad. It is life in a single draught. It frightens me."

The child was standing with her face hidden behind her hands. Old Peter, always very bad at lying, stood silent, not knowing what consolation to concoct. The shadow passed, and Tommy's laughing eyes looked out again.

"Haven't you anything to do, dad--outside, I mean?"

"You want to get rid of me?"

"Well, I've nothing else to occupy me till the proofs come in. I'm going to practise, hard."

"I think I'll turn over my article on the Embankment," said Peter.

"There's one thing you all of you ought to be grateful to me for," laughed Tommy, as she seated herself at the piano. "I do induce you all to take more fresh air than otherwise you would."

Tommy, left alone, set herself to her task with the energy and thoroughness that were characteristic of her. Struggling with complicated scales, Tommy bent her eyes closer and closer over the pages of Czerny's Exercises. Glancing up to turn a page, Tommy, to her surprise, met the eyes of a stranger. They were brown eyes, their expression sympathetic. Below them, looking golden with the sunlight falling on it, was a moustache and beard cut short in

Vandyke fashion, not altogether hiding a pleasant mouth, about the corners of which lurked a smile.

"I beg your pardon," said the stranger. "I knocked three times. Perhaps you did not hear me?"

"No, I didn't," confessed Tommy, closing the book of Czerny's Exercises, and rising with chin at an angle that, to anyone acquainted with the chart of Tommy's temperament, might have suggested the advisability of seeking shelter.

"This is the editorial office of Good Humour, is it not?" inquired the stranger.

"It is."

"Is the editor in?"

"The editor is out."

"The sub-editor?" suggested the stranger.

"I am the sub-editor."

The stranger raised his eyebrows. Tommy, on the contrary, lowered hers.

"Would you mind glancing through that?" The stranger drew from his pocket a folded manuscript. "It will not take you a moment. I ought, of course, to have sent it through the post; but I am so tired of sending things through the post."

The stranger's manner was compounded of dignified impudence combined with pathetic humility. His eyes both challenged and pleaded. Tommy held out her hand for the paper and retired with it behind the protection of the big editorial desk that, flanked on one side by a screen and on the other by a formidable revolving bookcase, stretched fortress-like across the narrow room. The stranger remained standing.

"Yes. It's pretty," criticised the sub-editor. "Worth printing, perhaps, not worth paying for."

"Not merely a--a nominal sum, sufficient to distinguish it from the work of the amateur?"

Tommy pursed her lips. "Poetry is quite a drug in the market. We can get as much as we want of it for nothing."

"Say half a crown," suggested the stranger.

Tommy shot a swift glance across the desk, and for the first time saw the whole of him. He was clad in a threadbare, long, brown ulster--long, that is, it would have been upon an ordinary man, but the stranger happening to be remarkably tall, it appeared on him ridiculously short, reaching only to his knees. Round his neck and tucked into his waistcoat, thus completely hiding the shirt and collar he may have been wearing or may not, was carefully arranged a blue silk muffler. His hands, which were bare, looked blue and cold. Yet the black frock-coat and waistcoat and French grey trousers bore the unmistakable cut of a first-class tailor and fitted him to perfection. His hat, which he had rested on the desk, shone resplendent, and the handle of his silk umbrella was an eagle's head in gold, with two small rubies for the eyes.

"You can leave it if you like," consented Tommy. "I'll speak to the editor about it when he returns."

"You won't forget it?" urged the stranger.

"No," answered Tommy. "I shall not forget it."

Her black eyes were fixed upon the stranger without her being aware of it. She had dropped unconsciously into her "stocktaking" attitude.

"Thank you very much," said the stranger. "I will call again to-morrow."

The stranger, moving backward to the door, went out.

Tommy sat with her face between her hands. Czerny's Exercises lay neglected.

"Anybody called?" asked Peter Hope.

"No," answered Tommy. "Oh, just a man. Left this--not bad."

"The old story," mused Peter, as he unfolded the manuscript. "We all of us begin with poetry. Then we take to prose romances; poetry doesn't pay. Finally, we write articles: 'How to be Happy though Married,' 'What shall we do with our Daughters?' It is life summarised. What is it all about?"

"Oh, the usual sort of thing," explained Tommy. "He wants half a crown for it."

"Poor devil! Let him have it."

"That's not business," growled Tommy.

"Nobody will ever know," said Peter. "We'll enter it as 'telegrams.'"

The stranger called early the next day, pocketed his half-crown, and left another manuscript--an essay. Also he left behind him his gold-handled umbrella, taking away with him instead an old alpaca thing Clodd kept in reserve for exceptionally dirty weather. Peter pronounced the essay usable.

"He has a style," said Peter; "he writes with distinction. Make an appointment for me with him."

Clodd, on missing his umbrella, was indignant.

"What's the good of this thing to me?" commented Clodd. "Sort of thing for a dude in a pantomime! The fellow must be a blithering ass!"

Tommy gave to the stranger messages from both when next he called. He appeared more grieved than surprised concerning the umbrellas.

"You don't think Mr. Clodd would like to keep this umbrella in exchange for his own?" he suggested.

"Hardly his style," explained Tommy.

"It's very peculiar," said the stranger, with a smile. "I have been trying to get rid of this umbrella for the last three weeks. Once upon a time, when I preferred to keep my own umbrella, people used to take it by mistake, leaving all kinds of shabby things behind them in exchange. Now, when I'd really like to get quit of it, nobody will have it."

"Why do you want to get rid of it?" asked Tommy. "It looks a very good umbrella."

"You don't know how it hampers me," said the stranger. "I have to live up to it. It requires a certain amount of resolution to enter a cheap restaurant accompanied by that umbrella. When I do, the waiters draw my attention to the most expensive dishes and recommend me special brands of their so-called champagne. They seem quite surprised if I only want a chop and a glass of beer. I haven't always got the courage to disappoint them. It is really becoming quite a curse to me. If I use it to stop a 'bus, three or four hansoms dash up and quarrel over me. I can't do anything I want to do. I want to live simply and inexpensively: it will not let me."

Tommy laughed. "Can't you lose it?"

The stranger laughed also. "Lose it! You have no idea how honest people are. I hadn't myself. The whole world has gone up in my estimation within the last few weeks. People run after me for quite long distances and force it into my hand--people on rainy days who haven't got umbrellas of their own. It is the same with this hat." The stranger sighed as he took it up. "I am always trying to get OFF with something reasonably shabby in exchange for it. I am always found out and stopped."

"Why don't you pawn them?" suggested the practicable Tommy.

The stranger regarded her with admiration.

"Do you know, I never thought of that," said the stranger. "Of course. What a good idea! Thank you so much."

The stranger departed, evidently much relieved.

"Silly fellow," mused Tommy. "They won't give him a quarter of the value, and he will say: 'Thank you so much,' and be quite contented." It worried Tommy a good deal that day, the thought of that stranger's helplessness.

The stranger's name was Richard Danvers. He lived the other side of Holborn, in Featherstone Buildings, but much of his time came to be spent in the offices of Good Humour.

Peter liked him. "Full of promise," was Peter's opinion. "His criticism of that article of mine on 'The Education of Woman' showed both sense and feeling. A scholar and a thinker."

Flipp, the office-boy (spelt Philip), liked him; and Flipp's attitude, in general, was censorial. "He's all right," pronounced Flipp; "nothing stuck-up about him. He's got plenty of sense, lying hidden away."

Miss Ramsbotham liked him. "The men--the men we think about at all," explained Miss Ramsbotham--"may be divided into two classes: the men we ought to like, but don't; and the men there is no particular reason for our liking, but that we do. Personally I could get very fond of your friend Dick. There is nothing whatever attractive about him except himself."

Even Tommy liked him in her way, though at times she was severe with him.

"If you mean a big street," grumbled Tommy, who was going over proofs, "why not say a big street? Why must you always call it a 'main artery'?"

"I am sorry," apologised Danvers. "It is not my own idea. You told me to study the higher-class journals."

"I didn't tell you to select and follow all their faults. Here it is again. Your crowd is always a 'hydra-headed monster'; your tea 'the cup that cheers but not inebriates.'"

"I am afraid I am a deal of trouble to you," suggested the staff.

"I am afraid you are," agreed the sub-editor.

"Don't give me up," pleaded the staff. "I misunderstood you, that is all. I will write English for the future."

"Shall be glad if you will," growled the sub-editor.

Dick Danvers rose. "I am so anxious not to get what you call 'the sack' from here."

The sub-editor, mollified, thought the staff need be under no apprehension, provided it showed itself teachable.

"I have been rather a worthless fellow, Miss Hope," confessed Dick Danvers. "I was beginning to despair of myself till I came across you and your father. The atmosphere here--I don't mean the material atmosphere of Crane Court--is so invigorating: its simplicity, its sincerity. I used to have ideals. I tried to stifle them. There is a set that sneers at all that sort of thing. Now I see that they are good. You will help me?"

Every woman is a mother. Tommy felt for the moment that she wanted to take this big boy on her knee and talk to him for his good. He was only an overgrown lad. But so exceedingly overgrown! Tommy had to content herself with holding out her hand. Dick Danvers grasped it tightly.

Clodd was the only one who did not approve of him.

"How did you get hold of him?" asked Clodd one afternoon, he and Peter alone in the office.

"He came. He came in the usual way," explained Peter.

"What do you know about him?"

"Nothing. What is there to know? One doesn't ask for a character with a journalist."

"No, I suppose that wouldn't work. Found out anything about him since?"

"Nothing against him. Why so suspicious of everybody?"

"Because you are just a woolly lamb and want a dog to look after you. Who is he? On a first night he gives away his stall and sneaks into the pit. When you send him to a picture-gallery, he dodges the private view and goes on the first shilling day. If an invitation comes to a public dinner, he asks me to go and eat it for him and tell him what it's all about. That doesn't suggest the frank and honest journalist, does it?"

"It is unusual, it certainly is unusual," Peter was bound to admit.

"I distrust the man," said Clodd. "He's not our class. What is he doing here?"

"I will ask him, Clodd; I will ask him straight out."

"And believe whatever he tells you."

"No, I shan't."

"Then what's the good of asking him?"

"Well, what am I to do?" demanded the bewildered Peter.

"Get rid of him," suggested Clodd.

"Get rid of him?"

"Get him away! Don't have him in and out of the office all day long-looking at her with those collie-dog eyes of his, arguing art and poetry with her in that cushat-dove voice of his. Get him clean away-- if it isn't too late already."

"Nonsense," said Peter, who had turned white, however. "She's not that sort of girl."

"Not that sort of girl!" Clodd had no patience with Peter Hope, and told him so. "Why are there never inkstains on her fingers now? There used to be. Why does she always keep a lemon in her drawer? When did she last have her hair cut? I'll tell you if you care to know-- the week before he came, five months ago. She used to have it cut once a fortnight: said it tickled her neck. Why does she jump on people when they call her Tommy and tell them that her name is Jane? It never used to be Jane. Maybe when you're a bit older you'll begin to notice things for yourself."

Clodd jammed his hat on his head and flung himself down the stairs.

Peter, slipping out a minute later, bought himself an ounce of snuff.

"Fiddle-de-dee!" said Peter as he helped himself to his thirteenth pinch. "Don't believe it. I'll sound her. I shan't say a word-- I'll just sound her."

Peter stood with his back to the fire. Tommy sat at her desk, correcting proofs of a fanciful story: The Man Without a Past.

"I shall miss him," said Peter; "I know I shall."

"Miss whom?" demanded Tommy.

"Danvers," sighed Peter. "It always happens so. You get friendly with a man; then he goes away--abroad, back to America, Lord knows where. You never see him again."

Tommy looked up. There was trouble in her face.

"How do you spell 'harassed'?" questioned Tommy! "two r's or one."

"One r," Peter informed her, "two s's."

"I thought so." The trouble passed from Tommy's face.

"You don't ask when he's going, you don't ask where he's going," complained Peter. "You don't seem to be interested in the least."

"I was going to ask, so soon as I had finished correcting this sheet," explained Tommy. "What reason does he give?"

Peter had crossed over and was standing where he could see her face illumined by the lamplight.

"It doesn't upset you--the thought of his going away, of your never seeing him again?"

"Why should it?" Tommy answered his searching gaze with a slightly puzzled look. "Of course, I'm sorry. He was becoming useful. But we couldn't expect him to stop with us always, could we?"

Peter, rubbing his hands, broke into a chuckle. "I told him 'twas all fiddlesticks. Clodd, he would have it you were growing to care for the fellow."

"For Dick Danvers?" Tommy laughed. "Whatever put that into his head?"

"Oh, well, there were one or two little things that we had noticed."

"We?"

"I mean that Clodd had noticed."

I'm glad it was Clodd that noticed them, not you, dad, thought Tommy to herself. They'd have been pretty obvious if you had noticed them.

"It naturally made me anxious," confessed Peter. "You see, we know absolutely nothing of the fellow."

"Absolutely nothing," agreed Tommy.

"He may be a man of the highest integrity. Personally, I think he is. I like him. On the other hand, he may be a thorough-paced scoundrel. I don't believe for a moment that he is, but he may be. Impossible to say."

"Quite impossible," agreed Tommy.

"Considered merely as a journalist, it doesn't matter. He writes well. He has brains. There's an end of it."

"He is very painstaking," agreed Tommy.

"Personally," added Peter, "I like the fellow." Tommy had returned to her work.

Of what use was Peter in a crisis of this kind? Peter couldn't scold. Peter couldn't bully. The only person to talk to Tommy as Tommy knew she needed to be talked to was one Jane, a young woman of dignity with sense of the proprieties.

"I do hope that at least you are feeling ashamed of yourself," remarked Jane to Tommy that same night, as the twain sat together in their little bedroom.

"Done nothing to be ashamed of," growled Tommy.

"Making a fool of yourself openly, for everybody to notice."

"Clodd ain't everybody. He's got eyes at the back of his head. Sees things before they happen."

"Where's your woman's pride: falling in love with a man who has never spoken to you, except in terms of the most ordinary courtesy."

"I'm not in love with him."

"A man about whom you know absolutely nothing."

"Not in love with him."

"Where does he come from? Who is he?"

"I don't know, don't care; nothing to do with me."

"Just because of his soft eyes, and his wheedling voice, and that half-caressing, half-devotional manner of his. Do you imagine he keeps it specially for you? I gave you credit for more sense."

"I'm not in love with him, I tell you. He's down on his luck, and I'm sorry for him, that's all."

"And if he is, whose fault was it, do you think?"

"It doesn't matter. We are none of us saints. He's trying to pull himself together, and I respect him for it. It's our duty to be charitable and kind to one another in this world!"

"Oh, well, I'll tell you how you can be kind to him: by pointing out to him that he is wasting his time. With his talents, now that he knows his business, he could be on the staff of some big paper, earning a good income. Put it nicely to him, but be firm. Insist on his going. That will be showing true kindness to him--and to yourself, too, I'm thinking, my dear."

And Tommy understood and appreciated the sound good sense underlying Jane's advice, and the very next day but one, seizing the first opportunity, acted upon it; and all would have gone as contemplated if only Dick Danvers had sat still and listened, as it had been arranged in Tommy's programme that he should.

"But I don't want to go," said Dick.

"But you ought to want to go. Staying here with us you are doing yourself no good."

He rose and came to where she stood with one foot upon the fender, looking down into the fire. His doing this disconcerted her. So long as he remained seated at the other end of the room, she was the sub-editor, counselling the staff for its own good. Now that she could not raise her eyes without encountering his, she felt painfully conscious of being nothing more important than a little woman who was trembling.

"It is doing me all the good in the world," he told her, "being near to you."

"Oh, please do sit down again," she urged him. "I can talk to you so much better when you're sitting down."

But he would not do anything he should have done that day. Instead he took her hands in his, and would not let them go; and the reason and the will went out of her, leaving her helpless.

"Let me be with you always," he pleaded. "It means the difference between light and darkness to me. You have done so much for me. Will you not finish your work? Will you not trust me? It is no hot passion that can pass away, my love for you. It springs from all that is best in me--from the part of me that is wholesome and joyous and strong, the part of me that belongs to you."

Releasing her, he turned away.

"The other part of me--the blackguard--it is dead, dear,--dead and buried. I did not know I was a blackguard, I thought myself a fine fellow, till one day it came home to me. Suddenly I saw myself as I really was. And the sight of the thing frightened me and I ran away from it. I said to myself I would begin life afresh, in a new country, free of every tie that could bind me to the past. It would mean poverty--privation, maybe, in the beginning. What of that? The struggle would brace me. It would be good sport. Ah, well, you can guess the result: the awakening to the cold facts, the reaction of feeling. In what way was I worse than other men? Who was I, to play the prig in a world where others were laughing and dining? I had tramped your city till my boots were worn into holes. I had but to abandon my quixotic ideals--return to where shame lay waiting for me, to be welcomed with the fatted calf. It would have ended so had I not chanced to pass by your door that afternoon and hear you strumming on the piano."

So Billy was right, after all, thought Tommy to herself, the piano does help.

"It was so incongruous--a piano in Crane Court--I looked to see where the noise came from. I read the name of the paper on the doorpost. 'It will be my last chance,' I said to myself. 'This shall decide it.'"

He came back to her. She had not moved. "I am not afraid to tell you all this. You are so big-hearted, so human; you will understand, you can forgive. It is all past. Loving you tells a man that he has done with evil. Will you not trust me?"

She put her hands in his. "I am trusting you," she said, "with all my life. Don't make a muddle of it, dear, if you can help it."

It was an odd wooing, as Tommy laughingly told herself when she came to think it over in her room that night. But that is how it shaped itself.

What troubled her most was that he had not been quite frank with Peter, so that Peter had to defend her against herself.

"I attacked you so suddenly," explained Peter, "you had not time to think. You acted from instinct. A woman seeks to hide her love even from herself."

"I expect, after all, I am more of a girl than a boy," feared Tommy: "I seem to have so many womanish failings."

Peter took himself into quite places and trained himself to face the fact that another would be more to her than he had ever been, and Clodd went about his work like a bear with a sore head; but they neither of them need have troubled themselves so much. The marriage did not take place till nearly fifteen years had passed away, and much water had to flow beneath old London Bridge before that day.

The past is not easily got rid of. A tale was once written of a woman who killed her babe and buried it in a lonely wood, and later stole back in the night and saw there, white in the moonlight, a child's hand calling through the earth, and buried it again and yet again; but always that white baby hand called upwards through the earth, trample it down as she would. Tommy read the story one evening in an old miscellany, and sat long before the dead fire, the book open on her lap, and shivered; for now she knew the fear that had been haunting her.

Tommy lived expecting her. She came one night when Tommy

was alone, working late in the office. Tommy knew her the moment she entered the door, a handsome woman, with snake-like, rustling skirts. She closed the door behind her, and drawing forward a chair, seated herself the other side of the desk, and the two looked long and anxiously at one another.

"They told me I should find you here alone," said the woman. "It is better, is it not?"

"Yes," said Tommy, "it is better."

"Tell me," said the woman, "are you very much in love with him?"

"Why should I tell you?"

"Because, if not--if you have merely accepted him thinking him a good catch--which he isn't, my dear; hasn't a penny to bless himself with, and never will if he marries you--why, then the matter is soon settled. They tell me you are a business-like young lady, and I am prepared to make a business-like proposition."

There was no answer. The woman shrugged her shoulders.

"If, on the other hand, you are that absurd creature, a young girl in love--why, then, I suppose we shall have to fight for him."

"It would be more sporting, would it not?" suggested Tommy.

"Let me explain before you decide," continued the woman. "Dick Danvers left me six months ago, and has kept from me ever since, because he loved me."

"It sounds a curious reason."

"I was a married woman when Dick Danvers and I first met. Since he left me--for my sake and his own--I have received information of my husband's death."

"And does Dick--does he know?" asked the girl.

"Not yet. I have only lately learnt the news myself."

"Then if it is as you say, when he knows he will go back to you."

"There are difficulties in the way."

"What difficulties?"

"My dear, this. To try and forget me, he has been making love to you. Men do these things. I merely ask you to convince yourself of the truth. Go away for six months--disappear entirely. Leave him free--uninfluenced. If he loves you--if it be not merely a sense of honour that binds him--you will find him here on your return. If not--if in the interval I have succeeded in running off with him, well, is not the two or three thousand pounds I am prepared to put into this paper of yours a fair price for such a lover?"

Tommy rose with a laugh of genuine amusement. She could never altogether put aside her sense of humour, let Fate come with what terrifying face it would.

"You may have him for nothing--if he is that man," the girl told her; "he shall be free to choose between us."

"You mean you will release him from his engagement?"

"That is what I mean."

"Why not take my offer? You know the money is needed. It will save your father years of anxiety and struggle. Go away--travel, for a couple of months, if you're afraid of the six. Write him that you must be alone, to think things over."

The girl turned upon her.

"And leave you a free field to lie and trick?"

The woman, too, had risen. "Do you think he really cares for you? At the moment you interest him. At nineteen every woman is a mystery. When the mood is past--and do you know how long a man's mood lasts, you poor chit? Till he has caught what he is running after, and has tasted it--then he will think not of what he has won, but of what he has lost: of the society from which he has cut himself adrift; of all the old pleasures and pursuits he can no longer enjoy; of the luxuries--necessities to a man of his stamp-- that marriage with you has deprived him of. Then your face will be a perpetual reminder to him of what he has paid for it, and he will curse it every time he sees it."

"You don't know him," the girl cried. "You know just a part of him--the part you would know. All the rest of him is a good man, that would rather his self-respect than all the luxuries you mention--you included."

"It seems to resolve itself into what manner of man he is," laughed the woman.

The girl looked at her watch. "He will be here shortly; he shall tell us himself."

"How do you mean?"

"That here, between the two of us, he shall decide--this very night." She showed her white face to the woman. "Do you think I could live through a second day like to this?"

"The scene would be ridiculous."

"There will be none here to enjoy the humour of it."

"He will not understand."

"Oh, yes, he will," the girl laughed. "Come, you have all the advantages; you are rich, you are clever; you belong to his class. If he elects to stop with me, it will be because he is my man-- mine. Are you afraid?"

The woman shivered. She wrapped her fur cloak about her closer and sat down again, and Tommy returned to her proofs. It was press-night, and there was much to be done.

He came a little later, though how long the time may have seemed to the two women one cannot say. They heard his footstep on the stair. The woman rose and went forward, so that when he opened the door she was the first he saw. But he made no sign. Possibly he had been schooling himself for this moment, knowing that sooner or later it must come. The woman held out her hand to him with a smile.

"I have not the honour," he said.

The smile died from her face. "I do not understand," she said.

"I have not the honour," he repeated. "I do not know you."

The girl was leaning with her back against the desk in a somewhat mannish attitude. He stood between them. It will always remain Life's chief comic success: the man between two women. The situation has amused the world for so many years. Yet, somehow, he contrived to maintain a certain dignity.

"Maybe," he continued, "you are confounding me with a Dick Danvers who lived in New York up to a few months ago. I knew him well--a worthless scamp you had done better never to have met."

"You bear a wonderful resemblance to him," laughed the woman.

"The poor fool is dead," he answered. "And he left for you, my dear lady, this dying message: that, from the bottom of his soul, he was sorry for the wrong he had done you. He asked you to forgive him--and forget him."

"The year appears to be opening unfortunately for me," said the woman. "First my lover, then my husband."

He had nerved himself to fight the living. This was a blow from the dead. The man had been his friend.

"Dead?"

"He was killed, it appears, in that last expedition in July," answered the woman. "I received the news from the Foreign Office only a fortnight ago."

An ugly look came into his eyes--the look of a cornered creature fighting for its life. "Why have you followed me here? Why do I find you here alone with her? What have you told her?"

The woman shrugged her shoulders. "Only the truth."

"All the truth?" he demanded--"all? Ah! be just. Tell her it was not all my fault. Tell her all the truth."

"What would you have me tell her? That I played Potiphar's wife to your Joseph?"

"Ah, no! The truth--only the truth. That you and I were a pair of idle fools with the devil dancing round us. That we played a fool's game, and that it is over."

"Is it over? Dick, is it over?" She flung her arms towards him; but he threw her from him almost brutally. "The man is dead, I tell you. His folly and his sin lie dead with him. I have nothing to do with you, nor you with me."

"Dick!" she whispered. "Dick, cannot you understand? I must speak with you alone."

But they did not understand, neither the man nor the child.

"Dick, are you really dead?" she cried. "Have you no pity for me? Do you think that I have followed you here to grovel at your feet for mere whim? Am I acting like a woman sane and sound? Don't you see that I am mad, and why I am mad? Must I tell you before her? Dick--" She staggered towards him, and the fine cloak slipped from her shoulders; and then it was that Tommy changed from a child into a woman, and raised the other woman from the ground with crooning words of encouragement such as mothers use, and led her to the inner room. "Do not go," she said, turning to Dick; "I shall be back in a few minutes."

He crossed to one of the windows against which beat the City's roar, and it seemed to him as the throb of passing footsteps beating down through the darkness to where he lay in his grave.

She re-entered, closing the door softly behind her. "It is true?" she asked.

"It can be. I had not thought of it."

They spoke in low, matter-of-fact tones, as people do who have grown weary of their own emotions.

"When did he go away--her husband?"

"About--it is February now, is it not? About eighteen months ago."

"And died just eight months ago. Rather conveniently, poor fellow."

"Yes, I'm glad he is dead--poor Lawrence."

"What is the shortest time in which a marriage can be arranged?"

"I do not know," he answered listlessly. "I do not intend to marry her."

"You would leave her to bear it alone?"

"It is not as if she were a poor woman. You can do anything with money."

"It will not mend reputation. Her position in society is everything to that class of woman."

"My marrying her now," he pointed out, "would not save her."

"Practically speaking it would," the girl pleaded. "The world does not go out of its way to find out things it does not want to know. Marry her as quietly as possible and travel for a year or two."

"Why should I? Ah! it is easy enough to call a man a coward for defending himself against a woman. What is he to do when he is fighting for his life? Men do not sin with good women."

"There is the child to be considered," she urged--"your child. You see, dear, we all do wrong sometimes. We must not let others suffer for our fault more--more than we can help."

He turned to her for the first time. "And you?"

"I? Oh, I shall cry for a little while, but later on I shall laugh, as often. Life is not all love. I have my work."

He knew her well by this time. And also it came to him that it would be a finer thing to be worthy of her than even to possess her.

So he did her bidding and went out with the other woman. Tommy was glad it was press-night. She would not be able to think for hours to come, and then, perhaps, she would be feeling too tired. Work can be very kind.

Were this an artistic story, here, of course, one would write "Finis." But in the workaday world one never knows the ending till it comes. Had it been otherwise, I doubt I could have found courage to tell you this story of Tommy. It is not all true--at least, I do not suppose so. One drifts unconsciously a little way into dream-land when one sits oneself down to recall the happenings of long ago; while Fancy, with a sly wink, whispers ever and again to Memory: "Let me tell this incident--picture that scene: I can make it so much more interesting than you would." But Tommy--how can I put it without saying too much: there is someone I think of when I speak of her? To remember only her dear wounds, and not the healing of them, would have been a task too painful. I love to dwell on their next meeting. Flipp, passing him on the steps, did not know him, the tall, sunburnt gentleman with the sweet, grave-faced little girl.

"Seen that face somewhere before," mused Flipp, as at the corner of Bedford Street he climbed into a hansom, "seen it somewhere on a thinner man."

For Dick Danvers, that he did not recognise Flipp, there was more excuse. A very old young man had Flipp become at thirty. Flipp no longer enjoyed popular journalism. He produced it.

The gold-bound doorkeeper feared the mighty Clodd would be unable to see so insignificant an atom as an unappointed stranger, but would let the card of Mr. Richard Danvers plead for itself. To the gold-bound keeper's surprise came down the message that Mr. Danvers was to be at once shown up.

"I thought, somehow, you would come to me first," said the portly Clodd, advancing with out-stretched hand. "And this is--?"

"My little girl, Honor. We have been travelling for the last few months."

Clodd took the grave, small face between his big, rough hands:

"Yes. She is like you. But looks as if she were going to have more sense. Forgive me, I knew your father my dear," laughed Clodd; "when he was younger."

They lit their cigars and talked.

"Well, not exactly dead; we amalgamated it," winked Clodd in answer to Danvers' inquiry. "It was just a trifle TOO high-class. Besides, the old gentleman was not getting younger. It hurt him a little at first. But then came Tommy's great success, and that has reconciled him to all things. Do they know you are in England?"

"No," explained Danvers; "we arrived only last night."

Clodd called directions down the speaking-tube.

"You will find hardly any change in her. One still has to keep one's eye upon her chin. She has not even lost her old habit of taking stock of people. You remember." Clodd laughed.

They talked a little longer, till there came a whistle, and Clodd put his ear to the tube.

"I have to see her on business," said Clodd, rising; "you may as well come with me. They are still in the old place, Gough Square."

Tommy was out, but Peter was expecting her every minute.

Peter did not know Dick, but would not admit it. Forgetfulness was a sign of age, and Peter still felt young.

"I know your face quite well," said Peter; "can't put a name to it, that's all."

Clodd whispered it to him, together with information bringing history up to date. And then light fell upon the old lined face. He came towards Dick, meaning to take him by both hands, but, perhaps because he had become somewhat feeble, he seemed glad when the younger man put his arms around him and held him for a moment. It was un-English, and both of them felt a little ashamed of themselves afterwards.

"What we want," said Clodd, addressing Peter, "we three--you, I, and Miss Danvers--is tea and cakes, with cream in them; and I know a shop where they sell them. We will call back for your father in half an hour." Clodd explained to Miss Danvers; "he has to talk over a matter of business with Miss Hope."

"I know," answered the grave-faced little person. She drew Dick's face down to hers and kissed it. And then the three went out together, leaving Dick standing by the window.

"Couldn't we hide somewhere till she comes?" suggested Miss Danvers. "I want to see her."

So they waited in the open doorway of a near printing-house till Tommy drove up. Both Peter and Clodd watched the child's face with some anxiety. She nodded gravely to herself three times, then slipped her hand into Peter's.

Tommy opened the door with her latchkey and passed in.

THE END

THE OBSERVATIONS OF HENRY

THE GHOST OF THE MARCHIONESS OF APPLEFORD

This is the story, among others, of Henry the waiter--or, as he now prefers to call himself, Henri--told to me in the long dining-room of the Riffel Alp Hotel, where I once stayed for a melancholy week "between seasons," sharing the echoing emptiness of the place with two maiden ladies, who talked all day to one another in frightened whispers. Henry's construction I have discarded for its amateurishness; his method being generally to commence a story at the end, and then, working backwards to the beginning, wind up with the middle. But in all other respects I have endeavoured to retain his method, which was individual; and this, I think, is the story as he would have told it to me himself, had he told it in this order:

My first place--well to be honest, it was a coffee shop in the Mile End Road--I'm not ashamed of it. We all have our beginnings. Young "Kipper," as we called him--he had no name of his own, not that he knew of anyhow, and that seemed to fit him down to the ground--had fixed his pitch just outside, between our door and the music hall at the corner; and sometimes, when I might happen to have a bit on, I'd get a paper from him, and pay him for it, when the governor was not about, with a mug of coffee, and odds and ends that the other customers had left on their plates--an arrangement that suited both of us. He was just about as sharp as they make boys, even in the Mile End Road, which is saying a good deal; and now and then, spying around among the right sort, and keeping his ears open, he would put me up to a good thing, and I would tip him a bob or a tanner as the case might be. He was the sort that gets on--you know.

One day in he walks, for all the world as if the show belonged to him, with a young imp of a girl on his arm, and down they sits at one of the tables.

"Garsong," he calls out, "what's the menoo to-day?"

"The menoo to-day," I says, "is that you get outside 'fore I clip you over the ear, and that you take that back and put it where you found it;" meaning o' course, the kid.

She was a pretty little thing, even then, in spite of the dirt, with those eyes like saucers, and red hair. It used to be called "carrots" in those days. Now all the swells have taken it up--or as near as they can get to it--and it's auburn.

"'Enery," he replied to me, without so much as turning a hair, "I'm afraid you're forgetting your position. When I'm on the kerb shouting 'Speshul!' and you comes to me with yer 'a'penny in yer 'and, you're master an' I'm man. When I comes into your shop to order refreshments, and to pay for 'em, I'm boss. Savey? You can bring me a rasher and two eggs, and see that they're this season's. The lidy will have a full-sized haddick and a cocoa."

Well, there was justice in what he said. He always did have sense, and I took his order. You don't often see anybody put it away like that girl did. I took it she hadn't had a square meal for many a long day. She polished off a ninepenny haddick, skin and all, and after that she had two penny rashers, with six slices of bread and butter--"doorsteps," as we used to call them--and two half pints of cocoa, which is a meal in itself the way we used to make it. "Kipper" must have had a bit of luck that day. He couldn't have urged her on more had it been a free feed.

"'Ave an egg," he suggested, the moment the rashers had disappeared. "One of these eggs will just about finish yer."

"I don't really think as I can," says she, after considering like.

"Well, you know your own strength," he answers. "Perhaps you're best without it. Speshully if yer not used to 'igh living."

I was glad to see them finish, 'cause I was beginning to get a bit nervous about the coin, but he paid up right enough, and giv me a ha'penny for myself.

That was the first time I ever waited upon those two, but it wasn't to be the last by many a long chalk, as you'll see. He often used to bring her in after that. Who she was and what she was he didn't know, and she didn't know, so there was a pair of them. She'd run away from an old woman down Limehouse way, who used to beat her. That was all she could tell him. He got her a lodging with an old woman, who had an attic in the same house where he slept--when it would run to that--taught her to yell "Speshul!" and found a corner for her. There ain't room for boys and girls in the Mile-End Road. They're either kids down there or they're grown-ups. "Kipper" and "Carrots"--as we named her--looked upon themselves as sweethearts, though he couldn't have been more than fifteen, and she barely twelve; and that he was regular gone on her anyone could see with half an eye. Not that he was soft about it--that wasn't his style. He kept her in order, and she had just to mind, which I guess was a good thing for her, and when she wanted it he'd use his hand on her, and make no bones about it. That's the way among that class. They up and give the old woman a friendly clump, just as you or me would swear at the missus, or fling a boot-jack at her. They don't mean anything more.

I left the coffee shop later on for a place in the city, and saw nothing more of them for five years. When I did it was at a restaurant in Oxford Street--one of those amatoor shows run by a lot of women, who know nothing about the business, and spend the whole day gossiping and flirting--"love-shops," I call 'em. There was a yellow-haired lady manageress who never heard you when you spoke to her, 'cause she was always trying to hear what some seedy old fool would be whispering to her across the counter. Then there were waitresses, and their notion of waiting was to spend an hour talking to a twopenny cup of coffee, and to look haughty and insulted whenever anybody as really wanted something ventured to ask for it. A frizzle-haired cashier used to make love all day out of her pigeon-hole with the two box-office boys from the Oxford Music Hall, who took it turn and turn about. Sometimes she'd leave off to take a customer's money, and sometimes she wouldn't. I've been to some rummy places in my time; and a waiter ain't the blind owl as he's supposed to be. But never in my life have I seen so much love-making, not all at once, as used to go on in that place. It was a dismal, gloomy sort of hole, and spoony couples seemed to scent it out by instinct, and would spend hours there over a pot of tea and assorted pastry. "Idyllic," some folks would have thought it: I used to get the fair dismals watching it. There was one girl--a weird-looking creature, with red eyes and long thin hands, that gave you the creeps to look at. She'd come in regular with her young man, a pale-faced nervous sort of chap, at three o'clock every afternoon. Theirs was the funniest love-making I ever saw. She'd pinch him under the table, and run pins into him, and he'd sit with his eyes glued on her as if she'd been a steaming dish of steak and onions and he a starving beggar the other side of the window. A strange story that was--as I came to learn it later on. I'll tell you that, one day.

I'd been engaged for the "heavy work," but as the heaviest order I ever heard given there was for a cold ham and chicken, which I had to slip out for to the nearest cook-shop, I must have been chiefly useful from an ornamental point of view.

I'd been there about a fortnight, and was feeling pretty sick of it, when in walked young "Kipper." I didn't know him at first, he'd changed so. He was swinging a silver-mounted crutch stick, which was the kind that was fashionable just then, and was dressed in a showy check suit and a white hat. But the thing that struck me most was his gloves. I suppose I hadn't improved quite so much myself, for he knew me in a moment, and held out his hand.

"What, 'Enery!" he says, "you've moved on, then!"

"Yes," I says, shaking hands with him, "and I could move on again from this shop without feeling sad. But you've got on a bit?" I says.

"So-so," he says, "I'm a journalist."

"Oh," I says, "what sort?" for I'd seen a good many of that lot during six months I'd spent at a house in Fleet Street, and their get-up hadn't sumptuousness about it, so to speak. "Kipper's" rig-out must have totted up to a tidy little sum. He had a diamond pin in his tie that must have cost somebody fifty quid, if not him.

"Well," he answers, "I don't wind out the confidential advice to old Beaky, and that sort of thing. I do the tips, yer know. 'Cap'n Kit,' that's my name."

"What, the Captain Kit?" I says. O' course I'd heard of him.

"Be'old!" he says.

"Oh, it's easy enough," he goes on. "Some of 'em's bound to come out right, and when one does, you take it from me, our paper mentions the fact. And when it is a wrong 'un--well, a man can't always be shouting about himself, can 'e?"

He ordered a cup of coffee. He said he was waiting for someone, and we got to chatting about old times.

"How's Carrots?" I asked.

"Miss Caroline Trevelyan," he answered, "is doing well."

"Oh," I says, "you've found out her fam'ly name, then?"

"We've found out one or two things about that lidy," he replies. "D'yer remember 'er dancing?"

"I have seen her flinging her petticoats about outside the shop, when the copper wasn't by, if that's what you mean," I says.

"That's what I mean," he answers. "That's all the rage now, 'skirt-dancing' they calls it. She's a-coming out at the Oxford to-morrow. It's 'er I'm waiting for. She's a-coming on, I tell you she is," he says.

"Shouldn't wonder," says I; "that was her disposition."

"And there's another thing we've found out about 'er," he says. He leant over the table, and whispered it, as if he was afraid that anybody else might hear: "she's got a voice."

"Yes," I says, "some women have."

"Ah," he says, "but 'er voice is the sort of voice yer want to listen to."

"Oh," I says, "that's its speciality, is it?"

"That's it, sonny," he replies.

She came in a little later. I'd a' known her anywhere for her eyes, and her red hair, in spite of her being that clean you might have eaten your dinner out of her hand. And as for her clothes! Well, I've mixed a good deal with the toffs in my time, and I've seen duchesses dressed more showily and maybe more expensively, but her clothes seemed to be just a framework to show her up. She was a beauty, you can take it from me; and it's not to be wondered that the La-De-Das were round her when they did see her, like flies round an open jam tart.

Before three months were up she was the rage of London--leastways of the music-hall part of it--with her portrait in all the shop windows, and interviews with her in half the newspapers. It seems she was the daughter of an officer who had died in India when she was a baby, and the niece of a bishop somewhere in Australia. He was dead too. There didn't seem to be any of her ancestry as wasn't dead, but they had all been swells. She had been educated privately, she had, by a relative; and had early displayed an aptitude for dancing, though her friends at first had much opposed her going upon the stage. There was a lot more of it--you know the sort of thing. Of course, she was a connection of one of our best known judges--they all are--and she merely acted in order to support a grandmother, or an invalid sister, I forget which. A wonderful talent for swallowing, these newspaper chaps has, some of 'em!

"Kipper" never touched a penny of her money, but if he had been her agent at twenty-five per cent. he couldn't have worked harder, and he just kept up the hum about her, till if you didn't want to hear anything more about Caroline Trevelyan, your only chance would have been to lie in bed, and never look at a newspaper. It was Caroline Trevelyan at Home, Caroline Trevelyan at Brighton, Caroline Trevelyan and the Shah of Persia, Caroline Trevelyan and the Old Apple-woman. When it wasn't Caroline Trevelyan herself it would be Caroline Trevelyan's dog as would be doing something out of the common, getting himself lost or summoned or drowned--it didn't matter much what.

I moved from Oxford Street to the new "Horseshoe" that year--it had just been rebuilt--and there I saw a good deal of them, for they came in to lunch there or supper pretty regular. Young "Kipper"--or the "Captain" as everybody called him--gave out that he was her half-brother.

"I'ad to be some sort of a relation, you see," he explained to me. "I'd a' been 'er brother out and out; that would have been simpler, only the family likeness wasn't strong enough. Our styles o' beauty ain't similar." They certainly wasn't.

"Why don't you marry her?" I says, "and have done with it?"

He looked thoughtful at that. "I did think of it," he says, "and I know, jolly well, that if I 'ad suggested it 'fore she'd found herself, she'd have agreed, but it don't seem quite fair now."

"How d'ye mean fair?" I says.

"Well, not fair to 'er," he says. "I've got on all right, in a small way; but she--well, she can just 'ave 'er pick of the nobs. There's one on 'em as I've made inquiries about. 'E'll be a dook, if a kid pegs out as is expected to, and anyhow 'e'll be a markis, and 'e means the straight thing--no errer. It ain't fair for me to stand in 'er way."

"Well," I says, "you know your own business, but it seems to me she wouldn't have much way to stand in if it hadn't been for you."

"Oh, that's all right," he says. "I'm fond enough of the gell, but I shan't clamour for a tombstone with wiolets, even if she ain't ever Mrs. Capt'n Kit. Business is business; and I ain't going to queer 'er pitch for 'er."

I've often wondered what she'd a' said, if he'd up and put the case to her plain, for she was a good sort; but, naturally enough, her head was a bit swelled, and she'd read so much rot about herself in the papers that she'd got at last to half believe some of it. The thought of her connection with the well-known judge seemed to hamper her at times, and she wasn't quite so chummy with "Kipper" as used to be the case in the Mile-End Road days, and he wasn't the sort as is slow to see a thing.

One day when he was having lunch by himself, and I was waiting on him, he says, raising his glass to his lips, "Well, 'Enery, here's luck to yer! I won't be seeing you agen for some time."

"Oh," I says. "What's up now?"

"I am," he says, "or rather my time is. I'm off to Africa."

"Oh," I says, "and what about--"

"That's all right," he interrupts. "I've fixed up that--a treat. Truth, that's why I'm going."

I thought at first he meant she was going with him.

"No," he says, "she's going to be the Duchess of Ridingshire with the kind consent o' the kid I spoke about. If not, she'll be the Marchioness of Appleford. 'E's doing the square thing. There's going to be a quiet marriage to-morrow at the Registry Office, and then I'm off."

"What need for you to go?" I says.

"No need," he says; "it's a fancy o' mine. You see, me gone, there's nothing to 'amper 'er--nothing to interfere with 'er settling down as a quiet, respectable toff. With a 'alf-brother, who's always got to be spry with some fake about 'is lineage and 'is ancestral estates, and who drops 'is 'h's,' complications are sooner or later bound to a-rise. Me out of it--everything's simple. Savey?"

Well, that's just how it happened. Of course, there was a big row when the family heard of it, and a smart lawyer was put up to try and undo the thing. No expense was spared, you bet; but it was all no go. Nothing could be found out against her. She just sat tight and said nothing. So the thing had to stand. They went and lived quietly in the country and abroad for a year or two, and then folks forgot a bit, and they came back to London. I often used to see her name in print, and then the papers always said as how she was charming and graceful and beautiful, so I suppose the family had made up its mind to get used to her.

One evening in she comes to the Savoy. My wife put me up to getting that job, and a good job it is, mind you, when you know your way about. I'd never have had the cheek to try for it, if it hadn't been for the missis. She's a clever one--she is. I did a good day's work when I married her.

"You shave off that moustache of yours--it ain't an ornament," she says to me, "and chance it. Don't get attempting the lingo. Keep to the broken English, and put in a shrug or two. You can manage that all right."

I followed her tip. Of course the manager saw through me, but I got in a "Oui, monsieur" now and again, and they, being short handed at the time, could not afford to be strict, I suppose. Anyhow I got took on, and there I stopped for the whole season, and that was the making of me.

Well, as I was saying, in she comes to the supper rooms, and toffy enough she looked in her diamonds and furs, and as for haughtiness there wasn't a born Marchioness she couldn't have given points to. She comes straight up to my table and sits down. Her husband was with her, but he didn't seem to have much to say, except to repeat her orders. Of course I looked as if I'd never set eyes on her before in all my life, though all the time she was a-pecking at the mayonnaise and a-sipping at the Giessler, I was thinking of the coffee-shop and of the ninepenny haddick and the pint of cocoa.

"Go and fetch my cloak," she says to him after a while. "I am cold."

And up he gets and goes out.

She never moved her head, and spoke as though she was merely giving me some order, and I stands behind her chair, respectful like, and answers according to the same tip,

"Ever hear from 'Kipper'?" she says to me.

"I have had one or two letters from him, your ladyship," I answers.

"Oh, stow that," she says. "I am sick of 'your ladyship.' Talk English; I don't hear much of it. How's he getting on?"

"Seems to be doing himself well," I says. "He's started an hotel, and is regular raking it in, he tells me."

"Wish I was behind the bar with him!" says she.

"Why, don't it work then?" I asks.

"It's just like a funeral with the corpse left out," says she. "Serves me jolly well right for being a fool!"

The Marquis, he comes back with her cloak at that moment, and I says: "Certainement, madame," and gets clear.

I often used to see her there, and when a chance occurred she would talk to me. It seemed to be a relief to her to use her own tongue, but it made me nervous at times for fear someone would hear her.

Then one day I got a letter from "Kipper" to say he was over for a holiday and was stopping at Morley's, and asking me to look him up.

He had not changed much except to get a bit fatter and more prosperous- looking. Of course, we talked about her ladyship, and I told him what she said.

"Rum things, women," he says; "never know their own minds."

"Oh, they know them all right when they get there," I says. "How could she tell what being a Marchioness was like till she'd tried it?"

"Pity," he says, musing like. "I reckoned it the very thing she'd tumble to. I only come over to get a sight of 'er, and to satisfy myself as she was getting along all right. Seems I'd better a' stopped away."

"You ain't ever thought of marrying yourself?" I asks.

"Yes, I have," he says. "It's slow for a man over thirty with no wife and kids to bustle him, you take it from me, and I ain't the talent for the Don Juan fake."

"You're like me," I says, "a day's work, and then a pipe by your own fireside with your slippers on. That's my swarry. You'll find someone as will suit you before long."

"No I shan't," says he. "I've come across a few as might, if it 'adn't been for 'er. It's like the toffs as come out our way. They've been brought up on 'ris de veau a la financier,' and sich like, and it just spoils 'em for the bacon and greens."

I give her the office the next time I see her, and they met accidental like in Kensington Gardens early one morning. What they said to one another I don't know, for he sailed that same evening, and, it being the end of the season, I didn't see her ladyship again for a long while.

When I did it was at the Hotel Bristol in Paris, and she was in widow's weeds, the Marquis having died eight months before. He never dropped into that dukedom, the kid turning out healthier than was expected, and hanging on; so she was still only a Marchioness, and her fortune, though tidy, was nothing very big--not as that class reckons. By luck I was told off to wait on her, she having asked for someone as could speak English. She seemed glad to see me and to talk to me.

"Well," I says, "I suppose you'll be bossing that bar in Capetown now before long?"

"Talk sense," she answers. "How can the Marchioness of Appleford marry a hotel keeper?"

"Why not," I says, "if she fancies him? What's the good of being a Marchioness if you can't do what you like?"

"That's just it," she snaps out; "you can't. It would not be doing the straight thing by the family. No," she says, "I've spent their money, and I'm spending it now. They don't love me, but they shan't say as I have disgraced them. They've got their feelings same as I've got mine."

"Why not chuck the money?" I says. "They'll be glad enough to get it back," they being a poor lot, as I heard her say.

"How can I?" she says. "It's a life interest. As long as I live I've got to have it, and as long as I live I've got to remain the Marchioness of Appleford."

She finishes her soup, and pushes the plate away from her. "As long as I live," she says, talking to herself.

"By Jove!" she says, starting up "why not?"

"Why not what?" I says.

"Nothing," she answers. "Get me an African telegraph form, and be quick about it!"

I fetched it for her, and she wrote it and gave it to the porter then and there; and, that done, she sat down and finished her dinner.

She was a bit short with me after that; so I judged it best to keep my own place.

In the morning she got an answer that seemed to excite her, and that afternoon she left; and the next I heard of her was a paragraph in the newspaper, headed--"Death of the Marchioness of Appleford. Sad accident." It seemed she had gone for a row on one of the Italian lakes with no one but a boatman. A squall had come on, and the boat had capsized. The boatman had swum ashore, but he had been unable to save his passenger, and her body had never been recovered. The paper reminded its readers that she had formerly been the celebrated tragic actress, Caroline Trevelyan, daughter of the well-known Indian judge of that name.

It gave me the blues for a day or two--that bit of news. I had known her from a baby as you might say, and had taken an interest in her. You can call it silly, but hotels and restaurants seemed to me less interesting now there was no chance of ever seeing her come into one again.

I went from Paris to one of the smaller hotels in Venice. The missis thought I'd do well to pick up a bit of Italian, and perhaps she fancied Venice for herself. That's one of the advantages of our profession. You can go about. It was a second-rate sort of place, and one evening, just before lighting-up time, I had the salle-a-manger all to myself, and had just taken up a paper when I hears the door open, and I turns round.

I saw "her" coming down the room. There was no mistaking her. She wasn't that sort.

I sat with my eyes coming out of my head till she was close to me, and then I says:

"Carrots!" I says, in a whisper like. That was the name that come to me.

"'Carrots' it is," she says, and down she sits just opposite to me, and then she laughs.

I could not speak, I could not move, I was that took aback, and the more frightened I looked the more she laughed till "Kipper" comes into the room. There was nothing ghostly about him. I never see a man look more as if he had backed the winner.

"Why, it's 'Enery," he says; and he gives me a slap on the back, as knocks the life into me again.

"I heard you was dead," I says, still staring at her. "I read it in the paper--'death of the Marchioness of Appleford.'"

"That's all right," she says. "The Marchioness of Appleford is as dead as a door-nail, and a good job too. Mrs. Captain Kit's my name, nee 'Carrots.'"

"You said as 'ow I'd find someone to suit me 'fore long," says "Kipper" to me, "and, by Jove! you were right; I 'ave. I was waiting till I found something equal to her ladyship, and I'd 'ave 'ad to wait a long time, I'm thinking, if I 'adn't come across this one 'ere"; and he tucks her up under his arm just as I remember his doing that day he first brought her into the coffee-shop, and Lord, what a long time ago that was!

∼

That is the story, among others, told me by Henry, the waiter. I have, at his request, substituted artificial names for real ones. For Henry tells me that at Capetown Captain Kit's First-class Family and Commercial Hotel still runs, and that the landlady is still a beautiful woman with fine eyes and red hair, who might almost be taken for a duchess--until she opens her mouth, when her accent is found to be still slightly reminiscent of the Mile-End Road.

THE USES AND ABUSES OF JOSEPH

"It is just the same with what you may call the human joints," observed Henry. He was in one of his philosophic moods that evening. "It all depends upon the cooking. I never see a youngster hanging up in the refrigerator, as one may put it, but I says to myself: 'Now I wonder what the cook is going to make of you! Will you be minced and devilled and fricasseed till you are all sauce and no meat? Will you be hammered tender and grilled over a slow fire till you are a blessing to mankind? Or will you be spoilt in the boiling, and come out a stringy rag, an immediate curse, and a permanent injury to those who have got to swallow you?'

"There was a youngster I knew in my old coffee-shop days," continued Henry, "that in the end came to be eaten by cannibals. At least, so the newspapers said. Speaking for myself, I never believed the report: he wasn't that sort. If anybody was eaten, it was more likely the cannibal. But that is neither here nor there. What I am thinking of is what happened before he and the cannibals ever got nigh to one another. He was fourteen when I first set eyes on him-- Mile End fourteen, that is; which is the same, I take it, as City eighteen and West End five-and-twenty--and he was smart for his age into the bargain: a trifle too smart as a matter of fact. He always came into the shop at the same time--half-past two; he always sat in the seat next the window; and three days out of six, he would order the same dinner: a fourpenny beef-steak pudding--we called it beef-steak, and, for all practical purposes, it was beef-steak--a penny plate of potatoes, and a penny slice of roly-poly pudding--'chest expander' was the name our customers gave it--to follow. That showed sense, I always thought, that dinner alone; a more satisfying menu, at the price, I defy any human being to work out. He always had a book with him, and he generally read during his meal; which is not a bad plan if you don't want to think too much about what you are eating. There was a seedy chap, I remember, used to dine at a cheap restaurant where I once served, just off the Euston Road. He would stick a book up in front of him--Eppy something or other--and read the whole time. Our four-course shilling table d'hote with Eppy, he would say, was a banquet fit for a prince; without Eppy he was of opinion that a policeman wouldn't touch it. But he was one of those men that report things for the newspapers, and was given to exaggeration.

"A coffee-shop becomes a bit of a desert towards three o'clock; and, after a while, young Tidelman, for that was his name, got to putting down his book and chatting to me. His father was dead; which, judging from what he told me about the old man, must have been a bit of luck for everybody; and his mother, it turned out, had come from my own village in Suffolk; and that constituted a sort of bond between us, seeing I had known all her people pretty intimately. He was earning good money at a dairy, where his work was scouring milk-cans; and his Christian name--which was the only thing Christian about him, and that, somehow or another, didn't seem to fit him--was Joseph.

"One afternoon he came into the shop looking as if he had lost a shilling and found sixpence, as the saying is; and instead of drinking water as usual, sent the girl out for a pint of ale. The moment it came he drank off half of it at a gulp, and then sat staring out of the window.

"'What's up?' I says. 'Got the shove?'

"'Yes,' he answers; 'but, as it happens, it's a shove up. I've been taken off the yard and put on the walk, with a rise of two bob a week.' Then he took another pull at the beer and looked more savage than ever.

"'Well,' I says, 'that ain't the sort of thing to be humpy about.'

"'Yes it is,' he snaps back; 'it means that if I don't take precious good care I'll drift into being a blooming milkman, spending my life yelling "Milk ahoi!" and spooning smutty-faced servant-gals across area railings.'

"'Oh!' I says, 'and what may you prefer to spoon--duchesses?'

"'Yes,' he answers sulky-like; 'duchesses are right enough--some of 'em.'

"'So are servant-gals,' I says, 'some of 'em. Your hat's feeling a bit small for you this morning, ain't it?'

"'Hat's all right,' says he; 'it's the world as I'm complaining of-- beastly place; there's nothing to do in it.'

"'Oh!' I says; 'some of us find there's a bit too much.' I'd been up since five that morning myself; and his own work, which was scouring milk- cans for twelve hours a day, didn't strike me as suggesting a life of leisured ease.

"'I don't mean that,' he says. 'I mean things worth doing.'

"'Well, what do you want to do,' I says, 'that this world ain't big enough for?'

"'It ain't the size of it,' he says; 'it's the dulness of it. Things used to be different in the old days.'

"'How do you know?' I says.

"'You can read about it,' he answers.

"'Oh,' I says, 'and what do they know about it--these gents that sit down and write about it for their living! You show me a book cracking up the old times, writ by a chap as lived in 'em, and I'll believe you. Till then I'll stick to my opinion that the old days were much the same as these days, and maybe a trifle worse.'

"'From a Sunday School point of view, perhaps yes,' says he; 'but there's no gainsaying--'

"'No what?' I says.

"'No gainsaying,' repeats he; 'it's a common word in literatoor.'

"'Maybe,' says I, 'but this happens to be "The Blue Posts Coffee House," established in the year 1863. We will use modern English here, if you don't mind.' One had to take him down like that at times. He was the sort of boy as would talk poetry to you if you weren't firm with him.

"'Well then, there's no denying the fact,' says he, 'if you prefer it that way, that in the old days there was more opportunity for adventure.'

"'What about Australia?' says I.

"'Australia!' retorts he; 'what would I do there? Be a shepherd, like you see in the picture, wear ribbons, and play the flute?'

"'There's not much of that sort of shepherding over there,' says I, 'unless I've been deceived; but if Australia ain't sufficiently uncivilised for you, what about Africa?'

"'What's the good of Africa?' replies he; 'you don't read advertisements in the "Clerkenwell News": "Young men wanted as explorers." I'd drift into a barber's shop at Cape Town more likely than anything else.'

"'What about the gold diggings?' I suggests. I like to see a youngster with the spirit of adventure in him. It shows grit as a rule.

"'Played out,' says he. 'You are employed by a company, wages ten dollars a week, and a pension for your old age. Everything's played out,' he continues. 'Men ain't wanted nowadays. There's only room for clerks, and intelligent artisans, and shopboys.'

"'Go for a soldier,' says I; 'there's excitement for you.'

"'That would have been all right,' says he, 'in the days when there was real fighting.'

"'There's a good bit of it going about nowadays,' I says. 'We are generally at it, on and off, between shouting about the blessings of peace.'

"'Not the sort of fighting I mean,' replies he; 'I want to do something myself, not be one of a row.'

"'Well,' I says, 'I give you up. You've dropped into the wrong world it seems to me. We don't seem able to cater for you here.'

"'I've come a bit too late,' he answers; 'that's the mistake I've made.

Two hundred years ago there were lots of things a fellow might have done.'

"'Yes, I know what's in your mind,' I says: 'pirates.'

"'Yes, pirates would be all right,' says he; 'they got plenty of sea-air and exercise, and didn't need to join a blooming funeral club.'

"'You've got ideas above your station,' I says. 'You work hard, and one day you'll have a milk-shop of your own, and be walking out with a pretty housemaid on your arm, feeling as if you were the Prince of Wales himself.'

"'Stow it!' he says; 'it makes me shiver for fear it might come true. I'm not cut out for a respectable cove, and I won't be one neither, if I can help it!'

"'What do you mean to be, then?' I says; 'we've all got to be something, until we're stiff 'uns.'

"'Well,' he says, quite cool-like, 'I think I shall be a burglar.'

"I dropped into the seat opposite and stared at him. If any other lad had said it I should have known it was only foolishness, but he was just the sort to mean it.

"'It's the only calling I can think of,' says he, 'that has got any element of excitement left in it.'

"'You call seven years at Portland "excitement," do you?' says I, thinking of the argument most likely to tell upon him.

"'What's the difference,' answers he, 'between Portland and the ordinary labouring man's life, except that at Portland you never need fear being out of work?' He was a rare one to argue. 'Besides,' says he, 'it's only the fools as gets copped. Look at that diamond robbery in Bond Street, two years ago. Fifty thousand pounds' worth of jewels stolen, and never a clue to this day! Look at the Dublin Bank robbery,' says he, his eyes all alight, and his face flushed like a girl's. 'Three thousand pounds in golden sovereigns walked away with in broad daylight, and never so much as the flick of a coat-tail seen. Those are the sort of men I'm thinking of, not the bricklayer out of work, who smashes a window and gets ten years for breaking open a cheesemonger's till with nine and fourpence ha'penny in it.'

"'Yes,' says I, 'and are you forgetting the chap who was nabbed at

Birmingham only last week? He wasn't exactly an amatoor. How long do think he'll get?'

"'A man like that deserves what he gets,' answers he; 'couldn't hit a police-man at six yards.'

"'You bloodthirsty young scoundrel,' I says; 'do you mean you wouldn't stick at murder?'

"'It's all in the game,' says he, not in the least put out. 'I take my risks, he takes his. It's no more murder than soldiering is.'

"'It's taking a human creature's life,' I says.

"'Well,' he says, 'what of it? There's plenty more where he comes from.'

"I tried reasoning with him from time to time, but he wasn't a sort of boy to be moved from a purpose. His mother was the only argument that had any weight with him. I believe so long as she had lived he would have kept straight; that was the only soft spot in him. But unfortunately she died a couple of years later, and then I lost sight of Joe altogether. I made enquiries, but no one could tell me anything. He had just disappeared, that's all.

"One afternoon, four years later, I was sitting in the coffee-room of a City restaurant where I was working, reading the account of a clever robbery committed the day before. The thief, described as a well-dressed young man of gentlemanly appearance, wearing a short black beard and moustache, had walked into a branch of the London and Westminster Bank during the dinner-hour, when only the manager and one clerk were there. He had gone straight through to the manager's room at the back of the bank, taken the key from the inside of the door, and before the man could get round his desk had locked him in. The clerk, with a knife to his throat, had then been persuaded to empty all the loose cash in the bank, amounting in gold and notes to nearly five hundred pounds, into a bag which the thief had thoughtfully brought with him. After which, both of them--for the thief seems to have been of a sociable disposition--got into a cab which was waiting outside, and drove away. They drove straight to the City: the clerk, with a knife pricking the back of his neck all the time, finding it, no doubt, a tiresome ride. In the middle of Threadneedle

Street, the gentlemanly young man suddenly stopped the cab and got out, leaving the clerk to pay the cabman.

"Somehow or other, the story brought back Joseph to my mind. I seemed to see him as that well-dressed gentlemanly young man; and, raising my eyes from the paper, there he stood before me. He had scarcely changed at all since I last saw him, except that he had grown better looking, and seemed more cheerful. He nodded to me as though we had parted the day before, and ordered a chop and a small hock. I spread a fresh serviette for him, and asked him if he cared to see the paper.

"'Anything interesting in it, Henry?' says he.

"'Rather a daring robbery committed on the Westminster Bank yesterday,' I answers.

"'Oh, ah! I did see something about that,' says he.

"'The thief was described as a well-dressed young man of gentlemanly appearance, wearing a black beard and moustache,' says I.

"He laughs pleasantly.

"'That will make it awkward for nice young men with black beards and moustaches,' says he.

"'Yes,' I says. 'Fortunately for you and me, we're clean shaved.'

"I felt as certain he was the man as though I'd seen him do it.

"He gives me a sharp glance, but I was busy with the cruets, and he had to make what he chose out of it.

"'Yes,' he replies, 'as you say, it was a daring robbery. But the man seems to have got away all right.'

"I could see he was dying to talk to somebody about it.

"'He's all right to-day,' says I; 'but the police ain't the fools they're reckoned. I've noticed they generally get there in the end.'

"'There's some very intelligent men among them,' says he: 'no question of it. I shouldn't be surprised if they had a clue!'

"'No,' I says, 'no more should I; though no doubt he's telling himself there never was such a clever thief.'

"'Well, we shall see,' says he.

"'That's about it,' says I.

"We talked a bit about old acquaintances and other things, and then, having finished, he handed me a sovereign and rose to go.

"'Wait a minute,' I says, 'your bill comes to three-and-eight. Say fourpence for the waiter; that leaves sixteen shillings change, which I'll ask you to put in your pocket.'

"'As you will,' he says, laughing, though I could see he didn't like it.

"'And one other thing,' says I. 'We've been sort of pals, and it's not my business to talk unless I'm spoken to. But I'm a married man,' I says, 'and I don't consider you the sort worth getting into trouble for. If I never see you, I know nothing about you. Understand?'

"He took my tip, and I didn't see him again at that restaurant. I kept my eye on the paper, but the Westminster Bank thief was never discovered, and success, no doubt, gave him confidence. Anyhow, I read of two or three burglaries that winter which I unhesitatingly put down to Mr. Joseph--I suppose there's style in housebreaking, as in other things--and early the next spring an exciting bit of business occurred, which I knew to be his work by the description of the man.

"He had broken into a big country house during the servants' supper-hour, and had stuffed his pockets with jewels. One of the guests, a young officer, coming upstairs, interrupted him just as he had finished. Joseph threatened the man with his revolver; but this time it was not a nervous young clerk he had to deal with. The man sprang at him, and a desperate struggle followed, with the result that in the end the officer was left with a bullet in his leg, while Joseph jumped clean through the window, and fell thirty feet. Cut and bleeding, if not broken, he would never have got away but that, fortunately for him, a tradesman's cart happened to be standing at the servants' entrance. Joe was in it, and off like a flash of greased lightning. How he managed to escape, with all the country in an uproar, I can't tell you; but he did it. The horse and cart, when found sixteen miles off, were neither worth much.

"That, it seems, sobered him down for a bit, and nobody heard any more of him till nine months later, when he walked into the Monico, where I was then working, and held out his hand to me as bold as brass.

"'It's all right,' says he, 'it's the hand of an honest man.'

"'It's come into your possession very recently then,' says I.

"He was dressed in a black frock-coat and wore whiskers. If I hadn't known him, I should have put him down for a parson out of work.

"He laughs. 'I'll tell you all about it,' he says.

"'Not here,' I answers, 'because I'm too busy; but if you like to meet me this evening, and you're talking straight--'

"'Straight as a bullet,' says he. 'Come and have a bit of dinner with me at the Craven; it's quiet there, and we can talk. I've been looking for you for the last week.'

"Well, I met him; and he told me. It was the old story: a gal was at the bottom of it. He had broken into a small house at Hampstead. He was on the floor, packing up the silver, when the door opens, and he sees a gal standing there. She held a candle in one hand and a revolver in the other.

"'Put your hands up above your head,' says she.

"'I looked at the revolver,' said Joe, telling me; 'it was about eighteen inches off my nose; and then I looked at the gal. There's lots of 'em will threaten to blow your brains out for you, but you've only got to look at 'em to know they won't.

"'They are thinking of the coroner's inquest, and wondering how the judge will sum up. She met my eyes, and I held up my hands. If I hadn't I wouldn't have been here.

"'Now you go in front,' says she to Joe, and he went. She laid her candle down in the hall and unbolted the front door.

"'What are you going to do?' says Joe, 'call the police? Because if so, my dear, I'll take my chance of that revolver being loaded and of your pulling the trigger in time. It will be a more dignified ending.'

"'No,' says she, 'I had a brother that got seven years for forgery. I don't want to think of another face like his when he came out. I'm going to see you outside my master's house, and that's all I care about.'

"She went down the garden-path with him, and opened the gate.

"'You turn round,' says she, 'before you reach the bottom of the lane and I give the alarm.' And Joe went straight, and didn't look behind him.

"Well, it was a rum beginning to a courtship, but the end was rummer. The girl was willing to marry him if he would turn honest. Joe wanted to turn honest, but didn't know how.

"'It's no use fixing me down, my dear, to any quiet, respectable calling,' says Joe to the gal, 'because, even if the police would let me alone, I wouldn't be able to stop there. I'd break out, sooner or later, try as I might.'

"The girl went to her master, who seems to have been an odd sort of a cove, and told him the whole story. The old gent said he'd see Joe, and Joe called on him.

"'What's your religion?' says the old gent to Joe.

"'I'm not particular, sir; I'll leave it to you,' says Joe.

"'Good!' says the old gent. 'You're no fanatic. What are your principles?'

"At first Joe didn't think he'd got any, but, the old gent leading, he found to his surprise as he had.

"'I believe,' says Joe, 'in doing a job thoroughly.'

"'What your hand finds to do, you believe in doing with all your might, eh?' says the old gent.

"'That's it, sir,' says Joe. 'That's what I've always tried to do.'

"'Anything else?' asks the old gent.

"'Yes; stick to your pals,' said Joe.

"'Through thick and thin,' suggests the old gent.

"'To the blooming end,' agrees Joe.

"'That's right,' says the old gent. 'Faithful unto death. And you really want to turn over a new leaf--to put your wits and your energy and your courage to good use instead of bad?'

"'That's the idea,' says Joe.

"The old gent murmurs something to himself about a stone which the builders wouldn't have at any price; and then he turns and puts it straight:

"'If you undertake the work,' says he, 'you'll go through with it without faltering--you'll devote your life to it?'

"'If I undertake the job, I'll do that,' says Joe. 'What may it be?'

"'To go to Africa,' says the old gent, 'as a missionary.'

"Joe sits down and stares at the old gent, and the old gent looks him back.

"'It's a dangerous station,' says the old gent. 'Two of our people have lost their lives there. It wants a man there--a man who will do something besides preach, who will save these poor people we have gathered together there from being scattered and lost, who will be their champion, their protector, their friend.'

"In the end, Joe took on the job, and went out with his wife. A better missionary that Society never had and never wanted. I read one of his early reports home; and if the others were anything like it his life must have been exciting enough, even for him. His station was a small island of civilisation, as one may say, in the middle of a sea of savages. Before he had been there a month the place had been attacked twice. On the first occasion Joe's 'flock' had crowded into the Mission House, and commenced to pray, that having been the plan of defence adopted by his predecessor. Joe cut the prayer short, and preached to them from the text, 'Heaven helps them as helps themselves'; after which he proceeded to deal out axes and old rifles. In his report he mentioned that he had taken a hand himself, merely as an example to the flock; I bet he had never enjoyed an evening more in all his life. The second fight began, as usual, round the Mission, but seems to have ended two miles off. In less than six months he had rebuilt the school-house, organised a police force, converted all that was left of one tribe, and started a tin church. He added (but I don't think they read that part of his report aloud) that law and order was going to be respected, and life and property secure in his district so long as he had a bullet left.

"Later on the Society sent him still further inland, to open up a fresh station; and there it was that, according to the newspapers, the cannibals got hold of him and ate him. As I said, personally I don't believe it. One of these days he'll turn up, sound and whole; he is that sort."

THE SURPRISE OF MR. MILBERRY

"It's not the sort of thing to tell 'em," remarked Henry, as, with his napkin over his arm, he leant against one of the pillars of the verandah, and sipped the glass of Burgundy I had poured out for him; "and they wouldn't believe it if you did tell 'em, not one of 'em. But it's the truth, for all that. Without the clothes they couldn't do it."

"Who wouldn't believe what?" I asked. He had a curious habit, had Henry, of commenting aloud upon his own unspoken thoughts, thereby bestowing upon his conversation much of the quality of the double acrostic. We had been discussing the question whether sardines served their purpose better as a hors d'oeuvre or as a savoury; and I found myself wondering for the moment why sardines, above all other fish, should be of an unbelieving nature; while endeavouring to picture to myself the costume best adapted to display the somewhat difficult figure of a sardine. Henry put down his glass, and came to my rescue with the necessary explanation.

"Why, women--that they can tell one baby from another, without its clothes. I've got a sister, a monthly nurse, and she will tell you for a fact, if you care to ask her, that up to three months of age there isn't really any difference between 'em. You can tell a girl from a boy and a Christian child from a black heathen, perhaps; but to fancy you can put your finger on an unclothed infant and say: 'That's a Smith, or that's a Jones,' as the case may be--why, it's sheer nonsense. Take the things off 'em, and shake them up in a blanket, and I'll bet you what you like that which is which you'd never be able to tell again so long as you lived."

I agreed with Henry, so far as my own personal powers of discrimination might be concerned, but I suggested that to Mrs. Jones or Mrs. Smith there would surely occur some means of identification.

"So they'd tell you themselves, no doubt," replied Henry; "and of course, I am not thinking of cases where the child might have a mole or a squint, as might come in useful. But take 'em in general, kids are as much alike as sardines of the same age would be. Anyhow, I knew a case where a fool of a young nurse mixed up two children at an hotel, and to this day neither of those women is sure that she's got her own."

"Do you mean," I said, "there was no possible means of distinguishing?"

"There wasn't a flea-bite to go by," answered Henry. "They had the same bumps, the same pimples, the same scratches; they were the same age to within three days; they weighed the same to an ounce; and they measured the same to an inch. One father was tall and fair, and the other was short and dark. The tall, fair man had a dark, short wife; and the short, dark man had married a tall, fair woman. For a week they changed those kids to and fro a dozen times a day, and cried and quarrelled over them. Each woman felt sure she was the mother of the one that was crowing at the moment, and when it yelled she was positive it was no child of hers. They thought they would trust to the instinct of the children. Neither child, so long as it wasn't hungry, appeared to care a curse for anybody; and when it was hungry it always wanted the mother that the other kid had got. They decided, in the end, to leave it to time. It's three years ago now, and possibly enough some likeness to the parents will develop that will settle the question. All I say is, up to three months old you can't tell 'em, I don't care who says you can."

He paused, and appeared to be absorbed in contemplation of the distant Matterhorn, then clad in its rosy robe of evening. There was a vein of poetry in Henry, not uncommon among cooks and waiters. The perpetual atmosphere of hot food I am inclined to think favourable to the growth of the softer emotions. One of the most sentimental men I ever knew kept a ham-and-beef shop just off the Farringdon Road. In the early morning he could be shrewd and business-like, but when hovering with a knife and fork above the mingled steam of bubbling sausages and hissing peas-pudding, any whimpering tramp with any impossible tale of woe could impose upon him easily.

"But the rummiest go I ever recollect in connection with a baby," continued Henry after a while, his gaze still fixed upon the distant snow- crowned peaks, "happened to me at Warwick in the Jubilee year. I'll never forget that."

"Is it a proper story," I asked, "a story fit for me to hear?"

On consideration, Henry saw no harm in it, and told it to me accordingly.

~

He came by the 'bus that meets the 4.52. He'd a handbag and a sort of hamper: it looked to me like a linen-basket. He wouldn't let the Boots touch the hamper, but carried it up into his bedroom himself. He carried it in front of him by the handles, and grazed his knuckles at every second step. He slipped going round the bend of the stairs, and knocked his head a rattling good thump against the balustrade; but he never let go that hamper--only swore and plunged on. I could see he was nervous and excited, but one gets used to nervous and excited people in hotels. Whether a man's running away from a thing, or running after a thing, he stops at a hotel on his way; and so long as he looks as if he could pay his bill one doesn't trouble much about him. But this man interested me: he was so uncommonly young and innocent-looking. Besides, it was a dull hole of a place after the sort of jobs I'd been used to; and when you've been doing nothing for three months but waiting on commercial gents as are having an exceptionally bad season, and spoony couples with guide-books, you get a bit depressed, and welcome any incident, however slight, that promises to be out of the common.

I followed him up into his room, and asked him if I could do anything for him. He flopped the hamper on the bed with a sigh of relief, took off his hat, wiped his head with his handkerchief, and then turned to answer me.

"Are you a married man?" says he.

It was an odd question to put to a waiter, but coming from a gent there was nothing to be alarmed about.

"Well, not exactly," I says--I was only engaged at that time, and that not to my wife, if you understand what I mean--"but I know a good deal about it," I says, "and if it's a matter of advice--"

"It isn't that," he answers, interrupting me; "but I don't want you to laugh at me. I thought if you were a married man you would be able to understand the thing better. Have you got an intelligent woman in the house?"

"We've got women," I says. "As to their intelligence, that's a matter of opinion; they're the average sort of women. Shall I call the chambermaid?"

"Ah, do," he says. "Wait a minute," he says; "we'll open it first."

He began to fumble with the cord, then he suddenly lets go and begins to chuckle to himself.

"No," he says, "you open it. Open it carefully; it will surprise you."

I don't take much stock in surprises myself. My experience is that they're mostly unpleasant.

"What's in it?" I says.

"You'll see if you open it," he says: "it won't hurt you." And off he goes again, chuckling to himself.

"Well," I says to myself, "I hope you're a harmless specimen." Then an idea struck me, and I stopped with the knot in my fingers.

"It ain't a corpse," I says, "is it?"

He turned as white as the sheet on the bed, and clutched the mantlepiece. "Good God! don't suggest such a thing," he says; "I never thought of that. Open it quickly."

"I'd rather you came and opened it yourself, sir," I says. I was beginning not to half like the business.

"I can't," he says, "after that suggestion of yours--you've put me all in a tremble. Open it quick, man; tell me it's all right."

Well, my own curiosity helped me. I cut the cord, threw open the lid, and looked in. He kept his eyes turned away, as if he were frightened to look for himself.

"Is it all right?" he says. "Is it alive?"

"It's about as alive," I says, "as anybody'll ever want it to be, I should say."

"Is it breathing all right?" he says.

"If you can't hear it breathing," I says, "I'm afraid you're deaf."

You might have heard its breathing outside in the street. He listened, and even he was satisfied.

"Thank Heaven!" he says, and down he plumped in the easy-chair by the fireplace. "You know, I never thought of that," he goes on. "He's been shut up in that basket for over an hour, and if by any chance he'd managed to get his head entangled in the clothes--I'll never do such a fool's trick again!"

"You're fond of it?" I says.

He looked round at me. "Fond of it," he repeats. "Why, I'm his father." And then he begins to laugh again.

"Oh!" I says. "Then I presume I have the pleasure of addressing Mr. Coster King?"

"Coster King?" he answers in surprise. "My name's Milberry."

I says: "The father of this child, according to the label inside the cover, is Coster King out of Starlight, his mother being Jenny Deans out of Darby the Devil."

He looks at me in a nervous fashion, and puts the chair between us. It was evidently his turn to think as how I was mad. Satisfying himself, I suppose, that at all events I wasn't dangerous, he crept closer till he could get a look inside the basket. I never heard a man give such an unearthly yell in all my life. He stood on one side of the bed and I on the other. The dog, awakened by the noise, sat up and grinned, first at one of us and then at the other. I took it to be a bull-pup of about nine months old, and a fine specimen for its age.

"My child!" he shrieks, with his eyes starting out of his head, "That thing isn't my child. What's happened? Am I going mad?"

"You're on that way," I says, and so he was. "Calm yourself," I says; "what did you expect to see?"

"My child," he shrieks again; "my only child--my baby!"

"Do you mean a real child?" I says, "a human child?" Some folks have such a silly way of talking about their dogs--you never can tell.

"Of course I do," he says; "the prettiest child you ever saw in all your life, just thirteen weeks old on Sunday. He cut his first tooth yesterday."

The sight of the dog's face seemed to madden him. He flung himself upon the basket, and would, I believe, have strangled the poor beast if I hadn't interposed between them.

"'Tain't the dog's fault," I says; "I daresay he's as sick about the whole business as you are. He's lost, too. Somebody's been having a lark with you. They've took your baby out and put this in--that is, if there ever was a baby there."

"What do you mean?" he says.

"Well, sir," I says, "if you'll excuse me, gentlemen in their sober senses don't take their babies about in dog-baskets. Where do you come from?"

"From Banbury," he says; "I'm well known in Banbury."

"I can quite believe it," I says; "you're the sort of young man that would be known anywhere."

"I'm Mr. Milberry," he says, "the grocer, in the High Street."

"Then what are you doing here with this dog?" I says.

"Don't irritate me," he answers. "I tell you I don't know myself. My wife's stopping here at Warwick, nursing her mother, and in every letter she's written home for the last fortnight she's said, 'Oh, how I do long to see Eric! If only I could see Eric for a moment!'"

"A very motherly sentiment," I says, "which does her credit."

"So this afternoon," continues he, "it being early-closing day, I thought I'd bring the child here, so that she might see it, and see that it was all right. She can't leave her mother for more than about an hour, and I can't go up to the house, because the old lady doesn't like me, and I excite her. I wish to wait here, and Milly--that's my wife--was to come to me when she could get away. I meant this to be a surprise to her."

"And I guess," I says, "it will be the biggest one you have ever given her."

"Don't try to be funny about it," he says; "I'm not altogether myself, and I may do you an injury."

He was right. It wasn't a subject for joking, though it had its humorous side.

"But why," I says, "put it in a dog-basket?"

"It isn't a dog-basket," he answers irritably; "it's a picnic hamper. At the last moment I found I hadn't got the face to carry the child in my arms: I thought of what the street-boys would call out after me. He's a rare one to sleep, and I thought if I made him comfortable in that he couldn't hurt, just for so short a journey. I took it in the carriage with me, and carried it on my knees; I haven't let it out of my hands a blessed moment. It's witchcraft, that's what it is. I shall believe in the devil after this."

"Don't be ridiculous," I says, "there's some explanation; it only wants finding. You are sure this is the identical hamper you packed the child in?"

He was calmer now. He leant over and examined it carefully. "It looks like it," he says; "but I can't swear to it."

"You tell me," I says, "you never let it go out of your hands. Now think."

"No," he says, "it's been on my knees all the time."

"But that's nonsense," I says; "unless you packed the dog yourself in mistake for your baby. Now think it over quietly. I'm not your wife, I'm only trying to help you. I shan't say anything even if you did take your eyes off the thing for a minute."

He thought again, and a light broke over his face. "By Jove!" he says, "you're right. I did put it down for a moment on the platform at Banbury while I bought a 'Tit-Bits.'"

"There you are," I says; "now you're talking sense. And wait a minute; isn't to-morrow the first day of the Birmingham Dog Show?"

"I believe you're right," he says.

"Now we're getting warm," I says. "By a coincidence this dog was being taken to Birmingham, packed in a hamper exactly similar to the one you put your baby in. You've got this man's bull-pup, he's got your baby; and I wouldn't like to say off-hand at this moment which of you's feeling the madder. As likely as not, he thinks you've done it on purpose."

He leant his head against the bed-post and groaned. "Milly may be here at any moment," says he, "and I'll have to tell her the baby's been sent by mistake to a Dog Show! I daresn't do it," he says, "I daresn't do it."

"Go on to Birmingham," I says, "and try and find it. You can catch the quarter to six and be back here before eight."

"Come with me," he says; "you're a good man, come with me. I ain't fit to go by myself."

He was right; he'd have got run over outside the door, the state he was in then.

"Well," I says, "if the guv'nor don't object--"

"Oh! he won't, he can't," cries the young fellow, wringing his hands. "Tell him it's a matter of a life's happiness. Tell him--"

"I'll tell him it's a matter of half sovereign extra on to the bill," I says. "That'll more likely do the trick."

And so it did, with the result that in another twenty minutes me and young Milberry and the bull-pup in its hamper were in a third-class carriage on our way to Birmingham. Then the difficulties of the chase began to occur to me. Suppose by luck I was right; suppose the pup was booked for the Birmingham Dog Show; and suppose by a bit more luck a gent with a hamper answering description had been noticed getting out of the 5.13 train; then where were we? We might have to interview every cabman in the town. As likely as not, by the time we did find the kid, it wouldn't be worth the trouble of unpacking. Still, it wasn't my cue to blab my thoughts. The father, poor fellow, was feeling, I take it, just about as bad as he wanted to feel. My business was to put hope into him; so when he asked me for about the twentieth time if I thought as he would ever see his child alive again, I snapped him up shortish.

"Don't you fret yourself about that," I says. "You'll see a good deal of that child before you've done with it. Babies ain't the sort of things as gets lost easily. It's only on the stage that folks ever have any particular use for other people's children. I've known some bad characters in my time, but I'd have trusted the worst of 'em with a wagon-load of other people's kids. Don't you flatter yourself you're going to lose it! Whoever's got it, you take it from me, his idea is to do the honest thing, and never rest till he's succeeded in returning it to the rightful owner."

Well, my talking like that cheered him, and when we reached Birmingham he was easier. We tackled the station-master, and he tackled all the porters who could have been about the platform when the 5.13 came in. All of 'em agreed that no gent got out of that train carrying a hamper. The station-master was a family man himself, and when we explained the case to him he sympathised and telegraphed to Banbury. The booking-clerk at Banbury remembered only three gents booking by that particular train. One had been Mr. Jessop, the corn-chandler; the second was a stranger, who had booked to Wolverhampton; and the third had been young Milberry himself. The business began to look hopeless, when one of Smith's newsboys, who was hanging around, struck in:

"I see an old lady," says he, "hovering about outside the station, and a-hailing cabs, and she had a hamper with her as was as like that one there as two peas."

I thought young Milberry would have fallen upon the boy's neck and kissed him. With the boy to help us, we started among the cabmen. Old ladies with dog-baskets ain't so difficult to trace. She had gone to a small second-rate hotel in the Aston Road. I heard all particulars from the chambermaid, and the old girl seems to have had as bad a time in her way as my gent had in his. They couldn't get the hamper into the cab, it had to go on the top. The old lady was very worried, as it was raining at the time, and she made the cabman cover it with his apron. Getting it off the cab they dropped the whole thing in the road; that woke the child up, and it began to cry.

"Good Lord, Ma'am! what is it?" asks the chambermaid, "a baby?"

"Yes, my dear, it's my baby," answers the old lady, who seems to have been a cheerful sort of old soul--leastways, she was cheerful up to then. "Poor dear, I hope they haven't hurt him."

The old lady had ordered a room with a fire in it. The Boots took the hamper up, and laid it on the hearthrug. The old lady said she and the chambermaid would see to it, and turned him out. By this time, according to the girl's account, it was roaring like a steam-siren.

"Pretty dear!" says the old lady, fumbling with the cord, "don't cry; mother's opening it as fast as she can." Then she turns to the chambermaid--"If you open my bag," says she, "you will find a bottle of milk and some dog-biscuits."

"Dog-biscuits!" says the chambermaid.

"Yes," says the old lady, laughing, "my baby loves dog-biscuits."

The girl opened the bag, and there, sure enough, was a bottle of milk and half a dozen Spratt's biscuits. She had her back to the old lady, when she heard a sort of a groan and a thud as made her turn round. The old lady was lying stretched dead on the hearthrug--so the chambermaid thought. The kid was sitting up in the hamper yelling the roof off. In her excitement, not knowing what she was doing, she handed it a biscuit, which it snatched at greedily and began sucking.

Then she set to work to slap the old lady back to life again. In about a minute the poor old soul opened her eyes and looked round. The baby was quiet now, gnawing the dog-biscuit. The old lady looked at the child, then turned and hid her face against the chambermaid's bosom.

"What is it?" she says, speaking in an awed voice. "The thing in the hamper?"

"It's a baby, Ma'am," says the maid.

"You're sure it ain't a dog?" says the old lady. "Look again."

The girl began to feel nervous, and to wish that she wasn't alone with the old lady.

"I ain't likely to mistake a dog for a baby, Ma'am," says the girl. "It's a child--a human infant."

The old lady began to cry softly. "It's a judgment on me," she says. "I used to talk to that dog as if it had been a Christian, and now this thing has happened as a punishment."

"What's happened?" says the chambermaid, who was naturally enough growing more and more curious.

"I don't know," says the old lady, sitting up on the floor. "If this isn't a dream, and if I ain't mad, I started from my home at Farthinghoe, two hours ago, with a one-year-old bulldog packed in that hamper. You saw me open it; you see what's inside it now."

"But bulldogs," says the chambermaid, "ain't changed into babies by magic."

"I don't know how it's done," says the old lady, "and I don't see that it matters. I know I started with a bulldog, and somehow or other it's got turned into that."

"Somebody's put it there," says the chambermaid; "somebody as wanted to get rid of a child. They've took your dog out and put that in its place."

"They must have been precious smart," says the old lady; "the hamper hasn't been out of my sight for more than five minutes, when I went into the refreshment-room at Banbury for a cup of tea."

"That's when they did it," says the chambermaid, "and a clever trick it was."

The old lady suddenly grasped her position, and jumped up from the floor. "And a nice thing for me," she says. "An unmarried woman in a scandal-mongering village! This is awful!"

"It's a fine-looking child," says the chambermaid.

"Would you like it?" says the old lady.

The chambermaid said she wouldn't. The old lady sat down and tried to think, and the more she thought the worse she felt. The chambermaid was positive that if we hadn't come when we did the poor creature would have gone mad. When the Boots appeared at the door to say there was a gent and a bulldog downstairs enquiring after a baby, she flung her arms round the man's neck and hugged him.

We just caught the train to Warwick, and by luck got back to the hotel ten minutes before the mother turned up. Young Milberry carried the child in his arms all the way. He said I could have the hamper for myself, and gave me half-a-sovereign extra on the understanding that I kept my mouth shut, which I did.

I don't think he ever told the child's mother what had happened--leastways, if he wasn't a fool right through, he didn't.

THE PROBATION OF JAMES WRENCH

"There are two sorts of men as gets hen-pecked," remarked Henry--I forgot how the subject had originated, but we had been discussing the merits of Henry VIII., considered as a father and a husband,--"the sort as likes it and the sort as don't, and I wouldn't be too cocksure that the sort as does isn't on the whole in the majority.

"You see," continued Henry argumentatively, "it gives, as it were, a kind of interest to life which nowadays, with everything going smoothly, and no chance of a row anywhere except in your own house, is apt to become a bit monotonous. There was a chap I got to know pretty well one winter when I was working in Dresden at the Europaischer Hof: a quiet, meek little man he was, a journeyman butcher by trade; and his wife was a dressmaker, a Schneiderin, as they call them over there, and ran a fairly big business in the Praguer Strasse. I've always been told that German husbands are the worst going, treating their wives like slaves, or, at the best, as mere upper servants. But my experience is that human nature don't alter so much according to distance from London as we fancy it does, and that husbands have their troubles same as wives all the world over. Anyhow, I've come across a German husband or two as didn't carry about with him any sign of the slave driver such as you might notice, at all events not in his own house; and I know for a fact that Meister Anton, which was the name of the chap I'm telling you about, couldn't have been much worse off, not even if he'd been an Englishman born and bred. There were no children to occupy her mind, so she just devoted herself to him and the work-girls, and made things hum, as they say in America, for all of them. As for the girls, they got away at six in the evening, and not many of them stopped more than the first month. But the old man, not being able to give notice, had to put up with an average of eighteen hours a day of it. And even when, as was sometimes the case, he managed to get away for an hour or two in the evening for a quiet talk with a few of us over a glass of beer, he could never be quite happy, thinking of what was accumulating for him at home. Of course everybody as knew him knew of his troubles--for a scolding wife ain't the sort of thing as can be hid under a bushel,--and was sorry for him, he being as amiable and good-tempered a fellow as ever lived, and most of us spent our time with him advising him for his good. Some of the more ardent would give him recipes for managing her, but they, being generally speaking bachelors, their suggestions lacked practicability, as you might say. One man bored his life out persuading him to try a bucket of cold water. He was one of those cold-water enthusiasts, this fellow; took it himself for everything, and always went to a hydropathic establishment for his holidays. Rumour had it that Meister Anton really did try this experiment on one unfortunate occasion--worried into it, I suppose, by the other chap's persistency. Anyhow, we didn't see him again for a week, he being confined to his bed with a chill on the liver. And the next suggestion made to him he rejected quite huffily, explaining that he had no intention of putting any fresh ideas into his wife's head.

"She wasn't a bad woman, mind you--merely given to fits of temper. At times she could be quite pleasant: but when she wasn't life with her must have been exciting. He had stood it for about seven years; and then one day, without a word of warning to anyone, he went away and left her. As she was quite able to keep herself, this seemed to be the best arrangement possible, and everybody wondered why he had never thought of it before, I did not see him again for nine months, until I ran against him by pure chance on the Koln platform, where I was waiting for a train to Paris. He told me they had made up all their differences by correspondence, and that he was then on his way back to her. He seemed quite cheerful and expectant.

"'Do you think she's really reformed?' I says. 'Do you think nine months is long enough to have taught her a lesson?' I didn't want to damp him, but personally I have never known but one case of a woman being cured of nagging, and that being brought about by a fall from a third-story window, resulting in what the doctors called permanent paralysis of the vocal organs, can hardly be taken as a precedent.

"'No,' he answers, 'nor nine years. But it's been long enough to teach me a lesson.'

"'You know me,' he goes on. 'I ain't a quarrelsome sort of chap. If nobody says a word to me, I never says a word to anybody; and it's been like that ever since I left her, day in and day out, all just the same. Up in the morning, do your bit of work, drink your glass of beer, and to bed in the evening; nothing to excite you, nothing to rouse you. Why, it's a mere animal existence.'

"He was a rum sort of chap, always thought things out from his own point of view as it were."

"Yes, a curious case," I remarked to Henry; "not the sort of story to put about, however. It might give women the idea that nagging is attractive, and encourage them to try it upon husbands who do not care for that kind of excitement."

"Not much fear of that," replied Henry. "The nagging woman is born, as they say, not made; and she'll nag like the roses bloom, not because she wants to, but because she can't help it. And a woman to whom it don't come natural will never be any real good at it, try as she may. And as for the men, why we'll just go on selecting wives according to the old rule, so that you never know what you've got till it's too late for you to do anything but make the best or the worst of it, according as your fancy takes you.

"There was a fellow," continued Henry, "as used to work with me a good many years ago now at a small hotel in the City. He was a waiter, like myself--not a bad sort of chap, though a bit of a toff in his off-hours. He'd been engaged for some two or three years to one of the chambermaids. A pretty, gentle-looking little thing she was, with big childish eyes, and a voice like the pouring out of water. They are strange things, women; one can never tell what they are made of from the taste of them. And while I was there, it having been a good season for both of them, they thought they'd risk it and get married. They did the sensible thing, he coming back to his work after the week's holiday, and she to hers; the only difference being that they took a couple of rooms of their own in Middleton Row, from where in summer-time you can catch the glimpse of a green tree or two, and slept out.

"The first few months they were as happy as a couple in a play, she thinking almost as much of him as he thought of himself, which must have been a comfort to both of them, and he as proud of her as if he made her himself. And then some fifteenth cousin or so of his, a man he had never heard of before, died in New Zealand and left him a fortune.

"That was the beginning of his troubles, and hers too. I don't say it was enough to buy a peerage, but to a man accustomed to dream of half-crown tips it seemed an enormous fortune. Anyhow, it was sufficient to turn his head and give him ideas above his station. His first move, of course, was to chuck his berth and set fire to his dress suit, which, being tolerably greasy, burned well. Had he stopped there nobody could have blamed him. I've often thought myself that I would willingly give ten years of my life, provided anybody wanted them, which I don't see how they should, to put my own behind the fire. But he didn't. He took a house in a mews, with the front door in a street off Grosvenor Square, furnished it like a second-class German restaurant, dressed himself like a bookmaker, and fancied that with the help of a few shady City chaps and a broken-down swell or two he had gathered round him, he was fairly on the road to Park Lane and the House of Lords.

"And the only thing that struck him as being at all in his way was his wife. In her cap and apron, or her Sunday print she had always looked as dainty and fetching a little piece of goods as a man could wish to be seen out with. Dressed according to the advice of his new-found friends, of course she looked like nothing else so much as a barn-yard chicken in turkey-cock's feathers. He was shocked to find that her size in gloves was seven-and-a-quarter, and in boots something over four, and that sort of thing naturally irritates a woman more even than finding fault with her immortal soul. I guess for about a year he made her life pretty well a burden for her, trying to bring her up to the standard of the Saturday- to-Monday-at-Brighton set with which he had surrounded himself, or which, to speak more correctly, had got round him. She'd a precious sight more gumption than he had ever possessed, and if he had listened to her instead of insisting upon her listening to him it would have been better for him. But there are some men who think that if you have a taste for champagne and the ballet that proves you are intended by nature for a nob, and he was one of them; and any common-sense suggestion of hers only convinced him of her natural unfitness for an exalted station.

"He grumbled at her accent, which, seeing that his own was acquired in Lime-house and finished off in the Minories, was just the sort of thing a fool would do. And he insisted on her reading all the society novels as they came out--you know the sort I mean,--where everybody snaps everybody else's head off, and all the proverbs are upside down; people leave them about the hotels when they've done with them, and one gets into the habit of dipping into them when one's nothing better to do. His hope was that she might, with pains, get to talk like these books. That was his ideal.

"She did her best, but of course the more she got away from herself the more absurd she became; and the rubbish and worse that he had about him would ridicule her more or less openly. And he, instead of kicking them out into the mews--which could have been done easily without Grosvenor Square knowing anything about it, and thereby having its high-class feelings hurt--he would blame her when they had all gone, just as if it was her fault that she was the daughter of a respectable bootmaker in the Mile End Road instead of something more likely than not turned out of the third row of the ballet because it couldn't dance, and didn't want to learn.

"He played a bit in the City, and won at first, and that swelled his head worse than ever. It also brought him a good deal of sympathy from an Italian Countess, the sort you find at Homburg, and that generally speaking is a widow. Her chief sorrow was for society--that in him was losing an ornament. She explained to him how an accomplished and experienced woman could help a man to gain admittance into the tiptop circles, which, according to her, were just thirsting for him. As a waiter, he had his share of brains, and it's a business that requires more insight than perhaps you'd fancy, if you don't want to waste your time on a rabbit-skin coat and a paste ring, and give the burnt sole to the real gent. But in the hands of this swell mob he was, of course, just the young man from the country; and the end of it was that he played the game down pretty low.

"She--not the Countess, I shouldn't like you to have that idea, but his wife--came to be pretty friendly with my missus later on, and that's how I got to know the details. He comes to her one day looking pretty sheepish-like, as one can well believe, and maybe he'd been drinking a bit to give himself courage.

"'We ain't been getting along too well together of late, have we, Susan?' says he.

"'We ain't seen much of one another,' she answers; 'but I agree with you, we don't seem to enjoy it much when we do.'

"'It ain't your fault,' says he.

"'I'm glad you think that,' she answers; 'it shows me you ain't quite as foolish as I was beginning to think you.'

"'Of course, I didn't know when I married you,' he goes on, 'as I was going to come into this money.'

"'No, nor I either,' says she, 'or you bet it wouldn't have happened.'

"'It seems to have been a bit of a mistake,' says he, 'as things have turned out.'

"'It would have been a mistake, and more than a bit of a one in any case,' answers she.

"'I'm glad you agree with me,' says he; 'there'll be no need to quarrel.'

"'I've always tried to agree with you,' says she. 'We've never quarrelled yet, and that ought to be sufficient proof to you that we never shall.'

"'It's a mistake that can be rectified,' says he, 'if you are sensible, and that without any harm to anyone.'

"'Oh!' says she, 'it must be a new sort of mistake, that kind.'

"'We're not fitted for one another,' says he.

"'Out with it,' says she. 'Don't you be afraid of my feelings; they are well under control, as I think I can fairly say by this time.'

"'With a man in your own station of life,' says he, 'you'd be happier.'

"'There's many a man I might have been happier with,' replies she. 'That ain't the thing to be discussed, seeing as I've got you.'

"'You might get rid of me,' says he.

"'You mean you might get rid of me,' she answers.

"'It comes to the same thing,' he says.

"'No, it don't,' she replies, 'nor anything like it. I shouldn't have got rid of you for my pleasure, and I'm not going to do it for yours. You can live like a decent man, and I'll go on putting up with you; or you can live like a fool, and I shan't stand in your way. But you can't do both, and I'm not going to help you try.'

"Well, he argued with her, and he tried the coaxing dodge, and he tried the bullying dodge, but it didn't work, neither of it.

"'I've done my duty by you,' says she, 'so far as I've been able, and that I'll go on doing or not, just as you please; but I don't do more.'

"'We can't go on living like this,' says he, 'and it isn't fair to ask me to. You're hammering my prospects.'

"'I don't want to do that,' says she. 'You take your proper position in society, whatever that may be, and I'll take mine. I'll be glad enough to get back to it, you may rest assured.'

"'What do you mean?' says he.

"'It's simple enough,' she answers. 'I was earning my living before I married you, and I can earn it again. You go your way, I go mine.'

"It didn't satisfy him; but there was nothing else to be done, and there was no moving her now in any other direction whatever, even had he wanted to. He offered her anything in the way of money--he wasn't a mean chap,--but she wouldn't touch a penny. She had kept her old clothes--I'm not sure that some idea of needing them hadn't always been in her head,--applied for a place under her former manager, who was then bossing a hotel in Kensington, and got it. And there was an end of high life so far as she was concerned.

"As for him, he went the usual way. It always seems to me as if men and women were just like water; sooner or later they get back to the level from which they started--that is, of course, generally speaking. Here and there a drop clings where it climbs; but, taking them on the whole, pumping-up is a slow business. Lord! I have seen them, many of them, jolly clever they've thought themselves, with their diamond rings and big cigars. 'Wait a bit,' I've always said to myself, 'there'll come a day when you'll walk in and be glad enough of your chop and potatoes again with your half-pint of bitter.' And nine cases out of ten I've been right. James Wrench followed the course of the majority, only a little more so: tried to do others a precious sight sharper than himself, and got done; tried a dozen times to scramble up again, each time coming down heavier than before, till there wasn't another spring left in him, and his only ambition victuals. Then, of course, he thought of his wife--it's a wonderful domesticator, ill luck--and wondered what she was doing.

"Fortunately for him, she'd been doing well. Her father died and left her a bit, just a couple of hundred or so, and with this and her own savings she started with a small inn in a growing town, and had sold out again three years later at four times what she had paid for it. She had done even better than that for herself. She had developed a talent for cooking--that was a settled income in itself,--and at this time was running a small hotel in Brighton, and making it pay to a tune that would have made the shareholders of some of its bigger rivals a bit envious could they have known.

"He came to me, having found out, I don't know how--necessity smartens the wits, I suppose,--that my missis still kept up a sort of friendship with her, and begged me to try and arrange a meeting between them, which I did, though I told him frankly that from what I knew his welcome wouldn't be much more enthusiastic than what he'd any right to expect. But he was always of a sanguine disposition; and borrowing his fare and an old greatcoat of mine, he started off, evidently thinking that all his troubles were over.

"But they weren't exactly. The Married Women's Property Act had altered things a bit, and Master James found himself greeted without any suggestion of tenderness by a business-like woman of thirty-six or thereabouts, and told to wait in the room behind the bar till she could find time to talk to him.

"She kept him waiting there for three-quarters of an hour, just sufficient time to take the side out of him; and then she walks in and closes the door behind her.

"'I'd say you hadn't changed hardly a day, Susan,' says he, 'if it wasn't that you'd grown handsomer than ever.'

"I guess he'd been turning that over in his mind during the three-quarters of an hour. It was his fancy that he knew a bit about women.

"'My name's Mrs. Wrench,' says she; 'and if you take your hat off and stand up while I'm talking to you it will be more what I'm accustomed to.'

"Well, that staggered him a bit; but there didn't seem anything else to be done, so he just made as if he thought it funny, though I doubt if at the time he saw the full humour of it.

"'And now, what do you want?' says she, seating herself in front of her desk, and leaving him standing, first on one leg and then on the other, twiddling his hat in his hands.

"'I've been a bad husband to you, Susan,' begins he.

"'I could have told you that,' she answers. 'What I asked you was what you wanted.'

"'I want for us to let bygones be bygones,' says he.

"'That's quite my own idea,' says she, 'and if you don't allude to the past, I shan't.'

"'You're an angel, Susan,' says he.

"'I've told you once,' answers she, 'that my name's Mrs. Wrench. I'm Susan to my friends, not to every broken-down tramp looking for a job.'

"'Ain't I your husband?' says he, trying a bit of dignity.

"She got up and took a glance through the glass-door to see that nobody was there to overhear her.

"'For the first and last time,' says she, 'let you and me understand one another. I've been eleven years without a husband, and I've got used to it. I don't feel now as I want one of any kind, and if I did it wouldn't be your sort. Eleven years ago I wasn't good enough for you, and now you're not good enough for me.'

"'I want to reform,' says he.

"'I want to see you do it,' says she.

"'Give me a chance,' says he.

"'I'm going to,' says she; 'but it's going to be my experiment this time, not yours. Eleven years ago I didn't give you satisfaction, so you turned me out of doors.'

"'You went, Susan,' says he; 'you know it was your own idea.'

"'Don't you remind me too much of the circumstances,' replies she, turning on him with a look in her eyes that was probably new to him, 'I went because there wasn't room for two of us; you know that. The other kind suited you better. Now I'm going to see whether you suit me,' and she sits herself again in her landlady's chair.

"'In what way?' says he.

"'In the way of earning your living,' says she, 'and starting on the road to becoming a decent member of society.'

"He stood for a while cogitating.

"'Don't you think,' says he at last, 'as I could manage this hotel for you?'

"'Thanks,' says she; 'I'm doing that myself.'

"'What about looking to the financial side of things,' says he, 'and keeping the accounts? It's hardly your work.'

"'Nor yours either,' answers she drily, 'judging by the way you've been keeping your own.'

"'You wouldn't like me to be head-waiter, I suppose?' says he. 'It would be a bit of a come-down.'

"'You're thinking of the hotel, I suppose,' says she. 'Perhaps you are right. My customers are mostly an old-fashioned class; it's probable enough they might not like you. You had better suggest something else.'

"'I could hardly be an under-waiter,' says he.

"'Perhaps not,' says she; 'your manners strike me as a bit too familiar for that.'

"Then he thought he'd try sarcasm.

"'Perhaps you'd fancy my being the boots,' says he.

"'That's more reasonable,' says she. 'You couldn't do much harm there, and I could keep an eye on you.'

"'You really mean that?' says he, starting to put on his dignity.

"But she cut him short by ringing the bell.

"'If you think you can do better for yourself,' she says, 'there's an end of it. By a curious coincidence the place is just now vacant. I'll keep it open for you till to-morrow night; you can turn it over in your mind.' And one of the page boys coming in she just says 'Good-morning,' and the interview was at an end.

"Well, he turned it over, and he took the job. He thought she'd relent after the first week or two, but she didn't. He just kept that place for over fifteen months, and learnt the business. In the house he was James the boots, and she Mrs. Wrench the landlady, and she saw to it that he didn't forget it. He had his wages and he made his tips, and the food was plentiful; but I take it he worked harder during that time than he'd ever worked before in his life, and found that a landlady is just twice as difficult to please as the strictest landlord it can be a man's misfortune to get under, and that Mrs. Wrench was no exception to the rule.

"At the end of the fifteen months she sends for him into the office. He didn't want telling by this time; he just stood with his hat in his hand and waited respectful like.

"'James,' says she, after she had finished what she was doing, 'I find I shall want another waiter for the coffee-room this season. Would you care to try the place?'

"'Thank you, Mrs. Wrench,' he answers; 'it's more what I've been used to, and I think I'll be able to give satisfaction.'

"'There's no wages attached, as I suppose you know,' continues she; 'but the second floor goes with it, and if you know your business you ought to make from twenty-five to thirty shillings a week.'

"'Thank you, Mrs. Wrench; that'll suit me very well,' replies he; and it was settled.

"He did better as a waiter; he'd got it in his blood, as you might say; and so after a time he worked up to be head-waiter. Now and then, of course, it came about that he found himself waiting on the very folks that he'd been chums with in his classy days, and that must have been a bit rough on him. But he'd taken in a good deal of sense since then; and when one of the old sort, all rings and shirt-front, dining there one Sunday evening, started chaffing him, Jimmy just shut him up with a quiet: 'Yes, I guess we were both a bit out of our place in those days. The difference between us now is that I have got back to mine,' which cost him his tip, but must nave been a satisfaction to him.

"Altogether he worked in that hotel for some three and a half years, and then Mrs. Wrench sends for him again into the office.

"'Sit down, James,' says she.

"'Thank you, Mrs. Wrench,' says James, and sat.

"'I'm thinking of giving up this hotel, James,' says she, 'and taking another near Dover, a quiet place with just such a clientele as I shall like. Do you care to come with me?'

"'Thank you,' says he, 'but I'm thinking, Mrs. Wrench, of making a change myself.'

"'Oh,' says she, 'I'm sorry to hear that, James. I thought we'd been getting on very well together.'

"'I've tried to do my best, Mrs. Wrench,' says he, 'and I hope as I've given satisfaction.'

"'I've nothing to complain of, James,' says she.

"'I thank you for saying it,' says he, 'and I thank you for the opportunity you gave me when I wanted it. It's been the making of me.'

"She didn't answer for about a minute. Then says she: 'You've been meeting some of your old friends, James, I'm afraid, and they've been persuading you to go back into the City.'

"'No, Mrs. Wrench,' says he; 'no more City for me, and no more neighbourhood of Grosvenor Square, unless it be in the way of business; and that couldn't be, of course, for a good long while to come.'

"'What do you mean by business?' asks she.

"'The hotel business,' replies he. 'I believe I know the bearings by now. I've saved a bit, thanks to you, Mrs. Wrench, and a bit's come in from the wreck that I never hoped for.'

"'Enough to start you?' asks she.

"'Not quite enough for that,' answers he. 'My idea is a small partnership.'

"'How much is it altogether?' says she, 'if it's not an impertinent question.'

"'Not at all,' answers he. 'It tots up to 900 pounds about.'

"She turns back to her desk and goes on with her writing.

"'Dover wouldn't suit you, I suppose?' says she without looking round.

"'Dover's all right,' says he, 'if the business is a good one.'

"'It can be worked up into one of the best things going,' says she, 'and I'm getting it dirt cheap. You can have a third share for a thousand pounds, that's just what it's costing, and owe me the other hundred."

"'And what position do I take?' says he.

"'If you come in on those terms,' says she, 'then, of course, it's a partnership.'

"He rose and came over to her. 'Life isn't all business, Susan,' says he.

"'I've found it so mostly,' says she.

"'Fourteen years ago,' says he, 'I made the mistake; now you're making it.'

"'What mistake am I making?' says she.

"'That man's the only thing as can't learn a lesson,' says he.

"'Oh,' says she, 'and what's the lesson that you've learnt?'

"'That I never get on without you, Susan,' says he.

"'Well,' says she, 'you suggested a partnership, and I agreed to it. What more do you want?'

"'I want to know the name of the firm,' says he.

"'Mr. and Mrs. Wrench,' says she, turning round to him and holding out her hand. 'How will that suit you?'

"'That'll do me all right,' answers he. 'And I'll try and give satisfaction,' adds he.

"'I believe you,' says she.

"And in that way they made a fresh start, as it were."

THE WOOING OF TOM SLEIGHT'S WIFE

"It's competition," replied Henry, "that makes the world go round. You never want a thing particularly until you see another fellow trying to get it; then it strikes you all of a sudden that you've a better right to it than he has. Take barmaids: what's the attraction about 'em? In looks they're no better than the average girl in the street; while as for their temper, well that's a bit above the average--leastways, so far as my experience goes. Yet the thinnest of 'em has her dozen, making sheep's-eyes at her across the counter. I've known girls that on the level couldn't have got a policeman to look at 'em. Put 'em behind a row of tumblers and a shilling's-worth of stale pastry, and nothing outside a Lincoln and Bennett is good enough for 'em. It's the competition that's the making of 'em.

"Now, I'll tell you a story," continued Henry, "that bears upon the subject. It's a pretty story, if you look at it from one point of view; though my wife maintains--and she's a bit of a judge, mind you--that it's not yet finished, she arguing that there's a difference between marrying and being married. You can have a fancy for the one, without caring much about the other. What I tell her is that a boy isn't a man, and a man isn't a boy. Besides, it's five years ago now, and nothing has happened since: though of course one can never say."

"I would like to hear the story," I ventured to suggest; "I'll be able to judge better afterwards."

"It's not a long one," replied Henry, "though as a matter of fact it began seventeen years ago in Portsmouth, New Hampshire. He was a wild young fellow, and always had been."

"Who was?" I interrupted.

"Tom Sleight," answered Henry, "the chap I'm telling you about. He belonged to a good family, his father being a Magistrate for Monmouthshire; but there had been no doing anything with young Tom from the very first. At fifteen he ran away from school at Clifton, and with everything belonging to him tied up in a pocket-handkerchief made his way to Bristol Docks. There he shipped as boy on board an American schooner, the Cap'n not pressing for any particulars, being short-handed, and the boy himself not volunteering much. Whether his folks made much of an effort to get him back, or whether they didn't, I can't tell you. Maybe, they thought a little roughing it would knock some sense into him. Anyhow, the fact remains that for the next seven or eight years, until the sudden death of his father made him a country gentleman, a more or less jolly sailor-man he continued to be. And it was during that period--to be exact, three years after he ran away and four years before he returned--that, as I have said, at Portsmouth, New Hampshire, he married, after ten days' courtship, Mary Godselle, only daughter of Jean Godselle, saloon keeper of that town."

"That makes him just eighteen," I remarked; "somewhat young for a bridegroom."

"But a good deal older than the bride," was Henry's comment, "she being at the time a few months over fourteen."

"Was it legal?" I enquired.

"Quite legal," answered Henry. "In New Hampshire, it would seem, they encourage early marriages. 'Can't begin a good thing too soon,' is, I suppose, their motto."

"How did the marriage turn out?" was my next question. The married life of a lady and gentleman, the united ages of whom amounted to thirty-two, promised interesting developments.

"Practically speaking," replied Henry, "it wasn't a marriage at all. It had been a secret affair from the beginning, as perhaps you can imagine. The old man had other ideas for his daughter, and wasn't the sort of father to be played with. They separated at the church door, intending to meet again in the evening. Two hours later Master Tom Sleight got knocked on the head in a street brawl. If a row was to be had anywhere within walking distance he was the sort of fellow to be in it. When he came to his senses he found himself lying in his bunk, and the 'Susan Pride'--if that was the name of the ship; I think it was--ten miles out to sea. The Captain declined to put the vessel about to please either a loving seaman or a loving seaman's wife; and to come to the point, the next time Mr. Tom Sleight saw Mrs. Tom Sleight was seven years later at the American bar of the Grand Central in Paris; and then he didn't know her."

"But what had she been doing all the time?" I queried. "Do you mean to tell me that she, a married woman, had been content to let her husband disappear without making any attempt to trace him?"

"I was making it short," retorted Henry, in an injured tone, "for your benefit; if you want to have the whole of it, of course you can. He wasn't a scamp; he was just a scatterbrain--that was the worst you could say against him. He tried to communicate with her, but never got an answer. Then he wrote to the father, and told him frankly the whole story. The letter came back six months later, marked--'Gone away; left no address.' You see, what had happened was this: the old man died suddenly a month or two after the marriage, without ever having heard a word about it. The girl hadn't a relative or friend in the town, all her folks being French Canadians. She'd got her pride, and she'd got a sense of humour not common in a woman. I was with her at the Grand Central for over a year, and came to know her pretty well. She didn't choose to advertise the fact that her husband had run away from her, as she thought, an hour after he had married her. She knew he was a gentleman with rich relatives somewhere in England; and as the months went by without bringing word or sign of him, she concluded he'd thought the matter over and was ashamed of her. You must remember she was merely a child at the time, and hardly understood her position. Maybe later on she would have seen the necessity of doing something. But Chance, as it were, saved her the trouble; for she had not been serving in the Cafe more than a month when, early one afternoon, in walked her Lord and Master. 'Mam'sell Marie,' as of course we called her over there, was at that moment busy talking to two customers, while smiling at a third; and our hero, he gave a start the moment he set eyes on her."

"You told me that when he saw her there he didn't know her," I reminded Henry.

"Quite right, sir," replied Henry, "so I did; but he knew a pretty girl when he saw one anywhere at any time--he was that sort, and a prettier, saucier looking young personage than Marie, in spite of her misfortunes, as I suppose you'd call 'em, you wouldn't have found had you searched Paris from the Place de la Bastille to the Arc de Triomphe."

"Did she," I asked, "know him, or was the forgetfulness mutual?"

"She recognised him," returned Henry, "before he entered the Cafe, owing to catching sight of his face through the glass door while he was trying to find the handle. Women on some points have better memories than men. Added to which, when you come to think of it, the game was a bit one-sided. Except that his moustache, maybe, was a little more imposing, and that he wore the clothes of a gentleman in place of those of an able- bodied seaman before the mast, he was to all intents and purposes the same as when they parted six years ago outside the church door; while she had changed from a child in a short muslin frock and a 'flapper,' as I believe they call it, tied up in blue ribbon, to a self-possessed young woman in a frock that might have come out of a Bond Street show window, and a Japanese coiffure, that being then the fashion.

"She finished with her French customers, not hurrying herself in the least--that wasn't her way; and then strolling over to her husband, asked him in French what she could have the pleasure of doing for him. His education on board the 'Susan Pride' and others had, I take it, gone back rather than forward. He couldn't understand her, so she translated it for him into broken English, with an accent. He asked her how she knew he was English. She told him it was because Englishmen had such pretty moustaches, and came back with his order, which was rum punch. She kept him waiting about a quarter of an hour before she returned with it. He filled up the time looking into the glass behind him when he thought nobody was observing him.

"One American drink, as they used to concoct it in that bar, was generally enough for most of our customers, but he, before he left, contrived to put away three; also contriving, during the same short space of time, to inform 'Mam'sel Marie' that Paris, since he had looked into her eyes, had become the only town worth living in, so far as he was concerned, throughout the whole universe. He had his failings, had Master Tom Sleight, but shyness wasn't one of them. She gave him a smile when he left that would have brought a less impressionable young man than he back again to that Cafe; but for the rest of the day I noticed 'Mam'sel Marie' frowned to herself a good deal, and was quite unusually cynical in her view of things in general.

"Next afternoon he found his way to us again, and much the same sort of thing went on, only a little more of it. A sailor-man, so I am told, makes love with his hour of departure always before his mind, and so gets into the habit of not wasting time. He gave her short lessons in English, for which she appeared to be grateful, and she at his request taught him the French for 'You are just charming! I love you!' with which, so he explained, it was his intention, on his return to England, to surprise his mother. He turned up again after dinner, and the next day before lunch, when after that I looked up and missed him at his usual table, the feeling would come to me that business was going down. Marie always appeared delighted to see him, and pouted when he left; but what puzzled me at the time was, that though she fooled him to the top of his bent, she flirted every bit as much, if not more, with her other customers--leastways with the nicer ones among them. There was one young Frenchman in particular--a good-looking chap, a Monsieur Flammard, son of the painter. Up till then he'd been making love pretty steadily to Miss Marie, as, indeed, had most of 'em, without ever getting much forrarder; for hitherto a chat about the weather, and a smile that might have meant she was in love with you or might have meant she was laughing at you--no man could ever tell which,--was all the most persistent had got out of her. Now, however, and evidently to his own surprise, young Monsieur Flammard found himself in clover. Provided his English rival happened to be present and not too far removed, he could have as much flirtation as he wanted, which, you may take it, worked out at a very tolerable amount. Master Tom could sit and scowl, and for the matter of that did; but as Marie would explain to him, always with the sweetest of smiles, her business was to be nice to all her customers, and to this, of course, he had nothing to reply: that he couldn't understand a word of what she and Flammard talked and laughed about didn't seem to make him any the happier.

"Well, this sort of thing went on for perhaps a fortnight, and then one morning over our dejeune, when she and I had the Cafe entirely to ourselves, I took the opportunity of talking to Mam'sel Marie like a father.

"She heard me out without a murmur, which showed her sense; for liking the girl sincerely, I didn't mince matters with her, but spoke plainly for her good. The result was, she told me her story much as I have told it to you.

"'It's a funny tale,' says I when she'd finished, 'though maybe you yourself don't see the humour of it.'

"'Yes, I do,' was her answer. 'But there's a serious side to it also,' says she, 'and that interests me more.'

"'You're sure you're not making a mistake?' I suggested.

"'He's been in my thoughts too much for me to forget him,' she replied. 'Besides, he's told me his name and all about himself.'

"'Not quite all,' says I.

"'No, and that's why I feel hard toward him,' answers she.

"'Now you listen to me,' says I. 'This is a very pretty comedy, and the way you've played it does you credit up till now. Don't you run it on too long, and turn it into a problem play.'

"'How d'ye mean?' says she.

"'A man's a man,' says I; 'anyhow he's one. He fell in love with you six years ago when you were only a child, and now you're a woman he's fallen in love with you again. If that don't convince you of his constancy, nothing will. You stop there. Don't you try to find out any more.'

"'I mean to find out one thing, answers she: 'whether he's a man-- or a cad.'

"'That's a severe remark,' says I, 'to make about your own husband.'

"'What am I to think?' says she. 'He fooled me into loving him when, as you say, I was only a child. Do you think I haven't suffered all these years? It's the girl that cries her eyes out for her lover; we learn to take 'em for what they're worth later on.'

"'But he's in love with you still,' I says. I knew what was in her mind, but I wanted to lead her away from it if I could.

"'That's a lie,' says she, 'and you know it.' She wasn't choosing her words; she was feeling, if you understand. 'He's in love with a pretty waitress that he met for the first time a fortnight ago.'

"'That's because she reminds him of you,' I replied, 'or because you remind him of her, whichever you prefer. It shows you're the sort of woman he'll always be falling in love with.'

"She laughed at that, but the next moment she was serious again. 'A man's got to fall out of love before he falls into it again,' she replied. 'I want a man that'll stop there. Besides,' she goes on, 'a woman isn't always young and pretty: we've got to remember that. We want something else in a husband besides eyes.'

"'You seem to know a lot about it,' says I.

"'I've thought a lot about it,' says she.

"'What sort of husband do you want?' says I.

"'I want a man of honour,' says she.

"That was sense. One don't often find a girl her age talking it, but her life had made her older than she looked. All I could find to say was that he appeared to be an honest chap, and maybe was one.

"'Maybe,' says she; 'that's what I mean to find out. And if you'll do me a kindness,' she adds, 'you won't mind calling me Marie Luthier for the future, instead of Godselle. It was my mother's name, and I've a fancy for it.'

"Well, there I left her to work out the thing for herself, having come to the conclusion she was capable of doing it; and so for another couple of weeks I merely watched. There was no doubt about his being in love with her. He had entered that Cafe at the beginning of the month with as good an opinion of himself as a man can conveniently carry without tumbling down and falling over it. Before the month was out he would sit with his head between his hands, evidently wondering why he had been born. I've seen the game played before, and I've seen it played since. A waiter has plenty of opportunities if he only makes use of them; for if it comes to a matter of figures, I suppose there's more love-making done in a month under the electric light of the restaurant than the moon sees in a year--leastways, so far as concerns what we call the civilised world. I've seen men fooled, from boys without hair on their faces, to old men without much on their heads. I've seen it done in a way that was pretty to watch, and I've seen it done in a manner that has made me feel that given a wig and a petticoat I could do it better myself. But never have I seen it neater played than Marie played it on that young man of hers. One day she would greet him for all the world like a tired child that at last has found its mother, and the next day respond to him in a style calculated to give you the idea of a small-sized empress in misfortune compelled to tolerate the familiarities of an anarchist. One moment she would throw him a pout that said as clearly as words: 'What a fool you are not to put your arms round me and kiss me'; and five minutes later chill him with a laugh that as good as told him he must be blind not to see that she was merely playing with him. What happened outside the Cafe--for now and then she would let him meet her of a morning in the Tuileries and walk down to the Cafe with her, and once or twice had allowed him to see her part of the way home--I cannot tell you: I only know that before strangers it was her instinct to be reserved. I take it that on such occasions his experiences were interesting; but whether they left him elated or depressed I doubt if he could have told you himself.

"But all the time Marie herself was just going from bad to worse. She had come to the Cafe a light-hearted, sweet-tempered girl; now, when she wasn't engaged in her play-acting--for that's all it was, I could see plainly enough--she would go about her work silent and miserable-looking, or if she spoke at all it would be to say something bitter. Then one morning after a holiday she had asked for, and which I had given her without any questions, she came to business more like her old self than I had seen her since the afternoon Master Tom Sleight had appeared upon the scene. All that day she went about smiling to herself; and young Flammard, presuming a bit too far maybe upon past favours, found himself sharply snubbed: it was a bit rough on him, the whole thing.

"'It's come to a head,' says I to myself; 'he has explained everything, and has managed to satisfy her. He's a cleverer chap than I took him for.'

"He didn't turn up at the Cafe that day, however, at all, and she never said a word until closing time, when she asked me to walk part of the way home with her.

"'Well,' I says, so soon as we had reached a quieter street, 'is the comedy over?'

"'No,' says she, 'so far as I'm concerned it's commenced. To tell you the truth, it's been a bit too serious up to now to please me. I'm only just beginning to enjoy myself,' and she laughed, quite her old light-hearted laugh.

"'You seem to be a bit more cheerful,' I says.

"'I'm feeling it,' says she; 'he's not as bad as I thought. We went to Versailles yesterday.'

"'Pretty place, Versailles,' says I; 'paths a bit complicated if you don't know your way among 'em.'

"'They do wind,' says she.

"'And there he told you that he loved you, and explained everything?'

"'You're quite right,' says she, 'that's just what happened. And then he kissed me for the first and last time, and now he's on his way to America.'

"'On his way to America?' says I, stopping still in the middle of the street.

"'To find his wife,' she says. 'He's pretty well ashamed of himself for not having tried to do it before. I gave him one or two hints how to set about it--he's not over smart--and I've got an idea he will discover her.' She dropped her joking manner, and gave my arm a little squeeze. She'd have flirted with her own grandfather--that's my opinion of her.

"'He was really nice,' she continues. 'I had to keep lecturing myself, or I'd have been sorry for him. He told me it was his love for me that had shown him what a wretch he had been. He said he knew I didn't care for him two straws--and there I didn't contradict him--and that he respected me all the more for it. I can't explain to you how he worked it out, but what he meant was that I was so good myself that no one but a thoroughly good fellow could possibly have any chance with me, and that any other sort of fellow ought to be ashamed of himself for daring even to be in love with me, and that he couldn't rest until he had proved to himself that he was worthy to have loved me, and then he wasn't going to love me any more.'

"'It's a bit complicated,' says I. 'I suppose you understood it?'

"'It was perfectly plain,' says she, somewhat shortly, 'and, as I told him, made me really like him for the first time.'

"'It didn't occur to him to ask you why you had been flirting like a volcano with a chap you didn't like,' says I.

"'He didn't refer to it as flirtation,' says she. 'He regarded it as kindness to a lonely man in a strange land.'

"'I think you'll be all right,' says I. 'There's all the makings of a good husband in him--seems to be simple-minded enough, anyhow.'

"'He has a very lovable personality when you once know him,' says she. 'All sailors are apt to be thoughtless.'

"'I should try and break him of it later on,' says I.

"'Besides, she was a bit of a fool herself, going away and leaving no address,' adds she; and having reached her turning, we said good-night to one another.

"About a month passed after that without anything happening.

For the first week Marie was as merry as a kitten, but as the days went by, and no sign came, she grew restless and excited. Then one morning she came into the Cafe twice as important as she had gone out the night before, and I could see by her face that her little venture was panning out successfully. She waited till we had the Cafe to ourselves, which usually happened about mid-day, and then she took a letter out of her pocket and showed it me. It was a nice respectful letter containing sentiments that would have done honour to a churchwarden. Thanks to Marie's suggestions, for which he could never be sufficiently grateful, and which proved her to be as wise as she was good and beautiful, he had traced Mrs. Sleight, nee Mary Godselle, to Quebec. From Quebec, on the death of her uncle, she had left to take a situation as waitress in a New York hotel, and he was now on his way there to continue his search. The result he would, with Miss Marie's permission, write and inform her. If he obtained happiness he would owe it all to her. She it was who had shown him his duty; there was a good deal of it, but that's what it meant.

"A week later came another letter, dated from New York this time. Mary could not be discovered anywhere; her situation she had left just two years ago, but for what or for where nobody seemed to know. What was to be done?

"Mam'sel Marie sat down and wrote him by return of post, and wrote him somewhat sharply--in broken English. It seemed to her he must be strangely lacking in intelligence. Mary, as he knew, spoke French as well as she did English. Such girls--especially such waitresses--he might know, were sought after on the Continent. Very possibly there were agencies in New York whose business it was to offer good Continental engagements to such young ladies. Even she herself had heard of one such--Brathwaite, in West Twenty-third Street, or maybe Twenty-fourth. She signed her new name, Marie Luthier, and added a P.S. to the effect that a right-feeling husband who couldn't find his wife would have written in a tone less suggestive of resignation.

"That helped him considerably, that suggestion of Marie's about the agent Brathwaite. A fortnight later came a third letter. Wonderful to relate, his wife was actually in Paris, of all places in the world! She had taken a situation in the Hotel du Louvre. Master Tom expected to be in Paris almost as soon as his letter.

"'I think I'll go round to the Louvre if you can spare me for quarter of an hour,' said Marie, 'and see the manager.'

"Two days after, at one o'clock precisely, Mr. Tom Sleight walked into the Cafe. He didn't look cheerful and he didn't look sad. He had been to the 'Louvre'; Mary Godselle had left there about a year ago; but he had obtained her address in Paris, and had received a letter from her that very morning. He showed it to Marie. It was short, and not well written. She would meet him in the Tuileries that evening at seven, by the Diana and the Nymph; he would know her by her wearing the onyx brooch he had given her the day before their wedding. She mentioned it was onyx, in case he had forgotten. He only stopped a few minutes, and both he and Marie spoke gravely and in low tones. He left a small case in her hands at parting; he said he hoped she would wear it in remembrance of one in whose thoughts she would always remain enshrined. I can't tell you what he meant; I only tell you what he said. He also gave me a very handsome walking-stick with a gold handle--what for, I don't know; I take it he felt like that.

"Marie asked to leave that evening at half-past six. I never saw her looking prettier. She called me into the office before she went. She wanted my advice. She had in one hand a beautiful opal brooch set in diamonds--it was what he had given her that morning--and in her other hand the one of onyx.

"'Shall I wear them both?' asked she, 'or only the one?' She was half laughing, half crying, already.

"I thought for a bit. 'I should wear the onyx to-night,' I said, 'by itself.'"

THE END

JOHN INGERFIELD AND OTHER STORIES

TO THE GENTLE READER

ALSO

TO THE GENTLE CRITIC

Once upon a time, I wrote a little story of a woman who was crushed to death by a python. A day or two after its publication, a friend stopped me in the street. "Charming little story of yours," he said, "that about the woman and the snake; but it's not as funny as some of your things!" The next week, a newspaper, referring to the tale, remarked, "We have heard the incident related before with infinitely greater humour."

With this--and many similar experiences--in mind, I wish distinctly to state that "John Ingerfield," "The Woman of the Saeter," and "Silhouettes," are not intended to be amusing. The two other items--"Variety Patter," and "The Lease of the Cross Keys"--I give over to the critics of the new humour to rend as they will; but "John Ingerfield," "The Woman of the Saeter," and "Silhouettes," I repeat, I should be glad if they would judge from some other standpoint than that of humour, new or old.

IN REMEMBRANCE OF JOHN INGERFIELD, AND OF ANNE, HIS WIFE

A STORY OF OLD LONDON, IN TWO CHAPTERS

CHAPTER 1

If you take the Underground Railway to Whitechapel Road (the East station), and from there take one of the yellow tramcars that start from that point, and go down the Commercial Road, past the George, in front of which starts--or used to stand-- a high flagstaff, at the base of which sits--or used to sit--an elderly female purveyor of pigs' trotters at three-ha'pence apiece, until you come to where a railway arch crosses the road obliquely, and there get down and turn to the right up a narrow, noisy street leading to the river, and then to the right again up a still narrower street, which you may know by its having a public-house at one corner (as is in the nature of things) and a marine store-dealer's at the other, outside which strangely stiff and unaccommodating garments of gigantic size flutter ghost-like in the wind, you will come to a dingy railed-in churchyard, surrounded on all sides by cheerless, many-peopled houses. Sad-looking little old houses they are, in spite of the tumult of life about their ever open doors. They and the ancient church in their midst seem weary of the ceaseless jangle around them. Perhaps, standing there for so many years, listening to the long silence of the dead, the fretful voices of the living sound foolish in their ears.

Peering through the railings on the side nearest the river, you will see beneath the shadow of the soot-grimed church's soot-grimed porch--that is, if the sun happen, by rare chance, to be strong enough to cast any shadow at all in that region of grey light--a curiously high and narrow headstone that once was white and straight, not tottering and bent with age as it is now. There is upon this stone a carving in bas-relief, as you will see for yourself if you will make your way to it through the gateway on the opposite side of the square. It represents, so far as can be made out, for it is much worn by time and dirt, a figure lying on the ground with another figure bending over it, while at a little distance stands a third object. But this last is so indistinct that it might be almost anything, from an angel to a post.

And below the carving are the words (already half obliterated) that I have used for the title of this story.

Should you ever wander of a Sunday morning within sound of the cracked bell that calls a few habit-bound, old-fashioned folk to worship within those damp-stained walls, and drop into talk with the old men who on such days sometimes sit, each in his brass-buttoned long brown coat, upon the low stone coping underneath those broken railings, you might hear this tale from them, as I did, more years ago than I care to recollect.

But lest you do not choose to go to all this trouble, or lest the old men who could tell it you have grown tired of all talk, and are not to be roused ever again into the telling of tales, and you yet wish for the story, I will here set it down for you.

But I cannot recount it to you as they told it to me, for to me it was only a tale that I heard and remembered, thinking to tell it again for profit, while to them it was a thing that had been, and the threads of it were interwoven with the woof of their own life. As they talked, faces that I did not see passed by among the crowd and turned and looked at them, and voices that I did not hear spoke to them below the clamour of the street, so that through their thin piping voices there quivered the deep music of life and death, and my tale must be to theirs but as a gossip's chatter to the story of him whose breast has felt the press of battle.

JOHN INGERFIELD, oil and tallow refiner, of Lavender Wharf, Limehouse, comes of a hard-headed, hard-fisted stock. The first of the race that the eye of Record, piercing the deepening mists upon the centuries behind her, is able to discern with any clearness is a long-haired, sea-bronzed personage, whom men call variously Inge or Unger. Out of the wild North Sea he has come. Record observes him, one of a small, fierce group, standing on the sands of desolate Northumbria, staring landward, his worldly wealth upon his back. This consists of a two-handed battle-axe, value perhaps some forty stycas in the currency of the time. A careful man, with business capabilities, may, however, manipulate a small capital to great advantage. In what would appear, to those accustomed to our slow modern methods, an incredibly short space of time, Inge's two-handed battle-axe has developed into wide lands and many head of cattle; which latter continue to multiply with a rapidity beyond the dreams of present- day breeders. Inge's descendants would seem to have inherited the genius of their ancestor, for they prosper and their worldly goods increase. They are a money-making race. In all times, out of all things, by all means, they make money. They fight for money, marry for money, live for money, are ready to die for money.

In the days when the most saleable and the highest priced article in the markets of Europe was a strong arm and a cool head, then each Ingerfield (as "Inge," long rooted in Yorkshire soil, had grown or been corrupted to) was a soldier of fortune, and offered his strong arm and his cool head to the highest bidder. They fought for their price, and they took good care that they obtained their price; but, the price settled, they fought well, for they were staunch men and true, according to their lights, though these lights may have been placed somewhat low down, near the earth.

Then followed the days when the chief riches of the world lay tossed for daring hands to grasp upon the bosom of the sea, and the sleeping spirit of the old Norse Rover stirred in their veins, and the lilt of a wild sea- song they had never heard kept ringing in their ears;

and they built them ships and sailed for the Spanish Main, and won much wealth, as was their wont.

Later on, when Civilisation began to lay down and enforce sterner rules for the game of life, and peaceful methods promised to prove more profitable than violent, the Ingerfields became traders and merchants of grave mien and sober life; for their ambition from generation to generation remains ever the same, their various callings being but means to an end.

A hard, stern race of men they would seem to have been, but just--so far as they understood justice. They have the reputation of having been good husbands, fathers, and masters; but one cannot help thinking of them as more respected than loved.

They were men to exact the uttermost farthing due to them, yet not without a sense of the thing due from them, their own duty and responsibility--nay, not altogether without their moments of heroism, which is the duty of great men. History relates how a certain Captain Ingerfield, returning with much treasure from the West Indies--how acquired it were, perhaps, best not to inquire too closely--is overhauled upon the high seas by King's frigate. Captain of King's frigate sends polite message to Captain Ingerfield requesting him to be so kind as to promptly hand over a certain member of his ship's company, who, by some means or another, has made himself objectionable to King's friends, in order that he (the said objectionable person) may be forthwith hanged from the yard-arm.

Captain Ingerfield returns polite answer to Captain of King's frigate that he (Captain Ingerfield) will, with much pleasure, hang any member of his ship's company that needs hanging, but that neither the King of England nor any one else on God Almighty's sea is going to do it for him. Captain of King's frigate sends back word that if objectionable person be not at once given up he shall be compelled with much regret to send Ingerfield and his ship to the bottom of the Atlantic. Replies Captain Ingerfield, "That is just what he will have to do before I give up one of my people," and fights the big frigate--fights it so fiercely that after three hours Captain of King's frigate thinks it will be good to try argument again, and sends therefore a further message, courteously acknowledging Captain Ingerfield's courage and skill, and suggesting that, he having done sufficient to vindicate his honour and renown, it would be politic to now hand over the unimportant cause of contention, and so escape with his treasure.

"Tell your Captain," shouts back this Ingerfield, who has discovered there are sweeter things to fight for than even money, "that the *Wild Goose* has flown the seas with her belly full of treasure before now, and will, if it be God's pleasure, so do again, but that master and man in her sail together, fight together, and die together."

Whereupon King's frigate pounds away more vigorously than ever, and succeeds eventually in carrying out her threat. Down goes the *Wild Goose*, her last chase ended--down she goes with a plunge, spit foremost with her colours flying; and down with her goes every man left standing on her decks; and at the bottom of the Atlantic they lie to this day, master and man side by side, keeping guard upon their treasure.

Which incident, and it is well authenticated, goes far to prove that the Ingerfields, hard men and grasping men though they be--men caring more for the getting of money than for the getting of love--loving more the cold grip of gold than the grip of kith or kin, yet bear buried in their hearts the seeds of a nobler manhood, for which, however, the barren soil of their ambition affords scant nourishment.

The John Ingerfield of this story is a man very typical of his race. He has discovered that the oil and tallow refining business, though not a pleasant one, is an exceedingly lucrative one. These are the good days when George the Third is king, and London is rapidly becoming a city of bright night. Tallow and oil and all materials akin thereto are in ever- growing request, and young John Ingerfield builds himself a large refining house and warehouse in the growing suburb of Limehouse, which lies between the teeming river and the quiet fields, gathers many people round about him, puts his strong heart into his work, and prospers.

All the days of his youth he labours and garners, and lays out and garners yet again. In early middle age he finds himself a wealthy man. The chief business of life, the getting of money, is practically done; his enterprise is firmly established, and will continue to grow with ever less need of husbandry. It is time for him to think about the secondary business of life, the getting together of a wife and home, for the Ingerfields have ever been good citizens, worthy heads of families, openhanded hosts, making a brave show among friends and neighbours.

John Ingerfield, sitting in his stiff, high-backed chair, in his stiffly, but solidly, furnished dining-room, above his counting-house, sipping slowly his one glass of port, takes counsel with himself.

What shall she be?

He is rich, and can afford a good article. She must be young and handsome, fit to grace the fine house he will take for her in fashionable Bloomsbury, far from the odour and touch of oil and tallow. She must be well bred, with a gracious, noble manner, that will charm his guests and reflect honour and credit upon himself; she must, above all, be of good family, with a genealogical tree sufficiently umbrageous to hide Lavender Wharf from the eyes of Society.

What else she may or may not be he does not very much care. She will, of course, be virtuous and moderately pious, as it is fit and proper that women should be. It will also be well that her disposition be gentle and yielding, but that is of minor importance, at all events so far as he is concerned: the Ingerfield husbands are not the class of men upon whom wives vent their tempers.

Having decided in his mind *what* she shall be, he proceeds to discuss with himself *who* she shall be. His social circle is small. Methodically, in thought, he makes the entire round of it, mentally scrutinising every maiden that he knows. Some are charming, some are fair, some are rich; but no one of them approaches near to his carefully considered ideal.

He keeps the subject in his mind, and muses on it in the intervals of business. At odd moments he jots down names as they occur to him upon a slip of paper, which he pins for the purpose on the inside of the cover of his desk. He arranges them alphabetically, and when it is as complete as his memory can make it, he goes critically down the list, making a few notes against each. As a result, it becomes clear to him that he must seek among strangers for his wife.

He has a friend, or rather an acquaintance, an old school-fellow, who has developed into one of those curious social flies that in all ages are to be met with buzzing contentedly within the most exclusive circles, and concerning whom, seeing that they are neither rare nor rich, nor extraordinarily clever nor well born, one wonders "how the devil they got there!" Meeting this man by chance one afternoon, he links his arm in his and invites him home to dinner.

So soon as they are left alone, with the walnuts and wine between them, John Ingerfield says, thoughtfully cracking a hard nut between his fingers--

"Will, I'm going to get married."

"Excellent idea--delighted to hear it, I'm sure," replies Will, somewhat less interested in the information than in the delicately flavoured Madeira he is lovingly sipping. "Who's the lady?"

"I don't know, yet," is John Ingerfield's answer.

His friend glances slyly at him over his glass, not sure whether he is expected to be amused or sympathetically helpful.

"I want you to find one for me."

Will Cathcart puts down his glass and stares at his host across the table.

"Should be delighted to help you, Jack," he stammers, in an alarmed tone--"'pon my soul I should; but really don't know a damned woman I could recommend--'pon my soul I don't."

"You must see a good many: I wish you'd look out for one that you *could* recommend."

"Certainly I will, my dear Jack!" answers the other, in a relieved voice. "Never thought about 'em in that way before. Daresay I shall come across the very girl to suit you. I'll keep my eyes open and let you know."

"I shall be obliged to you if you will," replies John Ingerfield, quietly; "and it's your turn, I think, to oblige me, Will. I have obliged you, if you recollect."

"Shall never forget it, my dear Jack," murmurs Will, a little uneasily. "It was uncommonly good of you. You saved me from ruin, Jack: shall think about it to my dying day--'pon my soul I shall."

"No need to let it worry you for so long a period as that," returns John, with the faintest suspicion of a smile playing round his firm mouth. "The bill falls due at the end of next month. You can discharge the debt then, and the matter will be off your mind."

Will finds his chair growing uncomfortable under him, while the Madeira somehow loses its flavour. He gives a short, nervous laugh.

"By Jove," he says: "so soon as that? The date had quite slipped my memory."

"Fortunate that I reminded you," says John, the smile round his lips deepening.

Will fidgets on his seat. "I'm afraid, my dear Jack," he says, "I shall have to get you to renew it, just for a month or two,--deuced awkward thing, but I'm remarkably short of money this year. Truth is, I can't get what's owing to myself."

"That's very awkward, certainly," replies his friend, "because I am not at all sure that I shall be able to renew it."

Will stares at him in some alarm. "But what am I to do if I hav'n't the money?"

John Ingerfield shrugs his shoulders.

"You don't mean, my dear Jack, that you would put me in prison?"

"Why not? Other people have to go there who can't pay their debts."

Will Cathcart's alarm grows to serious proportions. "But our friendship," he cries, "our--"

"My dear Will," interrupts the other, "there are few friends I would lend three hundred pounds to and make no effort to get it back. You, certainly, are not one of them."

"Let us make a bargain," he continues. "Find me a wife, and on the day of my marriage I will send you back that bill with, perhaps, a couple of hundred added. If by the end of next month you have not introduced me to a lady fit to be, and willing to be, Mrs. John Ingerfield, I shall decline to renew it."

John Ingerfield refills his own glass and hospitably pushes the bottle towards his guest--who, however, contrary to his custom, takes no notice of it, but stares hard at his shoe-buckles.

"Are you serious?" he says at length.

"Quite serious," is the answer. "I want to marry. My wife must be a lady by birth and education. She must be of good family--of family sufficiently good, indeed, to compensate for the refinery. She must be young and beautiful and charming. I am purely a business man. I want a woman capable of conducting the social department of my life. I know of no such lady myself. I appeal to you, because you, I know, are intimate with the class among whom she must be sought."

"There may be some difficulty in persuading a lady of the required qualifications to accept the situation," says Cathcart, with a touch of malice.

"I want you to find one who will," says John Ingerfield.

Early in the evening Will Cathcart takes leave of his host, and departs thoughtful and anxious; and John Ingerfield strolls contemplatively up and down his wharf, for the smell of oil and tallow has grown to be very sweet to him, and it is pleasant to watch the moonbeams shining on the piled-up casks.

Six weeks go by. On the first day of the seventh John takes Will Cathcart's acceptance from its place in the large safe, and lays it in the smaller box beside his desk, devoted to more pressing and immediate business. Two days later Cathcart picks his way across the slimy yard, passes through the counting-house, and enters his friend's inner sanctum, closing the door behind him.

He wears a jubilant air, and slaps the grave John on the back. "I've got her, Jack," he cries. "It's been hard work, I can tell you: sounding suspicious old dowagers, bribing confidential servants, fishing for information among friends of the family. By Jove, I shall be able to join the Duke's staff as spy-in-chief to His Majesty's entire forces after this!"

"What is she like?" asks John, without stopping his writing.

"Like! My dear Jack, you'll fall over head and ears in love with her the moment you see her. A little cold, perhaps, but that will just suit you."

"Good family?" asks John, signing and folding the letter he has finished.

"So good that I was afraid at first it would be useless thinking of her. But she's a sensible girl, no confounded nonsense about her, and the family are poor as church mice. In fact--well, to tell the truth, we have become most excellent friends, and she told me herself frankly that she meant to marry a rich man, and didn't much care whom."

"That sounds hopeful," remarks the would-be bridegroom, with his peculiar dry smile: "when shall I have the pleasure of seeing her?"

"I want you to come with me to-night to the Garden," replies the other; "she will be in Lady Heatherington's box, and I will introduce you."

So that evening John Ingerfield goes to Covent Garden Theatre, with the blood running a trifle quicker in his veins, but not much, than would be the case were he going to the docks to purchase tallow--examines, covertly, the proposed article from the opposite side of the house, and approves her--is introduced to her, and, on closer inspection, approves her still more--receives an invitation to visit--visits frequently, and each time is more satisfied of the rarity, serviceableness, and quality of the article.

If all John Ingerfield requires for a wife is a beautiful social machine, surely here he has found his ideal. Anne Singleton, only daughter of that persistently unfortunate but most charming of baronets, Sir Harry Singleton (more charming, it is rumoured, outside his family circle than within it), is a stately graceful, high-bred woman. Her portrait, by Reynolds, still to be seen above the carved wainscoting of one of the old City halls, shows a wonderfully handsome and clever face, but at the same time a wonderfully cold and heartless one. It is the face of a woman half weary of, half sneering at the world. One reads in old family letters, whereof the ink is now very faded and the paper very yellow, long criticisms of this portrait. The writers complain that if the picture is at all like her she must have greatly changed since her girlhood, for they remember her then as having a laughing and winsome expression.

They say--they who knew her in after-life--that this earlier face came back to her in the end, so that the many who remembered opening their eyes and seeing her bending down over them could never recognise the portrait of the beautiful sneering lady, even when they were told whom it represented.

But at the time of John Ingerfield's strange wooing she was the Anne Singleton of Sir Joshua's portrait, and John Ingerfield liked her the better that she was.

He had no feeling of sentiment in the matter himself, and it simplified the case that she had none either. He offered her a plain bargain, and she accepted it. For all he knew or cared, her attitude towards this subject of marriage was the usual one assumed by women. Very young girls had their heads full of romantic ideas. It was better for her and for him that she had got rid of them.

"Ours will be a union founded on good sense," said John Ingerfield.

"Let us hope the experiment will succeed," said Anne Singleton.

CHAPTER 2.

BUT THE EXPERIMENT does not succeed. The laws of God decree that man shall purchase woman, that woman shall give herself to man, for other coin than that of good sense. Good sense is not a legal tender in the marriage mart. Men and women who enter therein with only sense in their purse have no right to complain if, on reaching home, they find they have concluded an unsatisfactory bargain.

John Ingerfield, when he asked Anne Singleton to be his wife, felt no more love for her than he felt for any of the other sumptuous household appointments he was purchasing about the same time, and made no pretence of doing so. Nor, had he done so, would she have believed him; for Anne Singleton has learned much in her twenty-two summers and winters, and knows that love is only a meteor in life's sky, and that the true lodestar of this world is gold. Anne Singleton has had her romance and buried it deep down in her deep nature and over its grave, to keep its ghost from rising, has piled the stones of indifference and contempt, as many a woman has done before and since. Once upon a time Anne Singleton sat dreaming out a story. It was a story old as the hills--older than some of them--but to her, then, it was quite new and very wonderful. It contained all the usual stock material common to such stories: the lad and the lass, the plighted troth, the richer suitors, the angry parents, the love that was worth braving all the world for. One day into this dream there fell from the land of the waking a letter, a poor, pitiful letter: "You know I love you and only you," it ran; "my heart will always be yours till I die. But my father threatens to stop my allowance, and, as you know, I have nothing of my own except debts. Some would call her handsome, but how can I think of her beside you? Oh, why was money ever let to come into the world to curse us?" with many other puzzling questions of a like character, and much severe condemnation of Fate and Heaven and other parties generally, and much self-commiseration.

Anne Singleton took long to read the letter. When she had finished it, and had read it through again, she rose, and, crushing it her hand, flung it in the fire with a laugh, and as the flame burnt up and died away felt that her life had died with it, not knowing that bruised hearts can heal.

So when John Ingerfield comes wooing, and speaks to her no word of love but only of money, she feels that here at last is a genuine voice that she can trust. Love of the lesser side of life is still left to her. It will be pleasant to be the wealthy mistress of a fine house, to give great receptions, to exchange the secret poverty of home for display and luxury. These things are offered to her on the very terms she would have suggested herself. Accompanied by love she would have refused them, knowing she could give none in return.

But a woman finds it one thing not to desire affection and another thing not to possess it. Day by day the atmosphere of the fine house in Bloomsbury grows cold and colder about her heart. Guests warm it at times for a few hours, then depart, leaving it chillier than before.

For her husband she attempts to feel indifference, but living creatures joined together cannot feel indifference for each other. Even two dogs in a leash are compelled to think of one another. A man and wife must love or hate, like or dislike, in degree as the bond connecting them is drawn tight or allowed to hang slack. By mutual desire their chains of wedlock have been fastened as loosely as respect for security will permit, with the happy consequence that her aversion to him does not obtrude itself beyond the limits of politeness.

Her part of the contract she faithfully fulfils, for the Singletons also have their code of honour. Her beauty, her tact, her charm, her influence, are devoted to his service--to the advancement of his position, the furtherance of his ambition. Doors that would otherwise remain closed she opens to him. Society, that would otherwise pass by with a sneer, sits round his table. His wishes and pleasures are hers. In all things she yields him wifely duty, seeks to render herself agreeable to him, suffers in silence his occasional caresses. Whatever was implied in the bargain, that she will perform to the letter.

He, on his side, likewise performs his part with businesslike conscientiousness--nay, seeing that the pleasing of her brings no personal gratification to himself--not without generosity. He is ever thoughtful of and deferential to her, awarding her at all times an unvarying courteousness that is none the less sincere for being studied. Her every expressed want is gratified, her every known distaste respected. Conscious of his presence being an oppression to her, he is even careful not to intrude it upon her oftener than is necessary.

At times he asks himself, somewhat pertinently, what he has gained by marriage--wonders whether this social race was quite the most interesting game he could have elected to occupy his leisure--wonders whether, after all, he would not have been happier over his counting-house than in these sumptuous, glittering rooms, where he always seems, and feels himself to be, the uninvited guest.

The only feeling that a closer intimacy has created in him for his wife is that of indulgent contempt. As there is no equality between man and woman, so there can be no respect. She is a different being. He must either look up to her as superior to himself, or down upon her as inferior. When a man does the former he is more or less in love, and love to John Ingerfield is an unknown emotion. Her beauty, her charm, her social tact--even while he makes use of them for his own purposes, he despises as the weapons of a weak nature.

So in their big, cold mansion John Ingerfield and Anne, his wife, sit far apart, strangers to one another, neither desiring to know the other nearer.

About his business he never speaks to her, and she never questions him. To compensate for the slight shrinkage of time he is able to devote to it, he becomes more strict and exacting; grows a harsher master to his people, a sterner creditor, a greedier dealer, squeezing the uttermost out of every one, feverish to grow richer, so that he may spend more upon the game that day by day he finds more tiresome and uninteresting.

And the piled-up casks upon his wharves increase and multiply; and on the dirty river his ships and barges lie in ever-lengthening lines; and round his greasy cauldrons sweating, witch-like creatures swarm in ever-denser numbers, stirring oil and tallow into gold.

Until one summer, from its nest in the far East, there flutters westward a foul thing. Hovering over Limehouse suburb, seeing it crowded and unclean, liking its fetid smell, it settles down upon it.

Typhus is the creature's name. At first it lurks there unnoticed, battening upon the rich, rank food it finds around it, until, grown too big to hide longer, it boldly shows its hideous head, and the white face of Terror runs swiftly through alley and street, crying as it runs, forces itself into John Ingerfield's counting-house, and tells its tale. John Ingerfield sits for a while thinking. Then he mounts his horse and rides home at as hard a pace as the condition of the streets will allow. In the hall he meets Anne going out, and stops her.

"Don't come too near me," he says quietly. "Typhus fever has broken out at Limehouse, and they say one can communicate it, even without having it oneself. You had better leave London for a few weeks. Go down to your father's: I will come and fetch you when it is all over."

He passes her, giving her a wide berth, and goes upstairs, where he remains for some minutes in conversation with his valet. Then, coming down, he remounts and rides off again.

After a little while Anne goes up into his room. His man is kneeling in the middle of the floor, packing a valise.

"Where are you to take it?" she asks.

"Down to the wharf, ma'am," answers the man: "Mr. Ingerfield is going to be there for a day or two."

Then Anne sits in the great empty drawing-room, and takes *her* turn at thinking.

John Ingerfield finds, on his return to Limehouse, that the evil has greatly increased during the short time he has been away. Fanned by fear and ignorance, fed by poverty and dirt, the scourge is spreading through the district like a fire. Long smouldering in secret, it has now burst forth at fifty different points at once. Not a street, not a court but has its "case." Over a dozen of John's hands are down with it already. Two more have sunk prostrate beside their work within the last hour. The panic grows grotesque. Men and women tear their clothes off, looking to see if they have anywhere upon them a rash or a patch of mottled skin, find that they have, or imagine that they have, and rush, screaming, half- undressed, into the street. Two men, meeting in a narrow passage, both rush back, too frightened to pass each other. A boy stoops down and scratches his leg--not an action that under ordinary circumstances would excite much surprise in that neighbourhood. In an instant there is a wild stampede from the room, the strong trampling on the weak in their eagerness to escape.

These are not the days of organised defence against disease. There are kind hearts and willing hands in London town, but they are not yet closely enough banded together to meet a swift foe such as this. There are hospitals and charities galore, but these are mostly in the City, maintained by the City Fathers for the exclusive benefit of poor citizens and members of the guilds. The few free hospitals are already over-crowded and ill-prepared. Squalid, outlying Limehouse, belonging to nowhere, cared for by nobody, must fight for itself.

John Ingerfield calls the older men together, and with their help attempts to instil some sense and reason into his terrified people.

Standing on the step of his counting-house, and addressing as many of them as are not too scared to listen, he tells them of the danger of fear and of the necessity for calmness and courage.

"We must face and fight this thing like men," he cries, in that deep, din- conquering voice that has served the Ingerfields in good stead on many a steel-swept field, on many a storm-struck sea; "there must be no cowardly selfishness, no faint-hearted despair. If we've got to die we'll die; but please God we'll live. Anyhow, we will stick together, and help each other. I mean to stop here with you, and do what I can for you. None of my people shall want."

John Ingerfield ceases, and as the vibrations of his strong tones roll away a sweet voice from beside him rises clear and firm:--

"I have come down to be with you also, and to help my husband. I shall take charge of the nursing and tending of your sick, and I hope I shall be of some real use to you. My husband and I are so sorry for you in your trouble. I know you will be brave and patient. We will all do our best, and be hopeful."

He turns, half expecting to see only the empty air and to wonder at the delirium in his brain. She puts her hand in his, and their eyes meet; and in that moment, for the first time in their lives, these two see one another.

They speak no word. There is no opportunity for words. There is work to be done, and done quickly, and Anne grasps it with the greed of a woman long hungry for the joy of doing. As John watches her moving swiftly and quietly through the bewildered throng, questioning, comforting, gently compelling, the thought comes to him, Ought he to allow her to be here, risking her life for his people? followed by the thought, How is he going to prevent it? For in this hour the knowledge is born within him that Anne is not his property; that he and she are fellow hands taking their orders from the same Master; that though it be well for them to work together and help each other, they must not hinder one another.

As yet John does not understand all this. The idea is new and strange to him. He feels as the child in a fairy story on suddenly discovering that the trees and flowers has he passed by carelessly a thousand times can think and talk. Once he whispers to her of the labour and the danger, but she answers simply, "They are my people too, John: it is my work"; and he lets her have her way.

Anne has a true woman's instinct for nursing, and her strong sense stands her in stead of experience. A glance into one or two of the squalid dens where these people live tells her that if her patients are to be saved they must be nursed away from their own homes; and she determines to convert the large counting-house--a long, lofty room at the opposite end of the wharf to the refinery--into a temporary hospital. Selecting some seven or eight of the most reliable women to assist her, she proceeds to prepare it for its purpose. Ledgers might be volumes of poetry, bills of lading mere street ballads, for all the respect that is shown to them. The older clerks stand staring aghast, feeling that the end of all things is surely at hand, and that the universe is rushing down into space, until, their idleness being detected, they are themselves promptly impressed for the sacrilegious work, and made to assist in the demolition of their own temple.

Anne's commands are spoken very sweetly, and are accompanied by the sweetest of smiles; but they are nevertheless commands, and somehow it does not occur to any one to disobey them. John--stern, masterful, authoritative John, who has never been approached with anything more dictatorial than a timid request since he left Merchant Taylors' School nineteen years ago, who would have thought that something had suddenly gone wrong with the laws of Nature if he had been--finds himself hurrying along the street on his way to a druggist's shop, slackens his pace an instant to ask himself why and wherefore he is doing so, recollects that he was told to do so and to make haste back, marvels who could have dared to tell him to do anything and to make haste back, remembers that it was Anne, is not quite sure what to think about it, but hurries on. He "makes haste back," is praised for having been so quick, and feels pleased with himself; is sent off again in another direction, with instructions what to say when he gets there. He starts off (he is becoming used to being ordered about now). Halfway there great alarm seizes him, for on attempting to say over the message to himself, to be sure that he has it quite right, he discovers he has forgotten it. He pauses, nervous and excited; cogitates as to whether it will be safe for him to concoct a message of his own, weighs anxiously the chances--supposing that he does so--of being found out. Suddenly, to his intense surprise and relief, every word of what he was told to say comes back to him; and he hastens on, repeating it over and over to himself as he walks, lest it should escape him again.

And then a few hundred yards farther on there occurs one of the most extraordinary events that has ever happened in that street before or since: John Ingerfield laughs.

John Ingerfield, of Lavender Wharf, after walking two-thirds of Creek Lane, muttering to himself with his eyes on the ground, stops in the middle of the road and laughs; and one small boy, who tells the story to his dying day, sees him and hears him, and runs home at the top of his speed with the wonderful news, and is conscientiously slapped by his mother for telling lies.

All that day Anne works like a heroine, John helping her, and occasionally getting in the way. By night she has her little hospital prepared and three beds already up and occupied; and, all now done that can be done, she and John go upstairs to his old rooms above the counting-house.

John ushers her into them with some misgiving, for by contrast with the house at Bloomsbury they are poor and shabby. He places her in the arm-chair near the fire, begging her to rest quiet, and then assists his old housekeeper, whose wits, never of the strongest, have been scared by the day's proceeding, to lay the meal.

Anne's eyes follow him as he moves about the room. Perhaps here, where all the real part of his life has been passed, he is more his true self than amid the unfamiliar surroundings of fashion; perhaps this simpler frame shows him to greater advantage; but Anne wonders how it is she has never noticed before that he is a well-set, handsome man. Nor, indeed, is he so very old-looking. Is it a trick of the dim light, or what? He looks almost young. But why should he not look young, seeing he is only thirty-six, and at thirty-six a man is in his prime? Anne wonders why she has always thought of him as an elderly person.

A portrait of one of John's ancestors hangs over the great mantelpiece--of that sturdy Captain Ingerfield who fought the King's frigate rather than give up one of his people. Anne glances from the dead face to the living and notes the strong likeness between them. Through her half-closed eyes she sees the grim old captain hurling back his message of defiance, and his face is the face she saw a few hours ago, saying, "I mean to stop here with you and do what I can for you. None of my people shall want."

John is placing a chair for her at the table, and the light from the candles falls upon him. She steals another glance at his face--a strong, stern, handsome face, capable of becoming a noble face. Anne wonders if it has ever looked down tenderly at anyone; feels a sudden fierce pain at the thought; dismisses the thought as impossible; wonders, nevertheless, how tenderness would suit it; thinks she would like to see a look of tenderness upon it, simply out of curiosity; wonders if she ever will.

She rouses herself from her reverie as John, with a smile, tells her supper is ready, and they seat themselves opposite each other, an odd air of embarrassment pervading.

Day by day their work grows harder; day by day the foe grows stronger, fiercer, more all-conquering; and day by day, fighting side by side against it, John Ingerfield and Anne, his wife, draw closer to each other. On the battle-field of life we learn the worth of strength. Anne feels it good, when growing weary, to glance up and find him near her; feels it good, amid the troubled babel round her, to hear the deep, strong music of his voice.

And John, watching Anne's fair figure moving to and fro among the stricken and the mourning; watching her fair, fluttering hands, busy with their holy work, her deep, soul-haunting eyes, changeful with the light and shade of tenderness; listening to her sweet, clear voice, laughing with the joyous, comforting the comfortless, gently commanding, softly pleading, finds creeping into his brain strange new thoughts concerning women--concerning this one woman in particular.

One day, rummaging over an old chest, he comes across a coloured picture- book of Bible stories. He turns the torn pages fondly, remembering the Sunday afternoons of long ago. At one picture, wherein are represented many angels, he pauses; for in one of the younger angels of the group--one not quite so severe of feature as her sisters--he fancies he can trace resemblance to Anne. He lingers long over it. Suddenly there rushes through his brain the thought, How good to stoop and kiss the sweet feet of such a woman! and, thinking it, he blushes like a boy.

So from the soil of human suffering spring the flowers of human love and joy, and from the flowers there fall the seeds of infinite pity for human pain, God shaping all things to His ends.

Thinking of Anne, John's face grows gentler, his hand kinder; dreaming of him, her heart grows stronger, deeper, fuller. Every available room in the warehouse has been turned into a ward, and the little hospital is open free to all, for John and Anne feel that the whole world are their people. The piled-up casks are gone--shipped to Woolwich and Gravesend, bundled anywhere out of the way, as though oil and tallow and the gold they can be stirred into were matters of small moment in this world, not to be thought of beside such a thing as the helping of a human brother in sore strait.

All the labour of the day seems light to them, looking forward to the hour when they sit together in John's old shabby dining-room above the counting-house. Yet a looker-on might imagine such times dull to them; for they are strangely shy of one another, strangely sparing of words--fearful of opening the floodgates of speech, feeling the pressure of the pent-up thought.

One evening, John, throwing out words, not as a sop to the necessity for talk, but as a bait to catch Anne's voice, mentions girdle-cakes, remembers that his old housekeeper used to be famous for the making of them, and wonders if she has forgotten the art.

Anne, answering tremulously, as though girdle-cakes were a somewhat delicate topic, claims to be a successful amateur of them herself. John, having been given always to understand that the talent for them was exceedingly rare, and one usually hereditary, respectfully doubts Anne's capabilities, deferentially suggesting that she is thinking of scones. Anne indignantly repudiates the insinuation, knows quite well the difference between girdle-cakes and scones, offers to prove her powers by descending into the kitchen and making some then and there, if John will accompany her and find the things for her.

John accepts the challenge, and, guiding Anne with one shy, awkward hand, while holding aloft a candle in the other, leads the way. It is past ten o'clock, and the old housekeeper is in bed. At each creaking stair they pause, to listen if the noise has awakened her; then, finding all silent, creep forward again, with suppressed laughter, wondering with alarm, half feigned, half real, what the prim, methodical dame would say were she to come down and catch them.

They reach the kitchen, thanks more to the suggestions of a friendly cat than to John's acquaintanceship with the geography of his own house; and Anne rakes together the fire and clears the table for her work. What possible use John is to her--what need there was for her stipulating that he should accompany her, Anne might find it difficult, if examined, to explain satisfactorily. As for his "finding the things" for her, he has not the faintest notion where they are, and possesses no natural aptitude for discovery. Told to find flour, he industriously searches for it in the dresser drawers; sent for the rolling-pin--the nature and characteristics of rolling-pins being described to him for his guidance--he returns, after a prolonged absence, with the copper stick. Anne laughs at him; but really it would seem as though she herself were almost as stupid, for not until her hands are covered with flour does it occur to her that she has not taken that preliminary step in all cooking operations of rolling up her sleeves.

She holds out her arms to John, first one and then the other, asking him sweetly if he minds doing it for her. John is very slow and clumsy, but Anne stands very patient. Inch by inch he peels the black sleeve from the white round arm. Hundreds of times must he have seen those fair arms, bare to the shoulder, sparkling with jewels; but never before has he seen their wondrous beauty. He longs to clasp them round his neck, yet is fearful lest his trembling fingers touching them as he performs his tantalising task may offend her. Anne thanks him, and apologises for having given him so much trouble, and he murmurs some meaningless reply, and stands foolishly silent, watching her.

Anne seems to find one hand sufficient for her cake-making, for the other rests idly on the table--very near to one of John's, as she would see were not her eyes so intent upon her work. How the impulse came to him, where he--grave, sober, business-man John--learnt such story-book ways can never be known; but in one instant he is down on both knees, smothering the floury hand with kisses, and the next moment Anne's arms are round his neck and her lips against his, and the barrier between them is swept away, and the deep waters of their love rush together.

With that kiss they enter a new life whereinto one may not follow them. One thinks it must have been a life made strangely beautiful by self-forgetfulness, strangely sweet by mutual devotion--a life too ideal, perhaps, to have remained for long undimmed by the mists of earth.

They who remember them at that time speak of them in hushed tones, as one speaks of visions. It would almost seem as though from their faces in those days there shone a radiance, as though in their voices dwelt a tenderness beyond the tenderness of man.

They seem never to rest, never to weary. Day and night, through that little stricken world, they come and go, bearing healing and peace, till at last the plague, like some gorged beast of prey, slinks slowly back towards its lair, and men raise their heads and breathe.

One afternoon, returning from a somewhat longer round than usual, John feels a weariness creeping into his limbs, and quickens his step, eager to reach home and rest. Anne, who has been up all the previous night, is asleep, and not wishing to disturb her, he goes into the dining-room and sits down in the easy chair before the fire. The room strikes cold. He stirs the logs, but they give out no greater heat.

He draws his chair right in front of them, and sits leaning over them with his feet on the hearth and his hands outstretched towards the blaze; yet he still shivers.

Twilight fills the room and deepens into dusk. He wonders listlessly how it is that Time seems to be moving with such swift strides. After a while he hears a voice close to him, speaking in a slow, monotonous tone--a voice curiously familiar to him, though he cannot tell to whom it belongs. He does not turn his head, but sits listening to it drowsily. It is talking about tallow: one hundred and ninety-four casks of tallow, and they must all stand one inside the other. It cannot be done, the voice complains pathetically. They will not go inside each other. It is no good pushing them. See! they only roll out again.

The voice grows wearily fretful. Oh! why do they persist when they see it is impossible? What fools they all are!

Suddenly he recollects the voice, and starts up and stares wildly about him, trying to remember where he is. With a fierce straining of his will he grips the brain that is slipping away from him, and holds it. As soon as he feels sure of himself he steals out of the room and down the stairs.

In the hall he stands listening; the house is very silent. He goes to the head of the stairs leading to the kitchen and calls softly to the old housekeeper, and she comes up to him, panting and grunting as she climbs each step. Keeping some distance from her, he asks in a whisper where Anne is. The woman answers that she is in the hospital.

"Tell her I have been called away suddenly on business," he says, speaking in quick, low tones: "I shall be away for some days. Tell her to leave here and return home immediately. They can do without her here now. Tell her to go back home at once. I will join her there."

He moves toward the door but stops and faces round again.

"Tell her I beg and entreat her not to stop in this place an hour longer. There is nothing to keep her now. It is all over: there is nothing that cannot be done by any one. Tell her she must go home-- this very night. Tell her if she loves me to leave this place at once."

The woman, a little bewildered by his vehemence, promises, and disappears down the stairs. He takes his hat and cloak from the chair on which he had thrown them, and turns once more to cross the hall. As he does so, the door opens and Anne enters.

He darts back into the shadow, squeezing himself against the wall. Anne calls to him laughingly, then, as he does not answer, with a frightened accent:

"John,--John, dear. Was not that you? Are not you there?"

He holds his breath, and crouches still closer into the dark corner; and Anne, thinking she must have been mistaken in the dim light, passes him and goes upstairs.

Then he creeps stealthily to the door, lets himself out and closes it softly behind him.

After the lapse of a few minutes the old housekeeper plods upstairs and delivers John's message. Anne, finding it altogether incomprehensible, subjects the poor dame to severe examination, but fails to elicit anything further. What is the meaning of it? What "business" can have compelled John, who for ten weeks has never let the word escape his lips, to leave her like this--without a word! without a kiss! Then suddenly she remembers the incident of a few moments ago, when she had called to him, thinking she saw him, and he did not answer; and the whole truth strikes her full in the heart.

She refastens the bonnet-strings she has been slowly untying, and goes down and out into the wet street.

She makes her way rapidly to the house of the only doctor resident in the neighbourhood--a big, brusque-mannered man, who throughout these terrible two months has been their chief stay and help. He meets her on her entrance with an embarrassed air that tells its own tale, and at once renders futile his clumsy attempts at acting:--

How should he know where John is? Who told her John had the fever--a great, strong, hulking fellow like that? She has been working too hard, and has got fever on the brain. She must go straight back home, or she will be having it herself. She is more likely to take it than John.

Anne, waiting till he has finished jerking out sentences while stamping up and down the room, says gently, taking no notice of his denials,--"If you will not tell me I must find out from some one else--that is all." Then, her quick eyes noting his momentary hesitation, she lays her little hand on his rough paw, and, with the shamelessness of a woman who loves deeply, wheedles everything out of him that he has promised to keep secret.

He stops her, however, as she is leaving the room. "Don't go in to him now," he says; "he will worry about you. Wait till to-morrow."

So, while John lies counting endless casks of tallow, Anne sits by his side, tending her last "case."

Often in his delirium he calls her name, and she takes his fevered hand in hers and holds it, and he falls asleep.

Each morning the doctor comes and looks at him, asks a few questions and gives a few commonplace directions, but makes no comment. It would be idle his attempting to deceive her.

The days move slowly through the darkened room. Anne watches his thin hands grow thinner, his sunken eyes grow bigger; yet remains strangely calm, almost contented.

Very near the end there comes an hour when John wakes as from a dream, and remembers all things clearly.

He looks at her half gratefully, half reproachfully.

"Anne, why are you here?" he asks, in a low, laboured voice. "Did they not give you my message?"

For answer she turns her deep eyes upon him.

"Would you have gone away and left me here to die?" she questions him, with a faint smile.

She bends her head down nearer to him, so that her soft hair falls about his face.

"Our lives were one, dear," she whispers to him. "I could not have lived without you; God knew that. We shall be together always."

She kisses him, and laying his head upon her breast, softly strokes it as she might a child's; and he puts his weak arms around her.

Later on she feels them growing cold about her, and lays him gently back upon the bed, looks for the last time into his eyes, then draws the lids down over them.

His people ask that they may bury him in the churchyard hard by, so that he may always be among them; and, Anne consenting, they do all things needful with their own hands, wishful that no unloving labour may be mingled with their work. They lay him close to the porch, where, going in and out the church, their feet will pass near to him; and one among them who is cunning with the graver's chisel shapes the stone.

At the head he carves in bas-relief the figure of the good Samaritan tending the brother fallen by the way, and underneath the letters, "In Remembrance of John Ingerfield."

He thinks to put a verse of Scripture immediately after; but the gruff doctor says, "Better leave a space, in case you want to add another name."

So the stone remains a little while unfinished; till the same hand carves thereon, a few weeks later, "And of Anne, his Wife."

THE WOMAN OF THE SAETER

Wild-reindeer stalking is hardly so exciting a sport as the evening's verandah talk in Norroway hotels would lead the trustful traveller to suppose. Under the charge of your guide, a very young man with the dreamy, wistful eyes of those who live in valleys, you leave the farmstead early in the forenoon, arriving towards twilight at the desolate hut which, for so long as you remain upon the uplands, will be your somewhat cheerless headquarters.

Next morning, in the chill, mist-laden dawn, you rise; and, after a breakfast of coffee and dried fish, shoulder your Remington, and step forth silently into the raw, damp air; the guide locking the door behind you, the key grating harshly in the rusty lock.

For hour after hour you toil over the steep, stony ground, or wind through the pines, speaking in whispers, lest your voice reach the quick ears of your prey, that keeps its head ever pressed against the wind. Here and there, in the hollows of the hills lie wide fields of snow, over which you pick your steps thoughtfully, listening to the smothered thunder of the torrent, tunnelling its way beneath your feet, and wondering whether the frozen arch above it be at all points as firm as is desirable. Now and again, as in single file you walk cautiously along some jagged ridge, you catch glimpses of the green world, three thousand feet below you; though you gaze not long upon the view, for your attention is chiefly directed to watching the footprints of the guide, lest by deviating to the right or left you find yourself at one stride back in the valley--or, to be more correct, are found there.

These things you do, and as exercise they are healthful and invigorating. But a reindeer you never see, and unless, overcoming the prejudices of your British-bred conscience, you care to take an occasional pop at a fox, you had better have left your rifle at the hut, and, instead, have brought a stick which would have been helpful. Notwithstanding which the guide continues sanguine, and in broken English, helped out by stirring gesture, tells of the terrible slaughter generally done by sportsmen under his superintendence, and of the vast herds that generally infest these fields; and when you grow sceptical upon the subject of Reins he whispers alluringly of Bears.

Once in a way you will come across a track, and will follow it breathlessly for hours, and it will lead to a sheer precipice. Whether the explanation is suicide, or a reprehensible tendency on the part of the animal towards practical joking, you are left to decide for yourself. Then, with many rough miles between you and your rest, you abandon the chase.

But I speak from personal experience merely.

All day long we had tramped through the pitiless rain, stopping only for an hour at noon to eat some dried venison and smoke a pipe beneath the shelter of an overhanging cliff. Soon afterwards Michael knocked over a ryper (a bird that will hardly take the trouble to hop out of your way) with his gun-barrel, which incident cheered us a little; and, later on, our flagging spirits were still further revived by the discovery of apparently very recent deer-tracks. These we followed, forgetful, in our eagerness, of the lengthening distance back to the hut, of the fading daylight, of the gathering mist. The track led us higher and higher, farther and farther into the mountains, until on the shores of a desolate rock-bound vand it abruptly ended, and we stood staring at one another, and the snow began to fall.

Unless in the next half-hour we could chance upon a saeter, this meant passing the night upon the mountain. Michael and I looked at the guide; but though, with characteristic Norwegian sturdiness, he put a bold face upon it, we could see that in that deepening darkness he knew no more than we did. Wasting no time on words, we made straight for the nearest point of descent, knowing that any human habitation must be far below us.

Down we scrambled, heedless of torn clothes and bleeding hands, the darkness pressing closer round us. Then suddenly it became black--black as pitch--and we could only hear each other. Another step might mean death. We stretched out our hands, and felt each other. Why we spoke in whispers, I do not know, but we seemed afraid of our own voices. We agreed there was nothing for it but to stop where we were till morning, clinging to the short grass; so we lay there side by side, for what may have been five minutes or may have been an hour. Then, attempting to turn, I lost my grip and rolled. I made convulsive efforts to clutch the ground, but the incline was too steep. How far I fell I could not say, but at last something stopped me. I felt it cautiously with my foot: it did not yield, so I twisted myself round and touched it with my hand. It seemed planted firmly in the earth. I passed my arm along to the right, then to the left. I shouted with joy. It was a fence.

Rising and groping about me, I found an opening, and passed through, and crept forward with palms outstretched until I touched the logs of a hut; then, feeling my way round, discovered the door, and knocked. There came no response, so I knocked louder; then pushed, and the heavy woodwork yielded, groaning. But the darkness within was even darker than the darkness without. The others had contrived to crawl down and join me. Michael struck a wax vesta and held it up, and slowly the room came out of the darkness and stood round us.

Then something rather startling happened. Giving one swift glance about him, our guide uttered a cry, and rushed out into the night. We followed to the door, and called after him, but only a voice came to us out of the blackness, and the only words that we could catch, shrieked back in terror, were: "*Saetervronen! Saetervronen!*" ("The woman of the saeter").

"Some foolish superstition about the place, I suppose," said Michael. "In these mountain solitudes men breed ghosts for company. Let us make a fire. Perhaps, when he sees the light, his desire for food and shelter may get the better of his fears."

We felt about in the small enclosure round the house, and gathered juniper and birch-twigs, and kindled a fire upon the open stove built in the corner of the room. Fortunately, we had some dried reindeer and bread in our bag, and on that and the ryper and the contents of our flasks we supped. Afterwards, to while away the time, we made an inspection of the strange eyrie we had lighted on.

It was an old log-built saeter. Some of these mountain farmsteads are as old as the stone ruins of other countries. Carvings of strange beasts and demons were upon its blackened rafters, and on the lintel, in runic letters, ran this legend: "Hund built me in the days of Haarfager." The house consisted of two large apartments. Originally, no doubt, these had been separate dwellings standing beside one another, but they were now connected by a long, low gallery. Most of the scanty furniture was almost as ancient as the walls themselves, but many articles of a comparatively recent date had been added. All was now, however, rotting and falling into decay.

The place appeared to have been deserted suddenly by its last occupants. Household utensils lay as they were left, rust and dirt encrusted on them. An open book, limp and mildewed, lay face downwards on the table, while many others were scattered about both rooms, together with much paper, scored with faded ink. The curtains hung in shreds about the windows; a woman's cloak, of an antiquated fashion, drooped from a nail behind the door. In an oak chest we found a tumbled heap of yellow letters. They were of various dates, extending over a period of four months; and with them, apparently intended to receive them, lay a large envelope, inscribed with an address in London that has since disappeared.

Strong curiosity overcoming faint scruples, we read them by the dull glow of the burning juniper twigs, and, as we lay aside the last of them, there rose from the depths below us a wailing cry, and all night long it rose and died away, and rose again, and died away again; whether born of our brain or of some human thing, God knows.

And these, a little altered and shortened, are the letters:--

Extract from first letter:

"I cannot tell you, my dear Joyce, what a haven of peace this place is to me after the racket and fret of town. I am almost quite recovered already, and am growing stronger every day; and, joy of joys, my brain has come back to me, fresher and more vigorous, I think, for its holiday. In this silence and solitude my thoughts flow freely, and the difficulties of my task are disappearing as if by magic. We are perched upon a tiny plateau halfway up the mountain. On one side the rock rises almost perpendicularly, piercing the sky; while on the other, two thousand feet below us, the torrent hurls itself into the black waters of the fiord. The house consists of two rooms--or, rather, it is two cabins connected by a passage. The larger one we use as a living room, and the other is our sleeping apartment. We have no servant, but do everything for ourselves. I fear sometimes Muriel must find it lonely. The nearest human habitation is eight miles away, across the mountain, and not a soul comes near us. I spend as much time as I can with her, however, during the day, and make up for it by working at night after she has gone to sleep; and when I question her, she only laughs, and answers that she loves to have me all to herself. (Here you will smile cynically, I know, and say, 'Humph, I wonder will she say the same when they have been married six years instead of six months.') At the rate I am working now I shall have finished my first volume by the spring, and then, my dear fellow, you must try and come over, and we will walk and talk together 'amid these storm-reared temples of the gods.' I have felt a new man since I arrived here. Instead of having to 'cudgel my brains,' as we say, thoughts crowd upon me. This work will make my name."

Part of the third letter, the second being mere talk about the book (a history apparently) that the man was writing:

"MY DEAR JOYCE,--I have written you two letters--this will make the third--but have been unable to post them. Every day I have been expecting a visit from some farmer or villager, for the Norwegians are kindly people towards strangers--to say nothing of the inducements of trade. A fortnight having passed, however, and the commissariat question having become serious, I yesterday set out before dawn, and made my way down to the valley; and this gives me something to tell you. Nearing the village, I met a peasant woman. To my intense surprise, instead of returning my salutation, she stared at me, as if I were some wild animal, and shrank away from me as far as the width of the road would permit. In the village the same experience awaited me. The children ran from me, the people avoided me. At last a grey-haired old man appeared to take pity on me, and from him I learnt the explanation of the mystery. It seems there is a strange superstition attaching to this house in which we are living. My things were brought up here by the two men who accompanied me from Drontheim, but the natives are afraid to go near the place, and prefer to keep as far as possible from any one connected with it.

"The story is that the house was built by one Hund, 'a maker of runes' (one of the old saga writers, no doubt), who lived here with his young wife. All went peacefully until, unfortunately for him, a certain maiden stationed at a neighbouring saeter grew to love him.

"Forgive me if I am telling you what you know, but a 'saeter' is the name given to the upland pastures to which, during the summer, are sent the cattle, generally under the charge of one or more of the maids. Here for three months these girls will live in their lonely huts, entirely shut off from the world. Customs change little in this land. Two or three such stations are within climbing distance of this house, at this day, looked after by the farmers' daughters, as in the days of Hund, 'maker of runes.'

"Every night, by devious mountain paths, the woman would come and tap lightly at Hund's door. Hund had built himself two cabins, one behind the other (these are now, as I think I have explained to you, connected by a passage); the smaller one was the homestead; in the other he carved and wrote, so that while the young wife slept the 'maker of runes' and the saeter woman sat whispering.

"One night, however, the wife learnt all things, but said no word.

Then, as now, the ravine in front of the enclosure was crossed by a slight bridge of planks, and over this bridge the woman of the saeter passed and repassed each night. On a day when Hund had gone down to fish in the fiord, the wife took an axe, and hacked and hewed at the bridge, yet it still looked firm and solid; and that night, as Hund sat waiting in his workshop, there struck upon his ears a piercing cry, and a crashing of logs and rolling rock, and then again the dull roaring of the torrent far below.

"But the woman did not die unavenged; for that winter a man, skating far down the fiord, noticed a curious object embedded in the ice; and when, stooping, he looked closer, he saw two corpses, one gripping the other by the throat, and the bodies were the bodies of Hund and his young wife.

"Since then, they say, the woman of the saeter haunts Hund's house, and if she sees a light within she taps upon the door, and no man may keep her out. Many, at different times, have tried to occupy the house, but strange tales are told of them. 'Men do not live at Hund's saeter,' said my old grey-haired friend, concluding his tale,-- 'they die there.'

"I have persuaded some of the braver of the villagers to bring what provisions and other necessaries we require up to a plateau about a mile from the house and leave them there. That is the most I have been able to do. It comes somewhat as a shock to one to find men and women--fairly educated and intelligent as many of them are--slaves to fears that one would expect a child to laugh at. But there is no reasoning with superstition."

Extract from the same letter, but from a part seemingly written a day or two later:

"At home I should have forgotten such a tale an hour after I had heard it, but these mountain fastnesses seem strangely fit to be the last stronghold of the supernatural. The woman haunts me already. At night instead of working, I find myself listening for her tapping at the door; and yesterday an incident occurred that makes me fear for my own common sense. I had gone out for a long walk alone, and the twilight was thickening into darkness as I neared home. Suddenly looking up from my reverie, I saw, standing on a knoll the other side of the ravine, the figure of a woman. She held a cloak about her head, and I could not see her face. I took off my cap, and called out a good-night to her, but she never moved or spoke. Then--God knows why, for my brain was full of other thoughts at the time--a clammy chill crept over me, and my tongue grew dry and parched. I stood rooted to the spot, staring at her across the yawning gorge that divided us; and slowly she moved away, and passed into the gloom, and I continued my way. I have said nothing to Muriel, and shall not. The effect the story has had upon myself warns me not to do so."

From a letter dated eleven days later:

"She has come. I have known she would, since that evening I saw her on the mountain; and last night she came, and we have sat and looked into each other's eyes. You will say, of course, that I am mad--that I have not recovered from my fever--that I have been working too hard--that I have heard a foolish tale, and that it has filled my over-strung brain with foolish fancies: I have told myself all that. But the thing came, nevertheless--a creature of flesh and blood? a creature of air? a creature of my own imagination?--what matter? it was real to me.

"It came last night, as I sat working, alone. Each night I have waited for it, listened for it--longed for it, I know now. I heard the passing of its feet upon the bridge, the tapping of its hand upon the door, three times--tap, tap, tap. I felt my loins grow cold, and a pricking pain about my head; and I gripped my chair with both hands, and waited, and again there came the tapping--tap, tap, tap. I rose and slipped the bolt of the door leading to the other room, and again I waited, and again there came the tapping--tap, tap, tap. Then I opened the heavy outer door, and the wind rushed past me, scattering my papers, and the woman entered in, and I closed the door behind her. She threw her hood back from her head, and unwound a kerchief from about her neck, and laid it on the table. Then she crossed and sat before the fire, and I noticed her bare feet were damp with the night dew.

"I stood over against her and gazed at her, and she smiled at me--a strange, wicked smile, but I could have laid my soul at her feet. She never spoke or moved, and neither did I feel the need of spoken words, for I understood the meaning of those upon the Mount when they said, 'Let us make here tabernacles: it is good for us to be here.'

"How long a time passed thus I do not know, but suddenly the woman held her hand up, listening, and there came a faint sound from the other room. Then swiftly she drew her hood about her face and passed out, closing the door softly behind her; and I drew back the bolt of the inner door and waited, and hearing nothing more, sat down, and must have fallen asleep in my chair.

"I awoke, and instantly there flashed through my mind the thought of the kerchief the woman had left behind her, and I started from my chair to hide it. But the table was already laid for breakfast, and my wife sat with her elbows on the table and her head between her hands, watching me with a look in her eyes that was new to me.

"She kissed me, though her lips were cold; and I argued to myself that the whole thing must have been a dream. But later in the day, passing the open door when her back was towards me, I saw her take the kerchief from a locked chest and look at it.

"I have told myself it must have been a kerchief of her own, and that all the rest has been my imagination; that, if not, then my strange visitant was no spirit, but a woman; and that, if human thing knows human thing, it was no creature of flesh and blood that sat beside me last night. Besides, what woman would she be? The nearest saeter is a three-hours' climb to a strong man, and the paths are dangerous even in daylight: what woman would have found them in the night? What woman would have chilled the air around her, and have made the blood flow cold through all my veins? Yet if she come again I will speak to her. I will stretch out my hand and see whether she be mortal thing or only air."

The fifth letter:

"MY DEAR JOYCE,--Whether your eyes will ever see these letters is doubtful. From this place I shall never send them. They would read to you as the ravings of a madman. If ever I return to England I may one day show them to you, but when I do it will be when I, with you, can laugh over them. At present I write them merely to hide away,-- putting the words down on paper saves my screaming them aloud.

"She comes each night now, taking the same seat beside the embers, and fixing upon me those eyes, with the hell-light in them, that burn into my brain; and at rare times she smiles, and all my being passes out of me, and is hers. I make no attempt to work. I sit listening for her footsteps on the creaking bridge, for the rustling of her feet upon the grass, for the tapping of her hand upon the door. No word is uttered between us. Each day I say: 'When she comes to-night I will speak to her. I will stretch out my hand and touch her.' Yet when she enters, all thought and will goes out from me.

"Last night, as I stood gazing at her, my soul filled with her wondrous beauty as a lake with moonlight, her lips parted, and she started from her chair; and, turning, I thought I saw a white face pressed against the window, but as I looked it vanished. Then she drew her cloak about her, and passed out. I slid back the bolt I always draw now, and stole into the other room, and, taking down the lantern, held it above the bed. But Muriel's eyes were closed as if in sleep."

Extract from the sixth letter:

"It is not the night I fear, but the day. I hate the sight of this woman with whom I live, whom I call 'wife.' I shrink from the blow of her cold lips, the curse of her stony eyes. She has seen, she has learnt; I feel it, I know it. Yet she winds her arms around my neck, and calls me sweetheart, and smoothes my hair with her soft, false hands. We speak mocking words of love to one another, but I know her cruel eyes are ever following me. She is plotting her revenge, and I hate her, I hate her, I hate her!"

Part of the seventh letter:

"This morning I went down to the fiord. I told her I should not be back until the evening. She stood by the door watching me until we were mere specks to one another, and a promontory of the mountain shut me from view. Then, turning aside from the track, I made my way, running and stumbling over the jagged ground, round to the other side of the mountain, and began to climb again. It was slow, weary work. Often I had to go miles out of my road to avoid a ravine, and twice I reached a high point only to have to descend again. But at length I crossed the ridge, and crept down to a spot from where, concealed, I could spy upon my own house. She--my wife--stood by the flimsy bridge. A short hatchet, such as butchers use, was in her hand. She leant against a pine trunk, with her arm behind her, as one stands whose back aches with long stooping in some cramped position; and even at that distance I could see the cruel smile about her lips.

"Then I recrossed the ridge, and crawled down again, and, waiting until evening, walked slowly up the path. As I came in view of the house she saw me, and waved her handkerchief to me, and in answer I waved my hat, and shouted curses at her that the wind whirled away into the torrent. She met me with a kiss, and I breathed no hint to her that I had seen. Let her devil's work remain undisturbed. Let it prove to me what manner of thing this is that haunts me. If it be a spirit, then the bridge wilt bear it safely; if it be woman--

"But I dismiss the thought. If it be human thing, why does it sit gazing at me, never speaking? why does my tongue refuse to question it? why does all power forsake me in its presence, so that I stand as in a dream? Yet if it be spirit, why do I hear the passing of her feet? and why does the night-rain glisten on her hair?

"I force myself back into my chair. It is far into the night, and I am alone, waiting, listening. If it be spirit, she will come to me; and if it be woman, I shall hear her cry above the storm--unless it be a demon mocking me.

"I have heard the cry. It rose, piercing and shrill, above the storm, above the riving and rending of the bridge, above the downward crashing of the logs and loosened stones. I hear it as I listen now. It is cleaving its way upward from the depths below. It is wailing through the room as I sit writing.

"I have crawled upon my belly to the utmost edge of the still standing pier, until I could feel with my hand the jagged splinters left by the fallen planks, and have looked down. But the chasm was full to the brim with darkness. I shouted, but the wind shook my voice into mocking laughter. I sit here, feebly striking at the madness that is creeping nearer and nearer to me. I tell myself the whole thing is but the fever in my brain. The bridge was rotten. The storm was strong. The cry is but a single one among the many voices of the mountain. Yet still I listen; and it rises, clear and shrill, above the moaning of the pines, above the sobbing of the waters. It beats like blows upon my skull, and I know that she will never come again."

Extract from the last letter:

"I shall address an envelope to you, and leave it among these letters. Then, should I never come back, some chance wanderer may one day find and post them to you, and you will know.

"My books and writings remain untouched. We sit together of a night--this woman I call 'wife' and I--she holding in her hands some knitted thing that never grows longer by a single stitch, and I with a volume before me that is ever open at the same page. And day and night we watch each other stealthily, moving to and fro about the silent house; and at times, looking round swiftly, I catch the smile upon her lips before she has time to smooth it away.

"We speak like strangers about this and that, making talk to hide our thoughts. We make a pretence of busying ourselves about whatever will help us to keep apart from one another.

"At night, sitting here between the shadows and the dull glow of the smouldering twigs, I sometimes think I hear the tapping I have learnt to listen for, and I start from my seat, and softly open the door and look out. But only the Night stands there. Then I close-to the latch, and she--the living woman--asks me in her purring voice what sound I heard, hiding a smile as she stoops low over her work; and I answer lightly, and, moving towards her, put my arm about her, feeling her softness and her suppleness, and wondering, supposing I held her close to me with one arm while pressing her from me with the other, how long before I should hear the cracking of her bones.

"For here, amid these savage solitudes, I also am grown savage. The old primeval passions of love and hate stir within me, and they are fierce and cruel and strong, beyond what you men of the later ages could understand. The culture of the centuries has fallen from me as a flimsy garment whirled away by the mountain wind; the old savage instincts of the race lie bare. One day I shall twine my fingers about her full white throat, and her eyes will slowly come towards me, and her lips will part, and the red tongue creep out; and backwards, step by step, I shall push her before me, gazing the while upon her bloodless face, and it will be my turn to smile. Backwards through the open door, backwards along the garden path between the juniper bushes, backwards till her heels are overhanging the ravine, and she grips life with nothing but her little toes, I shall force her, step by step, before me. Then I shall lean forward, closer, closer, till I kiss her purpling lips, and down, down, down, past the startled sea- birds, past the white spray of the foss, past the downward peeping pines, down, down, down, we will go together, till we find the thing that lies sleeping beneath the waters of the fiord."

With these words ended the last letter, unsigned. At the first streak of dawn we left the house, and, after much wandering, found our way back to the valley. But of our guide we heard no news. Whether he remained still upon the mountain, or whether by some false step he had perished upon that night, we never learnt.

VARIETY PATTER

My first appearance at a Music Hall was in the year one thousand eight hundred and s---. Well, I would rather not mention the exact date. I was fourteen at the time. It was during the Christmas holidays, and my aunt had given me five shillings to go and see Phelps--I think it was Phelps--in *Coriolanus*--I think it was *Coriolanus*. Anyhow, it was to see a high-class and improving entertainment, I know.

I suggested that I should induce young Skegson, who lived in our road, to go with me. Skegson is a barrister now, and could not tell you the difference between a knave of clubs and a club of knaves. A few years hence he will, if he works hard, be innocent enough for a judge. But at the period of which I speak he was a red-haired boy of worldly tastes, notwithstanding which I loved him as a brother. My dear mother wished to see him before consenting to the arrangement, so as to be able to form her own opinion as to whether he was a fit and proper companion for me; and, accordingly, he was invited to tea. He came, and made a most favourable impression upon both my mother and my aunt. He had a way of talking about the advantages of application to study in early life, and the duties of youth towards those placed in authority over it, that won for him much esteem in grown-up circles. The spirit of the Bar had descended upon Skegson at a very early period of his career.

My aunt, indeed, was so much pleased with him that she gave him two shillings towards his own expenses ("sprung half a dollar" was how he explained the transaction when we were outside), and commended me to his especial care.

Skegson was very silent during the journey. An idea was evidently maturing in his mind. At the Angel he stopped and said: "Look here, I'll tell you what we'll do. Don't let's go and see that rot. Let's go to a Music Hall."

I gasped for breath. I had heard of Music Halls. A stout lady had denounced them across our dinner table on one occasion--fixing the while a steely eye upon her husband, who sat opposite and seemed uncomfortable--as low, horrid places, where people smoked and drank, and wore short skirts, and had added an opinion that they ought to be put down by the police--whether the skirts or the halls she did not explain. I also recollected that our charwoman, whose son had lately left London for a protracted stay in Devonshire, had, in conversation with my mother, dated his downfall from the day when he first visited one of these places; and likewise that Mrs. Philcox's nursemaid, upon her confessing that she had spent an evening at one with her young man, had been called a shameless hussy, and summarily dismissed as being no longer a fit associate for the baby.

But the spirit of lawlessness was strong within me in those days, so that I hearkened to the voice of Skegson, the tempter, and he lured my feet from the paths that led to virtue and Sadler's Wells, and we wandered into the broad and crowded ways that branch off from the Angel towards Merry Islington.

Skegson insisted that we should do the thing in style, so we stopped at a shop near the Agricultural Hall and purchased some big cigars. A huge card in the window claimed for these that they were "the most satisfactory twopenny smokes in London." I smoked two of them during the evening, and never felt more satisfied--using the word in its true sense, as implying that a person has had enough of a thing, and does not desire any more of it, just then--in all my life. Where we went, and what we saw, my memory is not very clear upon. We sat at a little marble table. I know it was marble because it was so hard, and cool to the head. From out of the smoky mist a ponderous creature of strange, undefined shape floated heavily towards us, and deposited a squat tumbler in front of me containing a pale yellowish liquor, which subsequent investigation has led me to believe must have been Scotch whisky. It seemed to me then the most nauseous stuff I had ever swallowed. It is curious to look back and notice how one's tastes change.

I reached home very late and very sick. That was my first dissipation, and, as a lesson, it has been of more practical use to me than all the good books and sermons in the world could have been. I can remember to this day standing in the middle of the room in my nightshirt, trying to catch my bed as it came round.

Next morning I confessed everything to my mother, and, for several months afterwards, was a reformed character. Indeed, the pendulum of my conscience swung too far the other way, and I grew exaggeratedly remorseful and unhealthily moral.

There was published in those days, for the edification of young people, a singularly pessimistic periodical, entitled *The Children's Band of Hope Review*. It was a magazine much in favour among grown-up people, and a bound copy of Vol. IX. had lately been won by my sister as a prize for punctuality (I fancy she must have exhausted all the virtue she ever possessed, in that direction, upon the winning of that prize. At all events, I have noticed no ostentatious display of the quality in her later life.) I had formerly expressed contempt for this book, but now, in my regenerate state, I took a morbid pleasure in poring over its denunciations of sin and sinners. There was one picture in it that appeared peculiarly applicable to myself. It represented a gaudily costumed young man, standing on the topmost of three steep steps, smoking a large cigar. Behind him was a very small church, and below, a bright and not altogether uninviting looking hell. The picture was headed "The Three Steps to Ruin," and the three stairs were labelled respectively "Smoking," "Drinking," "Gambling." I had already travelled two-thirds of the road! Was I going all the way, or should I be able to retrace those steps? I used to lie awake at night and think about it till I grew half crazy. Alas! since then I have completed the descent, so where my future will be spent I do not care to think.

Another picture in the book that troubled me was the frontispiece. This was a highly-coloured print, illustrating the broad and narrow ways. The narrow way led upward past a Sunday-school and a lion to a city in the clouds. This city was referred to in the accompanying letterpress as a place of "Rest and Peace," but inasmuch as the town was represented in the illustration as surrounded by a perfect mob of angels, each one blowing a trumpet twice his own size, and obviously blowing it for all he was worth, a certain confusion of ideas would seem to have crept into the allegory.

The other path--the "broad way"--which ended in what at first glance appeared to be a highly successful display of fireworks, started from the door of a tavern, and led past a Music Hall, on the steps of which stood a gentleman smoking a cigar. All the wicked people in this book smoked cigars--all except one young man who had killed his mother and died raving mad. He had gone astray on short pipes.

This made it uncomfortably clear to me which direction I had chosen, and I was greatly alarmed, until, on examining the picture more closely, I noticed, with much satisfaction, that about midway the two paths were connected by a handy little bridge, by the use of which it seemed feasible, starting on the one path and ending up on the other, to combine the practical advantages of both roads. From subsequent observation I have come to the conclusion that a good many people have made a note of that little bridge.

My own belief in the possibility of such convenient compromise must, I fear, have led to an ethical relapse, for there recurs to my mind a somewhat painful scene of a few months' later date, in which I am seeking to convince a singularly unresponsive landed proprietor that my presence in his orchard is solely and entirely due to my having unfortunately lost my way.

It was not until I was nearly seventeen that the idea occurred to me to visit a Music Hall again. Then, having regard to my double capacity of "Man About Town" and journalist (for I had written a letter to *The Era*, complaining of the way pit doors were made to open, and it had been inserted), I felt I had no longer any right to neglect acquaintanceship with so important a feature in the life of the people. Accordingly, one Saturday night, I wended my way to the "Pav."; and there the first person that I ran against was my uncle. He laid a heavy hand upon my shoulder, and asked me, in severe tones, what I was doing there. I felt this to be an awkward question, for it would have been useless trying to make him understand my real motives (one's own relations are never sympathetic), and I was somewhat nonplussed for an answer, until the reflection occurred to me: What was *he* doing there? This riddle I, in my turn, propounded to him, with the result that we entered into treaty, by the terms of which it was agreed that no future reference should be made to the meeting by either of us--especially not in the presence of my aunt--and the compact was ratified according to the usual custom, my uncle paying the necessary expenses.

In those days, we sat, some four or six of us, round a little table, on which were placed our drinks. Now we have to balance them upon a narrow ledge; and ladies, as they pass, dip the ends of their cloaks into them, and gentlemen stir them up for us with the ferrules of their umbrellas, or else sweep them off into our laps with their coat tails, saying as they do so, "Oh, I beg your pardon."

Also, in those days, there were "chairmen"--affable gentlemen, who would drink anything at anybody's expense, and drink any quantity of it, and never seem to get any fuller. I was introduced to a Music Hall chairman once, and when I said to him, "What is your drink?" he took up the "list of beverages" that lay before him, and, opening it, waved his hand lightly across its entire contents, from clarets, past champagnes and spirits, down to liqueurs. "That's my drink, my boy," said he. There was nothing narrow-minded or exclusive about his tastes.

It was the chairman's duty to introduce the artists. "Ladies and gentlemen," he would shout, in a voice that united the musical characteristics of a foghorn and a steam saw, "Miss 'Enerietta Montressor, the popular serio-comic, will now happear." These announcements were invariably received with great applause by the chairman himself, and generally with chilling indifference by the rest of the audience.

It was also the privilege of the chairman to maintain order, and reprimand evil-doers. This he usually did very effectively, employing for the purpose language both fit and forcible. One chairman that I remember seemed, however, to be curiously deficient in the necessary qualities for this part of his duty. He was a mild and sleepy little man, and, unfortunately, he had to preside over an exceptionally rowdy audience at a small hall in the South-East district. On the night that I was present, there occurred a great disturbance. "Joss Jessop, the Monarch of Mirth," a gentleman evidently high in local request was, for some reason or other, not forthcoming, and in his place the management proposed to offer a female performer on the zithern, one Signorina Ballatino.

The little chairman made the announcement in a nervous, deprecatory tone, as if he were rather ashamed of it himself. "Ladies and gentlemen," he began,--the poor are staunch sticklers for etiquette: I overheard a small child explaining to her mother one night in Three Colts Street, Limehouse, that she could not get into the house because there was a "lady" on the doorstep, drunk,--"Signorina Ballatino, the world-renowned--"

Here a voice from the gallery requested to know what had become of "Old Joss," and was greeted by loud cries of "'Ear, 'ear."

The chairman, ignoring the interruption, continued:

"--the world-renowned performer on the zither--"

"On the whoter?" came in tones of plaintive inquiry from the back of the hall.

"*Hon* the zither," retorted the chairman, waxing mildly indignant; he meant zithern, but he called it a zither. "A hinstrument well-known to anybody as 'as 'ad any learning."

This sally was received with much favour, and a gentleman who claimed to be acquainted with the family history of the interrupter begged the chairman to excuse that ill-bred person on the ground that his mother used to get drunk with the twopence a week and never sent him to school.

Cheered by this breath of popularity, our little president endeavoured to complete his introduction of the Signorina. He again repeated that she was the world-renowned performer on the zithern; and, undeterred by the audible remark of a lady in the pit to the effect that she'd "never 'eard on 'er," added:

"She will now, ladies and gentlemen, with your kind permission, give you examples of the--"

"Blow yer zither!" here cried out the gentleman who had started the agitation; "we want Joss Jessop."

This was the signal for much cheering and shrill whistling, in the midst of which a wag with a piping voice suggested as a reason for the favourite's non-appearance that he had not been paid his last week's salary.

A temporary lull occurred at this point; and the chairman, seizing the opportunity to complete his oft-impeded speech, suddenly remarked, "songs of the Sunny South"; and immediately sat down and began hammering upon the table.

Then Signora Ballatino, clothed in the costume of the Sunny South, where clothes are less essential than in these colder climes, skipped airily forward, and was most ungallantly greeted with a storm of groans and hisses. Her beloved instrument was unfeelingly alluded to as a pie-dish, and she was advised to take it back and get the penny on it. The chairman, addressed by his Christian name of "Jimmee," was told to lie down and let her sing him to sleep. Every time she attempted to start playing, shouts were raised for Joss.

At length the chairman, overcoming his evident disinclination to take any sort of hand whatever in the game, rose and gently hinted at the desirability of silence. The suggestion not meeting with any support, he proceeded to adopt sterner measures. He addressed himself personally to the ringleader of the rioters, the man who had first championed the cause of the absent Joss. This person was a brawny individual, who, judging from appearances, followed in his business hours the calling of a coalheaver. "Yes, sir," said the chairman, pointing a finger towards him, where he sat in the front row of the gallery; "you, sir, in the flannel shirt. I can see you. Will you allow this lady to give her entertainment?"

"No," answered he of the coalheaving profession, in stentorian tones.

"Then, sir," said the little chairman, working himself up into a state suggestive of Jove about to launch a thunderbolt--"then, sir, all I can say is that you are no gentleman."

This was a little too much, or rather a good deal too little, for the Signora Ballatino. She had hitherto been standing in a meek attitude of pathetic appeal, wearing a fixed smile of ineffable sweetness but she evidently felt that she could go a bit farther than that herself, even if she was a lady. Calling the chairman "an old messer," and telling him for Gawd's sake to shut up if that was all he could do for his living, she came down to the front, and took the case into her own hands.

She did not waste time on the rest of the audience. She went direct for that coalheaver, and thereupon ensued a slanging match the memory of which sends a trill of admiration through me even to this day. It was a battle worthy of the gods. He was a heaver of coals, quick and ready beyond his kind. During many years sojourn East and South, in the course of many wanderings from Billingsgate to Limehouse Hole, from Petticoat Lane to Whitechapel Road; out of eel-pie shop and penny gaff; out of tavern and street, and court and doss-house, he had gathered together slang words and terms and phrases, and they came back to him now, and he stood up against her manfully.

But as well might the lamb stand up against the eagle, when the shadow of its wings falls across the green pastures, and the wind flies before its dark oncoming. At the end of two minutes he lay gasping, dazed, and speechless.

Then she began.

She announced her intention of "wiping down the bloomin' 'all" with him, and making it respectable; and, metaphorically speaking, that is what she did. Her tongue hit him between the eyes, and knocked him down and trampled on him. It curled round and round him like a whip, and then it uncurled and wound the other way. It seized him by the scruff of his neck, and tossed him up into the air, and caught him as he descended, and flung him to the ground, and rolled him on it. It played around him like forked lightning, and blinded him. It danced and shrieked about him like a host of whirling fiends, and he tried to remember a prayer, and could not. It touched him lightly on the sole of his foot and the crown of his head, and his hair stood up straight, and his limbs grew stiff. The people sitting near him drew away, not feeling it safe to be near, and left him alone, surrounded by space, and language.

It was the most artistic piece of work of its kind that I have ever heard. Every phrase she flung at him seemed to have been woven on purpose to entangle him and to embrace in its choking folds his people and his gods, to strangle with its threads his every hope, ambition, and belief. Each term she put upon him clung to him like a garment, and fitted him without a crease. The last name that she called him one felt to be, until one heard the next, the one name that he ought to have been christened by.

For five and three-quarter minutes by the clock she spoke, and never for one instant did she pause or falter; and in the whole of that onslaught there was only one weak spot.

That was when she offered to make a better man than he was out of a Guy Fawkes and a lump of coal. You felt that one lump of coal would not have been sufficient.

At the end, she gathered herself together for one supreme effort, and hurled at him an insult so bitter with scorn so sharp with insight into his career and character, so heavy with prophetic curse, that strong men drew and held their breath while it passed over them, and women hid their faces and shivered.

Then she folded her arms, and stood silent; and the house, from floor to ceiling, rose and cheered her until there was no more breath left in its lungs.

In that one night she stepped from oblivion into success. She is now a famous "artiste."

But she does not call herself Signora Ballatino, and she does not play upon the zithern. Her name has a homelier sound, and her speciality is the delineation of coster character.

SILHOUETTES

I fear I must be of a somewhat gruesome turn of mind. My sympathies are always with the melancholy side of life and nature. I love the chill October days, when the brown leaves lie thick and sodden underneath your feet, and a low sound as of stifled sobbing is heard in the damp woods--the evenings in late autumn time, when the white mist creeps across the fields, making it seem as though old Earth, feeling the night air cold to its poor bones, were drawing ghostly bedclothes round its withered limbs. I like the twilight of the long grey street, sad with the wailing cry of the distant muffin man. One thinks of him, as, strangely mitred, he glides by through the gloom, jangling his harsh bell, as the High Priest of the pale spirit of Indigestion, summoning the devout to come forth and worship. I find a sweetness in the aching dreariness of Sabbath afternoons in genteel suburbs--in the evil-laden desolateness of waste places by the river, when the yellow fog is stealing inland across the ooze and mud, and the black tide gurgles softly round worm-eaten piles.

I love the bleak moor, when the thin long line of the winding road lies white on the darkening heath, while overhead some belated bird, vexed with itself for being out so late, scurries across the dusky sky, screaming angrily. I love the lonely, sullen lake, hidden away in mountain solitudes. I suppose it was my childhood's surroundings that instilled in me this affection for sombre hues. One of my earliest recollections is of a dreary marshland by the sea. By day, the water stood there in wide, shallow pools. But when one looked in the evening they were pools of blood that lay there.

It was a wild, dismal stretch of coast. One day, I found myself there all alone--I forget how it came about--and, oh, how small I felt amid the sky and the sea and the sandhills! I ran, and ran, and ran, but I never seemed to move; and then I cried, and screamed, louder and louder, and the circling seagulls screamed back mockingly at me. It was an "unken" spot, as they say up North.

In the far back days of the building of the world, a long, high ridge of stones had been reared up by the sea, dividing the swampy grassland from the sand. Some of these stones--"pebbles," so they called them round about--were as big as a man, and many as big as a fair-sized house; and when the sea was angry--and very prone he was to anger by that lonely shore, and very quick to wrath; often have I known him sink to sleep with a peaceful smile on his rippling waves, to wake in fierce fury before the night was spent--he would snatch up giant handfuls of these pebbles and fling and toss them here and there, till the noise of their rolling and crashing could be heard by the watchers in the village afar off.

"Old Nick's playing at marbles to-night," they would say to one another, pausing to listen. And then the women would close tight their doors, and try not to hear the sound.

Far out to sea, by where the muddy mouth of the river yawned wide, there rose ever a thin white line of surf, and underneath those crested waves there dwelt a very fearsome thing, called the Bar. I grew to hate and be afraid of this mysterious Bar, for I heard it spoken of always with bated breath, and I knew that it was very cruel to fisher folk, and hurt them so sometimes that they would cry whole days and nights together with the pain, or would sit with white scared faces, rocking themselves to and fro.

Once when I was playing among the sandhills, there came by a tall, grey woman, bending beneath a load of driftwood. She paused when nearly opposite to me, and, facing seaward, fixed her eyes upon the breaking surf above the Bar. "Ah, how I hate the sight of your white teeth!" she muttered; then turned and passed on.

Another morning, walking through the village, I heard a low wailing come from one of the cottages, while a little farther on a group of women were gathered in the roadway, talking. "Ay," said one of them, "I thought the Bar was looking hungry last night."

So, putting one and the other together, I concluded that the "Bar" must be an ogre, such as a body reads of in books, who lived in a coral castle deep below the river's mouth, and fed upon the fishermen as he caught them going down to the sea or coming home.

From my bedroom window, on moonlight nights, I could watch the silvery foam, marking the spot beneath where he lay hid; and I would stand on tip- toe, peering out, until at length I would come to fancy I could see his hideous form floating below the waters. Then, as the little white-sailed boats stole by him, tremblingly, I used to tremble too, lest he should suddenly open his grim jaws and gulp them down; and when they had all safely reached the dark, soft sea beyond, I would steal back to the bedside, and pray to God to make the Bar good, so that he would give up eating the poor fishermen.

Another incident connected with that coast lives in my mind. It was the morning after a great storm--great even for that stormy coast--and the passion-worn waters were still heaving with the memory of a fury that was dead. Old Nick had scattered his marbles far and wide, and there were rents and fissures in the pebbly wall such as the oldest fisherman had never known before. Some of the hugest stones lay tossed a hundred yards away, and the waters had dug pits here and there along the ridge so deep that a tall man might stand in some of them, and yet his head not reach the level of the sand.

Round one of these holes a small crowd was pressing eagerly, while one man, standing in the hollow, was lifting the few remaining stones off something that lay there at the bottom. I pushed my way between the straggling legs of a big fisher lad, and peered over with the rest. A ray of sunlight streamed down into the pit, and the thing at the bottom gleamed white. Sprawling there among the black pebbles it looked like a huge spider. One by one the last stones were lifted away, and the thing was left bare, and then the crowd looked at one another and shivered.

"Wonder how he got there," said a woman at length; "somebody must ha' helped him."

"Some foreign chap, no doubt," said the man who had lifted off the stones; "washed ashore and buried here by the sea."

"What, six foot below the water-mark, wi' all they stones atop of him?" said another.

"That's no foreign chap," cried a grizzled old woman, pressing forward. "What's that that's aside him?"

Some one jumped down and took it from the stone where it lay glistening, and handed it up to her, and she clutched it in her skinny hand. It was a gold earring, such as fishermen sometimes wear. But this was a somewhat large one, and of rather unusual shape.

"That's young Abram Parsons, I tell 'ee, as lies down there," cried the old creature, wildly. "I ought to know. I gave him the pair o' these forty year ago."

It may be only an idea of mine, born of after brooding upon the scene. I am inclined to think it must be so, for I was only a child at the time, and would hardly have noticed such a thing. But it seems to my remembrance that as the old crone ceased, another woman in the crowd raised her eyes slowly, and fixed them on a withered, ancient man, who leant upon a stick, and that for a moment, unnoticed by the rest, these two stood looking strangely at each other.

From these sea-scented scenes, my memory travels to a weary land where dead ashes lie, and there is blackness--blackness everywhere. Black rivers flow between black banks; black, stunted trees grow in black fields; black withered flowers by black wayside. Black roads lead from blackness past blackness to blackness; and along them trudge black, savage-looking men and women; and by them black, old-looking children play grim, unchildish games.

When the sun shines on this black land, it glitters black and hard; and when the rain falls a black mist rises towards heaven, like the hopeless prayer of a hopeless soul.

By night it is less dreary, for then the sky gleams with a lurid light, and out of the darkness the red flames leap, and high up in the air they gambol and writhe--the demon spawn of that evil land, they seem.

Visitors who came to our house would tell strange tales of this black land, and some of the stories I am inclined to think were true. One man said he saw a young bull-dog fly at a boy and pin him by the throat. The lad jumped about with much sprightliness, and tried to knock the dog away. Whereupon the boy's father rushed out of the house, hard by, and caught his son and heir roughly by the shoulder. "Keep still, thee young ---, can't 'ee!" shouted the man angrily; "let 'un taste blood."

Another time, I heard a lady tell how she had visited a cottage during a strike, to find the baby, together with the other children, almost dying for want of food. "Dear, dear me!" she cried, taking the wee wizened mite from the mother's arms, "but I sent you down a quart of milk, yesterday. Hasn't the child had it?"

"Theer weer a little coom, thank 'ee kindly, ma'am," the father took upon himself to answer; "but thee see it weer only just enow for the poops."

We lived in a big lonely house on the edge of a wide common. One night, I remember, just as I was reluctantly preparing to climb into bed, there came a wild ringing at the gate, followed by a hoarse, shrieking cry, and then a frenzied shaking of the iron bars.

Then hurrying footsteps sounded through the house, and the swift opening and closing of doors; and I slipped back hastily into my knickerbockers and ran out. The women folk were gathered on the stairs, while my father stood in the hall, calling to them to be quiet. And still the wild ringing of the bell continued, and, above it, the hoarse, shrieking cry.

My father opened the door and went out, and we could hear him striding down the gravel path, and we clung to one another and waited.

After what seemed an endless time, we heard the heavy gate unbarred, and quickly clanged to, and footsteps returning on the gravel. Then the door opened again, and my father entered, and behind him a crouching figure that felt its way with its hands as it crept along, as a blind man might. The figure stood up when it reached the middle of the hall, and mopped its eyes with a dirty rag that it carried in its hand; after which it held the rag over the umbrella-stand and wrung it out, as washerwomen wring out clothes, and the dark drippings fell into the tray with a dull, heavy splut.

My father whispered something to my mother, and she went out towards the back; and, in a little while, we heard the stamping of hoofs--the angry plunge of a spur-startled horse--the rhythmic throb of the long, straight gallop, dying away into the distance.

My mother returned and spoke some reassuring words to the servants. My father, having made fast the door and extinguished all but one or two of the lights, had gone into a small room on the right of the hall; the crouching figure, still mopping that moisture from its eyes, following him. We could hear them talking there in low tones, my father questioning, the other voice thick and interspersed with short panting grunts.

We on the stairs huddled closer together, and, in the darkness, I felt my mother's arm steal round me and encompass me, so that I was not afraid. Then we waited, while the silence round our frightened whispers thickened and grew heavy till the weight of it seemed to hurt us.

At length, out of its depths, there crept to our ears a faint murmur. It gathered strength like the sound of the oncoming of a wave upon a stony shore, until it broke in a Babel of vehement voices just outside. After a few moments, the hubbub ceased, and there came a furious ringing--then angry shouts demanding admittance.

Some of the women began to cry. My father came out into the hall, closing the room door behind him, and ordered them to be quiet, so sternly that they were stunned into silence. The furious ringing was repeated; and, this time, threats mingled among the hoarse shouts. My mother's arm tightened around me, and I could hear the beating of her heart.

The voices outside the gate sank into a low confused mumbling. Soon they died away altogether, and the silence flowed back.

My father turned up the hall lamp, and stood listening.

Suddenly, from the back of the house, rose the noise of a great crashing, followed by oaths and savage laughter.

My father rushed forward, but was borne back; and, in an instant, the hall was full of grim, ferocious faces. My father, trembling a little (or else it was the shadow cast by the flickering lamp), and with lips tight pressed, stood confronting them; while we women and children, too scared to even cry, shrank back up the stairs.

What followed during the next few moments is, in my memory, only a confused tumult, above which my father's high, clear tones rise every now and again, entreating, arguing, commanding. I see nothing distinctly until one of the grimmest of the faces thrusts itself before the others, and a voice which, like Aaron's rod, swallows up all its fellows, says in deep, determined bass, "Coom, we've had enow chatter, master. Thee mun give 'un up, or thee mun get out o' th' way an' we'll search th' house for oursel'."

Then a light flashed into my father's eyes that kindled something inside me, so that the fear went out of me, and I struggled to free myself from my mother's arm, for the desire stirred me to fling myself down upon the grimy faces below, and beat and stamp upon them with my fists. Springing across the hall, he snatched from the wall where it hung an ancient club, part of a trophy of old armour, and planting his back against the door through which they would have to pass, he shouted, "Then be damned to you all, he's in this room! Come and fetch him out."

(I recollect that speech well. I puzzled over it, even at that time, excited though I was. I had always been told that only low, wicked people ever used the word "damn," and I tried to reconcile things, and failed.)

The men drew back and muttered among themselves. It was an ugly-looking weapon, studded with iron spikes. My father held it secured to his hand by a chain, and there was an ugly look about him also, now, that gave his face a strange likeness to the dark faces round him.

But my mother grew very white and cold, and underneath her breath she kept crying, "Oh, will they never come--will they never come?" and a cricket somewhere about the house began to chirp.

Then all at once, without a word, my mother flew down the stairs, and passed like a flash of light through the crowd of dusky figures. How she did it I could never understand, for the two heavy bolts had both been drawn, but the next moment the door stood wide open; and a hum of voices, cheery with the anticipation of a period of perfect bliss, was borne in upon the cool night air.

My mother was always very quick of hearing.

∽

Again, I see a wild crowd of grim faces, and my father's, very pale, amongst them. But this time the faces are very many, and they come and go like faces in a dream. The ground beneath my feet is wet and sloppy, and a black rain is falling. There are women's faces in the crowd, wild and haggard, and long skinny arms stretch out threateningly towards my father, and shrill, frenzied voices call out curses on him. Boys' faces also pass me in the grey light, and on some of them there is an impish grin.

I seem to be in everybody's way; and to get out of it, I crawl into a dark, draughty corner and crouch there among cinders. Around me, great engines fiercely strain and pant like living things fighting beyond their strength. Their gaunt arms whirl madly above me, and the ground rocks with their throbbing. Dark figures flit to and fro, pausing from time to time to wipe the black sweat from their faces.

The pale light fades, and the flame-lit night lies red upon the land. The flitting figures take strange shapes. I hear the hissing of wheels, the furious clanking of iron chains, the hoarse shouting of many voices, the hurrying tread of many feet; and, through all, the wailing and weeping and cursing that never seem to cease. I drop into a restless sleep, and dream that I have broken a chapel window, stone-throwing, and have died and gone to hell.

At length, a cold hand is laid upon my shoulder, and I awake. The wild faces have vanished and all is silent now, and I wonder if the whole thing has been a dream. My father lifts me into the dog-cart, and we drive home through the chill dawn.

My mother opens the door softly as we alight. She does not speak, only looks her question. "It's all over, Maggie," answers my father very quietly, as he takes off his coat and lays it across a chair; "we've got to begin the world afresh."

My mother's arms steal up about his neck; and I, feeling heavy with a trouble I do not understand, creep off to bed.

THE LEASE OF THE «CROSS KEYS»

This story is about a shop: many stories are. One Sunday evening this Bishop had to preach a sermon at St. Paul's Cathedral. The occasion was a very special and important one, and every God-fearing newspaper in the kingdom sent its own special representative to report the proceedings.

Now, of the three reporters thus commissioned, one was a man of appearance so eminently respectable that no one would have thought of taking him for a journalist. People used to put him down for a County Councillor or an Archdeacon at the very least. As a matter of fact, however, he was a sinful man, with a passion for gin. He lived at Bow, and, on the Sabbath in question, he left his home at five o'clock in the afternoon, and started to walk to the scene of his labours. The road from Bow to the City on a wet and chilly Sunday evening is a cheerless one; who can blame him if on his way he stopped once or twice to comfort himself with "two" of his favourite beverage? On reaching St. Paul's he found he had twenty minutes to spare--just time enough for one final "nip." Half way down a narrow court leading out of the Churchyard he found a quiet little hostelry, and, entering the private bar, whispered insinuatingly across the counter:

"Two of gin hot, if you please, my dear."

His voice had the self-satisfied meekness of the successful ecclesiastic, his bearing suggested rectitude tempered by desire to avoid observation. The barmaid, impressed by his manner and appearance, drew the attention of the landlord to him. The landlord covertly took stock of so much of him as could be seen between his buttoned-up coat and his drawn-down hat, and wondered how so bland and innocent-looking a gentleman came to know of gin.

A landlord's duty, however, is not to wonder, but to serve. The gin was given to the man, and the man drank it. He liked it. It was good gin: he was a connoisseur, and he knew. Indeed, so good did it seem to him that he felt it would be a waste of opportunity not to have another twopen'orth. Therefore he had a second "go"; maybe a third. Then he returned to the Cathedral, and sat himself down with his notebook on his knee and waited.

As the service proceeded there stole over him that spirit of indifference to all earthly surroundings that religion and drink are alone able to bestow. He heard the good Bishop's text and wrote it down. Then he heard the Bishop's "sixthly and lastly," and took that down, and looked at his notebook and wondered in a peaceful way what had become of the "firstly" to "fifthly" inclusive. He sat there wondering until the people round him began to get up and move away, whereupon it struck him swiftly and suddenly that be had been asleep, and had thereby escaped the main body of the discourse.

What on earth was he to do? He was representing one of the leading religious papers. A full report of the sermon was wanted that very night. Seizing the robe of a passing wandsman, he tremulously inquired if the Bishop had yet left the Cathedral. The wandsman answered that he had not, but that he was just on the point of doing so.

"I must see him before he goes!" exclaimed the reporter, excitedly.

"You can't," replied the wandsman. The journalist grew frantic.

"Tell him," he cried, "a penitent sinner desires to speak with him about the sermon he has just delivered. To-morrow it will be too late."

The wandsman was touched; so was the Bishop. He said he would see the poor fellow.

As soon as the door was shut the man, with tears in his eyes, told the Bishop the truth--leaving out the gin. He said that he was a poor man, and not in good health, that he had been up half the night before, and had walked all the way from Bow that evening. He dwelt on the disastrous results to himself and his family should he fail to obtain a report of the sermon. The Bishop felt sorry for the man. Also, he was anxious that his sermon should be reported.

"Well, I trust it will be a warning to you against going to sleep in church," he said, with an indulgent smile. "Luckily, I have brought my notes with me, and if you will promise to be very careful of them, and to bring them back to me the first thing in the morning, I will lend them to you."

With this, the Bishop opened and handed to the man a neat little black leather bag, inside which lay a neat little roll of manuscript.

"Better take the bag to keep it in," added the Bishop. "Be sure and let me have them both back early to-morrow."

The reporter, when he examined the contents of the bag under a lamp in the Cathedral vestibule, could hardly believe his good fortune. The careful Bishop's notes were so full and clear that for all practical purposes they were equal to a report. His work was already done. He felt so pleased with himself that he determined to treat himself to another "two" of gin, and, with this intent, made his way across to the little "public" before-mentioned.

"It's really excellent gin you sell here," he said to the barmaid when he had finished; "I think, my dear, I'll have just one more."

At eleven the landlord gently but firmly insisted on his leaving, and he went, assisted, as far as the end of the court, by the potboy. After he was gone, the landlord noticed a neat little black bag on the seat where he had been lying. Examining it closely, he discovered a brass plate between the handles, and upon the brass plate were engraved the owner's name and title. Opening the bag, the landlord saw a neat little roll of manuscript, and across a corner of the manuscript was written the Bishop's name and address.

The landlord blew a long, low whistle, and stood with his round eyes wide open gazing down at the open bag. Then he put on his hat and coat, and taking the bag, went out down the court, chuckling hugely as he walked. He went straight to the house of the Resident Canon and rang the bell.

"Tell Mr. ---," he said to the servant, "that I must see him to-night. I wouldn't disturb him at this late hour if it wasn't something very important."

The landlord was ushered up. Closing the door softly behind him, he coughed deferentially.

"Well, Mr. Peters" (I will call him "Peters"), said the Canon, "what is it?"

"Well, sir," said Mr. Peters, slowly and deliberately, "it's about that there lease o' mine. I do hope you gentlemen will see your way to makin' it twenty-one year instead o' fourteen."

"God bless the man!" cried the Canon, jumping up indignantly, "you don't mean to say you've come to me at eleven o'clock on a Sunday night to talk about your lease?"

"Well, not entirely, sir," answered Peters, unabashed; "there's another little thing I wished to speak to you about, and that's this"--saying which, he laid the Bishop's bag before the Canon and told his story.

The Canon looked at Mr. Peters, and Mr. Peters looked at the Canon.

"There must be some mistake," said the Canon.

"There's no mistake," said the landlord. "I had my suspicions when I first clapped eyes on him. I seed he wasn't our usual sort, and I seed how he tried to hide his face. If he weren't the Bishop, then I don't know a Bishop when I sees one, that's all. Besides, there's his bag, and there's his sermon."

Mr. Peters folded his arms and waited. The Canon pondered. Such things had been known to happen before in Church history. Why not again?

"Does any one know of this besides yourself?" asked the Canon.

"Not a livin' soul," replied Mr. Peters, "as yet."

"I think--I think, Mr. Peters," said the Canon, "that we may be able to extend your lease to twenty-one years."

"Thank you kindly, sir," said the landlord, and departed. Next morning the Canon waited on the Bishop and laid the bag before him.

"Oh," said the Bishop cheerfully, "he's sent it back by you, has he?"

"He has, sir," replied the Canon; "and thankful I am that it was to me he brought it. It is right," continued the Canon, "that I should inform your lordship that I am aware of the circumstances under which it left your hands."

The Canon's eye was severe, and the Bishop laughed uneasily.

"I suppose it wasn't quite the thing for me to do," he answered apologetically; "but there, all's well that ends well," and the Bishop laughed.

This stung the Canon. "Oh, sir," he exclaimed, with a burst of fervour, "in Heaven's name--for the sake of our Church, let me entreat--let me pray you never to let such a thing occur again."

The Bishop turned upon him angrily.

"Why, what a fuss you make about a little thing!" he cried; then, seeing the look of agony upon the other's face, he paused.

"How did you get that bag?" he asked.

"The landlord of the Cross Keys brought it me," answered the Canon; "you left it there last night."

The Bishop gave a gasp, and sat down heavily. When he recovered his breath, he told the Canon the real history of the case; and the Canon is still trying to believe it.

THE END

MALVINA OF BRITTANY
AND OTHER STORIES

MALVINA OF BRITTANY

THE PREFACE

The Doctor never did believe this story, but claims for it that, to a great extent, it has altered his whole outlook on life.

"Of course, what actually happened--what took place under my own nose," continued the Doctor, "I do not dispute. And then there is the case of Mrs. Marigold. That was unfortunate, I admit, and still is, especially for Marigold. But, standing by itself, it proves nothing. These fluffy, giggling women--as often as not it is a mere shell that they shed with their first youth--one never knows what is underneath. With regard to the others, the whole thing rests upon a simple scientific basis. The idea was 'in the air,' as we say--a passing brainwave. And when it had worked itself out there was an end of it. As for all this Jack-and-the-Beanstalk tomfoolery--"

There came from the darkening uplands the sound of a lost soul. It rose and fell and died away.

"Blowing stones," explained the Doctor, stopping to refill his pipe. "One finds them in these parts. Hollowed out during the glacial period. Always just about twilight that one hears it. Rush of air caused by sudden sinking of the temperature. That's how all these sort of ideas get started."

The Doctor, having lit his pipe, resumed his stride.

"I don't say," continued the Doctor, "that it would have happened without her coming. Undoubtedly it was she who supplied the necessary psychic conditions. There was that about her--a sort of atmosphere. That quaint archaic French of hers--King Arthur and the round table and Merlin; it seemed to recreate it all. An artful minx, that is the only explanation. But while she was looking at you, out of that curious aloofness of hers--"

The Doctor left the sentence uncompleted.

"As for old Littlecherry," the Doctor began again quite suddenly, "that's his speciality--folklore, occultism, all that flummery. If you knocked at his door with the original Sleeping Beauty on your arm he'd only fuss round her with cushions and hope that she'd had a good night. Found a seed once--chipped it out of an old fossil, and grew it in a pot in his study. About the most dilapidated weed you ever saw. Talked about it as if he had re-discovered the Elixir of Life. Even if he didn't say anything in actually so many words, there was the way he went about. That of itself was enough to have started the whole thing, to say nothing of that loony old Irish housekeeper of his, with her head stuffed full of elves and banshees and the Lord knows what."

Again the Doctor lapsed into silence. One by one the lights of the village peeped upward out of the depths. A long, low line of light, creeping like some luminous dragon across the horizon, showed the track of the Great Western express moving stealthily towards Swindon.

"It was altogether out of the common," continued the Doctor, "quite out of the common, the whole thing. But if you are going to accept old Littlecherry's explanation of it--"

The Doctor struck his foot against a long grey stone, half hidden in the grass, and only just saved himself from falling.

"Remains of some old cromlech," explained the Doctor. "Somewhere about here, if we were to dig down, we should find a withered bundle of bones crouching over the dust of a prehistoric luncheon-basket. Interesting neighbourhood!"

The descent was rough. The Doctor did not talk again until we had reached the outskirts of the village.

"I wonder what's become of them?" mused the Doctor. "A rum go, the whole thing. I should like to have got to the bottom of it."

We had reached the Doctor's gate. The Doctor pushed it open and passed in. He seemed to have forgotten me.

"A taking little minx," I heard him muttering to himself as he fumbled with the door. "And no doubt meant well. But as for that cock-and-bull story--"

I pieced it together from the utterly divergent versions furnished me by the Professor and the Doctor, assisted, so far as later incidents are concerned, by knowledge common to the village.

I. THE STORY

It commenced, so I calculate, about the year 2OOO B.C., or, to be more precise--for figures are not the strong point of the old chroniclers--when King Heremon ruled over Ireland and Harbundia was Queen of the White Ladies of Brittany, the fairy Malvina being her favourite attendant. It is with Malvina that this story is chiefly concerned. Various quite pleasant happenings are recorded to her credit. The White Ladies belonged to the "good people," and, on the whole, lived up to their reputation. But in Malvina, side by side with much that is commendable, there appears to have existed a most reprehensible spirit of mischief, displaying itself in pranks that, excusable, or at all events understandable, in, say, a pixy or a pigwidgeon, strike one as altogether unworthy of a well-principled White Lady, posing as the friend and benefactress of mankind. For merely refusing to dance with her--at midnight, by the shores of a mountain lake; neither the time nor the place calculated to appeal to an elderly gentleman, suffering possibly from rheumatism--she on one occasion transformed an eminently respectable proprietor of tin mines into a nightingale, necessitating a change of habits that to a business man must have been singularly irritating. On another occasion a quite important queen, having had the misfortune to quarrel with Malvina over some absurd point of etiquette in connection with a lizard, seems, on waking the next morning, to have found herself changed into what one judges, from the somewhat vague description afforded by the ancient chroniclers, to have been a sort of vegetable marrow.

Such changes, according to the Professor, who is prepared to maintain that evidence of an historical nature exists sufficient to prove that the White Ladies formed at one time an actual living community, must be taken in an allegorical sense. Just as modern lunatics believe themselves to be china vases or poll-parrots, and think and behave as such, so it must have been easy, the Professor argues, for beings of superior intelligence to have exerted hypnotic influence upon the superstitious savages by whom they were surrounded, and who, intellectually considered, could have been little more than children.

"Take Nebuchadnezzar." I am still quoting the Professor. "Nowadays we should put him into a strait-waistcoat. Had he lived in Northern Europe instead of Southern Asia, legend would have told us how some Kobold or Stromkarl had turned him into a composite amalgamation of a serpent, a cat and a kangaroo." Be that as it may, this passion for change--in other people--seems to have grown upon Malvina until she must have become little short of a public nuisance, and eventually it landed her in trouble.

The incident is unique in the annals of the White Ladies, and the chroniclers dwell upon it with evident satisfaction. It came about through the betrothal of King Heremon's only son, Prince Gerbot, to the Princess Berchta of Normandy. Malvina seems to have said nothing, but to have bided her time. The White Ladies of Brittany, it must be remembered, were not fairies pure and simple. Under certain conditions they were capable of becoming women, and this fact, one takes it, must have exerted a disturbing influence upon their relationships with eligible male mortals. Prince Gerbot may not have been altogether blameless. Young men in those sadly unenlightened days may not, in their dealings with ladies, white or otherwise, have always been the soul of discretion and propriety. One would like to think the best of her.

But even the best is indefensible. On the day appointed for the wedding she seems to have surpassed herself. Into what particular shape or form she altered the wretched Prince Gerbot; or into what shape or form she persuaded him that he had been altered, it really, so far as the moral responsibility of Malvina is concerned, seems to be immaterial; the chronicle does not state: evidently something too indelicate for a self-respecting chronicler to even hint at. As, judging from other passages in the book, squeamishness does not seem to have been the author's literary failing, the sensitive reader can feel only grateful for the omission. It would have been altogether too harrowing.

It had, of course, from Malvina's point of view, the desired effect. The Princess Berchta appears to have given one look and then to have fallen fainting into the arms of her attendants. The marriage was postponed indefinitely, and Malvina, one sadly suspects, chortled. Her triumph was short-lived.

Unfortunately for her, King Heremon had always been a patron of the arts and science of his period. Among his friends were to be reckoned magicians, genii, the Nine Korrigans or Fays of Brittany--all sorts of parties capable of exerting influence, and, as events proved, only too willing. Ambassadors waited upon Queen Harbundia; and Harbundia, even had she wished, as on many previous occasions, to stand by her favourite, had no alternative. The fairy Malvina was called upon to return to Prince Gerbot his proper body and all therein contained.

She flatly refused. A self-willed, obstinate fairy, suffering from swelled head. And then there was that personal note. Merely that he should marry the Princess Berchta! She would see King Heremon, and Anniamus, in his silly old wizard's robe, and the Fays of Brittany, and all the rest of them--! A really nice White Lady may not have cared to finish the sentence, even to herself. One imagines the flash of the fairy eye, the stamp of the fairy foot. What could they do to her, any of them, with all their clacking of tongues and their wagging of heads? She, an immortal fairy! She would change Prince Gerbot back at a time of her own choosing. Let them attend to their own tricks and leave her to mind hers. One pictures long walks and talks between the distracted Harbundia and her refractory favourite-- appeals to reason, to sentiment: "For my sake." "Don't you see?" "After all, dear, and even if he did."

It seems to have ended by Harbundia losing all patience. One thing there was she could do that Malvina seems either not to have known of or not to have anticipated. A solemn meeting of the White Ladies was convened for the night of the midsummer moon. The place of meeting is described by the ancient chroniclers with more than their usual exactitude. It was on the land that the magician Kalyb had, ages ago, raised up above all Brittany to form the grave of King Taramis. The "Sea of the Seven Islands" lay to the north. One guesses it to be the ridge formed by the Arree Mountains. "The Lady of the Fountain" appears to have been present, suggesting the deep green pool from which the river D'Argent takes its source. Roughly speaking, one would place it halfway between the modern towns of Morlaix and Callac. Pedestrians, even of the present day, speak of the still loneliness of that high plateau, treeless, houseless, with no sign of human hand there but that high, towering monolith round which the shrill winds moan incessantly. There, possibly on some broken fragment of those great grey stones, Queen Harbundia sat in judgment. And the judgment was--and from it there was no appeal--that the fairy Malvina should be cast out from among the community of the White Ladies of Brittany. Over the face of the earth she should wander, alone and unforgiven. Solemnly from the book of the roll-call of the White Ladies the name of Malvina was struck out for ever.

The blow must have fallen upon Malvina as heavily as it was unexpected. Without a word, without one backward look, she seems to have departed. One pictures the white, frozen face, the wide-open, unseeing eyes, the trembling, uncertain steps, the groping hands, the deathlike silence clinging like grave-clothes round about her.

From that night the fairy Malvina disappears from the book of the chroniclers of the White Ladies of Brittany, from legend and from folklore whatsoever. She does not appear again in history till the year A.D. 1914.

II. HOW IT CAME ABOUT

It was on an evening towards the end of June, 1914, that Flight Commander Raffleton, temporarily attached to the French Squadron then harboured at Brest, received instructions by wireless to return at once to the British Air Service Headquarters at Farnborough, in Hampshire. The night, thanks to a glorious full moon, would afford all the light he required, and young Raffleton determined to set out at once. He appears to have left the flying ground just outside the arsenal at Brest about nine o'clock. A little beyond Huelgoat he began to experience trouble with the carburettor. His idea at first was to push on to Lannion, where he would be able to secure expert assistance; but matters only getting worse, and noticing beneath him a convenient stretch of level ground, he decided to descend and attend to it himself. He alighted without difficulty and proceeded to investigate. The job took him, unaided, longer than he had anticipated. It was a warm, close night, with hardly a breath of wind, and when he had finished he was feeling hot and tired. He had drawn on his helmet and was on the point of stepping into his seat, when the beauty of the night suggested to him that it would be pleasant, before starting off again, to stretch his legs and cool himself a little. He lit a cigar and looked round about him.

The plateau on which he had alighted was a table-land standing high above the surrounding country. It stretched around him, treeless, houseless. There was nothing to break the lines of the horizon but a group of gaunt grey stones, the remains, so he told himself, of some ancient menhir, common enough to the lonely desert lands of Brittany. In general the stones lie overthrown and scattered, but this particular specimen had by some strange chance remained undisturbed through all the centuries. Mildly interested, Flight Commander Raffleton strolled leisurely towards it. The moon was at its zenith. How still the quiet night must have been was impressed upon him by the fact that he distinctly heard, and counted, the strokes of a church clock which must have been at least six miles away. He remembers looking at his watch and noting that there was a slight difference between his own and the church time. He made it eight minutes past twelve. With the dying away of the last vibrations of the distant bell the silence and the solitude of the place seemed to return and settle down upon it with increased insistence. While he was working it had not troubled him, but beside the black shadows thrown by those hoary stones it had the effect almost of a presence. It was with a sense of relief that he contemplated returning to his machine and starting up his engine. It would whir and buzz and give back to him a comfortable feeling of life and security. He would walk round the stones just once and then be off. It was wonderful how they had defied old Time. As they had been placed there, quite possibly ten thousand years ago, so they still stood, the altar of that vast, empty sky-roofed temple. And while he was gazing at them, his cigar between his lips, struggling with a strange forgotten impulse that was tugging at his knees, there came from the very heart of the great grey stones the measured rise and fall of a soft, even breathing.

Young Raffleton frankly confesses that his first impulse was to cut and run. Only his soldier's training kept his feet firm on the heather. Of course, the explanation was simple. Some animal had made the place its nest. But then what animal was ever known to sleep so soundly as not to be disturbed by human footsteps? If wounded, and so unable to escape, it would not be breathing with that quiet, soft regularity, contrasting so strangely with the stillness and the silence all round. Possibly an owl's nest. Young owlets make that sort of noise--the "snorers," so country people call them. Young Raffleton threw away his cigar and went down upon his knees to grope among the shadows, and, doing so, he touched something warm and soft and yielding.

But it wasn't an owl. He must have touched her very lightly, for even then she did not wake. She lay there with her head upon her arm. And now close to her, his eyes growing used to the shadows, he saw her quite plainly, the wonder of the parted lips, the gleam of the white limbs beneath their flimsy covering.

Of course, what he ought to have done was to have risen gently and moved away. Then he could have coughed. And if that did not wake her he might have touched her lightly, say, on the shoulder, and have called to her, first softly, then a little louder, "Mademoiselle," or "Mon enfant." Even better, he might have stolen away on tiptoe and left her there sleeping.

This idea does not seem to have occurred to him. One makes the excuse for him that he was but three-and-twenty, that, framed in the purple moonlight, she seemed to him the most beautiful creature his eyes had ever seen. And then there was the brooding mystery of it all, that atmosphere of far-off primeval times from which the roots of life still draw their sap. One takes it he forgot that he was Flight Commander Raffleton, officer and gentleman; forgot the proper etiquette applying to the case of ladies found sleeping upon lonely moors without a chaperon. Greater still, the possibility that he never thought of anything at all, but, just impelled by a power beyond himself, bent down and kissed her.

Not a platonic kiss upon the brow, not a brotherly kiss upon the cheek, but a kiss full upon the parted lips, a kiss of worship and amazement, such as that with which Adam in all probability awakened Eve.

Her eyes opened, and, just a little sleepily, she looked at him. There could have been no doubt in her mind as to what had happened. His lips were still pressing hers. But she did not seem in the least surprised, and most certainly not angry. Raising herself to a sitting posture, she smiled and held out her hand that he might help her up. And, alone in that vast temple, star-roofed and moon- illumined, beside that grim grey altar of forgotten rites, hand in hand they stood and looked at one another.

"I beg your pardon," said Commander Raffleton. "I'm afraid I have disturbed you."

He remembered afterwards that in his confusion he had spoken to her in English. But she answered him in French, a quaint, old-fashioned French such as one rarely finds but in the pages of old missals. He would have had some difficulty in translating it literally, but the meaning of it was, adapted to our modern idiom:

"Don't mention it. I'm so glad you've come."

He gathered she had been expecting him. He was not quite sure whether he ought not to apologise for being apparently a little late. True, he had no recollection of any such appointment. But then at that particular moment Commander Raffleton may be said to have had no consciousness of anything beyond just himself and the wondrous other beside him. Somewhere outside was moonlight and a world; but all that seemed unimportant. It was she who broke the silence.

"How did you get here?" she asked.

He did not mean to be enigmatical. He was chiefly concerned with still gazing at her.

"I flew here," he answered. Her eyes opened wider at that, but with interest, not doubt.

"Where are your wings?" she asked. She was leaning sideways, trying to get a view of his back.

He laughed. It made her seem more human, that curiosity about his back.

"Over there," he answered. She looked, and for the first time saw the great shimmering sails gleaming like silver under the moonlight.

She moved towards it, and he followed, noticing without surprise that the heather seemed to make no sign of yielding to the pressure of her white feet.

She halted a little away from it, and he came and stood beside her. Even to Commander Raffleton himself it looked as if the great wings were quivering, like the outstretched pinions of a bird preening itself before flight.

"Is it alive?" she asked.

"Not till I whisper to it," he answered. He was losing a little of his fear of her. She turned to him.

"Shall we go?" she asked.

He stared at her. She was quite serious, that was evident. She was to put her hand in his and go away with him. It was all settled. That is why he had come. To her it did not matter where. That was his affair. But where he went she was to go. That was quite clearly the programme in her mind.

To his credit, let it be recorded, he did make an effort. Against all the forces of nature, against his twenty-three years and the red blood pulsing in his veins, against the fumes of the midsummer moonlight encompassing him and the voices of the stars, against the demons of poetry and romance and mystery chanting their witches' music in his ears, against the marvel and the glory of her as she stood beside him, clothed in the purple of the night, Flight Commander Raffleton fought the good fight for common sense.

Young persons who, scantily clad, go to sleep on the heather, five miles from the nearest human habitation, are to be avoided by well-brought-up young officers of His Majesty's Aerial Service. The incidence of their being uncannily beautiful and alluring should serve as an additional note of warning. The girl had had a row with her mother and wanted to get away. It was this infernal moonlight that was chiefly responsible. No wonder dogs bayed at it. He almost fancied he could hear one now. Nice, respectable, wholesome-minded things, dogs. No damned sentiment about them. What if he had kissed her! One is not bound for life to every woman one kisses. Not the first time she had been kissed, unless all the young men in Brittany were blind or white blooded. All this pretended innocence and simplicity! It was just put on. If not, she must be a lunatic. The proper thing to do was to say good-bye with a laugh and a jest, start up his machine and be off to England--dear old practical, merry England, where he could get breakfast and a bath.

It wasn't a fair fight; one feels it. Poor little prim Common Sense, with her defiant, turned-up nose and her shrill giggle and her innate vulgarity. And against her the stillness of the night, and the music of the ages, and the beating of his heart.

So it all fell down about his feet, a little crumbled dust that a passing breath of wind seemed to scatter, leaving him helpless, spellbound by the magic of her eyes.

"Who are you?" he asked her.

"Malvina," she answered him. "I am a fairy."

III. HOW COUSIN CHRISTOPHER BECAME MIXED UP WITH IT

It did just occur to him that maybe he had not made that descent quite as successfully as he had thought he had; that maybe he had come down on his head; that in consequence he had done with the experiences of Flight Commander Raffleton and was now about to enter on a new and less circumscribed existence. If so, the beginning, to an adventuresome young spirit, seemed promising. It was Malvina's voice that recalled him from this train of musing.

"Shall we go?" she repeated, and this time the note in her voice suggested command rather than question.

Why not? Whatever had happened to him, at whatever plane of existence he was now arrived, the machine apparently had followed him. Mechanically he started it up. The familiar whir of the engine brought back to him the possibility of his being alive in the ordinary acceptation of the term. It also suggested to him the practical advisability of insisting that Malvina should put on his spare coat. Malvina being five feet three, and the coat having been built for a man of six feet one, the effect under ordinary circumstances would have been comic. What finally convinced Commander Raffleton that Malvina really was a fairy was that, in that coat, with the collar standing up some six inches above her head, she looked more like one than ever.

Neither of them spoke. Somehow it did not seem to be needed. He helped her to climb into her seat and tucked the coat about her feet. She answered by the same smile with which she had first stretched out her hand to him. It was just a smile of endless content, as if all her troubles were now over. Commander Raffleton sincerely hoped they were. A momentary flash of intelligence suggested to him that his were just beginning.

Commander Raffleton's subconscious self it must have been that took charge of the machine. He seems, keeping a few miles inland, to have followed the line of the coast to a little south of the Hague lighthouse. Thereabouts he remembers descending for the purpose of replenishing his tank. Not having anticipated a passenger, he had filled up before starting with a spare supply of petrol, an incident that was fortunate. Malvina appears to have been interested in watching what she probably regarded as some novel breed of dragon being nourished from tins extricated from under her feet, but to have accepted this, together with all other details of the flight, as in the natural scheme of things. The monster refreshed, tugged, spurned the ground, and rose again with a roar; and the creeping sea rushed down.

One has the notion that for Flight Commander Raffleton, as for the rest of us, there lies in wait to test the heart of him the ugly and the commonplace. So large a portion of the years will be for him a business of mean hopes and fears, of sordid struggle, of low cares and vulgar fret. But also one has the conviction that there will always remain with him, to make life wonderful, the memory of that night when, godlike, he rode upon the winds of heaven crowned with the glory of the world's desire. Now and again he turned his head to look at her, and still, as ever, her eyes answered him with that strange deep content that seemed to wrap them both around as with a garment of immortality. One gathers dimly something of what he felt from the look that would unconsciously come into his eyes when speaking of that enchanted journey, from the sudden dumbness with which the commonplace words would die away upon his lips. Well for him that his lesser self kept firm hold upon the wheel or maybe a few broken spars, tossing upon the waves, would have been all that was left to tell of a promising young aviator who, on a summer night of June, had thought he could reach the stars.

Half-way across the dawn came flaming up over the Needles, and later there stole from east to west a long, low line of mist-enshrouded land. One by one headland and cliff, flashing with gold, rose out of the sea, and the white-winged gulls flew out to meet them. Almost he expected them to turn into spirits, circling round Malvina with cries of welcome.

Nearer and nearer they drew, while gradually the mist rose upward as the moonlight grew fainter. And all at once the sweep of the Chesil Bank stood out before them, with Weymouth sheltering behind it.

It may have been the bathing-machines, or the gasometer beyond the railway station, or the flag above the Royal Hotel. The curtains of the night fell suddenly away from him. The workaday world came knocking at the door.

He looked at his watch. It was a little after four. He had wired them at the camp to expect him in the morning. They would be looking out for him. By continuing his course he and Malvina could be there about breakfast-time. He could introduce her to the colonel: "Allow me, Colonel Goodyer, the fairy Malvina." It was either that or dropping Malvina somewhere between Weymouth and Farnborough. He decided, without much consideration, that this latter course would be preferable. But where? What was he to do with her? There was Aunt Emily. Hadn't she said something about wanting a French governess for Georgina? True, Malvina's French was a trifle old-fashioned in form, but her accent was charming. And as for salary--- There presented itself the thought of Uncle Felix and the three elder boys. Instinctively he felt that Malvina would not be Aunt Emily's idea. His father, had the dear old gentleman been alive, would have been a safe refuge. They had always understood one another, he and his father. But his mother! He was not at all sure. He visualised the scene: the drawing-room at Chester Terrace. His mother's soft, rustling entrance. Her affectionate but well-bred greeting. And then the disconcerting silence with which she would await his explanation of Malvina. The fact that she was a fairy he would probably omit to mention. Faced by his mother's gold-rimmed pince-nez, he did not see himself insisting upon that detail: "A young lady I happened to find asleep on a moor in Brittany. And seeing it was a fine night, and there being just room in the machine. And she--I mean I--well, here we are." There would follow such a painful silence, and then the raising of the delicately arched eyebrows: "You mean, my dear lad, that you have allowed this"--there would be a slight hesitation here--"this young person to leave her home, her people, her friends and relations in Brittany, in order to attach herself to you. May I ask in what capacity?"

For that was precisely how it would look, and not only to his mother. Suppose by a miracle it really represented the facts. Suppose that, in spite of the overwhelming evidence in her favour--of the night and the moon and the stars, and the feeling that had come to him from the moment he had kissed her--suppose that, in spite of all this, it turned out that she wasn't a fairy. Suppose that suggestion of vulgar Common Sense, that she was just a little minx that had run away from home, had really hit the mark. Suppose inquiries were already on foot. A hundred horse-power aeroplane does not go about unnoticed. Wasn't there a law about this sort of thing--something about "decoying" and "young girls"? He hadn't "decoyed" her. If anything, it was the other way about. But would her consent be a valid defence? How old was she? That would be the question. In reality he supposed about a thousand years or so. Possibly more. Unfortunately, she didn't look it. A coldly suspicious magistrate would probably consider sixteen a much better guess. Quite possibly he was going to get into a devil of a mess over this business. He cast a glance behind him. Malvina responded with her changeless smile of ineffable content. For the first time it caused him a distinct feeling of irritation.

They were almost over Weymouth by this time. He could read plainly the advertisement posters outside the cinema theatre facing the esplanade: "Wilkins and the Mermaid. Comic Drama." There was a picture of the lady combing her hair; also of Wilkins, a stoutish gentleman in striped bathing costume.

That mad impulse that had come to him with the first breath of dawn, to shake the dwindling world from his pinions, to plunge upward towards the stars never to return--he wished to Heaven he had yielded to it.

And then suddenly there leapt to him the thought of Cousin Christopher.

Dear old Cousin Christopher, fifty-eight and a bachelor. Why had it not occurred to him before? Out of the sky there appeared to Commander Raffleton the vision of "Cousin Christopher" as a plump, rubicund angel in a panama hat and a pepper-and-salt tweed suit holding out a lifebelt. Cousin Christopher would take to Malvina as some motherly hen to an orphaned duckling. A fairy discovered asleep beside one of the ancient menhirs of Brittany. His only fear would be that you might want to take her away before he had written a paper about her. He would be down from Oxford at his cottage. Commander Raffleton could not for the moment remember the name of the village. It would come to him. It was northwest of Newbury. You crossed Salisbury Plain and made straight for Magdalen Tower. The Downs reached almost to the orchard gate. There was a level stretch of sward nearly half a mile long. It seemed to Commander Raffleton that Cousin Christopher had been created and carefully preserved by Providence for this particular job.

He was no longer the moonstruck youth of the previous night, on whom phantasy and imagination could play what pranks they chose. That part of him the keen, fresh morning air had driven back into its cell. He was Commander Raffleton, an eager and alert young engineer with all his wits about him. At this point that has to be remembered. Descending on a lonely reach of shore he proceeded to again disturb Malvina for the purpose of extracting tins. He expected his passenger would in broad daylight prove to be a pretty, childish-looking girl, somewhat dishevelled, with, maybe, a tinge of blue about the nose, the natural result of a three-hours' flight at fifty miles an hour. It was with a startling return of his original sensations when first she had come to life beneath his kiss that he halted a few feet away and stared at her. The night was gone, and the silence. She stood there facing the sunlight, clad in a Burberry overcoat half a dozen sizes too large for her. Beyond her was a row of bathing-machines, and beyond that again a gasometer. A goods train half a mile away was noisily shunting trucks.

And yet the glamour was about her still; something indescribable but quite palpable--something out of which she looked at you as from another world.

He took her proffered hand, and she leapt out lightly. She was not in the least dishevelled. It seemed as if the air must be her proper element. She looked about her, interested, but not curious. Her first thought was for the machine.

"Poor thing!" she said. "He must be tired."

That faint tremor of fear that had come to him when beneath the menhir's shadow he had watched the opening of her eyes, returned to him. It was not an unpleasant sensation. Rather it added a piquancy to their relationship. But it was distinctly real. She watched the feeding of the monster; and then he came again and stood beside her on the yellow sands.

"England!" he explained with a wave of his hand. One fancies she had the impression that it belonged to him. Graciously she repeated the name. And somehow, as it fell from her lips, it conjured up to Commander Raffleton a land of wonder and romance.

"I have heard of it," she added. "I think I shall like it."

He answered that he hoped she would. He was deadly serious about it. He possessed, generally speaking, a sense of humour; but for the moment this must have deserted him. He told her he was going to leave her in the care of a wise and learned man called "Cousin Christopher"; his description no doubt suggesting to Malvina a friendly magician. He himself would have to go away for a little while, but would return.

It did not seem to matter to Malvina, these minor details. It was evident--the idea in her mind--that he had been appointed to her.

Whether as master or servant it was less easy to conjecture: probably a mixture of both, with preference towards the latter.

He mentioned again that he would not be away for longer than he could help. There was no necessity for this repetition. She wasn't doubting it.

Weymouth with its bathing machines and its gasometer faded away. King Rufus was out a-hunting as they passed over the New Forest, and from Salisbury Plain, as they looked down, the pixies waved their hands and laughed. Later, they heard the clang of the anvil, telling them they were in the neighbourhood of Wayland Smith's cave; and so planed down sweetly and without a jar just beyond Cousin Christopher's orchard gate.

A shepherd's boy was whistling somewhere upon the Downs, and in the valley a ploughman had just harnessed his team; but the village was hidden from them by the sweep of the hills, and no other being was in sight. He helped Malvina out, and leaving her seated on a fallen branch beneath a walnut tree, proceeded cautiously towards the house. He found a little maid in the garden. She had run out of the house on hearing the sound of his propeller and was staring up into the sky, so that she never saw him until he put his hand upon her shoulder, and then was fortunately too frightened to scream. He gave her hasty instructions. She was to knock at the Professor's door and tell him that his cousin, Commander Raffleton, was there, and would he come down at once, by himself, into the orchard. Commander Raffleton would rather not come in. Would the Professor come down at once and speak to Commander Raffleton in the orchard.

She went back into the house, repeating it all to herself, a little scared.

"Good God!" said Cousin Christopher from beneath the bedclothes. "He isn't hurt, is he?"

The little maid, through the jar of the door, thought not. Anyhow, he didn't look it. But would the Professor kindly come at once? Commander Raffleton was waiting for him--in the orchard.

So Cousin Christopher, in bedroom slippers, without socks, wearing a mustard-coloured dressing-gown and a black skull cap upon his head-- the very picture of a friendly magician--trotted hastily downstairs and through the garden, talking to himself about "foolhardy boys" and "knowing it would happen"; and was much relieved to meet young Arthur Raffleton coming towards him, evidently sound in wind and limb. And then began to wonder why the devil he had been frightened out of bed at six o'clock in the morning if nothing was the matter.

But something clearly was. Before speaking Arthur Raffleton looked carefully about him in a manner suggestive of mystery, if not of crime; and still without a word, taking Cousin Christopher by the arm, led the way to the farther end of the orchard. And there, on a fallen branch beneath the walnut tree, Cousin Christopher saw apparently a khaki coat, with nothing in it, which, as they approached it, rose up.

But it did not rise very high. The back of the coat was towards them. Its collar stood out against the sky line. But there wasn't any head. Standing upright, it turned round, and peeping out of its folds Cousin Christopher saw a child's face. And then looking closer saw that it wasn't a child. And then wasn't quite sure what it was; so that coming to a sudden halt in front of it, Cousin Christopher stared at it with round wide eyes, and then at Flight Commander Raffleton.

It was to Malvina that Flight Commander Raffleton addressed himself.

"This," he said, "is Professor Littlecherry, my Cousin Christopher, about whom I told you."

It was obvious that Malvina regarded the Professor as a person of importance. Evidently her intention was to curtsy, an operation that, hampered by those trailing yards of clinging khaki, might prove--so it flashed upon the Professor--not only difficult but dangerous.

"Allow me," said the Professor.

His idea was to help Malvina out of Commander Raffleton's coat, and Malvina was preparing to assist him. Commander Raffleton was only just in time.

"I don't think," said Commander Raffleton. "If you don't mind I think we'd better leave that for Mrs. Muldoon."

The Professor let go the coat. Malvina appeared a shade disappointed. One opines that not unreasonably she may have thought to make a better impression without it. But a smiling acquiescence in all arrangements made for her welfare seems to have been one of her charms.

"Perhaps," suggested Commander Raffleton to Malvina while refastening a few of the more important buttons, "if you wouldn't mind explaining yourself to my Cousin Christopher just exactly who and what you are--you'd do it so much better than I should." (What Commander Raffleton was saying to himself was: "If I tell the dear old Johnny, he'll think I'm pulling his leg. It will sound altogether different the way she will put it.") "You're sure you don't mind?"

Malvina hadn't the slightest objection. She accomplished her curtsy--or rather it looked as if the coat were curtsying--quite gracefully, and with a dignity one would not have expected from it.

"I am the fairy Malvina," she explained to the Professor. "You may have heard of me. I was the favourite of Harbundia, Queen of the White Ladies of Brittany. But that was long ago."

The friendly magician was staring at her with a pair of round eyes that in spite of their amazement looked kindly and understanding. They probably encouraged Malvina to complete the confession of her sad brief history.

"It was when King Heremon ruled over Ireland," she continued. "I did a very foolish and a wicked thing, and was punished for it by being cast out from the companionship of my fellows. Since then"-- the coat made the slightest of pathetic gestures--"I have wandered alone."

It ought to have sounded so ridiculous to them both; told on English soil in the year One Thousand Nine Hundred and Fourteen to a smart young officer of Engineers and an elderly Oxford Professor. Across the road the doctor's odd man was opening garage doors; a noisy milk cart was clattering through the village a little late for the London train; a faint odour of eggs and bacon came wafted through the garden, mingled with the scent of lavender and pinks. For Commander Raffleton, maybe, there was excuse. This story, so far as it has gone, has tried to make that clear. But the Professor! He ought to have exploded in a burst of Homeric laughter, or else to have shaken his head at her and warned her where little girls go to who do this sort of thing.

Instead of which he stared from Commander Raffleton to Malvina, and from Malvina back to Commander Raffleton with eyes so astonishingly round that they might have been drawn with a compass.

"God bless my soul!" said the Professor. "But this is most extraordinary!"

"Was there a King Heremon of Ireland?" asked Commander Raffleton. The Professor was a well-known authority on these matters.

"Of course there was a King Heremon of Ireland," answered the Professor quite petulantly--as if the Commander had wanted to know if there had ever been a Julius Caesar or a Napoleon. "And so there was a Queen Harbundia. Malvina is always spoken of in connection with her."

"What did she do?" inquired Commander Raffleton. They both of them seemed to be oblivious of Malvina's presence.

"I forget for the moment," confessed the professor. "I must look it up. Something, if I remember rightly, in connection with the daughter of King Dancrat. He founded the Norman dynasty. William the Conqueror and all that lot. Good Lord!"

"Would you mind her staying with you for a time until I can make arrangements," suggested Commander Raffleton. "I'd be awfully obliged if you would."

What the Professor's answer might have been had he been allowed to exercise such stock of wits as he possessed, it is impossible to say. Of course he was interested--excited, if you will. Folklore, legend, tradition; these had been his lifelong hobbies. Apart from anything else, here at least was a kindred spirit. Seemed to know a thing or two. Where had she learned it? Might not there be sources unknown to the Professor?

But to take her in! To establish her in the only spare bedroom. To introduce her--as what? to English village society. To the new people at the Manor House. To the member of Parliament with his innocent young wife who had taken the vicarage for the summer. To Dawson, R.A., and the Calthorpes!

He might, had he thought it worth his while, have found some respectable French family and boarded her out. There was a man he had known for years at Oxford, a cabinetmaker; the wife a most worthy woman. He could have gone over there from time to time, his notebook in his pocket, and have interviewed her.

Left to himself, he might have behaved as a sane and rational citizen; or he might not. There are records favouring the latter possibility. The thing is not certain. But as regards this particular incident in his career he must be held exonerated. The decision was taken out of his hands.

To Malvina, on first landing in England, Commander Raffleton had stated his intention of leaving her temporarily in the care of the wise and learned Christopher. To Malvina, regarding the Commander as a gift from the gods, that had settled the matter. The wise and learned Christopher, of course, knew of this coming. In all probability it was he--under the guidance of the gods--who had arranged the whole sequence of events. There remained only to tender him her gratitude. She did not wait for the Professor's reply. The coat a little hindered her but, on the other hand, added perhaps an appealing touch of its own. Taking the wise and learned Christopher's hand in both her own, she knelt and kissed it.

And in that quaint archaic French of hers, that long study of the Chronicles of Froissart enabled the Professor to understand:

"I thank you," she said, "for your noble courtesy and hospitality."

In some mysterious way the whole affair had suddenly become imbued with the dignity of an historical event. The Professor had the sudden impression--and indeed it never altogether left him so long as Malvina remained--that he was a great and powerful personage. A sister potentate; incidentally--though, of course, in high politics such points are immaterial--the most bewilderingly beautiful being he had ever seen; had graciously consented to become his guest. The Professor, with a bow that might have been acquired at the court of King Rene, expressed his sense of the honour done to him. What else could a self-respecting potentate do? The incident was closed.

Flight Commander Raffleton seems to have done nothing in the direction of re-opening it. On the contrary, he appears to have used this precise moment for explaining to the Professor how absolutely necessary it was that he should depart for Farnborough without another moment's loss of time. Commander Raffleton added that he would "look them both up again" the first afternoon he could get away; and was sure that if the Professor would get Malvina to speak slowly, he would soon find her French easy to understand.

It did occur to the Professor to ask Commander Raffleton where he had found Malvina--that is, if he remembered. Also what he was going to do about her--that is, if he happened to know. Commander Raffleton, regretting his great need of haste, explained that he had found Malvina asleep beside a menhir not far from Huelgoat, in Brittany, and was afraid that he had woke her up. For further particulars, would the Professor kindly apply to Malvina? For himself, he would never, he felt sure, be able to thank the professor sufficiently.

In conclusion, and without giving further opportunity for discussion, the Commander seems to have shaken his Cousin Christopher by the hand with much enthusiasm; and then to have turned to Malvina. She did not move, but her eyes were fixed on him. And he came to her slowly. And without a word he kissed her full upon the lips.

"That is twice you have kissed me," said Malvina--and a curious little smile played round her mouth. "The third time I shall become a woman."

IV. HOW IT WAS KEPT FROM MRS. ARLINGTON

What surprised the Professor himself, when he came to think of it, was that, left alone with Malvina, and in spite of all the circumstances, he felt neither embarrassment nor perplexity. It was as if, so far as they two were concerned, the whole thing was quite simple--almost humorous. It would be the other people who would have to worry.

The little serving maid was hovering about the garden. She was evidently curious and trying to get a peep. Mrs. Muldoon's voice could be heard calling to her from the kitchen. There was this question of clothes.

"You haven't brought anything with you?" asked the Professor. "I mean, in the way of a frock of any sort."

Malvina, with a smile, gave a little gesture. It implied that all there was of her and hers stood before him.

"We shall have to find you something," said the Professor. "Something in which you can go about--"

The Professor had intended to say "our world," but hesitated, not feeling positive at the moment to which he himself belonged; Malvina's or Mrs. Muldoon's. So he made it "the" world instead. Another gesture conveyed to him that Malvina was entirely in his hands.

"What really have you got on?" asked the Professor. "I mean underneath. Is it anything possible--for a day or two?"

Now Commander Raffleton, for some reason of his own not at all clear to Malvina, had forbidden the taking off of the coat. But had said nothing about undoing it. So by way of response Malvina undid it.

Upon which the Professor, to Malvina's surprise, acted precisely as Commander Raffleton had done. That is to say, he hastily re-closed the coat, returning the buttons to their buttonholes.

The fear may have come to Malvina that she was doomed never to be rid of Commander Raffleton's coat.

"I wonder," mused the Professor, "if anyone in the village--" The little serving maid flittering among the gooseberry bushes--she was pretending to be gathering goose-berries--caught the Professor's eye.

"We will consult my chatelaine, Mrs. Muldoon," suggested the Professor. "I think we shall be able to manage."

The Professor tendered Malvina his arm. With her other hand she gathered up the skirts of the Commander's coat.

"I think," said the Professor with a sudden inspiration as they passed through the garden, "I think I shall explain to Mrs. Muldoon that you have just come straight from a fancy-dress ball."

They found Mrs. Muldoon in the kitchen. A less convincing story than that by which the Professor sought to account to Mrs. Muldoon for the how and the why of Malvina it would be impossible to imagine. Mrs. Muldoon out of sheer kindness appears to have cut him short.

"I'll not be asking ye any questions," said Mrs. Muldoon, "so there'll be no need for ye to imperil your immortal soul. If ye'll just give a thought to your own appearance and leave the colleen to me and Drusilla, we'll make her maybe a bit dacent.

The reference to his own appearance disconcerted the Professor. He had not anticipated, when hastening into his dressing gown and slippers and not bothering about his socks, that he was on his way to meet the chief lady-in-waiting of Queen Harbundia. Demanding that shaving water should be immediately sent up to him, he appears to have retired into the bathroom.

It was while he was shaving that Mrs. Muldoon, knocking at the door, demanded to speak to him. From her tone the Professor came to the conclusion that the house was on fire. He opened the door, and Mrs. Muldoon, seeing he was respectable, slipped in and closed it behind her.

"Where did ye find her? How did she get here?" demanded Mrs. Muldoon. Never before had the Professor seen Mrs. Muldoon other than a placid, good-humoured body. She was trembling from head to foot.

"I told you," explained the Professor. "Young Arthur--"

"I'm not asking ye what ye told me," interrupted Mrs. Muldoon. "I'm asking ye for the truth, if ye know it."

The Professor put a chair for Mrs. Muldoon, and Mrs. Muldoon dropped down upon it.

"What's the matter?" questioned the Professor. "What's happened?"

Mrs. Muldoon glanced round her, and her voice was an hysterical whisper.

"It's no mortal woman ye've brought into the house," said Mrs. Muldoon. "It's a fairy."

Whether up to that moment the Professor had really believed Malvina's story, or whether lurking at the back of his mind there had all along been an innate conviction that the thing was absurd, the Professor himself is now unable to say. To the front of the Professor lay Oxford--political economy, the higher criticism, the rise and progress of rationalism. Behind him, fading away into the dim horizon of humanity, lay an unmapped land where for forty years he had loved to wander; a spirit-haunted land of buried mysteries, lost pathways, leading unto hidden gates of knowledge.

And now upon the trembling balance descended Mrs. Muldoon plump.

"How do you know?" demanded the Professor.

"Shure, don't I know the mark?" replied Mrs. Muldoon almost contemptuously. "Wasn't my own sister's child stolen away the very day of its birth and in its place--"

The little serving maid tapped at the door.

Mademoiselle was "finished." What was to be done with her?

"Don't ask me," protested Mrs. Muldoon, still in a terrified whisper. "I couldn't do it. Not if all the saints were to go down upon their knees and pray to me."

Common-sense argument would not have prevailed with Mrs. Muldoon. The Professor felt that; added to which he had not any handy. He directed, through the door, that "Mademoiselle" should be shown into the dining-room, and listened till Drusilla's footsteps had died away.

"Have you ever heard of the White Ladies?" whispered the Professor to Mrs. Muldoon.

There was not much in the fairy line, one takes it, that Mrs. Muldoon had not heard of and believed. Was the Professor sure?

The Professor gave Mrs. Muldoon his word of honour as a gentleman. The "White Ladies," as Mrs. Muldoon was of course aware, belonged to the "good people." Provided nobody offended her there was nothing to fear.

"Shure, it won't be meself that'll cross her," said Mrs. Muldoon.

"She won't be staying very long," added the Professor. "We will just be nice to her."

"She's got a kind face," admitted Mrs. Muldoon, "and a pleasant way with her." The good body's spirits were perceptibly rising. The favour of a "White Lady" might be worth cultivating.

"We must make a friend of her," urged the Professor, seizing his opportunity.

"And mind," whispered the Professor as he opened the door for Mrs. Muldoon to slip out, "not a word. She doesn't want it known."

One is convinced that Mrs. Muldoon left the bathroom resolved that, so far as she could help it, no breath of suspicion that Malvina was other than what in Drusilla's holiday frock she would appear to be should escape into the village. It was quite a pleasant little frock of a summery character, with short sleeves and loose about the neck, and fitted Malvina, in every sense, much better than the most elaborate confection would have done. The boots were not so successful. Malvina solved the problem by leaving them behind her, together with the stockings, whenever she went out. That she knew this was wrong is proved by the fact that invariably she tried to hide them. They would be found in the most unlikely places; hidden behind books in the Professor's study, crammed into empty tea canisters in Mrs. Muldoon's storeroom. Mrs. Muldoon was not to be persuaded even to abstract them. The canister with its contents would be placed in silence upon the Professor's table. Malvina on returning would be confronted by a pair of stern, unsympathetic boots. The corners of the fairy mouth would droop in lines suggestive of penitence and contrition.

Had the Professor been firm she would have yielded. But from the black accusing boots the Professor could not keep his eyes from wandering to the guilty white feet, and at once in his heart becoming "counsel for the defence." Must get a pair of sandals next time he went to Oxford. Anyhow, something more dainty than those grim, uncompromising boots.

Besides, it was not often that Malvina ventured beyond the orchard. At least not during the day time--perhaps one ought to say not during that part of the day time when the village was astir. For Malvina appears to have been an early riser. Somewhere about the middle of the night, as any Christian body would have timed it, Mrs. Muldoon--waking and sleeping during this period in a state of high nervous tension--would hear the sound of a softly opened door; peeping from a raised corner of the blind, would catch a glimpse of fluttering garments that seemed to melt into the dawn; would hear coming fainter and fainter from the uplands an unknown song, mingling with the answering voices of the birds.

It was on the uplands between dawn and sunrise that Malvina made the acquaintance of the Arlington twins.

They ought, of course, to have been in bed--all three of them, for the matter of that. The excuse for the twins was their Uncle George. He had been telling them all about the Uffington spectre and Wayland Smith's cave, and had given them "Puck" as a birthday present. They were always given their birthday presents between them, because otherwise they did not care for them. They had retired to their respective bedrooms at ten o'clock and taken it in turns to lie awake. At the first streak of dawn Victoria, who had been watching by her window, woke Victor, as arranged. Victor was for giving it up and going to sleep again, but Victoria reminding him of the "oath," they dressed themselves quite simply, and let themselves down by the ivy.

They came across Malvina close to the tail of the White Horse. They knew she was a fairy the moment they saw her. But they were not frightened--at least not very much. It was Victor who spoke first. Taking off his hat and going down on one knee, he wished Malvina good morning and hoped she was quite well. Malvina, who seemed pleased to see them, made answer, and here it was that Victoria took charge of the affair. The Arlington twins until they were nine had shared a French nurse between them; and then

Victor, going to school, had gradually forgotten; while Victoria, remaining at home, had continued her conversations with "madame."

"Oh!" said Victoria. "Then you must be a French fairy."

Now the Professor had impressed upon Malvina that for reasons needless to be explained--anyhow, he never had explained them--she was not to mention that she was a fairy. But he had not told her to deny it. Indeed how could she? The most that could be expected from her was that she should maintain silence on the point. So in answer to Victoria she explained that her name was Malvina, and that she had flown across from Brittany in company with "Sir Arthur," adding that she had often heard of England and had wished to see it.

"How do you like it?" demanded Victoria.

Malvina confessed herself charmed with it. Nowhere had she ever met so many birds. Malvina raised her hand and they all three stood in silence, listening. The sky was ablaze and the air seemed filled with their music. The twins were sure that there were millions of them. They must have come from miles and miles and miles, to sing to Malvina.

Also the people. They were so good and kind and round. Malvina for the present was staying with--accepting the protection, was how she put it, of the wise and learned Christopher. The "habitation" could be seen from where they stood, its chimneys peeping from among the trees. The twins exchanged a meaning glance. Had they not all along suspected the Professor! His black skull cap, and his big hooked nose, and the yellow-leaved, worm-eaten books--of magic: all doubts were now removed--that for hours he would sit poring over through owlish gold-rimmed spectacles!

Victor's French was coming back to him. He was anxious to know if Malvina had ever met Sir Launcelot--"to talk to."

A little cloud gathered upon Malvina's face. Yes, she had known them all: King Uthur and Igraine and Sir Ulfias of the Isles. Talked with them, walked with them in the fair lands of France. (It ought to have been England, but Malvina shook her head. Maybe they had travelled.) It was she who had saved Sir Tristram from the wiles of

Morgan le Fay. "Though that, of course," explained Malvina, "was never known."

The twins were curious why it should have been "of course," but did not like to interrupt again. There were others before and after. Most of them the twins had never heard of until they came to Charlemagne, beyond which Malvina's reminiscences appeared to fade.

They had all of them been very courteous to her, and some of them indeed quite charming. But...

One gathers they had never been to Malvina more than mere acquaintances, such as one passes the time with while waiting--and longing.

"But you liked Sir Launcelot," urged Victor. He was wishful that Malvina should admire Sir Launcelot, feeling how much there was in common between that early lamented knight and himself. That little affair with Sir Bedivere. It was just how he would have behaved himself.

Ah! yes, admitted Malvina. She had "liked" him. He was always so-- so "excellent."

"But he was not--none of them were my own people, my own dear companions." The little cloud had settled down again.

It was Bruno who recalled the three of them to the period of contemporary history.

Polley the cowman's first duty in the morning was to let Bruno loose for a run. He arrived panting and breathless, and evidently offended at not having been included in the escapade. He could have given them both away quite easily if he had not been the most forgiving of black-and-tan collies. As it was, he had been worrying himself crazy for the last half-hour, feeling sure they had forgotten the time. "Don't you know it's nearly six o'clock? That in less than half an hour Jane will be knocking at your doors with glasses of hot milk, and will probably drop them and scream when she finds your beds empty and the window wide open." That is what he had intended should be his first words, but on scenting Malvina they went from him entirely. He gave her one look and flopped down flat, wriggling towards her, whining and wagging his tail at the same time. Malvina acknowledged his homage by laughing and patting his head with her foot, and that sent him into the seventh heaven of delight. They all four descended the hill together and parted at the orchard gate. The twins expressed a polite but quite sincere hope that they would have the pleasure of seeing Malvina again; but Malvina, seized maybe with sudden doubts as to whether she had behaved with discretion, appears to have replied evasively. Ten minutes later she was lying asleep, the golden head pillowed on the round white arm; as Mrs. Muldoon on her way down to the kitchen saw for herself. And the twins, fortunate enough to find a side door open, slipped into the house unnoticed and scrambled back into their beds.

It was quarter past nine when Mrs. Arlington came in herself and woke them up. She was short-tempered with them both and had evidently been crying. They had their breakfast in the kitchen.

During lunch hardly a word was spoken. And there was no pudding. Mr. Arlington, a stout, florid gentleman, had no time for pudding. The rest might sit and enjoy it at their leisure, but not so Mr. Arlington. Somebody had to see to things--that is, if they were not to be allowed to go to rack and ruin. If other people could not be relied upon to do their duty, so that everything inside the house and out of it was thrown upon one pair of shoulders, then it followed as a natural consequence that that pair of shoulders could not spare the necessary time to properly finish its meals. This it was that was at the root of the decay of English farming. When farmers' wives, to say nothing of sons and daughters old enough one might imagine to be anxious to do something in repayment for the money and care lavished upon them, had all put their shoulders to the wheel, then English farming had prospered. When, on the other hand, other people shirked their fair share of labour and responsibility, leaving to one pair of hands ...

It was the eldest Arlington girl's quite audible remark that pa could have eaten two helpings of pudding while he had been talking, that caused Mr. Arlington to lose the thread of his discourse. To put it quite bluntly, what Mr. Arlington meant to say was this: He had never wanted to be a farmer--at least not in the beginning. Other men in his position, having acquired competency by years of self-sacrificing labour, would have retired to a well-earned leisure. Having yielded to persuasion and taken on the job, he was going to see it through; and everybody else was going to do their share or there would be trouble.

Mr. Arlington, swallowing the remains of his glass in a single gulp, spoilt a dignified exit by violently hiccoughing, and Mrs. Arlington rang the bell furiously for the parlourmaid to clear away. The pudding passed untouched from before the very eyes of the twins. It was a black-currant pudding with brown sugar.

That night Mrs. Arlington appears to have confided in the twins, partly for her own relief and partly for their moral benefit. If Mrs. Arlington had enjoyed the blessing in disguise of a less indulgent mother, all might have been well. By nature Mrs. Arlington had been endowed with an active and energetic temperament. "Miss Can't-sit-still-a-minute," her nurse had always called her. Unfortunately it had been allowed to sink into disuse; was now in all probability beyond hope of recovery. Their father was quite right. When they had lived in Bayswater and the business was in Mincing Lane it did not matter. Now it was different. A farmer's wife ought to be up at six; she ought to see that everybody else was up at six; servants looked after, kept up to the mark; children encouraged by their mother's example. Organisation. That was what was wanted. The day mapped out; to every hour its appointed task. Then, instead of the morning being gone before you could turn yourself round, and confusion made worse confounded by your leaving off what you were doing and trying to do six things at once that you couldn't remember whether you had done or whether you hadn't...

Here Mrs. Arlington appears to have dissolved into tears. Generally speaking, she was a placid, smiling, most amiable lady, quite delightful to have about the house provided all you demanded of her were pleasant looks and a sunny disposition. The twins appear to have joined their tears to hers. Tucked in and left to themselves, one imagines the problem being discussed with grave seriousness, much whispered conversation, then slept upon, the morning bringing with it ideas. The result being that the next evening, between high tea and supper, Mrs. Muldoon, answering herself the knock at the door, found twin figures standing hand in hand on the Professor's step.

They asked her if "the Fairy" was in.

V. HOW IT WAS TOLD TO MRS. MARIGOLD

There was no need of the proverbial feather. Mrs. Muldoon made a grab at the settle but missed it. She caught at a chair, but that gave way. It was the floor that finally stopped her.

"We're so sorry," apologised Victor. "We thought you knew. We ought to have said Mademoiselle Malvina."

Mrs. Muldoon regained her feet, and without answering walked straight into the study.

"They want to know," said Mrs. Muldoon, "if the Fairy's in." The Professor, with his back to the window, was reading. The light in the room was somewhat faint.

"Who wants to know?" demanded the Professor.

"The twins from the Manor House," explained Mrs. Muldoon.

"But what?--but who?" began the Professor.

"Shall I say 'not at home'?" suggested Mrs. Muldoon. "Or hadn't you better see them yourself."

"Show them in," directed the Professor.

They came in, looking a little scared and still holding one another by the hand. They wished the Professor good evening, and when he rose they backed away from him. The Professor shook hands with them, but they did not let go, so that Victoria gave him her right hand and Victor his left, and then at the Professor's invitation they sat themselves down on the extreme edge of the sofa.

"I hope we do not disturb you," said Victor. "We wanted to see Mademoiselle Malvina."

"Why do you want to see Mademoiselle Malvina?" inquired the Professor.

"It is something very private," said Victor.

"We wanted to ask her a great favour," said Victoria.

"I'm sorry," said the Professor, "but she isn't in. At least, I don't think so." (The Professor never was quite sure. "She slips in and out making no more noise than a wind-driven rose leaf," was Mrs. Muldoon's explanation.) "Hadn't you better tell me? Leave me to put it to her."

They looked at one another. It would never do to offend the wise and learned Christopher. Besides, a magician, it is to be assumed, has more ways than one of learning what people are thinking.

"It is about mamma," explained Victoria. "We wondered if Malvina would mind changing her."

The Professor had been reading up Malvina. It flashed across him that this had always been her speciality: Changing people. How had the Arlington twins discovered it? And why did they want their mother changed? And what did they want her changed into? It was shocking when you come to think of it! The Professor became suddenly so stern, that if the twins could have seen his expression--which, owing to the fading light, they couldn't--they would have been too frightened to answer.

"Why do you want your mother changed?" demanded the Professor. Even as it was his voice alarmed them.

"It's for her own good," faltered Victoria.

"Of course we don't mean into anything," explained Victor.

"Only her inside," added Victoria.

"We thought that Malvina might be able to improve her," completed Victor.

It was still very disgraceful. What were we coming to when children went about clamouring for their mothers to be "improved"! The atmosphere was charged with indignation. The twins felt it.

"She wants to be," persisted Victoria. "She wants to be energetic and to get up early in the morning and do things."

"You see," added Victor, "she was never properly brought up."

The Professor maintains stoutly that his only intention was a joke. It was not even as if anything objectionable had been suggested.

The Professor himself had on occasions been made the confidant of both.

"Best woman that ever lived, if only one could graft a little energy upon her. No sense of time. Too easy-going. No idea of keeping people up to the mark." So Mr. Arlington, over the nuts and wine.

"It's pure laziness. Oh, yes, it is. My friends say I'm so 'restful'; but that's the proper explanation of it--born laziness. And yet I try. You have no idea, Professor Littlecherry, how much I try." So Mrs. Arlington, laughingly, while admiring the Professor's roses.

Besides, how absurd to believe that Malvina could possibly change anybody! Way back, when the human brain was yet in process of evolution, such things may have been possible. Hypnotic suggestion, mesmeric influence, dormant brain cells quickened into activity by magnetic vibration. All that had been lost. These were the days of George the Fifth, not of King Heremon. What the Professor was really after was: How would Malvina receive the proposal? Of course she would try to get out of it. A dear little thing. But could any sane man, professor of mathematics ...

Malvina was standing beside him. No one had remarked her entrance. The eyes of the twins had been glued upon the wise and learned Christopher. The Professor, when he was thinking, never saw anything. Still, it was rather startling.

"We should never change what the good God has once fashioned," said Malvina. She spoke very gravely. The childishness seemed to have fallen from her.

"You didn't always think so," said the Professor. It nettled the Professor that all idea of this being a good joke had departed with the sound of Malvina's voice. She had that way with her.

She made a little gesture. It conveyed to the Professor that his remark had not been altogether in good taste.

"I speak as one who has learned," said Malvina.

"I beg your pardon," said the Professor. "I ought not to have said that."

Malvina accepted the Professor's apology with a bow.

"But this is something very different," continued the Professor.

Quite another interest had taken hold of the Professor. It was easy enough to summon Dame Commonsense to one's aid when Malvina was not present. Before those strange eyes the good lady had a habit of sneaking away. Suppose--of course the idea was ridiculous, but suppose--something did happen! As a psychological experiment was not one justified? What was the beginning of all science but applied curiosity? Malvina might be able--and willing--to explain how it was done. That is, if anything did happen, which, of course, it wouldn't, and so much the better. This thing had got to be ended.

"It would be using a gift not for one's own purposes, but to help others," urged the Professor.

"You see," urged Victor, "mamma really wants to be changed."

"And papa wants it too," urged Victoria.

"It seems to me, if I may so express it," added the Professor, "that really it would be in the nature of making amends for--well, for- -for our youthful follies," concluded the Professor a little nervously.

Malvina's eyes were fixed on the Professor. In the dim light of the low-ceilinged room, those eyes seemed all of her that was visible.

"You wish it?" said Malvina.

It was not at all fair, as the Professor told himself afterwards, her laying the responsibility on him. If she really was the original Malvina, lady-in-waiting to Queen Harbundia, then she was quite old enough to have decided for herself. From the Professor's calculations she must now be about three thousand eight hundred. The Professor himself was not yet sixty; in comparison a mere babe! But Malvina's eyes were compelling.

"Well, it can't do any harm," said the Professor. And Malvina seems to have accepted that as her authority.

"Let her come to the Cross Stones at sundown," directed Malvina.

The Professor saw the twins to the door. For some reason the Professor could not have explained, they all three walked out on tiptoe. Old Mr. Brent, the postman, was passing, and the twins ran after him and each took a hand. Malvina was still standing where the Professor had left her. It was very absurd, but the Professor felt frightened. He went into the kitchen, where it was light and cheerful, and started Mrs. Muldoon on Home Rule. When he returned to the parlour Malvina was gone.

The twins did not talk that night, and decided next morning not to say a word, but just to ask their mother to come for an evening walk with them. The fear was that she might demand reasons. But, quite oddly, she consented without question. It seemed to the twins that it was Mrs. Arlington herself who took the pathway leading past the cave, and when they reached the Cross Stones she sat down and apparently had forgotten their existence. They stole away without her noticing them, but did not quite know what to do with themselves. They ran for half a mile till they came to the wood; there they remained awhile, careful not to venture within; and then they crept back. They found their mother sitting just as they had left her. They thought she was asleep, but her eyes were wide open. They were tremendously relieved, though what they had feared they never knew. They sat down, one on each side of her, and each took a hand, but in spite of her eyes being open, it was quite a time before she seemed conscious of their return. She rose and slowly looked about her, and as she did so the church clock struck nine. She could not at first believe it was so late. Convinced by looking at her watch--there was just light enough for her to see it--she became all at once more angry than the twins had ever known her, and for the first time in their lives they both experienced the sensation of having their ears boxed. Nine o'clock was the proper time for supper and they were half an hour from home, and it was all their fault. It did not take them half an hour. It took them twenty minutes, Mrs. Arlington striding ahead and the twins panting breathless behind her. Mr. Arlington had not yet returned. He came in five minutes afterwards, and Mrs. Arlington told him what she thought of him. It was the shortest supper within the twins' recollection. They found themselves in bed ten minutes in advance of the record. They could hear their mother's voice from the kitchen. A jug of milk had been overlooked and had gone sour. She had given Jane a week's notice before the clock struck ten.

It was from Mr. Arlington that the Professor heard the news. Mr.

Arlington could not stop an instant, dinner being at twelve sharp and it wanting but ten minutes to; but seems to have yielded to temptation. The breakfast hour at the Manor Farm was now six a.m., had been so since Thursday; the whole family fully dressed and Mrs. Arlington presiding. If the Professor did not believe it he could come round any morning and see for himself. The Professor appears to have taken Mr. Arlington's word for it. By six-thirty everybody at their job and Mrs. Arlington at hers, consisting chiefly of seeing to it for the rest of the day that everybody was. Lights out at ten and everybody in bed; most of them only too glad to be there. "Quite right; keeps us all up to the mark," was Mr. Arlington's opinion (this was on Saturday). Just what was wanted. Not perhaps for a permanency; and, of course, there were drawbacks. The strenuous life--seeing to it that everybody else leads the strenuous life; it does not go with unmixed amiability. Particularly in the beginning. New-born zeal: must expect it to outrun discretion. Does not do to discourage it. Modifications to be suggested later. Taken all round, Mr. Arlington's view was that the thing must be regarded almost as the answer to a prayer. Mr. Arlington's eyes on their way to higher levels, appear to have been arrested by the church clock. It decided Mr. Arlington to resume his homeward way without further loss of time. At the bend of the lane the Professor, looking back, observed that Mr. Arlington had broken into a trot.

This seems to have been the end of the Professor, regarded as a sane and intelligent member of modern society. He had not been sure at the time, but it was now revealed to him that when he had urged Malvina to test her strength, so to express it, on the unfortunate Mrs. Arlington, it was with the conviction that the result would restore him to his mental equilibrium. That Malvina with a wave of her wand--or whatever the hocus-pocus may have been--would be able to transform the hitherto incorrigibly indolent and easy-going Mrs. Arlington into a sort of feminine Lloyd George, had not really entered into his calculations.

Forgetting his lunch, he must have wandered aimlessly about, not returning home until late in the afternoon. During dinner he appears to have been rather restless and nervous--"jumpy," according to the evidence of the little serving maid. Once he sprang out of his chair as if shot when the little serving maid accidentally let fall a table-spoon; and twice he upset the salt. It was at mealtime that, as a rule, the Professor found his attitude towards Malvina most sceptical. A fairy who could put away quite a respectable cut from the joint, followed by two helpings of pie, does take a bit of believing in. To-night the Professor found no difficulty. The White Ladies had never been averse to accepting mortal hospitality. There must always have been a certain adaptability. Malvina, since that fateful night of her banishment, had, one supposes, passed through varied experiences. For present purposes she had assumed the form of a jeune fille of the twentieth century (anno Domini). An appreciation of Mrs. Muldoon's excellent cooking, together with a glass of light sound claret, would naturally go with it.

One takes it that he could not for a moment get Mrs. Arlington out of his mind. More than once, stealing a covert glance across the table, it seemed to him that Malvina was regarding him with a mocking smile. Some impish spirit it must have been that had prompted him. For thousands of years Malvina had led--at all events so far as was known--a reformed and blameless existence; had subdued and put behind her that fatal passion of hers for change: in other people. What madness to have revived it! And no Queen Harbundia handy now to keep her in check. The Professor had a distinct sensation, while peeling a pear, that he was being turned into a guinea-pig--a curious feeling of shrinking about the legs. So vivid was the impression, that involuntarily the Professor jumped off his chair and ran to look at himself in the mirror over the sideboard. He was not fully relieved even then. It may have been the mirror. It was very old; one of those things with little gilt balls all round it; and it looked to the Professor as if his nose was growing straight out of his face. Malvina, trusting he had not been taken suddenly ill, asked if there was anything she could do for him. He seems to have earnestly begged her not to think of it.

The Professor had taught Malvina cribbage, and usually of an evening they played a hand or two. But to-night the Professor was not in the mood, and Malvina had contented herself with a book. She was particularly fond of the old chroniclers. The Professor had an entire shelf of them, many in the original French. Making believe to be reading himself, he heard Malvina break into a cheerful laugh, and went and looked over her shoulder. She was reading the history of her own encounter with the proprietor of tin mines, an elderly gentleman disliking late hours, whom she had turned into a nightingale. It occurred to the Professor that prior to the Arlington case the recalling of this incident would have brought to her shame and remorse. Now she seemed to think it funny.

"A silly trick," commented the Professor. He spoke quite heatedly. "No one has any right to go about changing people. Muddling up things they don't understand. No right whatever."

Malvina looked up. She gave a little sigh.

"Not for one's own pleasure or revenge," she made answer. Her tone was filled with meekness. It had a touch of self-reproach. "That is very wrong, of course. But changing them for their own good--at least, not changing, improving."

"Little hypocrite!" muttered the Professor to himself. "She's got back a taste for her old tricks, and Lord knows now where she'll stop."

The Professor spent the rest of the evening among his indexes in search of the latest information regarding Queen Harbundia.

Meanwhile the Arlington affair had got about the village. The twins in all probability had been unable to keep their secret. Jane, the dismissed, had looked in to give Mrs. Muldoon her version of Thursday night's scene in the Arlington kitchen, and Mrs. Muldoon, with a sense of things impending, may unconsciously have dropped hints.

The Marigolds met the Arlingtons on Sunday, after morning service, and heard all about it. That is to say, they met Mr. Arlington and the other children; Mrs. Arlington, with the two elder girls, having already attended early communion at seven. Mrs. Marigold was a pretty, fluffy, engaging little woman, ten years younger than her husband. She could not have been altogether a fool, or she would not have known it. Marigold, rising politician, ought, of course, to have married a woman able to help him; but seems to have fallen in love with her a few miles out of Brussels, over a convent wall. Mr. Arlington was not a regular church-goer, but felt on this occasion that he owed it to his Maker. He was still in love with his new wife. But not blindly. Later on a guiding hand might be necessary. But first let the new seed get firmly rooted. Marigold's engagements necessitated his returning to town on Sunday afternoon, and Mrs. Marigold walked part of the way with him to the station. On her way back across the fields she picked up the Arlington twins. Later, she seems to have called in at the cottage and spoken to Mrs. Muldoon about Jane, who, she had heard, was in want of a place. A little before sunset she was seen by the Doctor climbing the path to the Warren. Malvina that evening was missing for dinner. When she returned she seemed pleased with herself.

VI. AND HOW IT WAS FINISHED TOO SOON

Some days later--it may have been the next week; the exact date appears to have got mislaid--Marigold, M.P., looked in on the Professor. They talked about Tariff Reform, and then Marigold got up and made sure for himself that the door was tight closed.

"You know my wife," he said. "We've been married six years, and there's never been a cloud between us except one. Of course, she's not brainy. That is, at least . . ."

The Professor jumped out of his chair.

"If you take my advice," he said, "you'll leave her alone." He spoke with passion and conviction.

Marigold looked up.

"It's just what I wish to goodness I had done," he answered. "I blame myself entirely."

"So long as we see our own mistakes," said the Professor, "there is hope for us all. You go straight home, young man, and tell her you've changed your mind. Tell her you don't want her with brains. Tell her you like her best without. You get that into her head before anything else happens."

"I've tried to," said Marigold. "She says it's too late. That the light has come to her and she can't help it."

It was the Professor's turn to stare. He had not heard anything of Sunday's transactions. He had been hoping against hope that the Arlington affair would remain a locked secret between himself and the twins, and had done his best to think about everything else.

"She's joined the Fabian Society," continued Marigold gloomily. "They've put her in the nursery. And the W.S.P.U. If it gets about before the next election I'll have to look out for another constituency--that's all."

"How did you hear about her?" asked the Professor.

"I didn't hear about her," answered Marigold. "If I had I mightn't have gone up to town. You think it right," he added, "to--to encourage such people?"

"Who's encouraging her?" demanded the professor. "If fools didn't go about thinking they could improve every other fool but themselves, this sort of thing wouldn't happen. Arlington had an amiable, sweet-tempered wife, and instead of thanking God and keeping quiet about it, he worries her out of her life because she is not the managing woman. Well, now he's got the managing woman. I met him on Wednesday with a bump on his forehead as big as an egg. Says he fell over the mat. It can't be done. You can't have a person changed just as far as you want them changed and there stop. You let 'em alone or you change them altogether, and then they don't know themselves what they're going to turn out. A sensible man in your position would have been only too thankful for a wife who didn't poke her nose into his affairs, and with whom he could get away from his confounded politics. You've been hinting to her about once a month, I expect, what a tragedy it was that you hadn't married a woman with brains. Well, now she's found her brains and is using them. Why shouldn't she belong to the Fabian Society and the

W.S.P.U? Shows independence of character. Best thing for you to do is to join them yourself. Then you'll be able to work together."

"I'm sorry," said Marigold rising. "I didn't know you agreed with her."

"Who said I agreed with her?" snapped the Professor. "I'm in a very awkward position."

"I suppose," said Marigold--he was hesitating with the door in his hand--"it wouldn't be of any use my seeing her myself?"

"I believe," said the Professor, "that she is fond of the neighbourhood of the Cross Stones towards sundown. You can choose for yourself, but if I were you I should think twice about it."

"I was wondering," said Marigold, "whether, if I put it to her as a personal favour, she might not be willing to see Edith again and persuade her that she was only joking?"

A light began to break upon the Professor.

"What do you think has happened?" he asked.

"Well," explained Marigold, "I take it that your young foreign friend has met my wife and talked politics to her, and that what has happened is the result. She must be a young person of extraordinary ability; but it would be only losing one convert, and I could make it up to her in--in other ways." He spoke with unconscious pathos. It rather touched the Professor.

"It might mean," said the Professor--"that is, assuming that it can be done at all--Mrs. Marigold's returning to her former self entirely, taking no further interest in politics whatever."

"I should be so very grateful," answered Marigold.

The Professor had mislaid his spectacles, but thinks there was a tear in Marigold's eye.

"I'll do what I can," said the Professor. "Of course, you mustn't count on it. It may be easier to start a woman thinking than to stop her, even for a--" The Professor checked himself just in time. "I'll talk to her," he said; and Marigold gripped his hand and departed.

It was about time he did. The full extent of Malvina's activities during those few midsummer weeks, till the return of Flight Commander Raffleton, will never perhaps be fully revealed.

According to the Doctor, the whole business has been grossly exaggerated. There are those who talk as if half the village had been taken to pieces, altered and improved and sent back home again in a mental state unrecognisable by their own mothers. Certain it is that Dawson, R.A., generally described by everybody except his wife as "a lovable little man," and whose only fault was an incurable habit of punning, both in season--if such a period there be--and more often out, suddenly one morning smashed a Dutch interior, fifteen inches by nine, over the astonished head of Mrs. Dawson. It clung round her neck, recalling biblical pictures of the head of John the Baptist, and the frame-work had to be sawn through before she could get it off. As to the story about his having been caught by Mrs. Dawson's aunt kissing the housemaid behind the waterbutt, that, as the Doctor admits, is a bit of bad luck that might have happened to anyone. But whether there was really any evidence connecting him with Dolly Calthorpe's unaccountable missing of the last train home, is of course, a more serious matter. Mrs. Dawson, a handsome, high-spirited woman herself, may have found Dawson, as originally fashioned, trying to the nerves; though even then the question arises: Why have married him? But there is a difference, as Mrs. Dawson has pointed out, between a husband who hasn't enough of the natural man in him and a husband who has a deal too much. It is difficult to regulate these matters.

Altogether, and taking an outside estimate, the Doctor's opinion is that there may have been half a dozen, who, with Malvina's assistance, succeeded in hypnotising themselves into temporary insanity. When Malvina, a little disappointed, but yielding quite sweetly her own judgment to that of the wise and learned Christopher, consented to "restore" them, the explanation was that, having spent their burst of ill-acquired energy, they fell back at the first suggestion to their former selves.

Mrs. Arlington does not agree with the Doctor. She had been trying to reform herself for quite a long time and had miserably failed. There was something about them--it might almost be described as an aroma--that prompted her that evening to take the twins into her confidence; a sort of intuition that in some way they could help her. It remained with her all the next day; and when the twins returned in the evening, in company with the postman, she knew instinctively that they had been about her business. It was this same intuitive desire that drew her to the Downs. She is confident she would have taken that walk to the Cross Stones even if the twins had not proposed it. Indeed, according to her own account, she was not aware that the twins had accompanied her. There was something about the stones; a sense as of a presence. She knew when she reached them that she had arrived at the appointed place; and when there appeared to her--coming from where she could not tell--a diminutive figure that seemed in some mysterious way as if it were clothed merely in the fading light, she remembered distinctly that she was neither surprised nor alarmed. The diminutive lady sat down beside her and took Mrs. Arlington's hands in both her own. She spoke in a strange language, but Mrs. Arlington at the time understood it, though now the meaning of it had passed from her. Mrs. Arlington felt as if her body were being taken away from her. She had a sense of falling, a feeling that she must make some desperate effort to rise again. The strange little lady was helping her, assisting her to make this supreme effort. It was as if ages were passing. She was wrestling with unknown powers. Suddenly she seemed to slip from them. The little lady was holding her up. Clasping each other, they rose and rose and rose. Mrs. Arlington had a firm conviction that she must always be struggling upward, or they would overtake her and drag her down again. When she awoke the little lady had gone, but that feeling remained with her; that passionate acceptance of ceaseless struggle, activity, contention, as now the end and aim of her existence. At first she did not recollect where she was. A strange colourless light was around her, and a strange singing as of myriads of birds. And then the clock struck nine and life came back to her with a rush. But with it still that conviction that she must seize hold of herself and everybody else and get things done. Its immediate expression, as already has been mentioned, was experienced by the twins.

When, after a talk with the Professor, aided and abetted by Mr. Arlington and the eldest Arlington girl, she consented to pay that second visit to the stones, it was with very different sensations that she climbed the grass-grown path. The little lady had met her as before, but the curious deep eyes looked sadly, and Mrs. Arlington had the impression, generally speaking, that she was about to assist at her own funeral. Again the little lady took her by the hands, and again she experienced that terror of falling. But instead of ending with contest and effort she seemed to pass into a sleep, and when she opened her eyes she was again alone. Feeling a little chilly and unreasonably tired, she walked slowly home, and not being hungry, retired supperless to bed. Quite unable to explain why, she seems to have cried herself to sleep.

One supposes that something of a similar nature may have occurred to the others--with the exception of Mrs. Marigold. It was the case of Mrs. Marigold that, as the Doctor grudgingly admits, went far to weaken his hypothesis. Mrs. Marigold, having emerged, was spreading herself, much to her own satisfaction. She had discarded her wedding ring as a relic of barbarism--of the days when women were mere goods and chattels, and had made her first speech at a meeting in favour of marriage reform. Subterfuge, in her case, had to be resorted to. Malvina had tearfully consented, and Marigold, M.P., was to bring Mrs. Marigold to the Cross Stones that same evening and there leave her, explaining to her that Malvina had expressed a wish to see her again--"just for a chat."

All might have ended well if only Commander Raffleton had not appeared framed in the parlour door just as Malvina was starting. His Cousin Christopher had written to the Commander. Indeed, after the Arlington affair, quite pressingly, and once or twice had thought he heard the sound of Flight Commander Raffleton's propeller, but on each occasion had been disappointed. "Affairs of State," Cousin Christopher had explained to Malvina, who, familiar one takes it with the calls upon knights and warriors through all the ages, had approved.

He stood there with his helmet in his hand.

"Only arrived this afternoon from France," he explained. "Haven't a moment to spare."

But he had just time to go straight to Malvina. He laughed as he took her in his arms and kissed her full upon the lips.

When last he had kissed her--it had been in the orchard; the Professor had been witness to it--Malvina had remained quite passive, only that curious little smile about her lips. But now an odd thing happened. A quivering seemed to pass through all her body, so that it swayed and trembled. The Professor feared she was going to fall; and, maybe to save herself, she put up her arms about Commander Raffleton's neck, and with a strange low cry--it sounded to the Professor like the cry one sometimes hears at night from some little dying creature of the woods--she clung to him sobbing.

It must have been a while later when the chiming of the clock recalled to the Professor the appointment with Mrs. Marigold.

"You will only just have time," he said, gently seeking to release her. "I'll promise to keep him till you come back." And as Malvina did not seem to understand, he reminded her.

But still she made no movement, save for a little gesture of the hands as if she were seeking to lay hold of something unseen. And then she dropped her arms and looked from one of them to the other. The Professor did not think of it at the time, but remembered afterwards; that strange aloofness of hers, as if she were looking at you from another world. One no longer felt it.

"I am so sorry," she said. "It is too late. I am only a woman."

And Mrs. Marigold is still thinking.

THE PROLOGUE

And here follows the Prologue. It ought, of course, to have been written first, but nobody knew of it until quite the end entirely. It was told to Commander Raffleton by a French comrade, who in days of peace had been a painter, mingling with others of his kind, especially such as found their inspiration in the wide horizons and legend-haunted dells of old-world Brittany. Afterwards the Commander told it to the Professor, and the Professor's only stipulation was that it should not be told to the Doctor, at least for a time. For the Doctor would see in it only confirmation for his own narrow sense-bound theories, while to the Professor it confirmed beyond a doubt the absolute truth of this story.

It commenced in the year Eighteen hundred and ninety-eight (anno Domini), on a particularly unpleasant evening in late February--"a stormy winter's night," one would describe it, were one writing mere romance. It came to the lonely cottage of Madame Lavigne on the edge of the moor that surrounds the sunken village of Aven-a-Christ. Madame Lavigne, who was knitting stockings--for she lived by knitting stockings--heard, as she thought, a passing of feet, and what seemed like a tap at the door. She dismissed the idea, for who would be passing at such an hour, and where there was no road? But a few minutes later the tapping came again, and Madame Lavigne, taking her candle in her hand, went to see who was there. The instant she released the latch a gust of wind blew out the candle, and Madame Lavigne could see no one. She called, but there was no answer. She was about to close the door again when she heard a faint sound. It was not exactly a cry. It was as if someone she could not see, in the tiniest of voices, had said something she could not understand.

Madame Lavigne crossed herself and muttered a prayer, and then she heard it again. It seemed to come from close at her feet, and feeling with her hands--for she thought it might be a stray cat--she found quite a large parcel, It was warm and soft, though, of course, a bit wet, and Madame Lavigne brought it in, and having closed the door and re-lit her candle, laid it on the table. And then she saw it was the tiniest of babies.

It must always be a difficult situation. Madame Lavigne did what most people would have done in the case. She unrolled the wrappings, and taking the little thing on her lap, sat down in front of the dull peat fire and considered. It seemed wonderfully contented, and Madame Lavigne thought the best thing to do would be to undress it and put it to bed, and then go on with her knitting. She would consult Father Jean in the morning and take his advice. She had never seen such fine clothes. She took them off one by one, lovingly feeling their texture, and when she finally removed the last little shift and the little white thing lay exposed, Madame Lavigne sprang up with a cry and all but dropped it into the fire. For she saw by the mark that every Breton peasant knows that it was not a child but a fairy.

Her proper course, as she well knew, was to have opened the door and flung it out into the darkness. Most women of the village would have done so, and spent the rest of the night on their knees. But someone must have chosen with foresight. There came to Madame Lavigne the memory of her good man and her three tall sons, taken from her one by one by the jealous sea, and, come what might of it, she could not do it. The little thing understood, that was clear, for it smiled quite knowingly and stretched out its little hands, touching Madame Lavigne's brown withered skin, and stirring forgotten beatings of her heart.

Father Jean--one takes him to have been a tolerant, gently wise old gentleman--could see no harm. That is, if Madame Lavigne could afford the luxury. Maybe it was a good fairy. Would bring her luck. And certain it is that the cackling of Madame's hens was heard more often than before, and the weeds seemed fewer in the little patch of garden that Madame Lavigne had rescued from the moor.

Of course, the news spread. One gathers that Madame Lavigne rather gave herself airs. But the neighbours shook their heads, and the child grew up lonely and avoided. Fortunately, the cottage was far from other houses, and there was always the great moor with its deep hiding-places. Father Jean was her sole playmate. He would take her with him on his long tramps through his scattered district, leaving her screened among the furze and bracken near to the solitary farmsteads where he made his visitations.

He had learnt it was useless: all attempt of Mother Church to scold out of this sea and moor-girt flock their pagan superstitions. He would leave it to time. Later, perhaps opportunity might occur to place the child in some convent, where she would learn to forget, and grow into a good Catholic. Meanwhile, one had to take pity on the little lonely creature. Not entirely for her own sake maybe; a dear affectionate little soul strangely wise; so she seemed to Father Jean. Under the shade of trees or sharing warm shelter with the soft-eyed cows, he would teach her from his small stock of knowledge. Every now and then she would startle him with an intuition, a comment strangely unchildlike. It was as if she had known all about it, long ago. Father Jean would steal a swift glance at her from under his shaggy eyebrows and fall into a silence. It was curious also how the wild things of the field and wood seemed unafraid of her. At times, returning to where he had left her hidden, he would pause, wondering to whom she was talking, and then as he drew nearer would hear the stealing away of little feet, the startled flutter of wings. She had elfish ways, of which it seemed impossible to cure her. Often the good man, returning from some late visit of mercy with his lantern and his stout oak cudgel, would pause and listen to a wandering voice. It was never near enough for him to hear the words, and the voice was strange to him, though he knew it could be no one else. Madame Lavigne would shrug her shoulders. How could she help it? It was not for her to cross the "child," even supposing bolts and bars likely to be of any use. Father Jean gave it up in despair. Neither was it for him either to be too often forbidding and lecturing. Maybe the cunning tender ways had wove their web about the childless old gentleman's heart, making him also somewhat afraid. Perhaps other distractions! For Madame Lavigne would never allow her to do anything but the lightest of work. He would teach her to read. So quickly she learnt that it seemed to Father Jean she must be making believe not to have known it already. But he had his reward in watching the joy with which she would devour, for preference, the quaint printed volumes of romance and history that he would bring home to her from his rare journeyings to the distant town.

It was when she was about thirteen that the ladies and gentlemen came from Paris. Of course they were not real ladies and gentlemen. Only a little company of artists seeking new fields. They had "done" the coast and the timbered houses of the narrow streets, and one of them had suggested exploring the solitary, unknown inlands. They came across her seated on an old grey stone reading from an ancient-looking book, and she had risen and curtsied to them. She was never afraid. It was she who excited fear. Often she would look after the children flying from her, feeling a little sad. But, of course, it could not be helped. She was a fairy. She would have done them no harm, but this they could not be expected to understand. It was a delightful change; meeting human beings who neither screamed nor hastily recited their paternosters, but who, instead, returned one's smile. They asked her where she lived, and she showed them. They were staying at Aven-a-Christ; and one of the ladies was brave enough even to kiss her. Laughing and talking they all walked down the hill together. They found Madame Lavigne working in her garden. Madame Lavigne washed her hands of all responsibility. It was for Suzanne to decide. It seemed they wanted to make a picture of her, sitting on the grey stone where they had found her. It was surely only kind to let them; so next morning she was there again waiting for them. They gave her a five- franc piece. Madame Lavigne was doubtful of handling it, but Father Jean vouched for it as being good Republican money; and as the days went by Madame Lavigne's black stocking grew heavier and heavier as she hung it again each night in the chimney.

It was the lady who had first kissed her that discovered who she was. They had all of them felt sure from the beginning that she was a fairy, and that "Suzanne" could not be her real name. They found it in the "Heptameron of Friar Bonnet. In which is recorded the numerous adventures of the valiant and puissant King Ryence of Bretagne," which one of them had picked up on the Quai aux Fleurs and brought with him. It told all about the White Ladies, and therein she was described. There could be no mistaking her; the fair body that was like to a willow swayed by the wind. The white feet that could pass, leaving the dew unshaken from the grass. The eyes blue and deep as mountain lakes. The golden locks of which the sun was jealous.

It was all quite clear. She was Malvina, once favourite to Harbundia, Queen of the White Ladies of Brittany. For reasons-- further allusion to which politeness forbade--she had been a wanderer, no one knowing what had become of her. And now the whim had taken her to reappear as a little Breton peasant girl, near to the scene of her past glories. They knelt before her, offering her homage, and all the ladies kissed her. The gentlemen of the party thought their turn would follow. But it never did. It was not their own shyness that stood in their way: one must do them that justice. It was as if some youthful queen, exiled and unknown amongst strangers, had been suddenly recognised by a little band of her faithful subjects, passing by chance that way. So that, instead of frolic and laughter, as had been intended, they remained standing with bared heads; and no one liked to be the first to speak.

She put them at their ease--or tried to--with a gracious gesture. But enjoined upon them all her wish for secrecy. And so dismissed they seem to have returned to the village a marvellously sober little party, experiencing all the sensations of honest folk admitted to their first glimpse of high society.

They came again next year--at least a few of them--bringing with them a dress more worthy of Malvina's wearing. It was as near as Paris could achieve to the true and original costume as described by the good Friar Bonnet, the which had been woven in a single night by the wizard spider Karai out of moonlight. Malvina accepted it with gracious thanks, and was evidently pleased to find herself again in fit and proper clothes. It was hidden away for rare occasions where only Malvina knew. But the lady who had first kissed her, and whose speciality was fairies, craving permission, Malvina consented to wear it while sitting for her portrait. The picture one may still see in the Palais des Beaux Arts at Nantes (the Bretonne Room). It represents her standing straight as an arrow, a lone little figure in the centre of a treeless moor. The painting of the robe is said to be very wonderful. "Malvina of Brittany" is the inscription, the date being Nineteen Hundred and Thirteen.

The next year Malvina was no longer there. Madame Lavigne, folding knotted hands, had muttered her last paternoster. Pere Jean had urged the convent. But for the first time, with him, she had been frankly obstinate. Some fancy seemed to have got into the child's head. Something that she evidently connected with the vast treeless moor rising southward to where the ancient menhir of King Taramis crowned its summit. The good man yielded, as usual. For the present there were Madame Lavigne's small savings. Suzanne's wants were but few. The rare shopping necessary Father Jean could see to himself. With the coming of winter he would broach the subject again, and then be quite firm. Just these were the summer nights when Suzanne loved to roam; and as for danger! there was not a lad for ten leagues round who would not have run a mile to avoid passing, even in daylight, that cottage standing where the moor dips down to the sealands.

But one surmises that even a fairy may feel lonesome. Especially a banished fairy, hanging as it were between earth and air, knowing mortal maidens kissed and courted, while one's own companions kept away from one in hiding. Maybe the fancy came to her that, after all these years, they might forgive her. Still, it was their meeting place, so legend ran, especially of midsummer nights. Rare it was now for human eye to catch a glimpse of the shimmering robes, but high on the treeless moor to the music of the Lady of the Fountain, one might still hear, were one brave enough to venture, the rhythm of their dancing feet. If she sought them, softly calling, might they not reveal themselves to her, make room for her once again in the whirling circle? One has the idea that the moonlight frock may have added to her hopes. Philosophy admits that feeling oneself well dressed gives confidence.

If all of them had not disappeared--been kissed three times upon the lips by mortal man and so become a woman? It seems to have been a possibility for which your White Lady had to be prepared. That is, if she chose to suffer it. If not, it was unfortunate for the too daring mortal. But if he gained favour in her eyes! That he was brave, his wooing proved. If, added thereto, he were comely, with kind strong ways, and eyes that drew you? History proves that such dreams must have come even to White Ladies. Maybe more especially on midsummer nights when the moon is at its full. It was on such a night that Sir Gerylon had woke Malvina's sister Sighile with a kiss. A true White Lady must always dare to face her fate.

It seems to have befallen Malvina. Some told Father Jean how he had arrived in a chariot drawn by winged horses, the thunder of his passing waking many in the sleeping villages beneath. And others how he had come in the form of a great bird. Father Jean had heard strange sounds himself, and certain it was that Suzanne had disappeared.

Father Jean heard another version a few weeks later, told him by an English officer of Engineers who had ridden from the nearest station on a bicycle and who arrived hot and ravenously thirsty. And Father Jean, under promise of seeing Suzanne on the first opportunity, believed it. But to most of his flock it sounded an impossible rigmarole, told for the purpose of disguising the truth.

So ends my story--or rather the story I have pieced together from information of a contradictory nature received. Whatever you make of it; whether with the Doctor you explain it away; or whether with Professor Littlecherry, LL.D., F.R.S., you believe the world not altogether explored and mapped, the fact remains that Malvina of Brittany has passed away. To the younger Mrs. Raffleton, listening on the Sussex Downs to dull, distant sounds that make her heart beat, and very nervous of telegraph boys, has come already some of the disadvantages attendant on her new rank of womanhood. And yet one gathers, looking down into those strange deep eyes, that she would not change anything about her, even if now she could.

THE STREET OF THE BLANK WALL

I had turned off from the Edgware Road into a street leading west, the atmosphere of which had appealed to me. It was a place of quiet houses standing behind little gardens. They had the usual names printed on the stuccoed gateposts. The fading twilight was just sufficient to enable one to read them. There was a Laburnum Villa, and The Cedars, and a Cairngorm, rising to the height of three storeys, with a curious little turret that branched out at the top, and was crowned with a conical roof, so that it looked as if wearing a witch's hat. Especially when two small windows just below the eaves sprang suddenly into light, and gave one the feeling of a pair of wicked eyes suddenly flashed upon one.

The street curved to the right, ending in an open space through which passed a canal beneath a low arched bridge. There were still the same quiet houses behind their small gardens, and I watched for a while the lamplighter picking out the shape of the canal, that widened just above the bridge into a lake with an island in the middle. After that I must have wandered in a circle, for later on I found myself back in the same spot, though I do not suppose I had passed a dozen people on my way; and then I set to work to find my way back to Paddington.

I thought I had taken the road by which I had come, but the half light must have deceived me. Not that it mattered. They had a lurking mystery about them, these silent streets with their suggestion of hushed movement behind drawn curtains, of whispered voices behind the flimsy walls. Occasionally there would escape the sound of laughter, suddenly stifled as it seemed, and once the sudden cry of a child.

It was in a short street of semi-detached villas facing a high blank wall that, as I passed, I saw a blind move half-way up, revealing a woman's face. A gas lamp, the only one the street possessed, was nearly opposite. I thought at first it was the face of a girl, and then, as I looked again, it might have been the face of an old woman. One could not distinguish the colouring. In any case, the cold, blue gaslight would have made it seem pallid.

The remarkable feature was the eyes. It might have been, of course, that they alone caught the light and held it, rendering them uncannily large and brilliant. Or it might have been that the rest of the face was small and delicate, out of all proportion to them. She may have seen me, for the blind was drawn down again, and I passed on.

There was no particular reason why, but the incident lingered with me. The sudden raising of the blind, as of the curtain of some small theatre, the barely furnished room coming dimly into view, and the woman standing there, close to the footlights, as to my fancy it seemed. And then the sudden ringing down of the curtain before the play had begun. I turned at the corner of the street. The blind had been drawn up again, and I saw again the slight, girlish figure silhouetted against the side panes of the bow window.

At the same moment a man knocked up against me. It was not his fault. I had stopped abruptly, not giving him time to avoid me. We both apologised, blaming the darkness. It may have been my fancy, but I had the feeling that, instead of going on his way, he had turned and was following me. I waited till the next corner, and then swung round on my heel. But there was no sign of him, and after a while I found myself back in the Edgware Road.

Once or twice, in idle mood, I sought the street again, but without success; and the thing would, I expect, have faded from my memory, but that one evening, on my way home from Paddington, I came across the woman in the Harrow Road. There was no mistaking her. She almost touched me as she came out of a fishmonger's shop, and unconsciously, at the beginning, I found myself following her. This time I noticed the turnings, and five minutes' walking brought us to the street. Half a dozen times I must have been within a hundred yards of it. I lingered at the corner. She had not noticed me, and just as she reached the house a man came out of the shadows beyond the lamp-post and joined her.

I was due at a bachelor gathering that evening, and after dinner, the affair being fresh in my mind, I talked about it. I am not sure, but I think it was in connection with a discussion on Maeterlinck. It was that sudden lifting of the blind that had caught hold of me. As if, blundering into an empty theatre, I had caught a glimpse of some drama being played in secret. We passed to other topics, and when I was leaving a fellow guest asked me which way I was going. I told him, and, it being a fine night, he proposed that we should walk together. And in the quiet of Harley Street he confessed that his desire had not been entirely the pleasure of my company.

"It is rather curious," he said, "but today there suddenly came to my remembrance a case that for nearly eleven years I have never given a thought to. And now, on top of it, comes your description of that woman's face. I am wondering if it can be the same."

"It was the eyes," I said, "that struck me as so remarkable."

"It was the eyes that I chiefly remember her by," he replied. "Would you know the street again?"

We walked a little while in silence.

"It may seem, perhaps, odd to you," I answered, "but it would trouble me, the idea of any harm coming to her through me. What was the case?"

"You can feel quite safe on that point," he assured me. "I was her counsel--that is, if it is the same woman. How was she dressed?"

I could not see the reason for his question. He could hardly expect her to be wearing the clothes of eleven years ago.

"I don't think I noticed," I answered. "Some sort of a blouse, I suppose." And then I recollected. "Ah, yes, there was something uncommon," I added. "An unusually broad band of velvet, it looked like, round her neck."

"I thought so," he said. "Yes. It must be the same."

We had reached Marylebone Road, where our ways parted.

"I will look you up to-morrow afternoon, if I may," he said. "We might take a stroll round together."

He called on me about half-past five, and we reached the street just as the one solitary gas-lamp had been lighted. I pointed out the house to him, and he crossed over and looked at the number.

"Quite right," he said, on returning. "I made inquiries this morning. She was released six weeks ago on ticket-of-leave."

He took my arm.

"Not much use hanging about," he said. "The blind won't go up to-night. Rather a clever idea, selecting a house just opposite a lamp-post."

He had an engagement that evening; but later on he told me the story--that is, so far as he then knew it.

∼

It was in the early days of the garden suburb movement. One of the first sites chosen was off the Finchley Road. The place was in the building, and one of the streets--Laleham Gardens--had only some half a dozen houses in it, all unoccupied save one. It was a lonely, loose end of the suburb, terminating suddenly in open fields. From the unfinished end of the road the ground sloped down somewhat steeply to a pond, and beyond that began a small wood. The one house occupied had been bought by a young married couple named Hepworth.

The husband was a good-looking, pleasant young fellow. Being clean-shaven, his exact age was difficult to judge. The wife, it was quite evident, was little more than a girl. About the man there was a suggestion of weakness. At least, that was the impression left on the mind of the house-agent. To-day he would decide, and to-morrow he changed his mind. Jetson, the agent, had almost given up hope of bringing off a deal. In the end it was Mrs. Hepworth who, taking the matter into her own hands, fixed upon the house in Laleham Gardens. Young Hepworth found fault with it on the ground of its isolation. He himself was often away for days at a time, travelling on business, and was afraid she would be nervous. He had been very persistent on this point; but in whispered conversations she had persuaded him out of his objection. It was one of those pretty, fussy little houses; and it seemed to have taken her fancy. Added to which, according to her argument, it was just within their means, which none of the others were. Young Hepworth may have given the usual references, but if so they were never taken up. The house was sold on the company's usual terms. The deposit was paid by a cheque, which was duly cleared, and the house itself was security for the rest. The company's solicitor, with Hepworth's consent, acted for both parties.

It was early in June when the Hepworths moved in. They furnished only one bedroom; and kept no servant, a charwoman coming in every morning and going away about six in the evening. Jetson was their nearest neighbour. His wife and daughters called on them, and confess to have taken a liking to them both. Indeed, between one of the Jetson girls, the youngest, and Mrs. Hepworth there seems to have sprung up a close friendship. Young Hepworth, the husband, was always charming, and evidently took great pains to make himself agreeable. But with regard to him they had the feeling that he was never altogether at his ease. They described him--though that, of course, was after the event--as having left upon them the impression of a haunted man.

There was one occasion in particular. It was about ten o'clock. The Jetsons had been spending the evening with the Hepworths, and were just on the point of leaving, when there came a sudden, clear knock at the door. It turned out to be Jetson's foreman, who had to leave by an early train in the morning, and had found that he needed some further instructions. But the terror in Hepworth's face was unmistakable. He had turned a look towards his wife that was almost of despair; and it had seemed to the Jetsons--or, talking it over afterwards, they may have suggested the idea to each other--that there came a flash of contempt into her eyes, though it yielded the next instant to an expression of pity. She had risen, and already moved some steps towards the door, when young Hepworth had stopped her, and gone out himself. But the curious thing was that, according to the foreman's account, Hepworth never opened the front door, but came upon him stealthily from behind. He must have slipped out by the back and crept round the house.

The incident had puzzled the Jetsons, especially that involuntary flash of contempt that had come into Mrs. Hepworth's eyes. She had always appeared to adore her husband, and of the two, if possible, to be the one most in love with the other. They had no friends or acquaintances except the Jetsons. No one else among their neighbours had taken the trouble to call on them, and no stranger to the suburb had, so far as was known, ever been seen in Laleham Gardens.

Until one evening a little before Christmas.

Jetson was on his way home from his office in the Finchley Road. There had been a mist hanging about all day, and with nightfall it had settled down into a whitish fog. Soon after leaving the Finchley Road, Jetson noticed in front of him a man wearing a long, yellow mackintosh, and some sort of soft felt hat. He gave Jetson the idea of being a sailor; it may have been merely the stiff, serviceable mackintosh. At the corner of Laleham Gardens the man turned, and glanced up at the name upon the lamp-post, so that Jetson had a full view of him. Evidently it was the street for which he was looking. Jetson, somewhat curious, the Hepworths' house being still the only one occupied, paused at the corner, and watched. The Hepworths' house was, of course, the only one in the road that showed any light. The man, when he came to the gate, struck a match for the purpose of reading the number. Satisfied it was the house he wanted, he pushed open the gate and went up the path.

But, instead of using the bell or knocker, Jetson was surprised to hear him give three raps on the door with his stick. There was no answer, and Jetson, whose interest was now thoroughly aroused, crossed to the other corner, from where he could command a better view. Twice the man repeated his three raps on the door, each time a little louder, and the third time the door was opened. Jetson could not tell by whom, for whoever it was kept behind it.

He could just see one wall of the passage, with a pair of old naval cutlasses crossed above the picture of a three-masted schooner that he knew hung there. The door was opened just sufficient, and the man slipped in, and the door was closed behind him. Jetson had turned to continue his way, when the fancy seized him to give one glance back. The house was in complete darkness, though a moment before Jetson was positive there had been a light in the ground floor window.

It all sounded very important afterwards, but at the time there was nothing to suggest to Jetson anything very much out of the common. Because for six months no friend or relation had called to see them, that was no reason why one never should. In the fog, a stranger may have thought it simpler to knock at the door with his stick than to fumble in search of a bell. The Hepworths lived chiefly in the room at the back. The light in the drawing-room may have been switched off for economy's sake. Jetson recounted the incident on reaching home, not as anything remarkable, but just as one mentions an item of gossip. The only one who appears to have attached any meaning to the affair was Jetson's youngest daughter, then a girl of eighteen. She asked one or two questions about the man, and, during the evening, slipped out by herself and ran round to the Hepworths. She found the house empty. At all events, she could obtain no answer, and the place, back and front, seemed to her to be uncannily silent.

Jetson called the next morning, something of his daughter's uneasiness having communicated itself to him. Mrs. Hepworth herself opened the door to him. In his evidence at the trial, Jetson admitted that her appearance had startled him. She seems to have anticipated his questions by at once explaining that she had had news of an unpleasant nature, and had been worrying over it all night. Her husband had been called away suddenly to America, where it would be necessary for her to join him as soon as possible. She would come round to Jetson's office later in the day to make arrangements about getting rid of the house and furniture.

The story seemed to reasonably account for the stranger's visit, and Jetson, expressing his sympathy and promising all help in his power, continued his way to the office. She called in the afternoon and handed him over the keys, retaining one for herself. She wished the furniture to be sold by auction, and he was to accept almost any offer for the house. She would try and see him again before sailing; if not, she would write him with her address. She was perfectly cool and collected. She had called on his wife and daughters in the afternoon, and had wished them good-bye.

Outside Jetson's office she hailed a cab, and returned in it to Laleham Gardens to collect her boxes. The next time Jetson saw her she was in the dock, charged with being an accomplice in the murder of her husband.

∽

The body had been discovered in a pond some hundred yards from the unfinished end of Laleham Gardens. A house was in course of erection on a neighbouring plot, and a workman, in dipping up a pail of water, had dropped in his watch. He and his mate, worrying round with a rake, had drawn up pieces of torn clothing, and this, of course, had led to the pond being properly dragged. Otherwise the discovery might never have been made.

The body, heavily weighted with a number of flat-irons fastened to it by a chain and padlock, had sunk deep into the soft mud, and might have remained there till it rotted. A valuable gold repeater, that Jetson remembered young Hepworth having told him had been a presentation to his father, was in its usual pocket, and a cameo ring that Hepworth had always worn on his third finger was likewise fished up from the mud. Evidently the murder belonged to the category of crimes passionel. The theory of the prosecution was that it had been committed by a man who, before her marriage, had been Mrs. Hepworth's lover.

The evidence, contrasted with the almost spiritually beautiful face of the woman in the dock, came as a surprise to everyone in court. Originally connected with an English circus troupe touring in Holland, she appears, about seventeen, to have been engaged as a "song and dance artiste" at a particularly shady cafe chantant in Rotterdam, frequented chiefly by sailors. From there a man, an English sailor known as Charlie Martin, took her away, and for some months she had lived with him at a small estaminet the other side of the river. Later, they left Rotterdam and came to London, where they took lodgings in Poplar, near to the docks.

It was from this address in Poplar that, some ten months before the murder, she had married young Hepworth. What had become of Martin was not known. The natural assumption was that, his money being exhausted, he had returned to his calling, though his name, for some reason, could not be found in any ship's list.

That he was one and the same with the man that Jetson had watched till the door of the Hepworths' house had closed upon him there could be no doubt. Jetson described him as a thick-set, handsome-looking man, with a reddish beard and moustache. Earlier in the day he had been seen at Hampstead, where he had dined at a small coffee-shop in the High Street. The girl who had waited on him had also been struck by the bold, piercing eyes and the curly red beard. It had been an off-time, between two and three, when he had dined there, and the girl admitted that she had found him a "pleasant-spoken gentleman," and "inclined to be merry." He had told her that he had arrived in England only three days ago, and that he hoped that evening to see his sweetheart. He had accompanied the words with a laugh, and the girl thought--though, of course, this may have been after-suggestion--that an ugly look followed the laugh.

One imagines that it was this man's return that had been the fear constantly haunting young Hepworth. The three raps on the door, it was urged by the prosecution, was a pre-arranged or pre-understood signal, and the door had been opened by the woman. Whether the husband was in the house, or whether they waited for him, could not be said. He had been killed by a bullet entering through the back of the neck; the man had evidently come prepared.

Ten days had elapsed between the murder and the finding of the body, and the man was never traced. A postman had met him coming from the neighbourhood of Laleham Gardens at about half-past nine. In the fog, they had all but bumped into one another, and the man had immediately turned away his face.

About the soft felt hat there was nothing to excite attention, but the long, stiff, yellow mackintosh was quite unusual. The postman had caught only a momentary glimpse of the face, but was certain it was clean shaven. This made a sensation in court for the moment, but only until the calling of the next witness. The charwoman usually employed by the Hepworths had not been admitted to the house on the morning of Mrs. Hepworth's departure. Mrs. Hepworth had met her at the door and paid her a week's money in lieu of notice, explaining to her that she would not be wanted any more. Jetson, thinking he might possibly do better by letting the house furnished, had sent for this woman, and instructed her to give the place a thorough cleaning. Sweeping the carpet in the dining-room with a dustpan and brush, she had discovered a number of short red hairs. The man, before leaving the house, had shaved himself.

That he had still retained the long, yellow mackintosh may have been with the idea of starting a false clue. Having served its purpose, it could be discarded. The beard would not have been so easy. What roundabout way he may have taken one cannot say, but it must have been some time during the night or early morning that he reached young Hepworth's office in Fenchurch Street. Mrs. Hepworth had evidently provided him with the key.

There he seems to have hidden the hat and mackintosh and to have taken in exchange some clothes belonging to the murdered man. Hepworth's clerk, Ellenby, an elderly man--of the type that one generally describes as of gentlemanly appearance--was accustomed to his master being away unexpectedly on business, which was that of a ships' furnisher. He always kept an overcoat and a bag ready packed in the office. Missing them, Ellenby had assumed that his master had been called away by an early train. He would have been worried after a few days, but that he had received a telegram--as he then supposed from his master--explaining that young Hepworth had gone to Ireland and would be away for some days. It was nothing unusual for Hepworth to be absent, superintending the furnishing of a ship, for a fortnight at a time, and nothing had transpired in the office necessitating special instructions. The telegram had been handed in at Charing Cross, but the time chosen had been a busy period of the day, and no one had any recollection of the sender. Hepworth's clerk unhesitatingly identified the body as that of his employer, for whom it was evident that he had entertained a feeling of affection. About Mrs. Hepworth he said as little as he could. While she was awaiting her trial it had been necessary for him to see her once or twice with reference to the business. Previous to this, he knew nothing about her.

The woman's own attitude throughout the trial had been quite unexplainable. Beyond agreeing to a formal plea of "Not guilty," she had made no attempt to defend herself. What little assistance her solicitors had obtained had been given them, not by the woman herself, but by Hepworth's clerk, more for the sake of his dead master than out of any sympathy towards the wife. She herself appeared utterly indifferent. Only once had she been betrayed into a momentary emotion. It was when her solicitors were urging her almost angrily to give them some particulars upon a point they thought might be helpful to her case.

"He's dead!" she had cried out almost with a note of exultation. "Dead! Dead! What else matters?"

The next moment she had apologised for her outburst.

"Nothing can do any good," she had said. "Let the thing take its course."

It was the astounding callousness of the woman that told against her both with the judge and the jury. That shaving in the dining-room, the murdered man's body not yet cold! It must have been done with Hepworth's safety-razor. She must have brought it down to him, found him a looking-glass, brought him soap and water and a towel, afterwards removing all traces. Except those few red hairs that had clung, unnoticed, to the carpet. That nest of flat-irons used to weight the body! It must have been she who had thought of them. The idea would never have occurred to a man. The chain and padlock with which to fasten them. She only could have known that such things were in the house. It must have been she who had planned the exchange of clothes in Hepworth's office, giving him the key. She it must have been who had thought of the pond, holding open the door while the man had staggered out under his ghastly burden; waited, keeping watch, listening to hear the splash.

Evidently it had been her intention to go off with the murderer--to live with him! That story about America. If all had gone well, it would have accounted for everything. After leaving Laleham Gardens she had taken lodgings in a small house in Kentish Town under the name of Howard, giving herself out to be a chorus singer, her husband being an actor on tour. To make the thing plausible, she had obtained employment in one of the pantomimes. Not for a moment had she lost her head. No one had ever called at her lodgings, and there had come no letters for her. Every hour of her day could be accounted for. Their plans must have been worked out over the corpse of her murdered husband. She was found guilty of being an "accessory after the fact," and sentenced to fifteen years' penal servitude.

That brought the story up to eleven years ago. After the trial, interested in spite of himself, my friend had ferreted out some further particulars. Inquiries at Liverpool had procured him the information that Hepworth's father, a shipowner in a small way, had been well known and highly respected. He was retired from business when he died, some three years previous to the date of the murder. His wife had survived him by only a few months. Besides Michael, the murdered son, there were two other children--an elder brother, who was thought to have gone abroad to one of the colonies, and a sister who had married a French naval officer. Either they had not heard of the case or had not wished to have their names dragged into it. Young Michael had started life as an architect, and was supposed to have been doing well, but after the death of his parents had disappeared from the neighbourhood, and, until the trial, none of his acquaintances up North ever knew what had become of him.

But a further item of knowledge that my friend's inquiries had elicited had somewhat puzzled him. Hepworth's clerk, Ellenby, had been the confidential clerk of Hepworth's father! He had entered the service of the firm as a boy; and when Hepworth senior retired, Ellenby--with the old gentleman's assistance--had started in business for himself as a ships' furnisher! Nothing of all this came out at the trial. Ellenby had not been cross-examined. There was no need for it. But it seemed odd, under all the circumstances, that he had not volunteered the information. It may, of course, have been for the sake of the brother and sister. Hepworth is a common enough name in the North. He may have hoped to keep the family out of connection with the case.

As regards the woman, my friend could learn nothing further beyond the fact that, in her contract with the music-hall agent in Rotterdam, she had described herself as the daughter of an English musician, and had stated that both her parents were dead. She may have engaged herself without knowing the character of the hall, and the man, Charlie Martin, with his handsome face and pleasing sailor ways, and at least an Englishman, may have seemed to her a welcome escape.

She may have been passionately fond of him, and young Hepworth- -crazy about her, for she was beautiful enough to turn any man's head--may in Martin's absence have lied to her, told her he was dead--lord knows what!--to induce her to marry him. The murder may have seemed to her a sort of grim justice.

But even so, her cold-blooded callousness was surely abnormal! She had married him, lived with him for nearly a year. To the Jetsons she had given the impression of being a woman deeply in love with her husband. It could not have been mere acting kept up day after day.

"There was something else." We were discussing the case in my friend's chambers. His brief of eleven years ago was open before him. He was pacing up and down with his hands in his pockets, thinking as he talked. "Something that never came out. There was a curious feeling she gave me in that moment when sentence was pronounced upon her. It was as if, instead of being condemned, she had triumphed. Acting! If she had acted during the trial, pretended remorse, even pity, I could have got her off with five years. She seemed to be unable to disguise the absolute physical relief she felt at the thought that he was dead, that his hand would never again touch her. There must have been something that had suddenly been revealed to her, something that had turned her love to hate.

"There must be something fine about the man, too." That was another suggestion that came to him as he stood staring out of the window across the river. "She's paid and has got her receipt, but he is still 'wanted.' He is risking his neck every evening he watches for the raising of that blind."

His thought took another turn.

"Yet how could he have let her go through those ten years of living death while he walked the streets scot free? Some time during the trial--the evidence piling up against her day by day--why didn't he come forward, if only to stand beside her? Get himself hanged, if only out of mere decency?"

He sat down, took the brief up in his hand without looking at it.

"Or was that the reward that she claimed? That he should wait, keeping alive the one hope that would make the suffering possible to her? Yes," he continued, musing, "I can see a man who cared for a woman taking that as his punishment."

Now that his interest in the case had been revived he seemed unable to keep it out of his mind. Since our joint visit I had once or twice passed through the street by myself, and on the last occasion had again seen the raising of the blind. It obsessed him--the desire to meet the man face to face. A handsome, bold, masterful man, he conceived him. But there must be something more for such a woman to have sold her soul--almost, one might say--for the sake of him.

There was just one chance of succeeding. Each time he had come from the direction of the Edgware Road. By keeping well out of sight at the other end of the street, and watching till he entered it, one might time oneself to come upon him just under the lamp. He would hardly be likely to turn and go back; that would be to give himself away. He would probably content himself with pretending to be like ourselves, merely hurrying through, and in his turn watching till we had disappeared.

Fortune seemed inclined to favour us. About the usual time the blind was gently raised, and very soon afterwards there came round the corner the figure of a man. We entered the street ourselves a few seconds later, and it seemed likely that, as we had planned, we should come face to face with him under the gaslight. He walked towards us, stooping and with bent head. We expected him to pass the house by. To our surprise he stopped when he came to it, and pushed open the gate. In another moment we should have lost all chance of seeing anything more of him except his bent back. With a couple of strides my friend was behind him. He laid his hand on the man's shoulder and forced him to turn round. It was an old, wrinkled face with gentle, rather watery eyes.

We were both so taken aback that for a moment we could say nothing. My friend stammered out an apology about having mistaken the house, and rejoined me. At the corner we burst out laughing almost simultaneously. And then my friend suddenly stopped and stared at me.

"Hepworth's old clerk!" he said. "Ellenby!"

∼

It seemed to him monstrous. The man had been more than a clerk. The family had treated him as a friend. Hepworth's father had set him up in business. For the murdered lad he had had a sincere attachment; he had left that conviction on all of them. What was the meaning of it?

A directory was on the mantelpiece. It was the next afternoon. I had called upon him in his chambers. It was just an idea that came to me. I crossed over and opened it, and there was his name, "Ellenby and Co., Ships' Furnishers," in a court off the Minories.

Was he helping her for the sake of his dead master--trying to get her away from the man. But why? The woman had stood by and watched the lad murdered. How could he bear even to look on her again?

Unless there had been that something that had not come out-- something he had learnt later--that excused even that monstrous callousness of hers.

Yet what could there be? It had all been so planned, so cold-blooded. That shaving in the dining-room! It was that seemed most to stick in his throat. She must have brought him down a looking-glass; there was not one in the room. Why couldn't he have gone upstairs into the bathroom, where Hepworth always shaved himself, where he would have found everything to his hand?

He had been moving about the room, talking disjointedly as he paced, and suddenly he stopped and looked at me.

"Why in the dining-room?" he demanded of me.

He was jingling some keys in his pocket. It was a habit of his when cross-examining, and I felt as if somehow I knew; and, without thinking--so it seemed to me--I answered him.

"Perhaps," I said, "it was easier to bring a razor down than to carry a dead man up."

He leant with his arms across the table, his eyes glittering with excitement.

"Can't you see it?" he said. "That little back parlour with its fussy ornaments. The three of them standing round the table, Hepworth's hands nervously clutching a chair. The reproaches, the taunts, the threats. Young Hepworth--he struck everyone as a weak man, a man physically afraid--white, stammering, not knowing which way to look. The woman's eyes turning from one to the other. That flash of contempt again--she could not help it--followed, worse still, by pity. If only he could have answered back, held his own! If only he had not been afraid! And then that fatal turning away with a sneering laugh one imagines, the bold, dominating eyes no longer there to cower him.

"That must have been the moment. The bullet, if you remember, entered through the back of the man's neck. Hepworth must always have been picturing to himself this meeting--tenants of garden suburbs do not carry loaded revolvers as a habit--dwelling upon it till he had worked himself up into a frenzy of hate and fear. Weak men always fly to extremes. If there was no other way, he would kill him.

"Can't you hear the silence? After the reverberations had died away! And then they are both down on their knees, patting him, feeling for his heart. The man must have gone down like a felled ox; there were no traces of blood on the carpet. The house is far from any neighbour; the shot in all probability has not been heard. If only they can get rid of the body! The pond--not a hundred yards away!"

He reached for the brief, still lying among his papers; hurriedly turned the scored pages.

"What easier? A house being built on the very next plot. Wheelbarrows to be had for the taking. A line of planks reaching down to the edge. Depth of water where the body was discovered four feet six inches. Nothing to do but just tip up the barrow.

"Think a minute. Must weigh him down, lest he rise to accuse us; weight him heavily, so that he will sink lower and lower into the soft mud, lie there till he rots.

"Think again. Think it out to the end. Suppose, in spite of all our precautions, he does rise? Suppose the chain slips? The workmen going to and fro for water--suppose they do discover him?

"He is lying on his back, remember. They would have turned him over to feel for his heart. Have closed his eyes, most probably, not liking their stare.

"It would be the woman who first thought of it. She has seen them both lying with closed eyes beside her. It may have always been in her mind, the likeness between them. With Hepworth's watch in his pocket, Hepworth's ring on his finger! If only it was not for the beard--that fierce, curling, red beard!

"They creep to the window and peer out. Fog still thick as soup. Not a soul, not a sound. Plenty of time.

"Then to get away, to hide till one is sure. Put on the mackintosh. A man in a yellow mackintosh may have been seen to enter; let him be seen to go away. In some dark corner or some empty railway carriage take it off and roll it up. Then make for the office. Wait there for Ellenby. True as steel, Ellenby; good business man. Be guided by Ellenby."

He flung the brief from him with a laugh.

"Why, there's not a missing link!" he cried. "And to think that not a fool among us ever thought of it!"

"Everything fitting into its place," I suggested, "except young Hepworth. Can you see him, from your description of him, sitting down and coolly elaborating plans for escape, the corpse of the murdered man stretched beside him on the hearthrug?"

"No," he answered. "But I can see her doing it, a woman who for week after week kept silence while we raged and stormed at her, a woman who for three hours sat like a statue while old Cutbush painted her to a crowded court as a modern Jezebel, who rose up from her seat when that sentence of fifteen years' penal servitude was pronounced upon her with a look of triumph in her eyes, and walked out of court as if she had been a girl going to meet her lover.

"I'll wager," he added, "it was she who did the shaving. Hepworth would have cut him, even with a safety-razor."

"It must have been the other one, Martin," I said, "that she loathed. That almost exultation at the thought that he was dead," I reminded him.

"Yes," he mused. "She made no attempt to disguise it. Curious there having been that likeness between them." He looked at his watch. "Do you care to come with me?" he said.

"Where are you going?" I asked him.

"We may just catch him," he answered. "Ellenby and Co."

The office was on the top floor of an old-fashioned house in a cul-de-sac off the Minories. Mr. Ellenby was out, so the lanky office-boy informed us, but would be sure to return before evening; and we sat and waited by the meagre fire till, as the dusk was falling, we heard his footsteps on the creaking stairs.

He halted a moment in the doorway, recognising us apparently without surprise; and then, with a hope that we had not been kept waiting long, he led the way into an inner room.

"I do not suppose you remember me," said my friend, as soon as the door was closed. "I fancy that, until last night, you never saw me without my wig and gown. It makes a difference. I was Mrs. Hepworth's senior counsel."

It was unmistakable, the look of relief that came into the old, dim eyes. Evidently the incident of the previous evening had suggested to him an enemy.

"You were very good," he murmured. "Mrs. Hepworth was overwrought at the time, but she was very grateful, I know, for all your efforts."

I thought I detected a faint smile on my friend's lips.

"I must apologise for my rudeness to you of last night," he continued. "I expected, when I took the liberty of turning you round, that I was going to find myself face to face with a much younger man."

"I took you to be a detective," answered Ellenby, in his soft, gentle voice. "You will forgive me, I'm sure. I am rather short-sighted. Of course, I can only conjecture, but if you will take my word, I can assure you that Mrs. Hepworth has never seen or heard from the man Charlie Martin since the date of"--he hesitated a moment--"of the murder."

"It would have been difficult," agreed my friend, "seeing that Charlie Martin lies buried in Highgate Cemetery."

Old as he was, he sprang from his chair, white and trembling.

"What have you come here for?" he demanded.

"I took more than a professional interest in the case," answered my friend. "Ten years ago I was younger than I am now. It may have been her youth--her extreme beauty. I think Mrs. Hepworth, in allowing her husband to visit her--here where her address is known to the police, and watch at any moment may be set upon her--is placing him in a position of grave danger. If you care to lay before me any facts that will allow me to judge of the case, I am prepared to put my experience, and, if need be, my assistance, at her service."

His self-possession had returned to him.

"If you will excuse me," he said, "I will tell the boy that he can go."

We heard him, a moment later, turn the key in the outer door; and when he came back and had made up the fire, he told us the beginning of the story.

The name of the man buried in Highgate Cemetery was Hepworth, after all. Not Michael, but Alex, the elder brother.

From boyhood he had been violent, brutal, unscrupulous. Judging from Ellenby's story, it was difficult to accept him as a product of modern civilisation. Rather he would seem to have been a throwback to some savage, buccaneering ancestor. To expect him to work, while he could live in vicious idleness at somebody else's expense, was found to be hopeless. His debts were paid for about the third or fourth time, and he was shipped off to the Colonies. Unfortunately, there were no means of keeping him there. So soon as the money provided him had been squandered, he returned, demanding more by menaces and threats. Meeting with unexpected firmness, he seems to have regarded theft and forgery as the only alternative left to him. To save him from punishment and the family name from disgrace, his parents' savings were sacrificed. It was grief and shame that, according to Ellenby, killed them both within a few months of one another.

Deprived by this blow of what he no doubt had come to consider his natural means of support, and his sister, fortunately for herself, being well out of his reach, he next fixed upon his brother Michael as his stay-by. Michael, weak, timid, and not perhaps without some remains of boyish affection for a strong, handsome, elder brother, foolishly yielded. The demands, of course, increased, until, in the end, it came almost as a relief when the man's vicious life led to his getting mixed up with a crime of a particularly odious nature. He was anxious now for his own sake to get away, and Michael, with little enough to spare for himself, provided him with the means, on the solemn understanding that he would never return.

But the worry and misery of it all had left young Michael a broken man. Unable to concentrate his mind any longer upon his profession, his craving was to get away from all his old associations--to make a fresh start in life. It was Ellenby who suggested London and the ship furnishing business, where Michael's small remaining capital would be of service. The name of Hepworth would be valuable in shipping circles, and Ellenby, arguing this consideration, but chiefly with the hope of giving young Michael more interest in the business, had insisted that the firm should be Hepworth and Co.

They had not been started a year before the man returned, as usual demanding more money. Michael, acting under Ellenby's guidance, refused in terms that convinced his brother that the game of bullying was up. He waited a while, and then wrote pathetically that he was ill and starving. If only for the sake of his young wife, would not Michael come and see them?

This was the first they had heard of his marriage. There was just a faint hope that it might have effected a change, and Michael, against Ellenby's advice, decided to go. In a miserable lodging-house in the East End he found the young wife, but not his brother, who did not return till he was on the point of leaving. In the interval the girl seems to have confided her story to Michael.

She had been a singer, engaged at a music-hall in Rotterdam. There Alex Hepworth, calling himself Charlie Martin, had met her and made love to her. When he chose, he could be agreeable enough, and no doubt her youth and beauty had given to his protestations, for the time being, a genuine ring of admiration and desire. It was to escape from her surroundings, more than anything else, that she had consented. She was little more than a child, and anything seemed preferable to the nightly horror to which her life exposed her.

He had never married her. At least, that was her belief at the time.

During his first drunken bout he had flung it in her face that the form they had gone through was mere bunkum. Unfortunately for her, this was a lie. He had always been coolly calculating. It was probably with the idea of a safe investment that he had seen to it that the ceremony had been strictly legal.

Her life with him, so soon as the first novelty of her had worn off, had been unspeakable. The band that she wore round her neck was to hide where, in a fit of savagery, because she had refused to earn money for him on the streets, he had tried to cut her throat. Now that she had got back to England she intended to leave him. If he followed and killed her she did not care.

It was for her sake that young Hepworth eventually offered to help his brother again, on the condition that he would go away by himself. To this the other agreed. He seems to have given a short display of remorse. There must have been a grin on his face as he turned away. His cunning eyes had foreseen what was likely to happen. The idea of blackmail was no doubt in his mind from the beginning. With the charge of bigamy as a weapon in his hand, he might rely for the rest of his life upon a steady and increasing income.

Michael saw his brother off as a second-class passenger on a ship bound for the Cape. Of course, there was little chance of his keeping his word, but there was always the chance of his getting himself knocked on the head in some brawl. Anyhow, he would be out of the way for a season, and the girl, Lola, would be left. A month later he married her, and four months after that received a letter from his brother containing messages to Mrs. Martin, "from her loving husband, Charlie," who hoped before long to have the pleasure of seeing her again.

Inquiries through the English Consul in Rotterdam proved that the threat was no mere bluff. The marriage had been legal and binding.

What happened on the night of the murder, was very much as my friend had reconstructed it. Ellenby, reaching the office at his usual time the next morning, had found Hepworth waiting for him. There he had remained in hiding until one morning, with dyed hair and a slight moustache, he had ventured forth.

Had the man's death been brought about by any other means, Ellenby would have counselled his coming forward and facing his trial, as he himself was anxious to do; but, viewed in conjunction with the relief the man's death must have been to both of them, that loaded revolver was too suggestive of premeditation. The isolation of the house, that conveniently near pond, would look as if thought of beforehand. Even if pleading extreme provocation, Michael escaped the rope, a long term of penal servitude would be inevitable.

Nor was it certain that even then the woman would go free. The murdered man would still, by a strange freak, be her husband; the murderer--in the eye of the law--her lover.

Her passionate will had prevailed. Young Hepworth had sailed for America. There he had no difficulty in obtaining employment--of course, under another name--in an architects office; and later had set up for himself. Since the night of the murder they had not seen each other till some three weeks ago.

∼

I never saw the woman again. My friend, I believe, called on her. Hepworth had already returned to America, and my friend had succeeded in obtaining for her some sort of a police permit that practically left her free.

Sometimes of an evening I find myself passing through the street. And always I have the feeling of having blundered into an empty theatre--where the play is ended.

HIS EVENING OUT

The evidence of the park-keeper, David Bristow, of Gilder Street, Camden Town, is as follows:

I was on duty in St. James's Park on Thursday evening, my sphere extending from the Mall to the northern shore of the ornamental water east of the suspension bridge. At five-and-twenty to seven I took up a position between the peninsula and the bridge to await my colleague. He ought to have relieved me at half-past six, but did not arrive until a few minutes before seven, owing, so he explained, to the breaking down of his motor-'bus--which may have been true or may not, as the saying is.

I had just come to a halt, when my attention was arrested by a lady. I am unable to explain why the presence of a lady in St. James's Park should have seemed in any way worthy of notice except that, for certain reasons, she reminded me of my first wife. I observed that she hesitated between one of the public seats and two vacant chairs standing by themselves a little farther to the east. Eventually she selected one of the chairs, and, having cleaned it with an evening paper--the birds in this portion of the Park being extremely prolific--sat down upon it. There was plenty of room upon the public seat close to it, except for some children who were playing touch; and in consequence of this I judged her to be a person of means.

I walked to a point from where I could command the southern approaches to the bridge, my colleague arriving sometimes by way of Birdcage Walk and sometimes by way of the Horse Guards Parade. Not seeing any signs of him in the direction of the bridge, I turned back. A little way past the chair where the lady was sitting I met Mr. Parable. I know Mr. Parable quite well by sight. He was wearing the usual grey suit and soft felt hat with which the pictures in the newspapers have made us all familiar. I judged that Mr. Parable had come from the Houses of Parliament, and the next morning my suspicions were confirmed by reading that he had been present at a tea-party given on the terrace by Mr. Will Crooks. Mr. Parable conveyed to me the suggestion of a man absorbed in thought, and not quite aware of what he was doing; but in this, of course, I may have been mistaken. He paused for a moment to look over the railings at the pelican. Mr. Parable said something to the pelican which I was not near enough to overhear; and then, still apparently in a state of abstraction, crossed the path and seated himself on the chair next to that occupied by the young lady.

From the tree against which I was standing I was able to watch the subsequent proceedings unobserved. The lady looked at Mr. Parable and then turned away and smiled to herself. It was a peculiar smile, and, again in some way I am unable to explain, reminded me of my first wife. It was not till the pelican put down his other leg and walked away that Mr. Parable, turning his gaze westward, became aware of the lady's presence.

From information that has subsequently come to my knowledge, I am prepared to believe that Mr. Parable, from the beginning, really thought the lady was a friend of his. What the lady thought is a matter for conjecture; I can only speak to the facts. Mr. Parable looked at the lady once or twice. Indeed, one might say with truth that he kept on doing it. The lady, it must be admitted, behaved for a while with extreme propriety; but after a time, as I felt must happen, their eyes met, and then it was I heard her say:

"Good evening, Mr. Parable."

She accompanied the words with the same peculiar smile to which I have already alluded. The exact words of Mr. Parable's reply I cannot remember. But it was to the effect that he had thought from the first that he had known her but had not been quite sure. It was at this point that, thinking I saw my colleague approaching, I went to meet him. I found I was mistaken, and slowly retraced my steps. I passed Mr. Parable and the lady. They were talking together with what I should describe as animation. I went as far as the southern extremity of the suspension bridge, and must have waited there quite ten minutes before returning eastward. It was while I was passing behind them on the grass, partially screened by the rhododendrons, that I heard Mr. Parable say to the lady:

"Why shouldn't we have it together?"

To which the lady replied:

"But what about Miss Clebb?"

I could not overhear what followed, owing to their sinking their voices. It seemed to be an argument. It ended with the young lady laughing and then rising. Mr. Parable also rose, and they walked off together. As they passed me I heard the lady say:

"I wonder if there's any place in London where you're not likely to be recognised."

Mr. Parable, who gave me the idea of being in a state of growing excitement, replied quite loudly:

"Oh, let 'em!"

I was following behind them when the lady suddenly stopped.

"I know!" she said. "The Popular Cafe."

The park-keeper said he was convinced he would know the lady again, having taken particular notice of her. She had brown eyes and was wearing a black hat supplemented with poppies.

∼

Arthur Horton, waiter at the Popular Cafe, states as follows:

I know Mr. John Parable by sight. Have often heard him speak at public meetings. Am a bit of a Socialist myself. Remember his dining at the Popular Cafe on the evening of Thursday. Didn't recognise him immediately on his entrance for two reasons. One was his hat, and the other was his girl. I took it from him and hung it up. I mean, of course, the hat. It was a brand-new bowler, a trifle ikey about the brim. Have always associated him with a soft grey felt. But never with girls. Females, yes, to any extent. But this was the real article. You know what I mean--the sort of girl that you turn round to look after. It was she who selected the table in the corner behind the door. Been there before, I should say.

I should, in the ordinary course of business, have addressed Mr. Parable by name, such being our instructions in the case of customers known to us. But, putting the hat and the girl together, I decided not to. Mr. Parable was all for our three-and-six-penny table d'hote; he evidently not wanting to think. But the lady wouldn't hear of it.

"Remember Miss Clebb," she reminded him.

Of course, at the time I did not know what was meant. She ordered thin soup, a grilled sole, and cutlets au gratin. It certainly couldn't have been the dinner. With regard to the champagne, he would have his own way. I picked him out a dry '94, that you might have weaned a baby on. I suppose it was the whole thing combined.

It was after the sole that I heard Mr. Parable laugh. I could hardly credit my ears, but half-way through the cutlets he did it again.

There are two kinds of women. There is the woman who, the more she eats and drinks, the stodgier she gets, and the woman who lights up after it. I suggested a peche Melba between them, and when I returned with it, Mr. Parable was sitting with his elbows on the table gazing across at her with an expression that I can only describe as quite human. It was when I brought the coffee that he turned to me and asked:

"What's doing? Nothing stuffy," he added. "Is there an Exhibition anywhere--something in the open air?"

"You are forgetting Miss Clebb," the lady reminded him.

"For two pins," said Mr. Parable, "I would get up at the meeting and tell Miss Clebb what I really think about her."

I suggested the Earl's Court Exhibition, little thinking at the time what it was going to lead to; but the lady at first wouldn't hear of it, and the party at the next table calling for their bill (they had asked for it once or twice before, when I came to think of it), I had to go across to them.

When I got back the argument had just concluded, and the lady was holding up her finger.

"On condition that we leave at half-past nine, and that you go straight to Caxton Hall," she said.

"We'll see about it," said Mr. Parable, and offered me half a crown.

Tips being against the rules, I couldn't take it. Besides, one of the jumpers had his eye on me. I explained to him, jocosely, that I was doing it for a bet. He was surprised when I handed him his hat, but, the lady whispering to him, he remembered himself in time.

As they went out together I heard Mr. Parable say to the lady:

"It's funny what a shocking memory I have for names."

To which the lady replied:

"You'll think it funnier still to-morrow." And then she laughed.

Mr. Horton thought he would know the lady again. He puts down her age at about twenty-six, describing her--to use his own piquant expression--as "a bit of all right." She had brown eyes and a taking way with her.

∼

Miss Ida Jenks, in charge of the Eastern Cigarette Kiosk at the Earl's Court Exhibition, gives the following particulars:

From where I generally stand I can easily command a view of the interior of the Victoria Hall; that is, of course, to say when the doors are open, as on a warm night is usually the case.

On the evening of Thursday, the twenty-seventh, it was fairly well occupied, but not to any great extent. One couple attracted my attention by reason of the gentleman's erratic steering. Had he been my partner I should have suggested a polka, the tango not being the sort of dance that can be picked up in an evening. What I mean to say is, that he struck me as being more willing than experienced. Some of the bumps she got would have made me cross; but we all have our fancies, and, so far as I could judge, they both appeared to be enjoying themselves. It was after the "Hitchy Koo" that they came outside.

The seat to the left of the door is popular by reason of its being partly screened by bushes, but by leaning forward a little it is quite possible for me to see what goes on there. They were the first couple out, having had a bad collision near the bandstand, so easily secured it. The gentleman was laughing.

There was something about him from the first that made me think I knew him, and when he took off his hat to wipe his head it came to me all of a sudden, he being the exact image of his effigy at Madame Tussaud's, which, by a curious coincidence, I happened to have visited with a friend that very afternoon. The lady was what some people would call good-looking, and others mightn't.

I was watching them, naturally a little interested. Mr. Parable, in helping the lady to adjust her cloak, drew her--it may have been by accident--towards him; and then it was that a florid gentleman with a short pipe in his mouth stepped forward and addressed the lady. He raised his hat and, remarking "Good evening," added that he hoped she was "having a pleasant time." His tone, I should explain, was sarcastic.

The young woman, whatever else may be said of her, struck me as behaving quite correctly. Replying to his salutation with a cold and distant bow, she rose, and, turning to Mr. Parable, observed that she thought it was perhaps time for them to be going.

The gentleman, who had taken his pipe from his mouth, said-- again in a sarcastic tone--that he thought so too, and offered the lady his arm.

"I don't think we need trouble you," said Mr. Parable, and stepped between them.

To describe what followed I, being a lady, am hampered for

words. I remember seeing Mr. Parable's hat go up into the air, and then the next moment the florid gentleman's head was lying on my counter smothered in cigarettes. I naturally screamed for the police, but the crowd was dead against me; and it was only after what I believe in technical language would be termed "the fourth round" that they appeared upon the scene.

The last I saw of Mr. Parable he was shaking a young constable who had lost his helmet, while three other policemen had hold of him from behind. The florid gentleman's hat I found on the floor of my kiosk and returned to him; but after a useless attempt to get it on his head, he disappeared with it in his hand. The lady was nowhere to be seen.

Miss Jenks thinks she would know her again. She was wearing a hat trimmed with black chiffon and a spray of poppies, and was slightly freckled.

∼

Superintendent S. Wade, in answer to questions put to him by our representative, vouchsafed the following replies:

Yes. I was in charge at the Vine Street Police Station on the night of Thursday, the twenty-seventh.

No. I have no recollection of a charge of any description being preferred against any gentleman of the name of Parable.

Yes. A gentleman was brought in about ten o'clock charged with brawling at the Earl's Court Exhibition and assaulting a constable in the discharge of his duty.

The gentleman gave the name of Mr. Archibald Quincey, Harcourt Buildings, Temple.

No. The gentleman made no application respecting bail, electing to pass the night in the cells. A certain amount of discretion is permitted to us, and we made him as comfortable as possible.

Yes. A lady.

No. About a gentleman who had got himself into trouble at the Earl's Court Exhibition. She mentioned no name.

I showed her the charge sheet. She thanked me and went away.

That I cannot say. I can only tell you that at nine-fifteen on Friday morning bail was tendered, and, after inquiries, accepted in the person of Julius Addison Tupp, of the Sunnybrook Steam Laundry, Twickenham.

That is no business of ours.

The accused who, I had seen to it, had had a cup of tea and a little toast at seven-thirty, left in company with Mr. Tupp soon after ten.

Superintendent Wade admitted he had known cases where accused parties, to avoid unpleasantness, had stated their names to be other than their own, but declined to discuss the matter further.

Superintendent Wade, while expressing his regret that he had no more time to bestow upon our representative, thought it highly probable that he would know the lady again if he saw her.

Without professing to be a judge of such matters, Superintendent Wade thinks she might be described as a highly intelligent young woman, and of exceptionally prepossessing appearance.

⁂

From Mr. Julius Tupp, of the Sunnybrook Steam Laundry, Twickenham, upon whom our representative next called, we have been unable to obtain much assistance, Mr. Tupp replying to all questions put to him by the one formula, "Not talking."

Fortunately, our representative, on his way out through the drying ground, was able to obtain a brief interview with Mrs. Tupp.

Mrs. Tupp remembers admitting a young lady to the house on the morning of Friday, the twenty-eighth, when she opened the door to take in the milk. The lady, Mrs. Tupp remembers, spoke in a husky voice, the result, as the young lady explained with a pleasant laugh, of having passed the night wandering about Ham Common, she having been misdirected the previous evening by a fool of a railway porter, and not wishing to disturb the neighbourhood by waking people up at two o'clock in the morning, which, in Mrs. Tupp's opinion, was sensible of her.

Mrs. Tupp describes the young lady as of agreeable manners, but looking, naturally, a bit washed out. The lady asked for Mr. Tupp, explaining that a friend of his was in trouble, which did not in the least surprise Mrs. Tupp, she herself not holding with Socialists and such like. Mr. Tupp, on being informed, dressed hastily and went downstairs, and he and the young lady left the house together. Mr. Tupp, on being questioned as to the name of his friend, had called up that it was no one Mrs. Tupp would know, a Mr. Quince--it may have been Quincey.

Mrs. Tupp is aware that Mr. Parable is also a Socialist, and is acquainted with the saying about thieves hanging together. But has worked for Mr. Parable for years and has always found him a most satisfactory client; and, Mr. Tupp appearing at this point, our representative thanked Mrs. Tupp for her information and took his departure.

~

Mr. Horatius Condor, Junior, who consented to partake of luncheon in company with our representative at the Holborn Restaurant, was at first disinclined to be of much assistance, but eventually supplied our representative with the following information:

My relationship to Mr. Archibald Quincey, Harcourt Buildings, Temple, is perhaps a little difficult to define.

How he himself regards me I am never quite sure. There will be days together when we will be quite friendly like, and at other times he will be that offhanded and peremptory you might think I was his blooming office boy.

On Friday morning, the twenty-eighth, I didn't get to Harcourt Buildings at the usual time, knowing that Mr. Quincey would not be there himself, he having arranged to interview Mr. Parable for the Daily Chronicle at ten o'clock. I allowed him half an hour, to be quite safe, and he came in at a quarter past eleven.

He took no notice of me. For about ten minutes--it may have been less--he walked up and down the room, cursing and swearing and kicking the furniture about. He landed an occasional walnut table in the middle of my shins, upon which I took the opportunity of wishing him "Good morning," and he sort of woke up, as you might say.

"How did the interview go off?" I says. "Got anything interesting?"

"Yes," he says; "quite interesting. Oh, yes, decidedly interesting."

He was holding himself in, if you understand, speaking with horrible slowness and deliberation.

"D'you know where he was last night?" he asks me.

"Yes," I says; "Caxton Hall, wasn't it?--meeting to demand the release of Miss Clebb."

He leans across the table till his face was within a few inches of mine.

"Guess again," he says.

I wasn't doing any guessing. He had hurt me with the walnut table, and I was feeling a bit short-tempered.

"Oh! don't make a game of it," I says. "It's too early in the morning."

"At the Earl's Court Exhibition," he says; "dancing the tango with a lady that he picked up in St. James's Park."

"Well," I says, "why not? He don't often get much fun." I thought it best to treat it lightly.

He takes no notice of my observation.

"A rival comes upon the scene," he continues--"a fatheaded ass, according to my information--and they have a stand-up fight. He gets run in and spends the night in a Vine Street police cell."

I suppose I was grinning without knowing it.

"Funny, ain't it?" he says.

"Well," I says, "it has its humorous side, hasn't it? What'll he get?"

"I am not worrying about what HE is going to get," he answers back. "I am worrying about what *I* am going to get."

I thought he had gone dotty.

"What's it got to do with you?" I says.

"If old Wotherspoon is in a good humour," he continues, "and the constable's head has gone down a bit between now and Wednesday, I may get off with forty shillings and a public reprimand.

"On the other hand," he goes on--he was working himself into a sort of fit--"if the constable's head goes on swelling, and old Wotherspoon's liver gets worse, I've got to be prepared for a month without the option. That is, if I am fool enough--"

He had left both the doors open, which in the daytime we generally do, our chambers being at the top. Miss Dorton--that's Mr. Parable's secretary--barges into the room. She didn't seem to notice me. She staggers to a chair and bursts into tears.

"He's gone," she says; "he's taken cook with him and gone."

"Gone!" says the guv'nor. "Where's he gone?"

"To Fingest," she says through her sobs--"to the cottage. Miss Bulstrode came in just after you had left," she says. "He wants to get away from everyone and have a few days' quiet. And then he is coming back, and he is going to do it himself."

"Do what?" says the guv'nor, irritable like.

"Fourteen days," she wails. "It'll kill him."

"But the case doesn't come on till Wednesday," says the guv'nor. "How do you know it's going to be fourteen days?"

"Miss Bulstrode," she says, "she's seen the magistrate. He says he always gives fourteen days in cases of unprovoked assault."

"But it wasn't unprovoked," says the guv'nor. "The other man began it by knocking off his hat. It was self-defence."

"She put that to him," she says, "and he agreed that that would alter his view of the case. But, you see," she continues, "we can't find the other man. He isn't likely to come forward of his own accord."

"The girl must know," says the guv'nor--"this girl he picks up in St. James's Park, and goes dancing with. The man must have been some friend of hers."

"But we can't find her either," she says. "He doesn't even know her name--he can't remember it."

"You will do it, won't you?" she says.

"Do what?" says the guv'nor again.

"The fourteen days," she says.

"But I thought you said he was going to do it himself?" he says.

"But he mustn't," she says. "Miss Bulstrode is coming round to see you. Think of it! Think of the headlines in the papers," she says. "Think of the Fabian Society. Think of the Suffrage cause. We mustn't let him."

"What about me?" says the guv'nor. "Doesn't anybody care for me?"

"You don't matter," she says. "Besides," she says, "with your influence you'll be able to keep it out of the papers. If it comes out that it was Mr. Parable, nothing on earth will be able to."

The guv'nor was almost as much excited by this time as she was.

"I'll see the Fabian Society and the Women's Vote and the Home for Lost Cats at Battersea, and all the rest of the blessed bag of tricks--"

I'd been thinking to myself, and had just worked it out.

"What's he want to take his cook down with him for?" I says.

"To cook for him," says the guv'nor. "What d'you generally want a cook for?"

"Rats!" I says. "Does he usually take his cook with him?"

"No," answered Miss Dorton. "Now I come to think of it, he has always hitherto put up with Mrs. Meadows."

"You will find the lady down at Fingest," I says, "sitting opposite him and enjoying a recherche dinner for two."

The guv'nor slaps me on the back, and lifts Miss Dorton out of her chair.

"You get on back," he says, "and telephone to Miss Bulstrode. I'll be round at half-past twelve."

Miss Dorton went out in a dazed sort of condition, and the guv'nor gives me a sovereign, and tells me I can have the rest of the day to myself.

Mr. Condor, Junior, considers that what happened subsequently goes to prove that he was right more than it proves that he was wrong.

Mr. Condor, Junior, also promised to send us a photograph of himself for reproduction, but, unfortunately, up to the time of going to press it had not arrived.

∽

From Mrs. Meadows, widow of the late Corporal John Meadows, V.C., Turberville, Bucks, the following further particulars were obtained by our local representative:

I have done for Mr. Parable now for some years past, my cottage being only a mile off, which makes it easy for me to look after him.

Mr. Parable likes the place to be always ready so that he can drop in when he chooses, he sometimes giving me warning and sometimes not. It was about the end of last month--on a Friday, if I remember rightly--that he suddenly turned up.

As a rule, he walks from Henley station, but on this occasion he arrived in a fly, he having a young woman with him, and she having a bag--his cook, as he explained to me. As a rule, I do everything for Mr. Parable, sleeping in the cottage when he is there; but to tell the truth, I was glad to see her. I never was much of a cook myself, as my poor dead husband has remarked on more than one occasion, and I don't pretend to be. Mr. Parable added, apologetic like, that he had been suffering lately from indigestion.

"I am only too pleased to see her," I says. "There are the two beds in my room, and we shan't quarrel." She was quite a sensible young woman, as I had judged from the first look at her, though suffering at the time from a cold. She hires a bicycle from Emma Tidd, who only uses it on a Sunday, and, taking a market basket, off she starts for Henley, Mr. Parable saying he would go with her to show her the way.

They were gone a goodish time, which, seeing it's eight miles, didn't so much surprise me; and when they got back we all three had dinner together, Mr. Parable arguing that it made for what he called "labour saving." Afterwards I cleared away, leaving them talking together; and later on they had a walk round the garden, it being a moonlight night, but a bit too cold for my fancy.

In the morning I had a chat with her before he was down. She seemed a bit worried.

"I hope people won't get talking," she says. "He would insist on my coming."

"Well," I says, "surely a gent can bring his cook along with him to cook for him. And as for people talking, what I always say is, one may just as well give them something to talk about and save them the trouble of making it up."

"If only I was a plain, middle-aged woman," she says, "it would be all right."

"Perhaps you will be, all in good time," I says, but, of course, I could see what she was driving at. A nice, clean, pleasant-faced young woman she was, and not of the ordinary class. "Meanwhile," I says, "if you don't mind taking a bit of motherly advice, you might remember that your place is the kitchen, and his the parlour. He's a dear good man, I know, but human nature is human nature, and it's no good pretending it isn't."

She and I had our breakfast together before he was up, so that when he came down he had to have his alone, but afterwards she comes into the kitchen and closes the door.

"He wants to show me the way to High Wycombe," she says. "He will have it there are better shops at Wycombe. What ought I to do?"

My experience is that advising folks to do what they don't want to do isn't the way to do it.

"What d'you think yourself?" I asked her.

"I feel like going with him," she says, "and making the most of every mile."

And then she began to cry.

"What's the harm!" she says. "I have heard him from a dozen platforms ridiculing class distinctions. Besides," she says, "my people have been farmers for generations. What was Miss Bulstrode's father but a grocer? He ran a hundred shops instead of one. What difference does that make?"

"When did it all begin?" I says. "When did he first take notice of you like?"

"The day before yesterday," she answers. "He had never seen me before," she says. "I was just 'Cook'--something in a cap and apron that he passed occasionally on the stairs. On Thursday he saw me in my best clothes, and fell in love with me. He doesn't know it himself, poor dear, not yet, but that's what he's done."

Well, I couldn't contradict her, not after the way I had seen him looking at her across the table.

"What are your feelings towards him," I says, "to be quite honest? He's rather a good catch for a young person in your position."

"That's my trouble," she says. "I can't help thinking of that. And then to be 'Mrs. John Parable'! That's enough to turn a woman's head."

"He'd be a bit difficult to live with," I says.

"Geniuses always are," she says; "it's easy enough if you just think of them as children. He'd be a bit fractious at times, that's all. Underneath, he's just the kindest, dearest--"

"Oh, you take your basket and go to High Wycombe," I says. "He might do worse."

I wasn't expecting them back soon, and they didn't come back soon. In the afternoon a motor stops at the gate, and out of it steps Miss Bulstrode, Miss Dorton--that's the young lady that writes for him--and Mr. Quincey. I told them I couldn't say when he'd be back, and they said it didn't matter, they just happening to be passing.

"Did anybody call on him yesterday?" asks Miss Bulstrode, careless like--"a lady?"

"No," I says; "you are the first as yet."

"He's brought his cook down with him, hasn't he?" says Mr. Quincey.

"Yes," I says, "and a very good cook too," which was the truth.

"I'd like just to speak a few words with her," says Miss Bulstrode.

"Sorry, m'am," I says, "but she's out at present; she's gone to Wycombe."

"Gone to Wycombe!" they all says together.

"To market," I says. "It's a little farther, but, of course, it stands to reason the shops there are better."

They looked at one another.

"That settles it," says Mr. Quincey. "Delicacies worthy to be set before her not available nearer than Wycombe, but must be had. There's going to be a pleasant little dinner here to-night."

"The hussy!" says Miss Bulstrode, under her breath.

They whispered together for a moment, then they turns to me.

"Good afternoon, Mrs. Meadows," says Mr. Quincey. "You needn't say we called. He wanted to be alone, and it might vex him."

I said I wouldn't, and I didn't. They climbed back into the motor and went off.

Before dinner I had call to go into the woodshed. I heard a scuttling as I opened the door. If I am not mistaken, Miss Dorton was hiding in the corner where we keep the coke. I didn't see any good in making a fuss, so I left her there. When I got back to the kitchen, cook asked me if we'd got any parsley.

"You'll find a bit in the front," I says, "to the left of the gate," and she went out. She came back looking scared.

"Anybody keep goats round here?" she asked me.

"Not that I know of, nearer than Ibstone Common," I says.

"I could have sworn I saw a goat's face looking at me out of the gooseberry bushes while I was picking the parsley," she says. "It had a beard."

"It's the half light," I says. "One can imagine anything."

"I do hope I'm not getting nervy," she says.

I thought I'd have another look round, and made the excuse that I wanted a pail of water. I was stooping over the well, which is just under the mulberry tree, when something fell close to me and lodged upon the bricks. It was a hairpin. I fixed the cover carefully upon the well in case of accident, and when I got in I went round myself and was careful to see that all the curtains were drawn.

Just before we three sat down to dinner again I took cook aside.

"I shouldn't go for any stroll in the garden to-night," I says. "People from the village may be about, and we don't want them gossiping." And she thanked me.

Next night they were there again. I thought I wouldn't spoil the dinner, but mention it afterwards. I saw to it again that the curtains were drawn, and slipped the catch of both the doors. And just as well that I did.

I had always heard that Mr. Parable was an amusing speaker, but on previous visits had not myself noticed it. But this time he seemed ten years younger than I had ever known him before; and during dinner, while we were talking and laughing quite merry like, I had the feeling more than once that people were meandering about outside. I had just finished clearing away, and cook was making the coffee, when there came a knock at the door.

"Who's that?" says Mr. Parable. "I am not at home to anyone."

"I'll see," I says. And on my way I slipped into the kitchen.

"Coffee for one, cook," I says, and she understood. Her cap and apron were hanging behind the door. I flung them across to her, and she caught them; and then I opened the front door.

They pushed past me without speaking, and went straight into the parlour. And they didn't waste many words on him either.

"Where is she?" asked Miss Bulstrode.

"Where's who?" says Mr. Parable.

"Don't lie about it," said Miss Bulstrode, making no effort to control herself. "The hussy you've been dining with?"

"Do you mean Mrs. Meadows?" says Mr. Parable.

I thought she was going to shake him.

"Where have you hidden her?" she says.

It was at that moment cook entered with the coffee.

If they had taken the trouble to look at her they might have had an idea. The tray was trembling in her hands, and in her haste and excitement she had put on her cap the wrong way round. But she kept control of her voice, and asked if she should bring some more coffee.

"Ah, yes! You'd all like some coffee, wouldn't you?" says Mr. Parable. Miss Bulstrode did not reply, but Mr. Quincey said he was cold and would like it. It was a nasty night, with a thin rain.

"Thank you, sir," says cook, and we went out together.

Cottages are only cottages, and if people in the parlour persist in talking loudly, people in the kitchen can't very well help overhearing.

There was a good deal of talk about "fourteen days," which Mr. Parable said he was going to do himself, and which Miss Dorton said he mustn't, because, if he did, it would be a victory for the enemies of humanity. Mr. Parable said something about "humanity," which I didn't rightly hear, but, whatever it was, it started Miss Dorton crying; and Miss Bulstrode called Mr. Parable a "blind Samson," who had had his hair cut by a designing minx who had been hired to do it.

It was all French to me, but cook was drinking in every word, and when she returned from taking them in their coffee she made no bones about it, but took up her place at the door with her ear to the keyhole.

It was Mr. Quincey who got them all quiet, and then he began to explain things. It seemed that if they could only find a certain gentleman and persuade him to come forward and acknowledge that he began a row, that then all would be well. Mr. Quincey would be fined forty shillings, and Mr. Parable's name would never appear. Failing that, Mr. Parable, according to Mr. Quincey, could do his fourteen days himself.

"I've told you once," says Mr. Parable, "and I tell you again, that I don't know the man's name, and can't give it you."

"We are not asking you to," says Mr. Quincey. "You give us the name of your tango partner, and we'll do the rest."

I could see cook's face; I had got a bit interested myself, and we were both close to the door. She hardly seemed to be breathing.

"I am sorry," says Mr. Parable, speaking very deliberate-like, "but I am not going to have her name dragged into this business."

"It wouldn't be," says Mr. Quincey. "All we want to get out of her is the name and address of the gentleman who was so anxious to see her home."

"Who was he?" says Miss Bulstrode. "Her husband?"

"No," says Mr. Parable; "he wasn't."

"Then who was he?" says Miss Bulstrode. "He must have been something to her--fiance?"

"I am going to do the fourteen days myself," says Mr. Parable. "I shall come out all the fresher after a fortnight's complete rest and change."

Cook leaves the door with a smile on her face that made her look quite beautiful, and, taking some paper from the dresser drawer, began to write a letter.

They went on talking in the other room for another ten minutes, and then Mr. Parable lets them out himself, and goes a little way with them. When he came back we could hear him walking up and down the other room.

She had written and stamped the envelope; it was lying on the table.

"'Joseph Onions, Esq.,'" I says, reading the address. "Auctioneer and House Agent, Broadway, Hammersmith.' Is that the young man?"

"That is the young man," she says, folding her letter and putting it in the envelope.

"And was he your fiance?" I asked.

"No," she says. "But he will be if he does what I'm telling him to do."

"And what about Mr. Parable?" I says.

"A little joke that will amuse him later on," she says, slipping a cloak on her shoulders. "How once he nearly married his cook."

"I shan't be a minute," she says. And, with the letter in her hand, she slips out.

Mrs. Meadows, we understand, has expressed indignation at our publication of this interview, she being under the impression that she was simply having a friendly gossip with a neighbour. Our representative, however, is sure he explained to Mrs. Meadows that his visit was official; and, in any case, our duty to the public must be held to exonerate us from all blame in the matter.

∽

Mr. Joseph Onions, of the Broadway, Hammersmith, auctioneer and house agent, expressed himself to our representative as most surprised at the turn that events had subsequently taken. The letter that Mr. Onions received from Miss Comfort Price was explicit and definite. It was to the effect that if he would call upon a certain Mr. Quincey, of Harcourt Buildings, Temple, and acknowledge that it was he who began the row at the Earl's Court Exhibition on the evening of the twenty-seventh, that then the engagement between himself and Miss Price, hitherto unacknowledged by the lady, might be regarded as a fact.

Mr. Onions, who describes himself as essentially a business man, decided before complying with Miss Price's request to take a few preliminary steps. As the result of judiciously conducted inquiries, first at the Vine Street Police Station, and secondly at Twickenham, Mr. Onions arrived later in the day at Mr. Quincey's chambers, with, to use his own expression, all the cards in his hand. It was Mr. Quincey who, professing himself unable to comply with Mr. Onion's suggestion, arranged the interview with Miss Bulstrode. And it was Miss Bulstrode herself who, on condition that Mr. Onions added to the undertaking the further condition that he would marry Miss Price before the end of the month, offered to make it two hundred. It was in their joint interest--Mr. Onions regarding himself and Miss Price as now one--that Mr. Onions suggested her making it three, using such arguments as, under the circumstances, naturally occurred to him--as, for example, the damage caused to the lady's reputation by the whole proceedings, culminating in a night spent by the lady, according to her own account, on Ham Common. That the price demanded was reasonable Mr. Onions considers as proved by Miss Bulstrode's eventual acceptance of his terms. That, having got out of him all that he wanted, Mr. Quincey should have "considered it his duty" to communicate the entire details of the transaction to Miss Price, through the medium of Mr. Andrews, thinking it "as well she should know the character of the man she proposed to marry," Mr. Onions considers a gross breach of etiquette as between gentlemen; and having regard to Miss Price's after behaviour, Mr. Onions can only say that she is not the girl he took her for.

Mr. Aaron Andrews, on whom our representative called, was desirous at first of not being drawn into the matter; but on our representative explaining to him that our only desire was to contradict false rumours likely to be harmful to Mr. Parable's reputation, Mr. Andrews saw the necessity of putting our representative in possession of the truth.

She came back on Tuesday afternoon, explained Mr. Andrews, and I had a talk with her.

"It is all right, Mr. Andrews," she told me; "they've been in communication with my young man, and Miss Bulstrode has seen the magistrate privately. The case will be dismissed with a fine of forty shillings, and Mr. Quincey has arranged to keep it out of the papers."

"Well, all's well that ends well," I answered; "but it might have been better, my girl, if you had mentioned that young man of yours a bit earlier."

"I did not know it was of any importance," she explained. "Mr. Parable told me nothing. If it hadn't been for chance, I should never have known what was happening."

I had always liked the young woman. Mr. Quincey had suggested my waiting till after Wednesday. But there seemed to me no particular object in delay.

"Are you fond of him?" I asked her.

"Yes," she answered. "I am fonder than--" And then she stopped herself suddenly and flared scarlet. "Who are you talking about?" she demanded.

"This young man of yours," I said. "Mr.--What's his name--Onions?"

"Oh, that?" she answered. "Oh, yes; he's all right."

"And if he wasn't?" I said, and she looked at me hard.

"I told him," she said, "that if he would do what I asked him to do, I'd marry him. And he seems to have done it."

"There are ways of doing everything," I said; and, seeing it wasn't going to break her heart, I told her just the plain facts. She listened without a word, and when I had finished she put her arms round my neck and kissed me. I am old enough to be her grandfather, but twenty years ago it might have upset me.

"I think I shall be able to save Miss Bulstrode that three hundred pounds," she laughed, and ran upstairs and changed her things. When later I looked into the kitchen she was humming.

Mr. John came up by the car, and I could see he was in one of his moods.

"Pack me some things for a walking tour," he said. "Don't forget the knapsack. I am going to Scotland by the eight-thirty."

"Will you be away long?" I asked him.

"It depends upon how long it takes me," he answered. "When I come back I am going to be married."

"Who is the lady?" I asked, though, of course, I knew.

"Miss Bulstrode," he said.

"Well," I said, "she--"

"That will do," he said; "I have had all that from the three of them for the last two days. She is a Socialist, and a Suffragist, and all the rest of it, and my ideal helpmate. She is well off, and that will enable me to devote all my time to putting the world to rights without bothering about anything else. Our home will be the nursery of advanced ideas. We shall share together the joys and delights of the public platform. What more can any man want?"

"You will want your dinner early," I said, "if you are going by the eight-thirty. I had better tell cook--"

He interrupted me again.

"You can tell cook to go to the devil," he said.

I naturally stared at him.

"She is going to marry a beastly little rotter of a rent collector that she doesn't care a damn for," he went on.

I could not understand why he seemed so mad about it.

"I don't see, in any case, what it's got to do with you," I said, "but, as a matter of fact, she isn't."

"Isn't what?" he said, stopping short and turning on me.

"Isn't going to marry him," I answered.

"Why not?" he demanded.

"Better ask her," I suggested.

I didn't know at the time that it was a silly thing to say, and I am not sure that I should not have said it if I had. When he is in one of his moods I always seem to get into one of mine. I have looked after Mr. John ever since he was a baby, so that we do not either of us treat the other quite as perhaps we ought to.

"Tell cook I want her," he said.

"She is just in the middle--" I began.

"I don't care where she is," he said. He seemed determined never to let me finish a sentence. "Send her up here."

She was in the kitchen by herself.

"He wants to see you at once," I said.

"Who does?" she asked.

"Mr. John," I said.

"What's he want to see me for?" she asked.

"How do I know?" I answered.

"But you do," she said. She always had an obstinate twist in her, and, feeling it would save time, I told her what had happened.

"Well," I said, "aren't you going?"

She was standing stock still staring at the pastry she was making. She turned to me, and there was a curious smile about her lips.

"Do you know what you ought to be wearing?" she said. "Wings, and a little bow and arrow."

She didn't even think to wipe her hands, but went straight upstairs. It was about half an hour later when the bell rang. Mr. John was standing by the window.

"Is that bag ready?" he said.

"It will be," I said.

I went out into the hall and returned with the clothes brush.

"What are you going to do?" he said.

"Perhaps you don't know it," I said, "but you are all over flour."

"Cook's going with me to Scotland," he said.

I have looked after Mr. John ever since he was a boy. He was forty-two last birthday, but when I shook hands with him through the cab window I could have sworn he was twenty-five again.

THE LESSON

The first time I met him, to my knowledge, was on an evil-smelling, one-funnelled steam boat that in those days plied between London Bridge and Antwerp. He was walking the deck arm-in-arm with a showily dressed but decidedly attractive young woman; both of them talking and laughing loudly. It struck me as odd, finding him a fellow-traveller by such a route. The passage occupied eighteen hours, and the first-class return fare was one pound twelve and six, including three meals each way; drinks, as the contract was careful to explain, being extra. I was earning thirty shillings a week at the time as clerk with a firm of agents in Fenchurch Street. Our business was the purchasing of articles on commission for customers in India, and I had learned to be a judge of values. The beaver lined coat he was wearing--for the evening, although it was late summer, was chilly--must have cost him a couple of hundred pounds, while his carelessly displayed jewellery he could easily have pawned for a thousand or more.

I could not help staring at him, and once, as they passed, he returned my look.

After dinner, as I was leaning with my back against the gunwale on the starboard side, he came out of the only private cabin that the vessel boasted, and taking up a position opposite to me, with his legs well apart and a big cigar between his thick lips, stood coolly regarding me, as if appraising me.

"Treating yourself to a little holiday on the Continent?" he inquired.

I had not been quite sure before he spoke, but his lisp, though slight, betrayed the Jew. His features were coarse, almost brutal; but the restless eyes were so brilliant, the whole face so suggestive of power and character, that, taking him as a whole, the feeling he inspired was admiration, tempered by fear. His tone was one of kindly contempt--the tone of a man accustomed to find most people his inferiors, and too used to the discovery to be conceited about it.

Behind it was a note of authority that it did not occur to me to dispute.

"Yes," I answered, adding the information that I had never been abroad before, and had heard that Antwerp was an interesting town.

"How long have you got?" he asked.

"A fortnight," I told him.

"Like to see a bit more than Antwerp, if you could afford it, wouldn't you?" he suggested. "Fascinating little country Holland. Just long enough--a fortnight--to do the whole of it. I'm a Dutchman, a Dutch Jew."

"You speak English just like an Englishman," I told him. It was somehow in my mind to please him. I could hardly have explained why.

"And half a dozen other languages equally well," he answered, laughing. "I left Amsterdam when I was eighteen as steerage passenger in an emigrant ship. I haven't seen it since."

He closed the cabin door behind him, and, crossing over, laid a strong hand on my shoulder.

"I will make a proposal to you," he said. "My business is not of the kind that can be put out of mind, even for a few days, and there are reasons"--he glanced over his shoulder towards the cabin door, and gave vent to a short laugh--"why I did not want to bring any of my own staff with me. If you care for a short tour, all expenses paid at slap-up hotels and a ten-pound note in your pocket at the end, you can have it for two hours' work a day."

I suppose my face expressed my acceptance, for he did not wait for me to speak.

"Only one thing I stipulate for," he added, "that you mind your own business and keep your mouth shut. You're by yourself, aren't you?"

"Yes," I told him.

He wrote on a sheet of his notebook, and, tearing it out, handed it to me.

"That's your hotel at Antwerp," he said. "You are Mr. Horatio Jones's secretary." He chuckled to himself as he repeated the name, which certainly did not fit him. "Knock at my sitting-room door at nine o'clock tomorrow morning. Good night!"

He ended the conversation as abruptly as he had begun it, and returned to his cabin.

I got a glimpse of him next morning, coming out of the hotel bureau. He was speaking to the manager in French, and had evidently given instructions concerning me, for I found myself preceded by an obsequious waiter to quite a charming bedroom on the second floor, while the "English breakfast" placed before me later in the coffee-room was of a size and character that in those days I did not often enjoy. About the work, also, he was as good as his word. I was rarely occupied for more than two hours each morning. The duties consisted chiefly of writing letters and sending off telegrams. The letters he signed and had posted himself, so that I never learnt his real name--not during that fortnight--but I gathered enough to be aware that he was a man whose business interests must have been colossal and world-wide.

He never introduced me to "Mrs. Horatio Jones," and after a few days he seemed to be bored with her, so that often I would take her place as his companion in afternoon excursions.

I could not help liking the man. Strength always compels the adoration of youth; and there was something big and heroic about him. His daring, his swift decisions, his utter unscrupulousness, his occasional cruelty when necessity seemed to demand it. One could imagine him in earlier days a born leader of savage hordes, a lover of fighting for its own sake, meeting all obstacles with fierce welcome, forcing his way onward, indifferent to the misery and destruction caused by his progress, his eyes never swerving from their goal; yet not without a sense of rough justice, not altogether without kindliness when it could be indulged in without danger.

One afternoon he took me with him into the Jewish quarter of Amsterdam, and threading his way without hesitation through its maze of unsavoury slums, paused before a narrow three-storeyed house overlooking a stagnant backwater.

"The room I was born in," he explained. "Window with the broken pane on the second floor. It has never been mended."

I stole a glance at him. His face betrayed no suggestion of sentiment, but rather of amusement. He offered me a cigar, which I was glad of, for the stench from the offal-laden water behind us was distracting, and for a while we both smoked in silence: he with his eyes half-closed; it was a trick of his when working out a business problem.

"Curious, my making such a choice," he remarked. "A butcher's assistant for my father and a consumptive buttonhole-maker for my mother. I suppose I knew what I was about. Quite the right thing for me to have done, as it turned out."

I stared at him, wondering whether he was speaking seriously or in grim jest. He was given at times to making odd remarks. There was a vein of the fantastic in him that was continually cropping out and astonishing me.

"It was a bit risky," I suggested. "Better choose something a little safer next time."

He looked round at me sharply, and, not quite sure of his mood, I kept a grave face.

"Perhaps you are right," he agreed, with a laugh. "We must have a talk about it one day."

After that visit to the Goortgasse he was less reserved with me, and would often talk to me on subjects that I should never have guessed would have interested him. I found him a curious mixture. Behind the shrewd, cynical man of business I caught continual glimpses of the visionary.

I parted from him at The Hague. He paid my fare back to London, and gave me an extra pound for travelling expenses, together with the ten-pound note he had promised me. He had packed off "Mrs. Horatio Jones" some days before, to the relief, I imagine, of both of them, and he himself continued his journey to Berlin. I never expected to see him again, although for the next few months I often thought of him, and even tried to discover him by inquiries in the City. I had, however, very little to go upon, and after I had left Fenchurch Street behind me, and drifted into literature, I forgot him.

Until one day I received a letter addressed to the care of my publishers. It bore the Swiss postmark, and opening it and turning to the signature I sat wondering for the moment where I had met "Horatio Jones." And then I remembered.

He was lying bruised and broken in a woodcutter's hut on the slopes of the Jungfrau. Had been playing a fool's trick, so he described it, thinking he could climb mountains at his age. They would carry him down to Lauterbrunnen as soon as he could be moved farther with safety, but for the present he had no one to talk to but the nurse and a Swiss doctor who climbed up to see him every third day. He begged me, if I could spare the time, to come over and spend a week with him. He enclosed a hundred-pound cheque for my expenses, making no apology for doing so. He was complimentary about my first book, which he had been reading, and asked me to telegraph him my reply, giving me his real name, which, as I had guessed it would, proved to be one of the best known in the financial world. My time was my own now, and I wired him that I would be with him the following Monday.

He was lying in the sun outside the hut when I arrived late in the afternoon, after a three-hours' climb followed by a porter carrying my small amount of luggage. He could not raise his hand, but his strangely brilliant eyes spoke their welcome.

"I am glad you were able to come," he said. "I have no near relations, and my friends--if that is the right term--are business men who would be bored to tears. Besides, they are not the people I feel I want to talk to, now."

He was entirely reconciled to the coming of death. Indeed, there were moments when he gave me the idea that he was looking forward to it with an awed curiosity. With the conventional notion of cheering him, I talked of staying till he was able to return with me to civilisation, but he only laughed.

"I am not going back," he said. "Not that way. What they may do afterwards with these broken bones does not much concern either you or me.

"It's a good place to die in," he continued. "A man can think up here."

It was difficult to feel sorry for him, his own fate appearing to make so little difference to himself. The world was still full of interest to him--not his own particular corner of it: that, he gave me to understand, he had tidied up and dismissed from his mind. It was the future, its coming problems, its possibilities, its new developments, about which he seemed eager to talk. One might have imagined him a young man with the years before him.

One evening--it was near the end--we were alone together. The woodcutter and his wife had gone down into the valley to see their children, and the nurse, leaving him in my charge, had gone for a walk. We had carried him round to his favourite side of the hut facing the towering mass of the Jungfrau. As the shadows lengthened it seemed to come nearer to us, and there fell a silence upon us.

Gradually I became aware that his piercing eyes were fixed on me, and in answer I turned and looked at him.

"I wonder if we shall meet again," he said, "or, what is more important, if we shall remember one another."

I was puzzled for the moment. We had discussed more than once the various religions of mankind, and his attitude towards the orthodox beliefs had always been that of amused contempt.

"It has been growing upon me these last few days," he continued.

"It flashed across me the first time I saw you on the boat. We were fellow-students. Something, I don't know what, drew us very close together. There was a woman. They were burning her. And then there was a rush of people and a sudden darkness, and your eyes close to mine."

I suppose it was some form of hypnotism, for, as he spoke, his searching eyes fixed on mine, there came to me a dream of narrow streets filled with a strange crowd, of painted houses such as I had never seen, and a haunting fear that seemed to be always lurking behind each shadow. I shook myself free, but not without an effort.

"So that's what you meant," I said, "that evening in the Goortgasse. You believe in it?"

"A curious thing happened to me," he said, "when I was a child. I could hardly have been six years old. I had gone to Ghent with my parents. I think it was to visit some relative. One day we went into the castle. It was in ruins then, but has since been restored. We were in what was once the council chamber. I stole away by myself to the other end of the great room and, not knowing why I did so, I touched a spring concealed in the masonry, and a door swung open with a harsh, grinding noise. I remember peering round the opening. The others had their backs towards me, and I slipped through and closed the door behind me. I seemed instinctively to know my way. I ran down a flight of steps and along dark corridors through which I had to feel my way with my hands, till I came to a small door in an angle of the wall. I knew the room that lay the other side. A photograph was taken of it and published years afterwards, when the place was discovered, and it was exactly as I knew it with its way out underneath the city wall through one of the small houses in the Aussermarkt.

"I could not open the door. Some stones had fallen against it, and fearing to get punished, I made my way back into the council room. It was empty when I reached it. They were searching for me in the other rooms, and I never told them of my adventure."

At any other time I might have laughed. Later, recalling his talk that evening, I dismissed the whole story as mere suggestion, based upon the imagination of a child; but at the time those strangely brilliant eyes had taken possession of me. They remained still fixed upon me as I sat on the low rail of the veranda watching his white face, into which the hues of death seemed already to be creeping.

I had a feeling that, through them, he was trying to force remembrance of himself upon me. The man himself--the very soul of him--seemed to be concentrated in them. Something formless and yet distinct was visualising itself before me. It came to me as a physical relief when a spasm of pain caused him to turn his eyes away from me.

"You will find a letter when I am gone," he went on, after a moment's silence. "I thought that you might come too late, or that I might not have strength enough to tell you. I felt that out of the few people I have met outside business, you would be the most likely not to dismiss the matter as mere nonsense. What I am glad of myself, and what I wish you to remember, is that I am dying with all my faculties about me. The one thing I have always feared through life was old age, with its gradual mental decay. It has always seemed to me that I have died more or less suddenly while still in possession of my will. I have always thanked God for that."

He closed his eyes, but I do not think he was sleeping; and a little later the nurse returned, and we carried him indoors. I had no further conversation with him, though at his wish during the following two days I continued to read to him, and on the third day he died.

I found the letter he had spoken of. He had told me where it would be. It contained a bundle of banknotes which he was giving me--so he wrote--with the advice to get rid of them as quickly as possible.

"If I had not loved you," the letter continued, "I would have left you an income, and you would have blessed me, instead of cursing me, as you should have done, for spoiling your life."

This world was a school, so he viewed it, for the making of men; and the one thing essential to a man was strength. One gathered the impression of a deeply religious man. In these days he would, no doubt, have been claimed as a theosophist; but his beliefs he had made for, and adapted to, himself--to his vehement, conquering temperament. God needed men to serve Him--to help Him. So, through many changes, through many ages, God gave men life: that by contest and by struggle they might ever increase in strength; to those who proved themselves most fit the sterner task, the humbler beginnings, the greater obstacles. And the crown of well-doing was ever victory. He appeared to have convinced himself that he was one of the chosen, that he was destined for great ends. He had been a slave in the time of the Pharaohs; a priest in Babylon; had clung to the swaying ladders in the sack of Rome; had won his way into the councils when Europe was a battlefield of contending tribes; had climbed to power in the days of the Borgias.

To most of us, I suppose, there come at odd moments haunting thoughts of strangely familiar, far-off things; and one wonders whether they are memories or dreams. We dismiss them as we grow older and the present with its crowding interests shuts them out; but in youth they were more persistent. With him they appeared to have remained, growing in reality. His recent existence, closed under the white sheet in the hut behind me as I read, was only one chapter of the story; he was looking forward to the next.

He wondered, so the letter ran, whether he would have any voice in choosing it. In either event he was curious of the result. What he anticipated confidently were new opportunities, wider experience. In what shape would these come to him?

The letter ended with a strange request. It was that, on returning to England, I should continue to think of him: not of the dead man I had known, the Jewish banker, the voice familiar to me, the trick of speech, of manner--all such being but the changing clothes--but of the man himself, the soul of him, that would seek and perhaps succeed in revealing itself to me.

A postscript concluded the letter, to which at the time I attached no importance. He had made a purchase of the hut in which he had died. After his removal it was to remain empty.

I folded the letter and placed it among other papers, and passing into the hut took a farewell glance at the massive, rugged face. The mask might have served a sculptor for the embodiment of strength. He gave one the feeling that having conquered death he was sleeping.

I did what he had requested of me. Indeed, I could not help it. I thought of him constantly. That may have been the explanation of it.

I was bicycling through Norfolk, and one afternoon, to escape a coming thunderstorm, I knocked at the door of a lonely cottage on the outskirts of a common. The woman, a kindly bustling person, asked me in; and hoping I would excuse her, as she was busy ironing, returned to her work in another room. I thought myself alone, and was standing at the window watching the pouring rain. After a while, without knowing why, I turned. And then I saw a child seated on a high chair behind a table in a dark corner of the room. A book of pictures was open before it, but it was looking at me. I could hear the sound of the woman at her ironing in the other room. Outside there was the steady thrashing of the rain. The child was looking at me with large, round eyes filled with a terrible pathos. I noticed that the little body was misshapen. It never moved; it made no sound; but I had the feeling that out of those strangely wistful eyes something was trying to speak to me. Something was forming itself before me--not visible to my sight; but it was there, in the room. It was the man I had last looked upon as, dying, he sat beside me in the hut below the Jungfrau. But something had happened to him. Moved by instinct I went over to him and lifted him out of his chair, and with a sob the little wizened arms closed round my neck and he clung to me crying--a pitiful, low, wailing cry.

Hearing his cry, the woman came back. A comely, healthy-looking woman. She took him from my arms and comforted him.

"He gets a bit sorry for himself at times," she explained. "At least, so I fancy. You see, he can't run about like other children, or do anything without getting pains."

"Was it an accident?" I asked.

"No," she answered, "and his father as fine a man as you would find in a day's march. Just a visitation of God, as they tell me. Sure I don't know why. There never was a better little lad, and clever, too, when he's not in pain. Draws wonderfully."

The storm had passed. He grew quieter in her arms, and when I had promised to come again and bring him a new picture-book, a little grateful smile flickered across the drawn face, but he would not talk.

I kept in touch with him. Mere curiosity would have made me do that. He grew more normal as the years went by, and gradually the fancy that had come to me at our first meeting faded farther into the background. Sometimes, using the very language of the dead man's letter, I would talk to him, wondering if by any chance some flash of memory would come back to him, and once or twice it seemed to me that into the mild, pathetic eyes there came a look that I had seen before, but it passed away, and indeed, it was difficult to think of this sad little human oddity, with its pleading helplessness, in connection with the strong, swift, conquering spirit that I had watched passing away amid the silence of the mountains.

The one thing that brought joy to him was his art. I cannot help thinking that, but for his health, he would have made a name for himself. His work was always clever and original, but it was the work of an invalid.

"I shall never be great," he said to me once. "I have such wonderful dreams, but when it comes to working them out there is something that hampers me. It always seems to me as if at the last moment a hand was stretched out that clutched me by the feet. I long so, but I have not the strength. It is terrible to be one of the weaklings."

It clung to me, that word he had used. For a man to know he is weak; it sounds a paradox, but a man must be strong to know that. And dwelling upon this, and upon his patience and his gentleness, there came to me suddenly remembrance of that postscript, the significance of which I had not understood.

He was a young man of about three- or four-and-twenty at the time. His father had died, and he was living in poor lodgings in the south of London, supporting himself and his mother by strenuous, ill-paid work.

"I want you to come with me for a few days' holiday," I told him.

I had some difficulty in getting him to accept my help, for he was very proud in his sensitive, apologetic way. But I succeeded eventually, persuading him it would be good for his work. Physically the journey must have cost him dear, for he could never move his body without pain, but the changing landscapes and the strange cities more than repaid him; and when one morning I woke him early and he saw for the first time the distant mountains clothed in dawn, there came a new light into his eyes.

We reached the hut late in the afternoon. I had made my arrangements so that we should be there alone. Our needs were simple, and in various wanderings I had learnt to be independent. I did not tell him why I had brought him there, beyond the beauty and stillness of the place. Purposely I left him much alone there, making ever-lengthening walks my excuse, and though he was always glad of my return I felt that the desire was growing upon him to be there by himself.

One evening, having climbed farther than I had intended, I lost my way. It was not safe in that neighbourhood to try new pathways in the dark, and chancing upon a deserted shelter, I made myself a bed upon the straw.

I found him seated outside the hut when I returned, and he greeted me as if he had been expecting me just at that moment and not before. He guessed just what had happened, he told me, and had not been alarmed. During the day I found him watching me, and in the evening, as we sat in his favourite place outside the hut, he turned to me.

"You think it true?" he said. "That you and I sat here years ago and talked?"

"I cannot tell," I answered. "I only know that he died here, if there be such a thing as death--that no one has ever lived here since. I doubt if the door has ever been opened till we came."

"They have always been with me," he continued, "these dreams. But I have always dismissed them. They seemed so ludicrous. Always there came to me wealth, power, victory. Life was so easy."

He laid his thin hand on mine. A strange new look came into his eyes--a look of hope, almost of joy.

"Do you know what it seems to me?" he said. "You will laugh perhaps, but the thought has come to me up here that God has some fine use for me. Success was making me feeble. He has given me weakness and failure that I may learn strength. The great thing is to be strong."

SYLVIA OF THE LETTERS

Old Ab Herrick, so most people called him. Not that he was actually old; the term was an expression of liking rather than any reflection on his years. He lived in an old-fashioned house--old-fashioned, that is, for New York--on the south side of West Twentieth Street: once upon a time, but that was long ago, quite a fashionable quarter. The house, together with Mrs. Travers, had been left him by a maiden aunt. An "apartment" would, of course, have been more suitable to a bachelor of simple habits, but the situation was convenient from a journalistic point of view, and for fifteen years Abner Herrick had lived and worked there.

Then one evening, after a three days' absence, Abner Herrick returned to West Twentieth Street, bringing with him a little girl wrapped up in a shawl, and a wooden box tied with a piece of cord. He put the box on the table; and the young lady, loosening her shawl, walked to the window and sat down facing the room.

Mrs. Travers took the box off the table and put it on the floor--it was quite a little box--and waited.

"This young lady," explained Abner Herrick, "is Miss Ann Kavanagh, daughter of--of an old friend of mine."

"Oh!" said Mrs. Travers, and remained still expectant.

"Miss Kavanagh," continued Abner Herrick, "will be staying with us for--" He appeared to be uncertain of the length of Miss Kavanagh's visit. He left the sentence unfinished and took refuge in more pressing questions.

"What about the bedroom on the second floor? Is it ready? Sheets aired--all that sort of thing?"

"It can be," replied Mrs. Travers. The tone was suggestive of judgment reserved.

"I think, if you don't mind, Mrs. Travers, that we'd like to go to bed as soon as possible." From force of habit Abner S. Herrick in speaking employed as a rule the editorial "we." "We have been travelling all day and we are very tired. To-morrow morning--"

"I'd like some supper," said Miss Kavanagh from her seat in the window, without moving.

"Of course," agreed Miss Kavanagh's host, with a feeble pretence that the subject had been on the tip of his tongue. As a matter of fact, he really had forgotten all about it. "We might have it up here while the room is being got ready. Perhaps a little--"

"A soft boiled egg and a glass of milk, if you please, Mrs. Travers," interrupted Miss Kavanagh, still from her seat at the window.

"I'll see about it," said Mrs. Travers, and went out, taking the quite small box with her.

Such was the coming into this story of Ann Kavanagh at the age of eight years; or, as Miss Kavanagh herself would have explained, had the question been put to her, eight years and seven months, for Ann Kavanagh was a precise young lady. She was not beautiful--not then. She was much too sharp featured; the little pointed chin protruding into space to quite a dangerous extent. Her large dark eyes were her one redeeming feature. But the level brows above them were much too ready with their frown. A sallow complexion and nondescript hair deprived her of that charm of colouring on which youth can generally depend for attraction, whatever its faults of form. Nor could it truthfully be said that sweetness of disposition afforded compensation.

"A self-willed, cantankerous little imp I call her," was Mrs.

Travers's comment, expressed after one of the many trials of strength between them, from which Miss Kavanagh had as usual emerged triumphant.

"It's her father," explained Abner Herrick, feeling himself unable to contradict.

"It's unfortunate," answered Mrs. Travers, "whatever it is."

To Uncle Ab himself, as she had come to call him, she could on occasion be yielding and affectionate; but that, as Mrs. Travers took care to point out to her, was a small thing to her credit.

"If you had the instincts of an ordinary Christian child," explained Mrs. Travers to her, "you'd be thinking twenty-four hours a day of what you could do to repay him for all his loving kindness to you; instead of causing him, as you know you do, a dozen heartaches in a week. You're an ungrateful little monkey, and when he's gone you'll--"

Upon which Miss Kavanagh, not waiting to hear more, flew upstairs and, locking herself in her own room, gave herself up to howling and remorse; but was careful not to emerge until she felt bad tempered again; and able, should opportunity present itself, to renew the contest with Mrs. Travers unhampered by sentiment.

But Mrs. Travers's words had sunk in deeper than that good lady herself had hoped for; and one evening, when Abner Herrick was seated at his desk penning a scathing indictment of the President for lack of firmness and decision on the tariff question, Ann, putting her thin arms round his neck and rubbing her little sallow face against his right-hand whisker, took him to task on the subject.

"You're not bringing me up properly--not as you ought to," explained Ann. "You give way to me too much, and you never scold me."

"Not scold you!" exclaimed Abner with a certain warmth of indignation. "Why, I'm doing it all--"

"Not what *I* call scolding," continued Ann. "It's very wrong of you. I shall grow up horrid if you don't help me."

As Ann with great clearness pointed out to him, there was no one else to undertake the job with any chance of success. If Abner failed her, then she supposed there was no hope for her: she would end by becoming a wicked woman, and everybody, including herself, would hate her. It was a sad prospect. The contemplation of it brought tears to Ann's eyes.

He saw the justice of her complaint and promised to turn over a new leaf. He honestly meant to do so; but, like many another repentant sinner, found himself feeble before the difficulties of performance. He might have succeeded better had it not been for her soft deep eyes beneath her level brows.

"You're not much like your mother," so he explained to her one day, "except about the eyes. Looking into your eyes I can almost see your mother."

He was smoking a pipe beside the fire, and Ann, who ought to have been in bed, had perched herself upon one of the arms of his chair and was kicking a hole in the worn leather with her little heels.

"She was very beautiful, my mother, wasn't she?" suggested Ann.

Abner Herrick blew a cloud from his pipe and watched carefully the curling smoke.

"In a way, yes," he answered. "Quite beautiful."

"What do you mean, 'In a way'?" demanded Ann with some asperity.

"It was a spiritual beauty, your mother's," Abner explained. "The soul looking out of her eyes. I don't think it possible to imagine a more beautiful disposition than your mother's. Whenever I think of your mother," continued Abner after a pause, "Wordsworth's lines always come into my mind."

He murmured the quotation to himself, but loud enough to be heard by sharp ears. Miss Kavanagh was mollified.

"You were in love with my mother, weren't you?" she questioned him kindly.

"Yes, I suppose I was," mused Abner, still with his gaze upon the curling smoke.

"What do you mean by 'you suppose you were'?" snapped Ann. "Didn't you know?"

The tone recalled him from his dreams.

"I was in love with your mother very much," he corrected himself, turning to her with a smile.

"Then why didn't you marry her?" asked Ann. "Wouldn't she have you?"

"I never asked her," explained Abner.

"Why not?" persisted Ann, returning to asperity.

He thought a moment.

"You wouldn't understand," he told her.

"Yes, I would," retorted Ann.

"No, you wouldn't," he contradicted her quite shortly. They were both beginning to lose patience with one another. "No woman ever could."

"I'm not a woman," explained Ann, "and I'm very smart. You've said so yourself."

"Not so smart as all that," growled Abner. "Added to which, it's time for you to go to bed."

Her anger with him was such that it rendered her absolutely polite. It had that occasional effect upon her. She slid from the arm of his chair and stood beside him, a rigid figure of frozen femininity.

"I think you are quite right, Uncle Herrick. Good night!" But at the door she could not resist a parting shot:

"You might have been my father, and then perhaps she wouldn't have died. I think it was very wicked of you."

After she was gone Abner sat gazing into the fire, and his pipe went out. Eventually the beginnings of a smile stole to the corners of his mouth, but before it could spread any farther he dismissed it with a sigh.

Abner, for the next day or two, feared a renewal of the conversation, but Ann appeared to have forgotten it; and as time went by it faded from Abner's own memory. Until one evening quite a while later.

The morning had brought him his English mail. It had been arriving with some regularity, and Ann had noticed that Abner always opened it before his other correspondence. One letter he read through twice, and Ann, who was pretending to be reading the newspaper, felt that he was looking at her.

"I have been thinking, my dear," said Abner, "that it must be rather lonely for you here, all by yourself."

"It would be," answered Ann, "if I were here all by myself."

"I mean," said Abner, "without any other young person to talk to and--and to play with."

"You forget," said Ann, "that I'm nearly thirteen."

"God bless my soul," said Abner. "How time does fly!"

"Who is she?" asked Ann.

"It isn't a 'she,'" explained Abner. "It's a 'he.' Poor little chap lost his mother two years ago, and now his father's dead. I thought--it occurred to me we might put him up for a time. Look after him a bit. What do you think? It would make the house more lively, wouldn't it?"

"It might," said Ann.

She sat very silent, and Abner, whose conscience was troubling him, watched her a little anxiously. After a time she looked up.

"What's he like?" she asked.

"Precisely what I am wondering myself," confessed Abner. "We shall have to wait and see. But his mother--his mother," repeated Abner, "was the most beautiful woman I have ever known. If he is anything like she was as a girl--" He left the sentence unfinished.

"You have not seen her since--since she was young?" questioned Ann.

Abner shook his head. "She married an Englishman. He took her back with him to London."

"I don't like Englishmen," said Ann.

"They have their points," suggested Abner. "Besides, boys take after their mothers, they say." And Abner rose and gathered his letters together.

Ann remained very thoughtful all that day. In the evening, when Abner for a moment laid down his pen for the purpose of relighting his pipe, Ann came to him, seating herself on the corner of the desk.

"I suppose," she said, "that's why you never married mother?"

Abner's mind at the moment was much occupied with the Panama Canal.

"What mother?" he asked. "Whose mother?"

"My mother," answered Ann. "I suppose men are like that."

"What are you talking about?" said Abner, dismissing altogether the Panama Canal.

"You loved my mother very much," explained Ann with cold deliberation. "She always made you think of Wordsworth's perfect woman."

"Who told you all that?" demanded Abner.

"You did."

"I did?"

"It was the day you took me away from Miss Carew's because she said she couldn't manage me," Ann informed him.

"Good Lord! Why, that must be two years ago," mused Abner.

"Three," Ann corrected him. "All but a few days."

"I wish you'd use your memory for things you're wanted to remember," growled Abner.

"You said you had never asked her to marry you," pursued Ann relentlessly; "you wouldn't tell me why. You said I shouldn't understand."

"My fault," muttered Abner. "I forget you're a child. You ask all sorts of questions that never ought to enter your head, and I'm fool enough to answer you."

One small tear that had made its escape unnoticed by her was stealing down her cheek. He wiped it away and took one of her small paws in both his hands.

"I loved your mother very dearly," he said gravely. "I had loved her from a child. But no woman will ever understand the power that beauty has upon a man. You see we're built that way. It's Nature's lure. Later on, of course, I might have forgotten; but then it was too late. Can you forgive me?"

"But you still love her," reasoned Ann through her tears, "or you wouldn't want him to come here."

"She had such a hard time of it," pleaded Abner. "It made things easier to her, my giving her my word that I would always look after the boy. You'll help me?"

"I'll try," said Ann. But there was not much promise in the tone.

Nor did Matthew Pole himself, when he arrived, do much to help matters. He was so hopelessly English. At least, that was the way Ann put it. He was shy and sensitive. It is a trying combination. It made him appear stupid and conceited. A lonely childhood had rendered him unsociable, unadaptable. A dreamy, imaginative temperament imposed upon him long moods of silence: a liking for long solitary walks. For the first time Ann and Mrs. Travers were in agreement.

"A sulky young dog," commented Mrs. Travers. "If I were your uncle I'd look out for a job for him in San Francisco."

"You see," said Ann in excuse for him, "it's such a foggy country, England. It makes them like that."

"It's a pity they can't get out of it," said Mrs. Travers.

Also, sixteen is an awkward age for a boy. Virtues, still in the chrysalis state, are struggling to escape from their parent vices. Pride, an excellent quality making for courage and patience, still appears in the swathings of arrogance. Sincerity still expresses itself in the language of rudeness. Kindness itself is apt to be mistaken for amazing impertinence and love of interference.

It was kindness--a genuine desire to be useful, that prompted him to point out to Ann her undoubted faults and failings, nerved him to the task of bringing her up in the way she should go. Mrs. Travers had long since washed her hands of the entire business. Uncle Ab, as Matthew also called him, had proved himself a weakling. Providence, so it seemed to Matthew, must have been waiting impatiently for his advent. Ann at first thought it was some new school of humour. When she found he was serious she set herself to cure him. But she never did. He was too conscientious for that. The instincts of the guide, philosopher, and friend to humanity in general were already too strong in him. There were times when Abner almost wished that Matthew Pole senior had lived a little longer.

But he did not lose hope. At the back of his mind was the fancy that these two children of his loves would come together.

Nothing is quite so sentimental as a healthy old bachelor. He pictured them making unity from his confusions; in imagination heard the patter on the stairs of tiny feet. To all intents and purposes he would be a grandfather. Priding himself on his cunning, he kept his dream to himself, as he thought, but underestimated Ann's smartness.

For days together she would follow Matthew with her eyes, watching him from behind her long lashes, listening in silence to everything he said, vainly seeking to find points in him. He was unaware of her generous intentions. He had a vague feeling he was being criticised. He resented it even in those days.

"I do try," said Ann suddenly one evening apropos of nothing at all. "No one will ever know how hard I try not to dislike him."

Abner looked up.

"Sometimes," continued Ann, "I tell myself I have almost succeeded. And then he will go and do something that will bring it all on again."

"What does he do?" asked Abner.

"Oh, I can't tell you," confessed Ann. "If I told you it would sound as if it was my fault. It's all so silly. And then he thinks such a lot of himself. If one only knew why! He can't tell you himself when you ask him."

"You have asked him?" queried Abner.

"I wanted to know," explained Ann. "I thought there might be something in him that I could like."

"Why do you want to like him?" asked Abner, wondering how much she had guessed.

"I know," wailed Ann. "You are hoping that when I am grown up I shall marry him. And I don't want to. It's so ungrateful of me."

"Well, you're not grown up yet," Abner consoled her. "And so long as you are feeling like that about it, I'm not likely to want you to marry him."

"It would make you so happy," sobbed Ann.

"Yes, but we've got to think of the boy, don't forget that," laughed Abner. "Perhaps he might object."

"He would. I know he would," cried Ann with conviction. "He's no better than I am."

"Have you been asking him to?" demanded Abner, springing up from his chair.

"Not to marry me," explained Ann. "But I told him he must be an unnatural little beast not to try to like me when he knew how you loved me."

"Helpful way of putting it," growled Abner. "And what did he say to that?"

"Admitted it," flashed Ann indignantly. "Said he had tried."

Abner succeeded in persuading her that the path of dignity and virtue lay in her dismissing the whole subject from her mind.

He had made a mistake, so he told himself. Age may be attracted by contrast, but youth has no use for its opposite. He would send Matthew away. He could return for week-ends. Continually so close to one another, they saw only one another's specks and flaws; there is no beauty without perspective. Matthew wanted the corners rubbed off him, that was all. Mixing more with men, his priggishness would be laughed out of him. Otherwise he was quite a decent youngster, clean minded, high principled. Clever, too: he often said quite unexpected things. With approaching womanhood, changes were taking place in Ann. Seeing her every day one hardly noticed them; but there were times when, standing before him flushed from a walk or bending over him to kiss him before starting for some friendly dance, Abner would blink his eyes and be puzzled. The thin arms were growing round and firm; the sallow complexion warming into olive; the once patchy, mouse-coloured hair darkening into a rich harmony of brown. The eyes beneath her level brows, that had always been her charm, still reminded Abner of her mother; but there was more light in them, more danger.

"I'll run down to Albany and talk to Jephson about him," decided Abner. "He can come home on Saturdays."

The plot might have succeeded: one never can tell. But a New York blizzard put a stop to it. The cars broke down, and Abner, walking home in thin shoes from a meeting, caught a chill, which, being neglected, proved fatal.

Abner was troubled as he lay upon his bed. The children were sitting very silent by the window. He sent Matthew out on a message, and then beckoned Ann to come to him. He loved the boy, too, but Ann was nearer to him.

"You haven't thought any more," he whispered, "about--"

"No," answered Ann. "You wished me not to."

"You must never think," he said, "to show your love for my memory by doing anything that would not make you happy. If I am anywhere around," he continued with a smile, "it will be your good I shall be watching for, not my own way. You will remember that?"

He had meant to do more for them, but the end had come so much sooner than he had expected. To Ann he left the house (Mrs. Travers had already retired on a small pension) and a sum that, judiciously invested, the friend and attorney thought should be sufficient for her needs, even supposing--The friend and attorney, pausing to dwell upon the oval face with its dark eyes, left the sentence unfinished.

To Matthew he wrote a loving letter, enclosing a thousand dollars. He knew that Matthew, now in a position to earn his living as a journalist, would rather have taken nothing. It was to be looked upon merely as a parting gift. Matthew decided to spend it on travel. It would fit him the better for his journalistic career, so he explained to Ann. But in his heart he had other ambitions. It would enable him to put them to the test.

So there came an evening when Ann stood waving a handkerchief as a great liner cast its moorings. She watched it till its lights grew dim, and then returned to West Twentieth Street. Strangers would take possession of it on the morrow. Ann had her supper in the kitchen in company with the nurse, who had stayed on at her request; and that night, slipping noiselessly from her room, she lay upon the floor, her head resting against the arm of the chair where Abner had been wont to sit and smoke his evening pipe; somehow it seemed to comfort her. And Matthew the while, beneath the stars, was pacing the silent deck of the great liner and planning out the future.

To only one other being had he ever confided his dreams. She lay in the churchyard; and there was nothing left to encourage him but his own heart. But he had no doubts. He would be a great writer. His two hundred pounds would support him till he had gained a foothold. After that he would climb swiftly. He had done right, so he told himself, to turn his back on journalism: the grave of literature. He would see men and cities, writing as he went. Looking back, years later, he was able to congratulate himself on having chosen the right road. He thought it would lead him by easy ascent to fame and fortune. It did better for him than that. It led him through poverty and loneliness, through hope deferred and heartache--through long nights of fear, when pride and confidence fell upon him, leaving him only the courage to endure.

His great poems, his brilliant essays, had been rejected so often that even he himself had lost all love for them. At the suggestion of an editor more kindly than the general run, and urged by need, he had written some short pieces of a less ambitious nature. It was in bitter disappointment he commenced them, regarding them as mere pot-boilers. He would not give them his name. He signed them "Aston Rowant." It was the name of the village in Oxfordshire where he had been born. It occurred to him by chance. It would serve the purpose as well as another. As the work progressed it grew upon him. He made his stories out of incidents and people he had seen; everyday comedies and tragedies that he had lived among, of things that he had felt; and when after their appearance in the magazine a publisher was found willing to make them into a book, hope revived in him.

It was but short-lived. The few reviews that reached him contained nothing but ridicule. So he had no place even as a literary hack!

He was living in Paris at the time in a noisy, evil-smelling street leading out of the Quai Saint-Michel. He thought of Chatterton, and would loaf on the bridges looking down into the river where the drowned lights twinkled.

And then one day there came to him a letter, sent on to him from the publisher of his one book. It was signed "Sylvia," nothing else, and bore no address. Matthew picked up the envelope. The postmark was "London, S.E."

It was a childish letter. A prosperous, well-fed genius, familiar with such, might have smiled at it. To Matthew in his despair it brought healing. She had found the book lying in an empty railway carriage; and undeterred by moral scruples had taken it home with her. It had remained forgotten for a time, until when the end really seemed to have come her hand by chance had fallen on it. She fancied some kind little wandering spirit--the spirit perhaps of someone who had known what it was to be lonely and very sad and just about broken almost--must have manoeuvred the whole thing. It had seemed to her as though some strong and gentle hand had been laid upon her in the darkness. She no longer felt friendless. And so on.

The book, he remembered, contained a reference to the magazine in which the sketches had first appeared. She would be sure to have noticed this. He would send her his answer. He drew his chair up to the flimsy table, and all that night he wrote.

He did not have to think. It came to him, and for the first time since the beginning of things he had no fear of its not being accepted. It was mostly about himself, and the rest was about her, but to most of those who read it two months later it seemed to be about themselves. The editor wrote a charming letter, thanking him for it; but at the time the chief thing that worried him was whether "Sylvia" had seen it. He waited anxiously for a few weeks, and then received her second letter. It was a more womanly letter than the first. She had understood the story, and her words of thanks almost conveyed to him the flush of pleasure with which she had read it. His friendship, she confessed, would be very sweet to her, and still more delightful the thought that he had need of her: that she also had something to give. She would write, as he wished, her real thoughts and feelings.

They would never know one another, and that would give her boldness. They would be comrades, meeting only in dreamland.

In this way commenced the whimsical romance of Sylvia and Aston Rowant; for it was too late now to change the name--it had become a name to conjure with. The stories, poems, and essays followed now in regular succession. The anxiously expected letters reached him in orderly procession. They grew in interest, in helpfulness. They became the letters of a wonderfully sane, broad-minded, thoughtful woman--a woman of insight, of fine judgment. Their praise was rare enough to be precious. Often they would contain just criticism, tempered by sympathy, lightened by humour. Of her troubles, sorrows, fears, she came to write less and less, and even then not until they were past and she could laugh at them. The subtlest flattery she gave him was the suggestion that he had taught her to put these things into their proper place. Intimate, self-revealing as her letters were, it was curious he never shaped from them any satisfactory image of the writer.

A brave, kind, tender woman. A self-forgetting, quickly-forgiving woman. A many-sided woman, responding to joy, to laughter: a merry lady, at times. Yet by no means a perfect woman. There could be flashes of temper, one felt that; quite often occasional unreasonableness; a tongue that could be cutting. A sweet, restful, greatly loving woman, but still a woman: it would be wise to remember that. So he read her from her letters. But herself, the eyes, and hair, and lips of her, the voice and laugh and smile of her, the hands and feet of her, always they eluded him.

He was in Alaska one spring, where he had gone to collect material for his work, when he received the last letter she ever wrote him. They neither of them knew then it would be the last. She was leaving London, so the postscript informed him, sailing on the following Saturday for New York, where for the future she intended to live.

It worried him that postscript. He could not make out for a long time why it worried him. Suddenly, in a waste of endless snows, the explanation flashed across him. Sylvia of the letters was a living woman! She could travel--with a box, he supposed, possibly with two or three, and parcels. Could take tickets, walk up a gangway, stagger about a deck feeling, maybe, a little seasick. All these years he had been living with her in dreamland she had been, if he had only known it, a Miss Somebody-or-other, who must have stood every morning in front of a looking-glass with hairpins in her mouth. He had never thought of her doing these things; it shocked him. He could not help feeling it was indelicate of her--coming to life in this sudden, uncalled-for manner.

He struggled with this new conception of her, and had almost forgiven her, when a further and still more startling suggestion arrived to plague him. If she really lived why should he not see her, speak to her? So long as she had remained in her hidden temple, situate in the vague recesses of London, S.E., her letters had contented him. But now that she had moved, now that she was no longer a voice but a woman! Well, it would be interesting to see what she was like. He imagined the introduction: "Miss Somebody- or-other, allow me to present you to Mr. Matthew Pole." She would have no idea he was Aston Rowant. If she happened to be young, beautiful, in all ways satisfactory, he would announce himself. How astonished, how delighted she would be.

But if not! If she were elderly, plain? The wisest, wittiest of women have been known to have an incipient moustache. A beautiful spirit can, and sometimes does, look out of goggle eyes. Suppose she suffered from indigestion and had a shiny nose! Would her letters ever again have the same charm for him? Absurd that they should not. But would they?

The risk was too great. Giving the matter long and careful consideration, he decided to send her back into dreamland.

But somehow she would not go back into dreamland, would persist in remaining in New York, a living, breathing woman.

Yet even so, how could he find her? He might, say, in a poem convey to her his desire for a meeting. Would she comply? And if she did, what would be his position, supposing the inspection to result unfavourably for her? Could he, in effect, say to her: "Thank you for letting me have a look at you; that is all I wanted. Good-bye"?

She must, she should remain in dreamland. He would forget her postscript; in future throw her envelopes unglanced at into the wastepaper basket. Having by this simple exercise of his will replaced her in London, he himself started for New York--on his way back to Europe, so he told himself. Still, being in New York, there was no reason for not lingering there a while, if merely to renew old memories.

Of course, if he had really wanted to find Sylvia it would have been easy from the date upon the envelope to have discovered the ship "sailing the following Saturday." Passengers were compelled to register their names in full, and to state their intended movements after arrival in America. Sylvia was not a common Christian name. By the help of a five-dollar bill or two--. The idea had not occurred to him before. He dismissed it from his mind and sought a quiet hotel up town.

New York was changed less than he had anticipated. West Twentieth Street in particular was precisely as, leaning out of the cab window, he had looked back upon it ten years ago. Business had more and more taken possession of it, but had not as yet altered its appearance. His conscience smote him as he turned the corner that he had never once written to Ann. He had meant to, it goes without saying, but during those first years of struggle and failure his pride had held him back. She had always thought him a fool; he had felt she did. He would wait till he could write to her of success, of victory. And then when it had slowly, almost imperceptibly, arrived--! He wondered why he never had. Quite a nice little girl, in some respects. If only she had been less conceited, less self-willed. Also rather a pretty girl she had shown signs of becoming. There were times-- He remembered an evening before the lamps were lighted. She had fallen asleep curled up in Abner's easy chair, one small hand resting upon the arm. She had always had quite attractive hands--a little too thin. Something had moved him to steal across softly without waking her. He smiled at the memory.

And then her eyes, beneath the level brows! It was surprising how Ann was coming back to him. Perhaps they would be able to tell him, the people of the house, what had become of her. If they were decent people they would let him wander round a while. He would explain that he had lived there in Abner Herrick's time. The room where they had sometimes been agreeable to one another while Abner, pretending to read, had sat watching them out of the corner of an eye. He would like to sit there for a few moments, by himself.

He forgot that he had rung the bell. A very young servant had answered the door and was staring at him. He would have walked in if the small servant had not planted herself deliberately in his way. It recalled him to himself.

"I beg pardon," said Matthew, "but would you please tell me who lives here?"

The small servant looked him up and down with growing suspicion.

"Miss Kavanagh lives here," she said. "What do you want?"

The surprise was so great it rendered him speechless. In another moment the small servant would have slammed the door.

"Miss Ann Kavanagh?" he inquired, just in time.

"That's her name," admitted the small servant, less suspicious.

"Will you please tell her Mr. Pole--Mr. Matthew Pole," he requested.

"I'll see first if she is in," said the small servant, and shut the door.

It gave Matthew a few minutes to recover himself, for which he was glad. Then the door opened again suddenly.

"You are to come upstairs," said the small servant.

It sounded so like Ann that it quite put him at his ease. He followed the small servant up the stairs.

"Mr. Matthew Pole," she announced severely, and closed the door behind him.

Ann was standing by the window and came to meet him. It was in front of Abner's empty chair that they shook hands.

"So you have come back to the old house," said Matthew.

"Yes," she answered. "It never let well. The last people who had it gave it up at Christmas. It seemed the best thing to do, even from a purely economical point of view.

"What have you been doing all these years?" she asked him.

"Oh, knocking about," he answered. "Earning my living." He was curious to discover what she thought of Matthew, first of all.

"It seems to have agreed with you," she commented, with a glance that took him in generally, including his clothes.

"Yes," he answered. "I have had more luck than perhaps I deserved."

"I am glad of that," said Ann.

He laughed. "So you haven't changed so very much," he said. "Except in appearance.

"Isn't that the most important part of a woman?" suggested Ann.

"Yes," he answered, thinking. "I suppose it is."

She was certainly very beautiful.

"How long are you stopping in New York?" she asked him.

"Oh, not long," he explained.

"Don't leave it for another ten years," she said, "before letting me know what is happening to you. We didn't get on very well together as children; but we mustn't let him think we're not friends. It would hurt him."

She spoke quite seriously, as if she were expecting him any moment to open the door and join them. Involuntarily Matthew glanced round the room. Nothing seemed altered. The worn carpet, the faded curtains, Abner's easy chair, his pipe upon the corner of the mantelpiece beside the vase of spills.

"It is curious," he said, "finding this vein of fancy, of tenderness in you. I always regarded you as such a practical, unsentimental young person."

"Perhaps we neither of us knew each other too well, in those days," she answered.

The small servant entered with the tea.

"What have you been doing with yourself?" he asked, drawing his chair up to the table.

She waited till the small servant had withdrawn.

"Oh, knocking about," she answered. "Earning my living."

"It seems to have agreed with you," he repeated, smiling.

"It's all right now," she answered. "It was a bit of a struggle at first."

"Yes," he agreed. "Life doesn't temper the wind to the human lamb. But was there any need in your case?" he asked. "I thought--"

"Oh, that all went," she explained. "Except the house."

"I'm sorry," said Matthew. "I didn't know."

"Oh, we have been a couple of pigs," she laughed, replying to his thoughts. "I did sometimes think of writing you. I kept the address you gave me. Not for any assistance; I wanted to fight it out for myself. But I was a bit lonely."

"Why didn't you?" he asked.

She hesitated for a moment.

"It's rather soon to make up one's mind," she said, "but you seem to me to have changed. Your voice sounds so different. But as a boy-- well, you were a bit of a prig, weren't you? I imagined you writing me good advice and excellent short sermons. And it wasn't that that I was wanting."

"I think I understand," he said. "I'm glad you got through.

"What is your line?" he asked. "Journalism?"

"No," she answered. "Too self-opinionated."

She opened a bureau that had always been her own and handed him a programme. "Miss Ann Kavanagh, Contralto," was announced on it as one of the chief attractions.

"I didn't know you had a voice," said Matthew.

"You used to complain of it," she reminded him.

"Your speaking voice," he corrected her. "And it wasn't the quality of that I objected to. It was the quantity."

She laughed.

"Yes, we kept ourselves pretty busy bringing one another up," she admitted.

They talked a while longer: of Abner and his kind, quaint ways; of old friends. Ann had lost touch with most of them. She had studied singing in Brussels, and afterwards her master had moved to London and she had followed him. She had only just lately returned to New York.

The small servant entered to clear away the tea things. She said she thought that Ann had rung. Her tone implied that anyhow it was time she had. Matthew rose and Ann held out her hand.

"I shall be at the concert," he said.

"It isn't till next week," Ann reminded him.

"Oh, I'm not in any particular hurry," said Matthew. "Are you generally in of an afternoon?"

"Sometimes," said Ann.

He thought as he sat watching her from his stall that she was one of the most beautiful women he had ever seen. Her voice was not great. She had warned him not to expect too much.

"It will never set the Thames on fire," she had said. "I thought at first that it would. But such as it is I thank God for it."

It was worth that. It was sweet and clear and had a tender quality.

Matthew waited for her at the end. She was feeling well disposed towards all creatures and accepted his suggestion of supper with gracious condescension.

He had called on her once or twice during the preceding days. It was due to her after his long neglect of her, he told himself, and had found improvement in her. But to-night she seemed to take a freakish pleasure in letting him see that there was much of the old Ann still left in her: the frank conceit of her; the amazing self-opinionatedness of her; the waywardness, the wilfulness, the unreasonableness of her; the general uppishness and dictatorialness of her; the contradictoriness and flat impertinence of her; the swift temper and exasperating tongue of her.

It was almost as if she were warning him. "You see, I am not changed, except, as you say, in appearance. I am still Ann with all the old faults and failings that once made life in the same house with me a constant trial to you. Just now my very imperfections appear charms. You have been looking at the sun--at the glory of my face, at the wonder of my arms and hands. Your eyes are blinded. But that will pass. And underneath I am still Ann. Just Ann."

They had quarrelled in the cab on the way home. He forgot what it was about, but Ann had said some quite rude things, and her face not being there in the darkness to excuse her, it had made him very angry. She had laughed again on the steps, and they had shaken hands. But walking home through the still streets Sylvia had plucked at his elbow.

What fools we mortals be--especially men! Here was a noble woman--a restful, understanding, tenderly loving woman; a woman as nearly approaching perfection as it was safe for a woman to go! This marvellous woman was waiting for him with outstretched arms (why should he doubt it?)--and just because Nature had at last succeeded in making a temporary success of Ann's skin and had fashioned a rounded line above her shoulder-blade! It made him quite cross with himself. Ten years ago she had been gawky and sallow-complexioned. Ten years hence she might catch the yellow jaundice and lose it all. Passages in Sylvia's letters returned to him. He remembered that far-off evening in his Paris attic when she had knocked at his door with her great gift of thanks. Recalled how her soft shadow hand had stilled his pain. He spent the next two days with Sylvia. He re-read all her letters, lived again the scenes and moods in which he had replied to them.

Her personality still defied the efforts of his imagination, but he ended by convincing himself that he would know her when he saw her. But counting up the women on Fifth Avenue towards whom he had felt instinctively drawn, and finding that the number had already reached eleven, began to doubt his intuition. On the morning of the third day he met Ann by chance in a bookseller's shop. Her back was towards him. She was glancing through Aston Rowant's latest volume.

"What I," said the cheerful young lady who was attending to her, "like about him is that he understands women so well."

"What I like about him," said Ann, "is that he doesn't pretend to."

"There's something in that," agreed the cheerful young lady. "They say he's here in New York."

Ann looked up.

"So I've been told," said the cheerful young lady.

"I wonder what he's like?" said Ann.

"He wrote for a long time under another name," volunteered the cheerful young lady. "He's quite an elderly man."

It irritated Matthew. He spoke without thinking.

"No, he isn't," he said. "He's quite young."

The ladies turned and looked at him.

"You know him?" queried Ann. She was most astonished, and appeared disbelieving. That irritated him further.

"If you care about it," he said. "I will introduce you to him."

Ann made no answer. He bought a copy of the book for himself, and they went out together. They turned towards the park.

Ann seemed thoughtful. "What is he doing here in New York?" she wondered.

"Looking for a lady named Sylvia," answered Matthew.

He thought the time was come to break it to her that he was a great and famous man. Then perhaps she would be sorry she had said what she had said in the cab. Seeing he had made up his mind that his relationship to her in the future would be that of an affectionate brother, there would be no harm in also letting her know about Sylvia. That also might be good for her.

They walked two blocks before Ann spoke. Matthew, anticipating a pleasurable conversation, felt no desire to hasten matters.

"How intimate are you with him?" she demanded. "I don't think he would have said that to a mere acquaintance."

"I'm not a mere acquaintance," said Matthew. "I've known him a long time."

"You never told me," complained Ann.

"Didn't know it would interest you," replied Matthew.

He waited for further questions, but they did not come. At Thirty-fourth Street he saved her from being run over and killed, and again at Forty-second Street. Just inside the park she stopped abruptly and held out her hand.

"Tell him," she replied, "that if he is really serious about finding Sylvia, I may--I don't say I can--but I may be able to help him."

He did not take her hand, but stood stock still in the middle of the path and stared at her.

"You!" he said. "You know her?"

She was prepared for his surprise. She was also prepared--not with a lie, that implies evil intention. Her only object was to have a talk with the gentleman and see what he was like before deciding on her future proceedings--let us say, with a plausible story.

"We crossed on the same boat," she said. "We found there was a good deal in common between us. She--she told me things." When you came to think it out it was almost the truth.

"What is she like?" demanded Matthew.

"Oh, just--well, not exactly--" It was an awkward question. There came to her relief the reflection that there was really no need for her to answer it.

"What's it got to do with you?" she said.

"I am Aston Rowant," said Matthew.

The Central Park, together with the universe in general, fell away and disappeared. Somewhere out of chaos was sounding a plaintive voice: "What is she like? Can't you tell me? Is she young or old?"

It seemed to have been going on for ages. She made one supreme gigantic effort, causing the Central Park to reappear, dimly, faintly, but it was there again. She was sitting on a seat. Matthew--Aston Rowant, whatever it was--was seated beside her.

"You've seen her? What is she like?"

"I can't tell you."

He was evidently very cross with her. It seemed so unkind of him.

"Why can't you tell me--or, why won't you tell me? Do you mean she's too awful for words?"

"No, certainly not--as a matter of fact--"

"Well, what?"

She felt she must get away or there would be hysterics somewhere. She sprang up and began to walk rapidly towards the gate. He followed her.

"I'll write you," said Ann.

"But why--?"

"I can't," said Ann. "I've got a rehearsal."

A car was passing. She made a dash for it and clambered on. Before he could make up his mind it had gathered speed.

Ann let herself in with her key. She called downstairs to the small servant that she wasn't to be disturbed for anything. She locked the door.

So it was to Matthew that for six years she had been pouring out her inmost thoughts and feelings! It was to Matthew that she had laid bare her tenderest, most sacred dreams! It was at Matthew's feet that for six years she had been sitting, gazing up with respectful admiration, with reverential devotion! She recalled her letters, almost passage for passage, till she had to hold her hands to her face to cool it. Her indignation, one might almost say fury, lasted till tea-time.

In the evening--it was in the evening time that she had always written to him--a more reasonable frame of mind asserted itself. After all, it was hardly his fault. He couldn't have known who she was. He didn't know now. She had wanted to write. Without doubt he had helped her, comforted her loneliness; had given her a charming friendship, a delightful comradeship. Much of his work had been written for her, to her. It was fine work. She had been proud of her share in it. Even allowing there were faults--irritability, shortness of temper, a tendency to bossiness!--underneath it all was a man. The gallant struggle, the difficulties overcome, the long suffering, the high courage--all that she, reading between the lines, had divined of his life's battle! Yes, it was a man she had worshipped. A woman need not be ashamed of that. As Matthew he had seemed to her conceited, priggish. As Aston Rowant she wondered at his modesty, his patience.

And all these years he had been dreaming of her; had followed her to New York; had--

There came a sudden mood so ludicrous, so absurdly unreasonable that Ann herself stopped to laugh at it. Yet it was real, and it hurt. He had come to New York thinking of Sylvia, yearning for Sylvia. He had come to New York with one desire: to find Sylvia. And the first pretty woman that had come across his path had sent Sylvia clean out of his head. There could be no question of that. When Ann Kavanagh stretched out her hand to him in that very room a fortnight ago he had stood before her dazzled, captured. From that moment Sylvia had been tossed aside and forgotten. Ann Kavanagh could have done what she liked with him. She had quarrelled with him that evening of the concert. She had meant to quarrel with him.

And then for the first time he had remembered Sylvia. That was her reward--Sylvia's: it was Sylvia she was thinking of--for six years' devoted friendship; for the help, the inspiration she had given him.

As Sylvia, she suffered from a very genuine and explainable wave of indignant jealousy. As Ann, she admitted he ought not to have done it, but felt there was excuse for him. Between the two she feared her mind would eventually give way. On the morning of the second day she sent Matthew a note asking him to call in the afternoon. Sylvia might be there, or she might not. She would mention it to her.

She dressed herself in a quiet, dark-coloured frock. It seemed uncommittal and suitable to the occasion. It also happened to be the colour that best suited her. She would not have the lamps lighted.

Matthew arrived in a dark serge suit and a blue necktie, so that the general effect was quiet. Ann greeted him with kindliness and put him with his face to what little light there was. She chose for herself the window-seat. Sylvia had not arrived. She might be a little late--that is, if she came at all.

They talked about the weather for a while. Matthew was of opinion they were going to have some rain. Ann, who was in one of her contradictory moods, thought there was frost in the air.

"What did you say to her?" he asked.

"Sylvia? Oh, what you told me," replied Ann. "That you had come to New York to--to look for her."

"What did she say?" he asked.

"Said you'd taken your time about it," retorted Ann.

Matthew looked up with an injured expression.

"It was her own idea that we should never meet," he explained.

"Um!" Ann grunted.

"What do you think yourself she will be like?" she continued. "Have you formed any notion?"

"It is curious," he replied. "I have never been able to conjure up any picture of her until just now."

"Why 'just now'?" demanded Ann.

"I had an idea I should find her here when I opened the door," he answered. "You were standing in the shadow. It seemed to be just what I had expected."

"You would have been satisfied?" she asked.

"Yes," he said.

There was silence for a moment.

"Uncle Ab made a mistake," he continued. "He ought to have sent me away. Let me come home now and then."

"You mean," said Ann, "that if you had seen less of me you might have liked me better?"

"Quite right," he admitted. "We never see the things that are always there."

"A thin, gawky girl with a bad complexion," she suggested. "Would it have been of any use?"

"You must always have been wonderful with those eyes," he answered. "And your hands were beautiful even then."

"I used to cry sometimes when I looked at myself in the glass as a child," she confessed. "My hands were the only thing that consoled me."

"I kissed them once," he told her. "You were asleep, curled up in Uncle Ab's chair."

"I wasn't asleep," said Ann.

She was seated with one foot tucked underneath her. She didn't look a bit grown up.

"You always thought me a fool," he said.

"It used to make me so angry with you," said Ann, "that you seemed to have no go, no ambition in you. I wanted you to wake up--do something. If I had known you were a budding genius--"

"I did hint it to you," said he.

"Oh, of course it was all my fault," said Ann.

He rose. "You think she means to come?" he asked. Ann also had risen.

"Is she so very wonderful?" she asked.

"I may be exaggerating to myself," he answered. "But I am not sure that I could go on with my work without her--not now."

"You forgot her," flashed Ann, "till we happened to quarrel in the cab."

"I often do," he confessed. "Till something goes wrong. Then she comes to me. As she did on that first evening, six years ago. You see, I have been more or less living with her since then," he added with a smile.

"In dreamland," Ann corrected.

"Yes, but in my case," he answered, "the best part of my life is passed in dreamland."

"And when you are not in dreamland?" she demanded. "When you're just irritable, short-tempered, cranky Matthew Pole. What's she going to do about you then?"

"She'll put up with me," said Matthew.

"No she won't," said Ann. "She'll snap your head off. Most of the 'putting up with' you'll have to do."

He tried to get between her and the window, but she kept her face close to the pane.

"You make me tired with Sylvia," she said. "It's about time you did know what she's like. She's just the commonplace, short-tempered, disagreeable-if-she-doesn't-get-her-own-way, unreasonable woman. Only more so."

He drew her away from the window by brute force.

"So you're Sylvia," he said.

"I thought that would get it into your head," said Ann.

It was not at all the way she had meant to break it to him. She had meant the conversation to be chiefly about Sylvia. She had a high opinion of Sylvia, a much higher opinion than she had of Ann Kavanagh. If he proved to be worthy of her--of Sylvia, that is, then, with the whimsical smile that she felt belonged to Sylvia, she would remark quite simply, "Well, what have you got to say to her?"

What had happened to interfere with the programme was Ann Kavanagh. It seemed that Ann Kavanagh had disliked Matthew Pole less than she had thought she did. It was after he had sailed away that little Ann Kavanagh had discovered this. If only he had shown a little more interest in, a little more appreciation of, Ann Kavanagh! He could be kind and thoughtful in a patronising sort of way. Even that would not have mattered if there had been any justification for his airs of superiority.

Ann Kavanagh, who ought to have taken a back seat on this occasion, had persisted in coming to the front. It was so like her.

"Well," she said, "what are you going to say to her?" She did get it in, after all.

"I was going," said Matthew, "to talk to her about Art and Literature, touching, maybe, upon a few other subjects. Also, I might have suggested our seeing each other again once or twice, just to get better acquainted. And then I was going away."

"Why going away?" asked Ann.

"To see if I could forget you."

She turned to him. The fading light was full upon her face.

"I don't believe you could--again," she said.

"No," he agreed. "I'm afraid I couldn't."

"You're sure there's nobody else," said Ann, "that you're in love with. Only us two?"

"Only you two," he said.

She was standing with her hand on old Abner's empty chair. "You've got to choose," she said. She was trembling. Her voice sounded just a little hard.

He came and stood beside her. "I want Ann," he said.

She held out her hand to him.

"I'm so glad you said Ann," she laughed.

THE FAWN GLOVES

Always he remembered her as he saw her first: the little spiritual face, the little brown shoes pointed downwards, their toes just touching the ground; the little fawn gloves folded upon her lap. He was not conscious of having noticed her with any particular attention: a plainly dressed, childish-looking figure alone on a seat between him and the setting sun. Even had he felt curious his shyness would have prevented his deliberately running the risk of meeting her eyes. Yet immediately he had passed her he saw her again, quite clearly: the pale oval face, the brown shoes, and, between them, the little fawn gloves folded one over the other. All down the Broad Walk and across Primrose Hill, he saw her silhouetted against the sinking sun. At least that much of her: the wistful face and the trim brown shoes and the little folded hands; until the sun went down behind the high chimneys of the brewery beyond Swiss Cottage, and then she faded.

She was there again the next evening, precisely in the same place. Usually he walked home by the Hampstead Road. Only occasionally, when the beauty of the evening tempted him, would he take the longer way by Regent Street and through the Park. But so often it made him feel sad, the quiet Park, forcing upon him the sense of his own loneliness.

He would walk down merely as far as the Great Vase, so he arranged with himself. If she were not there--it was not likely that she would be--he would turn back into Albany Street. The newsvendors' shops with their display of the cheaper illustrated papers, the second-hand furniture dealers with their faded engravings and old prints, would give him something to look at, to take away his thoughts from himself. But seeing her in the distance, almost the moment he had entered the gate, it came to him how disappointed he would have been had the seat in front of the red tulip bed been vacant. A little away from her he paused, turning to look at the flowers. He thought that, waiting his opportunity, he might be able to steal a glance at her undetected. Once for a moment he did so, but venturing a second time their eyes met, or he fancied they did, and blushing furiously he hurried past. But again she came with him, or, rather, preceded him. On each empty seat between him and the sinking sun he saw her quite plainly: the pale oval face and the brown shoes, and, between them, the fawn gloves folded one upon the other.

Only this evening, about the small, sensitive mouth there seemed to be hovering just the faintest suggestion of a timid smile. And this time she lingered with him past Queen's Crescent and the Malden Road, till he turned into Carlton Street. It was dark in the passage, and he had to grope his way up the stairs, but with his hand on the door of the bed-sitting room on the third floor he felt less afraid of the solitude that would rise to meet him.

All day long in the dingy back office in Abingdon Street, Westminster, where from ten to six each day he sat copying briefs and petitions, he thought over what he would say to her; tactful beginnings by means of which he would slide into conversation with her. Up Portland Place he would rehearse them to himself. But at Cambridge Gate, when the little fawn gloves came in view, the words would run away, to join him again maybe at the gate into the Chester Road, leaving him meanwhile to pass her with stiff, hurried steps and eyes fixed straight in front of him. And so it might have continued, but that one evening she was no longer at her usual seat. A crowd of noisy children swarmed over it, and suddenly it seemed to him as if the trees and flowers had all turned drab. A terror gnawed at his heart, and he hurried on, more for the need of movement than with any definite object. And just beyond a bed of geraniums that had hidden his view she was seated on a chair, and stopping with a jerk absolutely in front of her, he said, quite angrily:

"Oh! there you are!"

Which was not a bit the speech with which he had intended to introduce himself, but served his purpose just as well--perhaps better.

She did not resent his words or the tone.

"It was the children," she explained. "They wanted to play; so I thought I would come on a little farther."

Upon which, as a matter of course, he took the chair beside her, and it did not occur to either of them that they had not known one another since the beginning, when between St. John's Wood and Albany Street God planted a garden.

Each evening they would linger there, listening to the pleading passion of the blackbird's note, the thrush's call to joy and hope. He loved her gentle ways. From the bold challenges, the sly glances of invitation flashed upon him in the street or from some neighbouring table in the cheap luncheon room he had always shrunk confused and awkward. Her shyness gave him confidence. It was she who was half afraid, whose eyes would fall beneath his gaze, who would tremble at his touch, giving him the delights of manly dominion, of tender authority. It was he who insisted on the aristocratic seclusion afforded by the private chair; who, with the careless indifference of a man to whom pennies were unimportant, would pay for them both. Once on his way through Piccadilly Circus he had paused by the fountain to glance at a great basket of lilies of the valley, struck suddenly by the thought how strangely their little pale petals seemed suggestive of her.

"'Ere y' are, honey. Her favourite flower!" cried the girl, with a grin, holding a bunch towards him.

"How much?" he had asked, vainly trying to keep the blood from rushing to his face.

The girl paused a moment, a coarse, kindly creature.

"Sixpence," she demanded; and he bought them. She had meant to ask him a shilling, and knew he would have paid it. "Same as silly fool!" she called herself as she pocketed the money.

He gave them to her with a fine lordly air, and watched her while she pinned them to her blouse, and a squirrel halting in the middle of the walk watched her also with his head on one side, wondering what was the good of them that she should store them with so much care. She did not thank him in words, but there were tears in her eyes when she turned her face to his, and one of the little fawn gloves stole out and sought his hand. He took it in both his, and would have held it, but she withdrew it almost hurriedly.

They appealed to him, her gloves, in spite of their being old and much mended; and he was glad they were of kid. Had they been of cotton, such as girls of her class usually wore, the thought of pressing his lips to them would have put his teeth on edge. He loved the little brown shoes, that must have been expensive when new, for they still kept their shape. And the fringe of dainty petticoat, always so spotless and with never a tear, and the neat, plain stockings that showed below the closely fitting frock. So often he had noticed girls, showily, extravagantly dressed, but with red bare hands and sloppy shoes. Handsome girls, some of them, attractive enough if you were not of a finicking nature, to whom the little accessories are almost of more importance than the whole.

He loved her voice, so different from the strident tones that every now and then, as some couple, laughing and talking, passed them, would fall upon him almost like a blow; her quick, graceful movements that always brought back to his memory the vision of hill and stream. In her little brown shoes and gloves and the frock which was also of a shade of brown though darker, she was strangely suggestive to him of a fawn. The gentle look, the swift, soft movements that have taken place before they are seen; the haunting suggestion of fear never quite conquered, as if the little nervous limbs were always ready for sudden flight. He called her that one day. Neither of them had ever thought to ask one another's names; it did not seem to matter.

"My little brown fawn," he had whispered, "I am always expecting you to suddenly dig your little heels into the ground and spring away"; and she had laughed and drawn a little closer to him. And even that was just the movement of a fawn. He had known them, creeping near to them upon the hill-sides when he was a child.

There was much in common between them, so they found. Though he could claim a few distant relatives scattered about the North, they were both, for all practical purposes, alone in the world. To her, also, home meant a bed-sitting room--"over there," as she indicated with a wave of the little fawn glove embracing the north-west district generally; and he did not press her for any more precise address.

It was easy enough for him to picture it: the mean, close-smelling street somewhere in the neighbourhood of Lisson Grove, or farther on towards the Harrow Road. Always he preferred to say good-bye to her at some point in the Outer Circle, with its peaceful vista of fine trees and stately houses, watching her little fawn-like figure fading away into the twilight.

No friend or relative had she ever known, except the pale, girlish-looking mother who had died soon after they had come to London. The elderly landlady had let her stay on, helping in the work of the house; and when even this last refuge had failed her, well-meaning folk had interested themselves and secured her employment. It was light and fairly well paid, but there were objections to it, so he gathered, more from her halting silences than from what she said. She had tried for a time to find something else, but it was so difficult without help or resources. There was nothing really to complain about it, except-- And then she paused with a sudden clasp of the gloved hands, and, seeing the troubled look in her eyes, he had changed the conversation.

It did not matter; he would take her away from it. It was very sweet to him, the thought of putting a protective arm about this little fragile creature whose weakness gave him strength. He was not always going to be a clerk in an office. He was going to write poetry, books, plays. Already he had earned a little. He told her of his hopes, and her great faith in him gave him new courage. One evening, finding a seat where few people ever passed, he read to her. And she had understood. All unconsciously she laughed in the right places, and when his own voice trembled, and he found it difficult to continue for the lump in his own throat, glancing at her he saw the tears were in her eyes. It was the first time he had tasted sympathy.

And so spring grew to summer. And then one evening a great thing happened. He could not make out at first what it was about her: some little added fragrance that made itself oddly felt, while she herself seemed to be conscious of increased dignity. It was not until he took her hand to say good-bye that he discovered it. There was something different about the feel of her, and, looking down at the little hand that lay in his, he found the reason. She had on a pair of new gloves. They were still of the same fawn colour, but so smooth and soft and cool. They fitted closely without a wrinkle, displaying the slightness and the gracefulness of the hands beneath. The twilight had almost faded, and, save for the broad back of a disappearing policeman, they had the Outer Circle to themselves; and, the sudden impulse coming to him, he dropped on one knee, as they do in plays and story books and sometimes elsewhere, and pressed the little fawn gloves to his lips in a long, passionate kiss. The sound of approaching footsteps made him rise hurriedly. She did not move, but her whole body was trembling, and in her eyes was a look that was almost of fear. The approaching footsteps came nearer, but a bend of the road still screened them. Swiftly and in silence she put her arms about his neck and kissed him. It was a strange, cold kiss, but almost fierce, and then without a word she turned and walked away; and he watched her to the corner of Hanover Gate, but she did not look back.

It was almost as if it had raised a barrier between them, that kiss. The next evening she came to meet him with a smile as usual, but in her eyes was still that odd suggestion of lurking fear; and when, seated beside her, he put his hand on hers it seemed to him she shrank away from him. It was an unconscious movement. It brought back to him that haunting memory of hill and stream when some soft- eyed fawn, strayed from her fellows, would let him approach quite close to her, and then, when he put out his hand to caress her, would start away with a swift, quivering movement.

"Do you always wear gloves?" he asked her one evening a little later.

"Yes," she answered, speaking low; "when I'm out of doors."

"But this is not out of doors," he had pleaded. "We have come into the garden. Won't you take them off?"

She had looked at him from under bent brows, as if trying to read him. She did not answer him then. But on the way out, on the last seat close to the gate, she had sat down, motioning him to sit beside her. Quietly she unbuttoned the fawn gloves; drew each one off and laid them aside. And then, for the first time, he saw her hands.

Had he looked at her, seen the faint hope die out, the mute agony in the quiet eyes watching him, he would have tried to hide the disgust, the physical repulsion that showed itself so plainly in his face, in the involuntary movement with which he drew away from her. They were small and shapely with rounded curves, but raw and seared as with hot irons, with a growth of red, angry-coloured warts, and the nails all worn away.

"I ought to have shown them to you before," she said simply as she drew the gloves on again. "It was silly of me. I ought to have known."

He tried to comfort her, but his phrases came meaningless and halting.

It was the work, she explained as they walked on. It made your hands like that after a time. If only she could have got out of it earlier! But now! It was no good worrying about it now.

They parted near to the Hanover Gate, but to-night he did not stand watching her as he had always done till she waved a last good-bye to him just before disappearing; so whether she turned or not he never knew.

He did not go to meet her the next evening. A dozen times his footsteps led him unconsciously almost to the gate. Then he would hurry away again, pace the mean streets, jostling stupidly against the passers-by. The pale, sweet face, the little nymph-like figure, the little brown shoes kept calling to him. If only there would pass away the horror of those hands! All the artist in him shuddered at the memory of them. Always he had imagined them under the neat, smooth gloves as fitting in with all the rest of her, dreaming of the time when he would hold them in his own, caressing them, kissing them. Would it be possible to forget them, to reconcile oneself to them? He must think--must get away from these crowded streets where faces seemed to grin at him. He remembered that Parliament had just risen, that work was slack in the office. He would ask that he might take his holiday now--the next day. And they had agreed.

He packed a few things into a knapsack. From the voices of the hills and streams he would find counsel.

He took no count of his wanderings. One evening at a lonely inn he met a young doctor. The innkeeper's wife was expecting to be taken with child that night, and the doctor was waiting downstairs till summoned. While they were talking, the idea came to him. Why had he not thought of it? Overcoming his shyness, he put his questions. What work would it be that would cause such injuries? He described them, seeing them before him in the shadows of the dimly lighted room, those poor, pitiful little hands.

Oh! a dozen things might account for it--the doctor's voice sounded callous--the handling of flax, even of linen under certain conditions. Chemicals entered so much nowadays into all sorts of processes and preparations. All this new photography, cheap colour printing, dyeing and cleaning, metal work. Might all be avoided by providing rubber gloves. It ought to be made compulsory. The doctor seemed inclined to hold forth. He interrupted him.

But could it be cured? Was there any hope?

Cured? Hope? Of course it could be cured. It was only local--the effect being confined to the hands proved that. A poisoned condition of the skin aggravated by general poverty of blood. Take her away from it; let her have plenty of fresh air and careful diet, using some such simple ointment or another as any local man, seeing them, would prescribe; and in three or four months they would recover.

He could hardly stay to thank the young doctor. He wanted to get away by himself, to shout, to wave his arms, to leap. Had it been possible he would have returned that very night. He cursed himself for the fancifulness that had prevented his inquiring her address. He could have sent a telegram. Rising at dawn, for he had not attempted to sleep, he walked the ten miles to the nearest railway station, and waited for the train. All day long it seemed to creep with him through the endless country. But London came at last.

It was still the afternoon, but he did not care to go to his room. Leaving his knapsack at the station, he made his way to Westminster. He wanted all things to be unchanged, so that between this evening and their parting it might seem as if there had merely passed an ugly dream; and timing himself, he reached the park just at their usual hour.

He waited till the gates were closed, but she did not come. All day long at the back of his mind had been that fear, but he had driven it away. She was ill, just a headache, or merely tired.

And the next evening he told himself the same. He dared not whisper to himself anything else. And each succeeding evening again. He never remembered how many. For a time he would sit watching the path by which she had always come; and when the hour was long past he would rise and walk towards the gate, look east and west, and then return. One evening he stopped one of the park-keepers and questioned him. Yes, the man remembered her quite well: the young lady with the fawn gloves. She had come once or twice--maybe oftener, the park-keeper could not be sure--and had waited. No, there had been nothing to show that she was in any way upset. She had just sat there for a time, now and then walking a little way and then coming back again, until the closing hour, and then she had gone. He left his address with the park-keeper. The man promised to let him know if he ever saw her there again.

Sometimes, instead of the park, he would haunt the mean streets about Lisson Grove and far beyond the other side of the Edgware Road, pacing them till night fell. But he never found her.

He wondered, beating against the bars of his poverty, if money would have helped him. But the grim, endless city, hiding its million secrets, seemed to mock the thought. A few pounds he had scraped together he spent in advertisements; but he expected no response, and none came. It was not likely she would see them.

And so after a time the park, and even the streets round about it, became hateful to him; and he moved away to another part of London, hoping to forget. But he never quite succeeded. Always it would come back to him when he was not thinking: the broad, quiet walk with its prim trees and gay beds of flowers. And always he would see her seated there, framed by the fading light. At least, that much of her: the little spiritual face, and the brown shoes pointing downwards, and between them the little fawn gloves folded upon her lap.

THE END

SKETCHES IN LAVENDER, BLUE AND GREEN

SKETCHES IN LAVENDER, BLUE AND GREEN

La-ven-der's blue, did-dle, did-dle!
La-ven-der's green;
When I am king, did-dle, did-dle!
You shall be queen.
Call up your men, did-dle, did-dle!
Set them to work;
Some to the plough, did-dle, did-dle!
Some to the cart.
Some to make hay, did-dle, did-dle!
Some to cut corn;
While you and I, did-dle, did-dle!
Keep ourselves warm.

REGINALD BLAKE, FINANCIER AND CAD

The advantage of literature over life is that its characters are clearly defined, and act consistently. Nature, always inartistic, takes pleasure in creating the impossible. Reginald Blake was as typical a specimen of the well-bred cad as one could hope to find between Piccadilly Circus and Hyde Park Corner. Vicious without passion, and possessing brain without mind, existence presented to him no difficulties, while his pleasures brought him no pains. His morality was bounded by the doctor on the one side, and the magistrate on the other. Careful never to outrage the decrees of either, he was at forty-five still healthy, though stout; and had achieved the not too easy task of amassing a fortune while avoiding all risk of Holloway. He and his wife, Edith (nee Eppington), were as ill-matched a couple as could be conceived by any dramatist seeking material for a problem play. As they stood before the altar on their wedding morn, they might have been taken as symbolising satyr and saint. More than twenty years his junior, beautiful with the beauty of a Raphael's Madonna, his every touch of her seemed a sacrilege. Yet once in his life Mr. Blake played the part of a great gentleman; Mrs. Blake, on the same occasion, contenting herself with a singularly mean role--mean even for a woman in love.

The affair, of course, had been a marriage of convenience. Blake, to do him justice, had made no pretence to anything beyond admiration and regard. Few things grow monotonous sooner than irregularity. He would tickle his jaded palate with respectability, and try for a change the companionship of a good woman. The girl's face drew him, as the moonlight holds a man who, bored by the noise, turns from a heated room to press his forehead to the window-pane. Accustomed to bid for what he wanted, he offered his price. The Eppington family was poor and numerous. The girl, bred up to the false notions of duty inculcated by a narrow conventionality, and, feminine like, half in love with martyrdom for its own sake, let her father bargain for a higher price, and then sold herself.

To a drama of this description, a lover is necessary, if the complications are to be of interest to the outside world. Harry Sennett, a pleasant-looking enough young fellow, in spite of his receding chin, was possessed, perhaps, of more good intention than sense. Under the influence of Edith's stronger character he was soon persuaded to acquiesce meekly in the proposed arrangement. Both succeeded in convincing themselves that they were acting nobly. The tone of the farewell interview, arranged for the eve of the wedding, would have been fit and proper to the occasion had Edith been a modern Joan of Arc about to sacrifice her own happiness on the altar of a great cause; as the girl was merely selling herself into ease and luxury, for no higher motive than the desire to enable a certain number of more or less worthy relatives to continue living beyond their legitimate means, the sentiment was perhaps exaggerated. Many tears were shed, and many everlasting good-byes spoken, though, seeing that Edith's new home would be only a few streets off, and that of necessity their social set would continue to be the same, more experienced persons might have counselled hope. Three months after the marriage they found themselves side by side at the same dinner-table; and after a little melodramatic fencing with what they were pleased to regard as fate, they accommodated themselves to the customary positions.

Blake was quite aware that Sennett had been Edith's lover. So had half a dozen other men, some younger, some older than himself. He felt no more embarrassment at meeting them than, standing on the pavement outside the Stock Exchange, he would have experienced greeting his brother jobbers after a settling day that had transferred a fortune from their hands into his. Sennett, in particular, he liked and encouraged. Our whole social system, always a mystery to the philosopher, owes its existence to the fact that few men and women possess sufficient intelligence to be interesting to themselves. Blake liked company, but not much company liked Blake. Young Sennett, however, could always be relied upon to break the tediousness of the domestic dialogue. A common love of sport drew the two men together. Most of us improve upon closer knowledge, and so they came to find good in one another.

"That is the man you ought to have married," said Blake one night to his wife, half laughingly, half seriously, as they sat alone, listening to Sennett's departing footsteps echoing upon the deserted pavement. "He's a good fellow--not a mere money-grubbing machine like me."

And a week later Sennett, sitting alone with Edith, suddenly broke out with:

"He's a better man than I am, with all my high-falutin' talk, and, upon my soul, he loves you. Shall I go abroad?"

"If you like," was the answer.

"What would you do?"

"Kill myself," replied the other, with a laugh, "or run away with the first man that asked me."

So Sennett stayed on.

Blake himself had made the path easy to them. There was little need for either fear or caution. Indeed, their safest course lay in recklessness, and they took it. To Sennett the house was always open. It was Blake himself who, when unable to accompany his wife, would suggest Sennett as a substitute. Club friends shrugged their shoulders. Was the man completely under his wife's thumb; or, tired of her, was he playing some devil's game of his own? To most of his acquaintances the latter explanation seemed the more plausible.

The gossip, in due course, reached the parental home. Mrs. Eppington shook the vials of her wrath over the head of her son-in-law. The father, always a cautious man, felt inclined to blame his child for her want of prudence.

"She'll ruin everything," he said. "Why the devil can't she be careful?"

"I believe the man is deliberately plotting to get rid of her," said Mrs. Eppington. "I shall tell him plainly what I think."

"You're a fool, Hannah," replied her husband, allowing himself the licence of the domestic hearth. "If you are right, you will only precipitate matters; if you are wrong, you will tell him what there is no need for him to know. Leave the matter to me. I can sound him without giving anything away, and meanwhile you talk to Edith."

So matters were arranged, but the interview between mother and daughter hardly improved the position. Mrs. Eppington was conventionally moral; Edith had been thinking for herself, and thinking in a bad atmosphere. Mrs. Eppington, grew angry at the girl's callousness.

"Have you no sense of shame?" she cried.

"I had once," was Edith's reply, "before I came to live here. Do you know what this house is for me, with its gilded mirrors, its couches, its soft carpets? Do you know what I am, and have been for two years?"

The elder woman rose, with a frightened pleading look upon her face, and the other stopped and turned away towards the window.

"We all thought it for the best," continued Mrs. Eppington meekly.

The girl spoke wearily without looking round.

"Oh! every silly thing that was ever done, was done for the best. *I* thought it would be for the best, myself. Everything would be so simple if only we were not alive. Don't let's talk any more. All you can say is quite right."

The silence continued for a while, the Dresden-china clock on the mantelpiece ticking louder and louder as if to say, "I, Time, am here. Do not make your plans forgetting me, little mortals; I change your thoughts and wills. You are but my puppets."

"Then what do you intend to do?" demanded Mrs. Eppington at length.

"Intend! Oh, the right thing of course. We all intend that. I shall send Harry away with a few well-chosen words of farewell, learn to love my husband and settle down to a life of quiet domestic bliss. Oh, it's easy enough to intend!"

The girl's face wrinkled with a laugh that aged her. In that moment it was a hard, evil face, and with a pang the elder woman thought of that other face, so like, yet so unlike--the sweet pure face of a girl that had given to a sordid home its one touch of nobility. As under the lightning's flash we see the whole arc of the horizon, so Mrs. Eppington looked and saw her child's life. The gilded, over-furnished room vanished. She and a big-eyed, fair-haired child, the only one of her children she had ever understood, were playing wonderful games in the twilight among the shadows of a tiny attic. Now she was the wolf, devouring Edith, who was Red Riding Hood, with kisses. Now Cinderella's prince, now both her wicked sisters. But in the favourite game of all, Mrs. Eppington was a beautiful princess, bewitched by a wicked dragon, so that she seemed to be an old, worn woman. But curly-headed Edith fought the dragon, represented by the three-legged rocking- horse, and slew him with much shouting and the toasting-fork. Then Mrs. Eppington became again a beautiful princess, and went away with Edith back to her own people.

In this twilight hour the misbehaviour of the "General," the importunity of the family butcher, and the airs assumed by cousin Jane, who kept two servants, were forgotten.

The games ended. The little curly head would be laid against her breast "for five minutes' love," while the restless little brain framed the endless question that children are for ever asking in all its thousand forms, "What is life, mother? I am very little, and I think, and think, until I grow frightened. Oh, mother, tell me, what is life?"

Had she dealt with these questions wisely? Might it not have been better to have treated them more seriously? Could life after all be ruled by maxims learned from copy-books? She had answered as she had been answered in her own far-back days of questioning. Might it not have been better had she thought for herself?

Suddenly Edith was kneeling on the floor beside her.

"I will try to be good, mother."

It was the old baby cry, the cry of us all, children that we are, till mother Nature kisses us and bids us go to sleep.

Their arms were round each other now, and so they sat, mother and child once more. And the twilight of the old attic, creeping westward from the east, found them again.

The masculine duet had more result, but was not conducted with the finesse that Mr. Eppington, who prided himself on his diplomacy, had intended. Indeed, so evidently ill at ease was that gentleman, when the moment came for talk, and so palpably were his pointless remarks mere efforts to delay an unpleasant subject, that Blake, always direct bluntly though not ill-naturedly asked him, "How much?"

Mr. Eppington was disconcerted.

"It's not that--at least that's not what I have come about," he answered confusedly.

"What have you come about?"

Inwardly Mr. Eppington cursed himself for a fool, for the which he was perhaps not altogether without excuse. He had meant to act the part of a clever counsel, acquiring information while giving none; by a blunder, he found himself in the witness-box.

"Oh, nothing, nothing," was the feeble response, "merely looked in to see how Edith was."

"Much the same as at dinner last night, when you were here," answered Blake. "Come, out with it."

It seemed the best course now, and Mr. Eppington took the plunge.

"Don't you think," he said, unconsciously glancing round the room to be sure they were alone, "that young Sennett is a little too much about the house?"

Blake stared at him.

"Of course, we know it is all right--as nice a young fellow as ever lived--and Edith--and all that. Of course, it's absurd, but--"

"But what?"

"Well, people will talk."

"What do they say?"

The other shrugged his shoulders.

Blake rose. He had an ugly look when angry, and his language was apt to be coarse.

"Tell them to mind their own business, and leave me and my wife alone." That was the sense of what he said; he expressed himself at greater length, and in stronger language.

"But, my dear Blake," urged Mr. Eppington, "for your own sake, is it wise? There was a sort of boy and girl attachment between them--nothing of any moment, but all that gives colour to gossip. Forgive me, but I am her father; I do not like to hear my child talked about."

"Then don't open your ears to the chatter of a pack of fools," replied his son-in-law roughly. But the next instant a softer expression passed over his face, and he laid his hand on the older man's arm.

"Perhaps there are many more, but there's one good woman in the world," he said, "and that's your daughter. Come and tell me that the Bank of England is getting shaky on its legs, and I'll listen to you."

But the stronger the faith, the deeper strike the roots of suspicion. Blake said no further word on the subject, and Sennett was as welcome as before. But Edith, looking up suddenly, would sometimes find her husband's eyes fixed on her with a troubled look as of some dumb creature trying to understand; and often he would slip out of the house of an evening by himself, returning home hours afterwards, tired and mud-stained.

He made attempts to show his affection. This was the most fatal thing he could have done. Ill-temper, ill-treatment even, she might have borne. His clumsy caresses, his foolish, halting words of tenderness became a horror to her. She wondered whether to laugh or to strike at his upturned face. His tactless devotion filled her life as with some sickly perfume, stifling her. If only she could be by herself for a little while to think! But he was with her night and day. There were times when, as he would cross the room towards her, he grew monstrous until he towered above her, a formless thing such as children dream of. And she would sit with her lips tight pressed, clutching the chair lest she should start up screaming.

Her only thought was to escape from him. One day she hastily packed a few necessaries in a small hand-bag and crept unperceived from the house. She drove to Charing Cross, but the Continental Express did not leave for an hour, and she had time to think.

Of what use was it? Her slender stock of money would soon be gone; how could she live? He would find her and follow her. It was all so hopeless!

Suddenly a fierce desire of life seized hold of her, the angry answer of her young blood to despair. Why should she die, never having known what it was to live? Why should she prostrate herself before this juggernaut of other people's respectability? Joy called to her; only her own cowardice stayed her from stretching forth her hand and gathering it. She returned home a different woman, for hope had come to her.

A week later the butler entered the dining room, and handed Blake a letter addressed to him in his wife's handwriting. He took it without a word, as though he had been expecting it. It simply told him that she had left him for ever.

The world is small, and money commands many services. Sennett had gone out for a stroll; Edith was left in the tiny salon of their appartement at Fecamp. It was the third day of their arrival in the town. The door was opened and closed, and Blake stood before her.

She rose frightened, but by a motion he reassured her. There was a quiet dignity about the man that was strange to her.

"Why have you followed me?" she asked.

"I want you to return home."

"Home!" she cried. "You must be mad. Do you not know--"

He interrupted her vehemently. "I know nothing. I wish to know nothing. Go back to London at once. I have made everything right;

no one suspects. I shall not be there; you will never see me again, and you will have an opportunity of undoing your mistake-- our mistake."

She listened. Hers was not a great nature, and the desire to obtain happiness without paying the price was strong upon her. As for his good name, what could that matter? he urged. People would only say that he had gone back to the evil from which he had emerged, and few would be surprised. His life would go on much as it had done, and she would only be pitied.

She quite understood his plan; it seemed mean of her to accept his proposal, and she argued feebly against it. But he overcame all her objections. For his own sake, he told her, he would prefer the scandal to be connected with his name rather than with that of his wife. As he unfolded his scheme, she began to feel that in acquiescing she was conferring a favour. It was not the first deception he had arranged for the public, and he appeared to be half in love with his own cleverness. She even found herself laughing at his mimicry of what this acquaintance and that would say. Her spirits rose; the play that might have been a painful drama seemed turning out an amusing farce.

The thing settled, he rose to go, and held out his hand. As she looked up into his face, something about the line of his lips smote upon her.

"You will be well rid of me," she said. "I have brought you nothing but trouble."

"Oh, trouble," he answered. "If that were all! A man can bear trouble."

"What else?" she asked.

His eyes travelled aimlessly about the room. "They taught me a lot of things when I was a boy," he said, "my mother and others--they meant well--which as I grew older I discovered to be lies; and so I came to think that nothing good was true, and that everything and everybody was evil. And then--"

His wandering eyes came round to her and he broke off abruptly. "Good-bye," he said, and the next moment he was gone.

She sat wondering for a while what he had meant. Then Sennett returned, and the words went out of her head.

A good deal of sympathy was felt for Mrs. Blake. The man had a charming wife; he might have kept straight; but as his friends added, "Blake always was a cad."

AN ITEM OF FASHIONABLE INTELLIGENCE

Speaking personally, I do not like the Countess of --. She is not the type of woman I could love. I hesitate the less giving expression to this sentiment by reason of the conviction that the Countess of -- would not be unduly depressed even were the fact to reach her ears. I cannot conceive the Countess of --'s being troubled by the opinion concerning her of any being, human or divine, other than the Countess of --.

But to be honest, I must admit that for the Earl of -- she makes an ideal wife. She rules him as she rules all others, relations and retainers, from the curate to the dowager, but the rod, though firmly held, is wielded with justice and kindly intent. Nor is it possible to imagine the Earl of --'s living as contentedly as he does with any partner of a less dominating turn of mind. He is one of those weak-headed, strong-limbed, good-natured, childish men, born to be guided in all matters, from the tying of a neck-cloth to the choice of a political party, by their women folk. Such men are in clover when their proprietor happens to be a good and sensible woman, but are to be pitied when they get into the hands of the selfish or the foolish. As very young men, they too often fall victims to bad-tempered chorus girls or to middle-aged matrons of the class from which Pope judged all womankind. They make capital husbands when well managed; treated badly, they say little, but set to work, after the manner of a dissatisfied cat, to find a kinder mistress, generally succeeding. The Earl of -- adored his wife, deeming himself the most fortunate of husbands, and better testimonial than such no wife should hope for. Till the day she snatched him away from all other competitors, and claimed him for her own, he had obeyed his mother with a dutifulness bordering on folly. Were the countess to die to-morrow, he would be unable to tell you his mind on any single subject until his eldest daughter and his still unmarried sister, ladies both of strong character, attracted towards one another by a mutual antagonism, had settled between themselves which was to be mistress of him and of his house.

However, there is little fear (bar accidents) but that my friend the countess will continue to direct the hereditary vote of the Earl of -- towards the goal of common sense and public good, guide his social policy with judgment and kindness, and manage his estates with prudence and economy for many years to come. She is a hearty, vigorous lady, of generous proportions, with the blood of sturdy forebears in her veins, and one who takes the same excellent good care of herself that she bestows on all others dependent upon her guidance.

"I remember," said the doctor--we were dining with the doctor in homely fashion, and our wives had adjourned to the drawing-room to discuss servants and husbands and other domestic matters with greater freedom, leaving us to the claret and the twilight--"I remember when we had the cholera in the village--it must be twenty years ago now--that woman gave up the London season to stay down here and take the whole burden of the trouble upon her own shoulders. I do not feel any call to praise her; she liked the work, and she was in her element, but it was good work for all that. She had no fear. She would carry the children in her arms if time pressed and the little ambulance was not at hand. I have known her sit all night in a room not twelve feet square, between a dying man and his dying wife. But the thing never touched her. Six years ago we had the small-pox, and she went all through that in just the same way. I don't believe she has ever had a day's illness in her life. She will be physicking this parish when my bones are rattling in my coffin, and she will be laying down the laws of literature long after your statue has become a familiar ornament of Westminster Abbey. She's a wonderful woman, but a trifle masterful."

He laughed, but I detected a touch of irritation in his voice. My host looked a man wishful to be masterful himself. I do not think he quite relished the calm way in which this grand dame took possession of all things around her, himself and his work included.

"Did you ever hear the story of the marriage?" he asked.

"No," I replied, "whose marriage? The earl's?"

"I should call it the countess's," he answered. "It was the gossip of the county when I first came here, but other curious things have happened among us to push it gradually out of memory. Most people, I really believe, have quite forgotten that the Countess of -- once served behind a baker's counter."

"You don't say so," I exclaimed. The remark, I admit, sounds weak when written down; the most natural remarks always do.

"It's a fact," said the doctor, "though she does not suggest the shop-girl, does she? But then I have known countesses, descended in a direct line from William the Conqueror, who did, so things balance one another. Mary, Countess of --, was, thirty years ago, Mary Sewell, daughter of a Taunton linen-draper. The business, profitable enough as country businesses go, was inadequate for the needs of the Sewell family, consisting, as I believe it did, of seven boys and eight girls. Mary, the youngest, as soon as her brief schooling was over, had to shift for herself. She seems to have tried her hand at one or two things, finally taking service with a cousin, a baker and confectioner, who was doing well in Oxford Street. She must have been a remarkably attractive girl; she's a handsome woman now. I can picture that soft creamy skin when it was fresh and smooth, and the West of England girls run naturally to dimples and eyes that glisten as though they had been just washed in morning dew. The shop did a good trade in ladies' lunches--it was the glass of sherry and sweet biscuit period. I expect they dressed her in some neat-fitting grey or black dress, with short sleeves, showing her plump arms, and that she flitted around the marble-topped tables, smiling, and looking cool and sweet. There the present Earl of --, then young Lord C-, fresh from Oxford, and new to the dangers of London bachelordom, first saw her. He had accompanied some female relatives to the photographer's, and, hotels and restaurants being deemed impossible in those days for ladies, had taken them to Sewell's to lunch. Mary Sewell waited upon the party; and now as many of that party as are above ground wait upon Mary Sewell."

"He showed good sense in marrying her," I said, "I admire him for it." The doctor's sixty-four Lafitte was excellent. I felt charitably inclined towards all men and women, even towards earls and countesses.

"I don't think he had much to do with it," laughed the doctor, "beyond being, like Barkis, 'willing.' It's a queer story; some people profess not to believe it, but those who know her ladyship best think it is just the story that must be true, because it is so characteristic of her. And besides, I happen to know that it is true."

"I should like to hear it," I said.

"I am going to tell it you," said the doctor, lighting a fresh cigar, and pushing the box towards me.

I will leave you to imagine the lad's suddenly developed appetite for decantered sherry at sixpence a glass, and the familiar currant bun of our youth. He lunched at Sewell's shop, he tea'd at Sewell's, occasionally he dined at Sewell's, off cutlets, followed by assorted pastry. Possibly, merely from fear lest the affair should reach his mother's ears, for he was neither worldly-wise nor vicious, he made love to Mary under an assumed name; and to do the girl justice, it must be remembered that she fell in love with and agreed to marry plain Mr. John Robinson, son of a colonial merchant, a gentleman, as she must have seen, and a young man of easy means, but of a position not so very much superior to her own. The first intimation she received that her lover was none other than Lord C-, the future Earl of --, was vouchsafed her during a painful interview with his lordship's mother.

"I never knew it, madam," asserted Mary, standing by the window of the drawing-room above the shop, "upon my word of honour, I never knew it"

"Perhaps not," answered her ladyship coldly. "Would you have refused him if you had?"

"I cannot tell," was the girl's answer; "it would have been different from the beginning. He courted me and asked me to be his wife."

"We won't go into all that," interrupted the other; "I am not here to defend him. I do not say he acted well. The question is, how much will compensate you for your natural disappointment?"

Her ladyship prided herself upon her bluntness and practicability. As she spoke she took her cheque-book out of her reticule, and, opening it, dipped her pen into the ink. I am inclined to think that the flutter of that cheque-book was her ladyship's mistake. The girl had common sense, and must have seen the difficulties in the way of a marriage between the heir to an earldom and a linen- draper's daughter; and had the old lady been a person of discernment, the interview might have ended more to her satisfaction. She made the error of judging the world by one standard, forgetting there are individualities. Mary Sewell came from a West of England stock that, in the days of Drake and Frobisher, had given more than one able-bodied pirate to the service of the country, and that insult of the cheque-book put the fight into her. Her lips closed with a little snap, and the fear fell from her.

"I am sorry I don't see my way to obliging your ladyship," she said.

"What do you mean, girl?" asked the elder woman.

"I don't mean to be disappointed," answered the girl, but she spoke quietly and respectfully. "We have pledged our word to one another. If he is a gentleman, as I know he is, he will keep his, and I shall keep mine."

Then her ladyship began to talk reason, as people do when it is too late. She pointed out to the girl the difference of social position, and explained to her the miseries that come from marrying out of one's station. But the girl by this time had got over her surprise, and perhaps had begun to reflect that, in any case, a countess-ship was worth fighting for. The best of women are influenced by such considerations.

"I am not a lady, I know," she replied quietly, "but my people have always been honest folk, well known, and I shall try to learn. I am not wishing to speak disrespectfully of my betters, but I was in service before I came here, ma'am, as lady's maid, in a place where I saw much of what is called Society. I think I can be as good a lady as some I know, if not better."

The countess began to grow angry again. "And who do you think will receive you?" she cried, "a girl who has served in a pastry-cook's shop!"

"Lady L- came from behind the bar," Mary answered, "and that's not much better. And the Duchess of C-, I have heard, was a ballet girl, but nobody seems to remember it. I don't think the people whose opinion is worth having will object to me for very long." The girl was beginning rather to enjoy the contest.

"You profess to love my son," cried the countess fiercely, "and you are going to ruin his life. You will drag him down to your own level."

The girl must have looked rather fine at that moment, I should dearly love to have been present.

"There will be no dragging down, my lady," she replied, "on either side. I do love your son very dearly. He is one of the kindest and best of gentlemen. But I am not blind, and whatever amount of cleverness there may be between us belongs chiefly to me. I shall make it my duty to fit myself for the position of his wife, and to help him in his work. You need not fear, my lady, I shall be a good wife to him, and he shall never regret it. You might find him a richer wife, a better educated wife, but you will never find him a wife who will be more devoted to him and to his interests."

That practically brought the scene to a close. The countess had sense enough to see that she was only losing ground by argument. She rose and replaced her cheque-book in her bag.

"I think, my good girl, you must be mad," she said; "if you will not allow me to do anything for you, there's an end to the matter. I did not come here to quarrel with you. My son knows his duty to me and to his family. You must take your own course, and I must take mine."

"Very well, my lady," said Mary Sewell, holding the door open for her ladyship to pass out, "we shall see who wins."

But however brave a front Mary Sewell may have maintained before the enemy, I expect she felt pretty limp when thinking matters calmly over after her ladyship's departure. She knew her lover well enough to guess that he would be as wax in the firm hands of his mother, while she herself would not have a chance of opposing her influence against those seeking to draw him away from her. Once again she read through the few schoolboy letters he had written her, and then looked up at the framed photograph that hung above the mantelpiece of her little bedroom. The face was that of a frank, pleasant-looking young fellow, lightened by eyes somewhat large for a man, but spoiled by a painfully weak mouth. The more Mary Sewell thought, the more sure she felt in her own mind that he loved her, and had meant honestly by her. Did the matter rest with him, she might reckon on being the future Countess of --, but, unfortunately for her, the person to be considered was not Lord C-, but the present Countess of --. From childhood, through boyhood, into manhood it had never once occurred to Lord C- to dispute a single command of his mother's, and his was not the type of brain to readily receive new ideas. If she was to win in the unequal contest it would have to be by art, not by strength. She sat down and wrote a letter which under all the circumstances was a model of diplomacy. She knew that it would be read by the countess, and, writing it, she kept both mother and son in mind. She made no reproaches, and indulged in but little sentiment. It was the letter of a woman who could claim rights, but who asked only for courtesy. It stated her wish to see him alone and obtain from his own lips the assurance that he wished their engagement to cease. "Do not fear," Mary Sewell wrote, "that I shall be any annoyance to you. My own pride would not let me urge you to marry me against your desire, and I care for you too much to cause you any pain. Assure me with your own lips that you wish our engagement to be at an end, and I shall release you without another word."

The family were in town, and Mary sent her letter by a trusty hand. The countess read it with huge satisfaction, and, re-sealing it, gave it herself into her son's hands. It promised a happy solution of the problem. In imagination, she had all the night been listening to a vulgar breach of promise case. She herself had been submitted to a most annoying cross-examination by a pert barrister. Her son's assumption of the name of Robinson had been misunderstood and severely commented upon by the judge. A sympathetic jury had awarded thumping damages, and for the next six months the family title would be a peg on which music-hall singers and comic journalists would hang their ribald jokes. Lord C- read the letter, flushed, and dutifully handed it back to his mother. She made pretence to read it as for the first time, and counselled him to accord the interview.

"I am so glad," she said, "that the girl is taking the matter sensibly. We must really do something for her in the future, when everything is settled. Let her ask for me, and then the servants will fancy she's a lady's maid or something of that sort, come after a place, and won't talk."

So that evening Mary Sewell, addressed by the butler as "young woman," was ushered into the small drawing-room that connects the library of No. -- Grosvenor Square with the other reception rooms. The countess, now all amiability, rose to meet her.

"My son will be here in a moment," she explained, "he has informed me of the purport of your letter. Believe me, my dear Miss Sewell, no one can regret his thoughtless conduct more than I do. But young men will be young men, and they do not stop to reflect that what may be a joke to them may be taken quite seriously by others."

"I don't regard the matter as a joke, my lady," replied Mary somewhat curtly.

"Of course not, my dear," added the countess, "that's what I'm saying. It was very wrong of him altogether. But with your pretty face, you will not, I am sure, have long to wait for a husband; we must see what we can do for you."

The countess certainly lacked tact; it must have handicapped her exceedingly.

"Thank you," answered the girl, "but I prefer to choose my own."

Fortunately--or the interview might have ended in another quarrel-- the cause of all the trouble at this moment entered the room, and the countess, whispering a few final words of instruction to him as she passed out, left them together.

Mary took a chair in the centre of the room, at equal distance from both doors. Lord C-, finding any sort of a seat uncomfortable under the circumstances, preferred to stand with his back to the mantelpiece. Dead silence was maintained for a few seconds, and then Mary, drawing the daintiest of handkerchiefs from her pocket, began to cry. The countess must have been a poor diplomatist, or she might have thought of this; or she may have remembered her own appearance on the rare occasions when she herself, a big, raw-boned girl, had attempted the softening influence of tears, and have attached little importance to the possibility. But when these soft, dimpled women cry, and cry quietly, it is another matter. Their eyes grow brighter, and the tears, few and far between, lie like dewdrops on a rose leaf.

Lord C- was as tender-hearted a lout as ever lived. In a moment he was on his knees with his arm round the girl's waist, pouring out such halting words of love and devotion as came to his unready brain, cursing his fate, his earldom, and his mother, and assuring Mary that his only chance of happiness lay in his making her his countess. Had Mary liked to say the word at that moment, he would have caught her to his arms, and defied the whole world--for the time being. But Mary was a very practical young woman, and there are difficulties in the way of handling a lover, who, however ready he may be to do your bidding so long as your eyes are upon him, is liable to be turned from his purpose so soon as another influence is substituted for your own. His lordship suggested an immediate secret marriage. But you cannot run out into the street, knock up a clergyman, and get married on the spot, and Mary knew that the moment she was gone his lordship's will would revert to his mother's keeping. Then his lordship suggested flight, but flight requires money, and the countess knew enough to keep his lordship's purse in her own hands. Despair seized upon his lordship.

"It's no use," he cried, "it will end in my marrying her."

"Who's she?" exclaimed Mary somewhat quickly.

His lordship explained the position. The family estates were heavily encumbered. It was deemed advisable that his lordship should marry Money, and Money, in the person of the only daughter of rich and ambitious parvenus, had offered itself--or, to speak more correctly, had been offered.

"What's she like?" asked Mary.

"Oh, she's nice enough," was the reply, "only I don't care for her and she doesn't care for me. It won't be much fun for either of us," and his lordship laughed dismally.

"How do you know she doesn't care for you?" asked Mary. A woman may be critical of her lover's shortcomings, but at the very least he is good enough for every other woman.

"Well, she happens to care for somebody else," answered his lordship, "she told me so herself."

That would account for it.

"And is she willing to marry you?" inquired Mary.

His lordship shrugged his shoulders.

"Oh, well, you know, her people want it," he replied.

In spite of her trouble, the girl could not help a laugh. These young swells seemed to have but small wills of their own. Her ladyship, on the other side of the door, grew nervous. It was the only sound she had been able to hear.

"It's deuced awkward," explained his lordship, "when you're--well, when you are anybody, you know. You can't do as you like. Things are expected of you, and there's such a lot to be considered."

Mary rose and clasped her pretty dimpled hands, from which she had drawn her gloves, behind his neck.

"You do love me, Jack?" she said, looking up into his face.

For answer the lad hugged her to him very tightly, and there were tears in his eyes.

"Look here, Mary," he cried, "if I could only get rid of my position, and settle down with you as a country gentleman, I'd do it to-morrow. Damn the title, it's going to be the curse of my life."

Perhaps in that moment Mary also wished that the title were at the bottom of the sea, and that her lover were only the plain Mr. John Robinson she had thought him. These big, stupid men are often very loveable in spite of, or because of their weakness. They appeal to the mother side of a woman's heart, and that is the biggest side in all good women.

Suddenly however, the door opened. The countess appeared, and sentiment flew out. Lord C-, releasing Mary, sprang back, looking like a guilty school-boy.

"I thought I heard Miss Sewell go out," said her ladyship in the icy tones that had never lost their power of making her son's heart freeze within him. "I want to see you when you are free."

"I shan't be long," stammered his lordship. "Mary--Miss Sewell is just going."

Mary waited without moving until the countess had left and closed the door behind her. Then she turned to her lover and spoke in quick, low tones.

"Give me her address--the girl they want you to marry!"

"What are you going to do?" asked his lordship.

"I don't know," answered the girl, "but I'm going to see her."

She scribbled the name down, and then said, looking the boy squarely in the face:

"Tell me frankly, Jack, do you want to marry me, or do you not?"

"You know I do, Mary," he answered, and his eyes spoke stronger than his words. "If I weren't a silly ass, there would be none of this trouble. But I don't know how it is; I say to myself I'll do, a thing, but the mater talks and talks and--"

"I know," interrupted Mary with a smile. "Don't argue with her, fall in with all her views, and pretend to agree with her."

"If you could only think of some plan," said his lordship, catching at the hope of her words, "you are so clever."

"I am going to try," answered Mary, "and if I fail, you must run off with me, even if you have to do it right before your mother's eyes."

What she meant was, "I shall have to run off with you," but she thought it better to put it the other way about.

Mary found her involuntary rival a meek, gentle little lady, as much under the influence of her blustering father as was Lord C- under that of his mother. What took place at the interview one can only surmise; but certain it is that the two girls, each for her own ends, undertook to aid and abet one another.

Much to the surprised delight of their respective parents, there came about a change in the attitude hitherto assumed towards one another by Miss Clementina Hodskiss and Lord C-. All objections to his lordship's unwilling attentions were suddenly withdrawn by the lady. Indeed, so swift to come and go are the whims of women, his calls were actually encouraged, especially when, as generally happened, they coincided with the absence from home of Mr. and Mrs. Hodskiss. Quite as remarkable was the new-born desire of Lord C- towards Miss Clementina Hodskiss. Mary's name was never mentioned, and the suggestion of immediate marriage was listened to without remonstrance. Wiser folk would have puzzled their brains, but both her ladyship and ex-Contractor Hodskiss were accustomed to find all things yield to their wishes. The countess saw visions of a rehabilitated estate, and Clementina's father dreamed of a peerage, secured by the influence of aristocratic connections. All that the young folks stipulated for (and on that point their firmness was supernatural) was that the marriage should be quiet, almost to the verge of secrecy.

"No beastly fuss," his lordship demanded. "Let it be somewhere in the country, and no mob!" and his mother, thinking she understood his reason, patted his cheek affectionately.

"I should like to go down to Aunt Jane's and be married quietly from there," explained Miss Hodskiss to her father.

Aunt Jane resided on the outskirts of a small Hampshire village, and "sat under" a clergyman famous throughout the neighbourhood for having lost the roof to his mouth.

"You can't be married by that old fool," thundered her father--Mr. Hodskiss always thundered; he thundered even his prayers.

"He christened me," urged Miss Clementina.

"And Lord knows what he called you. Nobody can understand a word he says."

"I'd like him to marry me," reiterated Miss Clementina.

Neither her ladyship nor the contractor liked the idea. The latter in particular had looked forward to a big function, chronicled at length in all the newspapers. But after all, the marriage was the essential thing, and perhaps, having regard to some foolish love passages that had happened between Clementina and a certain penniless naval lieutenant, ostentation might be out of place.

So in due course Clementina departed for Aunt Jane's, accompanied only by her maid.

Quite a treasure was Miss Hodskiss's new maid.

"A clean, wholesome girl," said of her Contractor Hodskiss, who cultivated affability towards the lower orders; "knows her place, and talks sense. You keep that girl, Clemmy."

"Do you think she knows enough?" hazarded the maternal Hodskiss.

"Quite sufficient for any decent woman," retorted the contractor. "When Clemmy wants painting and stuffing, it will be time enough for her to think about getting one of your 'Ach Himmels' or 'Mon Dieus'."

"I like the girl myself immensely," agreed Clementina's mother. "You can trust her, and she doesn't give herself airs."

Her praises reached even the countess, suffering severely at the moment from the tyranny of an elderly Fraulein.

"I must see this treasure," thought the countess to herself. "I am tired of these foreign minxes."

But no matter at what cunning hour her ladyship might call, the "treasure" always happened for some reason or other to be abroad.

"Your girl is always out when I come," laughed the countess. "One would fancy there was some reason for it."

"It does seem odd," agreed Clementina, with a slight flush.

Miss Hodskiss herself showed rather than spoke her appreciation of the girl. She seemed unable to move or think without her. Not even from the interviews with Lord C- was the maid always absent.

The marriage, it was settled, should be by licence. Mrs. Hodskiss made up her mind at first to run down and see to the preliminaries, but really when the time arrived it hardly seemed necessary to take that trouble. The ordering of the whole affair was so very simple, and the "treasure" appeared to understand the business most thoroughly, and to be willing to take the whole burden upon her own shoulders. It was not, therefore, until the evening before the wedding that the Hodskiss family arrived in force, filling Aunt Jane's small dwelling to its utmost capacity. The swelling figure of the contractor, standing beside the tiny porch, compelled the passer-by to think of the doll's house in which the dwarf resides during fair-time, ringing his own bell out of his own first-floor window. The countess and Lord C- were staying with her ladyship's sister, the Hon. Mrs. J-, at G- Hall, some ten miles distant, and were to drive over in the morning. The then Earl of -- was in Norway, salmon fishing. Domestic events did not interest him.

Clementina complained of a headache after dinner, and went to bed early. The "treasure" also was indisposed. She seemed worried and excited.

"That girl is as eager about the thing," remarked Mrs. Hodskiss, "as though it was her own marriage."

In the morning Clementina was still suffering from her headache, but asserted her ability to go through the ceremony, provided everybody would keep away, and not worry her. The "treasure" was the only person she felt she could bear to have about her. Half an hour before it was time to start for church her mother looked her up again. She had grown still paler, if possible, during the interval, and also more nervous and irritable. She threatened to go to bed and stop there if she was not left quite alone. She almost turned her mother out of the room, locking the door behind her. Mrs. Hodskiss had never known her daughter to be like this before.

The others went on, leaving her to follow in the last carriage with her father. The contractor, forewarned, spoke little to her. Only once he had occasion to ask her a question, and then she answered in a strained, unnatural voice. She appeared, so far as could be seen under her heavy veil, to be crying.

"Well, this is going to be a damned cheerful wedding," said Mr. Hodskiss, and lapsed into sulkiness.

The wedding was not so quiet as had been anticipated. The village had got scent of it, and had spread itself upon the event, while half the house party from G- Hall had insisted on driving over to take part in the proceedings. The little church was better filled than it had been for many a long year past.

The presence of the stylish crowd unnerved the ancient clergyman, long unaccustomed to the sight of a strange face, and the first sound of the ancient clergyman's voice unnerved the stylish crowd. What little articulation he possessed entirely disappeared, no one could understand a word he said. He appeared to be uttering sounds of distress. The ancient gentleman's infliction had to be explained in low asides, and it also had to be explained why such an one had been chosen to perform the ceremony.

"It was a whim of Clementina's," whispered her mother. "Her father and myself were married from here, and he christened her. The dear child's full of sentiment. I think it so nice of her."

Everybody agreed it was charming, but wished it were over. The general effect was weird in the extreme.

Lord C- spoke up fairly well, but the bride's responses were singularly indistinct, the usual order of things being thus reversed. The story of the naval lieutenant was remembered, and added to, and some of the more sentimental of the women began to cry in sympathy.

In the vestry things assumed a brighter tone. There was no lack of witnesses to sign the register. The verger pointed out to them the place, and they wrote their names, as people in such cases do, without stopping to read. Then it occurred to some one that the bride had not yet signed. She stood apart, with her veil still down, and appeared to have been forgotten. Encouraged, she came forward meekly, and took the pen from the hand of the verger. The countess came and stood behind her.

"Mary," wrote the bride, in a hand that looked as though it ought to have been firm, but which was not.

"Dear me," said the countess, "I never knew there was a Mary in your name. How differently you write when you write slowly."

The bride did not answer, but followed with "Susannah."

"Why, what a lot of names you must have, my dear!" exclaimed the countess. "When are you going to get to the ones we all know?"

"Ruth," continued the bride without answering.

Breeding is not always proof against strong emotion. The countess snatched the bride's veil from her face, and Mary Susannah Ruth Sewell stood before her, flushed and trembling, but looking none the less pretty because of that. At this point the crowd came in useful.

"I am sure your ladyship does not wish a scene," said Mary, speaking low. "The thing is done."

"The thing can be undone, and will be," retorted the countess in the same tone. "You, you--"

"My wife, don't forget that, mother," said Lord C- coming between them, and slipping Mary's hand on to his arm. "We are both sorry to have had to go about the thing in this roundabout way, but we wanted to avoid a fuss. I think we had better be getting away. I'm afraid Mr. Hodskiss is going to be noisy."

The doctor poured himself out a glass of claret, and drank it off. His throat must have been dry.

"And what became of Clementina?" I asked. "Did the naval lieutenant, while the others were at church, dash up in a post-chaise and carry her off?"

"That's what ought to have happened, for the whole thing to be in keeping," agreed the doctor. "I believe as a matter of fact she did marry him eventually, but not till some years later, after the contractor had died."

"And did Mr. Hodskiss make a noise in the vestry?" I persisted. The doctor never will finish a story.

"I can't say for certain," answered my host, "I only saw the gentleman once. That was at a shareholders' meeting. I should incline to the opinion that he did."

"I suppose the bride and bridegroom slipped out as quietly as possible and drove straight off," I suggested.

"That would have been the sensible thing for them to do," agreed the doctor.

"But how did she manage about her travelling frock?" I continued. "She could hardly have gone back to her Aunt Jane's and changed her things." The doctor has no mind for minutiae.

"I cannot tell you about all that," he replied. "I think I mentioned that Mary was a practical girl. Possibly she had thought of these details."

"And did the countess take the matter quietly?" I asked.

I like a tidy story, where everybody is put into his or her proper place at the end. Your modern romance leaves half his characters lying about just anyhow.

"That also I cannot tell you for certain," answered the doctor, "but I give her credit for so much sense. Lord C- was of age, and with Mary at his elbow, quite knew his own mind. I believe they travelled for two or three years. The first time I myself set eyes on the countess (nee Mary Sewell) was just after the late earl's death. I thought she looked a countess, every inch of her, but then I had not heard the story. I mistook the dowager for the housekeeper."

BLASE BILLY

It was towards the end of August. He and I appeared to be the only two men left to the Club. He was sitting by an open window, the Times lying on the floor beside him. I drew my chair a little closer and remarked:- "Good morning."

He suppressed a yawn, and replied "Mornin'"--dropping the "g." The custom was just coming into fashion; he was always correct.

"Going to be a very hot day, I am afraid," I continued.

"'Fraid so," was the response, after which he turned his head away and gently closed his eyes.

I opined that conversation was not to his wish, but this only made me more determined to talk, and to talk to him above all others in London. The desire took hold of me to irritate him--to break down the imperturbable calm within which he moved and had his being; and I gathered myself together, and settled down to the task.

"Interesting paper the Times," I observed.

"Very," he replied, taking it from the floor and handing it to me. "Won't you read it?"

I had been careful to throw into my voice an aggressive cheeriness which I had calculated would vex him, but his manner remained that of a man who is simply bored. I argued with him politely concerning the paper; but he insisted, still with the same weary air, that he had done with it. I thanked him effusively. I judged that he hated effusiveness.

"They say that to read a Times leader," I persisted, "is a lesson in English composition."

"So I've been told," he answered tranquilly. "Personally I don't take them."

The Times, I could see, was not going to be of much assistance to me. I lit a cigarette, and remarked that he was not shooting. He admitted the fact. Under the circumstances, it would have taxed him to deny it, but the necessity for confession aroused him.

"To myself," he said, "a tramp through miles of mud, in company with four gloomy men in black velveteen, a couple of depressed-looking dogs, and a heavy gun, the entire cavalcade being organised for the purpose of killing some twelve-and-sixpence worth of poultry, suggests the disproportionate."

I laughed boisterously, and cried, "Good, good--very good!"

He was the type of man that shudders inwardly at the sound of laughter. I had the will to slap him on the back, but I thought maybe that would send him away altogether.

I asked him if he hunted. He replied that fourteen hours' talk a day about horses, and only about horses tired him, and that in consequence he had abandoned hunting.

"You fish?" I said.

"I was never sufficiently imaginative," he answered.

"You travel a good deal," I suggested.

He had apparently made up his mind to abandon himself to his fate, for he turned towards me with a resigned air. An ancient nurse of mine had always described me as the most "wearing" child she had ever come across. I prefer to speak of myself as persevering.

"I should go about more," he said, "were I able to see any difference between one place and another."

"Tried Central Africa?" I inquired.

"Once or twice," he answered. "It always reminds me of Kew Gardens."

"China?" I hazarded.

"Cross between a willow-pattern plate and a New York slum," was his comment.

"The North Pole?" I tried, thinking the third time might be lucky.

"Never got quite up to it," he returned. "Reached Cape Hakluyt once."

"How did that impress you?" I asked.

"It didn't impress me," he replied.

The talk drifted to women and bogus companies, dogs, literature, and such-like matters. I found him well informed upon and bored by all.

"They used to be amusing," he said, speaking of the first named, "until they began to take themselves seriously. Now they are merely silly."

I was forced into closer companionship with "Blase Billy" that autumn, for by chance a month later he and I found ourselves the guests of the same delightful hostess, and I came to liking him better. He was a useful man to have about one. In matters of fashion one could always feel safe following his lead. One knew that his necktie, his collar, his socks, if not the very newest departure, were always correct; and upon social paths, as guide, philosopher, and friend, he was invaluable. He knew every one, together with his or her previous convictions. He was acquainted with every woman's past, and shrewdly surmised every man's future. He could point you out the coal-shed where the Countess of Glenleman had gambolled in her days of innocence, and would take you to breakfast at the coffee-shop off the Mile End Road where "Sam. Smith, Estd. 1820," own brother to the world-famed society novelist, Smith-Stratford, lived an uncriticised, unparagraphed, unphotographed existence upon the profits of "rashers" at three- ha'pence and "door-steps" at two a penny. He knew at what houses it was inadvisable to introduce soap, and at what tables it would be bad form to denounce political jobbery. He could tell you offhand what trade-mark went with what crest, and remembered the price paid for every baronetcy created during the last twenty-five years.

Regarding himself, he might have made claim with King Charles never to have said a foolish thing, and never to have done a wise one. He despised, or affected to despise, most of his fellow-men, and those of his fellow-men whose opinion was most worth having unaffectedly despised him.

Shortly described, one might have likened him to a Gaiety Johnny with brains. He was capital company after dinner, but in the early morning one avoided him.

So I thought of him until one day he fell in love; or to put it in the words of Teddy Tidmarsh, who brought the news to us, "got mashed on Gerty Lovell."

"The red-haired one," Teddy explained, to distinguish her from her sister, who had lately adopted the newer golden shade.

"Gerty Lovell!" exclaimed the captain, "why, I've always been told the Lovell girls hadn't a penny among them."

"The old man's stone broke, I know for a certainty," volunteered Teddy, who picked up a mysterious but, in other respects, satisfactory income in an office near Hatton Garden, and who was candour itself concerning the private affairs of everybody but himself.

"Oh, some rich pork-packing or diamond-sweating uncle has cropped up in Australia, or America, or one of those places," suggested the captain, "and Billy's got wind of it in good time. Billy knows his way about."

We agreed that some such explanation was needed, though in all other respects Gerty Lovell was just the girl that Reason (not always consulted on these occasions) might herself have chosen for "Blasé Billy's" mate.

The sunlight was not too kind to her, but at evening parties, where the lighting has been well considered, I have seen her look quite girlish. At her best she was not beautiful, but at her worst there was about her an air of breeding and distinction that always saved her from being passed over, and she dressed to perfection. In character she was the typical society woman: always charming, generally insincere. She went to Kensington for her religion and to Mayfair for her morals; accepted her literature from Mudie's and her art from the

Grosvenor Gallery; and could and would gabble philanthropy, philosophy, and politics with equal fluency at every five-o'clock tea-table she visited. Her ideas could always be guaranteed as the very latest, and her opinion as that of the person to whom she was talking. Asked by a famous novelist one afternoon, at the Pioneer Club, to give him some idea of her, little Mrs. Bund, the painter's wife, had remained for a few moments with her pretty lips pursed, and had then said:

"She is a woman to whom life could bring nothing more fully satisfying than a dinner invitation from a duchess, and whose nature would be incapable of sustaining deeper suffering than that caused by an ill-fitting costume."

At the time I should have said the epigram was as true as it was cruel, but I suppose we none of us quite know each other.

I congratulated "Blase Billy," or to drop his Club nickname and give him the full benefit of his social label, "The Hon. William Cecil Wychwood Stanley Drayton," on the occasion of our next meeting, which happened upon the steps of the Savoy Restaurant, and I thought--unless a quiver of the electric light deceived me--that he blushed.

"Charming girl," I said. "You're a lucky dog, Billy."

It was the phrase that custom demands upon such occasions, and it came of its own accord to my tongue without costing me the trouble of composition, but he seized upon it as though it had been a gem of friendly sincerity.

"You will like her even more when you know her better," he said. "She is so different from the usual woman that one meets. Come and see her to-morrow afternoon, she will be so pleased. Go about four, I will tell her to expect you."

I rang the bell at ten minutes past five. Billy was there. She greeted me with a little tremor of embarrassment, which sat oddly upon her, but which was not altogether unpleasing. She said it was kind of me to come so early. I stayed for about half an hour, but conversation flagged, and some of my cleverest remarks attracted no attention whatever.

When I rose to take my leave, Billy said that he must be off too, and that he would accompany me. Had they been ordinary lovers, I should have been careful to give them an opportunity of making their adieus in secret; but in the case of the Honourable William Drayton and the eldest Miss Lovell I concluded that such tactics were needless, so I waited till he had shaken hands, and went downstairs with him.

But in the hall Billy suddenly ejaculated, "By Jove! Half a minute," and ran back up the stairs three at a time. Apparently he found what he had gone for on the landing, for I did not hear the opening of the drawing-room door. Then the Honourable Billy redescended with a sober, nonchalent air.

"Left my gloves behind me," he explained, as he took my arm. "I am always leaving my gloves about."

I did not mention that I had seen him take them from his hat and slip them into his coat-tail pocket.

We at the Club did not see very much of Billy during the next three months, but the captain, who prided himself upon his playing of the role of smoking-room cynic--though he would have been better in the part had he occasionally displayed a little originality--was of opinion that our loss would be more than made up to us after the marriage. Once in the twilight I caught sight of a figure that reminded me of Billy's, accompanied by a figure that might have been that of the eldest Miss Lovell; but as the spot was Battersea Park, which is not a fashionable evening promenade, and the two figures were holding each other's hands, the whole picture being suggestive of the closing chapter of a London Journal romance, I concluded I had made an error.

But I did see them in the Adelphi stalls one evening, rapt in a sentimental melodrama. I joined them between the acts, and poked fun at the play, as one does at the Adelphi, but Miss Lovell begged me quite earnestly not to spoil her interest, and Billy wanted to enter upon a serious argument as to whether a man was justified in behaving as Will Terriss had just behaved towards the woman he loved. I left them and returned to my own party, to the satisfaction, I am inclined to think, of all concerned.

They married in due course. We were mistaken on one point. She brought Billy nothing. But they both seemed quite content on his not too extravagant fortune. They took a tiny house not far from Victoria Station, and hired a brougham for the season. They did not entertain very much, but they contrived to be seen everywhere it was right and fashionable they should be seen. The Honourable Mrs. Drayton was a much younger and brighter person than had been the eldest Miss Lovell, and as she continued to dress charmingly, her social position rose rapidly. Billy went everywhere with her, and evidently took a keen pride in her success. It was even said that he designed her dresses for her, and I have myself seen him earnestly studying the costumes in Russell and Allen's windows.

The captain's prophecy remained unfulfilled. "Blase Billy"--if the name could still be applied to him--hardly ever visited the Club after his marriage. But I had grown to like him, and, as he had foretold, to like his wife. I found their calm indifference to the burning questions of the day a positive relief from the strenuous atmosphere of literary and artistic circles. In the drawing-room of their little house in Eaton Row, the comparative merits of George Meredith and George R. Sims were not considered worth discussion. Both were regarded as persons who afforded a certain amount of amusement in return for a certain amount of cash. And on any Wednesday afternoon, Henrick Ibsen and Arthur Roberts would have been equally welcome, as adding piquancy to the small gathering. Had I been compelled to pass my life in such a house, this Philistine attitude might have palled upon me; but, under the circumstances, it refreshed me, and I made use of my welcome, which I believe was genuine, to its full extent.

As months went by, they seemed to me to draw closer to one another, though I am given to understand that such is not the rule in fashionable circles. One evening I arrived a little before my time, and was shown up into the drawing-room by the soft-footed butler. They were sitting in the dusk with their arms round one another. It was impossible to withdraw, so I faced the situation and coughed. A pair of middle-class lovers could not have appeared more awkward or surprised.

But the incident established an understanding between us, and I came to be regarded as a friend before whom there was less necessity to act.

Studying them, I came to the conclusion that the ways and manners of love are very same-like throughout the world, as though the foolish boy, unheedful of human advance, kept but one school for minor poet and East End shop-boy, for Girton girl and little milliner; taught but the one lesson to the end-of-the-nineteenth- century Johnny that he taught to bearded Pict and Hun four thousand years ago.

Thus the summer and the winter passed pleasantly for the Honourable Billy, and then, as luck would have it, he fell ill just in the very middle of the London season, when invitations to balls and dinner parties, luncheons and "At Homes," were pouring in from every quarter; when the lawns at Hurlingham were at their smoothest, and the paddocks at their smartest.

It was unfortunate, too, that the fashions that season suited the Honourable Mrs. Billy as they had not suited her for years. In the early spring, she and Billy had been hard at work planning costumes calculated to cause a flutter through Mayfair, and the dresses and the bonnets--each one a work of art--were waiting on their stands to do their killing work. But the Honourable Mrs. Billy, for the first time in her life, had lost interest in such things.

Their friends were genuinely sorry, for society was Billy's element, and in it he was interesting and amusing. But, as Lady Gower said, there was no earthly need for his wife to constitute herself a prisoner. Her shutting herself off from the world could do him no good and it would look odd.

Accordingly the Honourable Mrs. Drayton, to whom oddness was a crime, and the voice of Lady Gower as the voice of duty, sacrificed her inclinations on the social shrine, laced the new costumes tight across her aching heart, and went down into society.

But the Honourable Mrs. Drayton achieved not the success of former seasons. Her small talk grew so very small, that even Park Lane found it unsatisfying. Her famous laugh rang mechanically. She smiled at the wisdom of dukes, and became sad at the funny stories of millionaires. Society voted her a good wife but bad company, and confined its attentions to cards of inquiry. And for this relief the Honourable Mrs. Drayton was grateful, for Billy waned weaker and weaker. In the world of shadows in which she moved, he was the one real thing. She was of very little practical use, but it comforted her to think that she was helping to nurse him.

But Billy himself it troubled.

"I do wish you would go out more," he would say. "It makes me feel that I'm such a selfish brute, keeping you tied up here in this dismal little house. Besides," he would add, "people miss you; they will hate me for keeping you away." For, where his wife was concerned, Billy's knowledge of the world availed him little. He really thought society craved for the Honourable Mrs. Drayton, and would not be comforted where she was not.

"I would rather stop with you, dear," would be the answer; "I don't care to go about by myself. You must get well quickly and take me."

And so the argument continued, until one evening, as she sat by herself, the nurse entered softly, closed the door behind her, and came over to her.

"I wish you would go out to-night, ma'am," said the nurse, "just for an hour or two. I think it would please the master; he is worrying himself because he thinks it is his fault that you do not; and just now"--the woman hesitated for a moment--"just now I want to keep him very quiet."

"Is he weaker, nurse?"

"Well, he is not stronger, ma'am, and I think--I think we must humour him."

The Honourable Mrs. Drayton rose, and, crossing to the window, stood for a while looking out.

"But where am I to go, nurse?" she said at length, turning with a smile. "I've no invitations anywhere."

"Can't you make believe to have one?" said the nurse. "It is only seven o'clock. Say you are going to a dinner-party; you can come home early then. Go and dress yourself, and come down and say good-bye to him, and then come in again about eleven, as though you had just returned."

"You think I must, nurse?"

"I think it would be better, ma'am. I wish you would try it."

The Honourable Mrs. Drayton went to the door, then paused.

"He has such sharp ears, nurse; he will listen for the opening of the door and the sound of the carriage."

"I will see to that," said the nurse. "I will tell them to have the carriage here at ten minutes to eight. Then you can drive to the end of the street, slip out, and walk back. I will let you in myself."

"And about coming home?" asked the other woman.

"You must slip out for a few minutes before eleven, and the carriage must be waiting for you at the corner again. Leave all that to me."

In half an hour the Honourable Mrs. Drayton entered the sick-room, radiant in evening dress and jewels. Fortunately the lights were low, or "Blase-Billy" might have been doubtful as to the effect his wife was likely to produce. For her face was not the face that one takes to dinner-parties.

"Nurse tells me you are going to the Grevilles this evening. I am so glad. I've been worrying myself about you, moped up here right through the season."

He took her hands in his and held her out at arm's length from him.

"How handsome you look, dear!" he said. "How they must have all been cursing me for keeping you shut up here, like a princess in an ogre's castle! I shall never dare to face them again."

She laughed, well pleased at his words.

"I shall not be late," she said. "I shall be so anxious to get back and see how my boy has behaved. If you have not been good I shan't go again."

They kissed and parted, and at eleven she returned to the room. She told him what a delightful evening it had been, and bragged a little of her own success.

The nurse told her that he had been more cheerful that evening than for many nights.

So every day the farce was played for him. One day it was to a luncheon that she went, in a costume by Redfern; the next night to a ball, in a frock direct from Paris; again to an "At Home," or concert, or dinner-party. Loafers and passers-by would stop to stare at a haggard, red-eyed woman, dressed as for a drawing-room, slipping thief-like in and out of her own door.

I heard them talking of her one afternoon, at a house where I called, and I joined the group to listen.

"I always thought her heartless, but I gave her credit for sense," a woman was saying. "One doesn't expect a woman to be fond of her husband, but she needn't make a parade of ignoring him when he is dying."

I pleaded absence from town to inquire what was meant, and from all lips I heard the same account. One had noticed her carriage at the door two or three evenings in succession. Another had seen her returning home. A third had seen her coming out, and so on.

I could not fit the fact in with my knowledge of her, so the next evening I called. The door was opened instantly by herself.

"I saw you from the window," she said. "Come in here; don't speak."

I followed her, and she closed the door behind her. She was dressed in a magnificent costume, her hair sparkling with diamonds, and I looked my questions.

She laughed bitterly.

"I am supposed to be at the opera to-night," she explained. "Sit down, if you have a few minutes to spare."

I said it was for a talk that I had come; and there, in the dark room, lighted only by the street lamp without, she told me all. And at the end she dropped her head on her bare arms; and I turned away and looked out of the window for a while.

"I feel so ridiculous," she said, rising and coming towards me. "I sit here all the evening dressed like this. I'm afraid I don't act my part very well; but, fortunately, dear Billy never was much of a judge of art, and it is good enough for him. I tell him the most awful lies about what everybody has said to me, and what I've said to everybody, and how my gowns were admired. What do you think of this one?"

For answer I took the privilege of a friend.

"I'm glad you think well of me," she said. "Billy has such a high opinion of you. You will hear some funny tales. I'm glad you know."

I had to leave London again, and Billy died before I returned. I heard that she had to be fetched from a ball, and was only just in time to touch his lips before they were cold. But her friends excused her by saying that the end had come very suddenly.

I called on her a little later, and before I left I hinted to her what people were saying, and asked her if I had not better tell them the truth.

"I would rather you didn't," she answered. "It seems like making public the secret side of one's life."

"But," I urged, "they will think--"

She interrupted me.

"Does it matter very much what they think?"

Which struck me as a very remarkable sentiment, coming from the Hon. Mrs. Drayton, nee the elder Miss Lovell.

THE CHOICE OF CYRIL HARJOHN

Between a junior resident master of twenty-one, and a backward lad of fifteen, there yawns an impassable gulf. Between a struggling journalist of one-and-thirty, and an M.D. of twenty-five, with a brilliant record behind him, and a career of exceptional promise before him, a close friendship is however permissible.

My introduction to Cyril Harjohn was through the Rev. Charles Fauerberg.

"Our young friend," said the Rev. Mr. Fauerberg, standing in the most approved tutorial attitude, with his hand upon his pupil's shoulder, "our young friend has been somewhat neglected, but I see in him possibilities warranting hope--warranting, I may say, very great hope. For the present he will be under my especial care, and you will not therefore concern yourself with his studies. He will sleep with Milling and the others in dormitory number two."

The lad formed a liking for me, and I think, and hope, I rendered his sojourn at "Alpha House" less irksome than otherwise it might have been. The Reverend Charles' method with the backward was on all fours with that adopted for the bringing on of geese; he cooped them up and crammed them. The process is profitable to the trainer, but painful to the goose.

Young Harjohn and myself left "Alpha House" at the end of the same term; he bound for Brasenose, I for Bloomsbury. He made a point of never coming up to London without calling on me, when we would dine together in one of Soho's many dingy, garlic-scented restaurants, and afterwards, over our bottle of cheap Beaune, discuss the coming of our lives; and when he entered Guy's I left John Street, and took chambers close to his in Staple Inn. Those were pleasant days. Childhood is an over-rated period, fuller of sorrow than of joy. I would not take my childhood back, were it a gift, but I would give the rest of my life to live the twenties over again.

To Cyril I was the man of the world, and he looked to me for wisdom, not seeing always, I fear, that he got it; while from him I gathered enthusiasm, and learnt the profit that comes to a man from the keeping of ideals.

Often as we have talked, I have felt as though a visible light came from him, framing his face as with the halo of some pictured saint. Nature had wasted him, putting him into this nineteenth century of ours. Her victories are accomplished. Her army of heroes, the few sung, the many forgotten, is disbanded. The long peace won by their blood and pain is settled on the land. She had fashioned Cyril Harjohn for one of her soldiers. He would have been a martyr, in the days when thought led to the stake, a fighter for the truth, when to speak one's mind meant death. To lead some forlorn hope for Civilisation would have been his true work; Fate had condemned him to sentry duty in a well-ordered barrack.

But there is work to be done in the world, though the labour lies now in the vineyard, not on the battlefield. A small but sufficient fortune purchased for him freedom. To most men an assured income is the grave of ambition; to Cyril it was the foundation of desire. Relieved from the necessity of working to live, he could afford the luxury of living to work. His profession was to him a passion; he regarded it, not with the cold curiosity of the scholar, but with the imaginative devotion of the disciple. To help to push its frontiers forward, to carry its flag farther into the untravelled desert that ever lies beyond the moving boundary of human knowledge, was his dream.

One summer evening, I remember, we were sitting in his rooms, and during a silence there came to us through the open window the moaning of the city, as of a tired child. He rose and stretched his arms out towards the darkening streets, as if he would gather to him all the toiling men and women and comfort them.

"Oh, that I could help you!" he cried, "my brothers and my sisters. Take my life, oh God, and spend it for me among your people."

The speech sounds theatrical, as I read it, written down, but to the young such words are not ridiculous, as to us older men.

In the natural order of events, he fell in love, and with just the woman one would expect him to be attracted by. Elspeth Grant was of the type from which the world, by instinct rather than by convention, has drawn its Madonnas and its saints. To describe a woman in words is impossible. Her beauty was not a possession to be catalogued, but herself. One felt it as one feels the beauty of a summer's dawn breaking the shadows of a sleeping city, but one cannot set it down. I often met her, and, when talking to her, I knew myself--I, hack-journalist, frequenter of Fleet Street bars, retailer of smoke-room stories--a great gentleman, incapable of meanness, fit for all noble deeds.

In her presence life became a thing beautiful and gracious; a school for courtesy, and tenderness, and simplicity.

I have wondered since, coming to see a little more clearly into the ways of men, whether it would not have been better had she been less spiritual, had her nature possessed a greater alloy of earth, making it more fit for the uses of this work-a-day world. But at the time, these two friends of mine seemed to me to have been created for one another.

She appealed to all that was highest in Cyril's character, and he worshipped her with an unconcealed adoration that, from any man less high-minded, would have appeared affectation, and which she accepted with the sweet content that Artemis might have accorded to the homage of Endymion.

There was no formal engagement between them. Cyril seemed to shrink from the materialising of his love by any thought of marriage. To him she was an ideal of womanhood rather than a flesh-and-blood woman. His love for her was a religion; it had no taint of earthly passion in its composition.

Had I known the world better I might have anticipated the result; for the red blood ran in my friend's veins; and, alas, we dream our poems, not live them. But at the time, the idea of any other woman coming between them would have appeared to me folly. The suggestion that that other woman might be Geraldine Fawley I should have resented as an insult to my intelligence: that is the point of the story I do not understand to this day.

That he should be attracted by her, that he should love to linger near her, watching the dark flush come and go across her face, seeking to call the fire into her dark eyes was another matter, and quite comprehensible; for the girl was wonderfully handsome, with a bold, voluptuous beauty which invited while it dared. But considered in any other light than that of an animal, she repelled. At times when, for her ends, it seemed worth the exertion, she would assume a certain wayward sweetness, but her acting was always clumsy and exaggerated, capable of deceiving no one but a fool.

Cyril, at all events, was not taken in by it. One evening, at a Bohemian gathering, the entree to which was notoriety rather than character, they had been talking together for some considerable time when, wishing to speak to Cyril, I strolled up to join them. As I came towards them she moved away, her dislike for me being equal to mine for her; a thing which was, perhaps, well for me.

"Miss Fawley prefers two as company to three," I observed, looking after her retreating figure.

"I am afraid she finds you what we should call an anti-sympathetic element," he replied, laughing.

"Do you like her?" I asked him, somewhat bluntly.

His eyes rested upon her as she stood in the doorway, talking to a small, black-bearded man who had just been introduced to her. After a few moments she went out upon his arm, and then Cyril turned to me.

"I think her," he replied, speaking, as was necessary, very low, "the embodiment of all that is evil in womanhood. In old days she would have been a Cleopatra, a Theodora, a Delilah. To-day, lacking opportunity, she is the 'smart woman' grubbing for an opening into society--and old Fawley's daughter. I'm tired; let us go home."

His allusion to her parentage was significant. Few people thought of connecting clever, handsome Geraldine Fawley with "Rogue Fawley," Jew renegade, ex-gaol bird, and outside broker; who, having expectations from his daughter, took care not to hamper her by ever being seen in her company. But no one who had once met the father could ever forget the relationship while talking to the daughter. The older face, with its cruelty, its cunning, and its greed stood reproduced, feature for feature, line for line. It was as though Nature, for an artistic freak, had set herself the task of fashioning hideousness and beauty from precisely the same materials. Between the leer of the man and the smile of the girl, where lay the difference? It would have puzzled any student of anatomy to point it out. Yet the one sickened, while to gain the other most men would have given much.

Cyril's answer to my question satisfied me for the time. He met the girl often, as was natural. She was a singer of some repute, and our social circle was what is commonly called "literary and artistic." To do her justice, however, she made no attempt to fascinate him, nor even to be particularly agreeable to him. Indeed, she seemed to be at pains to show him her natural--in other words, her most objectionable side.

Coming out of the theatre one first night, we met her in the lobby. I was following Cyril at some little distance, but as he stopped to speak to her the movement of the crowd placed me just behind them.

"Will you be at Leightons' to-morrow?" I heard him ask her in a low tone.

"Yes," she answered, "and I wish you wouldn't come."

"Why not?"

"Because you're a fool, and you bore me."

Under ordinary circumstances I should have taken the speech for badinage--it was the kind of wit the woman would have indulged in. But Cyril's face clouded with anger and vexation. I said nothing. I did not wish him to know that I had overheard. I tried to believe that he was amusing himself, but my own explanation did not satisfy me.

Next evening I went to Leightons' by myself. The Grants were in town, and Cyril was dining with them. I found I did not know many people, and cared little for those I did. I was about to escape when Miss Fawley's name was announced. I was close to the door, and she had to stop and speak to me. We exchanged a few commonplaces. She either made love to a man or was rude to him. She generally talked to me without looking at me, nodding and smiling meanwhile to people around. I have met many women equally ill-mannered, and without her excuse. For a moment, however, she turned her eyes to mine.

"Where's your friend, Mr. Harjohn?" she asked. "I thought you were inseparables."

I looked at her in astonishment.

"He is dining out to-night," I replied. "I do not think he will come."

She laughed. I think it was the worst part about the woman, her laugh; it suggested so much cruelty.

"I think he will," she said.

It angered me into an indiscretion. She was moving away. I stepped in front of her and stopped her.

"What makes you think so?" I asked, and my voice, I know, betrayed the anxiety I felt as to her reply. She looked me straight in the face. There was one virtue she possessed--the virtue that animals hold above mankind--truthfulness. She knew I disliked her--hate would be, perhaps, a more exact expression, did not the word sound out of date, and she made no pretence of not knowing it and returning the compliment.

"Because I am here," she answered. "Why don't you save him? Have you no influence over him? Tell the Saint to keep him; I don't want him. You heard what I said to him last night. I shall only marry him for the sake of his position, and the money he can earn if he likes to work and not play the fool. Tell him what I have said; I shan't deny it."

She passed on to greet a decrepit old lord with a languishing smile, and I stood staring after her with, I fear, a somewhat stupid expression, until some young fool came up grinning, to ask me whether I had seen a ghost or backed a "wrong 'un."

There was no need to wait; I felt no curiosity. Something told me the woman had spoken the truth. It was mere want of motive that made me linger. I saw him come in, and watched him hanging round her, like a dog, waiting for a kind word, or failing that, a look. I knew she saw me, and I knew it added to her zest that I was there. Not till we were in the street did I speak to him. He started as I touched him. We were neither of us good actors. He must have read much in my face, and I saw that he had read it; and we walked side by side in silence, I thinking what to say, wondering whether I should do good or harm, wishing that we were anywhere but in these silent, life-packed streets, so filled with the unseen. It was not until we had nearly reached the Albert Hall that we broke the silence. Then it was he who spoke:

"Do you think I haven't told myself all that?" he said. "Do you think I don't know I'm a damned fool, a cad, a liar! What the devil's the good of talking about it?"

"But I can't understand it," I said.

"No," he replied, "because you're a fool, because you have only seen one side of me. You think me a grand gentleman, because I talk big, and am full of noble sentiment. Why, you idiot, the Devil himself could take you in. HE has his fine moods, I suppose, talks like a saint, and says his prayers with the rest of us. Do you remember the first night at old Fauerberg's? You poked your silly head into the dormitory, and saw me kneeling by the bedside, while the other fellows stood by grinning. You closed the door softly--you thought I never saw you. I was not praying, I was trying to pray."

"It showed that you had pluck, if it showed nothing else," I answered. "Most boys would not have tried, and you kept it up."

"Ah, yes," he answered, "I promised the Mater I would, and I did. Poor old soul, she was as big a fool as you are. She believed in me. Don't you remember, finding me one Saturday afternoon all alone, stuffing myself with cake and jam?"

I laughed at the recollection, though Heaven knows I was in no laughing mood. I had found him with an array of pastry spread out before him, sufficient to make him ill for a week, and I had boxed his ears, and had thrown the whole collection into the road.

"The Mater gave me half-a-crown a week for pocket-money," he continued, "and I told the fellows I had only a shilling, so that I could gorge myself with the other eighteenpence undisturbed. Pah! I was a little beast even in those days!"

"It was only a schoolboy trick," I argued, "it was natural enough."

"Yes," he answered, "and this is only a man's trick, and is natural enough; but it is going to ruin my life, to turn me into a beast instead of a man. Good God! do you think I don't know what that woman will do for me? She will drag me down, down, down, to her own level. All my ideas, all my ambition, all my life's work will be bartered for a smug practice, among paying patients. I shall scheme and plot to make a big income that we may live like a couple of plump animals, that we may dress ourselves gaudily and parade our wealth. Nothing will satisfy her. Such women are leeches; their only cry is 'give, give, give.' So long as I can supply her with money she will tolerate me, and to get it for her I shall sell my heart, and my brain, and my soul. She will load herself with jewels, and go about from house to house, half naked, to leer at every man she comes across: that is 'life' to such women. And I shall trot behind her, the laughing stock of every fool, the contempt of every man."

His vehemence made any words I could say sound weak before they were uttered. What argument could I show stronger than that he had already put before himself? I knew his answer to everything I could urge.

My mistake had been in imagining him different from other men.

I began to see that he was like the rest of us: part angel, part devil. But the new point he revealed to me was that the higher the one, the lower the other. It seems as if nature must balance her work; the nearer the leaves to heaven, the deeper the roots striking down into the darkness. I knew that his passion for this woman made no change in his truer love. The one was a spiritual, the other a mere animal passion. The memory of incidents that had puzzled me came back to enlighten me. I remembered how often on nights when I had sat up late, working, I had heard his steps pass my door, heavy and uncertain; how once in a dingy quarter of London, I had met one who had strangely resembled him. I had followed him to speak, but the man's bleared eyes had stared angrily at me, and I had turned away, calling myself a fool for my mistake. But as I looked at the face beside me now, I understood.

And then there rose up before my eyes the face I knew better, the eager noble face that to merely look upon had been good. We had reached a small, evil-smelling street, leading from Leicester Square towards Holborn. I caught him by the shoulders and turned him round with his back against some church railings. I forget what I said. We are strange mixtures. I thought of the shy, backward boy I had coached and bullied at old Fauerberg's, of the laughing handsome lad I had watched grow into manhood. The very restaurant we had most frequented in his old Oxford days--where we had poured out our souls to one another, was in this very street where we were standing. For the moment I felt towards him as perhaps his mother might have felt; I wanted to scold him and to cry with him; to shake him and to put my arms about him. I pleaded with him, and urged him, and called him every name I could put my tongue to. It must have seemed an odd conversation. A passing policeman, making a not unnatural mistake, turned his bull's-eye upon us, and advised us sternly to go home. We laughed, and with that laugh Cyril came back to his own self, and we walked on to Staple Inn more soberly. He promised me to go away by the very first train the next morning, and to travel for some four or five months, and I undertook to make all the necessary explanations for him.

We both felt better for our talk, and when I wished him goodnight at his door, it was the real Cyril Harjohn whose hand I gripped -- the real Cyril, because the best that is in a man is his real self. If there be any future for man beyond this world, it is the good that is in him that will live. The other side of him is of the earth; it is that he will leave behind him.

He kept his word. In the morning he was gone, and I never saw him again. I had many letters from him, hopeful at first, full of strong resolves. He told me he had written to Elspeth, not telling her everything, for that she would not understand, but so much as would explain; and from her he had had sweet womanly letters in reply. I feared she might have been cold and unsympathetic, for often good women, untouched by temptation themselves, have small tenderness for those who struggle. But her goodness was something more than a mere passive quantity; she loved him the better because he had need of her. I believe she would have saved him from himself, had not fate interfered and taken the matter out of her hands. Women are capable of big sacrifices; I think this woman would have been content to lower herself, if by so doing she could have raised him.

But it was not to be. From India he wrote to me that he was coming home. I had not met the Fawley woman for some time, and she had gone out of my mind until one day, chancing upon a theatrical paper, some weeks old, I read that "Miss Fawley had sailed for Calcutta to fulfil an engagement of long standing."

I had his last letter in my pocket. I sat down and worked out the question of date. She would arrive in Calcutta the day before he left. Whether it was chance or intention on her part I never knew; as likely as not the former, for there is a fatalism in this world shaping our ends.

I heard no more from him, I hardly expected to do so, but three months later a mutual acquaintance stopped me on the Club steps.

"Have you heard the news," he said, "about young Harjohn?"

"No," I replied. "Is he married?"

"Married," he answered, "No, poor devil, he's dead!"

"Thank God," was on my lips, but fortunately I checked myself. "How did it happen?" I asked.

"At a shooting party, up at some Rajah's place. Must have caught his gun in some brambles, I suppose. The bullet went clean through his head."

"Dear me," I said, "how very sad!" I could think of nothing else to say at the moment.

THE MATERIALISATION OF CHARLES AND MIVANWAY

The fault that most people will find with this story is that it is unconvincing. Its scheme is improbable, its atmosphere artificial. To confess that the thing really happened--not as I am about to set it down, for the pen of the professional writer cannot but adorn and embroider, even to the detriment of his material--is, I am well aware, only an aggravation of my offence, for the facts of life are the impossibilities of fiction. A truer artist would have left this story alone, or at most have kept it for the irritation of his private circle. My lower instinct is to make use of it. A very old man told me the tale. He was landlord of the Cromlech Arms, the only inn of a small, rock-sheltered village on the north-east coast of Cornwall, and had been so for nine and forty years. It is called the Cromlech Hotel now, and is under new management, and during the season some four coachloads of tourists sit down each day to table d'hote lunch in the low-ceilinged parlour. But I am speaking of years ago, when the place was a mere fishing harbour, undiscovered by the guide books.

The old landlord talked, and I hearkened the while we both sat drinking thin ale from earthenware mugs, late one summer's evening, on the bench that runs along the wall just beneath the latticed windows. And during the many pauses, when the old landlord stopped to puff his pipe in silence, and lay in a new stock of breath, there came to us the murmuring voices of the Atlantic; and often, mingled with the pompous roar of the big breakers farther out, we would hear the rippling laugh of some small wave that, maybe, had crept in to listen to the tale the landlord told.

The mistake that Charles Seabohn, Junior partner of the firm of Seabohn & Son, civil engineers of London and Newcastle-upon-Tyne, and Mivanway Evans, youngest daughter of the Rev. Thomas Evans, Pastor of the Presbyterian Church at Bristol, made originally, was marrying too young. Charles Seabohn could hardly have been twenty years of age, and Mivanway could have been little more than seventeen, when they first met upon the cliffs, two miles beyond the Cromlech Arms. Young Charles Seabohn, coming across the village in the course of a walking tour, had decided to spend a day or two exploring the picturesque coast, and Mivanway's father had hired that year a neighbouring farmhouse wherein to spend his summer vacation.

Early one morning--for at twenty one is virtuous, and takes exercise before breakfast--as young Charles Seabohn lay upon the cliffs, watching the white waters coming and going upon the black rocks below, he became aware of a form rising from the waves. The figure was too far off for him to see it clearly, but judging from the costume, it was a female figure, and promptly the mind of Charles, poetically inclined, turned to thoughts of Venus--or Aphrodite, as he, being a gentleman of delicate taste would have preferred to term her. He saw the figure disappear behind a head- land, but still waited. In about ten minutes or a quarter of an hour it reappeared, clothed in the garments of the eighteen- sixties, and came towards him. Hidden from sight himself behind a group of rocks, he could watch it at his leisure, ascending the steep path from the beach, and an exceedingly sweet and dainty figure it would have appeared, even to eyes less susceptible than those of twenty. Sea-water--I stand open to correction--is not, I believe, considered anything of a substitute for curling tongs, but to the hair of the youngest Miss Evans it had given an additional and most fascinating wave. Nature's red and white had been most cunningly laid on, and the large childish eyes seemed to be searching the world for laughter, with which to feed a pair of delicious, pouting lips. Charles's upturned face, petrified into admiration, was just the sort of thing for which they were on the look-out. A startled "Oh!" came from the slightly parted lips, followed by the merriest of laughs, which in its turn was suddenly stopped by a deep blush. Then the youngest Miss Evans looked offended, as though the whole affair had been Charles's fault, which is the way of women. And Charles, feeling himself guilty under that stern gaze of indignation, rose awkwardly and apologised meekly, whether for being on the cliffs at all or for having got up too early, he would have been unable to explain.

The youngest Miss Evans graciously accepted the apology thus tendered with a bow, and passed on, and Charles stood staring after her till the valley gathered her into its spreading arms and hid her from his view.

That was the beginning of all things. I am speaking of the Universe as viewed from the standpoint of Charles and Mivanway.

Six months later they were man and wife, or perhaps it would be more correct to say boy and wifelet. Seabohn senior counselled delay, but was overruled by the impatience of his junior partner. The Reverend Mr. Evans, in common with most theologians, possessed a goodly supply of unmarried daughters, and a limited income. Personally he saw no necessity for postponement of the marriage.

The month's honeymoon was spent in the New Forest. That was a mistake to begin with. The New Forest in February is depressing, and they had chosen the loneliest spot they could find. A fortnight in Paris or Rome would have been more helpful. As yet they had nothing to talk about except love, and that they had been talking and writing about steadily all through the winter. On the tenth morning Charles yawned, and Mivanway had a quiet half-hour's cry about it in her own room. On the sixteenth evening, Mivanway, feeling irritable, and wondering why (as though fifteen damp, chilly days in the New Forest were not sufficient to make any woman irritable), requested Charles not to disarrange her hair; and Charles, speechless with astonishment, went out into the garden, and swore before all the stars that he would never caress Mivanway's hair again as long as he lived.

One supreme folly they had conspired to commit, even before the commencement of the honeymoon. Charles, after the manner of very young lovers, had earnestly requested Mivanway to impose upon him some task. He desired to do something great and noble to show his devotion. Dragons was the thing he had in mind, though he may not have been aware of it. Dragons also, no doubt, flitted through Mivanway's brain, but unfortunately for lovers the supply of dragons has lapsed. Mivanway, liking the conceit, however, thought over it, and then decided that Charles must give up smoking. She had discussed the matter with her favourite sister, and that was the only thing the girls could think of. Charles's face fell. He suggested some more Herculean labour, some sacrifice more worthy to lay at Mivanway's feet. But Mivanway had spoken. She might think of some other task, but the smoking prohibition would, in any case, remain. She dismissed the subject with a pretty hauteur that would have graced Marie Antoinette.

Thus tobacco, the good angel of all men, no longer came each day to teach Charles patience and amiability, and he fell into the ways of short temper and selfishness.

They took up their residence in a suburb of Newcastle, and this was also unfortunate for them, because there the society was scanty and middle-aged; and, in consequence, they had still to depend much upon their own resources. They knew little of life, less of each other, and nothing at all of themselves. Of course they quarrelled, and each quarrel left the wound a little more raw. No kindly, experienced friend was at hand to laugh at them. Mivanway would write down all her sorrows in a bulky diary, which made her feel worse; so that before she had written for ten minutes her pretty, unwise head would drop upon her dimpled arm, and the book-- the proper place for which was behind the fire--would become damp with her tears; and Charles, his day's work done and the clerks gone, would linger in his dingy office and hatch trifles into troubles.

The end came one evening after dinner, when, in the heat of a silly squabble, Charles boxed Mivanway's ears. That was very ungentlemanly conduct, and he was heartily ashamed of himself the moment he had done it, which was right and proper for him to be. The only excuse to be urged on his behalf is that girls sufficiently pretty to have been spoilt from childhood by everyone about them can at times be intensely irritating. Mivanway rushed up to her room, and locked herself in. Charles flew after her to apologise, but only arrived in time to have the door slammed in his face.

It had only been the merest touch. A boy's muscles move quicker than his thoughts. But to Mivanway it was a blow. This was what it had come to! This was the end of a man's love!

She spent half the night writing in the precious diary, with the result that in the morning she came down feeling more bitter than she had gone up. Charles had walked the streets of Newcastle all night, and that had not done him any good. He met her with an apology combined with an excuse, which was bad tactics. Mivanway, of course, fastened upon the excuse, and the quarrel recommenced. She mentioned that she hated him; he hinted that she had never loved him, and she retorted that he had never loved her. Had there been anybody by to knock their heads together and suggest breakfast, the thing might have blown over, but the combined effect of a sleepless night and an empty stomach upon each proved disastrous. Their words came poisoned from their brains, and each believed they meant what they said. That afternoon Charles sailed from Hull, on a ship bound for the Cape, and that evening Mivanway arrived at the paternal home in Bristol with two trunks and the curt information that she and Charles had separated for ever. The next morning both thought of a soft speech to say to the other, but the next morning was just twenty-four hours too late.

Eight days afterwards Charles's ship was run down in a fog, near the coast of Portugal, and every soul on board was supposed to have perished. Mivanway read his name among the list of lost; the child died within her, and she knew herself for a woman who had loved deeply, and will not love again.

Good luck intervening, however, Charles and one other man were rescued by a small trading vessel, and landed in Algiers. There Charles learnt of his supposed death, and the idea occurred to him to leave the report uncontradicted. For one thing, it solved a problem that had been troubling him. He could trust his father to see to it that his own small fortune, with possibly something added, was handed over to Mivanway, and she would be free if she wished to marry again. He was convinced that she did not care for him, and that she had read of his death with a sense of relief. He would make a new life for himself, and forget her.

He continued his journey to the Cape, and once there he soon gained for himself an excellent position. The colony was young, engineers were welcome, and Charles knew his business. He found the life interesting and exciting. The rough, dangerous up-country work suited him, and the time passed swiftly.

But in thinking he would forget Mivanway, he had not taken into consideration his own character, which at bottom was a very gentlemanly character. Out on the lonely veldt he found himself dreaming of her. The memory of her pretty face and merry laugh came back to him at all hours. Occasionally he would curse her roundly, but that only meant that he was sore because of the thought of her; what he was really cursing was himself and his own folly. Softened by the distance, her quick temper, her very petulance became mere added graces; and if we consider women as human beings and not as angels, it was certainly a fact that he had lost a very sweet and lovable woman. Ah! if she only were by his side now--now that he was a man capable of appreciating her, and not a foolish, selfish boy. This thought would come to him as he sat smoking at the door of his tent, and then he would regret that the stars looking down upon him were not the same stars that were watching her, it would have made him feel nearer to her. For, though young people may not credit it, one grows more sentimental as one grows older; at least, some of us do, and they perhaps not the least wise.

One night he had a vivid dream of her. She came to him and held out her hand, and he took it, and they said good-bye to one another.

They were standing on the cliff where he had first met her, and one of them was going upon a long journey, though he was not sure which.

In the towns men laugh at dreams, but away from civilisation we listen more readily to the strange tales that Nature whispers to us. Charles Seabohn recollected this dream when he awoke in the morning.

"She is dying," he said, "and she has come to wish me good-bye."

He made up his mind to return to England at once; perhaps if he made haste he would be in time to kiss her. But he could not start that day, for work was to be done; and Charles Seabohn, lover though he still was, had grown to be a man, and knew that work must not be neglected even though the heart may be calling. So for a day or two he stayed, and on the third night he dreamed of Mivanway again, and this time she lay within the little chapel at Bristol where, on Sunday mornings, he had often sat with her. He heard her father's voice reading the burial service over her, and the sister she had loved best was sitting beside him, crying softly. Then Charles knew that there was no need for him to hasten. So he remained to finish his work. That done, he would return to England. He would like again to stand upon the cliffs, above the little Cornish village, where they had first met.

Thus a few months later Charles Seabohn, or Charles Denning, as he called himself, aged and bronzed, not easily recognisable by those who had not known him well, walked into the Cromlech Arms, as six years before he had walked in with his knapsack on his back, and asked for a room, saying he would be stopping in the village for a short while.

In the evening he strolled out and made his way to the cliffs. It was twilight when he reached the place of rocks to which the fancy-loving Cornish folk had given the name of the Witches' Cauldron. It was from this spot that he had first watched Mivanway coming to him from the sea.

He took the pipe from his mouth, and leaning against a rock, whose rugged outline seemed fashioned into the face of an old friend, gazed down the narrow pathway now growing indistinct in the dim light. And as he gazed the figure of Mivanway came slowly up the pathway from the sea, and paused before him.

He felt no fear. He had half expected it. Her coming was the complement of his dreams. She looked older and graver than he remembered her, but for that the face was the sweeter.

He wondered if she would speak to him, but she only looked at him with sad eyes; and he stood there in the shadow of the rocks without moving, and she passed on into the twilight.

Had he on his return cared to discuss the subject with his landlord, had he even shown himself a ready listener--for the old man loved to gossip--he might have learnt that a young widow lady named Mrs. Charles Seabohn, accompanied by an unmarried sister, had lately come to reside in the neighbourhood, having, upon the death of a former tenant, taken the lease of a small farmhouse sheltered in the valley a mile beyond the village, and that her favourite evening's walk was to the sea and back by the steep footway leading past the Witches' Cauldron.

Had he followed the figure of Mivanway into the valley, he would have known that out of sight of the Witches' Cauldron it took to running fast till it reached a welcome door, and fell panting into the arms of another figure that had hastened out to meet it.

"My dear," said the elder woman, "you are trembling like a leaf. What has happened?"

"I have seen him," answered Mivanway.

"Seen whom?"

"Charles."

"Charles!" repeated the other, looking at Mivanway as though she thought her mad.

"His spirit, I mean," explained Mivanway, in an awed voice. "It was standing in the shadow of the rocks, in the exact spot where we first met. It looked older and more careworn; but, oh! Margaret, so sad and reproachful."

"My dear," said her sister, leading her in, "you are overwrought. I wish we had never come back to this house."

"Oh! I was not frightened," answered Mivanway, "I have been

expecting it every evening. I am so glad it came. Perhaps it will come again, and I can ask it to forgive me."

So next night Mivanway, though much against her sister's wishes and advice, persisted in her usual walk, and Charles at the same twilight hour started from the inn.

Again Mivanway saw him standing in the shadow of the rocks. Charles had made up his mind that if the thing happened again he would speak, but when the silent figure of Mivanway, clothed in the fading light, stopped and gazed at him, his will failed him.

That it was the spirit of Mivanway standing before him he had not the faintest doubt. One may dismiss other people's ghosts as the phantasies of a weak brain, but one knows one's own to be realities, and Charles for the last five years had mingled with a people whose dead dwell about them. Once, drawing his courage around him, he made to speak, but as he did so the figure of Mivanway shrank from him, and only a sigh escaped his lips, and hearing that the figure of Mivanway turned and again passed down the path into the valley, leaving Charles gazing after it.

But the third night both arrived at the trysting spot with determination screwed up to the sticking point.

Charles was the first to speak. As the figure of Mivanway came towards him, with its eyes fixed sadly on him, he moved from the shadow of the rocks, and stood before it.

"Mivanway!" he said.

"Charles!" replied the figure of Mivanway. Both spoke in an awed whisper suitable to the circumstances, and each stood gazing sorrowfully upon the other.

"Are you happy?" asked Mivanway.

The question strikes one as somewhat farcical, but it must be remembered that Mivanway was the daughter of a Gospeller of the old school, and had been brought up to beliefs that were not then out of date.

"As happy as I deserve to be," was the sad reply, and the answer-- the inference was not complimentary to Charles's deserts--struck a chill to Mivanway's heart.

"How could I be happy having lost you?" went on the voice of Charles.

Now this speech fell very pleasantly upon Mivanway's ears. In the first place it relieved her of her despair regarding Charles's future. No doubt his present suffering was keen, but there was hope for him. Secondly, it was a decidedly "pretty" speech for a ghost, and I am not at all sure that Mivanway was the kind of woman to be averse to a little mild flirtation with the spirit of Charles.

"Can you forgive me?" asked Mivanway.

"Forgive YOU!" replied Charles, in a tone of awed astonishment. "Can you forgive me? I was a brute--a fool--I was not worthy to love you."

A most gentlemanly spirit it seemed to be. Mivanway forgot to be afraid of it.

"We were both to blame," answered Mivanway. But this time there was less submission in her tones. "But I was the most at fault. I was a petulant child. I did not know how deeply I loved you."

"You loved me!" repeated the voice of Charles, and the voice lingered over the words as though it found them sweet.

"Surely you never doubted it," answered the voice of Mivanway. "I never ceased to love you. I shall love you always and ever."

The figure of Charles sprang forward as though it would clasp the ghost of Mivanway in its arms, but halted a step or two off.

"Bless me before you go," he said, and with uncovered head the figure of Charles knelt to the figure of Mivanway.

Really, ghosts could be exceedingly nice when they liked. Mivanway bent graciously towards her shadowy suppliant, and, as she did so, her eye caught sight of something on the grass beside it, and that something was a well-coloured meerschaum pipe. There was no mistaking it for anything else, even in that treacherous light; it lay glistening where Charles, in falling upon his knees had jerked it from his breast-pocket.

Charles, following Mivanway's eyes, saw it also, and the memory of the prohibition against smoking came back to him.

Without stopping to consider the futility of the action--nay, the direct confession implied thereby--he instinctively grabbed at the pipe, and rammed it back into his pocket; and then an avalanche of mingled understanding and bewilderment, fear and joy, swept Mivanway's brain before it. She felt she must do one of two things, laugh or scream and go on screaming, and she laughed. Peal after peal of laughter she sent echoing among the rocks, and Charles springing to his feet was just in time to catch her as she fell forward a dead weight into his arms.

Ten minutes later the eldest Miss Evans, hearing heavy footsteps, went to the door. She saw what she took to be the spirit of Charles Seabohn, staggering under the weight of the lifeless body of Mivanway, and the sight not unnaturally alarmed her. Charles's suggestion of brandy, however, sounded human, and the urgent need of attending to Mivanway kept her mind from dwelling upon problems tending towards insanity.

Charles carried Mivanway to her room, and laid her upon the bed.

"I'll leave her with you," he whispered to the eldest Miss Evans. "It will be better for her not to see me until she is quite recovered. She has had a shock."

Charles waited in the dark parlour for what seemed to him an exceedingly long time. But at last the eldest Miss Evans returned.

"She's all right now," were the welcome words he heard.

"I'll go and see her," he said.

"But she's in bed," exclaimed the scandalised Miss Evans.

And then as Charles only laughed, "Oh, ah--yes, I suppose--of course," she added.

And the eldest Miss Evans, left alone, sat down and wrestled with the conviction that she was dreaming.

PORTRAIT OF A LADY

My work pressed upon me, but the louder it challenged me--such is the heart of the timid fighter--the less stomach I felt for the contest. I wrestled with it in my study, only to be driven to my books. I walked out to meet it in the streets, only to seek shelter from it in music-hall or theatre. Thereupon it waxed importunate and over-bearing, till the shadow of it darkened all my doings. The thought of it sat beside me at the table, and spoilt my appetite. The memory of it followed me abroad, and stood between me and my friends, so that all talk died upon my lips, and I moved among men as one ghost-ridden.

Then the throbbing town, with its thousand distracting voices, grew maddening to me. I felt the need of converse with solitude, that master and teacher of all the arts, and I bethought me of the Yorkshire Wolds, where a man may walk all day, meeting no human creature, hearing no voice but the curlew's cry; where, lying prone upon the sweet grass, he may feel the pulsation of the earth, travelling at its eleven hundred miles a minute through the ether. So one morning I bundled many things, some needful, more needless, into a bag, hurrying lest somebody or something should happen to stay me, and that night I lay in a small northern town that stands upon the borders of smokedom at the gate of the great moors; and at seven the next morning I took my seat beside a one-eyed carrier behind an ancient piebald mare. The one-eyed carrier cracked his whip, the piebald horse jogged forward. The nineteenth century, with its turmoil, fell away behind us; the distant hills, creeping nearer, swallowed us up, and we became but a moving speck upon the face of the quiet earth.

Late in the afternoon we arrived at a village, the memory of which had been growing in my mind. It lies in the triangle formed by the sloping walls of three great fells, and not even the telegraph wire has reached it yet, to murmur to it whispers of the restless world- -or had not at the time of which I write. Nought disturbs it save, once a day, the one-eyed carrier--if he and his piebald mare have not yet laid their ancient bones to rest--who, passing through, leaves a few letters and parcels to be called for by the people of the scattered hill-farms round about. It is the meeting-place of two noisy brooks. Through the sleepy days and the hushed nights, one hears them ever chattering to themselves as children playing alone some game of make-believe. Coming from their far-off homes among the hills, they mingle their waters here, and journey on in company, and then their converse is more serious, as becomes those who have joined hands and are moving onward towards life together. Later they reach sad, weary towns, black beneath a never-lifted pall of smoke, where day and night the clang of iron drowns all human voices, where the children play with ashes, where the men and women have dull, patient faces; and so on, muddy and stained, to the deep sea that ceaselessly calls to them. Here, however, their waters are fresh and clear, and their passing makes the only stir that the valley has ever known. Surely, of all peaceful places, this was the one where a tired worker might find strength.

My one-eyed friend had suggested I should seek lodgings at the house of one Mistress Cholmondley, a widow lady, who resided with her only daughter in the white-washed cottage that is the last house in the village, if you take the road that leads over Coll Fell.

"Tha' can see th' house from here, by reason o' its standing so high above t'others," said the carrier, pointing with his whip. "It's theer or nowhere, aw'm thinking, for folks don't often coom seeking lodgings in these parts."

The tiny dwelling, half smothered in June roses, looked idyllic, and after a lunch of bread and cheese at the little inn I made my way to it by the path that passes through the churchyard. I had conjured up the vision of a stout, pleasant, comfort-radiating woman, assisted by some bright, fresh girl, whose rosy cheeks and sunburnt hands would help me banish from my mind all clogging recollections of the town; and hopeful, I pushed back the half- opened door and entered.

The cottage was furnished with a taste that surprised me, but in themselves my hosts disappointed me. My bustling, comely housewife turned out a wizened, blear-eyed dame. All day long she dozed in her big chair, or crouched with shrivelled hands spread out before the fire. My dream of winsome maidenhood vanished before the reality of a weary-looking, sharp-featured woman of between forty and fifty. Perhaps there had been a time when the listless eyes had sparkled with roguish merriment, when the shrivelled, tight- drawn lips had pouted temptingly; but spinsterhood does not sweeten the juices of a woman, and strong country air, though, like old ale, it is good when taken occasionally, dulls the brain if lived upon. A narrow, uninteresting woman I found her, troubled with a shyness that sat ludicrously upon her age, and that yet failed to save her from the landlady's customary failing of loquacity concerning "better days," together with an irritating, if harmless, affectation of youthfulness.

All other details were, however, most satisfactory; and at the window commanding the road that leads through the valley towards the distant world I settled down to face my work.

But the spirit of industry, once driven forth, returns with coy steps. I wrote for perhaps an hour, and then throwing down my halting pen I looked about the room, seeking distraction. A Chippendale book-case stood against the wall and I strolled over to it. The key was in the lock, and opening its glass doors, I examined the well-filled shelves. They held a curious collection: miscellanies with quaint, glazed bindings; novels and poems; whose authors I had never heard of; old magazines long dead, their very names forgotten;

"keepsakes" and annuals, redolent of an age of vastly pretty sentiments and lavender-coloured silks. On the top shelf, however, was a volume of Keats wedged between a number of the Evangelical Rambler and Young's Night Thoughts, and standing on tip-toe, I sought to draw it from its place.

The book was jambed so tightly that my efforts brought two or three others tumbling about me, covering me with a cloud of fine dust, and to my feet there fell, with a rattle of glass and metal, a small miniature painting, framed in black wood.

I picked it up, and, taking it to the window, examined it. It was the picture of a young girl, dressed in the fashion of thirty years ago--I mean thirty years ago then. I fear it must be nearer fifty, speaking as from now--when our grandmothers wore corkscrew curls, and low-cut bodices that one wonders how they kept from slipping down. The face was beautiful, not merely with the conventional beauty of tiresome regularity and impossible colouring such as one finds in all miniatures, but with soul behind the soft deep eyes. As I gazed, the sweet lips seemed to laugh at me, and yet there lurked a sadness in the smile, as though the artist, in some rare moment, had seen the coming shadow of life across the sunshine of the face. Even my small knowledge of Art told me that the work was clever, and I wondered why it should have lain so long neglected, when as a mere ornament it was valuable. It must have been placed in the book-case years ago by someone, and forgotten.

I replaced it among its dusty companions, and sat down once more to my work. But between me and the fading light came the face of the miniature, and would not be banished. Wherever I turned it looked out at me from the shadows. I am not naturally fanciful, and the work I was engaged upon--the writing of a farcical comedy--was not of the kind to excite the dreamy side of a man's nature. I grew angry with myself, and made a further effort to fix my mind upon the paper in front of me. But my thoughts refused to return from their wanderings. Once, glancing back over my shoulder, I could have sworn I saw the original of the picture sitting in the big chintz-covered chair in the far corner. It was dressed in a faded lilac frock, trimmed with some old lace, and I could not help noticing the beauty of the folded hands, though in the portrait only the head and shoulders had been drawn.

Next morning I had forgotten the incident, but with the lighting of the lamp the memory of it awoke within me, and my interest grew so strong that again I took the miniature from its hiding-place and looked at it.

And then the knowledge suddenly came to me that I knew the face. Where had I seen her, and when? I had met her and spoken to her. The picture smiled at me, as if rallying me on my forgetfulness. I put it back upon its shelf, and sat racking my brains trying to recollect. We had met somewhere--in the country--a long time ago, and had talked of common-place things. To the vision of her clung the scent of roses and the murmuring voices of haymakers. Why had I never seen her again? Why had she passed so completely out of my mind?

My landlady entered to lay my supper, and I questioned her assuming a careless tone. Reason with or laugh at myself as I would, this shadowy memory was becoming a romance to me. It was as though I were talking of some loved, dead friend, even to speak of whom to commonplace people was a sacrilege. I did not want the woman to question me in return.

"Oh, yes," answered my landlady. Ladies had often lodged with her. Sometimes people stayed the whole summer, wandering about the woods and fells, but to her thinking the great hills were lonesome. Some of her lodgers had been young ladies, but she could not remember any of them having impressed her with their beauty. But then it was said women were never a judge of other women. They had come and gone. Few had ever returned, and fresh faces drove out the old.

"You have been letting lodgings for a long time?" I asked. "I suppose it could be fifteen--twenty years ago that strangers to you lived in this room?"

"Longer than that," she said quietly, dropping for the moment all affectation. "We came here from the farm when my father died. He had had losses, and there was but little left. That is twenty- seven years ago now."

I hastened to close the conversation, fearing long-winded recollections of "better days." I have heard such so often from one landlady and another. I had not learnt much. Who was the original of the miniature, how it came to be lying forgotten in the dusty book-case were still mysteries; and with a strange perversity I could not have explained to myself I shrank from putting a direct question.

So two days more passed by. My work took gradually a firmer grip upon my mind, and the face of the miniature visited me less often. But in the evening of the third day, which was a Sunday, a curious thing happened.

I was returning from a stroll, and dusk was falling as I reached the cottage. I had been thinking of my farce, and I was laughing to myself at a situation that seemed to me comical, when, passing the window of my room, I saw looking out the sweet fair face that had become so familiar to me. It stood close to the latticed panes, a slim, girlish figure, clad in the old-fashioned lilac- coloured frock in which I had imagined it on the first night of my arrival, the beautiful hands clasped across the breast, as then they had been folded on the lap. Her eyes were gazing down the road that passes through the village and goes south, but they seemed to be dreaming, not seeing, and the sadness in them struck upon one almost as a cry. I was close to the window, but the hedge screened me, and I remained watching, until, after a minute I suppose, though it appeared longer, the figure drew back into the darkness of the room and disappeared.

I entered, but the room was empty. I called, but no one answered. The uncomfortable suggestion took hold of me that I must be growing a little crazy. All that had gone before I could explain to myself as a mere train of thought, but this time it had come to me suddenly, uninvited, while my thoughts had been busy elsewhere. This thing had appeared not to my brain but to my senses. I am not a believer in ghosts, but I am in the hallucinations of a weak mind, and my own explanation was in consequence not very satisfactory to myself.

I tried to dismiss the incident, but it would not leave me, and later that same evening something else occurred that fixed it still clearer in my thoughts. I had taken out two or three books at random with which to amuse myself, and turning over the leaves of one of them, a volume of verses by some obscure poet, I found its sentimental passages much scored and commented upon in pencil as was common fifty years ago--as may be common now, for your Fleet Street cynic has not altered the world and its ways to quite the extent that he imagines.

One poem in particular had evidently appealed greatly to the reader's sympathies. It was the old, old story of the gallant who woos and rides away, leaving the maiden to weep. The poetry was poor, and at another time its conventionality would have excited only my ridicule. But, reading it in conjunction with the quaint, naive notes scattered about its margins, I felt no inclination to jeer. These hackneyed stories that we laugh at are deep profundities to the many who find in them some shadow of their own sorrows, and she--for it was a woman's handwriting--to whom this book belonged had loved its trite verses, because in them she had read her own heart. This, I told myself, was her story also. A common enough story in life as in literature, but novel to those who live it.

There was no reason for my connecting her with the original of the miniature, except perhaps a subtle relationship between the thin nervous handwriting and the mobile features; yet I felt instinctively they were one and the same, and that I was tracing, link by link, the history of my forgotten friend.

I felt urged to probe further, and next morning while my landlady was clearing away my breakfast things, I fenced round the subject once again.

"By the way," I said, "while I think of it, if I leave any books or papers here behind me, send them on at once. I have a knack of doing that sort of thing. I suppose," I added, "your lodgers often do leave some of their belongings behind them."

It sounded to myself a clumsy ruse. I wondered if she would suspect what was behind it.

"Not often," she answered. "Never that I can remember, except in the case of one poor lady who died here."

I glanced up quickly.

"In this room?" I asked.

My landlady seemed troubled at my tone.

"Well, not exactly in this very room. We carried her upstairs, but she died immediately. She was dying when she came here. I should not have taken her in had I known. So many people are prejudiced against a house where death has occurred, as if there were anywhere it had not. It was not quite fair to us."

I did not speak for a while, and the rattle of the plates and knives continued undisturbed.

"What did she leave here?" I asked at length.

"Oh, just a few books and photographs, and such-like small things that people bring with them to lodgings," was the reply. "Her people promised to send for them, but they never did, and I suppose I forgot them. They were not of any value."

The woman turned as she was leaving the room.

"It won't drive you away, sir, I hope, what I have told you," she said. "It all happened a long while ago."

"Of course not," I answered. "It interested me, that was all." And the woman went out, closing the door behind her.

So here was the explanation, if I chose to accept it. I sat long that morning, wondering to myself whether things I had learnt to laugh at could be after all realities. And a day or two afterwards I made a discovery that confirmed all my vague surmises.

Rummaging through this same dusty book-case, I found in one of the ill-fitting drawers, beneath a heap of torn and tumbled books, a diary belonging to the fifties, stuffed with many letters and shapeless flowers, pressed between stained pages; and there--for the writer of stories, tempted by human documents, is weak--in faded ink, brown and withered like the flowers, I read the story I already knew.

Such a very old story it was, and so conventional. He was an artist--was ever story of this type written where the hero was not an artist?

They had been children together, loving each other without knowing it till one day it was revealed to them. Here is the entry:-

"May 18th.--I do not know what to say, or how to begin. Chris loves me. I have been praying to God to make me worthy of him, and dancing round the room in my bare feet for fear of waking them below. He kissed my hands and clasped them round his neck, saying they were beautiful as the hands of a goddess, and he knelt and kissed them again. I am holding them before me and kissing them myself. I am glad they are so beautiful. O God, why are you so good to me? Help me to be a true wife to him. Help me that I may never give him an instant's pain! Oh, that I had more power of loving, that I might love him better,"--and thus foolish thoughts for many pages, but foolish thoughts of the kind that has kept this worn old world, hanging for so many ages in space, from turning sour.

Later, in February, there is another entry that carries on the story:-

"Chris left this morning. He put a little packet into my hands at the last moment, saying it was the most precious thing he possessed, and that when I looked at it I was to think of him who loved it. Of course I guessed what it was, but I did not open it till I was alone in my room. It is the picture of myself that he has been so secret about, but oh, so beautiful. I wonder if I am really as beautiful as this. But I wish he had not made me look so sad. I am kissing the little lips. I love them, because he loved to kiss them. Oh, sweetheart! it will be long before you kiss them again. Of course it was right for him to go, and I am glad he has been able to manage it. He could not study properly in this quiet country place, and now he will be able to go to Paris and Rome and he will be great. Even the stupid people here see how clever he is. But, oh, it will be so long before I see him again, my love! my king!"

With each letter that comes from him, similar foolish rhapsodies are written down, but these letters of his, I gather, as I turn the pages, grow after a while colder and fewer, and a chill fear that dare not be penned creeps in among the words.

"March 12th. Six weeks and no letter from Chris, and, oh dear! I am so hungry for one, for the last I have almost kissed to pieces. I suppose he will write more often when he gets to London. He is working hard, I know, and it is selfish of me to expect him to write more often, but I would sit up all night for a week rather than miss writing to him. I suppose men are not like that. O God, help me, help me, whatever happens! How foolish I am to-night! He was always careless. I will punish him for it when he comes back, but not very much."

Truly enough a conventional story.

Letters do come from him after that, but apparently they are less and less satisfactory, for the diary grows angry and bitter, and the faded writing is blotted at times with tears. Then towards the end of another year there comes this entry, written in a hand of strange neatness and precision:-

"It is all over now. I am glad it is finished. I have written to him, giving him up. I have told him I have ceased to care for him, and that it is better we should both be free. It is best that way. He would have had to ask me to release him, and that would have given him pain. He was always gentle. Now he will be able to marry her with an easy conscience, and he need never know what I have suffered. She is more fitted for him than I am. I hope he will be happy. I think I have done the right thing."

A few lines follow, left blank, and then the writing is resumed, but in a stronger, more vehement hand.

"Why do I lie to myself? I hate her! I would kill her if I could. I hope she will make him wretched, and that he will come to hate her as I do, and that she will die! Why did I let them persuade me to send that lying letter? He will show it to her, and she will see through it and laugh at me. I could have held him to his promise; he could not have got out of it.

"What do I care about dignity, and womanliness, and right, and all the rest of the canting words! I want him. I want his kisses and his arms about me. He is mine! He loved me once! I have only given him up because I thought it a fine thing to play the saint. It is only an acted lie. I would rather be evil, and he loved me. Why do I deceive myself? I want him. I care for nothing else at the bottom of my heart--his love, his kisses!"

And towards the end. "My God, what am I saying? Have I no shame, no strength? O God, help me!"

And there the diary closes.

I looked among the letters lying between the pages of the book. Most of them were signed simply "Chris." or "Christopher." But one gave his name in full, and it was a name I know well as that of a famous man, whose hand I have often shaken. I thought of his hard-featured, handsome wife, and of his great chill place, half house, half exhibition, in Kensington, filled constantly with its smart, chattering set, among whom he seemed always to be the uninvited guest; of his weary face and bitter tongue. And thinking thus there rose up before me the sweet, sad face of the woman of the miniature, and, meeting her eyes as she smiled at me from out of the shadows, I looked at her my wonder.

I took the miniature from its shelf. There would be no harm now in learning her name. So I stood with it in my hand till a little later my landlady entered to lay the cloth.

"I tumbled this out of your book-case," I said, "in reaching down some books. It is someone I know, someone I have met, but I cannot think where. Do you know who it is?"

The woman took it from my hand, and a faint flush crossed her withered face. "I had lost it," she answered. "I never thought of looking there. It's a portrait of myself, painted years ago, by a friend."

I looked from her to the miniature, as she stood among the shadows, with the lamplight falling on her face, and saw her perhaps for the first time.

"How stupid of me," I answered. "Yes, I see the likeness now."

THE MAN WHO WOULD MANAGE

It has been told me by those in a position to know--and I can believe it--that at nineteen months of age he wept because his grandmother would not allow him to feed her with a spoon, and that at three and a half he was fished, in an exhausted condition, out of the water-butt, whither he had climbed for the purpose of teaching a frog to swim.

Two years later he permanently injured his left eye, showing the cat how to carry kittens without hurting them, and about the same period was dangerously stung by a bee while conveying it from a flower where, as it seemed to him, it was only wasting its time, to one more rich in honey-making properties.

His desire was always to help others. He would spend whole mornings explaining to elderly hens how to hatch eggs, and would give up an afternoon's black-berrying to sit at home and crack nuts for his pet squirrel. Before he was seven he would argue with his mother upon the management of children, and reprove his father for the way he was bringing him up.

As a child nothing could afford him greater delight than "minding" other children, or them less. He would take upon himself this harassing duty entirely of his own accord, without hope of reward or gratitude. It was immaterial to him whether the other children were older than himself or younger, stronger or weaker, whenever and wherever he found them he set to work to "mind" them. Once, during a school treat, piteous cries were heard coming from a distant part of the wood, and upon search being made, he was discovered prone upon the ground, with a cousin of his, a boy twice his own weight, sitting upon him and steadily whacking him. Having rescued him, the teacher said:

"Why don't you keep with the little boys? What are you doing along with him?"

"Please, sir," was the answer, "I was minding him."

He would have "minded" Noah if he had got hold of him.

He was a good-natured lad, and at school he was always willing for the whole class to copy from his slate--indeed he would urge them to do so. He meant it kindly, but inasmuch as his answers were invariably quite wrong--with a distinctive and inimitable wrongness peculiar to himself--the result to his followers was eminently unsatisfactory; and with the shallowness of youth that, ignoring motives, judges solely from results, they would wait for him outside and punch him.

All his energies went to the instruction of others, leaving none for his own purposes. He would take callow youths to his chambers and teach them to box.

"Now, try and hit me on the nose," he would say, standing before them in an attitude of defence. "Don't be afraid. Hit as hard as ever you can."

And they would do it. And so soon as he had recovered from his surprise, and a little lessened the bleeding, he would explain to them how they had done it all wrong, and how easily he could have stopped the blow if they had only hit him properly.

Twice at golf he lamed himself for over a week, showing a novice how to "drive"; and at cricket on one occasion I remember seeing his middle stump go down like a ninepin just as he was explaining to the bowler how to get the balls in straight. After which he had a long argument with the umpire as to whether he was in or out.

He has been known, during a stormy Channel passage, to rush excitedly upon the bridge in order to inform the captain that he had "just seen a light about two miles away to the left"; and if he is on the top of an omnibus he generally sits beside the driver, and points out to him the various obstacles likely to impede their progress.

It was upon an omnibus that my own personal acquaintanceship with him began. I was sitting behind two ladies when the conductor came up to collect fares. One of them handed him a sixpence telling him to take to Piccadilly Circus, which was twopence.

"No," said the other lady to her friend, handing the man a shilling, "I owe you sixpence, you give me fourpence and I'll pay for the two."

The conductor took the shilling, punched two twopenny tickets, and then stood trying to think it out.

"That's right," said the lady who had spoken last, "give my friend fourpence."

The conductor did so.

"Now you give that fourpence to me."

The friend handed it to her.

"And you," she concluded to the conductor, "give me eightpence, then we shall be all right."

The conductor doled out to her the eightpence--the sixpence he had taken from the first lady, with a penny and two halfpennies out of his own bag--distrustfully, and retired, muttering something about his duties not including those of a lightning calculator.

"Now," said the elder lady to the younger, "I owe you a shilling."

I deemed the incident closed, when suddenly a florid gentleman on the opposite seat called out in stentorian tones:-

"Hi, conductor! you've cheated these ladies out of fourpence."

"'Oo's cheated 'oo out 'o fourpence?" replied the indignant conductor from the top of the steps, "it was a twopenny fare."

"Two twopences don't make eightpence," retorted the florid gentleman hotly. "How much did you give the fellow, my dear?" he asked, addressing the first of the young ladies.

"I gave him sixpence," replied the lady, examining her purse. "And then I gave you fourpence, you know," she added, addressing her companion.

"That's a dear two pen'oth," chimed in a common-looking man on the seat behind.

"Oh, that's impossible, dear," returned the other, "because I owed you sixpence to begin with."

"But I did," persisted the first lady.

"You gave me a shilling," said the conductor, who had returned, pointing an accusing forefinger at the elder of the ladies.

The elder lady nodded.

"And I gave you sixpence and two pennies, didn't I?"

The lady admitted it.

"An' I give 'er"--he pointed towards the younger lady--"fourpence, didn't I?"

"Which I gave you, you know, dear," remarked the younger lady.

"Blow me if it ain't ME as 'as been cheated out of the fourpence," cried the conductor.

"But," said the florid gentleman, "the other lady gave you sixpence."

"Which I give to 'er," replied the conductor, again pointing the finger of accusation at the elder lady. "You can search my bag if yer like. I ain't got a bloomin' sixpence on me."

By this time everybody had forgotten what they had done, and contradicted themselves and one another. The florid man took it upon himself to put everybody right, with the result that before Piccadilly Circus was reached three passengers had threatened to report the conductor for unbecoming language. The conductor had called a policeman and had taken the names and addresses of the two ladies, intending to sue them for the fourpence (which they wanted to pay, but which the florid man would not allow them to do); the younger lady had become convinced that the elder lady had meant to cheat her, and the elder lady was in tears.

The florid gentleman and myself continued to Charing Cross Station. At the booking office window it transpired that we were bound for the same suburb, and we journeyed down together. He talked about the fourpence all the way.

At my gate we shook hands, and he was good enough to express delight at the discovery that we were near neighbours. What attracted him to myself I failed to understand, for he had bored me considerably, and I had, to the best of my ability, snubbed him. Subsequently I learned that it was a peculiarity of his to be charmed with anyone who did not openly insult him.

Three days afterwards he burst into my study unannounced--he appeared to regard himself as my bosom friend--and asked me to forgive him for not having called sooner, which I did.

"I met the postman as I was coming along," he said, handing me a blue envelope, "and he gave me this, for you."

I saw it was an application for the water-rate.

"We must make a stand against this," he continued. "That's for water to the 29th September. You've no right to pay it in June."

I replied to the effect that water-rates had to be paid, and that it seemed to me immaterial whether they were paid in June or September.

"That's not it," he answered, "it's the principle of the thing. Why should you pay for water you have never had? What right have they to bully you into paying what you don't owe?"

He was a fluent talker, and I was ass enough to listen to him. By the end of half an hour he had persuaded me that the question was bound up with the inalienable rights of man, and that if I paid that fourteen and tenpence in June instead of in September, I should be unworthy of the privileges my forefathers had fought and died to bestow upon me.

He told me the company had not a leg to stand upon, and at his instigation I sat down and wrote an insulting letter to the chairman.

The secretary replied that, having regard to the attitude I had taken up, it would be incumbent upon themselves to treat it as a test case, and presumed that my solicitors would accept service on my behalf.

When I showed him this letter he was delighted.

"You leave it to me," he said, pocketing the correspondence, "and we'll teach them a lesson."

I left it to him. My only excuse is that at the time I was immersed in the writing of what in those days was termed a comedy-drama. The little sense I possessed must, I suppose, have been absorbed by the play.

The magistrate's decision somewhat damped my ardour, but only inflamed his zeal. Magistrates, he said, were muddle-headed old fogies. This was a matter for a judge.

The judge was a kindly old gentleman, and said that bearing in mind the unsatisfactory wording of the sub-clause, he did not think he could allow the company their costs, so that, all told, I got off for something under fifty pounds, inclusive of the original fourteen and tenpence.

Afterwards our friendship waned, but living as we did in the same outlying suburb, I was bound to see a good deal of him; and to hear more.

At parties of all kinds he was particularly prominent, and on such occasions, being in his most good-natured mood, was most to be dreaded. No human being worked harder for the enjoyment of others, or produced more universal wretchedness.

One Christmas afternoon, calling upon a friend, I found some fourteen or fifteen elderly ladies and gentlemen trotting solemnly round a row of chairs in the centre of the drawing-room while Poppleton played the piano. Every now and then Poppleton would suddenly cease, and everyone would drop wearily into the nearest chair, evidently glad of a rest; all but one, who would thereupon creep quietly away, followed by the envying looks of those left behind. I stood by the door watching the weird scene. Presently an escaped player came towards me, and I enquired of him what the ceremony was supposed to signify.

"Don't ask me," he answered grumpily. "Some of Poppleton's damned tomfoolery." Then he added savagely, "We've got to play forfeits after this."

The servant was still waiting a favourable opportunity to announce me. I gave her a shilling not to, and got away unperceived.

After a satisfactory dinner, he would suggest an impromptu dance, and want you to roll up mats, or help him move the piano to the other end of the room.

He knew enough round games to have started a small purgatory of his own. Just as you were in the middle of an interesting discussion, or a delightful tete-a-tete with a pretty woman, he would swoop down upon you with: "Come along, we're going to play literary consequences," and dragging you to the table, and putting a piece of paper and a pencil before you, would tell you to write a description of your favourite heroine in fiction, and would see that you did it.

He never spared himself. It was always he who would volunteer to escort the old ladies to the station, and who would never leave them until he had seen them safely into the wrong train. He it was who would play "wild beasts" with the children, and frighten them into fits that would last all night.

So far as intention went, he was the kindest man alive. He never visited poor sick persons without taking with him in his pocket some little delicacy calculated to disagree with them and make them worse. He arranged yachting excursions for bad sailors, entirely at his own expense, and seemed to regard their subsequent agonies as ingratitude.

He loved to manage a wedding. Once he planned matters so that the bride arrived at the altar three-quarters of an hour before the groom, which led to unpleasantness upon a day that should have been filled only with joy, and once he forgot the clergyman. But he was always ready to admit when he made a mistake.

At funerals, also, he was to the fore, pointing out to the grief-stricken relatives how much better it was for all concerned that the corpse was dead, and expressing a pious hope that they would soon join it.

The chiefest delight of his life, however, was to be mixed up in other people's domestic quarrels. No domestic quarrel for miles round was complete without him. He generally came in as mediator, and finished as leading witness for the appellant.

As a journalist or politician his wonderful grasp of other people's business would have won for him esteem. The error he made was working it out in practice.

THE MAN WHO LIVED FOR OTHERS

The first time we met, to speak, he was sitting with his back against a pollard willow, smoking a clay pipe. He smoked it very slowly, but very conscientiously. After each whiff he removed the pipe from his mouth and fanned away the smoke with his cap.

"Feeling bad?" I asked from behind a tree, at the same time making ready for a run, big boys' answers to small boys' impertinences being usually of the nature of things best avoided.

To my surprise and relief--for at second glance I perceived I had under-estimated the length of his legs--he appeared to regard the question as a natural and proper one, replying with unaffected candour, "Not yet."

My desire became to comfort him--a sentiment I think he understood and was grateful for. Advancing into the open, I sat down over against him, and watched him for a while in silence. Presently he said:-

"Have you ever tried drinking beer?"

I admitted I had not.

"Oh, it is beastly stuff," he rejoined with an involuntary shudder.

Rendered forgetful of present trouble by bitter recollection of the past, he puffed away at his pipe carelessly and without judgment.

"Do you often drink it?" I inquired.

"Yes," he replied gloomily; "all we fellows in the fifth form drink beer and smoke pipes."

A deeper tinge of green spread itself over his face.

He rose suddenly and made towards the hedge. Before he reached it, however, he stopped and addressed me, but without turning round.

"If you follow me, young 'un, or look, I'll punch your head," he said swiftly, and disappeared with a gurgle.

He left at the end of the terms and I did not see him again until we were both young men. Then one day I ran against him in Oxford Street, and he asked me to come and spend a few days with his people in Surrey.

I found him wan-looking and depressed, and every now and then he sighed. During a walk across the common he cheered up considerably, but the moment we got back to the house door he seemed to recollect himself, and began to sigh again. He ate no dinner whatever, merely sipping a glass of wine and crumbling a piece of bread. I was troubled at noticing this, but his relatives--a maiden aunt, who kept house, two elder sisters, and a weak-eyed female cousin who had left her husband behind her in India--were evidently charmed. They glanced at each other, and nodded and smiled. Once in a fit of abstraction he swallowed a bit of crust, and immediately they all looked pained and surprised.

In the drawing-room, under cover of a sentimental song, sung by the female cousin, I questioned his aunt on the subject.

"What's the matter with him?" I said. "Is he ill?"

The old lady chuckled.

"You'll be like that one day," she whispered gleefully.

"When," I asked, not unnaturally alarmed.

"When you're in love," she answered.

"Is HE in love?" I inquired after a pause.

"Can't you see he is?" she replied somewhat scornfully.

I was a young man, and interested in the question.

"Won't he ever eat any dinner till he's got over it?" I asked.

She looked round sharply at me, but apparently decided that I was only foolish.

"You wait till your time comes," she answered, shaking her curls at me. "You won't care much about your dinner--not if you are REALLY in love."

In the night, about half-past eleven, I heard, as I thought, footsteps in the passage, and creeping to the door and opening it I saw the figure of my friend in dressing-gown and slippers, vanishing down the stairs. My idea was that, his brain weakened by trouble, he had developed sleep-walking tendencies. Partly out of curiosity, partly to watch over him, I slipped on a pair of trousers and followed him.

He placed his candle on the kitchen table and made a bee-line for the pantry door, from where he subsequently emerged with two pounds of cold beef on a plate and about a quart of beer in a jug; and I came away, leaving him fumbling for pickles.

I assisted at his wedding, where it seemed to me he endeavoured to display more ecstasy than it was possible for any human being to feel; and fifteen months later, happening to catch sight of an advertisement in the births column of The Times, I called on my way home from the City to congratulate him. He was pacing up and down the passage with his hat on, pausing at intervals to partake of an uninviting-looking meal, consisting of a cold mutton chop and a glass of lemonade, spread out upon a chair. Seeing that the cook and the housemaid were wandering about the house evidently bored for want of something to do, and that the dining-room, where he would have been much more out of the way, was empty and quite in order, I failed at first to understand the reason for his deliberate choice of discomfort. I, however, kept my reflections to myself, and inquired after the mother and child.

"Couldn't be better," he replied with a groan. "The doctor said he'd never had a more satisfactory case in all his experience."

"Oh, I'm glad to hear that," I answered; "I was afraid you'd been worrying yourself."

"Worried!" he exclaimed. "My dear boy, I don't know whether I'm standing on my head or my heels" (he gave one that idea). "This is the first morsel of food that's passed my lips for twenty-four hours."

At this moment the nurse appeared at the top of the stairs. He flew towards her, upsetting the lemonade in his excitement.

"What is it?" he asked hoarsely. "Is it all right?"

The old lady glanced from him to his cold chop, and smiled approvingly.

"They're doing splendidly," she answered, patting him on the shoulder in a motherly fashion. "Don't you worry."

"I can't help it, Mrs. Jobson," he replied, sitting down upon the bottom stair, and leaning his head against the banisters.

"Of course you can't," said Mrs. Jobson admiringly; "and you wouldn't be much of a man if you could." Then it was borne in upon me why he wore his hat, and dined off cold chops in the passage.

The following summer they rented a picturesque old house in Berkshire, and invited me down from a Saturday to Monday. Their place was near the river, so I slipped a suit of flannels in my bag, and on the Sunday morning I came down in them. He met me in the garden. He was dressed in a frock coat and a white waistcoat; and I noticed that he kept looking at me out of the corner of his eye, and that he seemed to have a trouble on his mind. The first breakfast bell rang, and then he said, "You haven't got any proper clothes with you, have you?"

"Proper clothes!" I exclaimed, stopping in some alarm. "Why, has anything given way?"

"No, not that," he explained. "I mean clothes to go to church in."

"Church," I said. "You're surely not going to church a fine day like this? I made sure you'd be playing tennis, or going on the river. You always used to."

"Yes," he replied, nervously flicking a rose-bush with a twig he had picked up. "You see, it isn't ourselves exactly. Maud and I would rather like to, but our cook, she's Scotch, and a little strict in her notions."

"And does she insist on your going to church every Sunday morning?" I inquired.

"Well," he answered, "she thinks it strange if we don't, and so we generally do, just in the morning--and evening. And then in the afternoon a few of the village girls drop in, and we have a little singing and that sort of thing. I never like hurting anyone's feelings if I can help it."

I did not say what I thought. Instead I said, "I've got that tweed suit I wore yesterday. I can put that on if you like."

He ceased flicking the rose-bush, and knitted his brows. He seemed to be recalling it to his imagination.

"No," he said, shaking his head, "I'm afraid it would shock her. It's my fault, I know," he added, remorsefully. "I ought to have told you."

Then an idea came to him.

"I suppose," he said, "you wouldn't care to pretend you were ill, and stop in bed just for the day?"

I explained that my conscience would not permit my being a party to such deception

"No, I thought you wouldn't," he replied. "I must explain it to her. I think I'll say you've lost your bag. I shouldn't like her to think bad of us."

Later on a fourteenth cousin died, leaving him a large fortune. He purchased an estate in Yorkshire, and became a "county family," and then his real troubles began.

From May to the middle of August, save for a little fly fishing, which generally resulted in his getting his feet wet and catching a cold, life was fairly peaceful; but from early autumn to late spring he found the work decidedly trying. He was a stout man, constitutionally nervous of fire-arms, and a six-hours' tramp with a heavy gun across ploughed fields, in company with a crowd of careless persons who kept blazing away within an inch of other people's noses, harassed and exhausted him. He had to get out of bed at four on chilly October mornings to go cub-hunting, and twice a week throughout the winter--except when a blessed frost brought him a brief respite--he had to ride to hounds. That he usually got off with nothing more serious than mere bruises and slight concussions of the spine, he probably owed to the fortunate circumstances of his being little and fat. At stiff timber he shut his eyes and rode hard; and ten yards from a river he would begin to think about bridges.

Yet he never complained.

"If you are a country gentleman," he would say, "you must behave as a country gentleman, and take the rough with the smooth."

As ill fate would have it a chance speculation doubled his fortune, and it became necessary that he should go into Parliament and start a yacht. Parliament made his head ache, and the yacht made him sick. Notwithstanding, every summer he would fill it with a lot of expensive people who bored him, and sail away for a month's misery in the Mediterranean.

During one cruise his guests built up a highly-interesting gambling scandal. He himself was confined to his cabin at the time, and knew nothing about it; but the Opposition papers, getting hold of the story, referred casually to the yacht as a "floating hell," and The Police News awarded his portrait the place of honour as the chief criminal of the week.

Later on he got into a cultured set, ruled by a thick-lipped undergraduate. His favourite literature had hitherto been of the Corelli and Tit-Bits order, but now he read Meredith and the yellow book, and tried to understand them; and instead of the Gaiety, he subscribed to the Independent Theatre, and fed "his soul," on Dutch Shakespeares. What he liked in art was a pretty girl by a cottage- door with an eligible young man in the background, or a child and a dog doing something funny. They told him these things were wrong and made him buy "Impressions" that stirred his liver to its deepest depths every time he looked at them--green cows on red hills by pink moonlight, or scarlet-haired corpses with three feet of neck.

He said meekly that such seemed to him unnatural, but they answered that nature had nothing to do with the question; that the artist saw things like that, and that whatever an artist saw--no matter in what condition he may have been when he saw it--that was art.

They took him to Wagner festivals and Burne-Jones's private views. They read him all the minor poets. They booked seats for him at all Ibsen's plays. They introduced him into all the most soulful circles of artistic society. His days were one long feast of other people's enjoyments.

One morning I met him coming down the steps of the Arts Club. He looked weary. He was just off to a private view at the New Gallery. In the afternoon he had to attend an amateur performance of "The Cenci," given by the Shelley Society. Then followed three literary and artistic At Homes, a dinner with an Indian nabob who couldn't speak a word of English, "Tristam and Isolde" at Covent Garden Theatre, and a ball at Lord Salisbury's to wind up the day.

I laid my hand upon his shoulder.

"Come with me to Epping Forest," I said. "There's a four-horse brake starts from Charing Cross at eleven. It's Saturday, and there's bound to be a crowd down there. I'll play you a game of skittles, and we will have a shy at the cocoa-nuts. You used to be rather smart at cocoa-nuts. We can have lunch there and be back at seven, dine at the Troc., spend the evening at the Empire, and sup at the Savoy. What do you say?"

He stood hesitating on the steps, a wistful look in his eyes.

His brougham drew up against the curb, and he started as if from a dream.

"My dear fellow," he replied, "what would people say?" And shaking me by the hand, he took his seat, and the footman slammed the door upon him.

A MAN OF HABIT

There were three of us in the smoke-room of the Alexandra--a very good friend of mine, myself, and, in the opposite corner, a shy-looking, unobtrusive man, the editor, as we subsequently learned, of a New York Sunday paper.

My friend and I were discussing habits, good and bad.

"After the first few months," said my friend, "it is no more effort for a man to be a saint than to be a sinner; it becomes a mere matter of habit."

"I know," I interrupted, "it is every whit as easy to spring out of bed the instant you are called as to say 'All Right,' and turn over for just another five minutes' snooze, when you have got into the way of it. It is no more trouble not to swear than to swear, if you make a custom of it. Toast and water is as delicious as champagne, when you have acquired the taste for it. Things are also just as easy the other way about. It is a mere question of making your choice and sticking to it."

He agreed with me.

"Now take these cigars of mine," he said, pushing his open case towards me.

"Thank you," I replied hurriedly, "I'm not smoking this passage."

"Don't be alarmed," he answered, "I meant merely as an argument. Now one of these would make you wretched for a week."

I admitted his premise.

"Very well," he continued. "Now I, as you know, smoke them all day long, and enjoy them. Why? Because I have got into the habit. Years ago, when I was a young man, I smoked expensive Havanas. I found that I was ruining myself. It was absolutely necessary that I should take a cheaper weed. I was living in Belgium at the time, and a friend showed me these. I don't know what they are--probably cabbage leaves soaked in guano; they tasted to me like that at first-- but they were cheap. Buying them by the five hundred, they cost me three a penny. I determined to like them, and started with one a day. It was terrible work, I admit, but as I said to myself, nothing could be worse than the Havanas themselves had been in the beginning. Smoking is an acquired taste, and it must be as easy to learn to like one flavour as another. I persevered and I conquered. Before the year was over I could think of them without loathing, at the end of two I could smoke them without positive discomfort. Now I prefer them to any other brand on the market. Indeed, a good cigar disagrees with me."

I suggested it might have been less painful to have given up smoking altogether.

"I did think of it," he replied, "but a man who doesn't smoke always seems to me bad company. There is something very sociable about smoke."

He leant back and puffed great clouds into the air, filling the small den with an odour suggestive of bilge water and cemeteries.

"Then again," he resumed after a pause, "take my claret. No, you don't like it." (I had not spoken, but my face had evidently betrayed me.) "Nobody does, at least no one I have ever met. Three years ago, when I was living in Hammersmith, we caught two burglars with it. They broke open the sideboard, and swallowed five bottlefuls between them. A policeman found them afterwards, sitting on a doorstep a hundred yards off, the 'swag' beside them in a carpet bag. They were too ill to offer any resistance, and went to the station like lambs, he promising to send the doctor to them the moment they were safe in the cells. Ever since then I have left out a decanterful upon the table every night.

"Well, I like that claret, and it does me good. I come in sometimes dead beat. I drink a couple of glasses, and I'm a new man. I took to it in the first instance for the same reason that I took to the cigars--it was cheap. I have it sent over direct from Geneva, and it costs me six shillings a dozen. How they do it I don't know. I don't want to know. As you may remember, it's fairly heady and there's body in it.

"I knew one man," he continued, "who had a regular Mrs. Caudle of a wife. All day long she talked to him, or at him, or of him, and at night he fell asleep to the rising and falling rhythm of what she thought about him. At last she died, and his friends congratulated him, telling him that now he would enjoy peace. But it was the peace of the desert, and the man did not enjoy it. For two-and- twenty years her voice had filled the house, penetrated through the conservatory, and floated in faint shrilly waves of sound round the garden, and out into the road beyond. The silence now pervading everywhere frightened and disturbed him. The place was no longer home to him. He missed the breezy morning insult, the long winter evening's reproaches beside the flickering fire. At night he could not sleep. For hours he would lie tossing restlessly, his ears aching for the accustomed soothing flow of invective.

"'Ah!' he would cry bitterly to himself, 'it is the old story, we never know the value of a thing until we have lost it.'

"He grew ill. The doctors dosed him with sleeping draughts in vain. At last they told him bluntly that his life depended upon his finding another wife, able and willing to nag him to sleep.

"There were plenty of wives of the type he wanted in the neighbourhood, but the unmarried women were, of necessity, inexperienced, and his health was such that he could not afford the time to train them.

"Fortunately, just as despair was about to take possession of him, a man died in the next parish, literally talked to death, the gossip said, by his wife. He obtained an introduction, and called upon her the day after the funeral. She was a cantankerous old woman, and the wooing was a harassing affair, but his heart was in his work, and before six months were gone he had won her for his own.

"She proved, however, but a poor substitute. The spirit was willing but the flesh was weak. She had neither that command of language nor of wind that had distinguished her rival. From his favourite seat at the bottom of the garden he could not hear her at all, so he had his chair brought up into the conservatory. It was all right for him there so long as she continued to abuse him; but every now and again, just as he was getting comfortably settled down with his pipe and his newspaper, she would suddenly stop.

"He would drop his paper and sit listening, with a troubled, anxious expression.

"'Are you there, dear?' he would call out after a while.

"'Yes, I'm here. Where do you think I am you old fool?' she would gasp back in an exhausted voice.

"His face would brighten at the sound of her words. 'Go on, dear,' he would answer. 'I'm listening. I like to hear you talk.'

"But the poor woman was utterly pumped out, and had not so much as a snort left.

"Then he would shake his head sadly. 'No, she hasn't poor dear Susan's flow,' he would say. 'Ah! what a woman that was!'

"At night she would do her best, but it was a lame and halting performance by comparison. After rating him for little over three-quarters of an hour, she would sink back on the pillow, and want to go to sleep. But he would shake her gently by the shoulder.

"'Yes, dear,' he would say, 'you were speaking about Jane, and the way I kept looking at her during lunch.'

"It's extraordinary," concluded my friend, lighting a fresh cigar, "what creatures of habit we are."

"Very," I replied. "I knew a man who told tall stories till when he told a true one nobody believed it."

"Ah, that was a very sad case," said my friend.

"Speaking of habit," said the unobtrusive man in the corner, "I can tell you a true story that I'll bet my bottom dollar you won't believe."

"Haven't got a bottom dollar, but I'll bet you half a sovereign I do," replied my friend, who was of a sporting turn. "Who shall be judge?"

"I'll take your word for it," said the unobtrusive man, and started straight away.

"He was a Jefferson man, this man I'm going to tell you of," he begun. "He was born in the town, and for forty-seven years he never slept a night outside it. He was a most respectable man--a drysalter from nine to four, and a Presbyterian in his leisure moments. He said that a good life merely meant good habits. He rose at seven, had family prayer at seven-thirty, breakfasted at eight, got to his business at nine, had his horse brought round to the office at four, and rode for an hour, reached home at five, had a bath and a cup of tea, played with and read to the children (he was a domesticated man) till half-past six, dressed and dined at seven, went round to the club and played whist till quarter after ten, home again to evening prayer at ten-thirty, and bed at eleven. For five-and-twenty years he lived that life with never a variation. It worked into his system and became mechanical. The church clocks were set by him. He was used by the local astronomers to check the sun.

"One day a distant connection of his in London, an East Indian Merchant and an ex-Lord Mayor died, leaving him sole legatee and executor. The business was a complicated one and needed management. He determined to leave his son by his first wife, now a young man of twenty-four, in charge at Jefferson, and to establish himself with his second family in England, and look after the East Indian business.

"He set out from Jefferson City on October the fourth, and arrived in London on the seventeenth. He had been ill during the whole of the voyage, and he reached the furnished house he had hired in Bayswater somewhat of a wreck. A couple of days in bed, however, pulled him round, and on the Wednesday evening he announced his intention of going into the City the next day to see to his affairs.

"On the Thursday morning he awoke at one o'clock. His wife told him she had not disturbed him, thinking the sleep would do him good. He admitted that perhaps it had. Anyhow, he felt very well, and he got up and dressed himself. He said he did not like the idea of beginning his first day by neglecting a religious duty, and his wife agreeing with him, they assembled the servants and the children in the dining-room, and had family prayer at half-past one. After which he breakfasted and set off, reaching the City about three.

"His reputation for punctuality had preceded him, and surprise was everywhere expressed at his late arrival. He explained the circumstances, however, and made his appointments for the following day to commence from nine-thirty.

"He remained at the office until late, and then went home. For dinner, usually the chief meal of the day, he could manage to eat only a biscuit and some fruit. He attributed his loss of appetite to want of his customary ride. He was strangely unsettled all the evening. He said he supposed he missed his game of whist, and determined to look about him without loss of time for some quiet, respectable club. At eleven he retired with his wife to bed, but could not sleep. He tossed and turned, and turned and tossed, but grew only more and more wakeful and energetic. A little after midnight an overpowering desire seized him to go and wish the children good-night. He slipped on a dressing-gown and stole into the nursery. He did not intend it, but the opening of the door awoke them, and he was glad. He wrapped them up in the quilt, and, sitting on the edge of the bed, told them moral stories till one o'clock.

"Then he kissed them, bidding them be good and go to sleep; and finding himself painfully hungry, crept downstairs, where in the back kitchen he made a hearty meal off cold game pie and cucumber.

"He retired to bed feeling more peaceful, yet still could not sleep, so lay thinking about his business affairs till five, when he dropped off.

"At one o'clock to the minute he awoke. His wife told him she had made every endeavour to rouse him, but in vain. The man was vexed and irritated. If he had not been a very good man indeed, I believe he would have sworn. The same programme was repeated as on the Thursday, and again he reached the City at three.

"This state of things went on for a month. The man fought against himself, but was unable to alter himself. Every morning, or rather every afternoon at one he awoke. Every night at one he crept down into the kitchen and foraged for food. Every morning at five he fell asleep.

"He could not understand it, nobody could understand it. The doctor treated him for water on the brain, hypnotic irresponsibility and hereditary lunacy. Meanwhile his business suffered, and his health grew worse. He seemed to be living upside down. His days seemed to have neither beginning nor end, but to be all middle. There was no time for exercise or recreation. When he began to feel cheerful and sociable everybody else was asleep.

"One day by chance the explanation came. His eldest daughter was preparing her home studies after dinner.

"'What time is it now in New York?' she asked, looking up from her geography book.

"'New York,' said her father, glancing at his watch, 'let me see. It's just ten now, and there's a little over four and a half hours' difference. Oh, about half-past five in the afternoon.'

"'Then in Jefferson,' said the mother, 'it would be still earlier, wouldn't it?'

"'Yes,' replied the girl, examining the map, 'Jefferson is nearly two degrees further west.'

"'Two degrees,' mused the father, 'and there's forty minutes to a degree. That would make it now, at the present moment in Jefferson--'

"He leaped to his feet with a cry:

"'I've got it!' he shouted, 'I see it.'

"'See what?' asked his wife, alarmed.

"'Why, it's four o'clock in Jefferson, and just time for my ride. That's what I'm wanting.'

"There could be no doubt about it. For five-and-twenty years he had lived by clockwork. But it was by Jefferson clockwork, not London clockwork. He had changed his longitude, but not himself. The habits of a quarter of a century were not to be shifted at the bidding of the sun.

"He examined the problem in all its bearings, and decided that the only solution was for him to return to the order of his old life. He saw the difficulties in his way, but they were less than those he was at present encountering. He was too formed by habit to adapt himself to circumstances. Circumstances must adapt themselves to him.

"He fixed his office hours from three till ten, leaving himself at half-past nine. At ten he mounted his horse and went for a canter in the Row, and on very dark nights he carried a lantern. News of it got abroad, and crowds would assemble to see him ride past.

"He dined at one o'clock in the morning, and afterwards strolled down to his club. He had tried to discover a quiet, respectable club where the members were willing to play whist till four in the morning, but failing, had been compelled to join a small Soho gambling-hell, where they taught him poker. The place was occasionally raided by the police, but thanks to his respectable appearance, he generally managed to escape.

"At half-past four he returned home, and woke up the family for evening prayers. At five he went to bed and slept like a top.

"The City chaffed him, and Bayswater shook its head over him, but that he did not mind. The only thing that really troubled him was loss of spiritual communion. At five o'clock on Sunday afternoons he felt he wanted chapel, but had to do without it. At seven he ate his simple mid-day meal. At eleven he had tea and muffins, and at midnight he began to crave again for hymns and sermons. At three he had a bread-and-cheese supper, and retired early at four a.m., feeling sad and unsatisfied.

"He was essentially a man of habit."

The unobtrusive stranger ceased, and we sat gazing in silence at the ceiling.

At length my friend rose, and taking half-a-sovereign from his pocket, laid it upon the table, and linking his arm in mine went out with me upon the deck.

THE ABSENT-MINDED MAN

You ask him to dine with you on Thursday to meet a few people who are anxious to know him.

"Now don't make a muddle of it," you say, recollectful of former mishaps, "and come on the Wednesday."

He laughs good-naturedly as he hunts through the room for his diary.

"Shan't be able to come Wednesday," he says, "shall be at the Mansion House, sketching dresses, and on Friday I start for Scotland, so as to be at the opening of the Exhibition on Saturday. It's bound to be all right this time. Where the deuce is that diary! Never mind, I'll make a note of it on this--you can see me do it."

You stand over him while he writes the appointment down on a sheet of foolscap, and watch him pin it up over his desk. Then you come away contented.

"I do hope he'll turn up," you say to your wife on the Thursday evening, while dressing.

"Are you sure you made it clear to him?" she replies, suspiciously, and you instinctively feel that whatever happens she is going to blame you for it.

Eight o'clock arrives, and with it the other guests. At half-past eight your wife is beckoned mysteriously out of the room, where the parlour-maid informs her that the cook has expressed a determination, in case of further delay, to wash her hands, figuratively speaking, of the whole affair.

Your wife, returning, suggests that if the dinner is to be eaten at all it had better be begun. She evidently considers that in pretending to expect him you have been merely playing a part, and that it would have been manlier and more straightforward for you to have admitted at the beginning that you had forgotten to invite him.

During the soup and the fish you recount anecdotes of his unpunctuality. By the time the entree arrives the empty chair has begun to cast a gloom over the dinner, and with the joint the conversation drifts into talk about dead relatives.

On Friday, at a quarter past eight, he dashes to the door and rings violently. Hearing his voice in the hall, you go to meet him.

"Sorry I'm late," he sings out cheerily. "Fool of a cabman took me to Alfred Place instead of--"

"Well, what do you want now you are come?" you interrupt, feeling anything but genially inclined towards him. He is an old friend, so you can be rude to him.

He laughs, and slaps you on the shoulder.

"Why, my dinner, my dear boy, I'm starving."

"Oh," you grunt in reply. "Well, you go and get it somewhere else, then. You're not going to have it here."

"What the devil do you mean?" he says. "You asked me to dinner."

"I did nothing of the kind," you tell him. "I asked you to dinner on Thursday, not on Friday."

He stares at you incredulously.

"How did I get Friday fixed in my mind?" inquiringly.

"Because yours is the sort of mind that would get Friday firmly fixed into it, when Thursday was the day," you explain. "I thought you had to be off to Edinburgh to-night," you add.

"Great Scott!" he cries, "so I have."

And without another word he dashes out, and you hear him rushing down the road, shouting for the cab he has just dismissed.

As you return to your study you reflect that he will have to travel all the way to Scotland in evening dress, and will have to send out the hotel porter in the morning to buy him a suit of ready-made clothes, and are glad.

Matters work out still more awkwardly when it is he who is the host. I remember being with him on his house-boat one day. It was a little after twelve, and we were sitting on the edge of the boat, dangling our feet in the river--the spot was a lonely one, half-way between Wallingford and Day's Lock. Suddenly round the bend appeared two skiffs, each one containing six elaborately-dressed persons. As soon as they caught sight of us they began waving handkerchiefs and parasols.

"Hullo!" I said, "here's some people hailing you."

"Oh, they all do that about here," he answered, without looking up. "Some beanfeast from Abingdon, I expect."

The boats draw nearer. When about two hundred yards off an elderly gentleman raised himself up in the prow of the leading one and shouted to us.

McQuae heard his voice, and gave a start that all but pitched him into the water.

"Good God!" he cried, "I'd forgotten all about it."

"About what?" I asked.

"Why, it's the Palmers and the Grahams and the Hendersons. I've asked them all over to lunch, and there's not a blessed thing on board but two mutton chops and a pound of potatoes, and I've given the boy a holiday."

Another day I was lunching with him at the Junior Hogarth, when a man named Hallyard, a mutual friend, strolled across to us.

"What are you fellows going to do this afternoon?" he asked, seating himself the opposite side of the table.

"I'm going to stop here and write letters," I answered.

"Come with me if you want something to do," said McQuae. "I'm going to drive Leena down to Richmond." ("Leena" was the young lady he recollected being engaged to. It transpired afterwards that he was engaged to three girls at the time. The other two he had forgotten all about.) "It's a roomy seat at the back."

"Oh, all right," said Hallyard, and they went away together in a hansom.

An hour and a half later Hallyard walked into the smoking-room looking depressed and worn, and flung himself into a chair.

"I thought you were going to Richmond with McQuae," I said.

"So did I," he answered.

"Had an accident?" I asked.

"Yes."

He was decidedly curt in his replies.

"Cart upset?" I continued.

"No, only me."

His grammar and his nerves seemed thoroughly shaken.

I waited for an explanation, and after a while he gave it.

"We got to Putney," he said, "with just an occasional run into a tram-car, and were going up the hill, when suddenly he turned a corner. You know his style at a corner--over the curb, across the road, and into the opposite lamp-post. Of course, as a rule one is prepared for it, but I never reckoned on his turning up there, and the first thing I recollect is finding myself sitting in the middle of the street with a dozen fools grinning at me.

"It takes a man a few minutes in such a case to think where he is and what has happened, and when I got up they were some distance away. I ran after them for a quarter of a mile, shouting at the top of my voice, and accompanied by a mob of boys, all yelling like hell on a Bank Holiday. But one might as well have tried to hail the dead, so I took the 'bus back.

"They might have guessed what had happened," he added, "by the shifting of the cart, if they'd had any sense. I'm not a light- weight."

He complained of soreness, and said he would go home. I suggested a cab, but he replied that he would rather walk.

I met McQuae in the evening at the St. James's Theatre. It was a first night, and he was taking sketches for The Graphic. The moment he saw me he made his way across to me.

"The very man I wanted to see," he said. "Did I take Hallyard with me in the cart to Richmond this afternoon?"

"You did," I replied.

"So Leena says," he answered, greatly bewildered, "but I'll swear he wasn't there when we got to the Queen's Hotel."

"It's all right," I said, "you dropped him at Putney."

"Dropped him at Putney!" he repeated. "I've no recollection of doing so."

"He has," I answered. "You ask him about it. He's full of it."

Everybody said he never would get married; that it was absurd to suppose he ever would remember the day, the church, and the girl, all in one morning; that if he did get as far as the altar he would forget what he had come for, and would give the bride away to his own best man. Hallyard had an idea that he was already married, but that the fact had slipped his memory. I myself felt sure that if he did marry he would forget all about it the next day.

But everybody was wrong. By some miraculous means the ceremony got itself accomplished, so that if Hallyard's idea be correct (as to which there is every possibility), there will be trouble. As for my own fears, I dismissed them the moment I saw the lady. She was a charming, cheerful little woman, but did not look the type that would let him forget all about it.

I had not seen him since his marriage, which had happened in the spring. Working my way back from Scotland by easy stages, I stopped for a few days at Scarboro'. After table d'hote I put on my mackintosh, and went out for a walk. It was raining hard, but after a month in Scotland one does not notice English weather, and I wanted some air. Struggling along the dark beach with my head against the wind, I stumbled over a crouching figure, seeking to shelter itself a little from the storm under the lee of the Spa wall.

I expected it to swear at me, but it seemed too broken-spirited to mind anything.

"I beg your pardon," I said. "I did not see you."

At the sound of my voice it started to its feet.

"Is that you, old man?" it cried.

"McQuae!" I exclaimed.

"By Jove!" he said, "I was never so glad to see a man in all my life before."

And he nearly shook my hand off.

"But what in thunder!" I said, "are you doing here? Why, you're drenched to the skin."

He was dressed in flannels and a tennis-coat.

"Yes," he answered. "I never thought it would rain. It was a lovely morning."

I began to fear he had overworked himself into a brain fever.

"Why don't you go home?" I asked.

"I can't," he replied. "I don't know where I live. I've forgotten the address."

"For heaven's sake," he said, "take me somewhere, and give me something to eat. I'm literally starving."

"Haven't you any money?" I asked him, as we turned towards the hotel.

"Not a sou," he answered. "We got in here from York, the wife and I, about eleven. We left our things at the station, and started to hunt for apartments. As soon as we were fixed, I changed my clothes and came out for a walk, telling Maud I should be back at one to lunch. Like a fool, I never took the address, and never noticed the way I was going.

"It's an awful business," he continued. "I don't see how I'm ever going to find her. I hoped she might stroll down to the Spa in the evening, and I've been hanging about the gates ever since six. I hadn't the threepence to go in."

"But have you no notion of the sort of street or the kind of house it was?" I enquired.

"Not a ghost," he replied. "I left it all to Maud, and didn't trouble."

"Have you tried any of the lodging-houses?" I asked.

"Tried!" he exclaimed bitterly. "I've been knocking at doors, and asking if Mrs. McQuae lives there steadily all the afternoon, and they slam the door in my face, mostly without answering. I told a policeman--I thought perhaps he might suggest something--but the idiot only burst out laughing, and that made me so mad that I gave him a black eye, and had to cut. I expect they're on the lookout for me now."

"I went into a restaurant," he continued gloomily, "and tried to get them to trust me for a steak. But the proprietress said she'd heard that tale before, and ordered me out before all the other customers. I think I'd have drowned myself if you hadn't turned up."

After a change of clothes and some supper, he discussed the case more calmly, but it was really a serious affair. They had shut up their flat, and his wife's relatives were travelling abroad. There was no one to whom he could send a letter to be forwarded; there was no one with whom she would be likely to communicate. Their chance of meeting again in this world appeared remote.

Nor did it seem to me--fond as he was of his wife, and anxious as he undoubtedly was to recover her--that he looked forward to the actual meeting, should it ever arrive, with any too pleasurable anticipation.

"She will think it strange," he murmured reflectively, sitting on the edge of the bed, and thoughtfully pulling off his socks. "She is sure to think it strange."

The following day, which was Wednesday, we went to a solicitor, and laid the case before him, and he instituted inquiries among all the lodging-house keepers in Scarborough, with the result that on Thursday afternoon McQuae was restored (after the manner of an Adelphi hero in the last act) to his home and wife.

I asked him next time I met him what she had said.

"Oh, much what I expected," he replied.

But he never told me what he had expected.

A CHARMING WOMAN

"Not THE MR. --, REALLY?"

In her deep brown eyes there lurked pleased surprise, struggling with wonder. She looked from myself to the friend who introduced us with a bewitching smile of incredulity, tempered by hope.

He assured her, adding laughingly, "The only genuine and original," and left us.

"I've always thought of you as a staid, middle-aged man," she said, with a delicious little laugh, then added in low soft tones, "I'm so very pleased to meet you, really."

The words were conventional, but her voice crept round one like a warm caress.

"Come and talk to me," she said, seating herself upon a small settee, and making room for me.

I sat down awkwardly beside her, my head buzzing just a little, as with one glass too many of champagne. I was in my literary childhood. One small book and a few essays and criticisms, scattered through various obscure periodicals had been as yet my only contributions to current literature. The sudden discovery that I was the Mr. Anybody, and that charming women thought of me, and were delighted to meet me, was a brain-disturbing thought.

"And it was really you who wrote that clever book?" she continued, "and all those brilliant things, in the magazines and journals. Oh, it must be delightful to be clever."

She gave breath to a little sigh of vain regret that went to my heart. To console her I commenced a laboured compliment, but she stopped me with her fan. On after reflection I was glad she had-- it would have been one of those things better expressed otherwise.

"I know what you are going to say," she laughed, "but don't. Besides, from you I should not know quite how to take it. You can be so satirical."

I tried to look as though I could be, but in her case would not.

She let her ungloved hand rest for an instant upon mine. Had she left it there for two, I should have gone down on my knees before her, or have stood on my head at her feet--have made a fool of myself in some way or another before the whole room full. She timed it to a nicety.

"I don't want YOU to pay me compliments," she said, "I want us to be friends. Of course, in years, I'm old enough to be your mother." (By the register I should say she might have been thirty- two, but looked twenty-six. I was twenty-three, and I fear foolish for my age.) "But you know the world, and you're so different to the other people one meets. Society is so hollow and artificial; don't you find it so? You don't know how I long sometimes to get away from it, to know someone to whom I could show my real self, who would understand me. You'll come and see me sometimes--I'm always at home on Wednesdays--and let me talk to you, won't you, and you must tell me all your clever thoughts."

It occurred to me that, maybe, she would like to hear a few of them there and then, but before I had got well started a hollow Society man came up and suggested supper, and she was compelled to leave me. As she disappeared, however, in the throng, she looked back over her shoulder with a glance half pathetic, half comic, that I understood. It said, "Pity me, I've got to be bored by this vapid, shallow creature," and I did.

I sought her through all the rooms before I went. I wished to assure her of my sympathy and support. I learned, however, from the butler that she had left early, in company with the hollow Society man.

A fortnight later I ran against a young literary friend in Regent Street, and we lunched together at the Monico.

"I met such a charming woman last night," he said, "a Mrs. Clifton Courtenay, a delightful woman."

"Oh, do YOU know her?" I exclaimed. "Oh, we're very old friends. She's always wanting me to go and see her. I really must."

"Oh, I didn't know YOU knew her," he answered. Somehow, the fact of my knowing her seemed to lessen her importance in his eyes. But soon he recovered his enthusiasm for her.

"A wonderfully clever woman," he continued. "I'm afraid I disappointed her a little though." He said this, however, with a laugh that contradicted his words. "She would not believe I was THE Mr. Smith. She imagined from my book that I was quite an old man."

I could see nothing in my friend's book myself to suggest that the author was, of necessity, anything over eighteen. The mistake appeared to me to display want of acumen, but it had evidently pleased him greatly.

"I felt quite sorry for her," he went on, "chained to that bloodless, artificial society in which she lives. 'You can't tell,' she said to me, 'how I long to meet someone to whom I could show my real self--who would understand me.' I'm going to see her on Wednesday."

I went with him. My conversation with her was not as confidential as I had anticipated, owing to there being some eighty other people present in a room intended for the accommodation of eight; but after surging round for an hour in hot and aimless misery--as very young men at such gatherings do, knowing as a rule only the man who has brought them, and being unable to find him--I contrived to get a few words with her.

She greeted me with a smile, in the light of which I at once forgot my past discomfort, and let her fingers rest, with delicious pressure, for a moment upon mine.

"How good of you to keep your promise," she said. "These people have been tiring me so. Sit here, and tell me all you have been doing."

She listened for about ten seconds, and then interrupted me with -

"And that clever friend of yours that you came with. I met him at dear Lady Lennon's last week. Has HE written anything?"

I explained to her that he had.

"Tell me about it?" she said. "I get so little time for reading, and then I only care to read the books that help me," and she gave me a grateful look more eloquent than words.

I described the work to her, and wishing to do my friend justice I even recited a few of the passages upon which, as I knew, he especially prided himself.

One sentence in particular seemed to lay hold of her. "A good woman's arms round a man's neck is a lifebelt thrown out to him from heaven."

"How beautiful!" she murmured. "Say it again."

I said it again, and she repeated it after me.

Then a noisy old lady swooped down upon her, and I drifted away into a corner, where I tried to look as if I were enjoying myself, and failed.

Later on, feeling it time to go, I sought my friend, and found him talking to her in a corner. I approached and waited. They were discussing the latest east-end murder. A drunken woman had been killed by her husband, a hard-working artizan, who had been maddened by the ruin of his home.

"Ah," she was saying, "what power a woman has to drag a man down or lift him up. I never read a case in which a woman is concerned without thinking of those beautiful lines of yours: 'A good woman's arms round a man's neck is a lifebelt thrown out to him from heaven.'"

Opinions differed concerning her religion and politics. Said the Low Church parson: "An earnest Christian woman, sir, of that unostentatious type that has always been the bulwark of our Church. I am proud to know that woman, and I am proud to think that poor words of mine have been the humble instrument to wean that true woman's heart from the frivolities of fashion, and to fix her thoughts upon higher things. A good Churchwoman, sir, a good Churchwoman, in the best sense of the word."

Said the pale aristocratic-looking young Abbe to the Comtesse, the light of old-world enthusiasm shining from his deep-set eyes: "I have great hopes for our dear friend. She finds it hard to sever the ties of time and love. We are all weak, but her heart turns towards our mother Church as a child, though suckled among strangers, yearns after many years for the bosom that has borne it. We have spoken, and I, even I, may be the voice in the wilderness leading the lost sheep back to the fold."

Said Sir Harry Bennett, the great Theosophist lecturer, writing to a friend: "A singularly gifted woman, and a woman evidently thirsting for the truth. A woman capable of willing her own life. A woman not afraid of thought and reason, a lover of wisdom. I have talked much with her at one time or another, and I have found her grasp my meaning with a quickness of perception quite unusual in my experience; and the arguments I have let fall, I am convinced, have borne excellent fruit. I look forward to her becoming, at no very distant date, a valued member of our little band. Indeed, without betraying confidence, I may almost say I regard her conversion as an accomplished fact."

Colonel Maxim always spoke of her as "a fair pillar of the State."

"With the enemy in our midst," said the florid old soldier, "it behoves every true man--aye, and every true woman--to rally to the defence of the country; and all honour, say I, to noble ladies such as Mrs. Clifton Courtenay, who, laying aside their natural shrinking from publicity, come forward in such a crisis as the present to combat the forces of disorder and disloyalty now rampant in the land."

"But," some listener would suggest, "I gathered from young Jocelyn that Mrs. Clifton Courtenay held somewhat advanced views on social and political questions."

"Jocelyn," the Colonel would reply with scorn; "pah! There may have been a short space of time during which the fellow's long hair and windy rhetoric impressed her. But I flatter myself I've put MY spoke in Mr. Jocelyn's wheel. Why, damme, sir, she's consented to stand for Grand Dame of the Bermondsey Branch of the Primrose League next year. What's Jocelyn to say to that, the scoundrel!"

What Jocelyn said was:-

"I know the woman is weak. But I do not blame her; I pity her. When the time comes, as soon it will, when woman is no longer a puppet, dancing to the threads held by some brainless man--when a woman is not threatened with social ostracism for daring to follow her own conscience instead of that of her nearest male relative-- then will be the time to judge her. It is not for me to betray the confidence reposed in me by a suffering woman, but you can tell that interesting old fossil, Colonel Maxim, that he and the other old women of the Bermondsey Branch of the Primrose League may elect Mrs. Clifton Courtenay for their President, and make the most of it; they have only got the outside of the woman. Her heart is beating time to the tramp of an onward-marching people; her soul's eyes are straining for the glory of a coming dawn."

But they all agreed she was a charming woman.

WHIBLEY'S SPIRIT

I never met it myself, but I knew Whibley very well indeed, so that I came to hear a goodish deal about it.

It appeared to be devoted to Whibley, and Whibley was extremely fond of it. Personally I am not interested in spirits, and no spirit has ever interested itself in me. But I have friends whom they patronise, and my mind is quite open on the subject. Of Whibley's Spirit I wish to speak with every possible respect. It was, I am willing to admit, as hard-working and conscientious a spirit as any one could wish to live with. The only thing I have to say against it is that it had no sense.

It came with a carved cabinet that Whibley had purchased in Wardour Street for old oak, but which, as a matter of fact, was chestnut wood, manufactured in Germany, and at first was harmless enough, saying nothing but "Yes!" or "No!" and that only when spoken to.

Whibley would amuse himself of an evening asking it questions, being careful to choose tolerably simple themes, such as, "Are you there?" (to which the Spirit would sometimes answer "Yes!" and sometimes "No!") "Can you hear me?" "Are you happy?"--and so on. The Spirit made the cabinet crack--three times for "Yes" and twice for "No." Now and then it would reply both "Yes!" and "No!" to the same question, which Whibley attributed to over-scrupulousness. When nobody asked it anything it would talk to itself, repeating "Yes!" "No!" "No!" "Yes!" over and over again in an aimless, lonesome sort of a way that made you feel sorry for it.

After a while Whibley bought a table, and encouraged it to launch out into more active conversation. To please Whibley, I assisted at some of the earlier seances, but during my presence it invariably maintained a reticence bordering on positive dulness. I gathered from Whibley that it disliked me, thinking that I was unsympathetic. The complaint was unjust; I was not unsympathetic, at least not at the commencement. I came to hear it talk, and I wanted to hear it talk; I would have listened to it by the hour. What tired me was its slowness in starting, and its foolishness when it had started, in using long words that it did not know how to spell. I remember on one occasion, Whibley, Jobstock (Whibley's partner), and myself, sitting for two hours, trying to understand what the thing meant by "H-e-s-t-u-r-n-e-m-y-s-f-e-a-r." It used no stops whatever. It never so much as hinted where one sentence ended and another began. It never even told us when it came to a proper name. Its idea of an evening's conversation was to plump down a hundred or so vowels and consonants in front of you and leave you to make whatever sense out of them you could.

We fancied at first it was talking about somebody named Hester (it had spelt Hester with a "u" before we allowed a margin for spelling), and we tried to work the sentence out on that basis, "Hester enemies fear," we thought it might be. Whibley had a niece named Hester, and we decided the warning had reference to her. But whether she was our enemy, and we were to fear her, or whether we had to fear her enemies (and, if so, who were they?), or whether it was our enemies who were to be frightened by Hester, or her enemies, or enemies generally, still remained doubtful. We asked the table if it meant the first suggestion, and it said "No." We asked what it did mean, and it said "Yes."

This answer annoyed me, but Whibley explained that the Spirit was angry with us for our stupidity (which seemed quaint). He informed us that it always said first "No," and then "Yes," when it was angry, and as it was his Spirit, and we were in his house, we kept our feelings to ourselves and started afresh.

This time we abandoned the "Hestur" theory altogether. Jobstock suggested "Haste" for the first word, and, thought the Spirit might have gone on phonetically.

"Haste! you are here, Miss Sfear!" was what he made of it.

Whibley asked him sarcastically if he'd kindly explain what that meant.

I think Jobstock was getting irritable. We had been sitting cramped up round a wretched little one-legged table all the evening, and this was almost the first bit of gossip we had got out of it. To further excuse him, it should also be explained that the gas had been put out by Whibley, and that the fire had gone out of its own accord. He replied that it was hard labour enough to find out what the thing said without having to make sense of it.

"It can't spell," he added, "and it's got a nasty, sulky temper. If it was my spirit I'd hire another spirit to kick it."

Whibley was one of the mildest little men I ever knew, but chaff or abuse of his Spirit roused the devil in him, and I feared we were going to have a scene. Fortunately, I was able to get his mind back to the consideration of "Hesturnemysfear" before anything worse happened than a few muttered remarks about the laughter of fools, and want of reverence for sacred subjects being the sign of a shallow mind.

We tried "He's stern," and "His turn," and the "fear of Hesturnemy," and tried to think who "Hesturnemy" might be. Three times we went over the whole thing again from the beginning, which meant six hundred and six tiltings of the table, and then suddenly the explanation struck me--"Eastern Hemisphere."

Whibley had asked it for any information it might possess concerning his wife's uncle, from whom he had not heard for months, and that apparently was its idea of an address.

The fame of Whibley's Spirit became noised abroad, with the result that Whibley was able to command the willing service of more congenial assistants, and Jobstock and myself were dismissed. But we bore no malice.

Under these more favourable conditions the Spirit plucked up wonderfully, and talked everybody's head off. It could never have been a cheerful companion, however, for its conversation was chiefly confined to warnings and prognostications of evil. About once a fortnight Whibley would drop round on me, in a friendly way, to tell me that I was to beware of a man who lived in a street beginning with a "C," or to inform me that if I would go to a town on the coast where there were three churches I should meet someone who would do me an irreparable injury, and, that I did not rush off then and there in search of that town he regarded as flying in the face of Providence.

In its passion for poking its ghostly nose into other people's affairs it reminded me of my earthly friend Poppleton. Nothing pleased it better than being appealed to for aid and advice, and Whibley, who was a perfect slave to it, would hunt half over the parish for people in trouble and bring them to it.

It would direct ladies, eager for divorce court evidence, to go to the third house from the corner of the fifth street, past such and such a church or public-house (it never would give a plain, straightforward address), and ring the bottom bell but one twice. They would thank it effusively, and next morning would start to find the fifth street past the church, and would ring the bottom bell but one of the third house from the corner twice, and a man in his shirt sleeves would come to the door and ask them what they wanted.

They could not tell what they wanted, they did not know themselves, and the man would use bad language, and slam the door in their faces.

Then they would think that perhaps the Spirit meant the fifth street the other way, or the third house from the opposite corner, and would try again, with still more unpleasant results.

One July I met Whibley, mooning disconsolately along Princes Street, Edinburgh.

"Hullo!" I exclaimed, "what are you doing here? I thought you were busy over that School Board case."

"Yes," he answered, "I ought really to be in London, but the truth is I'm rather expecting something to happen down here."

"Oh!" I said, "and what's that?"

"Well," he replied hesitatingly, as though he would rather not talk about it, "I don't exactly know yet."

"You've come from London to Edinburgh, and don't know what you've come for!" I cried.

"Well, you see," he said, still more reluctantly, as it seemed to me, "it was Maria's idea; she wished--"

"Maria!" I interrupted, looking perhaps a little sternly at him, "who's Maria?" (His wife's name I knew was Emily Georgina Anne.)

"Oh! I forgot," he explained; "she never would tell her name before you, would she? It's the Spirit, you know."

"Oh! that," I said, "it's she that has sent you here. Didn't she tell you what for?"

"No," he answered, "that's what worries me. All she would say was, 'Go to Edinburgh--something will happen.'"

"And how long are you going to remain here?" I inquired.

"I don't know," he replied. "I've been here a week already, and Jobstock writes quite angrily. I wouldn't have come if Maria hadn't been so urgent. She repeated it three evenings running."

I hardly knew what to do. The little man was so dreadfully in earnest about the business that one could not argue much with him.

"You are sure," I said, after thinking a while, "that this Maria is a good Spirit? There are all sorts going about, I'm told. You're sure this isn't the spirit of some deceased lunatic, playing the fool with you?"

"I've thought of that," he admitted. "Of course that might be so. If nothing happens soon I shall almost begin to suspect it."

"Well, I should certainly make some inquiries into its character before I trusted it any further," I answered, and left him.

About a month later I ran against him outside the Law Courts.

"It was all right about Maria; something did happen in Edinburgh while I was there. That very morning I met you one of my oldest clients died quite suddenly at his house at Queensferry, only a few miles outside the city."

"I'm glad of that," I answered, "I mean, of course, for Maria's sake. It was lucky you went then."

"Well, not altogether," he replied, "at least, not in a worldly sense. He left his affairs in a very complicated state, and his eldest son went straight up to London to consult me about them, and, not finding me there, and time being important, went to Kebble. I was rather disappointed when I got back and heard about it."

"Umph!" I said; "she's not a smart spirit, anyway."

"No," he answered, "perhaps not. But, you see, something did really happen."

After that his affection for "Maria" increased tenfold, while her attachment to himself became a burden to his friends. She grew too big for her table, and, dispensing with all mechanical intermediaries, talked to him direct. She followed him everywhere. Mary's lamb couldn't have been a bigger nuisance. She would even go with him into the bedroom, and carry on long conversations with him in the middle of the night. His wife objected; she said it seemed hardly decent, but there was no keeping her out.

She turned up with him at picnics and Christmas parties. Nobody heard her speak to him, but it seemed necessary for him to reply to her aloud, and to see him suddenly get up from his chair and slip away to talk earnestly to nothing in a corner disturbed the festivities.

"I should really be glad," he once confessed to me, "to get a little time to myself. She means kindly, but it IS a strain. And then the others don't like it. It makes them nervous. I can see it does."

One evening she caused quite a scene at the club. Whibley had been playing whist, with the Major for a partner. At the end of the game the Major, leaning across the table toward him, asked, in a tone of deadly calm, "May I inquire, sir, whether there was any earthly reason" (he emphasised "earthly") "for your following my lead of spades with your only trump?"

"I--I--am very sorry, Major," replied Whibley apologetically. "I-- I--somehow felt I--I ought to play that queen."

"Entirely your own inspiration, or suggested?" persisted the Major, who had, of course, heard of "Maria."

Whibley admitted the play had been suggested to him. The Major rose from the table.

"Then, sir," said he, with concentrated indignation, "I decline to continue this game. A human fool I can tolerate for a partner, but if I am to be hampered by a damned spirit--"

"You've no right to say that," cried Whibley hotly.

"I apologise," returned the Major coldly; "we will say a blessed spirit. I decline to play whist with spirits of any kind; and I advise you, sir, if you intend giving many exhibitions with the lady, first to teach her the rudiments of the game."

Saying which the Major put on his hat and left the club, and I made Whibley drink a stiff glass of brandy and water, and sent him and "Maria" home in a cab.

Whibley got rid of "Maria" at last. It cost him in round figures about eight thousand pounds, but his family said it was worth it.

A Spanish Count hired a furnished house a few doors from Whibley's, and one evening he was introduced to Whibley, and came home and had a chat with him. Whibley told him about "Maria," and the Count quite fell in love with her. He said that if only he had had such a spirit to help and advise him, it might have altered his whole life.

He was the first man who had ever said a kind word about the spirit, and Whibley loved him for it. The Count seemed as though he could never see enough of Whibley after that evening, and the three of them--Whibley, the Count, and "Maria"--would sit up half the night talking together.

The precise particulars I never heard. Whibley was always very reticent on the matter. Whether "Maria" really did exist, and the Count deliberately set to work to bamboozle her (she was fool enough for anything), or whether she was a mere hallucination of Whibley's, and the man tricked Whibley by "hypnotic suggestions" (as I believe it is called), I am not prepared to say. The only thing certain is that "Maria" convinced Whibley that the Count had discovered a secret gold mine in Peru. She said she knew all about it, and counselled Whibley to beg the Count to let him put a few thousands into the working of it. "Maria," it appeared, had known the Count from his boyhood, and could answer for it that he was the most honourable man in all South America. Possibly enough he was.

The Count was astonished to find that Whibley knew all about his mine. Eight thousand pounds was needed to start the workings, but he had not mentioned it to any one, as he wanted to keep the whole thing to himself, and thought he could save the money on his estates in Portugal. However, to oblige "Maria," he would let Whibley supply the money. Whibley supplied it--in cash, and no one has ever seen the Count since.

That broke up Whibley's faith in "Maria," and a sensible doctor, getting hold of him threatened to prescribe a lunatic asylum for him if ever he found him carrying on with any spirits again. That completed the cure.

THE MAN WHO WENT WRONG

I first met Jack Burridge nearly ten years ago on a certain North-country race-course.

The saddling bell had just rung for the chief event of the day. I was sauntering along with my hands in my pockets, more interested in the crowd than in the race, when a sporting friend, crossing on his way to the paddock, seized me by the arm and whispered hoarsely in my ear:-

"Put your shirt on Mrs. Waller."

"Put my -?" I began.

"Put your shirt on Mrs. Waller," he repeated still more impressively, and disappeared in the throng.

I stared after him in blank amazement. Why should I put my shirt on Mrs. Waller? Even if it would fit a lady. And how about myself?

I was passing the grand stand, and, glancing up, I saw "Mrs. Waller, twelve to one," chalked on a bookmaker's board. Then it dawned upon me that "Mrs. Waller" was a horse, and, thinking further upon the matter, I evolved the idea that my friend's advice, expressed in more becoming language, was "Back 'Mrs. Waller' for as much as you can possibly afford."

"Thank you," I said to myself, "I have backed cast-iron certainties before. Next time I bet upon a horse I shall make the selection by shutting my eyes and putting a pin through the card."

But the seed had taken root. My friend's words surged in my brain. The birds passing overhead twittered, "Put your shirt on 'Mrs. Waller.'"

I reasoned with myself. I reminded myself of my few former ventures. But the craving to put, if not my shirt, at all events half a sovereign on "Mrs. Waller" only grew the stronger the more strongly I battled against it. I felt that if "Mrs. Waller" won and I had nothing on her, I should reproach myself to my dying day.

I was on the other side of the course. There was no time to get back to the enclosure. The horses were already forming for the start. A few yards off, under a white umbrella, an outside bookmaker was shouting his final prices in stentorian tones. He was a big, genial-looking man, with an honest red face.

"What price 'Mrs. Waller'?" I asked him.

"Fourteen to one," he answered, "and good luck to you."

I handed him half a sovereign, and he wrote me out a ticket. I crammed it into my waistcoat pocket, and hurried off to see the race. To my intense astonishment "Mrs. Waller" won. The novel sensation of having backed the winner so excited me that I forgot all about my money, and it was not until a good hour afterwards that I recollected my bet.

Then I started off to search for the man under the white umbrella. I went to where I thought I had left him, but no white umbrella could I find.

Consoling myself with the reflection that my loss served me right for having been fool enough to trust an outside "bookie," I turned on my heel and began to make my way back to my seat. Suddenly a voice hailed me:-

"Here you are, sir. It's Jack Burridge you want. Over here, sir."

I looked round, and there was Jack Burridge at my elbow.

"I saw you looking about, sir," he said, "but I could not make you hear. You was looking the wrong side of the tent."

It was pleasant to find that his honest face had not belied him.

"It is very good of you," I said; "I had given up all hopes of seeing you. Or," I added with a smile, "my seven pounds."

"Seven pun' ten," he corrected me; "you're forgetting your own thin 'un."

He handed me the money and went back to his stand.

On my way into the town I came across him again. A small crowd was collected, thoughtfully watching a tramp knocking about a miserable-looking woman.

Jack, pushing to the front, took in the scene and took off his coat in the same instant.

"Now then, my fine old English gentleman," he sang out, "come and have a try at me for a change."

The tramp was a burly ruffian, and I have seen better boxers than Jack. He got himself a black eye, and a nasty cut over the lip, before he hardly knew where he was. But in spite of that--and a good deal more--he stuck to his man and finished him.

At the end, as he helped his adversary up, I heard him say to the fellow in a kindly whisper:-

"You're too good a sort, you know, to whollop a woman. Why, you very near give me a licking. You must have forgot yourself, matey."

The fellow interested me. I waited and walked on with him. He told me about his home in London, at Mile End--about his old father and mother, his little brothers and sisters--and what he was saving up to do for them. Kindliness oozed from every pore in his skin.

Many that we met knew him, and all, when they saw his round, red face, smiled unconsciously. At the corner of the High Street a pale-faced little drudge of a girl passed us, saying as she slipped by "Good-evening, Mr. Burridge."

He made a dart and caught her by the shoulder.

"And how is father?" he asked.

"Oh, if you please, Mr. Burridge, he is out again. All the mills is closed," answered the child.

"And mother?"

"She don't get no better, sir."

"And who's keeping you all?"

"Oh, if you please, sir, Jimmy's earning something now," replied the mite.

He took a couple of sovereigns from his waistcoat pocket, and closed the child's hand upon them.

"That's all right, my lass, that's all right," he said, stopping her stammering thanks. "You write to me if things don't get better. You know where to find Jack Burridge."

Strolling about the streets in the evening, I happened to pass the inn where he was staying. The parlour window was open, and out into the misty night his deep, cheery voice, trolling forth an old-fashioned drinking song, came rolling like a wind, cleansing the corners of one's heart with its breezy humanness. He was sitting at the head of the table surrounded by a crowd of jovial cronies. I lingered for a while watching the scene. It made the world appear a less sombre dwelling-place than I had sometimes pictured it.

I determined, on my return to London, to look him up, and accordingly one evening started to find the little by-street off the Mile End Road in which he lived. As I turned the corner he drove up in his dog-cart; it was a smart turn-out. On the seat beside him sat a neat, withered little old woman, whom he introduced to me as his mother.

"I tell 'im it's a fine gell as 'e oughter 'ave up 'ere aside 'im," said the old lady, preparing to dismount, "an old woman like me takes all the paint off the show."

"Get along with yer," he replied laughingly, jumping down and handing the reins to the lad who had been waiting, "you could give some of the young uns points yet, mother. I allus promised the old lady as she should ride behind her own 'oss one day," he continued, turning to me, "didn't I, mother?"

"Ay, ay," replied the old soul, as she hobbled nimbly up the steps, "ye're a good son, Jack, ye're a good son."

He led the way into the parlour. As he entered every face lightened up with pleasure, a harmony of joyous welcome greeted him. The old hard world had been shut out with the slam of the front door. I seemed to have wandered into Dickensland. The red-faced man with the small twinkling eyes and the lungs of leather loomed before me, a large, fat household fairy. From his capacious pockets came forth tobacco for the old father; a huge bunch of hot- house grapes for a neighbour's sickly child, who was stopping with them; a book of Henty's--beloved of boys--for a noisy youngster who called him "uncle"; a bottle of port wine for a wan, elderly woman with a swollen face--his widowed sister-in-law, as I subsequently learned; sweets enough for the baby (whose baby I don't know) to make it sick for a week; and a roll of music for his youngest sister.

"We're a-going to make a lady of her," he said, drawing the child's shy face against his gaudy waistcoat, and running his coarse hand through her pretty curls; "and she shall marry a jockey when she grows up."

After supper he brewed some excellent whisky punch, and insisted upon the old lady joining us, which she eventually did with much coughing and protestation; but I noticed that she finished the tumblerful. For the children he concocted a marvellous mixture, which he called an "eye-composer," the chief ingredients being hot lemonade, ginger wine, sugar, oranges, and raspberry vinegar. It had the desired effect.

I stayed till late, listening to his inexhaustible fund of stories. Over most of them he laughed with us himself--a great gusty laugh that made the cheap glass ornaments upon the mantelpiece to tremble; but now and then a recollection came to him that spread a sudden gravity across his jovial face, bringing a curious quaver into his deep voice.

Their tongues a little loosened by the punch, the old folks would have sung his praises to the verge of tediousness had he not almost sternly interrupted them.

"Shut up, mother," he cried at last, quite gruffly, "what I does I does to please myself. I likes to see people comfortable about me. If they wasn't, it's me as would be more upset than them."

I did not see him again for nearly two years. Then one October evening, strolling about the East End, I met him coming out of a little Chapel in the Burdett Road. He was so changed that I should not have known him had not I overheard a woman as she passed him say, "Good-evening, Mr. Burridge."

A pair of bushy side-whiskers had given to his red face an aggressively respectable appearance. He was dressed in an ill-fitting suit of black, and carried an umbrella in one hand and a book in the other.

In some mysterious way he managed to look both thinner and shorter than my recollection of him. Altogether, he suggested to me the idea that he himself--the real man--had by some means or other been extracted, leaving only his shrunken husk behind. The genial juices of humanity had been squeezed out of him.

"Not Jack Burridge!" I exclaimed, confronting him in astonishment.

His little eyes wandered shiftily up and down the street. "No, sir," he replied (his tones had lost their windy boisterousness--a hard, metallic voice spoke to me), "not the one as you used to know, praise be the Lord."

"And have you given up the old business?" I asked.

"Yes, sir," he replied, "that's all over; I've been a vile sinner in my time, God forgive me for it. But, thank Heaven, I have repented in time."

"Come and have a drink," I said, slipping my arm through his, "and tell me all about it."

He disengaged himself from me, firmly but gently. "You mean well, sir," he said, "but I have given up the drink."

Evidently he would have been rid of me, but a literary man, scenting material for his stockpot, is not easily shaken off. I asked after the old folks, and if they were still stopping with him.

"Yes," he said, "for the present. Of course, a man can't be expected to keep people for ever; so many mouths to fill is hard work these times, and everybody sponges on a man just because he's good-natured."

"And how are you getting on?" I asked.

"Tolerably well, thank you, sir. The Lord provides for His servants," he replied with a smug smile. "I have got a little shop now in the Commercial Road."

"Whereabouts?" I persisted. "I would like to call and see you."

He gave me the address reluctantly, and said he would esteem it a great pleasure if I would honour him by a visit, which was a palpable lie.

The following afternoon I went. I found the place to be a pawn-broker's shop, and from all appearances he must have been doing a very brisk business. He was out himself attending a temperance committee, but his old father was behind the counter, and asked me inside. Though it was a chilly day there was no fire in the parlour, and the two old folks sat one each side of the empty hearth, silent and sad. They seemed little more pleased to see me than their son, but after a while Mrs. Burridge's natural garrulity asserted itself, and we fell into chat.

I asked what had become of his sister-in-law, the lady with the swollen face.

"I couldn't rightly tell you, sir," answered the old lady, "she ain't livin' with us now. You see, sir," she continued, "John's got different notions to what 'e used to 'ave. 'E don't cotten much to them as ain't found grace, and poor Jane never did 'ave much religion!"

"And the little one?" I inquired. "The one with the curls?"

"What, Bessie, sir?" said the old lady. "Oh, she's out at service, sir; John don't think it good for young folks to be idle."

"Your son seems to have changed a good deal, Mrs. Burridge," I remarked.

"Ay, sir," she assented, "you may well say that. It nearly broke my 'art at fust; everythin' so different to what it 'ad been. Not as I'd stand in the boy's light. If our being a bit uncomfortable like in this world is a-going to do 'im any good in the next me and father ain't the ones to begrudge it, are we, old man?"

The "old man" concurred grumpily.

"Was it a sudden conversion?" I asked. "How did it come about?"

"It was a young woman as started 'im off," explained the old lady. "She come round to our place one day a-collectin' for somethin' or other, and Jack, in 'is free-'anded way, 'e give 'er a five-pun' note. Next week she come agen for somethin' else, and stopped and talked to 'im about 'is soul in the passage. She told 'im as 'e was a-goin' straight to 'ell, and that 'e oughter give up the bookmakin' and settle down to a respec'ble, God-fearin' business. At fust 'e only laughed, but she lammed in tracts at 'im full of the most awful language; and one day she fetched 'im round to one of them revivalist chaps, as fair settled 'im.

"'E ain't never been his old self since then. 'E give up the bettin' and bought this 'ere, though what's the difference blessed if I can see. It makes my 'eart ache, it do, to 'ear my Jack a- beatin' down the poor people--and it ain't like 'im. It went agen 'is grain at fust, I could see; but they told him as 'ow it was folks's own fault that they was poor, and as 'ow it was the will of God, because they was a drinkin', improvident lot.

"Then they made 'im sign the pledge. 'E'd allus been used to 'is glass, Jack 'ad, and I think as knockin' it off 'ave soured 'im a bit-- seems as if all the sperit 'ad gone out of 'im--and of course me and father 'ave 'ad to give up our little drop too. Then they told 'im as 'e must give up smokin'- that was another way of goin' straight to 'ell-- and that ain't made 'im any the more cheerful like, and father misses 'is little bit--don't ye, father?"

"Ay," answered the old fellow savagely; "can't say I thinks much of these 'ere folks as is going to heaven; blowed if I don't think they'll be a chirpier lot in t'other place."

An angry discussion in the shop interrupted us. Jack had returned, and was threatening an excited woman with the police. It seemed she had miscalculated the date, and had come a day too late with her interest.

Having got rid of her, he came into the parlour with the watch in his hand.

"It's providential she was late," he said, looking at it; "it's worth ten times what I lent on it."

He packed his father back into the shop, and his mother down into the kitchen to get his tea, and for a while we sat together talking.

I found his conversation a strange mixture of self-laudation, showing through a flimsy veil of self-disparagement, and of satisfaction at the conviction that he was "saved," combined with equally evident satisfaction that most other people weren't-- somewhat trying, however; and, remembering an appointment, rose to go.

He made no effort to stay me, but I could see that he was bursting to tell me something. At last, taking a religious paper from his pocket, and pointing to a column, he blurted out:

"You don't take any interest in the Lord's vineyard, I suppose, sir?"

I glanced at the part of the paper indicated. It announced a new mission to the Chinese, and heading the subscription list stood the name, "Mr. John Burridge, one hundred guineas."

"You subscribe largely, Mr. Burridge," I said, handing him back the paper.

He rubbed his big hands together. "The Lord will repay a hundredfold," he answered.

"In which case it's just as well to have a note of the advance down in black and white, eh?" I added.

His little eyes looked sharply at me; but he made no reply, and, shaking hands, I left him.

THE HOBBY RIDER

Bump. Bump. Bump-bump. Bump.

I sat up in bed and listened intently. It seemed to me as if someone with a muffled hammer were trying to knock bricks out of the wall.

"Burglars," I said to myself (one assumes, as a matter of course, that everything happening in this world after 1 a.m. is due to burglars), and I reflected what a curiously literal, but at the same time slow and cumbersome, method of housebreaking they had adopted.

The bumping continued irregularly, yet uninterruptedly.

My bed was by the window. I reached out my hand and drew aside a corner of the curtain. The sunlight streamed into the room. I looked at my watch: it was ten minutes past five.

A most unbusinesslike hour for burglars, I thought. Why, it will be breakfast-time before they get in.

Suddenly there came a crash, and some substance striking against the blind fell upon the floor. I sprang out of bed and threw open the window.

A red-haired young gentleman, scantily clad in a sweater and a pair of flannel trousers, stood on the lawn below me.

"Good morning," he said cheerily. "Do you mind throwing me back my ball?"

"What ball?" I said.

"My tennis ball," he answered. "It must be somewhere in the room; it went clean through the window."

I found the ball and threw it back to him,

*** Quick tidied and spell-checked to here--page 155 *** "What are you doing?" I asked. "Playing tennis?"

"No," he said. "I am just practising against the side of the house. It improves your game wonderfully."

"It don't improve my night's rest," I answered somewhat surlily I fear. "I came down here for peace and quiet. Can't you do it in the daytime?"

"Daytime!" he laughed. "Why it has been daytime for the last two hours. Never mind, I'll go round the other side."

He disappeared round the corner, and set to work at the back, where he woke up the dog. I heard another window smash, followed by a sound as of somebody getting up violently in a distant part of the house, and shortly afterwards I must have fallen asleep again.

I had come to spend a few weeks at a boarding establishment in Deal. He was the only other young man in the house, and I was naturally thrown a good deal upon his society. He was a pleasant, genial young fellow, but he would have been better company had he been a little less enthusiastic as regards tennis.

He played tennis ten hours a day on the average. He got up romantic parties to play it by moonlight (when half his time was generally taken up in separating his opponents), and godless parties to play it on Sundays. On wet days I have seen him practising services by himself in a mackintosh and goloshes.

He had been spending the winter with his people at Tangiers, and I asked him how he liked the place.

"Oh, a beast of a hole!" he replied. "There is not a court anywhere in the town. We tried playing on the roof, but the mater thought it dangerous."

Switzerland he had been delighted with. He counselled me next time I went to stay at Zermatt.

"There is a capital court at Zermatt," he said. "You might almost fancy yourself at Wimbledon."

A mutual acquaintance whom I subsequently met told me that at the top of the Jungfrau he had said to him, his eyes fixed the while upon a small snow plateau enclosed by precipices a few hundred feet below them -

"By Jove! That wouldn't make half a bad little tennis court--that flat bit down there. Have to be careful you didn't run back too far."

When he was not playing tennis, or practising tennis, or reading about tennis, he was talking about tennis. Renshaw was the prominent figure in the tennis world at that time, and he mentioned Renshaw until there grew up within my soul a dark desire to kill Renshaw in a quiet, unostentatious way, and bury him.

One drenching afternoon he talked tennis to me for three hours on end, referring to Renshaw, so far as I kept count, four thousand nine hundred and thirteen times. After tea he drew his chair to the window beside me, and commenced -

"Have you ever noticed how Renshaw--"

I said -

"Suppose someone took a gun--someone who could aim very straight-- and went out and shot Renshaw till he was quite dead, would you tennis players drop him and talk about somebody else?"

"Oh, but who would shoot Renshaw?" he said indignantly.

"Never mind," I said, "supposing someone did?"

"Well, then, there would be his brother," he replied.

I had forgotten that.

"Well, we won't argue about how many of them there are," I said. "Suppose someone killed the lot, should we hear less of Renshaw?"

"Never," he replied emphatically. "Renshaw will always be a name wherever tennis is spoken of."

I dread to think what the result might have been had his answer been other than it was.

The next year he dropped tennis completely and became an

ardent amateur photographer, whereupon all his friends implored him to return to tennis, and sought to interest him in talk about services and returns and volleys, and in anecdotes concerning Renshaw. But he would not heed them.

Whatever he saw, wherever he went, he took. He took his friends, and made them his enemies. He took babies, and brought despair to fond mothers' hearts. He took young wives, and cast a shadow on the home. Once there was a young man who loved not wisely, so his friends thought, but the more they talked against her the more he clung to her. Then a happy idea occurred to the father. He got Begglely to photograph her in seven different positions.

When her lover saw the first, he said -

"What an awful looking thing! Who did it?"

When Begglely showed him the second, he said -

"But, my dear fellow, it's not a bit like her. You've made her look an ugly old woman."

At the third he said -

"Whatever have you done to her feet? They can't be that size, you know. It isn't in nature!"

At the fourth he exclaimed -

"But, heavens, man! Look at the shape you've made her. Where on earth did you get the idea from?"

At the first glimpse of the fifth he staggered.

"Great Scott!" he cried with a shudder, "what a ghastly expression you've got into it! It isn't human!"

Begglely was growing offended, but the father, who was standing by, came to his defence.

"It's nothing to do with Begglely," exclaimed the old gentleman suavely. "It can't be HIS fault. What is a photographer? Simply an instrument in the hands of science. He arranges his apparatus, and whatever is in front of it comes into it."

"No," continued the old gentleman, laying a constrained hand upon Begglely, who was about to resume the exhibition, "don't--don't show him the other two."

I was sorry for the poor girl, for I believe she really cared for the youngster; and as for her looks, they were quite up to the average. But some evil sprite seemed to have got into Begglely's camera. It seized upon defects with the unerring instinct of a born critic, and dilated upon them to the obscuration of all virtues. A man with a pimple became a pimple with a man as background. People with strongly marked features became merely adjuncts to their own noses. One man in the neighbourhood had, undetected, worn a wig for fourteen years. Begglely's camera discovered the fraud in an instant, and so completely exposed it that the man's friends wondered afterwards how the fact ever could have escaped them. The thing seemed to take a pleasure in showing humanity at its very worst. Babies usually came out with an expression of low cunning. Most young girls had to take their choice of appearing either as simpering idiots or embryo vixens. To mild old ladies it generally gave a look of aggressive cynicism. Our vicar, as excellent an old gentleman as ever breathed, Begglely presented to us as a beetle-browed savage of a peculiarly low type of intellect; while upon the leading solicitor of the town he bestowed an expression of such thinly-veiled hypocrisy that few who saw the photograph cared ever again to trust him with their affairs.

As regards myself I should, perhaps, make no comment, I am possibly a prejudiced party. All I will say, therefore, is that if I in any way resemble Begglely's photograph of me, then the critics are fully justified in everything they have at any time, anywhere, said of me-- and more. Nor, I maintain--though I make no pretence of possessing the figure of Apollo--is one of my legs twice the length of the other, and neither does it curve upwards. This I can prove. Begglely allowed that an accident had occurred to the negative during the process of development, but this explanation does not appear on the picture, and I cannot help feeling that an injustice has been done me.

His perspective seemed to be governed by no law either human or divine. I have seen a photograph of his uncle and a windmill, judging from which I defy any unprejudiced person to say which is the bigger, the uncle or the mill.

On one occasion he created quite a scandal in the parish by exhibiting a well-known and eminently respectable maiden lady nursing a young man on her knee. The gentleman's face was indistinct, and he was dressed in a costume which, upon a man of his size--one would have estimated him as rising 6 ft. 4 in.-- appeared absurdly juvenile. He had one arm round her neck, and she was holding his other hand and smirking.

I, knowing something of Begglely's machine, willingly accepted the lady's explanation, which was to the effect that the male in question was her nephew, aged eleven; but the uncharitable ridiculed this statement, and appearances were certainly against her.

It was in the early days of the photographic craze, and an inexperienced world was rather pleased with the idea of being taken on the cheap. The consequence was that nearly everyone for three miles round sat or stood or leant or laid to Begglely at one time or another, with the result that a less conceited parish than ours it would have been difficult to discover. No one who had once looked upon a photograph of himself taken by Begglely ever again felt any pride in his personal appearance. The picture was invariably a revelation to him.

Later, some evil-disposed person invented Kodaks, and Begglely went everywhere slung on to a thing that looked like an overgrown missionary box, and that bore a legend to the effect that if Begglely would pull the button, a shameless Company would do the rest. Life became a misery to Begglely's friends. Nobody dared to do anything for fear of being taken in the act. He took an instantaneous photograph of his own father swearing at the gardener, and snapped his youngest sister and her lover at the exact moment of farewell at the garden gate. Nothing was sacred to him. He Kodaked his aunt's funeral from behind, and showed the chief mourner but one whispering a funny story into the ear of the third cousin as they stood behind their hats beside the grave.

Public indignation was at its highest when a new comer to the neighbourhood, a young fellow named Haynoth, suggested the getting together of a party for a summer's tour in Turkey. Everybody took up the idea with enthusiasm, and recommended Begglely as the "party." We had great hopes from that tour. Our idea was that

Begglely would pull his button outside a harem or behind a sultana, and that a Bashi Bazouk or a Janissary would do the rest for us.

We were, however, partly doomed to disappointment--I say, "partly," because, although Begglely returned alive, he came back entirely cured of his photographic craze. He said that every English-speaking man, woman, or child whom he met abroad had its camera with it, and that after a time the sight of a black cloth or the click of a button began to madden him.

He told us that on the summit of Mount Tutra, in the Carpathians, the English and American amateur photographers waiting to take "the grand panorama" were formed by the Hungarian police in queue, two abreast, each with his or her camera under his or her arm, and that a man had to stand sometimes as long as three and a half hours before his turn came round. He also told us that the beggars in Constantinople went about with placards hung round their necks, stating their charges for being photographed. One of these price lists he brought back with him as a sample.

It ran:-

One snap shot, back or front .. .. 2 frcs. " with expression ... ... 3 " " surprised in quaint attitude . 4 " " while saying prayers ... ... 5 " " while fighting ... ... 10 "

He said that in some instances where a man had an exceptionally villainous cast of countenance, or was exceptionally deformed, as much as twenty francs were demanded and readily obtained.

He abandoned photography and took to golf. He showed people how, by digging a hole here and putting a brickbat or two there, they could convert a tennis-lawn into a miniature golf link,--and did it for them. He persuaded elderly ladies and gentlemen that it was the mildest exercise going, and would drag them for miles over wet gorse and heather, and bring them home dead beat, coughing, and full of evil thoughts.

The last time I saw him was in Switzerland, a few months ago. He appeared indifferent to the subject of golf, but talked much about whist. We met by chance at Grindelwald, and agreed to climb the Faulhorn together next morning. Half-way up we rested, and I strolled on a little way by myself to gain a view. Returning, I found him with a "Cavendish" in his hand and a pack of cards spread out before him on the grass, solving a problem.

THE MAN WHO DID NOT BELIEVE IN LUCK

He got in at Ipswich with seven different weekly papers under his arm. I noticed that each one insured its reader against death or injury by railway accident. He arranged his luggage upon the rack above him, took off his hat and laid it on the seat beside him, mopped his bald head with a red silk handkerchief, and then set to work steadily to write his name and address upon each of the seven papers. I sat opposite to him and read Punch. I always take the old humour when travelling; I find it soothing to the nerves.

Passing over the points at Manningtree the train gave a lurch, and a horse-shoe he had carefully placed in the rack above him slipped through the netting, falling with a musical ring upon his head.

He appeared neither surprised nor angry. Having staunched the wound with his handkerchief, he stooped and picked the horse-shoe up, glanced at it with, as I thought, an expression of reproach, and dropped it gently out of the window.

"Did it hurt you?" I asked.

It was a foolish question. I told myself so the moment I had uttered it. The thing must have weighed three pounds at the least; it was an exceptionally large and heavy shoe. The bump on his head was swelling visibly before my eyes. Anyone but an idiot must have seen that he was hurt. I expected an irritable reply. I should have given one myself had I been in his place. Instead, however, he seemed to regard the inquiry as a natural and kindly expression of sympathy.

"It did, a little," he replied.

"What were you doing with it?" I asked. It was an odd sort of thing for a man to be travelling with.

"It was lying in the roadway just outside the station," he explained; "I picked it up for luck."

He refolded his handkerchief so as to bring a cooler surface in contact with the swelling, while I murmured something genial about the inscrutability of Providence.

"Yes," he said, "I've had a deal of luck in my time, but it's never turned out well."

"I was born on a Wednesday," he continued, "which, as I daresay you know, is the luckiest day a man can be born on. My mother was a widow, and none of my relatives would do anything for me. They said it would be like taking coals to Newcastle, helping a boy born on a Wednesday; and my uncle, when he died, left every penny of his money to my brother Sam, as a slight compensation to him for having been born on a Friday. All I ever got was advice upon the duties and responsibilities of wealth, when it arrived, and entreaties that I would not neglect those with claims upon me when I came to be a rich man."

He paused while folding up his various insurance papers and placing them in the inside breast-pocket of his coat.

"Then there are black cats," he went on; "they're said to be lucky. Why, there never was a blacker cat than the one that followed me into my rooms in Bolsover Street the very first night I took them."

"Didn't it bring you luck?" I enquired, finding that he had stopped.

A far-away look came into his eyes.

"Well, of course it all depends," he answered dreamily. "Maybe we'd never have suited one another; you can always look at it that way. Still, I'd like to have tried."

He sat staring out of the window, and for a while I did not care to intrude upon his evidently painful memories.

"What happened then?" I asked, however, at last.

He roused himself from his reverie.

"Oh," he said. "Nothing extraordinary. She had to leave London for a time, and gave me her pet canary to take charge of while she was away."

"But it wasn't your fault," I urged.

"No, perhaps not," he agreed; "but it created a coldness which others were not slow to take advantage of."

"I offered her the cat, too," he added, but more to himself than to me.

We sat and smoked in silence. I felt that the consolations of a stranger would sound weak.

"Piebald horses are lucky, too," he observed, knocking the ashes from his pipe against the window sash. "I had one of them once."

"What did it do to you?" I enquired.

"Lost me the best crib I ever had in my life," was the simple rejoinder. "The governor stood it a good deal longer than I had any right to expect; but you can't keep a man who is ALWAYS drunk. It gives a firm a bad name."

"It would," I agreed.

"You see," he went on, "I never had the head for it. To some men it would not have so much mattered, but the very first glass was enough to upset me. I'd never been used to it."

"But why did you take it?" I persisted. "The horse didn't make you drink, did he?"

"Well, it was this way," he explained, continuing to rub gently the lump which was now about the size of an egg. "The animal had belonged to a gentleman who travelled in the wine and spirit line, and who had been accustomed to visit in the way of business almost every public-house he came to. The result was you couldn't get that little horse past a public-house --at least I couldn't. He sighted them a quarter of a mile off, and made straight for the door. I struggled with him at first, but it was five to ten minutes' work getting him away, and folks used to gather round and bet on us. I think, maybe, I'd have stuck to it, however, if it hadn't been for a temperance chap who stopped one day and lectured the crowd about it from the opposite side of the street. He called me Pilgrim, and said the little horse was 'Pollion,' or some such name, and kept on shouting out that I was to fight him for a heavenly crown. After that they called us "Polly and the Pilgrim, fighting for the crown." It riled me, that did, and at the very next house at which he pulled up I got down and said I'd come for two of Scotch. That was the beginning. It took me years to break myself of the habit.

"But there," he continued, "it has always been the same. I hadn't been a fortnight in my first situation before my employer gave me a goose weighing eighteen pounds as a Christmas present."

"Well, that couldn't have done you any harm," I remarked. "That was lucky enough."

"So the other clerks said at the time," he replied. "The old gentleman had never been known to give anything away before in his life. 'He's taken a fancy to you,' they said; 'you are a lucky beggar!'"

He sighed heavily. I felt there was a story attached.

"What did you do with it?" I asked.

"That was the trouble," he returned. "I didn't know what to do with it. It was ten o'clock on Christmas Eve, just as I was leaving, that he gave it to me. 'Tiddling Brothers have sent me a goose, Biggles,' he said to me as I helped him on with his great-coat. 'Very kind of 'em, but I don't want it myself; you can have it!'

"Of course I thanked him, and was very grateful. He wished me a merry Christmas and went out. I tied the thing up in brown paper, and took it under my arm. It was a fine bird, but heavy.

"Under all the circumstances, and it being Christmas time, I thought I would treat myself to a glass of beer. I went into a quiet little house at the corner of the Lane and laid the goose on the counter.

"'That's a big 'un,' said the landlord; 'you'll get a good cut off him to-morrow.'

"His words set me thinking, and for the first time it struck me that I didn't want the bird--that it was of no use to me at all. I was going down to spend the holidays with my young lady's people in Kent."

"Was this the canary young lady?" I interrupted.

"No," he replied. "This was before that one. It was this goose I'm telling you of that upset this one. Well, her folks were big farmers; it would have been absurd taking a goose down to them, and I knew no one in London to give it to, so when the landlord came round again I asked him if he would care to buy it. I told him he could have it cheap,

"'I don't want it myself,' he answered. 'I've got three in the house already. Perhaps one of these gentlemen would like to make an offer.'

"He turned to a couple of chaps who were sitting drinking gin. They didn't look to me worth the price of a chicken between them. The seediest said he'd like to look at it, however, and I undid the parcel. He mauled the thing pretty considerably, and cross-examined me as to how I come by it, ending by upsetting half a tumbler of gin and water over it. Then he offered me half a crown for it. It made me so angry that I took the brown paper and the string in one hand and the goose in the other, and walked straight out without saying a word.

"I carried it in this way for some distance, because I was excited and didn't care how I carried it; but as I cooled, I began to reflect how ridiculous I must look. One or two small boys evidently noticed the same thing. I stopped under a lamp-post and tried to tie it up again. I had a bag and an umbrella with me at the same time, and the first thing I did was to drop the goose into the gutter, which is just what I might have expected to do, attempting to handle four separate articles and three yards of string with one pair of hands. I picked up about a quart of mud with that goose, and got the greater part of it over my hands and clothes and a fair quantity over the brown paper; and then it began to rain.

"I bundled everything up into my arm and made for the nearest pub, where I thought I would ask for a piece more string and make a neat job of it.

"The bar was crowded. I pushed my way to the counter and flung the goose down in front of me. The men nearest stopped talking to look at it; and a young fellow standing next to me said -

"'Well, you've killed it.' I daresay I did seem a bit excited.

"I had intended making another effort to sell it here, but they were clearly not the right sort. I had a pint of ale--for I was feeling somewhat tired and hot--scraped as much of the mud off the bird as I could, made a fresh parcel of it, and came out.

"Crossing the road a happy idea occurred to me. I thought I would raffle it. At once I set to work to find a house where there might seem to be a likely lot. It cost me three or four whiskies--for I felt I didn't want any more beer, which is a thing that easily upsets me--but at length I found just the crowd I wanted--a quiet domestic-looking set in a homely little place off the Goswell Road.

"I explained my views to the landlord. He said he had no objection; he supposed I would stand drinks round afterwards. I said I should be delighted to do so, and showed him the bird.

"'It looks a bit poorly,' he said. He was a Devonshire man.

"'Oh, that's nothing,' I explained. 'I happened to drop it. That will all wash off.'

"'It smells a bit queer, too,' he said.

"'That's mud,' I answered; 'you know what London mud is. And a gentleman spilled some gin over it. Nobody will notice that when it's cooked.'

"'Well,' he replied. 'I don't think I'll take a hand myself, but if any other gent likes to, that's his affair.'

"Nobody seemed enthusiastic. I started it at sixpence, and took a ticket myself. The potman had a free chance for superintending the arrangements, and he succeeded in inducing five other men, much against their will, to join us. I won it myself, and paid out three and twopence for drinks. A solemn-looking individual who had been snoring in a corner suddenly woke up as I was going out, and offered me sevenpence ha'penny for it--why sevenpence ha'penny I have never been able to understand. He would have taken it away, I should never have seen it again, and my whole life might have been different. But Fate has always been against me. I replied, with perhaps unnecessary hauteur, that I wasn't a Christmas dinner fund for the destitute, and walked out.

"It was getting late, and I had a long walk home to my lodgings. I was beginning to wish I had never seen the bird. I estimated its weight by this time to be thirty-six pounds.

"The idea occurred to me to sell it to a poulterer. I looked for a shop, I found one in Myddleton Street. There wasn't a customer near it, but by the way the man was shouting you might have thought that he was doing all the trade of Clerkenwell. I took the goose out of the parcel and laid it on the shelf before him.

"'What's this?' he asked.

"'It's a goose,' I said. 'You can have it cheap.'

"He just seized the thing by the neck and flung it at me. I dodged, and it caught the side of my head. You can have no idea, if you've never been hit on the head with a goose, how if hurts. I picked it up and hit him back with it, and a policeman came up with the usual, 'Now then, what's all this about?'

"I explained the facts. The poulterer stepped to the edge of the curb and apostrophised the universe generally.

"'Look at that shop,' he said. "It's twenty minutes to twelve, and there's seven dozen geese hanging there that I'm willing to give away, and this fool asks me if I want to buy another.'

"I perceived then that my notion had been a foolish one, and I followed the policeman's advice, and went away quietly, taking the bird with me.

"Then said I to myself, 'I will give it away. I will select some poor deserving person, and make him a present of the damned thing.' I passed a good many people, but no one looked deserving enough. It may have been the time or it may have been the neighbourhood, but those I met seemed to me to be unworthy of the bird. I offered it to a man in Judd Street, who I thought appeared hungry. He turned out to be a drunken ruffian. I could not make him understand what I meant, and he followed me down the road abusing me at the top of his voice, until, turning a corner without knowing it, he plunged down Tavistock Place, shouting after the wrong man. In the Euston Road I stopped a half-starved child and pressed it upon her. She answered 'Not me!' and ran away. I heard her calling shrilly after me, 'Who stole the goose?'

"I dropped it in a dark part of Seymour Street. A man picked it up and brought it after me. I was unequal to any more explanations or arguments. I gave him twopence and plodded on with it once more. The pubs were just closing, and I went into one for a final drink. As a matter of fact I had had enough already, being, as I am, unaccustomed to anything more than an occasional class of beer. But I felt depressed, and I thought it might cheer me. I think I had gin, which is a thing I loathe.

"I meant to fling it over into Oakley Square, but a policeman had his eye on me, and followed me twice round the railings. In Golding Road I sought to throw it down an area, but was frustrated in like manner. The whole night police of London seemed to have nothing else to do but prevent my getting rid of that goose.

"They appeared so anxious about it that I fancied they might like to have it. I went up to one in Camden Street. I called him 'Bobby,' and asked him if he wanted a goose.

"'I'll tell you what I don't want,' he replied severely, 'and that is none of your sauce.'

"He was very insulting, and I naturally answered him back. What actually passed I forget, but it ended in his announcing his intention of taking me in charge.

"I slipped out of his hands and bolted down King Street. He blew his whistle and started after me. A man sprang out from a doorway in College Street and tried to stop me. I tied him up with a butt in the stomach, and cut through the Crescent, doubling back into the Camden Road by Batt Street.

"At the Canal Bridge I looked behind me, and could see no one. I dropped the goose over the parapet, and it fell with a splash into the water.

"Heaving a sigh of relief, I turned and crossed into Randolph Street, and there a constable collared me. I was arguing with him when the first fool came up breathless. They told me I had better explain the matter to the Inspector, and I thought so too.

"The Inspector asked me why I had run away when the other constable wanted to take me in charge. I replied that it was because I did not desire to spend my Christmas holidays in the lock-up, which he evidently regarded as a singularly weak argument. He asked me what I had thrown into the canal. I told him a goose. He asked me why I had thrown a goose into the canal. I told him because I was sick and tired of the animal.

"At this stage a sergeant came in to say that they had succeeded in recovering the parcel. They opened it on the Inspector's table. It contained a dead baby.

"I pointed out to them that it wasn't my parcel, and that it wasn't my baby, but they hardly took the trouble to disguise the fact that they did not believe me.

"The Inspector said it was too grave a case for bail, which, seeing that I did not know a soul in London, was somewhat immaterial. I got them to send a telegram to my young lady to say that I was unavoidably detained in town, and passed as quiet and uneventful a Christmas Day and Boxing Day as I ever wish to spend.

"In the end the evidence against me was held to be insufficient to justify a conviction, and I got off on the minor charge of drunk and disorderly. But I lost my situation and I lost my young lady, and I don't care if I never see a goose again."

We were nearing Liverpool Street. He collected his luggage, and taking up his hat made an attempt to put it on his head. But in consequence of the swelling caused by the horseshoe it would not go anywhere near him, and he laid it sadly back upon the seat.

"No," he said quietly, "I can't say that I believe very much in luck."

DICK DUNKERMAN'S CAT

Richard Dunkerman and I had been old school-fellows, if a gentleman belonging to the Upper Sixth, and arriving each morning in a "topper" and a pair of gloves, and "a discredit to the Lower Fourth," in a Scotch cap, can by any manner of means be classed together. And though in those early days a certain amount of coldness existed between us, originating in a poem, composed and sung on occasions by myself in commemoration of an alleged painful incident connected with a certain breaking-up day, and which, if I remember rightly ran:-

Dicky, Dicky, Dunk, Always in a funk, Drank a glass of sherry wine, And went home roaring drunk,

and kept alive by his brutal criticism of the same, expressed with the bony part of the knee, yet in after life we came to know and like each other better. I drifted into journalism, while he for years had been an unsuccessful barrister and dramatist; but one spring, to the astonishment of us all, he brought out the play of the season, a somewhat impossible little comedy, but full of homely sentiment and belief in human nature. It was about a couple of months after its production that he first introduced me to "Pyramids, Esquire."

I was in love at the time. Her name was, I think, Naomi, and I wanted to talk to somebody about her. Dick had a reputation for taking an intelligent interest in other men's love affairs. He would let a lover rave by the hour to him, taking brief notes the while in a bulky red-covered volume labelled "Commonplace Book." Of course everybody knew that he was using them merely as raw material for his dramas, but we did not mind that so long as he would only listen. I put on my hat and went round to his chambers.

We talked about indifferent matters for a quarter of an hour or so, and then I launched forth upon my theme. I had exhausted her beauty and goodness, and was well into my own feelings--the madness of my ever imagining I had loved before, the utter impossibility of my ever caring for any other woman, and my desire to die breathing her name--before he made a move. I thought he had risen to reach down, as usual, the "Commonplace Book," and so waited, but instead he went to the door and opened it, and in glided one of the largest and most beautiful black tom-cats I have ever seen. It sprang on Dick's knee with a soft "cur-roo," and sat there upright, watching me, and I went on with my tale.

After a few minutes Dick interrupted me with:-

"I thought you said her name was Naomi?"

"So it is," I replied. "Why?"

"Oh, nothing," he answered, "only just now you referred to her as Enid."

This was remarkable, as I had not seen Enid for years, and had quite forgotten her. Somehow it took the glitter out of the conversation. A dozen sentences later Dick stopped me again with:-

"Who's Julia?"

I began to get irritated. Julia, I remembered, had been cashier in a city restaurant, and had, when I was little more than a boy, almost inveigled me into an engagement. I found myself getting hot at the recollection of the spooney rhapsodies I had hoarsely poured into her powder-streaked ear while holding her flabby hand across the counter.

"Did I really say 'Julia'?" I answered somewhat sharply, "or are you joking?"

"You certainly alluded to her as Julia," he replied mildly. "But never mind, you go on as you like, I shall know whom you mean."

But the flame was dead within me. I tried to rekindle it, but every time I glanced up and met the green eyes of the black Tom it flickered out again. I recalled the thrill that had penetrated my whole being when Naomi's hand had accidentally touched mine in the conservatory, and wondered whether she had done it on purpose. I thought how good and sweet she was to that irritatingly silly old frump her mother, and wondered if it really were her mother, or only hired. I pictured her crown of gold-brown hair as I had last seen it with the sunlight kissing its wanton waves, and felt I would like to be quite sure that it were all her own.

Once I clutched the flying skirts of my enthusiasm with sufficient firmness to remark that in my own private opinion a good woman was more precious than rubies; adding immediately afterwards--the words escaping me unconsciously before I was aware even of the thought-- "pity it's so difficult to tell 'em."

Then I gave it up, and sat trying to remember what I had said to her the evening before, and hoping I had not committed myself.

Dick's voice roused me from my unpleasant reverie.

"No," he said, "I thought you would not be able to. None of them can."

"None of them can what?" I asked. Somehow I was feeling angry with Dick and with Dick's cat, and with myself and most other things.

"Why talk love or any other kind of sentiment before old Pyramids here?" he replied, stroking the cat's soft head as it rose and arched its back.

"What's the confounded cat got to do with it?" I snapped.

"That's just what I can't tell you," he answered, "but it's very remarkable. Old Leman dropped in here the other evening and began in his usual style about Ibsen and the destiny of the human race, and the Socialistic idea and all the rest of it--you know his way. Pyramids sat on the edge of the table there and looked at him, just as he sat looking at you a few minutes ago, and in less than a quarter of an hour Leman had come to the conclusion that society would do better without ideals and that the destiny of the human race was in all probability the dust heap. He pushed his long hair back from his eyes and looked, for the first time in his life, quite sane. 'We talk about ourselves,' he said, 'as though we were the end of creation. I get tired listening to myself sometimes. Pah!' he continued, 'for all we know the human race may die out utterly and another insect take our place, as possibly we pushed out and took the place of a former race of beings. I wonder if the ant tribe may not be the future inheritors of the earth. They understand combination, and already have an extra sense that we lack. If in the courses of evolution they grow bigger in brain and body, they may become powerful rivals, who knows?' Curious to hear old Leman talking like that, wasn't it?"

"What made you call him 'Pyramids'?" I asked of Dick.

"I don't know," he answered, "I suppose because he looked so old. The name came to me."

I leaned across and looked into the great green eyes, and the creature, never winking, never blinking, looked back into mine, until the feeling came to me that I was being drawn down into the very wells of time. It seemed as though the panorama of the ages must have passed in review before those expressionless orbs--all the loves and hopes and desires of mankind; all the everlasting truths that have been found false; all the eternal faiths discovered to save, until it was discovered they damned. The strange black creature grew and grew till it seemed to fill the room, and Dick and I to be but shadows floating in the air.

I forced from myself a laugh, that only in part, however, broke the spell, and inquired of Dick how he had acquired possession of it.

"It came to me," he answered, "one night six months ago. I was down on my luck at the time. Two of my plays, on which I had built great hopes, had failed, one on top of the other--you remember them--and it appeared absurd to think that any manager would ever look at anything of mine again. Old Walcott had just told me that he did not consider it right of me under all the circumstances to hold Lizzie any longer to her engagement, and that I ought to go away and give her a chance of forgetting me, and I had agreed with him. I was alone in the world, and heavily in debt. Altogether things seemed about as hopeless as they could be, and I don't mind confessing to you now that I had made up my mind to blow out my brains that very evening. I had loaded my revolver, and it lay before me on the desk. My hand was toying with it when I heard a faint scratching at the door. I paid no attention at first, but it grew more persistent, and at length, to stop the faint noise which excited me more than I could account for, I rose and opened the door and IT walked in.

"It perched itself upon the corner of my desk beside the loaded pistol, and sat there bolt upright looking at me; and I, pushing back my chair, sat looking at it. And there came a letter telling me that a man of whose name I had never heard had been killed by a cow in Melbourne, and that under his will a legacy of three thousand pounds fell into the estate of a distant relative of my own who had died peacefully and utterly insolvent eighteen months previously, leaving me his sole heir and representative, and I put the revolver back into the drawer."

"Do you think Pyramids would come and stop with me for a week?" I asked, reaching over to stroke the cat as it lay softly purring on Dick's knee.

"Maybe he will some day," replied Dick in a low voice, but before the answer came--I know not why--I had regretted the jesting words.

"I came to talk to him as though he were a human creature," continued Dick, "and to discuss things with him. My last play I regard as a collaboration; indeed, it is far more his than mine."

I should have thought Dick mad had not the cat been sitting there before me with its eyes looking into mine. As it was, I only grew more interested in his tale.

"It was rather a cynical play as I first wrote it," he went on, "a truthful picture of a certain corner of society as I saw and knew it. From an artistic point of view I felt it was good; from the box-office standard it was doubtful. I drew it from my desk on the third evening after Pyramids' advent, and read it through. He sat on the arm of the chair and looked over the pages as I turned them.

"It was the best thing I had ever written. Insight into life ran through every line, I found myself reading it again with delight. Suddenly a voice beside me said:-

"'Very clever, my boy, very clever indeed. If you would just turn it topsy-turvy, change all those bitter, truthful speeches into noble sentiments; make your Under-Secretary for Foreign Affairs (who never has been a popular character) die in the last act instead of the Yorkshireman, and let your bad woman be reformed by her love for the hero and go off somewhere by herself and be good to the poor in a black frock, the piece might be worth putting on the stage.'

"I turned indignantly to see who was speaking. The opinions sounded like those of a theatrical manager. No one was in the room but I and the cat. No doubt I had been talking to myself, but the voice was strange to me.

"'Be reformed by her love for the hero!' I retorted, contemptuously, for I was unable to grasp the idea that I was arguing only with myself, 'why it's his mad passion for her that ruins his life.'

"'And will ruin the play with the great B.P.,' returned the other voice. 'The British dramatic hero has no passion, but a pure and respectful admiration for an honest, hearty English girl-- pronounced "gey-url." You don't know the canons of your art.'

"'And besides,' I persisted, unheeding the interruption, 'women born and bred and soaked for thirty years in an atmosphere of sin don't reform.'

"'Well, this one's got to, that's all,' was the sneering reply, 'let her hear an organ.'

"'But as an artist -,' I protested.

"'You will be always unsuccessful,' was the rejoinder. 'My dear fellow, you and your plays, artistic or in artistic, will be forgotten in a very few years hence. You give the world what it wants, and the world will give you what you want. Please, if you wish to live.'

"So, with Pyramids beside me day by day, I re-wrote the play, and whenever I felt a thing to be utterly impossible and false I put it down with a grin. And every character I made to talk clap-trap sentiment while Pyramids purred, and I took care that everyone of my puppets did that which was right in the eyes of the lady with the lorgnettes in the second row of the dress circle; and old Hewson says the play will run five hundred nights.

"But what is worst," concluded Dick, "is that I am not ashamed of myself, and that I seem content."

"What do you think the animal is?" I asked with a laugh, "an evil spirit"? For it had passed into the next room and so out through the open window, and its strangely still green eyes no longer drawing mine towards them, I felt my common sense returning to me.

"You have not lived with it for six months," answered Dick quietly, "and felt its eyes for ever on you as I have. And I am not the only one. You know Canon Whycherly, the great preacher?"

"My knowledge of modern church history is not extensive," I replied. "I know him by name, of course. What about him?"

"He was a curate in the East End," continued Dick, and for ten years he laboured, poor and unknown, leading one of those noble, heroic lives that here and there men do yet live, even in this age. Now he is the prophet of the fashionable up-to-date Christianity of South Kensington, drives to his pulpit behind a pair of thorough-bred Arabs, and his waistcoat is taking to itself the curved line of prosperity. He was in here the other morning on behalf of Princess --. They are giving a performance of one of my plays in aid of the Destitute Vicars' Fund."

"And did Pyramids discourage him?" I asked, with perhaps the suggestion of a sneer.

"No," answered Dick, "so far as I could judge, it approved the scheme. The point of the matter is that the moment Whycherly came into the room the cat walked over to him and rubbed itself affectionately against his legs. He stood and stroked it."

"'Oh, so it's come to you, has it?' he said, with a curious smile.

"There was no need for any further explanation between us. I understood what lay behind those few words."

I lost sight of Dick for some time, though I heard a good deal of him, for he was rapidly climbing into the position of the most successful dramatist of the day, and Pyramids I had forgotten all about, until one afternoon calling on an artist friend who had lately emerged from the shadows of starving struggle into the sunshine of popularity, I saw a pair of green eyes that seemed familiar to me gleaming at me from a dark corner of the studio.

"Why, surely," I exclaimed, crossing over to examine the animal more closely, "why, yes, you've got Dick Dunkerman's cat."

He raised his face from the easel and glanced across at me.

"Yes," he said, "we can't live on ideals," and I, remembering, hastened to change the conversation.

Since then I have met Pyramids in the rooms of many friends of mine. They give him different names, but I am sure it is the same cat, I know those green eyes. He always brings them luck, but they are never quite the same men again afterwards.

Sometimes I sit wondering if I hear his scratching at the door.

THE MINOR POET'S STORY

"It doesn't suit you at all," I answered.

"You're very disagreeable," said she, "I shan't ever ask your advice again."

"Nobody," I hastened to add, "would look well in it. You, of course, look less awful in it than any other woman would, but it's not your style."

"He means," exclaimed the Minor Poet, "that the thing itself not being pre-eminently beautiful, it does not suit, is not in agreement with you. The contrast between you and anything approaching the ugly or the commonplace, is too glaring to be aught else than displeasing."

"He didn't say it," replied the Woman of the World; "and besides it isn't ugly. It's the very latest fashion."

"Why is it," asked the Philosopher, "that women are such slaves to fashion? They think clothes, they talk clothes, they read clothes, yet they have never understood clothes. The purpose of dress, after the primary object of warmth has been secured, is to adorn, to beautify the particular wearer. Yet not one woman in a thousand stops to consider what colours will go best with her complexion, what cut will best hide the defects or display the advantages of her figure. If it be the fashion, she must wear it. And so we have pale-faced girls looking ghastly in shades suitable to dairy- maids, and dots waddling about in costumes fit and proper to six- footers. It is as if crows insisted on wearing cockatoo's feathers on their heads, and rabbits ran about with peacocks' tails fastened behind them."

"And are not you men every bit as foolish?" retorted the Girton Girl. "Sack coats come into fashion, and dumpy little men trot up and down in them, looking like butter-tubs on legs. You go about in July melting under frock-coats and chimney-pot hats, and because it is the stylish thing to do, you all play tennis in still shirts and stand-up collars, which is idiotic. If fashion decreed that you should play cricket in a pair of top-boots and a diver's helmet, you would play cricket in a pair of top-boots and a diver's helmet, and dub every sensible fellow who didn't a cad. It's worse in you than in us; men are supposed to think for themselves, and to be capable of it, the womanly woman isn't."

"Big women and little men look well in nothing," said the Woman of the World. "Poor Emily was five foot ten and a half, and never looked an inch under seven foot, whatever she wore. Empires came into fashion, and the poor child looked like the giant's baby in a pantomime. We thought the Greek might help her, but it only suggested a Crystal Palace statue tied up in a sheet, and tied up badly; and when puff-sleeves and shoulder-capes were in and Teddy stood up behind her at a water-party and sang 'Under the spreading chestnut-tree,' she took it as a personal insult and boxed his ears. Few men liked to be seen with her, and I'm sure George proposed to her partly with the idea of saving himself the expense of a step-ladder, she reaches down his boots for him from the top shelf."

"I," said the Minor Poet, "take up the position of not wanting to waste my brain upon the subject. Tell me what to wear, and I will wear it, and there is an end of the matter. If Society says, 'Wear blue shirts and white collars,' I wear blue shirts and white collars. If she says, 'The time has now come when hats should be broad-brimmed,' I take unto myself a broad-brimmed hat. The question does not interest me sufficiently for me to argue it. It is your fop who refuses to follow fashion. He wishes to attract attention to himself by being peculiar. A novelist whose books pass unnoticed, gains distinction by designing his own necktie; and many an artist, following the line of least resistance, learns to let his hair grow instead of learning to paint."

"The fact is," remarked the Philosopher, "we are the mere creatures of fashion. Fashion dictates to us our religion, our morality, our affections, our thoughts. In one age successful cattle-lifting is a virtue, a few hundred years later company-promoting takes its place as a respectable and legitimate business. In England and America Christianity is fashionable, in Turkey, Mohammedanism, and 'the crimes of Clapham are chaste in Martaban.' In Japan a woman dresses down to the knees, but would be considered immodest if she displayed bare arms. In Europe it is legs that no pure-minded woman is supposed to possess. In China we worship our mother-in-law and despise our wife; in England we treat our wife with respect, and regard our mother-in-law as the bulwark of comic journalism. The stone age, the iron age, the age of faith, the age of infidelism, the philosophic age, what are they but the passing fashions of the world? It is fashion, fashion, fashion wherever we turn. Fashion waits beside our cradle to lead us by the hand through life. Now literature is sentimental, now hopefully humorous, now psychological, now new-womanly. Yesterday's pictures are the laughing-stock of the up-to-date artist of to-day, and to-day's art will be sneered at to-morrow. Now it is fashionable to be democratic, to pretend that no virtue or wisdom can exist outside corduroy, and to abuse the middle classes. One season we go slumming, and the next we are all socialists. We think we are thinking; we are simply dressing ourselves up in words we do not understand for the gods to laugh at us."

"Don't be pessimistic," retorted the Minor Poet, "pessimism is going out. You call such changes fashions, I call them the footprints of progress. Each phase of thought is an advance upon the former, bringing the footsteps of the many nearer to the landmarks left by the mighty climbers of the past upon the mountain paths of truth. The crowd that was satisfied with The Derby Day now appreciates Millet. The public that were content to wag their heads to The Bohemian Girl have made Wagner popular."

"And the play lovers, who stood for hours to listen to Shakespeare," interrupted the Philosopher, "now crowd to music-halls."

"The track sometimes descends for a little way, but it will wind upwards again," returned the Poet. "The music-hall itself is improving; I consider it the duty of every intellectual man to visit such places. The mere influence of his presence helps to elevate the tone of the performance. I often go myself!"

"I was looking," said the Woman of the World, "at some old illustrated papers of thirty years ago, showing the men dressed in those very absurd trousers, so extremely roomy about the waist, and so extremely tight about the ankles. I recollect poor papa in them; I always used to long to fill them out by pouring in sawdust at the top."

"You mean the peg-top period," I said. "I remember them distinctly myself, but it cannot be more than three-and-twenty years ago at the outside."

"That is very nice of you," replied the Woman of the World, "and shows more tact than I should have given you credit for. It could, as you say, have been only twenty-three years ago. I know I was a very little girl at the time. I think there must be some subtle connection between clothes and thought. I cannot imagine men in those trousers and Dundreary whiskers talking as you fellows are talking now, any more than I could conceive of a woman in a crinoline and a poke bonnet smoking a cigarette. I think it must be so, because dear mother used to be the most easy-going woman in the world in her ordinary clothes, and would let papa smoke all over the house. But about once every three weeks she would put on a hideous old-fashioned black silk dress, that looked as if Queen Elizabeth must have slept in it during one of those seasons when she used to go about sleeping anywhere, and then we all had to sit up. 'Look out, ma's got her black silk dress on,' came to be a regular formula. We could always make papa take us out for a walk or a drive by whispering it to him."

"I can never bear to look at those pictures of by-gone fashions," said the Old Maid, "I see the by-gone people in them, and it makes me feel as though the faces that we love are only passing fashions with the rest. We wear them for a little while upon our hearts, and think so much of them, and then there comes a time when we lay them by, and forget them, and newer faces take their place, and we are satisfied. It seems so sad."

"I wrote a story some years ago," remarked the Minor Poet, "about a young Swiss guide, who was betrothed to a laughing little French peasant girl."

"Named Suzette," interrupted the Girton Girl. "I know her. Go on."

"Named Jeanne," corrected the Poet, "the majority of laughing French girls, in fiction, are named Suzette, I am well aware. But this girl's mother's family was English. She was christened Jeanne after an aunt Jane, who lived in Birmingham, and from whom she had expectations."

"I beg your pardon," apologised the Girton Girl, "I was not aware of that fact. What happened to her?"

"One morning, a few days before the date fixed for the wedding," said the Minor Poet, "she started off to pay a visit to a relative living in the village, the other side of the mountain. It was a dangerous track, climbing half-way up the mountain before it descended again, and skirting more than one treacherous slope, but the girl was mountain born and bred, sure-footed as a goat, and no one dreamed of harm."

"She went over, of course," said the Philosopher, "those sure-footed girls always do."

"What happened," replied the Minor Poet, "was never known. The girl was never seen again."

"And what became of her lover?" asked the Girton Girl. "Was he, when next year's snow melted, and the young men of the village went forth to gather Edelweiss, wherewith to deck their sweethearts, found by them dead, beside her, at the bottom of the crevasse?"

"No," said the Poet; "you do not know this story, you had better let me tell it. Her lover returned the morning before the wedding day, to be met with the news. He gave way to no sign of grief, he repelled all consolation. Taking his rope and axe he went up into the mountain by himself. All through the winter he haunted the track by which she must have travelled, indifferent to the danger that he ran, impervious apparently to cold, or hunger, or fatigue, undeterred by storm, or mist, or avalanche. At the beginning of the spring he returned to the village, purchased building utensils, and day after day carried them back with him up into the mountain. He hired no labour, he rejected the proffered assistance of his brother guides. Choosing an almost inaccessible spot, at the edge of the great glacier, far from all paths, he built himself a hut, with his own hands; and there for eighteen years he lived alone.

"In the 'season' he earned good fees, being known far and wide as one of the bravest and hardiest of all the guides, but few of his clients liked him, for he was a silent, gloomy man, speaking little, and with never a laugh or jest on the journey. Each fall, having provisioned himself, he would retire to his solitary hut, and bar the door, and no human soul would set eyes on him again until the snows melted.

"One year, however, as the spring days wore on, and he did not appear among the guides, as was his wont, the elder men, who remembered his story and pitied him, grew uneasy; and, after much deliberation, it was determined that a party of them should force their way up to his eyrie. They cut their path across the ice where no foot among them had trodden before, and finding at length the lonely snow-encompassed hut, knocked loudly with their axe-staves on the door; but only the whirling echoes from the glacier's thousand walls replied, so the foremost put his strong shoulder to the worn timber and the door flew open with a crash.

"They found him dead, as they had more than half expected, lying stiff and frozen on the rough couch at the farther end of the hut; and, beside him, looking down upon him with a placid face, as a mother might watch beside her sleeping child, stood Jeanne. She wore the flowers pinned to her dress that she had gathered when their eyes had last seen her. The girl's face that had laughed back to their good-bye in the village, nineteen years ago.

"A strange steely light clung round her, half illuminating, half obscuring her, and the men drew back in fear, thinking they saw a vision, till one, bolder than the rest, stretched out his hand and touched the ice that formed her coffin.

"For eighteen years the man had lived there with this face that he had loved. A faint flush still lingered on the fair cheeks, the laughing lips were still red. Only at one spot, above her temple, the wavy hair lay matted underneath a clot of blood."

The Minor Poet ceased.

"What a very unpleasant way of preserving one's love!" said the Girton Girl.

"When did the story appear?" I asked. "I don't remember reading it."

"I never published it," explained the Minor Poet. "Within the same week two friends of mine, one of whom had just returned from Norway and the other from Switzerland, confided to me their intention of writing stories about girls who had fallen into glaciers, and who had been found by their friends long afterwards, looking as good as new; and a few days later I chanced upon a book, the heroine of which had been dug out of a glacier alive three hundred years after she had fallen in. There seemed to be a run on ice maidens, and I decided not to add to their number."

"It is curious," said the Philosopher, "how there seems to be a fashion even in thought. An idea has often occurred to me that has seemed to me quite new, and taking up a newspaper I have found that some man in Russia or San Francisco has just been saying the very same thing in almost the very same words. We say a thing is 'in the air'; it is more true than we are aware of. Thought does not grow in us. It is a thing apart, we simply gather it. All truths, all discoveries, all inventions, they have not come to us from any one man. The time grows ripe for them, and from this corner of the earth and from that, hands, guided by some instinct, grope for and grasp them. Buddha and Christ seize hold of the morality needful to civilisation, and promulgate it, unknown to one another, the one on the shores of the Ganges, the other by the Jordan. A dozen forgotten explorers, FEELING America, prepared the way for Columbus to discover it. A deluge of blood is required to sweep away old follies, and Rousseau and Voltaire, and a myriad others are set to work to fashion the storm clouds. The steam-engine, the spinning loom is 'in the air.' A thousand brains are busy with them, a few go further than the rest. It is idle to talk of human thought; there is no such thing. Our minds are fed as our bodies with the food God has provided for us. Thought hangs by the wayside, and we pick it and cook it, and eat it, and cry out what clever 'thinkers' we are!"

"I cannot agree with you," replied the Minor Poet, "if we were simply automata, as your argument would suggest, what was the purpose of creating us?"

"The intelligent portion of mankind has been asking itself that question for many ages," returned the Philosopher.

"I hate people who always think as I do," said the Girton Girl; "there was a girl in our corridor who never would disagree with me. Every opinion I expressed turned out to be her opinion also. It always irritated me."

"That might have been weak-mindedness," said the Old Maid, which sounded ambiguous.

"It is not so unpleasant as having a person always disagreeing with you," said the Woman of the World. "My cousin Susan never would agree with any one. If I came down in red she would say, 'Why don't you try green, dear? every one says you look so well in green'; and when I wore green she would say, 'Why have you given up red dear? I thought you rather fancied yourself in red.' When I told her of my engagement to Tom, she burst into tears and said she couldn't help it. She had always felt that George and I were intended for one another; and when Tom never wrote for two whole months, and behaved disgracefully in--in other ways, and I told her I was engaged to George, she reminded me of every word I had ever said about my affection for Tom, and of how I had ridiculed poor George. Papa used to say, 'If any man ever tells Susan that he loves her, she will argue him out of it, and will never accept him until he has jilted her, and will refuse to marry him every time he asks her to fix the day.'"

"Is she married?" asked the Philosopher.

"Oh, yes," answered the Woman of the World, "and is devoted to her children. She lets them do everything they don't want to."

THE DEGENERATION OF THOMAS HENRY

The most respectable cat I have ever known was Thomas Henry. His original name was Thomas, but it seemed absurd to call him that. The family at Hawarden would as soon think of addressing Mr. Gladstone as "Bill." He came to us from the Reform Club, via the butcher, and the moment I saw him I felt that of all the clubs in London that was the club he must have come from. Its atmosphere of solid dignity and petrified conservatism seemed to cling to him. Why he left the club I am unable, at this distance of time, to remember positively, but I am inclined to think that it came about owing to a difference with the new chef, an overbearing personage who wanted all the fire to himself. The butcher, hearing of the quarrel, and knowing us as a catless family, suggested a way out of the impasse that was welcomed both by cat and cook. The parting between them, I believe, was purely formal, and Thomas arrived prejudiced in our favour.

My wife, the moment she saw him, suggested Henry as a more suitable name. It struck me that the combination of the two would be still more appropriate, and accordingly, in the privacy of the domestic circle, Thomas Henry he was called. When speaking of him to friends, we generally alluded to him as Thomas Henry, Esquire.

He approved of us in his quiet, undemonstrative way. He chose my own particular easy chair for himself, and stuck to it. An ordinary cat I should have shot out, but Thomas Henry was not the cat one chivvies. Had I made it clear to him that I objected to his presence in my chair, I feel convinced he would have regarded me much as I should expect to be regarded by Queen Victoria, were that gracious Lady to call upon me in a friendly way, and were I to inform her that I was busy, and request her to look in again some other afternoon. He would have risen, and have walked away, but he never would have spoken to me again so long as we lived under the same roof.

We had a lady staying with us at the time--she still resides with us, but she is now older, and possessed of more judgment--who was no respecter of cats. Her argument was that seeing the tail stuck up, and came conveniently to one's hand, that was the natural appendage by which to raise a cat. She also laboured under the error that the way to feed a cat was to ram things into its head, and that its pleasure was to be taken out for a ride in a doll's perambulator. I dreaded the first meeting of Thomas Henry with this lady. I feared lest she should give him a false impression of us as a family, and that we should suffer in his eyes.

But I might have saved myself all anxiety. There was a something about Thomas Henry that checked forwardness and damped familiarity. His attitude towards her was friendly but firm. Hesitatingly, and with a new-born respect for cats, she put out her hand timidly towards its tail. He gently put it on the other side, and looked at her. It was not an angry look nor an offended look. It was the expression with which Solomon might have received the advances of the Queen of Sheba. It expressed condescension, combined with distance.

He was really a most gentlemanly cat. A friend of mine, who believes in the doctrine of the transmigration of souls, was convinced that he was Lord Chesterfield. He never clamoured for food, as other cats do. He would sit beside me at meals, and wait till he was served. He would eat only the knuckle-end of a leg of mutton, and would never look at over-done beef. A visitor of ours once offered him a piece of gristle; he said nothing, but quietly left the room, and we did not see him again until our friend had departed.

But every one has his price, and Thomas Henry's price was roast duck. Thomas Henry's attitude in the presence of roast duck came to me as a psychological revelation. It showed me at once the lower and more animal side of his nature. In the presence of roast duck Thomas Henry became simply and merely a cat, swayed by all the savage instincts of his race. His dignity fell from him as a cloak. He clawed for roast duck, he grovelled for it. I believe he would have sold himself to the devil for roast duck.

We accordingly avoided that particular dish: it was painful to see a cat's character so completely demoralised. Besides, his manners, when roast duck was on the table, afforded a bad example to the children.

He was a shining light among all the eats of our neighbourhood. One might have set one's watch by his movements. After dinner he invariably took half an hour's constitutional in the square; at ten o'clock each night, precisely, he returned to the area door, and at eleven o'clock he was asleep in my easy chair. He made no friends among the other cats. He took no pleasure in fighting, and I doubt his ever having loved, even in youth; his was too cold and self-contained a nature, female society he regarded with utter indifference.

So he lived with us a blameless existence during the whole winter. In the summer we took him down with us into the country. We thought the change of air would do him good; he was getting decidedly stout. Alas, poor Thomas Henry! the country was his ruin. What brought about the change I cannot say: maybe the air was too bracing. He slid down the moral incline with frightful rapidity. The first night he stopped out till eleven, the second night he never came home at all, the third night he came home at six o'clock in the morning, minus half the fur on the top of his head. Of course, there was a lady in the case, indeed, judging by the riot that went on all night, I am inclined to think there must have been a dozen. He was certainly a fine cat, and they took to calling for him in the day time. Then gentleman cats who had been wronged took to calling also, and demanding explanations, which Thomas Henry, to do him justice, was always ready to accord.

The village boys used to loiter round all day to watch the fights, and angry housewives would be constantly charging into our kitchen to fling dead cats upon the table, and appeal to Heaven and myself for justice. Our kitchen became a veritable cat's morgue, and I had to purchase a new kitchen table. The cook said it would make her work simpler if she could keep a table entirely to herself. She said it quite confused her, having so many dead cats lying round among her joints and vegetables: she was afraid of making a mistake. Accordingly, the old table was placed under the window, and devoted to the cats; and, after that, she would never allow anyone to bring a cat, however dead, to her table.

"What do you want me to do with it," I heard her asking an excited lady on one occasion; "cook it?"

"It's my cat," said the lady; "that's what that is."

"Well, I'm not making cat pie to-day," answered our cook. "You take it to its proper table. This is my table."

At first, "Justice" was generally satisfied with half a crown, but as time went on cats rose. I had hitherto regarded cats as a cheap commodity, and I became surprised at the value attached to them. I began to think seriously of breeding cats as an industry. At the prices current in that village, I could have made an income of thousands.

"Look what your beast has done," said one irate female, to whom I had been called out in the middle of dinner.

I looked. Thomas Henry appeared to have "done" a mangy, emaciated animal, that must have been far happier dead than alive. Had the poor creature been mine I should have thanked him; but some people never know when they are well off.

"I wouldn't ha' taken a five-pun' note for that cat," said the lady.

"It's a matter of opinion," I replied, "but personally I think you would have been unwise to refuse it. Taking the animal as it stands, I don't feel inclined to give you more than a shilling for it. If you think you can do better by taking it elsewhere, you do so."

"He was more like a Christian than a cat," said the lady.

"I'm not taking dead Christians," I answered firmly, "and even if I were I wouldn't give more than a shilling for a specimen like that. You can consider him as a Christian, or you can consider him as a cat; but he's not worth more than a shilling in either case."

We settled eventually for eighteenpence.

The number of cats that Thomas Henry contrived to dispose of also surprised me. Quite a massacre of cats seemed to be in progress.

One evening, going into the kitchen, for I made it a practice now to visit the kitchen each evening, to inspect the daily consignment of dead cats, I found, among others, a curiously marked tortoiseshell cat, lying on the table.

"That cat's worth half a sovereign," said the owner, who was standing by, drinking beer.

I took up the animal, and examined it.

"Your cat killed him yesterday," continued the man. "It's a burning shame."

"My cat has killed him three times," I replied. "He was killed on Saturday as Mrs. Hedger's cat; on Monday he was killed for Mrs. Myers. I was not quite positive on Monday; but I had my suspicions, and I made notes. Now I recognise him. You take my advice, and bury him before he breeds a fever. I don't care how many lives a cat has got; I only pay for one."

We gave Thomas Henry every chance to reform; but he only went from bad to worse, and added poaching and chicken-stalking to his other crimes, and I grew tired of paying for his vices.

I consulted the gardener, and the gardener said he had known cats taken that way before.

"Do you know of any cure for it?" I asked.

"Well, sir," replied the gardener, "I have heard as how a dose of brickbat and pond is a good thing in a general way."

"We'll try him with a dose just before bed time," I answered. The gardener administered it, and we had no further trouble with him.

Poor Thomas Henry! It shows to one how a reputation for respectability may lie in the mere absence of temptation. Born and bred in the atmosphere of the Reform Club, what gentleman could go wrong? I was sorry for Thomas Henry, and I have never believed in the moral influence of the country since.

THE CITY OF THE SEA

They say, the chroniclers who have written the history of that low-lying, wind-swept coast, that years ago the foam fringe of the ocean lay further to the east; so that where now the North Sea creeps among the treacherous sand-reefs, it was once dry land. In those days, between the Abbey and the sea, there stood a town of seven towers and four rich churches, surrounded by a wall of twelve stones' thickness, making it, as men reckoned then, a place of strength and much import; and the monks, glancing their eyes downward from the Abbey garden on the hill, saw beneath their feet its narrow streets, gay with the ever passing of rich merchandise, saw its many wharves and water-ways, ever noisy with the babel of strange tongues, saw its many painted masts, wagging their grave heads above the dormer roofs and quaintly-carved oak gables.

Thus the town prospered till there came a night when it did evil in the sight of God and man. Those were troublous times to Saxon dwellers by the sea, for the Danish water-rats swarmed round each river mouth, scenting treasure from afar; and by none was the white flash of their sharp, strong teeth more often seen than by the men of Eastern Anglia, and by none in Eastern Anglia more often than by the watchers on the walls of the town of seven towers that once stood upon the dry land, but which now lies twenty fathom deep below the waters. Many a bloody fight raged now without and now within its wall of twelve stones' thickness. Many a groan of dying man, many a shriek of murdered woman, many a wail of mangled child, knocked at the Abbey door upon its way to Heaven, calling the trembling-monks from their beds, to pray for the souls that were passing by.

But at length peace came to the long-troubled land: Dane and Saxon agreeing to dwell in friendship side by side, East Anglia being wide, and there being room for both. And all men rejoiced greatly, for all were weary of a strife in which little had been gained on either side beyond hard blows, and their thoughts were of the ingle-nook. So the long-bearded Danes, their thirsty axes harmless on their backs, passed to and fro in straggling bands, seeking where undisturbed and undisturbing they might build their homes; and thus it came about that Haafager and his company, as the sun was going down, drew near to the town of seven towers, that in those days stood on dry land between the Abbey and the sea.

And the men of the town, seeing the Danes, opened wide their gates saying:-

"We have fought, but now there is peace. Enter, and make merry with us, and to-morrow go your way."

But Haafager made answer:-

"I am an old man, I pray you do not take my words amiss. There is peace between us, as you say, and we thank you for your courtesy, but the stains are still fresh upon our swords. Let us camp here without your walls, and a little later, when the grass has grown upon the fields where we have striven, and our young men have had time to forget, we will make merry together, as men should who dwell side by side in the same land."

But the men of the town still urged Haafager, calling his people neighbours; and the Abbot, who had hastened down, fearing there might be strife, added his words to theirs, saying:-

"Pass in, my children. Let there indeed be peace between you, that the blessing of God may be upon the land, and upon both Dane and Saxon"; for the Abbot saw that the townsmen were well disposed towards the Danes, and knew that men, when they have feasted and drunk together, think kinder of one another.

Then answered Haafager, who knew the Abbot for a holy man:-

"Hold up your staff, my father, that the shadow of the cross your people worship may fall upon our path, so we will pass into the town and there shall be peace between us, for though your gods are not our gods, faith between man and man is of all altars."

And the Abbot held his staff aloft between Haafager's people and the sun, it being fashioned in the form of a cross, and under its shadow the Danes passed by into the town of seven towers, there being of them, with the women and the children, nearly two thousand souls, and the gates were made fast behind them.

So they who had fought face to face, feasted side by side, pledging one another in the wine cup, as was the custom; and Haafager's men, knowing themselves amongst friends, cast aside their arms, and when the feast was done, being weary, they lay down to sleep.

Then an evil voice arose in the town, and said: "Who are these that have come among us to share our land? Are not the stones of our streets red with the blood of wife and child that they have slain? Do men let the wolf go free when they have trapped him with meat? Let us fall upon them now that they are heavy with food and wine, so that not one of them shall escape. Thus no further harm shall come to us from them nor from their children."

And the voice of evil prevailed, and the men of the town of seven towers fell upon the Danes with whom they had broken meat, even to the women and the little children; and the blood of the people of Haafager cried with a loud voice at the Abbey door, through the long night it cried, saying:-

"I trusted in your spoken word. I broke meat with you. I put my faith in you and in your God. I passed beneath the shadow of your cross to enter your doors. Let your God make answer!"

Nor was there silence till the dawn.

Then the Abbot rose from where he knelt and called to God, saying:-

"Thou hast heard, O God. Make answer."

And there came a great sound from the sea as though a tongue had been given to the deep, so that the monks fell upon their knees in fear; but the Abbot answered:-

"It is the voice of God speaking through the waters. He hath made answer."

And that winter a mighty storm arose, the like of which no man had known before; for the sea was piled upon the dry land until the highest tower of the town of seven towers was not more high; and the waters moved forward over the dry land. And the men of the town of seven towers fled from the oncoming of the waters, but the waters overtook them so that not one of them escaped. And the town of the seven towers and of the four churches, and of the many streets and quays, was buried underneath the waters, and the feet of the waters still moved till they came to the hill whereon the Abbey stood. Then the Abbot prayed to God that the waters might be stayed, and God heard, and the sea came no farther.

And that this tale is true, and not a fable made by the weavers of words, he who doubts may know from the fisher-folk, who to-day ply their calling amongst the reefs and sandbanks of that lonely coast. For there are those among them who, peering from the bows of their small craft, have seen far down beneath their keels a city of strange streets and many quays. But as to this, I, who repeat these things to you, cannot speak of my own knowledge, for this city of the sea is only visible when a rare wind, blowing from the north, sweeps the shadows from the waves; and though on many a sunny day I have drifted where its seven towers should once have stood, yet for me that wind has never blown, pushing back the curtains of the sea, and, therefore, I have strained my eyes in vain.

But this I do know, that the rumbling stones of that ancient Abbey, between which and the foam fringe of the ocean the town of seven towers once lay, now stand upon a wave-washed cliff, and that he who looks forth from its shattered mullions to-day sees only the marshland and the wrinkled waters, hears only the plaint of the circling gulls and the weary crying of the sea.

And that God's anger is not everlasting, and that the evil that there is in men shall be blotted out, he who doubts may also learn from the wisdom of the simple fisher-folk, who dwell about the borders of the marsh-land; for they will tell him that on stormy nights there speaks a deep voice from the sea, calling the dead monks to rise from their forgotten graves, and chant a mass for the souls of the men of the town of seven towers. Clothed in long glittering white, they move with slowly pacing feet around the Abbey's grass-grown aisles, and the music of their prayers is heard above the screaming of the storm. And to this I also can bear witness, for I have seen the passing of their shrouded forms behind the blackness of the shattered shafts; I have heard their sweet, sad singing above the wailing of the wind.

Thus for many ages have the dead monks prayed that the men of the town of seven towers may be forgiven. Thus, for many ages yet shall they so pray, till the day come when of their once fair Abbey not a single stone shall stand upon its fellow; and in that day it shall be known that the anger of God against the men of the town of seven towers has passed away; and in that day the feet of the waters shall move back, and the town of seven towers shall stand again upon the dry land.

There be some, I know, who say that this is but a legend; who will tell you that the shadowy shapes that you may see with your own eyes on stormy nights, waving their gleaming arms behind the ruined buttresses are but of phosphorescent foam, tossed by the raging waves above the cliffs; and that the sweet, sad harmony cleaving the trouble of the night is but the aeolian music of the wind.

But such are of the blind, who see only with their eyes. For myself I see the white-robed monks, and hear the chanting of their mass for the souls of the sinful men of the town of seven towers. For it has been said that when an evil deed is done, a prayer is born to follow it through time into eternity, and plead for it. Thus is the whole world clasped around with folded hands both of the dead and of the living, as with a shield, lest the shafts of God's anger should consume it.

Therefore, I know that the good monks of this nameless Abbey are still praying that the sin of those they love may be forgiven.

God grant good men may say a mass for us.

DRIFTWOOD

CHARACTERS

MR. TRAVERS. MRS. TRAVERS. MARION [their daughter]. DAN [a gentleman of no position].

SCENE: A room opening upon a garden. The shadows creep from their corners, driving before them the fading twilight.

MRS. TRAVERS sits in a wickerwork easy chair. MR. TRAVERS, smoking a cigar, sits the other side of the room. MARION stands by the open French window, looking out.

MR. TRAVERS. Nice little place Harry's got down here.

MRS. TRAVERS. Yes; I should keep this on if I were you, Marion. You'll find it very handy. One can entertain so cheaply up the river; one is not expected to make much of a show. [She turns to her husband.] Your poor cousin Emily used to work off quite half her list that way--relations and Americans, and those sort of people, you know--at that little place of theirs at Goring. You remember it--a poky hole I always thought it, but it had a lot of green stuff over the door--looked very pretty from the other side of the river. She always used to have cold meat and pickles for lunch--called it a picnic. People said it was so homely and simple.

MR. TRAVERS. They didn't stop long, I remember.

MRS. TRAVERS. And there was a special champagne she always kept for the river--only twenty-five shillings a dozen, I think she told me she paid for it, and very good it was too, for the price. That old Indian major--what was his name?--said it suited him better than anything else he had ever tried. He always used to drink a tumblerful before breakfast; such a funny thing to do. I've often wondered where she got it.

MR. TRAVERS. So did most people who tasted it. Marion wants to forget those lessons, not learn them. She is going to marry a rich man who will be able to entertain his guests decently.

MRS. TRAVERS. Oh, well, James, I don't know. None of us can afford to live up to the income we want people to think we've got. One must economise somewhere. A pretty figure we should cut in the county if I didn't know how to make fivepence look like a shilling. And, besides, there are certain people that one has to be civil to, that, at the same time, one doesn't want to introduce into one's regular circle. If you take my advice, Marion, you won't encourage those sisters of Harry's more than you can help. They're dear sweet girls, and you can be very nice to them; but don't have them too much about. Their manners are terribly old-fashioned, and they've no notion how to dress, and those sort of people let down the tone of a house.

MARION. I'm not likely to have many "dear sweet girls" on my visiting list. [With a laugh.] There will hardly be enough in common to make the company desired, on either side.

MRS. TRAVERS. Well, I only want you to be careful, my dear. So much depends on how you begin, and with prudence there's really no reason why you shouldn't do very well. I suppose there's no doubt about Harry's income. He won't object to a few inquiries?

MARION. I think you may trust me to see to that, mamma. It would be a bad bargain for me, if even the cash were not certain.

MR. TRAVERS [jumping up]. Oh, I do wish you women wouldn't discuss the matter in that horribly business-like way. One would think the girl was selling herself.

MRS. TRAVERS. Oh, don't be foolish, James. One must look at

the practical side of these things. Marriage is a matter of sentiment to a man--very proper that it should be. A woman has to remember that she's fixing her position for life.

MARION. You see, papa dear, it's her one venture. If she doesn't sell herself to advantage then, she doesn't get another opportunity--very easily.

MR. TRAVERS. Umph! When I was a young man, girls talked more about love and less about income.

MARION. Perhaps they had not our educational advantages.

[DAN enters from the garden. He is a man of a little over forty, his linen somewhat frayed about the edges.]

MRS. TRAVERS. Ah! We were just wondering where all you people had got to.

DAN. We've been out sailing. I've been sent up to fetch you. It's delightful on the river. The moon is just rising.

MRS. TRAVERS. But it's so cold.

MR. TRAVERS. Oh, never mind the cold. It's many a long year since you and I looked at the moon together. It will do us good.

MRS. TRAVERS. Ah, dear. Boys will be boys. Give me my wrap then.

[DAN places it about her. They move towards the window, where they stand talking. MARION has slipped out and returns with her father's cap. He takes her face between his hands and looks at her.]

MR. TRAVERS. Do you really care for Harry, Marion?

MARION. As much as one can care for a man with five thousand a year. Perhaps he will make it ten one day--then I shall care for him twice as much. [Laughs.]

MR. TRAVERS. And are you content with this marriage?

MARION. Quite.

[He shakes his head gravely at her.]

MRS. TRAVERS. Aren't you coming, Marion?

MARION. No. I'm feeling tired.

[MR. and MRS. TRAVERS go out.]

DAN. Are you going to leave Harry alone with two pairs of lovers?

MARION [with a laugh]. Yes--let him see how ridiculous they

look. I hate the night--it follows you and asks questions. Shut it out. Come and talk to me. Amuse me.

DAN. What shall I talk to you about?

MARION. Oh, tell me all the news. What is the world doing? Who has run away with whose wife? Who has been swindling whom? Which philanthropist has been robbing the poor? What saint has been discovered sinning? What is the latest scandal? Who has been found out? and what is it they have been doing? and what is everybody saying about it?

DAN. Would it amuse you?

MARION [she sits by the piano, softly touching the keys, idly recalling many memories]. What should it do? Make me weep? Should not one be glad to know one's friends better?

DAN. I wish you wouldn't be clever. Everyone one meets is clever nowadays. It came in when the sun-flower went out. I preferred the sun-flower; it was more amusing.

MARION. And stupid people, I suppose, will come in when the clever people go out. I prefer the clever. They have better manners. You're exceedingly disagreeable. [She leaves the piano, and, throwing herself upon the couch, takes up a book.]

DAN. I know I am. The night has been with me also. It follows one and asks questions.

MARION. What questions has it been asking you?

DAN. Many--and so many of them have no answer. Why am I a useless, drifting log upon the world's tide? Why have all the young men passed me? Why am I, at thirty-nine, let us say, with brain, with power, with strength--nobody thinks I am worth anything, but I am--I know it. I might have been an able editor, devoting every morning from ten till three to arranging the affairs of the Universe, or a popular politician, trying to understand what I was talking about, and to believe it. And what am I? A newspaper reporter, at three-ha'pence a line--I beg their pardon, its occasionally twopence.

MARION. Does it matter?

DAN. Does it matter! Does it matter whether a Union Jack or a Tricolor floats over the turrets of Badajoz? yet we pour our blood into its ditches to decide the argument. Does it matter whether one star more or less is marked upon our charts? yet we grow blind peering into their depths. Does it matter that one keel should slip through the grip of the Polar ice? yet nearer, nearer to it, we pile our whitening bones. And it's worth playing, the game of life. And there's a meaning in it. It's worth playing, if only that it strengthens the muscles of our souls. I'd like to have taken a hand in it.

MARION. Why didn't you?

DAN. No partner. Dull playing by oneself. No object.

MARION [after a silence]. What was she like?

DAN. So like you that there are times when I almost wish I had never met you. You set me thinking about myself, and that is a subject I find it pleasanter to forget.

MARION. And this woman that was like me--she could have made a man's life?

DAN. Ay!

MARION. Won't you tell me about her? Had she many faults?

DAN. Enough to love her by.

MARION. But she must have been good.

DAN. Good enough to be a woman.

MARION. That might mean so much or so little.

DAN. It should mean much to my thinking. There are few women.

MARION. Few! I thought the economists held that there were too many of us.

DAN. Not enough--not enough to go round. That is why a true woman has many lovers.

[There is a silence between them. Then MARION rises, but their eyes do not meet.]

MARION. How serious we have grown!

DAN. They say a dialogue between a man and woman always does.

MARION [she moves away, then, hesitating, half returns]. May I ask you a question?

DAN. That is an easy favour to grant.

MARION. If--if at any time you felt regard again for a woman, would you, for her sake, if she wished it, seek to gain, even now, that position in the world which is your right--which would make her proud of your friendship--would make her feel that even her life had not been altogether without purpose?

DAN. Too late! The old hack can only look over the hedge, and watch the field race by. The old ambition stirs within me at times--especially after a glass of good wine--and Harry's wine--God bless him--is excellent--but to-morrow morning--[with a shrug of his shoulders he finishes his meaning].

MARION. Then she could do nothing?

DAN. Nothing for his fortunes--much for himself. My dear young lady, never waste pity on a man in love--nor upon a child crying for the moon. The moon is a good thing to cry for.

MARION. I am glad I am like her. I am glad that I have met you.

[She gives him her hand, and for a moment he holds it. Then she goes out.]

[A flower has fallen from her breast, whether by chance or meaning, he knows not. He picks it up and kisses it; stands twirling it, undecided for a second, then lets it fall again upon the floor.]

THE END